Vivian Hollis Mayne

§

Whom God Loves

To Beatrice
Enjoy

V. Mayne

© Copyright 2006 Vivian Hollis Mayne.
All rights reserved. No part of this publication may be reproduced, stored in a retrieval system, or transmitted, in any form or by any means, electronic, mechanical, photocopying, recording, or otherwise, without the written prior permission of the author.

Note for Librarians: A cataloguing record for this book is available from Library and Archives Canada at www.collectionscanada.ca/amicus/index-e.html
ISBN 1-4251-0589-0

Printed in Victoria, BC, Canada. Printed on paper with minimum 30% recycled fibre.
Trafford's print shop runs on "green energy" from solar, wind and other environmentally-friendly power sources.

TRAFFORD
PUBLISHING
Offices in Canada, USA, Ireland and UK

Book sales for North America and international:
Trafford Publishing, 6E–2333 Government St.,
Victoria, BC V8T 4P4 CANADA
phone 250 383 6864 (toll-free 1 888 232 4444)
fax 250 383 6804; email to orders@trafford.com

Book sales in Europe:
Trafford Publishing (UK) Limited, 9 Park End Street, 2nd Floor
Oxford, UK OX1 1HH UNITED KINGDOM
phone +44 (0)1865 722 113 (local rate 0845 230 9601)
facsimile +44 (0)1865 722 868; info.uk@trafford.com

Order online at:
trafford.com/06-2347

10 9 8 7 6 5 4 3 2

...He persecutes.

To
Laura and Susan

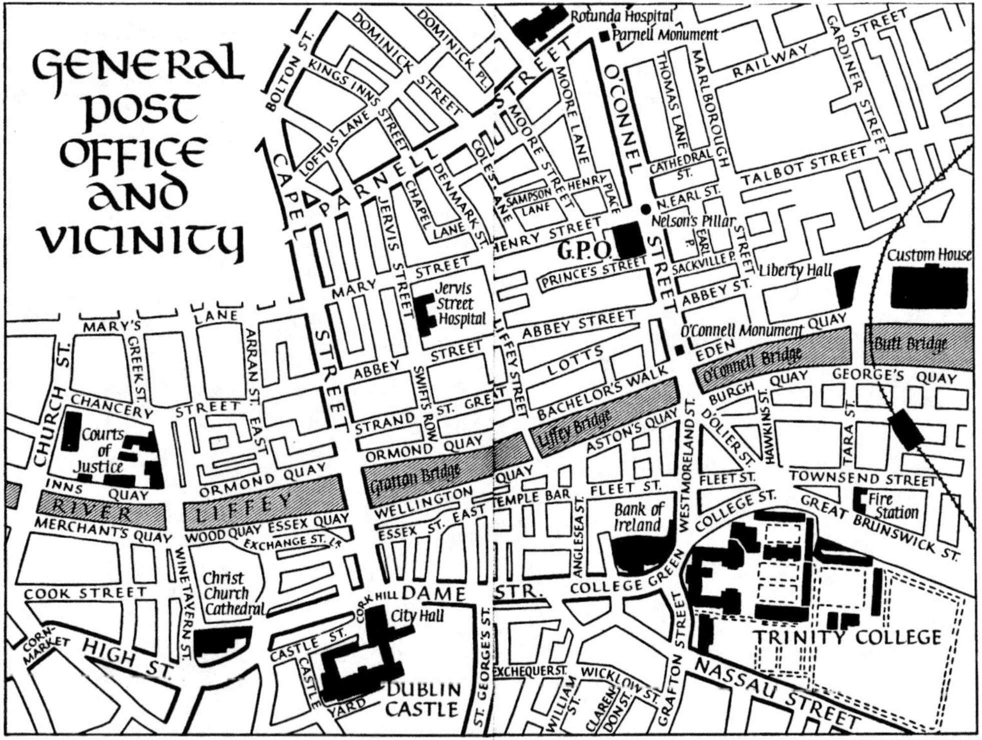
General Post Office and Vicinity
Rotunda Hospital
Parnell Monument
O'CONNELL STREET
Nelson's Pillar
G.P.O.
Custom House
Liberty Hall
Butt Bridge
O'Connell Bridge
O'Connell Monument
Liffey Bridge
Grattan Bridge
RIVER LIFFEY
Jervis Street Hospital
Courts of Justice
Christ Church Cathedral
City Hall
DUBLIN CASTLE
Bank of Ireland
Fire Station
TRINITY COLLEGE
PARNELL STREET
CAPEL STREET
BOLTON ST.
DOMINICK STREET
DOMINICK PL.
KINGS INNS STREET
LOFTUS LANE
DENMARK ST.
CHAPEL LANE
COLE'S LANE
MOORE STREET
MOORE LANE
HENRY PLACE
SAMPSON LANE
HENRY STREET
MARY STREET
JERVIS STREET
MARY'S LANE
GREEK ST.
ARRAN ST. EAST
CHURCH ST.
CHANCERY STREET
ABBEY STREET
SWIFT'S ROW
STRAND ST.
GREAT STRAND ST.
ORMOND QUAY
INNS QUAY
MERCHANT'S QUAY
WOOD QUAY
ESSEX QUAY
EXCHANGE ST. LR.
WELLINGTON QUAY
ESSEX ST. EAST
COOK STREET
WINETAVERN ST.
CORN-MARKET
HIGH ST.
CASTLE ST.
CASTLE YARD
CORK HILL
DAME STR.
ST. GEORGE'S ST.
LIFFEY STREET
PRINCE'S STREET
ABBEY STREET
LOTTS
BACHELOR'S WALK
ASTON'S QUAY
TEMPLE BAR
FLEET ST.
ANGLESEA ST.
COLLEGE GREEN
EXCHEQUER ST.
WILLIAM ST.
WICKLOW ST.
CLARENDON ST.
GRAFTON STREET
NASSAU STREET
WESTMORELAND ST.
COLLEGE ST.
D'OLIER ST.
HAWKINS ST.
TARA ST.
TOWNSEND STREET
GREAT BRUNSWICK ST.
BURGH QUAY
GEORGE'S QUAY
EDEN QUAY
ABBEY ST.
SACKVILLE P.
EARL P.
N. EARL ST.
CATHEDRAL ST.
THOMAS LANE
MARLBOROUGH STREET
TALBOT STREET
RAILWAY STREET
GARDINER STREET

1916

Chapter 1

Willie

On a tender July evening in 1911, Willie, observed the sunset while leaning on the rail of the Mail Boat bringing him to Liverpool. It was spectacular. Blazing along the horizon of the Irish Sea was a bar of golden light with a fiery orb at its center. For a while fingers of clouds crossed its radiance. Then moved away in time to show the orb dropping into the sea. With that came the darkness, turning crimson waves to metal, relieved only by shards of white.

Though the sunset was magnificent in its own right, Willie. a tall, rangy, young man, not yet eighteen, would have preferred to be witnessing the sunrise. Somehow the early morning sunshine brought a message of hope. Whereas the sunset brought darkness; a darkness that blended in with the bleakness of his mind and the loneliness he felt he was drowning in. Out there everything was black.

'You emigrating?' a kindly voice asked at his elbow.

Willie turned to see a young man about his own age, small in stature with a pleasant face; a face that radiated friendliness.

'Yeah,' Willie answered. 'How'd ye guess?'

'Your gloomy expression,' the young man replied. 'I know how you're feeling. I, too, am an emigrant bound for Liverpool.'

'Same here,' Willie said.

The young man proffered his hand. 'By the way,' he said, 'my name is Denis O'Dea.'

Willie shook is hand. 'Nice to meet you, Denis,' he said. Then added, 'mine's Willie MacNamee.'

'You on your own, Willie?' Denis asked.

Willie nodded his head. 'Yeah,' he said, surprised at how calm his voice sounded.

'How about joining me in some refreshments downstairs?' Denis suggested. 'Nothing like a bit of company to get rid of the doldrums.'

'Why not,' Willie answered.

The ship's bar, packed solid with drinkers, was the quintessential Irish bar scene. Masses of people converged on the counter where two barmen, dripping in perspiration, tried to cope with their orders. Tables, laden with debris — empty bottles, full glasses and spilt beer — were fully occupied. Not an inch of space remained where the lads could park themselves, much less hear themselves.

'Not the best place for a chat,' Willie said, observing the scene.

Denis pointed to an arrow on the wall indicating the café. 'A quiet cup of tea might be a better bet?' he said.

'Very definitely.'

Heading in the direction of the café, Denis said, laughing, 'If I got caught in the middle of that bar mob, I could be trampled to death.'

'I take it you're referring to your size?' Willie laughed with him.

'Naturally,' Denis grinned. 'Being small has its disadvantages.'

The café was a definite improvement on the frenetic bar. It held a much smaller crowd and tables were available. Armed with sandwiches and cups of tea, Willie and Denis found a table in a nice, quiet corner. But no sooner were they comfortably seated than some unruly children started a disturbance: a brother and a sister fought like cats and dogs, then four other children from another family started charging around yelling and screaming. Sedate couples looked at them like they could willingly kill them. Until a father, obviously sensing the chill in the atmosphere, volunteered to bring all the children on a tour of the ship. The silence they left behind was a blessing. People could at last hear their ears.

Gradually Willie and Denis began to share confidences about their very dissimilar backgrounds.

Unlike Willie's impecunious background rooted in the bogs of Mayo, Denis came from a well-to-do family who owned *the* hardware store in Waterford city.

'It's a business I can think of in a sentimental haze now that I'm away from it,' Denis told Willie, 'but I know if I were to return t'would suck me back into its meshes and have me running from morning till night.'

'Are you an only son?' Willie asked.

'No, I've two older brothers caught up in the family business who'd give their eye teeth to be doing what I'm doing.'

'Emigrating?' Willie said.

'Exactly,' Denis replied. Then reflected for a moment. 'How about yourself?' he asked. 'What lead you to this path?'

'Necessity.'

'Necessity?' Denis repeated.

'Yes,' Willie said. 'The place I come from in Mayo is bog and rock and totally barren.' He gave a wry smile. 'Nonetheless, with the help of a small, defiant, fertile patch of land producing vegetables and a bit of pasture for the few head a cattle, we just about manage to keep body and soul together.'

'You come from a large family?' Denis asked.

'Once upon a time there were five offspring at home,' Willie said, 'of which I'm the youngest. But three—two brothers and a sister—emigrated to America when they were my age. Which leaves my eldest brother, Martin, helping the parents to run the farm and doing the odd bit of carpentry work for the locals.'

The unruly children arrived back in the café putting an end to the peace and quiet.

'Do you have a bunk to sleep in on the boat?' Denis shouted at Willie over the din.

'No,' Willie shouted back, 'I thought I'd just curl up on an easy chair in one of the lounges.'

As conversation was impossible, the lads decided to leave. Outside Denis said, 'I booked a double bunk; you're more than welcome to share it with me.'

'Do you think we'd fit?' Willie asked, laughing.

'We're both pretty slim,' Denis answered. 'Truth to tell, I could do with the company.'

Comfortably settled in their bunk, the two lads talked well into the night about their hopes and dreams. During the course of the conversation Willie mentioned, 'my cousin, Eoin, who works in Liverpool, has arranged a job for me with his construction company.'

'You're very lucky,' Denis sounded unashamedly envious. 'First thing I have to do when I reach Liverpool, is find a job.'

'Maybe my cousin, could fix you up,' Willie said. 'I understand his employer is Irish.' Willie hesitated, then added, 'That is, of course, if you're up to doing that type of work?'

'I'll take anthin I can get,' Denis said humbly into the darkness.

From that day forward Willie and Denis became firm friends. Willie couldn't believe his good luck meeting someone like Denis. He was like a twin-soul. He appeared to be in tune with him all the time.

The cousin in Liverpool turned up trumps; he actually managed to arrange a job for Denis working on Willie's site.

One day, not long after Willie and Denis started work, the mates assembled as usual for the lunch break on the top floor of the building. When Willie and Denis arrived together, Brendan—a bit of a joker—who happened to be reading a comic strip, burst out laughing. 'Will you look at the pair of them!' he exclaimed for all to hear. 'Aren't they a perfect depiction of the 'Ham and Bud' characters in this comic strip.' He handed the paper to Willie to see for himself. Right enough; the characters in question had an uncanny resemblance in stature to Willie and Denis. Ham was long and lanky, just like Willie, and Bud was small and stocky, just like Denis. The other mates gathered round Willie and Denis studying the strip.

'That settles it then,' Con, the Clerk of Works, said, 'whether yis like it or not, from now on the pair of yis will be known as Ham and Bud.'

Midst all the laughter, Bud turned to Willie and said, 'I don't mind being Bud as long as you don't mind being Ham.'

'You're on,' Willie said cheerfully.

So from that day forward Willie and Denis became known as Ham and Bud. They were quite amenable to the change.

The difference in height never bothered them. In fact, the great joke was when Bud would strain his neck and ask, 'How's the weather up there, Ham?'

Ham would proudly pronounce, 'Begob! Isn't it warmer than down there. Amn't I nearer the sun.'

They shared the same lodgings and had many interests in common, chief among them being to further their education. 'The only way we'll rise above our station,' Ham maintained, 'is by acquiring a good education.'

So for the next couple of years the lads attended classes in the Polytechnic, two nights a week. For the time being it was convenient to be laborers. (Didn't it put money in their pockets?) But they were ambitious; they'd come to England to make their fortune and intended being laborers only as long as it was absolutely necessary.

Saturday nights the lads found recreation at the Parish Council's dances and ceilidhes. Though they were slow to ask the girls to dance, the girls weren't shy about asking them. But the real *craic* came afterwards when they recounted stories about their awkwardness on the dance floor and the lassies who fancied them. At one of these dances Bud met Alice, a fun-loving girl with red hair and freckles. It only took a few dates with Alice for Bud to realize he was in love.

It was during that first summer in Liverpool that Ham discovered the joys of opera. It happened in the strangest way. Regularly on warm Sunday evenings, a phonograph, belonging to an elderly Italian gentleman, played classical music, which wafted out through his open window, filling the air with wondrous sounds, transcending the last hours of Ham's day of rest. It brought joy to his heart and quite often tears to his eyes. It touched his soul as nothing before ever did. Back in Mayo the only music he'd ever heard was John Joe's fiddling for the ceilidhes at the crossroads of a Saturday night. He loved John Joe's music, but it couldn't be compared to this Italian stuff. As a result, Ham spent many a Sunday night on his own, refusing invitations to go out, liking nothing better than to open his bedroom window and bask in the Italian's music. Gradually, as the music became familiar, Ham found himself involuntarily whistling it.

From time to time, Geoff, the Works Manager on the job, overheard Ham's whistling. Quite the opera buff, Geoff wondered about this Irish laborer's amazingly good ear. Well, who would expect a Paddy fresh from Ireland to be so musically adept as to whistle a perfect rendition of 'Your Tiny Hand is Frozen' from *La Bohème*, beginning to end? Considering all the operas he'd attended himself in England and on the Continent, he couldn't even manage the first few bars.

As Ham knocked off work one evening, Geoff handed him a ticket to a performance of *La Bohème*, which was coming to the Liverpool Opera house the following week. 'It's a spare,' he explained, 'no sense in giving it to someone who won't appreciate it.' Then with a grin, he added, 'Your whistling of the score has been most entertaining.' The words were said with such good humor, it was impossible to take offense. Still, Ham was embarrassed. Apart from feeling self-conscious about being overheard whistling, he felt that out of courtesy he should offer to pay for the ticket. But the trouble was he didn't have the money. Geoff caught the doubt in his eyes. 'Maybe I'm jumping the gun,' he said. 'Perhaps you already have a ticket?'

'No, I definitely haven't,' Ham told him, 'it's just I don't have the money to pay for it.' He was tempted to add, no way could I afford such a luxury anyway.

'For God's sake, take it! It's a gift,' Geoff insisted. 'I can't think of anyone who'd appreciate seeing this opera more than yourself.'

Ham's heart lurched with pleasure at the prospect of attending a real, live opera. Thanking Geoff profusely, he graciously accepted the ticket.

Entering the Opera House a half an hour before curtain up time, Ham was surprised to find so many extra attractions attached to going to the opera. For instance, there was the foyer of the Opera House itself. The lavishness of it took his breath away; the inlaid marble floor covering its vastness and the sweeping, ornate staircase with every inch of wall covered in portraits of famous singers. Finally, there was the huge chandelier hanging from the center of the ceiling—a myriad of glass beads and petals, glittering and dancing in the light of countless candles.

Inside the theater more surprises awaited Ham. First, there was its unusual shape, which rose up to a vaulted ceiling at least four stories above him. Gracing each side were gilt-encrusted boxes, one over the other, rising to the ceiling. At the back, gilt-encrusted balconies were at different levels. Dominating the theater was an ocean of red seats. Up front, the red plush curtain covered the magical stage.

After lowering himself into his seat in the parterre, Ham took stock of what was happening around him. First thing he noticed was the symphony of French perfumes, exuded by the ladies, which seemed to float in the atmosphere. Next were the couples wearing evening dress sitting in the boxes and the Dress Circle; men cutting a dash in tailed-coats and black bow ties, some with colored cummerbunds. Not to be outdone, the ladies wore beautiful gowns, hats, gloves, jewelry; all very pretty and all very expensive. Some seemed preoccupied with choosing chocolates from luscious boxes, after which they'd train their binoculars on the lower classes above and below them.

After a while the house lights dimmed, the chatter ceased and the entire audience focused on the stage. Just then the conductor arrived in the Orchestra Pit. Taking up his position on the raised dais in front of the orchestra, he turned to the audience and bowed graciously, acknowledging their applause. Turning back to the orchestra, he tapped his baton and in the semi-darkness of the musicians' candlelight, the Overture commenced. It lasted about five minutes. Wonderful, mellifluous music. Coming near the end, however, an uneasy shuffling asserted itself around Ham, which bespoke the audience's impatience for the magical moment when the curtain would slowly rise.

What followed, was for Ham, a heavenly experience: hearing the full score of Puccini's arias sung by glorious voices, interspersed with the fabulous chorus. Adding to his enjoyment was the fact that he was close enough to see the actors' faces, their clothes and details of the realistic scenery. It was spellbinding; like being in another world. Ham wished it could go on forever. But apparently, halfway through the opera there had to be an intermission. The theater emptied. Most of the patrons adjourned to the beautiful foyer, the place where the well-dressed promenaded in their finery; another tradition associated with going to the opera. At the Refreshment Bar, Ham got talking to a student. They discussed the opera at length—the glorious music, the purity of the voices, the magnificence of the spectacle.

'Of course, if I hadn't got a present of the ticket, I could never have afforded this phenomenal experience,' Ham told him. 'This opera will have to keep me going for a long time.'

'Not necessarily!' the student remarked. 'There's always the Gods.'

'The Gods?'

'Yeah. You know. Those seats up there in the highest part of the Gallery.' He gave a ragged laugh. 'For the princely sum of sixpence you can enjoy the opera sitting on a hard seat.' Then with a grin he added, 'Mind you, the stage looks like a handkerchief and the artists like dolls, but they say up there the music sounds at its very best.'

From then on, whenever the opera came to Liverpool—about twice a year—Ham made a point of being one of the first in the mile long queue for 'The Gods.'

As time passed, Ham and Bud gravitated to things more Irish. Among these, was membership of the Liverpool Branch of the Gaelic League. Here they participated in activities and attended Irish classes for beginners.

Then in January, 1914, Frank, one of the students, lured Ham and Bud into going to a political meeting in the same building. At least a hundred people were in attendance. This was Ham and Bud's introduction to Irish politics. Ham was immediately captivated by the topics being discussed, particularly the one about Home Rule. He'd heard the expression many times, but never fully understood it. Listening to discussions and arguments, he was finally finding out what Home Rule was all about. Apparently, it would allow Ireland to have its own Parliament, with powers to legislate on Irish domestic matters only, under the overall sovereignty of the British Parliament. It would appear that the Home-Rule Bill had been on the British Parliament's Statute Books since 1885, but because of Protestant Northern Ireland's strong opposition to it, the British Government did not bring it in.

At a later meeting, the topic under discussion was Ireland's formation of its own National Volunteers under Redmond, the Leader of the Irish Parliamentary Party (the IPP) in Westminster. This discussion absorbed most of the meeting. Ham was surprised to learn that the prevailing Liberal Party depended solely on the IPP's support to keep the government in power.

When there was a lull, Ham asked the pertinent question, 'Why can't Liverpool do the same thing as Ireland and become part of the Irish National Volunteers under Redmond?'

Consensus was divided. Arguments for and against it abounded. Until Bud, sickened by the divergence, suggested, 'Why don't we have a show of hands?'

The Yes vote won. Liverpool would have its own National Volunteers under Redmond.

'You know something,' Bud said to Ham that evening on the way home, 'you should volunteer for that vacancy on the Council?'

'I don't know that I could stand those endless arguments,' Ham said, shaking his head.

'Well, it's patently obvious that what that crowd needs is a good, strong leader,' said Bud, looking appraisingly at Ham. 'Someone like yourself who would get things done.'

At the next meeting Bud proposed Ham to fill the vacancy on the Council. Eamonn, a council member, seconded it. A show of hands unanimously elected Ham to the position.

Some weeks later came the outbreak of the First World War. Not long afterwards, Redmond had the gall to stand up in Parliament and pledge the support of his National Volunteers—both in Ireland and in Liverpool—to fight in the war. Ham immediately summoned an emergency meeting of the Liverpool National Volunteers. He got a full house.

Shaking with anger, Ham opened the meeting saying, 'In the name of God, where did Redmond get the idea that we Irishmen would fight in England's war?'

Silence followed his question. No one had an answer.

Ham continued, 'Our mandate clearly states that the National Volunteer movement is a show of strength in the struggle for Home Rule. It has nothing whatsoever to do with fighting for England.'

'But,' someone roared, 'haven't you heard the news, Ham? Home Rule was passed into law a few days ago.'

'Yeah,' another added, 'the Act was actually signed by the King himself and placed on the Statute Books to come into force at the end of the war. T'was all in the newspapers.'

'The Bill has been passed all right,' Ham said, 'but it's not being implemented immediately. I can't accept that.'

'But it will be implemented eventually,' the first voice argued.

'Horse shit!' Ham said. 'The only reason that Bill was passed so quickly was to lure our Irish lads into joining the British Army. There's no guarantee that that Bill will ever come into effect.'

Philip Holmes, a member of the Council, asked, 'What should we do about Redmond's pledge to Prime Minister Asquith that we'd fight in the war?'

Ham had the answer ready. The day before the meeting, he and Bud had discussed the matter at length and finally came up with the solution. 'We'll tell Redmond, in no uncertain terms,' he said, 'that we have no intention of fighting in Britain's war.'

'But...' somebody tried to interrupt.

Still angry, Ham bulldozed through the interruption. 'No buts about it,' he said. 'If Redmond doesn't go along with it, those of us who are against going to war will pull out of the National Volunteers and form our own Volunteer movement. That would automatically rule out going to war.'

This statement stirred up powerful feelings in the room. Ham had anticipated a certain amount of disagreement, but nothing prepared him for the battle that now ensued. The chief offenders were a cadre in favor of going to war.

'You bloody Irish!' one of them said. 'Deadbeats! The lot of ye!'

'Yeah,' another added. 'When it comes to getting jobs in this country you jump at the opportunity. But let Britain ask for your support in the war and you slink away like bloody cowards.'

An anti-war member came back with, 'Why should we die for a country that has oppressed our nation for the last seven hundred years?'

'If you hate England so much, why are you here scrounging?' a hefty member of the cadre asked. Then added, 'Yes, that's what yis are, a pack of fecken scroungers!'

An anti-war member raised his voice and his fists. 'You'll take that back if you don't want your face pushed in.'

'Another anti-war member put in, 'We work hard for what we get. We're not slackers.'

'You're worse than slackers,' the hefty member said viciously, 'you're bloody cowards and spongers.'

This time the anti-war member who threatened to make a mess of this member's face, punched him on the nose. The fighting then started in earnest, with fisticuffs all around. Though Ham tried to intervene on numerous occasions, he got nowhere. Desperate to bring order back to the meeting, he walked across to the spot where The Liverpool Hurling Club had an advertisement on display. Its centerpiece was a hurling stick. It lay cushioned on red, shiny satin amid ribbons and bunting in the Club's colors. Angered now beyond words, Ham grabbed the hurling stick, came back and whacked the table so hard that it caused the head of the stick to split. This assuredly got everyone's attention.

'What the hell are yis doing here?' he bellowed at the group of dissidents. 'If ye can't be civil at an ordinary meeting, a fine army yis'd make fighting in a war.'

Ham's outburst shocked the room into silence. Then Desmond, one of the dissidents, broke the silence and brought some lightness to the situation. 'Sure don't ye know what brings us here, Ham,' he said snidely. 'Isn't it the sound of that lovely, lilting Irish voice of yours.'

The room rocked with laughter. The tension eased and a semblance of decorum was restored.

Taking his cue from Desmond, Ham brought his own brand of humor to bear on the meeting. Examining the markings on the smashed hurling stick, he said, 'I wouldn't mind only it scored the winning point when Liverpool won the championship.'

'Sure now that Liverpool no longer has its champion hurling stick,' Tom, another dissident, put in, 'won't they have a great excuse for not winning again.'

'Never mind, Ham,' Desmond chipped in with a lopsided grin, 'your secret is safe with us; not a word will we breathe about the part you played in destroying Liverpool's chances of winning the championship again.'

Again the room erupted in laughter. They were enjoying taking the mickey out of Ham. He took it well and laughed with them. Sure wasn't laughter the best medicine. Nevertheless, Ham continued pressing the point about the formation of another volunteer movement divorced from Redmond. Until slowly but surely he got the members to agree to put it to a vote. In a secret ballot, seventy-five per cent voted in favor of forming a new volunteer anti-war group. They also voted for the new name suggested by Ham—The Irish Volunteers.

Meanwhile, Irishmen all over Ireland, betrayed by the promise of Home Rule, flocked to the British army's colors. To get things moving Ham prevailed on the new Irish Volunteers to join The Irish Republican Brotherhood (IRB) based in Liverpool and participate in their activities. This lead to the company becoming very active. Nights were spent drilling in a rented hall in Araby Street.

Sometimes the training involved weaponry: taking guns apart, reassembling them. Sometimes climbing ropes and walls. Sometimes charging at bags with bayonets. Then when winter ended, maneuvers were conducted in the country. The men crawled under barbed wire with so-called machine guns clattering over their heads. They wrestled in the woods with men wearing white helmets — supposedly the enemy. They ran up hills with 50-caliber machine guns on their shoulders. Scrambled through mud. Slept all night in the woods with back packs for pillows. The group was now so dedicated they even made substantial contributions towards purchasing arms from America.

Meanwhile the British were so preoccupied with the war, they paid little or no attention to the clandestine activities of the Irish, both in Britain and in Ireland. Around this time a vacancy occurred in the company for an officer. (Appointments of officers were normally by election.) Among others, Ham's name was nominated. To his surprise, he was elected and became a second lieutenant.

Included in the company's activities in August, 1915, was attendance at the funeral in Dublin of Jeremiah O'Donovan Rossa. The group included Ham. Rossa had died in America after being in exile for forty years, before which he served a hard term in British jails for his part in the Fenian conspiracy; dynamiting British cities in the 1880's. Many memorable speeches were made over the grave of O'Donovan Rossa, but to Ham's mind, poet and teacher, Padraig Pearse's, was the most stirring. He ended his speech with the words,

'Life springs from death and from the graves of patriot men and women spring living nations. The British Government cannot realize the fact that the true future of Ireland lies in the inspiration of the past. The fools! The fools,' he railed, 'don't they know that while Ireland holds these graves, Ireland un free shall never be at peace.'

Talking to members of the Irish National Volunteers after the funeral, Ham got the impression that Pearse was obsessed with the need for a blood sacrifice for Ireland. One member remarked, 'This day is a memorial to Ireland's sad past, on the eve of a better future. If this funeral has proved anything, it's the fact that the volunteers are perfectly capable of secretly organizing when directed by the IRB inner councils.'

In the Fall of 1915, the war was doing badly. Casualties were heavy and the British Government was finding it increasingly difficult to replace the manpower by voluntary recruitment. One Sunday morning a strange man paid Ham and Bud a visit at their lodgings. He carried a briefcase.

'I'm from the War Recruiting Office,' he told them, 'here to find out what I can about you two.' With that he produced what looked like a dossier containing a list of names, together with relevant details. After recording information supplied by the two lads — names, dates of birth, place of birth, place of employment, how long resident in England — on the dossier, the recruitment officer announced, 'You two are fit enough and strong enough to serve in His Majesty's army.' Then studying the dossier further, he added, 'What I need now from both of you is a commitment to enlist within the next six weeks; if possible, the date.'

'Before you go any further,' Ham interjected angrily, 'I have to tell you that it's neither my intention nor my duty to give my services to the British army for the simple reason that I'm an Irishman and my country is not at war with anybody.'

'Well now, we'll have to see about that, won't we!' the recruitment officer said and left abruptly.

Soon after this incident, the British Government went ahead and passed the Military Service Act. (Mandatory conscription.) Now pressure was brought to bear on a number of the Liverpool volunteers to join up. They too were visited by Recruiting officers who threatened them with imprisonment if they didn't join up within the month.

Hurriedly, meetings were held. Schemes and solutions considered. But the only one that met with unanimous approval was the transfer of the company, intact, to Dublin. Philip Holmes, who appeared to have many connections with the IRB in Dublin, was deployed to Dublin to consult with Volunteer Headquarters about the transfer of the Liverpool Volunteers. Holmes came back from Dublin with a very favorable report. He told the meeting that Volunteer Headquarters there were in full agreement with the transfer of the Liverpool Volunteers; they would be more than happy to cooperate financially and otherwise. Better still, Count Plunkett had offered accommodation in a disused mill close to his home in Larchfield, Kimmage, at the foot of the Dublin Mountains.

By now, quite a number of volunteers were under notice of imprisonment if they didn't comply with the Act and enlist immediately. Because of their untenable positions, this meeting was charged with great urgency. As a result, Ham, unopposed, was selected to go to Dublin immediately to make arrangements about establishing a camp there. For obvious reasons, members would cross to Dublin in ones and twos. Those under threat of imprisonment would be the first to travel.

Ham arrived in Dublin on January 15, 1916. He wasted no time contacting the Volunteers' Headquarters at number 2 Dawson Street. But unfortunately for him, things did not go according to plan.

'Jesus, Bud!' Ham wrote, shortly after his arrival, 'the day I got here, that shower at Headquarters had me traipsing around all over Dublin on a wild goose chase. First, there was Thomas McDonagh sending me, with a note, to Eamonn Ceannt, who sent me with another note to a man called Kenny — Quartermaster of the 4th Battalion — who told me straight out there was nothing he could do to help. Consequently, I had to dig into my own pockets to purchase blankets; our accommodation was so totally devoid of any comforts. It consists of two rooms on the top floor of a derelict mill. The place reeks of dampness and has two broken windows. I was lucky I didn't get pneumonia. Barring the dust and cobwebs, except for a stove, a few forms and odds and ends of crockery, it's completely bare. And because that's not enough, it seems to be rat infested. So this was what I had to offer the first two lads — Paddy Caulwell and Paddy Sutton - arriving on the mail boat the following morning.

They couldn't believe their eyes when they saw the conditions at the mill. 'You wouldn't ask a dog to live in a place like this,' Paddy Caulwell said, 'much less human beings.' Decent enough, however, the two lads pooled their financial resources, rolled up their sleeves and set to work trying to make the placed habitable.'

In a later letter to Bud, Ham mentioned, 'I visited Headquarters again only to be told that neither McDonagh nor Bulmer Hobson, the Secretary, were available to talk to me. And nobody else could help. Putting it bluntly, I got the 'bum's rush.' I did, however, leave a letter for McDonagh reminding him about the promises made by Headquarters to the Liverpool Volunteers. But to date haven't heard a word from him or anybody else at Headquarters. Despite this situation,' Ham's letter went one, 'volunteers who arrive daily from England are directed by Headquarters to Larchfield. And to all intents and purposes, my appeals for the promised help and cooperation, continue to fall on deaf ears. Our survival now depends solely on the good will of our new arrivals. We now number thirty-five, and need I say that, as the quartermaster, I'm extremely embarrassed.'

After coping with this situation for four weeks, the one bright spot in Ham's life was Bud's arrival at the camp. At the outset it was decided that it would look too suspicious if the two of them quit work at the same time. So for appearances' sake, Bud delayed his departure. Within minutes of seeing Bud an adrenaline rush cut through Ham's fatigue and anxiety. Conversation flowed naturally between them. Bud was someone with whom Ham could be open and frank. He could spill his guts about the problems dogging the camp, the appalling conditions and the financial predicament. Even worse, the guilt he himself was feeling. He suspected that a lot of the members thought they'd been brought to Ireland under false pretenses. But his main concern was about the low morale of the camp.

Typical of Bud, the first thing he did was clear out his savings in an Irish bank and make a significant contribution to the camp.

Weeks passed without a word or a movement from Headquarters. Yet volunteers newly arrived from London, Manchester, Birmingham and Glasgow were directed by them to the Larchfield camp. It couldn't be more obvious that someone in that place was well-informed about the camp. Ham wondered who it could be? Did they think the Larchfield volunteers could live on fresh air? Then one night when Paddy Caulwell was having a quick pint in a pub in Terenure, he overheard the words, 'Larchfield camp' being bandied about by two men in conversation.

'Larchfield camp!' one laughed sarcastically, 'according to Bulmer Hobson, it's a joke! He calls them a gang of refugees and 'fly boys.' '

Though Paddy was bursting to butt in and defend his camp, he decided to keep quiet. 'Fly boys' was the term used to describe young Britons who sought refuge in Ireland rather than serve their country. So now the word was out. Bulmer Hobson, the Secretary of the Volunteer Headquarters, was the arch begrudger. Paddy couldn't wait to get back to tell his comrades what he'd heard.

This name calling was the last straw for the sixty-seven volunteers who were living under appalling conditions in the camp. A meeting was called by Ham to discuss how to deal with it.

Captain Craig, a new addition to the camp argued against making representation to Headquarters. 'It would appear too much like looking for charity,' he said. 'What we need to do is outsmart them.'

'How?' the chorus roared.

'I need a little time to think about it,' Craig said.

That night Ham and Craig put their heads together and came up with a bold strategy that they decided not to divulge to the rest of the camp. The plan had to do with the weekly Irish classes Ham and Craig attended: early on, a teacher named Liam O'Flaherty, had shown great interest in Ham's story about how he brought the Liverpool Volunteers to Dublin. Since then, whenever the opportunity presented itself, they had further discussions about politics. A recent conversation, however, enlightened Ham to the fact that O'Flaherty was on the Executive of the Irish Volunteers.

At the next Irish class, Ham made a point of talking to O'Flaherty. In the course of their conversation, he leaked some solid facts about the diabolical conditions prevailing in the Larchfield camp. When he saw O'Flaherty's shocked expression, he decided to bring the strategy arranged between himself and Craig into play.

'As a matter of fact,' he said casually, 'with the camp now bordering on mutiny, myself and Captain Craig have decided to accept the Citizens Army's offer to march down to Liberty Hall (Union Headquarters) where our company will be taken in and supported.'

Two days after this conversation with O'Flaherty, a Teleboy Dispatch Rider arrived at the camp with a telegram summoning Lieutenant MacNamee and Captain Craigh to report immediately to Headquarters to meet with Thomas McDonagh.

Glowering at the two men, McDonagh demanded aggressively, 'So what have you two buffs to say for yourselves?'

'Regarding what?' Ham inquired nonchalantly.

'Regarding this business of the Larchfield Volunteers joining the Irish Citizen Army?' McDonagh said. 'I thought you lads from across the water came to support the National Volunteers?'

'And so we did,' Ham said, striking an exaggerated pose of impatience. 'But Volunteer Headquarters left us no alternative.'

'What do you mean, left you no alternative?' McDonagh said, eying Ham suspiciously.

'Since the camp started up,' Ham said, 'despite the numerous appeals made by me personally to Headquarters for the financial aid and cooperation promised us in the beginning, Headquarters has totally ignored us. We received no money, no equipment, no recognition. As a consequence, day by day, the men are becoming more and more mutinous.'

With eyes hooded in contemplation, McDonagh gazed at his desk. Eventually he raised his head and summoned his most pleasant smile. 'Well, Lieutenant,' he said with emphasis, 'I've news for you; this most unhappy situation is about to change.' His face paraded a myriad of emotions as he entreated, 'For God's sake, don't do anything rash. Give me a day or two to sort things out.'

As they left the building, Ham and Craig exchanged smiles. Their ruse had succeeded; O'Flaherty obviously dropped the information in the right quarters.

The following day, McDonagh arrived at the camp and announced that the Volunteer Organization was now undertaking responsibility for the control and management of the camp, that George Plunkett, Count Plunkett's son, had been appointed the camp commandant and that from this day forward the camp would be known as the Kimmage Garrison. The camp had won.

The takeover of the camp made an enormous difference. With the Commandant in charge, discipline and orderliness were restored. And with the arrival of the necessary supplies — food, drink, bedding, equipment — the camp could finally get down to operating normally. McDonagh visited the camp on a regular basis. Early on he advised that, as most of the training took place at the weekends, anyone who could get employment during the week, should do so.

Ham and Bud secured employment in the city. Ham with an insurance company, Bud in Heitons, the coal people. Those who remained behind in the camp were given productive employment making munitions. One evening shortly afterwards, when Ham and Bud were having a pint in the local pub, Bud couldn't help noticing the way Ham seemed to be caught up in his own thoughts.

'Now that the camp is up and running,' he said to Ham, 'you don't look like someone who's overwhelmed with relief. What's bothering you?'

'Trust you to notice,' Ham said reflectively. 'To be honest with you, Bud, I'm worried about the lack of security at night in the camp: sure it's wide open to anyone who wishes to pry.'

'But there's always a sentry on duty,' Bud said, baffled.

'One sentry,' Ham replied, 'who spends the night snoozing beside the stove. What kind of security is that?'

'Why don't you have a word with the Commandant?' Bud asked.

'I did,' Ham said, his face stiffening. 'I actually said to him that it would be much wiser to have two men on sentry duty at night time. But I got the deaf ear.'

'Of course, it's all right for him,' Bud interjected, 'he sleeps in his own house down the road.' Then Bud's face suddenly beamed with animation. 'Perhaps I could fix it,' he said.

'How?'

'It's just an idea,' Bud said, 'But you know that fellow, Don, from Glasgow, who does sentry duty?'

'What about him?'

'Well, I was thinking,' Bud said, amused, 'that maybe I could ask him to do something to simulate a raid or intrusion into the camp the next night he's on duty. Then our dear Commander would have to listen.'

'If you could bring it off,' Ham said. 'sounds great. But do you think you can trust that lad to do the job and keep quiet about it?'

'Oh, definitely!' Bud said confidently. 'He's a real nice person and himself and myself have a very good rapport.'

'I suppose there's no harm in trying,' Ham said, warming to the idea.

Two nights later at two o'clock in the morning, Don, the sentry on duty, noisily pulled up the trap door, cursed and swore at a phantom intruder, then fired three shots down the stairs. The whole camp was aroused. Members bolted out of bed in their night attire and dashed down the stairs into the open with the intention of apprehending the intruder. Willie couldn't look at Bud for fear of bursting out laughing. Don's ruse not only succeeded in getting two sentries posted nightly, but the Commandant himself brought in his mattress and slept on the floor with the volunteers.

Meanwhile the camp had taken over the whole of the mill and was being run on strict, military lines, with guard duties, drill and the rest of the military paraphernalia. On Saint Patrick's Day, March 17th, 1916, members of the Kimmage Garrison took part with some 2,000 other minority volunteers in the Big Parade through the center of the city of Dublin, where they took the salute marching past Pearse and other officers.

When Ham and Bud had been working for a couple of weeks, it suddenly dawned on them that their lives could be made a lot easier if they were living closer to the city. As things stood, they spent hours, commuting mornings and evenings. Moreover, living elsewhere wouldn't interfere with their involvement in the Garrison activities at the weekends. So on the 1st of April the lads found digs in Ranelagh — a short tram ride to the city center.

On Palm Sunday (the Sunday before Easter), Commandant Plunkett spoke with unusual fervor to the members of the Garrison. He opened his remarks with the words, 'Listen now, lads, and listen well.' Then he continued, 'It has been decided by the Council of the Irish Republican Brotherhood to mobilize all the volunteers and hold all Ireland maneuvers on Easter Sunday morning.' Before he could go any further the questions started.

'Is this a preparation for the real thing?' someone asked.

'Does that mean the rising is imminent?' Bud asked.

'Depending on how the maneuvers go,' Plunkett interjected sharply, 'the Rising could take place as early as Easter Monday.'

'In other words,' Ham said, solemnly, 'the maneuvers planned for Easter Sunday are in fact a cover-up for the outbreak of armed rebellion against the British on the Monday?'

'You got it in one sentence, Ham,' Plunkett said with a jaded smile. Excitement pulsed through the room as members digested these facts.

'Now,' Plunkett went on, 'this coming week, apart from the week end, I want you all to make a special effort to be in attendance at the Garrison each evening.'

On Holy Thursday night to everybody's astonishment, including Plunkett's, the Garrison had a surprise visitor. It was none other than the Supreme Commander himself, Padraig Pearse. After congratulating the Garrison on its adherence to the Cause, Pearse went on to say in a calm, implacable tone, 'In my opinion, this Garrison constitutes the first standing army of the Republic.' Continuing, he said, 'The Council and I are in the process of forming a Headquarters Battalion consisting of one company from each of the four Dublin Battalions, including the Kimmage Garrison.' He ended by saying, 'We're hoping to make progress with this during the maneuvers on Easter Sunday.'

After early Mass in Rathmines Church on Easter Sunday, Ham and Bud were on their way back to the digs to get themselves togged out for that day's maneuvers when they ran into Kevin O'Rourke, a member of the Kimmage Garrison. Waving a copy of a newspaper, O'Rourke told them, 'You can forget about the maneuvers today, they've been canceled.' O'Rourke then showed them the brief paragraph published in that Sunday's Independent. It ran as follows:

NOTICE TO VOLUNTEERS

Owing to the very critical position, all orders given to Irish Volunteers for today, Easter Sunday, are hereby rescinded and no parades, marches or other movements of Irish Volunteers will take place. Each individual volunteer will obey this order strictly in every particular.
Eoin MacNeill, Chief of Staff.

'Well, that seems to be that,' Bud said.

'That means that tomorrow's action is probably off too,' Ham said.

'Certainly looks like it,' Kevin rejoined.

After the three debated whether or not to go out to the garrison, the decision was eventually taken to make the journey. All three agreed that the situation needed to be expeditiously investigated. To be left dangling like this was frustrating in the extreme. There had to be a rational explanation and the obvious place to get it was from the Kimmage Garrison. But the only information they could glean from the live-in members was that apparently Commandant Plunkett had got word of the decision to cancel the maneuvers through a telephone call to his home.

Afterwards, he made the bald statement to the company: 'You can stop gearing up for the maneuvers; they've been canceled.' Then he disappeared. It seemed the company were as much in the dark as themselves regarding the situation.

'Go out and enjoy yourselves,' Paddy Caulwell said to Ham. 'That's what I intend to do.'

'What about tomorrow?' Ham asked, concerned.

'I'd say that that's definitely off too,' Paddy said.

On Easter Monday morning, as was customary, Ham woke at first light. Throwing on his clothes, he went outside to study the weather. He saw a clear blue sky flushed with a few white foaming clouds which predicted a warm, sunny day. Back in the bedroom, he shook Bud awake. 'Okay, Bud,' he said, 'it's a day for the Fairy House Races.'

'It's a fine day?' Bud asked, jerking himself awake.

'More than fine,' Ham said. 'Not a black cloud in sight.'

'Right,' Bud said, 'Fairy House it is.'

As days like this were few and far between, the pair decided to walk into the city. Sauntering across O'Connell Bridge on their way to the Pillar (where trams were filling up with passengers going to the Races), at the junction of Eden Quay they stood with other pedestrians on the edge of the pavement waiting for the policeman on point duty to give them the beck to cross. Suddenly a car filled with a few familiar faces slowed down and pulled into the curb.

Barney Mellows leaned out of the window and shouted, 'It's on! Get yourselves to your Unit as quickly as possible.'

The car then sped away before any questions could be asked.

'Christ Almighty!' Bud's face registered consternation. 'What the hell do we do now?'

Ham said, 'Relax. Like Plunkett said during one of the sessions, 'any problems on the day, the thing to do is get yourself up to The Hibernian Rifles' Headquarters in North Frederick Street.''

At the Hibernian Rifles Headquarters there was no sign of life. The door was closed and locked. Ham rang the bell. They waited a few minutes, then Bud knocked the knocker. No answer. Ham rang the bell again. They waited. After what seemed an eternity they heard feet shuffling to the door. The door opened, barely. An elderly, frightened looking man poked his head through the small opening. 'What do yis want?' he asked.

'Instructions,' Ham said.

'Instructions for what?' the old man asked, his eyes squinting suspiciously.

'Who are you?' Bud butted in.

'I'm the Caretaker of this building.'

'Well, we're members of The Kimmage Garrison Unit, under the command of George Plunkett,' Ham told him. 'We've come to...'

'Oh! Don't tell me!' the old man groaned. 'I know, I know. Such confusion! Never, in me born days have I seen the likes.'

'So, do you know what we're supposed to do?' Bud asked. 'Obviously there's nothing happening here?'

'Have yis any identification?' the caretaker inquired. Ham produced 'the card.' It was enough to convince the caretaker. 'Right! Me instructions are to advise anyone with the right credentials to report immediately at The Liberty Hall.'

As they came down the steps Ham and Bud grinned at each other. Right enough it looked like the show was going ahead. 'Best return to the digs and get our arms and gear,' Bud suggested as a tram approached. 'No sense turning up at The Liberty Hall unprepared.'

They found the scene at The Liberty Hall most disappointing: about a hundred Volunteers — some in gray-green uniforms, some in their Sunday best — standing around looking lost. Nothing was happening. The only thing that suggested serious military action was the evidence of the machine guns and the ammunition. But as far as Ham and Bud were concerned, total confusion reigned; no one seemed to know anything, no one could tell them where to go nor what to do. Nor could they find any members of their own Garrison.

Eventually, they found an officer in a bright green uniform who told them the leaders, Connolly, Pearse, Clarke and Plunkett had been there earlier, but had already left on a march with their respective units. He couldn't say where they'd gone. 'We could do with your help doing surveillance in one of the rooms upstairs overlooking Eden Quay,' he told them.

'Right, at last, something to do,' Ham said to Bud.

As they were leaving, the officer said, 'Don't fire on anything or anybody without orders.'

Ham and Bud found a room upstairs with an empty window and took up their positions. There were about a dozen other young volunteers present. They were excited, but frightened. After a while, a young officer shouted, 'There's a company of British Fifth Lancers coming up the Quays; they're escorting horse-drawn lorries laden with munitions.'

It was the volunteers first encounter with the enemy. Gasps of fear rumbled through the room. The young volunteers were thinking, isn't this the real thing, not playacting?

Minutes later, the officer barked out, 'You're to hold your fire until you get the order.'

For a few seconds there was dead silence.

'I don't know about you,' Bud said to Ham, 'but I'm saying the Act of Contrition.' Both men turned their faces to the wall and recited, 'Oh, my God, I'm heartily sorry for having offended you...' out loud. One by one the other volunteers joined in the prayer and the Act of Contrition was recited in unison. Ham turned back to the window just in time to see the company of Lancers and the horse-drawn lorries stream by.

'Hold your fire,' the young officer barked. 'The Lancers are merely acting as an escort — they've no warlike intentions.' Tremendous relief washed over the room.

For the next hour or so, there was no further activity. Then around half past twelve, the voice of another officer could be heard as he moved through the building. 'Okay, Lads,' his voice boomed out authoritatively, 'we've received orders to vacate Liberty Hall. We're to transfer all war and other materials to the General Post Office.'

'What do we do for transport?' Ham inquired when the officer finally reached their room.

'We commandeer what we need from the traffic in the street,' the officer replied.

At that time the traffic was heavy in the lane that ran alongside the Liberty Hall. So it made life easier for the volunteers to stop suitable vehicles for the purpose of transporting war materials, gear and themselves to the General Post Office. When Ham and Bud got outside the building, the officer supervising the loading, recognized Ham's seniority from the badge on his cap. Indicating a group of fifteen volunteers standing around looking like spares, the officer said to Ham, 'You take charge here; give those lads their orders.'

'Certainly, sir.' Ham said, pleased to be doing something useful at last.

If he lived to be a hundred, Ham would never forget the expression of shock and disgust on the face of the driver whose lorry his group commandeered.

'A crowd of hooligans! Bloody gobshites! That's what yis are!' he shouted at them. Then tried to drive away. But the army of men blocking his path made it impossible; he'd no option but to surrender his lorry.

The officer who originally gave Ham instructions, arrived back. 'Your face isn't familiar,' he said to Ham. 'What unit are you with?'

'The Kimmage Garrison, Sir.'

'Oh, you should find them at the G.P.O.'

Ham split his group into two sections. He delegated Bud to supervise the group carrying the arms and ammunition from the building while he himself stayed behind with the second group supervising the stripping of the lorry, seeing to it that the boxes being removed were stacked into a nice, tidy pyramid on the pavement.

Meantime the hapless driver looked on in disbelief, and anger. 'Yis won't get away with this,' he yelled. 'The company'll sue yis right, left and center.'

As soon as the lorry was empty, the two groups joined forces heaving heavy arms and ammunition on to it. With that done, the volunteers climbed aboard. The lorry was now ready to take off.

The next task was to find a driver. Ham didn't drive. All along he'd taken it for granted that there would be at least one driver among the group, but not one of them, including Bud, had a notion about how to drive. Now he had the unenviable task of finding a driver elsewhere, which meant approaching the officer in charge. He felt terrible. It went against the grain for Ham to have to bother an officer with a petty problem the likes of this one. As a leader, he should be able to solve it himself. Wasn't that what leadership was about?

Bud noticed Ham's grim expression. 'Having problems?' he asked him. 'Anthin I can do to help?'

'I can't believe that among seventeen of us we haven't one driver, Ham told him, 'and I just hate having to approach the powers-that-be to get one.'

'You definitely can't do it yourself?'

'Never been in a car in my life.'

Bud could well understand Ham's feelings. It would be a terrible come-down for him now if he had to admit he couldn't drive. 'Well, I have been behind the wheel a few times,' Bud conceded limply. 'But nothing as big as that yoke. I never really learnt to drive.'

But sure that's great!' A look of supreme relief washed over Ham's face at the thought of solving the problem without fret or fuss. 'At least you've an idea about the procedure.'

Despite his total lack of driving skills, Bud decided this was no time to be making bones about it. 'Arrah, sure I might as well have a go anyways,' he said, climbing into the driver's seat, taking over the controls. 'Hold on to yer hats, lads,' he shouted gleefully to the volunteers in the back.

Feeling extremely grateful to Bud, Ham sat tall in the seat beside him. It was important that the lads in the back got the impression that he had complete confidence in his driver.

It was a rough start. As Bud pushed and shoved the gears he was inclined to let the clutch out too fast causing the engine to stall and cut out. Eventually he managed to coordinate the gear and the clutch and got the lorry moving, except that it lurched forward in a frog-leap missing a car by inches. The incident provoked an ear-splitting volley of horns — an unequivocal protest against the dirty *eejit* driving the lorry that was buck lepping all over the street. Needless to say, the jarring sound made Bud more flustered than ever; he kept repeating the same mistakes.

'Calm down, take it easy, you're doing fine,' Ham assured him. When there was a good solid break in the traffic, Ham told Bud, 'Right, now it's all right to go.' This time Bud let the clutch out slowly. Thankfully the lorry moved forward nice and smoothly.

Tensed out of his mind, Bud clung to the steering wheel like it was his life line. 'Pray to the Lord,' he muttered, 'we don't have any stops, because, by Jesus! t'would be the mercy a God if I'd ever got this yoke into gear again.'

By now they were halfway up Abbey Street slowly catching up on the motley convoy advancing on the General Post Office. Togged out as the volunteers were in ordinary clothes and traveling in ordinary lorries, vans and big expensive cars, the convoy attracted little or no attention from the pubic. Until Ham's lorry turned the corner into Sackville Street. (Now O'Connell Street.)

Suddenly there was a burst of cheering in the back. 'Hooray! Hooray! Hooray! Up the Republic!'

It came from the volunteers. There before their eyes was a sight they thought they could only dream about—THREE TRICOLOUR FLAGS - flying over the General Post Office. Some waved their arms in jubilation, some, too overcome with emotion, were silent. Ham felt a prickling sensation behind his eyes; before he could stop them the tears were trickling down his face. Looking sideways at Bud, he could see, midst his fumbling and foostering with the gears, Bud was similarly affected, surreptitiously whacking the tears away with the back of his hand.

Ham's lorry followed the convoy into Sackville Street. On the corner of Abbey Street a working-man recognized the volunteers. He cheered wildly as the lorry lurched and jerked its way across Sackville Street. Waving his cap he shouted, 'Good men, the best of luck to yis! Give it to the British bastards!'

Following the van ahead, the lorry eventually entered Prince's Street at the side of the General Post Office, then turned right into the lane behind it. Here volunteers were busy unloading ammunition from other vehicles, carrying it through a back door into the Post Office building. After giving a hand with emptying their lorry, Ham and Bud entered the Post Office. It was a hive of activity; ten times better organized than Liberty Hall. Members of both the volunteers and the brotherhood were present. Some volunteers were neatly attired in trim gray-green uniforms with soldierly caps on their heads; they were armed with service rifles and automatic pistols. The majority of the volunteers, however, were attired like Ham and Bud in everyday garb, crossed and inter crossed with shoulder straps and armed with shot guns or miniature rifles. Their left arms sported shiny yellow bands as distinctive badges.

The chief activity in the Post Office appeared to be the breaking of windows and the filling of mailbags with coal, nails, paper and any rubbish to hand to form makeshift sandbags. Some of the windows were barricaded with wax effigies taken from the Waxworks Show in Henry Street—King George the Fifth, Queen Mary and Kitchener were pushed into the windows. For Ham and Bud, the most comforting sight was their Commander, George Plunkett. He welcomed them and told them to join their comrades in the Main Hall. It was a happy reunion.

'What's going on?' Ham asked Paddy Caulwell.

'The story going round is apparently a lot of the battalions received no word from their officers. As a result, most of the companies didn't come out. Well, after reading Eoin MacNeill's Press Notice in yesterday morning's newspapers canceling the maneuvers, is it any wonder the leaders and volunteers were convinced that the show was off.' Paddy's lips twisted cynically. 'But the fight is on despite the mighty poor turn out.' Rolling his eyes, he added, 'To tell ye nothing but the truth, as I see it, total confusion seems to be the order of the day.'

'We got the same impression down at the Liberty Hall,' Ham told him.

'The Garrison did assemble there originally along with Plunkett,' Paddy said. 'A short while afterwards the order came through to march on the General Post Office.' Paddy's chest expanded with pride. 'Believe it or not, the Kimmage Garrison was the vanguard of the takeover of the G.P.O.'

'God, I'm sorry I missed that,' Ham said, feeling cheated. 'But it appears to have gone all right?'

'Oh, the takeover of the Post Office went smoothly enough,' Paddy answered. 'T'was them premises they seized as look-out posts that gave all the trouble.'

'What premises?'

'The Hotel Metropole next door, the Imperial Hotel opposite, Hopkins and Hopkins Jewelry Store beside the Bridge, Lawrences Toy Emporium in Upper Sackville Street, to mention but a few.' Paddy's eyes crinkled with amusement, 'Well, who in their right mind wants their premises taken over and pressed into service for war purposes?'

'So there was no class of opposition from the British?' Ham said.

'No, theory is that most of the British hierarchy and the Army Brass are away enjoying themselves at the Fairy House Races. We caught 'em napping, so to speak. So far we've been lucky.'

Just then the silence was broken by the distant sporadic rattle of rifle fire. 'Coming from the Liberty Hall,' Paddy said. 'Seems yis only got outa there in time.'

There were further rattles of long drawn-out rifle fire which seemed to fade into reports around the city. Answering Ham's inquiring look, Paddy announced, 'Coming from Dublin Castle.' (The seat of British rule in Ireland.) He appeared to be unusually *au fait* with where the different volleys were coming from.

The Commandant in charge, a slight, spare figure of a man in a green uniform, wearing the military cap complimented by the large badge, stood up on a counter in the main hall and addressed the volunteers.

'For those of you just arrived, I've an announcement,' he said. 'Today at twelve noon an Irish Republic was proclaimed by Patrick Pearse from the front of this building.' He pulled a piece of paper from his pocket. 'Here are some of his words:

'In the name of God and the dead generations from which she receives her old tradition of nationhood, Ireland, through us, summons her children to her flag and strikes for her freedom.''

The Commandant bowed his head for a moment, then continued. 'Communication with other positions are precarious and perhaps in less than an hour we may be in action.'

'Have we a ghost of a chance?' Ham whispered to Paddy.

'Aye,' Paddy said, 'of funerals and glory!'

It seemed the commandant's predictions about being in action were correct because shortly afterwards, a party of Lancers, came from behind the Parnell Monument at full gallop down Sackville Street.

'Hold your fire.' The order was bellowed in the main hall. This was followed by a fusillade ringing out from the roof of the Post Office and the look-out premises. It seemed to take the Lancers by surprise. Still they returned fire, concentrating on the 'look-out buildings' and the volunteers in the street on their way to the G.P.O: bullets splattered at the feet of thirty or so of them. The barrage coming from the buildings, however, convinced the Lancers they were outnumbered and they wheeled around to retreat, leaving four of their dead behind.

The volunteers' first taste of victory was short-lived because during the lull that followed the bodies of a number of volunteers — some dead, some casualties - involved in the fighting in the street, were carried up to the makeshift hospital in the Sorting Room on the second floor. Here the Cumann na Mban nurses had set up a dressing station.

In the street stray bullets smashed the windows of some of the shops; it was an opportunity not to be missed by Dublin's poor. They swarmed into Sackville Street from side streets, looting goods from shops with smashed windows, taking everything and anything they could lay hands on. Some made their way into Clery's Department Store whose windows had suffered the same fate. From their vantage point in the Post Office opposite Clerys, volunteers could see the looters filling sacks with all sorts of merchandise. They saw 'shawlie women' carrying and wearing fur coats. Also, a few men bent under the weight of great bales of materials. One man walked off wearing the tails part of a dress-suit carrying a bag of golf clubs. There was hair-pulling and snatching of sacks and a series of punch-ups.

'Dublin's poor are having a ball,' someone quipped. However, the leaders were not so good-humored about it.

'They've got to be stopped,' Sean MacDermott said. 'They're

bringing disgrace on the first days of the Republic.' He lead a unit of volunteers across the street to disperse them. But their pleas fell on deaf ears until MacDermott ordered the volunteers to fire three volleys over the looters' heads. The street emptied fast for the moment. But the looting continued throughout the rest of the week.

While the lull lasted, Ham told his comrades, 'In case you don't know, there's food and drink available in the room where they have the makeshift hospital.' Then with a wink, he added, 'If you're lucky, you might even get a bottle of Guinness.'

As nightfall came creeping in, a distinctive looking volunteer in a bright green uniform, piercing eyes and pointed mustache, moved among the men telling them that no British attack was expected that night.

'Who's yer man?' Ham asked Paddy.

'The O'Rahilly,' Paddy answered. 'He was dead against going ahead, but he's 'in' all the same.' The O'Rahilly joined MacDermott and Clarke.

'My sources tell me that despite little resistance at the Castle we failed to take it,' he said to them.

'Unfortunately, our intelligence got it wrong,' MacDermott answered. 'They were convinced the Castle was the stronghold most heavily guarded, that we'd suffer too many casualties.'

'Instead of which we could easily have taken it.'

'Put it down to misinformation,' Clarke said wearily. 'Seems to be the story of this rising — misinformation!'

The O'Reilly spoke in low tones, 'Another source tells me the British army are swarming up from the Curragh, plus there's a load of artillery on its way from Athlone.' There was no denying his despondency. 'But the big trouble is the country has not risen.'

'Is it any wonder,' MacDermott declared. 'Our people must've been totally confused; first, reading in Saturday's newspaper about the failure of the arms landing in Kerry on Good Friday and Casement (the organizer's) subsequent arrest. Then on its heels comes O'Neill's notice in Sunday's newspapers canceling the maneuvers.'

The O'Rahilly shook his head. He was sad, bewildered and disillusioned. 'Because of the terrible muddle of orders,' he said, 'only half the Dublin Brigade came out. Tomorrow the British will hold us in an iron grip. But our orders are to hold out as long as the building lasts.'

Soon darkness fell. Some of the volunteers dropped into an uneasy sleep.

Chapter II

Jane

In the year 1871, the O'Dwyer Family Dairy was one of the first and one of the finest premises to open its doors in Parnell Street (round the corner from Sackville Street.) Later, in its heyday, Parnell Street became a Mecca for shoppers in the city of Dublin. Situated North of the River Liffey, the dairy was widely known for its low prices and good value. So, apart from the steady trade provided by the locals, people came from far and near to avail of its many bargains. Another of the dairy's attractions was the late hours it kept; up to midnight, shoppers could always be sure of finding its doors open for business. In fact, between eleven and twelve at night it wasn't unusual to find the place jam-packed with customers because at this hour, perishable food was offered at half-price to people who could afford to pay, and free to the tenement-dwellers who lived close by. The dairy did more than its share for the poor of the city of Dublin.

In 1892, Mary Campbell, originally from County Louth, married the then proprietor John O'Dwyer and took on the duties of wife, mother and helper in the dairy. Then after fourteen years of marriage and the bearing of seven children, Mary went through the anguish of losing John when he died suddenly from pneumonia, handing her the torch of responsibility for running the business and rearing the family — one boy, Peter, the eldest, and six girls: Bridget, Nancy, Jane, Lily, Jody and Eileen — who ranged in age from thirteen down to two. Then because life hadn't dealt Mary a hard enough blow, the reading of the Will after the funeral revealed some shocking facts about her husband: he was a gambler and a big spender; worst of all, he had bequeathed to her a multiplicity of large debts — a millstone that would nearly destroy her and the family in the future.

The following years saw Mary wrestle with crisis after crisis trying to keep the roof over the family's head. It was a grueling challenge, like pushing a boulder up a mountain that kept crashing down. Yet somehow, Mary's stubborn determination helped her surmount the most intractable of obstacles. She was a survivor. Of course, had she not had John's debts, life could have been a lot easier: for instance, she could have engaged the services of a second young woman to help her in the dairy. Instead, she had to settle for just the one young one to mind the children while she slogged away in the dairy, standing on her feet some days for as long as sixteen hours. Be it midnight or otherwise, as long as the customers came, the doors of the dairy remained open. As a catholic and a daily communicant, Mary's most pressing mission in life was to pay off John's debts. It took three long, back breaking years.

As soon as the debts were paid off, Mary's business began to show a small profit, which made it possible to engage a second young woman to assist her in the dairy. Now, somewhat relieved of the full-time drudgery of selling over the counter, Mary began to explore ideas about expanding the business. She extended the line of dairy produce, offering a bigger, better and more expensive range at very competitive prices. This brought in the wealthier customers. Gradually the dairy began to show a tidy profit. Then one day when an affluent customer complained that it was impossible to get good quality milk in the city of Dublin, Mary had a brain wave.

Her Uncle Tom and Aunt Maggie in County Meath were the proud owners of a prize dairy herd whose milk was considered the best in the County. Recently their daughter, Nora, on a visit to the city to buy her trousseau, dropped in to see her cousin Mary. Nora was a sweet, gentle girl, frank and open and full of chat. During their discourse Mary learnt that in recent months Nora's parents' business had suffered a big setback: local farmers had lowered the price of milk, and because they couldn't afford to do likewise, the demand for their 'special' milk had decreased substantially. Frequently surpluses had to be dumped. Thinking she might be doing them a favor, while doing herself a service, Mary wrote a letter to her aunt and uncle. In it she explained a business venture she had in mind which could possibly benefit both of them.

What it boiled down to was this: *Would they consider letting her have a supply of their famous milk to sell in her dairy?* If they agreed to the arrangement, it would involve putting churns of milk on the train to Dublin each morning and collecting the empty churns each evening. She'd been in touch with the Broadstone Railway Station and they could take deliveries. At her end, she'd need to hire a horse-drawn milk dray and a driver. In conclusion, she stressed that she was prepared to pay top price for the milk and would cover all extraneous expenses. Not wanting to betray Nora's trust, she made no mention of their financial straits.

A short time afterwards, Aunt Maggie, Mary's mother's youngest sister (the only surviving member of that family) paid Mary a visit. The few times Mary had occasion to be in Maggie's company in the past, she found her a stiff, pompous woman with a cutting tongue, who made a big issue out of doing anything for anyone. On this occasion she was no less pompous nor difficult.

'If it was up to meself and Tom,' she said in her shifty way, the gimlet eyes scouring the parlor making sure they missed nothing, 'you could have all the milk you want.' She paused, 'But, ye see, now with the pair of us — meself and Tom — getting on in age, we have to depend more and more on Sean to do the work. He's a lazy hulk!' There was venom in her voice. 'It's all we can do to get him outa the bed in the mornings to do our own chores, and poor Tom is only crucified with the lumbago trying to cope.'

'Did you discuss the scheme with Sean at all?' Mary ventured to ask timorously.

'We did,' Maggie shook her head gloomily. 'Of course, he was very interested, particularly if it means making more money. But to get him to do the work — that's the problem; he's unreliable entirely, continually making promises he never keeps. Tom and I fully agree t'would be the rock we'd perish on were we to hand the farm over to him; we're determined he won't inherit till he starts acting responsibly.'

Mary suspected the war had started between the parents and the son about who was in charge. Maggie was no chicken; she must be now pushing seventy. However, knowing Maggie, she would be reluctant to relinquish the reins of power to the next generation, who happened to be Sean. (The three younger boys had emigrated and Nora, the youngest, was now about to be comfortably married.) Anyway, no matter how hard the work, wasn't it traditional for Maggie's generation to want to be in control until the day they dropped. Mary once overheard Maggie say at a relative's funeral, 'As long as there's breath in my body, I'll never be a visitor in my own home.'

More to the point was the damper Maggie was putting on Mary's cherished dream today; it was a crushing blow. A look of hopelessness washed over her face. Strangely, Maggie noticed it. Even more strange was the slight softening effect it had on her. After further hemming and hawing, her voice, though rasping with sarcasm, sounded a little more positive, 'Well, I suppose there's always the chance Sean might smarten up and surprise us all by making a success of the job.'

Her words gave Mary a smidgen of hope, enough to muscle up the courage to say, 'Sure if Sean's as interested as you say, why don't we give him the benefit of the doubt?'

Maggie's voice was now sugar-coated. 'Mary, you must know how much I admire the way you managed to keep the business afloat since John died, working your fingers to the bone. And needless to say, I'm only too anxious to do all I can to help you.' There was a pause while she weighed up the pros and cons further. 'You're probably right,' she said, sounding more decisive. 'I'll talk to Sean. I suppose he is entitled to the chance to prove himself.'

Three weeks passed without a word from Aunt Maggie and Mary had more or less given up all hope, when her cousin, Sean, middle-aged, tall, fat with a high color, paid her a visit. He sounded really enthusiastic about the scheme, wanted it to go ahead. More important, he wanted to be part of it. At first, remembering Maggie's derisive remarks, Mary was inclined to be non-committal. But Sean was so forthcoming and charming as he discussed the details from his point of view, it occurred to Mary that whatever about his shortcomings, today she was dealing with an altogether different Sean from the one his mother described. He asked numerous intelligent questions, showed enormous interest in Mary's answers and made suggestions about some vital things that needed to be done at her end; things that hadn't even crossed her mind. Then when Mary brought him to see the outhouse where the horse and dray would be housed, he noticed the dampness immediately and was quick to point out that the roof needed to be repaired.

'The condition this place is in,' he said jocularly, 'ye couldn't be after asking a poor horse to inhabit it.' Tracing his hands around the moldy walls, he added, 'First and foremost, you'll have to dry out the place.'

'So I get the roof repaired, how can the drying out be done?'

'Well, if it was my problem,' Sean said, 'as soon as the roof is fixed, I'd put an oil heater in here for a couple of days. Then I'd cover the floor with lots of good, quality, dry hay. (After the heater's been removed, of course.)' His eyes were smiling. 'That should do the trick.'

'Any other ideas or suggestions?' Mary asked.

'Yes, the door needs widening to let the dray in.'

Finally, when they finished going over all the arrangements, Sean surprised Mary even further by asserting, 'It'll take me about three weeks to get things up and running my end. How about yourself, Mary?' he asked. 'Do you think that'll be enough time for you to get yourself organized?'

'Perfect.'

Mary wasted no time getting a carpenter to do the jobs on outhouse roof and the door opening. Meanwhile, she decided to lease the horse and dray, rather than buy them. A lingering doubt still remained about Sean's reliability. However, three weeks later, to her enormous surprise and relief, Sean came through with flying colors. On the arranged Monday morning, not only did the milk arrive on time at Broadstone Station, but Sean himself accompanied it, making sure everything went smoothly. From that day forward there hadn't been a hitch in the deliveries.

But there was one problem. As soon as Dubliners discovered O'Dwyer's fine quality milk, they came in droves to buy it. By midday each day the milk was completely sold out. Mary now realized this could well be her 'golden nest egg.' She wondered if she could talk Sean into increasing the milk supply? Would the promise of extra money ever be enough to persuade him?

Leaving Bridget, now a young teenager, to stand in for her in the shop with Marie, the shop girl, Mary made the trip by bus on a Sunday to her aunt and uncle's farm in County Meath. On arrival she found Maggie and Tom on their own. Sean was missing. After exhausting the small talk with the cups of tea and the homemade scones, Mary eventually got round to the reason for her visit. Accentuating her need for the extra milk, she said, 'You've no idea how many customers I have to disappoint daily; they're even coming in from the suburbs to buy O'Dwyer's special milk.'

Before Tom could say a word, Maggie jumped in. 'It's out of the question!' she said aggressively, clearly demonstrating who ruled the roost in that house. 'T'would mean we'd have to increase the herd.' Tom tried to interject, but Maggie bulldozed through his every attempt to speak. 'Meself and himself are much too old to be taking on all that extra work.'

'But I thought Sean was looking after things for me?' Mary said, adding appreciatively, 'And a great job he's doing too.'

'Aye, while he neglects all our work.' Maggie's face contorted like she was sucking a lemon.

'Ah, now Maggie,' Tom intervened, 'don't be so hard on the lad; he's working his heart out. There's just so much he can do.' Tom spoke with quiet intensity. 'And I'm not exactly an invalid.'

'That's the trouble,' Maggie retorted. 'You're heading for an early grave.' The dirge continued, 'Tell me what's to become of me when you pass on and I'm left to fend for myself with that pair?'

At this point, the pair in question — Sean and his fiancee, Siobain, a fine, strapping, good-looking, country girl, quite a bit younger than Sean — arrived.

To his mother's chagrin, Sean made a great fuss of Mary. After introducing her to Siobain, he asked, 'What brings you to these parts, cousin Mary?'

Before Mary could answer, Maggie butted in, 'She's wants us to double her supply of milk, but I told her it's impossible.'

'Why so?' Sean asked.

'T'would mean increasing the herd; t'would be much to much work for your father.'

'But I'm looking after Mary's interests,' Sean asserted.

'So while you look after Mary's interests, your father has to work overtime doing your chores. Not to mention my back —I t's nearly broke coping with the work you should be doing.'

'Well, now, all that's going to change,' Sean said with a broad grin. Then sounding quite formal, added, 'Siobain and myself have an announcement to make.' He paused before taking the plunge. 'We've set the date.'

Maggie looked like she was about to have a seizure, but then she suddenly pulled herself together and assumed a puzzled expression. 'Date?' What date?' she exclaimed. It was obvious she was trying to save face.

'The date of our wedding,' Sean said. 'It's all arranged. The wedding is to take place the tenth of next month.' Maggie's face fell a foot. 'So when Siobain moves in here,' Sean continued undaunted, 'it should reduce everybody's work load.' He pointed to Maggie, 'Yours in particular, Mother; you'll be able to put your feet up and take things aisy.'

'Yes, of course, Maggie, Siobain added, grinning overly from ear to ear. 'Sure I'm big and strong and so used to doing the farm work at our own place.'

For the first time in her life Maggie was lost for words; the wind was taken completely out of her sails.

Sean then turned to Mary. 'Cousin Mary,' he said, 'don't worry you can have your extra milk. I'll see to everything.' He sounded masterful and in charge.

One didn't have to be a genius to guess why; the genial wink his father bestowed on him unbeknownst to Maggie was now explained. But now it was time to drink the health of the engaged couple, so Tom produced the customary bottle of whiskey.

While drinking the toast, of course, Maggie had to have the last word. 'Apart altogether from the herd,' she said, 'isn't it their fodder — County Meath's lush, green pasture land — that makes the milk so good.' There was much truth to it.

Now that all the arrangements were in place, Mary would need another horse and dray to carry the extra milk. She decided the time had come to buy them rather than lease them. It meant getting a loan from the bank. Shivers ran up and down her spine at the thought of approaching the bank manager with such a request. After all, she was a woman and her place (as she was reminded so often growing up) was in the kitchen, not at the Bank looking for a substantial loan. She could just picture the bank manager's eyebrows shooting up in surprise and disbelief when she made her request. A woman looking for a loan! It was unheard of! Preposterous! Didn't she realize that acquiring loans was the irrefutable prerogative of the male species? Wouldn't this request of hers be considered an encroachment on that sacrosanct financial arena which was exclusively theirs? Yet unless she obtained a loan, wouldn't all the hard work she'd put into organizing the extra milk be for nothing? Ah well, Mary said to herself in the mirror, as she adjusted the veil on the new hat getting ready to meet the demon bank manager, nothing ventured nothing gained.

As she entered the bank manager's office Mary's legs felt like putty.

'Well, now Mrs O'Dwyer,' the manager began after Mary was seated, 'how can I help you?' His voice sounded affable; Mary wondered if it would be quite so affable when she'd finished making her request. God! How she wished this ordeal was behind her. Trying to make it as brief as possible, Mary explained about what she termed her 'nest egg'— O'Dwyer's special milk — outlining her ideas for the future. She couldn't believe her ears when the manager said, 'You'll be wanting a loan, I expect?' still sounding quite affable.

'Yes,' she replied in a low tone, her eyes downcast afraid to meet his for fear of the rejection she would see in them. When he didn't answer for a couple of seconds, Mary rushed on, 'I know it isn't the bank's policy to give loans to women, but maybe you could bend the rules a little in this instance?'

The Manager took a deep breath, then spoke, 'In the name of God, Mrs. O'Dwyer,' he said, 'how could I possibly refuse a loan to a customer the likes of yerself?' He was affability itself. 'And you after paying off all those debts in such record time.' Rustling through his papers, until he found the right one, he said, 'Isn't your statement showing a fierce healthy balance.'

As she signed the papers he put in front of her sanctioning the loan, Mary could hardly believe it had been so easy. 'There you are now,' the manager said after she'd signed, 'you can put all your plans into action, and there's plenty more where that came from.' At the door, the manager shook Mary's hand warmly. 'Isn't it meself should be asking for advice from yerself, Mrs. O'Dwyer,' he said with a glint in his eye. 'Sure aren't you one of the shrewdest business women I ever met.'

The increase in the supply of milk met with the same fate as before. Word spread like wildfire about O'Dwyer's special milk and the rush on it was greater than ever. By early afternoon each day the churns were empty. Despite their disappointment, however, seldom did customers leave the shop empty-handed. So, if nothing else, the milk proved a godsend for trade.

Now at forty-nine, considering her many years of toil and turmoil, Mary was still a handsome woman; she was tall, ram-rod straight, with a face that was lean and handsome. Her dark hair streaked with white, rather than making her look older, tended to make her look distinctive. And though she gave the impression of hardness, it was well known that beneath that tough exterior was an overly generous heart.

As far as O'Dwyer's Family Dairy was concerned, this Easter Bank Holiday Monday would be the same as any other day: the dairy would open as usual after the milk drays arrived from The Broadstone Station at seven a.m. and would remain open until midnight. The only difference between bank holidays and other days was the two shop girls had the day off. Thankfully, bank holidays didn't happen too often, because shortage of staff meant longer hours and more work for Mary and her eldest daughter Bridget — now a full time employee. However, there would be a complication this Bank Holiday — Bridget was a patient.

On Holy Thursday she complained of a very sore throat and had symptoms of a high temperature. The doctor was called, he diagnosed a streptococcal throat and pronounced her unfit for work for at least five days. Mary would have no alternative now but to get the younger daughters to assist her in the shop on the Monday; she couldn't cope on her own. And the question of not opening didn't arise; not opening would be totally contrary to the dairy's tradition of being open all day, every day, all year round. The only exceptions being Christmas Day, from midday onwards and Good Friday, from midday until four o'clock — the first three hours out of respect for the crucified Jesus dying on the cross, the last hour to allow everyone to attend the three o'clock Church ceremonies of the Stations of the Cross. Good Friday, the one and only day in the year when shops, pubs, cinemas, restaurants, theaters, offices, everywhere, closed down, was the ideal day for Mary to solicit the help she would be needing on the Monday.

As anticipated, she found the three older daughters, our Nancy, Jane and Lily (home from their boarding school in Drogheda for the Easter holidays) lounging in the parlor, stranded, killing time until three o'clock, when they would wend their way, as a family, up to Dominick Street Church to attend 'the stations.'

Unceremoniously Mary announced, 'I'll need each one of the

three of you to do a five-hour shift in the shop on Easter Monday.' She could tell by their expressions her request was anything but popular. It came as no surprise: she was well aware of their lack of gra for working in the shop. Nevertheless she'd no qualms about making this request: when all was said and done, wasn't it the shop that gave them their high standard of living, that dressed them better than other children, that fed them better, that paid their school fees? Anyway, now that they were in their teens, it was time they started pulling their weight with the work. 'Who ever's on first,' she said matter of factly, 'will start at seven a.m.' Then as she was leaving she turned back, 'I'll leave it to yourselves to work out the details of the shifts — remember, three shifts, five hours each.'

Their mother had hardly left the room when our Nancy, the eldest of the three, started to carp and quibble. 'I can't do any of it,' she said, 'I've a date with Larry.' Then using the whining voice she adapted when things didn't suit her, she continued, 'He can't get to the city till Sunday night, which means I can't see him till Monday. If I don't see him then, it'll be the Summer holidays before we see each other again.'

Our Nancy, was called 'our' to differentiate between herself and their sister-in-law, Nancy Pete, married to their brother, Peter. With her lush blond hair, china blue eyes and trim, shapely figure, eighteen-year-old our Nancy was considered the beauty of the family. At the end of next term she would finish school. She was in love. She'd met Larry the previous Christmas at a party given by a friend. Unknown to her mother, she'd been walking out with him during the holidays. But Larry's recent transfer to Mullingar meant he could only get to the city at weekends. So the romance was suffering a bit of a set back.

'What about the early morning shift?' Jane asked our Nancy.

'We've planned to go to the Fairy House Races,' our Nancy's whine continued. 'If we're to be there on time, we'll have to leave early.' As only she could, our Nancy managed to look quite distraught. 'Well, you know how packed the buses and trams are going to Fairy House on an Easter Monday.'

If our Nancy's aim was to make her sisters feel guilty even discussing the subject, she was succeeding. They put up no argument. It would now be up to Jane and Lily to work out the hours between them. Not only that, they'd have to think up a suitable lie to explain Nancy's absence to the mother. Despite differences that might arise between them, it was an accepted code among the siblings that nobody snitched to the mother.

'I suppose t'will be the same old lame excuse that she's made plans to see a girlfriend for the day,' Lily remarked mockingly after our Nancy left the room.

Of all the girls in the family, Lily, at sixteen, was probably the plainest. Tall and big boned, with what she herself described as 'a big platter face with dark, stringy hair,' her redeeming features were her tender, bronze-colored eyes. When her face lit up with a smile she could look extraordinarily handsome.

Lily paused, thinking about the ordeal facing them on Monday. 'Jesus!' she spluttered resentfully, 'I hate that bloody shop! The work is pure slavery.'

'You took the words right out of my mouth,' Jane answered. 'But still, if we don't do it, Bridget will probably get out of her sick bed to do it.'

Unlike Lily, Jane was coltish. She was seventeen; a year older than Lily. With her dark, laughing eyes and a face that was framed with a riot of dark, wavy hair, Jane was now maturing into a real beauty.

'Ach, I suppose you're right,' Lily simmered down. 'Poor Bridget! She has my complete sympathy; it's awful the way Mother leans on her.'

'Isn't she lucky! She'll soon be out of it for good,' Jane said. Recently Bridget had confided in her two sisters, that if it wasn't for the fact that she and Michael were getting married next year when he got his law degree, she couldn't stick another minute slaving in that sweat shop. Jane continued despondently, 'T'will be our turn then when we finish school.'

'Not if I can help it,' Lily was most emphatic. 'The first man who says 'will you marry me?' I'll say Yes, even if he has a face on him like the back of a bus.'

Jane had to laugh. Lily was under the impression that marriage was the surefire cure for everything that ails you. 'Tell you what,' Jane said, getting back to the immediate problem, 'I'll do half the day starting at seven in the morning until say three o'clock. Then maybe you could do it from then onwards until whatever time Mother tells you to knock off. How'd that suit you?'

'Doesn't!' But I suppose I've no option,' Lily's big moon face registered extreme annoyance. 'That Nancy wan! God damn her!' she said angrily. 'She always manages to worm her way out of doing anything in the house or in the shop.'

'Isn't she *the lady*,' Jane said with a broad grin, 'We couldn't be asking her to dirty her hands.' Then laughing outright, 'Sure aren't you and I the two mugs.'

'True for you,' Lily said joining in the laughter.

On Easter Monday morning, Jane could well understand Bridget's feelings. You wouldn't get a minute to scratch yourself between the constant flow of customers and all that loose food that had to be weighed—tea, sugar, butter, margarine, cheese, flour, oatmeal, rice, corn flour, sago, tapioca—the list was endless. Every order had to be individually weighed. The people from the tenements were particularly difficult; depending on how much money they had to spend, they could order as little as two ounces of something. Then there was the milk and the buttermilk; that too had to be measured and poured into whatever containers the customers brought—jugs, cans, jars, bottles of every size and shape.

One thing was certain, Jane wasn't looking forward to the four weeks this coming summer when the staff took holidays and she'd have to fill in for them. She pushed the thought to the back of her mind; it was still months away. In a week's time there'd be the thrill of returning to school, to the things she loved most—the convent, the nuns, the music lessons. Herself and Sister Cecilia, her music teacher, had such a marvelous rapport, particularly when it came to ragtime, which Jane played deftly. The music lessons had become great fun since that day last year when Sister discovered Jane improvising 'Alexander's Ragtime Band' on the piano as she awaited her arrival. (She picked up the piece by ear after hearing it on the pantomime over Christmas.) Now routinely after each lesson Sister closed the windows in the Music Room and invited Jane to *let it rip*. 'Time to stir up dem decrepit, old bones with a bit of rhythm,' she'd say. Then to Jane's great rhythmic beat, while the beads clicked and clacked, Sister would tap out the footwork like a professional; holding up the skirts, swaggering the hips, twirling around, raising her arms with such abandonment, Jane would be in stitches laughing at her.

That Easter Monday morning there was a mad rush of people shopping early so as to get out and enjoy the sunshine. Then for a while the shop was relatively quiet. During the lull Mary decided to escape to her office at the back and sort out the cash flow. 'If you're rushed off your feet,' she told Jane before she disappeared, 'give me a shout.'

The job of counting the thousands of coins, putting them into bank bags, filling out the sheets was particularly arduous that day. It wasn't unexpected. Well, the dairy had been rather busy over the holiday. Along with that, having to fill in for Bridget meant Mary was behind with the banking business. Normally she did this job every evening, lodging the money the following morning. But this weekend was different, what with the Banks being closed for four days, not surprisingly, there was a huge glut of cash.

Around eleven o'clock, Mary appeared in the shop with the big black leather bag used for carrying the cash to the bank. It was absolutely bulging with coins and notes. 'I don't feel safe having all this cash in the house,' she said to Jane. 'Be an angel, hop round to the Post Office and lodge it for me.' Along with the bag, she handed Jane an envelope. 'Keep that separate from the bag,' she instructed, 'it contains the sheets and the Post Office pass book.'

Jane put the envelope safely into the pocket of her skirt. She was delighted to be getting out of the shop into the fresh air. However, outside the sun was unmercifully hot, beating down from a clear blue sky. She wished she'd left her cardigan behind. Then there was the bag full of money; God, it weighed a ton! Normally, Jane walked at a brisk pace, but not today, not carrying this load. Along with everything else, the fact that she had to keep passing the bag from one hand to the other every few minutes, was bound to attract attention. And because things weren't bad enough, at this particular moment, Parnell Street was deserted. (Probably on account of the shops being closed.)

An awful thought now prowled through Jane's mind: wouldn't it be quite within the realms of possibility that some strange man might jump out of a doorway, snatch the bag and disappear? She felt a knot tightening in her stomach. God! she thought, this is a terrible responsibility. What on earth was mother thinking about asking me to carry such a load of money on my own without an escort? Thank God, in Sackville Street there were lots of people around; it made her feel more secure. Nonetheless, though the Post Office was only about five hundred yards away, it felt like ten miles. Sweet Mother of God! she thought as she lumbered on, I can't wait to get rid of this money — the weight of it and the worry of it.

The nearest door of the Post Office was closed. That wasn't unusual on a bank holiday. Like their dairy, the post office was probably on a skeletal staff. She noticed the door on the other side was half-open. A crowd of about twenty people stood outside looking anxious and nervous. Jane inquired of one of the women at the door if they were queuing and when the answer was no, she pushed her way through the crowd to the half-open door. Here she was met by a young soldier carrying a rifle.

'Sorry!' he said, 'I'm afraid you can't come in. The Post Office isn't open for business today.' Behind him, inside, Jane could see armed men rushing around, and hear unintelligible orders being barked.

'But I've a lot of cash to lodge,' she said, her face showing the panic she was feeling. Sweet Jesus! she thought, I'll go crazy if I have to lug this load back to Parnell Street again. Out loud, she said to the soldier, 'The Post Office is always open on bank holidays.

Why is it closed today?'

'Because it's been taken over by the Irish Volunteers,' the soldier replied. 'You'd best be getting home immediately, Miss. You'd be far safer there.'

At this point, a middle-aged Dublin woman joined Jane, 'He's right, you know, Miss,' she said, 'there's no knowing what's going to happen here.' She lead Jane away from the door. 'These lads mean business.'

'Business?'

'Haven't they taken over the post office. I seen them with me very own eyes bringing in the guns and the ammunition.'

'But why?' Jane asked, baffled.

'Aren't they striking a blow for Irish freedom.'

Someone in the crowd started shouting, 'Up the Republic.'

Jane was beginning to get really annoyed. 'Where on earth are the police?' she asked. 'Why aren't they here doing their duty?' She was thinking, imagine these stupid Nationalists getting away with this?

'Their duty is it!' the woman laughed cynically. 'Weren't the police told in no uncertain terms if they as much as put a nose inside the door, they'd get their heads blown off.' She pointed to an elderly man in the crowd. 'That man over there, he knows all about it.'

The man overheard her remark. He joined them. He was very excited. 'Did ye see the three tricolor flags flying over the G.P.O.?' he asked Jane, his face glowing with pride.

'Can't say I did,' Jane answered indifferently. 'Besides, I couldn't care less what flag is flying over the G.P.O.' Now she sounded really annoyed. 'As far as I'm concerned those volunteers are making a damn nuisance of themselves.'

'No matter how ye feel at this moment, Miss,' the man said, 'I tell ye, this day — the day the rising began — will be a day Ireland won't forget in a hurry.'

Damn and blast those bloody volunteers! Jane thought as she staggered under the weight of the black bag trudging back through Sackville Street. Themselves and their stupid rising!

Coming up to the corner of Parnell Street, Seamus Moriarity, the publican's son from down the street, came from behind Jane and joined her. A cocky, pimply young fella a little older than herself, Seamus fancied himself as a great ladies man. Jane suspected he had designs on her on account of the way he acted on Sunday when he accompanied herself and Lily from Mass. The whole way home he'd flirted outrageously with her, trying to persuade her to have a date with him. 'Jesus above!' Jane burst out to Lily after he left, 'doesn't he have a great notion of himself.' Lily didn't answer. In fact, she looked quite grim and unhappy. Only then did it dawn on Jane that Lily herself had a crush on Seamus. She felt awful. Wasn't it bad enough that Lily had to suffer Seamus ignoring her without having to listen to him coaxing her sister to make a date with him. And, sure, Jane wouldn't have him for a wet Sunday.

Since then Jane decided to avoid Seamus like the plague; she wouldn't give him the light of day if she could help it. But today when he slapped her on the back and said 'how're ye, how're ye' she thought: A familiar face! Was it ever welcome! It didn't matter whose it was!

Seamus couldn't believe the change in Jane — she actually seemed pleased to see him. Walking along Jane was thinking, if he's ever to be turned off me, it'll be now. I must look a fright, with a face on me that's beetroot red, and the hair, so tacky with perspiration, looking like it hasn't been washed in weeks. No. Today she was definitely not at her best. Not that it bothered her one iota where Seamus was concerned.

Seamus was, as usual, impeccably dressed in a beautiful tailored suit, well-starched shirt, tasteful tie and shoes with a shine you could see your face in. One thing about Seamus, he always looked beautifully turned out. Jane wondered could it be this eejit's fine feathers that attracted Lily. As far as she herself was concerned, her ideal boyfriend would have to have an IQ that shone more than his shoes.

'You seem to be bowed down under the weight of that bag,' Seamus remarked.

'Oh, you noticed,' Jane smiled nervously.

'Give it here. I'll carry it,' Seamus said taking the bag out of her hand, then acting the clown pretending to fall over with the weight of it. 'What's in it? Rocks?'

'You guessed,' Jane laughed. Gosh, she thought, it's an almighty relief to get someone else to carry the load for a while. Changing the subject, Jane asked, 'Did you know the volunteers have taken over the General Post Office?'

'No, why would they do the likes of that?'

'It's a kind of protest, I think,' Jane answered.

'Strange,' Seamus said. He looked puzzled. 'So maybe the rumors are true after all.' He shook his head dispassionately. 'The poor eejits! That's one protest that'll get a short shift!'

In case Lily would be in the shop filling in for her, Jane tried to take the bag from Seamus when they reached his pub; the last thing she wanted was Lily to see them together. But Seamus insisted on being chivalrous seeing her right to the door. Thanks be to God there was no sign of Lily.

As soon as they reached the shop, Jane grabbed the bag out of Seamus' hand and with the abruptest 'good-bye and thanks for carrying the bag' dashed in the door, leaving him with his gob hanging open like a Dublin Bay herring's.

Chapter III

Peter

Peter O'Dwyer was the eldest and only son of Mary O'Dwyer. Broad-shouldered and just under six feet, this handsome young man of twenty-three years, with his soot-black hair, dark eyes and dark complexion bore a striking resemblance to the rest of the family. From his early years in the National school Peter was an inveterate reader, always seeking out books of serious content as opposed to the usual run of children's literature. Later as a border with the Dominican College, Newbridge (Mary's brother, Father Vincent — a teacher there — managed to get his nephew accepted at a token fee), Peter spent a lot of time in the school library devouring the classics. During vacation time as home, the family christened him *the book worm*. 'Sure there's no getting a word out of him,' they'd say, 'he might as well not be here, the way his head is always stuck in those books.'

After a couple of years in Newbridge, Peter demonstrated a flair for writing good essays, with the result that regularly the teacher asked him to read them out to the class. In the beginning, Peter was shy and diffident about the reading, but then the notion struck him that maybe he did have the potential to be writer after all. Though he invariably came first in English in the class, Peter's unpretentious nature prevented him from getting a swelled head. Not only that, he frequently helped classmates having trouble with their English preparation. However, it was his musical prowess that made him one of the most popular lads in the school. Many's the sing-songs he got going belting out Gilbert and Sullivan arias on the piano.

One day early in his final year, Father Quinn, Peter's English teacher, handed him a printed leaflet which gave details of a National Essay Competition. 'Why don't you capitalize on your writing, Peter,' he said, 'and enter one of your essays for that competition.'

Peter couldn't believe his good luck winning first prize, worth ten pounds — an absolute fortune. The win not only established his credibility as a writer, but lead to some of his articles being published in local magazines, thus yielding crucial financial assistance. To a young man who relied on his struggling Mother for every penny, the money was absolute mammon from heaven. More to the point was the fact that Peter was taking his first steps towards becoming a journalist — his chosen profession.

When Peter finished school as an honors student in June, 1911, little thinking about the consternation it would cause, he announced that he wanted to study journalism at Trinity College, Dublin. Anglo-Irish and Protestant, Trinity's reputation for producing celebrated Irish and English writers was legendary. But Peter was Catholic, and as such he couldn't be a student there without first obtaining permission from the Holy Father (The Pope) in Rome. It would be a long drawn-out process, with letters and references toing and froing between Dublin and Rome. And even after waiting months for the procedure to take its course, there was no guarantee that this permission would be granted.

These facts were related to Peter by a friend who'd gone through the whole bloody rigmarole the year before without success. So it would be a case of Peter hanging around maybe for months with nothing to do and, in all probability, the mother taking full advantage of the situation. He'd be herded into the family business, which was the last thing he needed. So, after much soul-searching and many arguments with the Mother about why he couldn't just bypass Rome, attend Trinity and get on with his career, his mother finally agreed to him taking his Diploma in the London College of Journalism.

After the sheltered, cosseted life Peter lead in Ireland under the ever watchful eye of his mother at home and the reverend fathers at school — an alter boy who once swung the censer for benediction — Peter's eventual discovery of London's Bohemian lifestyle couldn't be more of a contrast to his former life. At first the big novelty was not having to be accountable to anyone, even if he stayed out all night. Such freedom! Peter thought, it was the nearest thing to opening a window, letting fresh air into a mind that was stifled and stultified with rules and regulations. Slowly but surely Peter would discover a thrilling new world in London. This thrilling new world, however, didn't assert itself right away. First, Peter had to find his feet socially. Not an easy task when you're a stranger in a strange land.

On his first Saturday night, a group of six students, who, like himself, were away from home, invited Peter to accompany them on a night on the town. On first acquaintance the friends seemed friendly and sociable and Peter was glad to accept their invitation. It certainly beat going back to spend an evening in the dingy little terrace house in Shepherd's Bush where he had digs with his widowed English Aunt Elizabeth, whose husband — Mary's eldest brother — had been killed in the Boer War. Along with that, she was childless.

'Sure won't you be great company for your aunt,' Mary asserted after she'd arranged everything with the aunt through the mail. 'The poor unfortunate creature, she must be very lonely.' But like the saying goes: *the best laid plans of mice and men....*

Shortly after settling into his Aunt's house, Peter discovered she had no need whatsoever of his comfort. Wasn't she getting all she needed daily in the local pub. This was not to say that Peter had any complaints. His aunt was very conscientious and fervent about looking after his needs; making his bed, cleaning his room, doing his laundry, having a hot meal ready for him every evening. But it would appear while she cooked the meal, the gin got a great gait of going. By the time the meal was ready, the bottle was empty. With the meal served, it was time for the aunt to sprawl out on the sofa.

Then with open mouth and globs of saliva slithering down her chin, saturating her ample bosom, she'd raise the roof with snores that sounded the nearest thing to a chain saw.

The lads picked The Shakespeare pub, just beside the college as the watering hole. Within five minutes of entering that pub Peter knew he'd little or nothing in common with his friends or with the pub's clientele. They, the clientele, were a bookish clique of English bores with plummy accents; a coterie of pseudo-intellectuals who ventilated their endless lore of literature and poetry, whether anyone listened or not. And unless you were one of them, you couldn't get a word in edgeways. Peter's young friends, apparently dazzled by these phony scholars, hung on to their every word and syllable, lapping it up like it was a privilege to be in their company.

Not so Peter. To his mind these people were fakes. 'Spiffing and ripping' were the operative words; a book was either spiffing or ripping, a poem or person likewise. The words got completely on Peter's nerves.

On the second Saturday night, Peter tried to persuade his companions to go elsewhere so they could have some social discourse among themselves. But none of them wanted to change from 'The Shakespeare.' So he accompanied them hoping against hope it would be a different crowd. But no, it was the same crowd of stuffed shirts pontificating the same old literary refuse. What became the last straw for Peter that night was when one of the so-called poets started to recite Keats: 'My heart aches and a drowsy numbness pains my senses,' he recited dramatically, then stalled for seconds, apparently at a loss for the words.

'As though of hemlock I had drunk, or emptied some dull opiate to the drains,' Peter put in thinking he was helping out.

'Be gorra! An Oirish poet!' The so-called poet interjected in a phony Irish accent that oozed sarcasm. Doubtless, his remark was meant to deride the Irish and, of course, it evoked loud, guffaws from the others. Peter's face burned with embarrassment; he felt like crawling under a stone.

For the rest of the evening, the loud-mouthed, pompous arse-

63

holes (Peter's name for them) turned their backs on Peter totally ignoring him, concentrating their full attention on the wide-eyed students who thought they were so bloody marvelous. The idea of a thick, Oirish Paddy stealing their thunder evidently didn't sit well with them. One thing was certain: their manners left a lot to be desired.

After that second Saturday night Peter had enough. He decided to branch out on his own and seek pastures new. The following Saturday night he found The Diamond, a small pub a little ways further down the street from The Shakespeare. Despite the sly, laconic air of the regulars, the atmosphere was definitely more congenial. A memory stirred in Peter of the infamous Sunday afternoon the week before his schooldays ended, when himself and a gang of his classmates invaded a similar type of pub in the little town of Newbridge. That pub, too, was very congenial. But between the excitement of finishing school and the fact that the majority of them were unaccustomed to alcohol, they got very drunk and were capable of such obnoxious behavior as would incur the wrath the most patient of pub owners.

Practically frothing at the mouth, this angry Newbridge owner fell upon the offenders like a ton of bricks. 'I run an establishment befitting gentlemen here,' he bellowed at them. Then, to the intense relief of the clientele, he caught a couple of the smaller lads by the scruff of the neck and pushed them out through the entrance. After that he turned to the others, his face now blue with fury, 'Okay, the rest of you,' he barked, 'out, out this very minute and don't ever come back.'

But sure the craic was great.

'You new to this pub?' A friendly cockney accent asked Peter as he stood waiting for his glass of beer at the counter. The voice belonged to a friendly, middle-aged male Londoner standing beside him.

'How'd ye guess?'

'Haven't seen you here before.'

'Well, as it happens I am a stranger here. In fact, I'm a stranger to London.'

For a while they exchanged comments on the vagaries of the weather. Gradually, the man's two companions — very Cockney — joined in the conversation. When they heard Peter was new to London, they were full of advice.

A short while afterwards, Peter met Duncan (who would later become his best friend). Duncan arrived at the counter to get another pint. Pleasant featured with a shock of wild hair, Duncan was Scottish, friendly, articulate, witty and smiled a lot. Introducing himself to Peter, his handshake was strong, the palm warm and dry; Peter was immediately drawn to him. During the course of their conversation Peter discovered Duncan was a second year student with the London College of Journalism, and like himself, away from home. Straightaway, Peter knew they were kindred spirits. Duncan invited him to join a bunch of young people, students mostly, at a table in the corner. It was here that Peter discovered another dimension to Duncan — his art of storytelling. Peter couldn't decide whether it was Duncan's heather-drenched Scottish accent or the way he described things that made the telling of the story so hilarious.

'I'm glad you're enjoying it, Laddie,' Duncan said to Peter when he saw him laughing with the others. 'If I were to tell that yarn to those literary snobs above in The Shakespeare, t'would go down like a lead balloon, bringing forth lots of yawns.' Then he added with much sarcasm, 'however, you never know, with a bit of luck, they might even stretch to a humorless snigger. '

The remark boosted Peter's morale no end. No, he told himself, he hadn't imagined those incorrigible snobs in The Shakespeare. Here was someone else expressing the self same sentiments about those awful people. For someone like Peter given to loquacity, it was punishment in the extreme to have to keep his gob clamped shut for all those hours in that Shakespeare pub. It certainly had a terrible effect on his self esteem.

After a few more get-togethers, a strong kinship developed between Peter and Duncan. Peter discovered there was more to Duncan than his scintillating company and his flashing wit; for instance, he never tried to monopolize the conversation. He had a great way with people, drawing them out, asking them questions, more importantly, listening to their answers — qualities essential to a good journalist. Though Duncan would never know it, his friendship did a lot to restore Peter's confidence and self esteem.

The next time they met in The Diamond, Duncan slapped Peter on the back saying, 'Come on, Laddie, you're from Ireland — the land of the great storytellers — tell us an Irish yarn.' Surrounded by Duncan's collection of very amiable friends, Peter now felt confident enough to recount the story of his first incursion into a pub — the one in Newbridge. And though he wasn't in the same league as Duncan as a storyteller, he got lots of laughs.

One Monday night after Duncan returned from Glasgow where he'd attended his uncle's funeral, Peter and himself were having an unaccustomed drink on their own. They were really celebrating the fact that the uncle had left Duncan two hundred pounds in his will. As usual, Duncan was bubbling over with comical anecdotes about the funeral and the family. The pints were coming up fast.

'There am I,' he tells Peter, 'sitting on the lav upstairs in the mother's house with the trousers down round me ankles when in dashes this beautiful blond. Her head is down; she's in such a hurry to get to the John she's practically cutting a groove in the linoleum. The skirt is up and the knickers halfway down, before she realizes someone else occupies the seat. 'Jesus, Christ Almighty!' she screams at me, 'What the hell are you doing there?' She's now re-arranging her clothes as best she can. I was tempted to say, *I'm doing a hefty one,* but discretion being the better part of valor, I refrained.'

By now the two lads are doubled up with the laughter.

Duncan stopped long enough to regain his composure, then continued, 'Can't ye see what I'm doin, I says to her, I'm using me mother's lavatory. 'It's not your mother's lavatory,' says she, 'it's my lavatory.' Well you could have knocked me over with the proverbial feather. But I held my ground, I'd no option—wasn't the load ready to drop—and I assumed the best place to drop it was in the lav.'

By now Peter is in hysterics.

Duncan waits for him to stop laughing. 'How come it's your lav?'

I says to her, now that the load was comfortably in the bowl. 'These are my quarters,' says she. Since when? says I? 'Didn't your mother sub-let the upstairs to me,' says she, 'get to hell off that lavatory before I mess me drawers.' '

When Peter finally stopped laughing, he ordered another pint for the pair of them. It was their fourth. They were getting nicely sloshed.

Suddenly Duncan spontaneously came up with this great idea. 'Why don't we treat ourselves to a crawl of the Soho district tonight, Laddie?' Before Peter could throw in the word 'money,' Duncan was quick to reply, 'No need to worry about the money, Laddie, isn't it burning a hole in my pocket here this very minute.'

'You mean you got your inheritance in cash?'

'Out of an old sock under the mattress.'

'Beats Bannagher!' Peter took a fit of laughing. At the same time he wasn't too sure about this mad scheme of Duncan's He hesitated thinking about it.

Duncan butted in, 'From what I hear, it seems our education will never be complete, Laddie, until we've seen the sleazy side of London's night life.'

'Sleazy side?'

'Yeah, you know — the tits in tinsel bit.' Duncan laughed heartily.

'You mean naked ladies?' Peter's young bushy eyebrows shot up.

'Yeah. More or less.'

'What do you mean more or less?'

'Duncan rolled his eyes then suggestively drew his hand across his breast, then up between his legs. 'Well, I imagine that's where the tinsel comes in.' There was much merriment in his laughter. 'Covers all the 'you know what' areas!!!' His infectious laughter, got Peter going. He still wasn't a hundred per cent sure, however, but then quietly reasoned with himself, if I refuse to go, Duncan's bound to get the impression I'm insular and narrow-minded. As he weighed up the pros and cons, Duncan began to get impatient. 'Och, come on, Laddie,' he urged. ' How can we hope to be writers if we haven't seen life in the raw.' Obviously he couldn't wait to put a dent in his windfall. And of course he did have a point.

'Have you ever done it before?'

'No, but you know that American fellow, Hank, I think his name is?'

'The one they call the professor?'

'The very one. In the early days he filled me in on where to go and what to see in London. 'You ain't seen nothin, Buddy,' he says, 'till you've seen London's sleazy night life — you know all those fantastic clubs, shows and gambling joints in Soho.' Then he produces pen and paper an starts making a list. 'That's your card marked for you, Bud,' he says handing me the list. 'But if you're interested in a really, super show — one that'll have the hair standing up on the back of your neck — the one to see is at The Club Majestic.' Hank then pointed it out on the list and went on to give me directions about how to get there.'

'Ach, what have we got to lose?' Peter said. Having drained the fourth pint, emboldened by the Dutch courage, he was suddenly all agog to go. 'The worst that can happen is our minds might be broadened a bit.'

'You never know, laddie,' Duncan said with a mischievous grin, 'the experience could possibly help to embroider the old scribe; raise it to a higher plateau perhaps.'

They took a taxi to Soho. The first thing they noticed about the The Club Majestic were the illuminations; they were ten times brighter than any of the others. Then there were the pictures outside; though neither would admit it, they were quite shocked by them. Except for statues, never in their young lives had they seen the likes. God! Most of the women were naked or next to naked; bare bosoms all over the place, not a shred of tinsel where it was necessary. Topping off all this notoriety was the large brightly lit sign advertising, 'The Club Majestic — the best striptease in London.'

Duncan looked hard at Peter. 'Is it a bit much, do you think?' he said, his laughter sounding pretty hollow. Peter sensed he was getting cold feet.

It made two of them; Peter's feet were just as cold. He looked around. The place next door seemed much more modest; it was small and demure looking without all that garish, lighting. Even its name — The Pink Lady — was anything but showy.

'What about next door?' Peter suggested. 'It's less ostentatious and there's no sign of naked ladies.'

'Probably a high-class pub,' Duncan said. 'More our style.' Bouncing back, he added enthusiastically, 'Let's try it .'

'Why not,' Peter said. Now that naked women weren't involved, he felt more comfortable. 'Having ventured this far, t'would be a shame to turn back.'

The darkness inside The Pink Lady struck them as rather odd. Indeed, in the lobby where Duncan paid the cover charge of five shillings each (entitling each of them to one free drink) you could hardly see the hand in front of your face. After that to gain entrance to the pub proper, they had to pass through a pair of heavy, plush, black curtains.

Inside was small and intimate, it spelt bewitchment. A lot had to do with the dimness of the lighting, its sole supply coming from candles in pink glass globes on the tables. Then there was the pervasive aroma of pleasant-smelling incense and the soft Oriental music, all of which created a wonderful, exotic atmosphere.

Gradually, as the lads' eyes got used to the darkness, they began to understand from whence the club got its name, The Pink Lady — it was, of course, the decor. Everything was pink. First there were the walls spread with pinkish, purplish festoon curtains. Then the furniture and furnishings: couches and gilt chairs, padded in the plushest of pink velvet; tables — a half dozen or so — covered in pink damask table cloths; waitresses, two presently delivering drinks to two tables; dresses, a deep shade of pink covered by small frilly aprons. Even down to the trays, drinking glasses and ashtrays, everything was pink.

In the corner, barely discernible was a small bar; it too depended on candles in pink glass globes for its lighting. Peter decided this place filled with mystery and intrigue was well worth exploring.

'Let's have our free drinks anyway,' Peter said indicating the bar, taking the initiative, 'and see what happens.' Fast disappearing was his former hesitancy. After all, this experience was supposed to be an exercise in broadening the mind. Now they were here, it only made sense to stay a while and discover what was what.

The bar was deserted except for the barman, who was black, and was, of course, wearing a pink jacket. He gave them a warm welcome after which he announced good humouredly that the free drink was 'The Pink Lady Cocktail'— what else! The preparation of the drink was an education in itself. First, the barman poured a measure from a number of different bottles into a long silver container, added some sort of cordial, put the lid on, then shook the bejasus out of it.

'Such a mixture! Laddie!' Duncan remarked, rubbing his hands in anticipation. 'This has got to be a heck of a drink.'

The barman poured the concoction into two pink cocktail glasses, adding a cherry to each. 'Would you like the waitress to carry your drinks to a table?' the barman inquired.

'No!' They said it together; they were beginning to feel much more at ease leaning against a counter with a drink in their hands.

The cocktail tasted excellent, but unlike a pint, was gone in seconds. 'That went down nice and smooth,' Duncan said smacking his lips, feeling like he was six inches above the ground. 'Let's have another.'

'Why not,' Peter agreed. The whole experience was proving intensely interesting. Even the dimness of the place now seemed perfectly normal. The second two drinks cost ten shillings each. They tasted even more nectarous than the first ones. 'Mind you t'wouldn't take too many a' these to get addicted,' Peter remarked nodding his head at his empty glass.

With the pleasant fuel that sparks the intellect doing its job, Peter and Duncan were at their finest as they regaled each other and the friendly barman with streams of anecdotes and yarns. Being Monday night, business was slow, so the barman had time to chat. He exchanged witty stories about his life and travels since he left his native Kenya as a young man. With the jokes coming up fast and furious, it was only natural that Duncan would brag about his inheritance, which, by now, had become a fortune.

'Now it's my (hick) twist,' Peter addressed the barman between hiccups. 'When you're ready there (hick), ' he said to the barman, 'we'll have another two (hick) cocktails here.' The barman willingly obliged.

After the third drink it was time for the floozies (as Peter christened them afterwards) to move in. This was an upper-class brothel, after all, except that our two innocents were clueless. The two females appeared out of nowhere. Young (well, through a drunken haze and hardly any light they looked young), attractive, chic and chatty, they decided that these lads so green and nicely sloshed were now ripe for the picking. It didn't take much persuasion to get the lads to stagger upstairs to the so-called party. Innocence is guileless and trustful, the lads were in for a big surprise.

'She touched me, father.'

'Where, my Son?'

'In a house of disrepute,' Peter answered, sounding like a fool. He was stalling as he worked up to the telling of the big sin in confession.

'I meant where did she touch you on your person?' the priest asked.

Peter wished to God he'd keep his voice down. Weren't his mother and his sisters outside the confessional awaiting their turns to make the Christmas confessions. The last thing his Mother had said to him on the day he left for England was, 'Peter, I'm asking the Virgin Mother to throw her blessed mantle over you — to keep you pure and chaste.' If she were to overhear any of this confession wouldn't she go out her mind.

'Well, all over, Father,' Peter whispered.

'Your body?'

'Yes?'

'Every part.'

'Yes.'

'Including your privates?'

'Yes.' Why couldn't he have said penis? Peter thought, and be done with it. Of course, that was a word they never used in Ireland; probably t'was a sin to even utter it.

'And?'

'And what, Father?'

'What happened after that?'

'We went the whole way, Father.'

Peter thought the father had gone into shock he was that silent. Then he said in an even louder voice. 'You mean you had relations with her?'

'We had intercourse, father,' Peter whispered. There it was, out at last—the unmentionable. There was such a long pause, Peter thought, he's surely having a stroke from the shock.

'Well, my boy,' (It was a relief to hear the father's voice again.) 'every time you commit a sin of the flesh, you're committing a mortal sin.' Another pause. The father was breathing heavily. 'And you know what's in store for you if you die in the state of mortal sin?'

Here it comes, Peter thought. 'Yes, Father.'

'Now my boy, I can't give you absolution unless you give me your solemn promise never to frequent such a den of iniquity again or indulge in the likes of that behavior until you're married.'

'Oh sure, Father,' Peter whispered. 'I'll give the promise.'

'Now, if you break your promise you'll be in the state of mortal sin.'

'I understand, father.'

'When you pass from this world, my boy,' the father continued dramatically, 'do you want to hear the words, 'depart from me ye cursed into everlasting flames prepared for the devil and his angels?'' His voice had risen a few decibels. The father was determined to impress upon this young man how grievous his sin was.

'No, Father Osborne, I don't,' Peter answered, still whispering.

'What was that you said?' the father cocked his ear.

'No, Father, I don't.'

'You don't what?' The father was now shouting at the top of his voice.

'Want to hear those words.' Peter was convinced every blooming word the Father was saying could be heard outside. Wouldn't the people want to be stone deaf not to hear. In the name of God, he thought, what'll they be thinking?

There was another long pause before the father spoke again. 'And now, need I remind you that we know not the hour nor the day when death will come stalking like…a thief in the night.'

'Yes, Father, I know that.' Peter was thinking, will he ever stop jabbering, for God's sake give him his penance and let him go? Didn't he realize there were rows and rows of people outside waiting to be heard? Not to mention the poor sucker stuck in the box on the other side, kneeling there in the dark, probably thinking the father had gone home. This confession was taking much too long, what with himself holding forth at the top of his voice about hell and damnation for everyone to hear.

'And for your penance,' at last the Father had got to the point, 'I want you to say two Rosaries every day for two weeks. ' Then hurriedly he commanded, 'Now say the Act of Contrition.' Halfway through the prayer the Father uttered the words 'pray for me' and slammed the door of the hatch across.

Peter didn't mind the tough penance. But what he did mind was having to face the people outside. God only knows what they'd heard. Emerging from the confessional feeling like a criminal, Peter kept his chin stuck in his chest, rushed towards the alter and fell on his knees.

For the next four years, Peter made good progress in his course, exhibiting a natural flair for writing, from time to time having articles published in English newspapers and magazines. Though, he missed Duncan, who had returned to Scotland triumphantly flaunting his diploma the previous year, Peter continued to enjoy London and his freedom. With so many young men away fighting in the war, as an eligible bachelor his company was in constant demand. Invitations to theaters, concerts, operas, music hall revues, dances in hotels, wild-weekend parties were in abundance. Life was one continual merry-go-round.

Along with that, with Duncan's departure, Peter inherited his delightful, spacious flat in South Kensington. It was an absolute godsend. It meant he was able to entertain friends and return hospitality. On the study front too there were many excellent outlets helping with his studies: museums, art galleries, historical buildings, libraries, book stores — probably the best in the world — selling books which, if not totally banned in Ireland, would certainly be banned in his circles. One couldn't compare this free and easy lifestyle with the Irish one. For instance where, but in London would he meet, and mingle freely with, so many sophisticated literary people? Certainly not in Ireland. With the mother constantly looking over his shoulder, were she to get an inkling of his lifestyle, she'd be as righteous as be damned; without question, it (his lifestyle) would be labeled corrupt and immoral.

Now in his final year, Peter began to think seriously about staying on to work in London. He was so used to this hectic life he couldn't imagine giving it up for what awaited him back in Ireland. So in March he began to investigate the job situation. Going to interviews he got the distinct impression there was no shortage of jobs for writers. In fact, as a qualified journalist he could probably pick and choose where to work.

Then he met Nancy Hanrahan. Pretty, talented, and twenty-two, Nancy was an actress with the Irish Abbey Theater players. She'd just arrived in London from Dublin to appear nightly with the Abbey company at the Lyceum Theater, for a run of two weeks, after which the company would tour Britain. Peter and Nancy were introduced at the Abbey Theater's Opening Night Reception held at the Irish Club. For both it was love at first sight. And though the courtship was brief, before Nancy left London on tour, she was unofficially engaged to be married to Peter. Needless to say, many fervid letters traveled across the Irish Sea during their separation. Until the month of June, when Peter returned, wielding his diploma in Journalism. Nonetheless, it seemed jobs for journalists were not as plentiful in Dublin. So for a while it looked like Peter would have no option but to return to London.

At this juncture, Nancy Pete took matters into her own hands and approached her Uncle Colm, a Senior Editor with The Independent Newspapers. The actress in Nancy made her very persuasive; she acted the part of the lonely, deserted, bride-to-be so convincingly that her uncle capitulated finally and persuaded the boss of the Independent to give Peter a job as a Junior Reporter.

The following month, Peter and Nancy were married, with lots of pomp and ceremony. The reception was held in the palatial Gresham Hotel Dublin. It would be a memorable occasion for the O'Dwyer family on account of the fact that it was a big flashy affair. The assemblage consisted of numerous famous people associated with the Arts and politics: actors and actresses from the Abbey Theater, celebrities of the ilk of Sean O'Casey, Maude Gonne MacBride, Lady Gregory, William Butler Yates, Countess Markiewitz, to name but a few. But the person who made the biggest impression on Peter that day was Patrick Pearse — the poet and founder of Saint Enda's College.

Before his return to Ireland, Peter had never given any serious thought to Irish politics; like all news items, Irish politics had to be viewed impartially. As far as the country was concerned, he was happy the way things were. Why would he want change? Hadn't he and his family done extremely well under British rule? His mother's dairy business, though it had gone through difficult times in the early days, was now flourishing. He'd done all right for himself with education and with jobs. His sisters too attended the best schools. Putting it mildly, life couldn't have been kinder to the O'Dwyer clan. Not a single grievance could Peter dredge up against the British. Such was his thinking when he first met Pearse on the day of his wedding. A great admirer of the man's writings and poetry, Peter felt privileged to be talking to him. Their conversation finally drifted from literature to politics.

The subject of Home Rule came up. Pearse voiced his suspicions that it would never be honored.

'Pardon my ignorance,' Peter said, 'but my understanding of the situation is that when the Home Rule Act was passed in the British House of Parliament, it was expected to come into force within twelve months. Then, of course, the war intervened, which naturally set things back; Ireland would have to wait until after the war for Home Rule to be introduced.'

'A load of poppycock!' Pearse came on very strong. 'I'm afraid I regard Home Rule as a complete sell-out,' he sounded sardonic. 'And now that it's formally on the statute books in the British Parliament, the vast majority of Irishmen unfortunately see England's difficulty in the war against the Hun, as an opportunity to display Ireland's good faith. Haven't the men of the great Southern Irish regiments — the Dublin Fusiliers, The Munster Fusiliers, the Connaught Rangers — flocked into the British Army to fight in their war. But, mark my word, Peter, all this talk about Home Rule coming into force after the war is a myth! A fallacy! It will never come to pass after the war or any other time.' Strong words.

'So, you think Britain will renege on the promise to introduce Home Rule?'

'I don't think it, I know it!' Pearse said bitterly. 'If only the Irish Nation would wake up and recognize the fact, it might put an end to the slaughter of our young Irish men in the war.'

'I can't believe what you're telling me?' Peter's concern surprised even himself. Unfortunately since his return to Dublin, settling into the job and preparing for his forthcoming nuptials left little time to study the current political climate in Ireland. Now conversing with this soft-spoken poet he was hearing, for the first time, views about Home Rule he'd never heard before. He was also discovering this man's celebrated magnetism and charisma. He wished he was better informed on the subject of Home Rule and didn't sound such an amadaun. 'Would you think me very impudent if I were to ask you to expand on your theory about Home Rule?' he asked. 'Like,' Peter cocked his head, grinning genially to take the harm out of it, 'what are your sources?'

Pearse's face broke into a broad smile. 'This is your wedding day, Peter, he said. 'It's neither the time nor the place to be discussing such matters.'

'But I am genuinely interested in learning more about the Cause, Home Rule, your philosophy, future plans?' Peter said. 'You see, those four years I spent living in London, what with the war and everything, the British Press gave little or no coverage to Home Rule. Like everyone else over there I was convinced that the Irish question would be resolved as soon as the war was over and Home Rule was introduced. Now you're telling me it's not going to happen.'

Peter was thinking, he knew very little about Pearse the politician, except for the article he'd cursorily read recently in *The Statesman*: 'Despite the fact that the cream of Irish manhood is away fighting the British battle,' the article stated, 'and therefore not around to swell Pearse's volunteers, and in spite of the apathy existing throughout the country about the Cause, Pearse still shows extraordinary selflessness and perseverance in his efforts to build the special volunteer Irish force.'

Suddenly, welling up in Peter was the feeling that this was a moment not to be wasted in idle banter common to weddings; it was an opportunity to hear the facts from the horse's mouth, so to speak. Especially when that horse was convinced Home Rule would never be honored. He wondered, could Pearse be right after all? Was the Irish nation being lulled into a false sense of security?

Pearse interrupted his thoughts. 'Maybe when you get back from your honeymoon, you'd like to attend one of our meetings?' he suggested.

'Tell me where and when?' Peter produced the ubiquitous notebook from the inside pocket of his morning suit.'

'Leave it for the moment, 'Pearse said. 'I'll be in touch.'

Christ! Peter thought, when he parted company with Pearse, if anyone suggested to me last night that today I'd be arranging to attend one of Pearse's meetings, I'd have said they were balmy.

The next time Peter saw Pearse was when he was on assignment covering the funeral of the old Fenian—Jeremiah O'Donovan Rossa. It turned out to be a great public event. It brought thousands of ordinary moderate-minded people filing past the coffin where an armed guard of honor was provided by the minority Irish Volunteers, together with Redmond's Volunteers.

The Irish Republicans who organized the arrangements for the funeral made sure that it struck a firm military note. A volley was fired over the grave. As the coffin was lowered, Pearse, in the uniform of the minority Irish Volunteers, took a paper from his pocket and delivered what Peter considered an awe-inspiring speech. Awe-inspiring because Pearse's philosophy was beginning to make sense to Peter. Since his initial meeting with Pearse, Peter had undergone a conversion to the Cause. James Dolan, a well-seasoned, patriotic reporter with The Independent Newspapers, heavyset, a bit bald, with the beginnings of a paunch, had taken Peter under his wing and brought him up to date on the political situation in Ireland. Through his association with James, Peter began delving seriously into Irish history; he was shocked at how little he knew. The blame, of course, lay in the way history was taught in school.

'Come to think of it,' he said to James, 'in our history class, hardly any time was devoted to Irish history; it was skimmed over like it wasn't the slightest bit important. As long as you could rattle off a plethora of dates and titles of events, like parroting the Hail Mary, that was sufficient. The last historical event I can remember details of was Brian Boru and the battle of Clontarf in ten fourteen'

'The history books in the schools have a lot to answer for,' James remarked. 'Published by the British, what could you expect? Weren't they bound to be biased. It was exactly the same in my day; unless a teacher went out on a limb and secretly told his students the details of the different events, students never learnt the full facts from the history books. I was lucky to have such a teacher.'

'Well, I suppose as kids, none of us ever thought of questioning the system. Why would we? Wasn't international history, particularly British history, much more interesting. For heaven's sake, where but in an English history book would you get all the grisly details of the battles between the British, the French the Spanish and the Portuguese? Wasn't all that blood, guts and gore grist to the mill of a youngster's mind?'

Suddenly Peter began to feel irked. 'But it's a damn shame that the Irish people were kept in ignorance about their history — especially in the cities. A people have a right to know the full facts. Take me, for example I'm a complete ignoramus when it comes to Irish history.'

'I've a book I want you to read,' James ventured. 'It's a treasured Irish publication. In it you'll find a full, comprehensive, detailed account of Irish history. T'will open your eyes.' The following day James brought the book in and surreptitiously slipped it to Peter saying, 'Guard it with your life.'

Reading this exceptionally rare book which recorded the full, authentic history of Ireland, did indeed open Peter's eyes; it was a riveting revelation. He couldn't believe it had taken him till this stage of his life to learn about the atrocities the British committed against the Irish over the past seven hundred years. How they originally stole the land from the Irish, ruled and oppressed the people, the tyranny and brutality they practiced trying to prevent the Irish nation from preserving its heritage, its culture, its religion and its language. But despite the persecution, the resolute Irish people rose up regularly against the oppressor, only to be trampled into the dust by Britain's mighty armies roving the country savagely suppressing risings, insurrections, and executing leaders. So even before hearing Pearse's speech that faithful day at the O'Donovan Rossa funeral, Peter had had a big change of heart.

After the funeral ceremonies, Peter spoke with Pearse and arranged to attend a meeting the following week. At this meeting it was agreed that Peter's special talents would be best employed doing intelligence work. His contact would be Michael O'Rahilly (known as 'The O'Rahilly') in the Irish Republican Army. From then on — before and during the nineteen-sixteen Rising — Peter reported regularly to The O'Rahilly, sharing with him information he was privy to through James and other contacts in the press. Secretly too, Peter looked after printing some of the propaganda pamphlets for the volunteer movement.

So on this Tuesday of Easter week in the late afternoon, Peter slipped away from his office to put in an appearance at the General Post Office. Here he would pass on to The O'Rahilly his latest report, giving him the 'inside scoop' as he jestingly called it. To say the least, the news was anything but good.

'The British Army are on full alert,' Peter told The O'Rahilly. 'They've rapidly snapped out of their inertia of yesterday, which we all know they were lulled into by MacNeill's advertisement canceling the Sunday volunteer maneuvers.'

'That advertisement,' The O'Rahilly said, 'though it may have put the British off the scent, did more harm than good; it's the reason there was so much confusion among our own ranks.'

Peter continued making his report. 'Well, anyway, the British troops stationed here—all two thousand, five hundred of them—have been mobilized and are in the process of erecting a cordon of barricades around the city with the intent of gradually tightening the cordon till it surrounds the General Post Office.' Looking around the post office, he thought, God almighty! It's pitiful to see such a handful of fighters prepared to take on the might of the British army.

'Is that all of it?' the careworn O'Rahilly asked.

'No, I'm afraid it's not. There's further bad news.'

'Break it to me gently.'

'There was an urgent wireless message to London asking for reinforcements. As a result two infantry brigades are due to arrive at Kingstown Harbor first thing tomorrow morning, ready to march on Dublin.'

The O'Rahilly looked surprised. 'They can actually spare that number away from the Front?' He shrugged his shoulders and sighed. 'Well, we always knew it wouldn't be a picnic,' he said. 'All we ever hoped to do was make a statement and, with luck, rustle up a bit of sympathy abroad.' The O'Rahilly now noticed that Peter, the normally cheerful, looked quite dejected. 'You're holding something back?' he asked. 'More bad news?'

'There's another enemy abroad,' Peter sounded bitter. 'It's the Dublin people themselves — they're very hostile.'

'We were expecting that,' the O'Rahilly said wearily.

'Maybe we were. But not to the existing extent.' Peter seethed with rage. 'This morning I witnessed a disgusting incident outside the Jacobs' factory garrison; a crowd of angry Dubliners, each and every one of them carrying Union Jacks, jeering at the volunteers inside. 'Bloody slackers the lot of yis!' they were saying. 'If yis want to fight, yis should go out and fight with yer brothers in France.''

The O'Rahilly smiled whimsically, as Peter continued to look most unhappy. Peter had expected a certain amount of opposition in the city, but nothing as blatant as this anti-nationalism. For the past few months, though he had to keep quiet about his politics in the job, Peter had tried to enlist the support of people he was sure had leanings towards an independent Ireland, but his efforts met with little success; 'feckin posturing fence-sitters' he called them. The O'Rahilly had his head bent. He was looking down on his joined hands with his stretched fingers interplaying with each other as if intent on pulling them apart.

Peter observed him for a few seconds. He was thinking, I'm doing nothing to boost this man's morale bringing him so much bad news. He chuckled, trying to coax a bit of cheer back into his voice. 'More than likely that crowd of Dublin gurriers only represent a small minority of the Dublin people,' he said with a grin. 'Better to ignore their brand of horseshit.'

The O'Rahilly lifted his hand, palm upturned as if to indicate fate and its inexplicable mastery of events. 'You're so right, Peter,' he said, 'it would be better. Nonetheless, let's be factual. Dublin isn't the only place in Ireland where public opinion is dead against us.'

Chapter IV

While Peter was conversing with The O'Rahilly in the anteroom, the men in the main hall relaxed and had a light repast of food and drink. 'This is a mad bloody business,' Barry, one of the lads from the Kimmage Garrison, remarked to Ham and Bud as he downed his tea. 'We should've taken to the mountains, not shut ourselves up in here with the leaders and three bloody tricolor flags flying over our heads showing them exactly where we are.'

'We're only following Pearse's orders,' Ham said. 'How could we do otherwise after the speech he gave at the Garrison on Holy Thursday night?'

'I suppose you're right,' Barry said. 'That speech pretty well explains why our Garrison was chosen to be the vanguard in the takeover of the Post Office. Obviously, Pearse had complete confidence in us.'

'We've every reason to be very proud of the Kimmage Garrison's role in this Rising,' Bud said, 'even if meself and Ham did miss the beginning.'

Tuesday night passed without incident, uneventful, an opportunity for the men to snatch a few hours of uneasy kip. Wednesday morning started quietly. Then around ten o'clock the booming sound of machine guns and the rattle of rifle fire rang over the city. The machine gun fire coming from British guns seemed to be concentrating for the moment on putting the look-out posts out of action. The post office building itself didn't come under fire. Meantime the volunteers in the main hall were ordered to hold their fire and conserve ammunition: for the time being snipers on the roof and in the look-out posts would counter attack.

The British attack lasted about forty minutes. Then there was silence and a lull. Word was the British had sustained a number of casualties in the street. This news brought feelings of elation to the Post Office.

'Di ye think we might have routed the bastards?' Bud asked Ham, his eyes round as saucers.

'T'would appear we've won the first round anyways,' Ham said with a comforting wink.

Positioned close to an outside door Ham suddenly found himself coughing uncontrollably, then his eyes started to smart and stream. Close by Bud was similarly affected.

'God! It's smoke!' Ham exclaimed. There was no question about what the stench was. Soon all the volunteers around him were coughing, those with handkerchiefs held them to their faces.

'Jesus!' Bud said, 'the roof must be on fire.'

'No, it's not the roof,' Paddy Caulwell told him. 'I've just come from there. It's the hotel Metropole next door; it's on fire. A bloody inferno it is.'

Within minutes the clanging of the fire brigade bells were heard outside. Shortly afterwards a stream of dazed volunteers, some struggling with wounded comrades, staggered into the Post Office. Accounts were given of the fire raging along the two sides of Sackville Street. Fire brigades had arrived, but were unable to bring the flames under control. Hence, they retired to avoid loss of life.

Meanwhile deafening warlike noises and the rumble of gunfire sounding like thunder, continued to be heard in the distance, most of it coming from the direction of the Four Courts. Though there was still no direct attack on the Post Office, the inhabitants were convinced that the battle for independence had begun; a full-scale attack was imminent.

§

As the fire raged out of control down Sackville Street, getting closer to Parnell Street, chaos reigned in O'Dwyer's Dairy. Panic-stricken customers swarmed in buying all before them — stockpiling. It started as a trickle that became a flow that became a flood. As the crowding increased and the pushing, shoving and jostling intensified, it occurred to Mary that soon the staff (herself, Brigid and the two shop girls) would not be able to cope. Stock was fast running out and the more empty the shelves, barrels and churns became, the more hysterical and out of control the customers were getting.

In all her years serving the public, Mary had never seen anything like the behavior of these customers. 'For God's sake, we need help!' she said, in desperation to Bridget. 'Go to the back and rally whatever members of the family you can find and bring them here; even if it's only to control this unruly mob.'

'They're fighting a losing battle,' Jane said despondently to her sisters, Lily, Jody and Eileen, who were part of a group of onlookers outside O'Dwyer's back gate facing towards Sackville Street. Among the group were Moore Street 'shawlie' hawkers — complete with baskets and boxes of fruit and vegetables. The fire prevented them from vending. They gawked in awe at the big, brawny firemen towering above them on elongated ladders, hosing down the end of Sackville Street in a valiant attempt to prevent the fire from spreading into Parnell Street.

'Does that mean the fire is going to reach our house?' Thirteen-year-old Jody asked, wide-eyed. Though she was getting a great thrill out of all the excitement, if their home was threatened that'd be a different story — a very worrying one.

'We can only hope and pray it doesn't,' Jane answered, 'but it's not looking good. As you can see, the fire is still spreading; they don't seem to be able to contain it.'

'Sorry to encroach on your pleasure,' Bridget interposed putting her hands on Jane and Lily's shoulders, 'but we have great need of your services in the shop — it's awash with wild, hysterical customers.'

Jane and Lily couldn't believe the extent of the crush in the shop.

'Holy smoke! They're like sardines in a tin,' Jane remarked.

'Only sardines behave better,' Lily answered rolling up her sleeves getting ready for action. 'Okay, you lot,' she addressed about twenty people jockeying for position at the back of the shop. 'We'll have two lines at the counter and no more. The rest of you will form a queue outside the door.' No one budged.

Then an incident took place which brought things to a head. Lily saw a large, well-built Moore Street 'shawlie' intimidate a small genteel lady, elbowing her in the eye and bellowing, 'Just because you've got a posh accent, Missus, doesn't mean you get priority here.' The poor woman writhed in pain. Her hands wedged to her sides in the crush made it impossible to defend herself.

Seeing the incident, Lily, who couldn't abide bullies, was riled. She pushed her way through the crowd. The 'shawlie' didn't know what hit her when this big, strapping young one, grabbed her by her collar, dragged her to the door and pushed her into the street, saying, 'There y'are now! You can be first in the queue!' Re-entering the shop, Lily addressed the people at the back once more. 'Now unless the rest of you want similar treatment,' she said, 'I suggest you step outside and form an orderly queue.'

The customers needed no further persuasion; meekly they streamed out on to the street where Jane organized them. Lily's action brought grins to a few strained faces.

'Your sister doesn't put up with any nonsense, does she?' a customer remarked to Jane. Jane was having difficulty keeping a straight face. Well, the situation did call for strong-armed tactics: no better person than our Lily to oblige.

Lily, the tough one, supervised the head of the queue, allowing customers to enter the shop as soon as others left. Meantime, Jane kept an eye on the hordes joining the end. The queue now stretched quite a distance down Parnell Street. Then to everyone's surprise British armored vehicles began arriving in the Street. Soldiers erected barricades and put sandbags and machine guns in place, at each junction.

Coming from the dairy a woman stopped to speak to a lady near the front of the queue. 'I don't want to depress you, Phyllis,' she said, 'but I think you're wasting your time queuing.' She nudged her head in the direction of the dairy. 'They're practically out of everything.'

'Sweet Mother a God!' Phyllis exclaimed, 'How do you explain no food in the house to six starving childer.'

'Them blasted volunteers! Bloody hooligans! They deserve to be hanged, drawn and quartered,' the first lady said looking thunderous. 'Not satisfied with burning us out, now they're going to starve us out.' Then she noticed the barricades. 'Jesus, Mary and holy Saint Joseph!' she exclaimed, 'will ye look at that! Not even in our beds now will we be safe!'

'Jaysus, young one!' a shawlie at the back of the queue said to Jane, 'It won't be long now before the whole city's ablaze.' Her face was white with fear. 'Divil stiffen them volunteers! They'll be the ruination of our lovely city.'

Jane nodded her sympathy. Her mind was a mile away, thinking about what she'd overheard the Fire Chief say to her mother when she was on her way to the toilet a while ago. 'Missus, I've grave doubts we'll be able to save Parnell Street,' he'd said. 'With the wind blowing so strongly in that direction and the buildings so old, like matchwood, all t'will take is one spark.'

As word spread that all the dairy's bins were empty, people started leaving the queue. For the first time since commencing duty, Jane and Lily came into contact. Lily looked on edge. She drew Jane out of earshot of the remnants of the queue.

Nodding her head in the direction of Sackville Street, her voice dropped to a whisper, 'I suppose you know our brother, Peter, is up to the gills in that trouble?' she said.

'What trouble?'

'The volunteer movement,' Lily said. 'At this moment he's probably in the thick of things either in the Post Office or in one of the other buildings seized by the volunteers.'

Jane stared at Lily in disbelief. 'You're joking?'

'No, I'm not,' Lily whispered.

'Why are you whispering?'

'Haven't you noticed how totally anti-the-volunteers and the Cause these people in the queue are?' Lily mumbled under her breath, eying the queue. 'What do you think they'd do if they got wind of Peter O'Dwyer's part in it?'

The seriousness of the situation began to dawn on Jane. 'Is he a volunteer?' she whispered.

'I'm not sure.'

'Well then, how exactly is he involved?' Jane asked anxiously.

'As far as I know he prints and distributes illicit pamphlets,' Lily said. 'On Holy Thursday, when mother and the rest of ye were out doing the 'churches,' and I was helping out in the shop, I declare to God didn't I catch him in our basement churning out hundreds of pamphlets on his portable printer.'

'Mother doesn't know?' Jane gasped, breathless with shock.

'Course not,' Lily said. 'She'd probably have a stroke. He swore me to secrecy. But Christ Almighty! I had to tell someone.'

'How on earth did he get away with doing it in our basement?'

'According to him,' Lily said, 'he only operated there once in a while. Mostly he's on the move.'

'So what does he do with the pamphlets?' Jane asked.

'Hasn't he an army of minions outside churches on Sunday mornings handing them out to Mass-goers.'

'Oh, my God! I can't believe it! Did you read any of them?'

'Course I did. I kept one actually. I'll show it to you later. Can't remember the exact words, but it said something to the effect, *We Irish have been repressed long enough. It's time we took our country back from the British. Join the Irish Volunteers today. Have a word with the Agent handing you this leaflet.*'

'Sainted Mother!' Jane exclaimed. 'Not for one minute did I take those volunteers seriously. Sure they've little or no support from the people. I thought it was all a joke.'

'Joke or no joke,' Lily said, 'aren't they making their point — doing a massive job reducing our city to ruins.'

Just then, eleven-year-old Eileen arrived. 'Mother said to tell you and any customers left in the queue that we're closing down immediately,' she said ruefully. 'We have to leave on account of the fire.'

'Sweet Jesus! It really is serious!' Jane exclaimed. A knot began to build in her stomach.

After dismissing the queue, the girls returned to the shop. The door closed behind them.

'The flames are licking at the outhouses at the back,' Mary told Jane and Lily in a calm voice. Then handed them each a huge bag of coins. 'These are to be carried round your necks,' she said.

Earlier, when it became clear that the O'Dwyer premises would have to be evacuated, Mary was worried out of her mind about how to manage the huge glut of cash amassed over the past five days due to the Bank's closure and the situation in the G.P.O. With the safe anchored to the floor, immovable, she had an enormous problem. How could she possibly ask any one person, or for that matter, any two, to take responsibility for looking after those thousands of coins — halfpennies, pennies, sixpences, shillings, two shillings, half-crowns?

She eventually decided there was only one solution: the cash would have to be distributed among the family and the shop girls. For security reasons, somehow or other it would have to be disguised. Living up to her reputation as the great innovator, she solved the problem herself by working on her machine producing a dozen small bags from old sacking. She decided that each member of the family and the shop girls would be given a bag of coins to carry round their necks. The tightening drawstring formed loops large enough for bags to go over heads and down out of sight under dresses.

Suddenly the girls had enormous bosoms making them look like matrons. Our Nancy nearly had a fit when she saw what this bag of coins was doing to her beautiful figure. She was full of protests. 'I'll carry the bag in my hand,' she said to Bridget. 'There's no way I'm going to let people see me looking like this.'

Bridget boiled. 'Bad scant to you our Nancy!' she barked, 'Aren't things bad enough without you adding to them.' Typical! she thought. In time of troubles we can always depend on our Nancy to add to them. 'Put the damn thing round your neck and be done with it,' Bridget's eyes blazed. 'It's the only way we can be sure the money will be safe.'

The sight of sedate Bridget in such a tearing rage had a subduing effect on our Nancy: without further ado, the bag went back round her neck and inside her clothes. When Jane and Lily put their bags in place they couldn't stop laughing and giggling.

Looking down on her figure, Jane remarked, 'We have the bosoms, now all we need are the shawls and the baskets of fruit and vegetables and we'd pass for 'shawlies.''

In her special notebook, Mary kept a record of what each person was carrying. Jody and Eileen's bags carried the much less cumbersome bank notes.

Mary, wearing her most resolute expression, informed everyone, 'We're to remain in the shop until we get the order to leave from the Fire Chief.'

No one said anything. For the moment it was hard to grasp the fact that, like many of the shops in Sackville Street, soon their dairy would be a smoldering mass. The atmosphere was eerie. The more so because Mary was acting as if everything was perfectly normal: helped by the shop girls, she was washing down empty shelves. She even had one of them cleaning the windows. Then out of the blue Mary asked about Peter. She hadn't seen him for days. Lily's face went puce.

'The last time I saw Peter,' to everyone's amazement our Nancy was actually volunteering information, 'he told me he was going on assignment to Cork.'

'When was that?' Mary asked our Nancy.

'Sometime last week. ' Our Nancy was vague as ever.

'Well, maybe that explains his absence.' Mary looked relieved. She had been wondering all day where he was, fully expecting him to turn up any minute. If he was in the city surely he'd know about the fire?

'Do you think we might carry out some personal stuff?' Jane asked her mother. Though she didn't want to sound heartless, it was way of changing the subject from Peter.

'Each of you can take a small bag,' Mary said. 'Bring the minimum and make haste; any minute now we could get word to vacate the premises.' As they were leaving Mary added, 'You're to keep those bags of money round your necks, they're not to go into any carry bags.'

Except for Jane all the family rushed for the stairs. They were grateful to Jane for bringing up the matter of their personal stuff.

When the word came that they had to evacuate, Bridget was dead against broaching the subject to the mother. 'Well,' she reasoned, 'wouldn't it be very callous to be talking about things like trinkets and adornments at a time like this.'

'Where will we stay?' Jane asked her mother.

'With Aunt Jude in Manor Street for the time being.'

Jude was Mary's younger sister. Jane couldn't help noticing how her mother kept her back to her. The last thing Mary wanted at this moment was to let any member of the family witness her distress.

'What about food?' Jane was trying to be helpful.

'All taken care of.' Mary still stood with her back to Jane. She was now putting odds and ends away in boxes under the counter, issuing instructions to the shop girls about where to put things, and generally giving the impression she was busy. 'I sent a supply of food to Jude's place on the drays.'

'Oh, my God! The horses!' Jane's voice was filled with horror. The mention of drays brought the horses to mind. 'What's to become of them?'

'They'll be all right. Jude is providing shelter for them in the shed at the back of her place.'

Much as Jane despised the work in the dairy, she felt real anguish for her mother. But she could see her questions weren't helping. 'I suppose I'd better get my bag packed,' she said making for the door.

When Jane returned with her carry bag the family and staff, including the dray men, were on their knees ready to recite the Family Rosary. Halfway through the rosary, Peter arrived; it was touching to see the way Mary's face lit up at the sight of him. Giving his mother a knowing wink, Peter dropped to his knees, joined in the prayers and, on cue, recited the last of the Sorrowful Mysteries.

Peter was appalled when he heard about the seriousness of the situation. 'God!' he exclaimed, 'I'd no idea the fire was threatening Parnell Street. I've been in Maynooth all morning, just got back a while ago. Still Peter couldn't control his laughter at the sight of his sisters' comical appearances. 'Good God! I can't get over the big busts,' he exclaimed. 'Suddenly my sisters have become middle-aged spinsters!'

Our Nancy was not impressed.

'Surely you saw the stables on fire at the back?' Mary upbraided Peter.

'Saints be praised!' Peter was getting one shock after another. 'No,' he gasped, thunderstruck. Then hurriedly he made for the door leading to the back.

'Where are you going?' Mary screamed after him. Now that he was here she didn't want him out of her sight.

'To see the Fire Chief and get an update on the situation.'

Peter was gone so long the family began to have qualms about the outcome of his interview with the Fire Chief. They'd forgotten that being a newspaper man, Peter was a dab hand at getting the facts, no matter how long it took. So it was most reassuring to see him smiling as he came through the door. 'Now, I won't beat about the bush,' he said. 'The situation is still quite grave. I've been informed, however, by the Fire Chief that there's been a shift in the wind. So the firemen now feel more confident about bringing the fire under control. But then,' he added, with a spark of unease, 'of course, there's always the chance that the wind will shift again, in which case the smoldering embers could rekindle.'

'Please God!' Mary raised her hands beseechingly towards heaven, 'don't let the wind shift.'

'Anyway,' Peter continued, 'you're to stay put for the moment, but be on alert. The fire chief will keep you posted.'

The room echoed with sighs of relief.

Mercifully, the wind remained steady for the next twelve hours ensuring that the family didn't have to leave.

Later that evening Peter arrived in the Post Office to make his report to The O'Rahilly.

'Sorry I couldn't get in before now,' he said, 'Mother's dairy was in danger of being obliterated by the fire this afternoon. I had to rally round and give the family my support.'

'Of course. I forgot. It's in Parnell Street, isn't it?' The O'Rahilly seemed quite concerned. 'It escaped, I hope?'

'For the moment,' Peter said. Then changing the subject he got down to the business of the day. 'When I eventually got to the newspaper office this afternoon, I was given the low down on the British troops arrival at Kingstown Harbor this morning.' He hesitated, thinking that by now maybe the news was stale. 'Perhaps you already know what happened?' he said, raising an inquisitive eyebrow.

'Not the whole story. We got a few jumbled snippets,' The O'Rahilly smiled cynically, 'from which we gathered there was a bit of a barney with one of the columns at the Mount Street Bridge?'

'A bit of a barney would be putting it mildly!' Peter was brimming with pride. 'The battle lasted five hours. Believe it or not, seventeen of our brave lads took on the whole column, blasting them from a house in Northumberland Road. They picked them off with such precision that by late afternoon they were responsible for killing and wounding two hundred and fifty British soldiers.' Before the O'Rahilly could ask the question, Peter forestalled him, 'Yes, unfortunately all our lads were killed. But what a run for their money they gave those British bastards.' Peter was enjoying the telling of the tale. The O'Rahilly had to smile at his boyish levity. Peter continued proudly. 'At the very least it'll show the British that putting the Irish in their place won't be a pushover this time.' He grinned impishly. 'That victory at the Mount Street Bridge gave them a taste of what's to come.'

'You mean it might put off the evil moment?' The O'Rahilly turned his face away: he didn't want Peter to see how worried he was. How he wished he could share Peter's enthusiasm. Turning back he asked, 'How about the other column?'

'Met with no opposition. Got through without incident. Now they're bivouacked near Kilmainham: they intend to join up with the troops in charge of the cordon around the city.'

'To be honest with you,' the haggard and weary O'Rahilly said, 'This waiting is pure agony; I wish to God they'd get on with the attack.'

Chapter V

Coming from seven o'clock Mass the next morning, Thursday, Mary ran into Taigh Moriarity — a large florid man — the owner of the pub down the street on her side. During the fire he too had been under orders to evacuate his premises. As far as Mary knew Taigh had his account with the same bank as herself — the one that was burnt down yesterday in Sackville Street. So, he'd probably be in the same position as herself with regard to the cash flow. This would be a good opportunity to find out how he was managing?

'Well, now, I'll tell you what I did, Mrs O'Dwyer,' Taig said to Mary, 'when the bank in Sackville Street didn't open on Tuesday, I decided to go up to Dorset Street and open an account with The Commercial Bank there. His brow furrowed. 'Well, with the times that are in it, ye couldn't be having all that cash on the premises. So I reckoned Dorset Street was a good bet — far enough away from the fighting to be safe and only a short tram ride.'

'Oh! the trams are still running?' Mary hadn't seen a tram in days.

'Yeah,' Taigh said. 'Mind you, the service is a joke. The terminus is now at Findlater's Church if and when the friggin thing comes.'

'Maybe I should do the same thing?' Mary suggested.

'Oh, for God's sake do!' Taigh looked quite concerned. 'Get the money outa the house as quickly as possible. Sure we don't know from one minute to the next whether it's blown out of it or burnt out of it we'll be.'

'I'm so glad I ran into you, Taigh.' Mary's face showed enormous relief. 'I'll do it today — the Commercial Bank, you say?'

'Yeah.' Just as Mary was leaving, Taigh stopped her short, 'Oh,

Mrs O'D, there's one most important detail you should know.'

'What's that?'

'You'll be needing a Pass to get through all them British Army barricades on the way up to the Findlaters' Church. Otherwise you'll be stopped, challenged for your identity and searched.'

'Sweet Mother of God! That's all I'll need, to be searched carrying all that cash.' Mary's face was filled with consternation. 'In the name of God! where, do I get a Pass?'

Taigh put a comforting hand on Mary's arm. 'The officer in charge of the barricade at the junction of Parnell Street and Dominick Street gave me mine. He seems a decent sort a chap. Just tell him who you are, show him some identification—like a mailed enveloped addressed to yourself—tell him about your bank in Sackville Street being burnt down and that you need to lodge a large amount of cash in a bank in Dorset Street.' Taigh smiled, 'It did the trick for me anyways.'

'The blessing a God on ye, Taigh!' Mary said.

'Any problems,' Taigh stopped in his tracks, 'come and see me.'

'I'll do that. A million thanks,' Mary called over her shoulder as she rushed away in the direction of the Dominick Street barricade.

Luckily the officer in charge was there and was gracious and polite. After Mary told him about her dilemma with the money and he'd studied the envelope establishing her identity, he said, 'Certainly, Mam, you can have a pass. I know your premises.' He paused a second. 'There's just one difficulty, the pass has to have my Commanding Officer's signature on it—that could take a day or two.' Then seeing the raw anxiety on Mary's face, he mellowed. 'Tell you what,' he said, 'come at midday tomorrow, I'll do my best to have the pass here for you.'

§

Thursday morning Ham saw the dawn of another day. For a short while all was quiet in Sackville Street. The General Post Office still remained in a state of alert inactivity. Until the silence was broken by the sound of a strange and terrible clanking at the end of the street. Word came down from the volunteers on the roof that they could dimly make out what looked like a lorry with a boiler stuck on top, making its way towards the Post Office. As it got closer, they could see this was exactly what it was — an engine locomotive boiler with an entrance through the fire box at the back, rigged up as an improvised armored car. Slots had been cut in the side for observation, together with a number of dummy slots.

The order was given to the volunteers in the main hall to hold their fire, preserve ammunition at all costs, the volunteers on the roof would take care of it. Shots rang out and presumably one of the shots wounded the driver because a little while later another armored monster towed the mock armored vehicle away. This small victory brought forth wild cheers from the volunteers; the exhilaration they were feeling was very palpable. Some volunteers took advantage of the lull that followed to avail themselves of tea and nosh from the make shift kitchen. It was refreshing to hear the hum of light hearted chatter as they indulged themselves.

Paddy, always good for a laugh, excelled himself giving his comrades an exaggerated version of what happened to him in the kitchen. 'Ye know that fella, Louis O'Brien, the alleged poet, who's in charge of the food?' Paddy asked his comrades.

'The one with the accent ye could hang yer hat on,' Ham said, making the identity.

'The very one,' Paddy laughed. 'Well, didn't I arrive in the kitchen looking for something to eat. For the love of Jaysus, I says to him, give us a bottle a stout and something to eat. 'Drink watah,' says he, 'and ye can eat that crust there,' says he pointing to the heel of a loaf that'd blunt a crocodiles teeth. 'If ye never had a decent meal in yer life before,' says he, 'is that any reason why I should supply ye with a four course dinner before ye die for Kathleen NiHoulihaun?' '

There was a loud burst of laughter from his appreciative audience.

Not to be outdone, Bud started telling his most recent anecdote. 'Ye know that pub, O'Donovans, down the Quays — a yob called

Breffni runs it?'

'Yeah,' A chorus responded. Attracted by the roars of laughter, more volunteers had joined the group.

'Wasn't I in there a couple a weeks ago,' Bud continued, 'and this fella, a customer, says to me: 'I wouldn't touch the Guinness in here if I was you.' Why not? says I. 'I'll tell you why,' says he. 'Last night didn't I order a pint from Breffni there behind the bar. He hands me the pint and isn't there a dead mouse floating in it. Here, I says to Breffni, handin' him back the pint, take this back, there's a dead mouse in it. 'The divils!' says he, 'there's no knowin where they're going to turn up next.' With that doesn't he get a spoon and scoop the dead mouse outa the pint, throws it in the bin, pours the pint into another glass and hands it back to me. I'm thinkin it's coddin me he is and wait for him to pour me a fresh pint. But he ignores me. Just carries on pouring drinks for other people. Now I'm gettin annoyed. Here, I shouts at Breffni, I'm not drinkin this pint. No one should be expected to drink a pint the likes a this. 'The likes a what?' says Breffni. The likes a one that had a mouse swimmin in it, says I. 'How the hell can he swim when he's dead?' said Breffni. Well swimmin or not, says I, I'm not drinking this pint. 'Arrah, give it here,' says Breffni, 'yer the contrariest man I ever served a pint to — ye won't drink it with the mouse and now ye won't drink it without the mouse. There's no pleasin ye.' '

His appreciative audience howled with laughter.

Ham couldn't help thinking how wonderful it was to have lads the likes of Bud and Paddy in his group; the way they helped to keep up the spirits of their comrades with their funny yarns and anecdotes.

§

Friday on the stroke of twelve, Mary arrived at the barricade with the black leather bag bulging with cash, though it only represented a fraction of the full amount. Thankfully, the Pass was there as was the young officer in charge. He was most helpful. Pointing to two indecipherable signatures he said, 'In case you should be challenged, that's my signature, Charles Garland and that's my commanding officer's, Colonel David Briers.'

The Pass was a godsend: on her way to Findlater's Church, Mary sailed through the three barricades without hindrance. When she saw the hassle other people were having at the barricades, emptying their pockets, their handbags, even opening their parcels, she said a silent prayer for the young officer. At Findlater's Church she waited thirty minutes for the tram to come. Then, of course, there were further delays as the tram went through the complicated process of changing to the outgoing line.

Arriving at the bank, Mary took her place in a queue waiting in front of a mature bank clerk's window. Just as she reached the head of the queue, another clerk opened his window and beckoned to her. He was young, no more than eighteen or so. Reluctantly, Mary approached him. She'd much rather have dealt with the mature clerk. After all, as a new customer lodging a huge amount of cash she'd be expected to do a lot of explaining. So wouldn't an older, senior clerk be better qualified to deal with this unusual transaction?

Nevertheless, the young clerk appeared to listen attentively as Mary told him how the cash had accumulated over the bank holiday, how her bank in Sackville Street didn't opened on Tuesday and was finally burnt down on Wednesday, and now it was imperative that she deposit the money in another bank.

The clerk handed her the customary form saying, 'If you'll just fill out the details on this, Mrs. O'Dwyer, we can get started.' Finished filling out the form, Mary handed it back to him. He studied it for seconds, then asked, 'Have you the cash with you?'

'Of course.'

'Let's have it, so that I can record the amount.'

Before producing the cash, Mary gave him sheets of figures. After that, she lifted the black bag and piled dozens of small bank bags filled with coins on to the counter. Startled, seeing such an enormous amount of cash in one lot, quick as a flash, the young clerk put his arms around the pile and whisked it in out of sight. Assuming this was all the cash the lady was talking about, the young clerk applied himself to checking the bank bags against Mary's list. It was a complex task that took quite a while.

After filling the amount in on Mary's form and satisfied that everything was in order, the young clerk raised his head. The sight now confronting him made his eyes nearly pop out. Piled high on the counter were hundreds of bundles of notes in elastic bands. For seconds, all he could do was stare wordlessly at this mountain. The pinions of his imagination started to twitch. Not only was this transaction difficult, it was positively dangerous. During his six months with the bank he'd never seen so much cash in one transaction. Visibly shaken, he put his arms around the stack and hastily drew it in.

'Is that all of it?' he asked Mary timorously.

'No,' Mary answered, spilling the remaining thousands of loose coins on the counter while explaining that she had run out of bank bags.

It was too much for the young clerk to have to deal with; he was overwhelmed with anxiety. Nonetheless, after the initial shock, his reflexes responded positively to the urgency of the situation. Standing up, he leaned over the counter, his eyes spanning the bank premises to see if anyone was watching. 'Mrs O'Dwyer,' he whispered, 'please put that change back into your bag.'

Puzzled, Mary scooped the loose cash back into the bag. Then to her surprise, the young clerk pushed the bundles of notes, the bank bags and the sheets she'd already given him, towards her saying, 'Better put these back in the bag too.' Standing up, he indicated the waiting area. 'Mrs. O'Dwyer, would you be good enough to take a seat over there,' he said politely. 'It's important that I talk to the manager.' With that, he closed the window and hurried away in the direction of the manager's office.

En route he thought, this whole business is highly suspicious. I couldn't possibly take responsibility for accepting such a large amount of cash. Even if she does look highly respectable, for all I know she could've robbed a bank or a store. Aren't the papers full of reports about the looting and stealing that's going in Sackville Street and its surrounds.

Sitting in the waiting area, Mary clutched the bag of money in a vice like grip. It seemed like an eternity before the young clerk returned and opened his window. Mary fully expected him to call her over, but instead he just ignored her. Without as much as a glance in her direction he beckoned to the next customer in the queue. The snub heightened Mary's apprehension; her stomach started to flip with fear. Something was horribly wrong with the way she was being treated; she was being made to feel like a criminal. Surely they didn't think she'd come by this money dishonestly? Her blood ran cold as a terrifying thought suddenly assailed her; any minute now the police will arrive and arrest me. Panic-stricken, Mary decided, I've got to get out of here. She could see that the young clerk was preoccupied with his customer. If I leave now, she thought, no one will notice. On her way to the entrance, though her legs felt rickety as a broken gate, she held her head high determined to give the impression she was a regular customer.

About to pass the Manager's office, the door suddenly opened. A middle-aged, stiff-looking man, whom she assumed was the manager, motioned to her. Mary's mind ran riot. That's it! she thought. He's going to detain me in his office till the police arrive. What to do? Should she make a dash for it? No, most likely it would look suspicious. Ach, better do his bidding. The manager's bushy eyebrows raised querulously as he ushered Mary into his office. He indicated the chair at the table where she should sit, taking his place opposite her.

For the next few minutes, silence took possession of the room as the manager scrutinized a piece of paper. Then to Mary's intense relief his face cracked with what was probably his best attempt at a smile. 'Sorry, Mrs. O'Dwyer, for the delay,' he said in a distinct North of Ireland accent. 'Not surprisingly I had to make some circumspect phone calls to establish your bona fides.' This time his smile was a bit warmer. 'You understand the circumstances surrounding you're opening an account with us are, to say the least, quite unusual; we're dealing with such a huge amount of cash here.'

'I quite understand,' Mary tried to control the quiver in her voice. 'We're living in such frightful times.'

'Now,' the manager said matter-of-factly, 'I'm pleased to tell you that we're prepared to take you on as a new customer.' With that he picked up a telephone and spoke into it, 'Tell Searson to come to my office,' he said.

Searson turned out to be the young clerk Mary originally dealt with. 'I want you to count Mrs. O'Dwyer's money here in her presence,' the manager told Searson. Mary parted with the black bag and watched the young clerk go through the drudgery of counting millions of coins, while the manager did the paper work finally filling out the deposit slip. It took a full three-quarters of an hour to finalize everything.

On her way back, the tram didn't come. Mary walked the two miles to the city. As she got closer to Sackville Street the thunder of guns and artillery got louder and louder. Evidently, the tanks and armored cars she'd seen earlier filing past the end of Parnell Street, were now fully operational. At the junction of Parnell Street and Sackville Street people were being turned back. Mercifully, once again Mary's pass got her through without any trouble.

As she hurried along Parnell Street, a Moore Street hawker, Daisy, a customer, caught up with her. 'The Lord save us, Mrs O'Dwyer!' she gasped, 'What's to become of us all? There won't be a building left in the city with the damage that warship is doing.'

'What warship?' Mary stopped dead in her tracks.

'The one they've brought up the river Liffey. It's shelling the Quays and Sackville Street. Did ye not know?'

'No, I didn't know,' Mary said. 'My God! this is awful! It really is war! Better get home quickly, Daisy.'

§

In the General Post Office, Friday morning started quietly. Then around midday the bombardment started in earnest. It seemed to concentrate on the center of the city, leaving the Post Office to wait anxiously.

'I've just heard a rumor that the Germans have landed,' Paddy told Ham gleefully after arriving back from having relieved himself. 'That heavy shelling we're hearing could be the sound of German guns.'

'God! wouldn't it be wonderful if it was!' Ham's face lit up. 'T'would make up for all the cock-ups.' But then it dawned on him that it was probably a rumor, to be taken like all the others — with a grain of salt. 'To be on the safe side,' he said to Paddy, 'don't spread it around till I get it confirmed. No sense in raising people's hopes.'

The first chance Ham got, he discussed the matter with Plunkett.

'Sorry to disappoint you,' Plunkett told him, 'but it's definitely a rumor; what we're hearing is British artillery.' He sounded very despondent. 'No,' he continued, 'since they scuttled their submarine – the one that was carrying the arms to Ireland - in Dublin Bay, the Germans have made no attempt to help us any further.'

'Better get word to the lads that it's definitely a rumor,' Ham said. 'No sense in them living in a fool's paradise.'

'Absolutely right,' Plunkett said, 'but while you're here, I'm sure you'd like to be put in the picture about what's happening on the outside?'

'I'd certainly appreciate it, sir.'

'First of all, there's a British warship shelling Sackville Street from the river Liffey. Second, Intelligence informs us that the British infantry has started moving from the outskirts of the city into the center.' A pale smile nearly reached his eyes. 'Nonetheless, the British are not having it all their own way; their progress is being hampered by snipers and barricades erected, believe it or not, by Dublin nationalists.' Suddenly he couldn't contain the laughter any longer. 'God bless them! those Dublin rebels!' he said. 'Their barricades should definitely go down in history. You wouldn't believe the items they've used as obstructions; pianos, bedsteads, mattresses, tables, chairs, sideboards, china cabinets - everything but the kitchen sink.'

'Well, hooray for them!' Ham said, laughing. He was really pleased to hear about this unexpected support from Dubliners, no matter by which or what means.

When Ham arrived back to his unit he told Paddy that the story about the German invasion was a con. Luckily, Paddy hadn't mentioned a word to anyone.

By one o'clock the lull in the Post Office was at an end; the roar of heavy artillery grew and the British Army began to concentrate its attack on the building. They blasted it with artillery and machine-gun fire. There was a general call to arms and the garrison spurred itself to repel the long awaited assault. But the volunteers' machine guns and rifles were no match for the armory and the booming guns attacking from outside.

Pearse, his eyes appearing to burn with enthusiasm, came into the center of the main hall. Competing with the noise of the gunfire, the rumble of falling houses, the rattle of rifles overhead, he raised his voice as he addressed the volunteers. 'Lads,' he said, 'Dublin will be forever an heroic city like Paris of old.' His voice echoed the pride he was feeling. 'The main positions are in tact. Other Risings have taken place throughout the country. We Irish have defied England's might for four days now. We'll win through, though perhaps for many of us it will be in death.' It was evident he'd no intention of surrendering easily.

The men clapped their hands in applause.

Some shouted, 'Up the republic.'

Others, 'Eireann go brath.'

'It's looking bad,' Bud whispered to Ham as Pearse left the hall.

Ham nodded agreement.

The bombardment heightened. Plunkett walked down the line of volunteers at the front windows. 'Hold your fire,' he told the men. 'We must conserve ammunition.'

A fiery Ham said, 'Sir, I'd like to have a crack at them.'

'Wouldn't we all!' Plunkett replied. 'But it would be a waste of ammunition firing on those mechanized monsters. Anyway the lads on the roof are in a better position to retaliate; they're doing a fine job. We'll leave it to them for the moment.'

Boom, boom, boom. The walls and floors of the Post Office trembled. Holding their rifles at the ready, the dazed volunteers waited patiently. As time passed they could see the street outside had become one great big orange blaze lapping at a serene blue, sky.

'It's an absolute disgrace what the British have done to the city of Dublin,' Plunkett remarked to Ham the next time he passed. 'Not since Moscow has a capital city been burnt down.'

§

Friday afternoon Mary was in her office trying to work, hoping that in work she would find a diversion from her worries. The main one being the fierce war waging at this moment not seven hundred yards away. There was no guarantee that it wouldn't spill into Parnell Street, nor that a stray shell wouldn't hit her premises and raze it to the ground. The other big worry was the safety of her daughters, Jane and Lily.

When Mary arrived back from the bank fully intent on telling the family about the dangers in the streets and insisting that none of them venture out, she was appalled to discover that Jane and Lily had already gone to Clontarf to visit school friends for the afternoon. Thankfully, the rest of the family were accounted for: the two youngest, Jody and Eileen were in the parlor, dressed to the nines, rehearsing for the Easter Pageant to be staged at the school tomorrow and Sunday, while our Nancy was in her room writing a letter and Bridget — probably safest of all — above in Glasnevin spending the night with her in-laws-to-be.

After getting our Nancy to come out of her room and join the younger daughters, Mary gave the three of them a graphic description of what was happening in the streets outside, insisting they stay indoors. 'Listen to me, and listen good,' she said with an intensity they'd seldom seen, 'until peace and quiet is restored in the city, you're all housebound; don't any of you dare go out.' It was imperative that she drove home the message. The family's safety was sacrosanct. 'Oh, and by the way,' she added as they were leaving, 'keep away from all the windows.'

The reaction from the younger ones amazed her. 'Awe,' Jody said, 'Eileen and I were looking forward to going out to get a decco when we finished our rehearsal.'

'Are you out of your minds?' Mary screamed, 'Can't you hear that gunfire, those explosions? Don't you realize you could easily be killed.'

'Awe alright, we'll stay indoors,' Eileen said grudgingly.

Our Nancy just shrugged her shoulders disinterestedly and returned to her room and her writing. With the family sorted out, Mary drifted into her office. In a way she was glad the children were taking the situation so lightly — that they weren't shaking in their shoes the way she was. But now, if she wasn't to lose her reason, she needed something to occupy her mind. Work! In times of stress didn't it always prove therapeutic. And despite the fact that the dairy had remained closed for the past few days, there was still a lot to be done. The balance of the cash needed to be counted and organized. Now that she'd got the necessary bank bags, she'd no excuse for putting the job off any longer. Then there were hundreds of Order Forms she could start filling out, so as to be ready for the wholesalers when the troubles were over.

The shelling and the gunfire intensified, the house trembled, the noise was ear splitting. Mary became very jittery. How could anyone concentrate listening to that racket? At one stage the gunfire seemed so close she could have sworn the battle was raging right outside her door. Her curiosity got the better of her. Danger or no danger, she told herself dashing up the stairs to a front bedroom window, I need to find out what's happening outside? Apart from a column of British Infantry marching through Parnell Street to take up their position at the Parnell Monument, everything appeared to be normal.

On the landing Mary ran into our Nancy dressed for the street. 'I'm going to the post box in Capel Street to post this letter,' she hastened to explain. 'On the way back I'll probably drop in to see

Carmel.' Carmel, her one and only friend, lived a few doors away.

'For God's sake don't stay away too long,' Mary pleaded with her. When she was gone, Mary was thinking, I wonder if I hadn't met our Nancy on the landing, would she have slipped out without saying a word? More than likely she would. Tight-lipped and secretive, our Nancy was the one member of the family who was so different from the rest.

As Mary struggled to concentrate on the Order Forms, she began to smell smoke. Goodness, she thought, just when that cloying, sickly smell that clung to everything in the house since the big fire is on the wane, here it is back again. She was distracted by a loud knock on the outside door. Thank God! she thought, our Nancy's back.

Shortly afterwards, Jody, dressed as an angel in a white dress with large wings on her shoulders, stuck her head around the door. 'It's two men to see you, Mother,' she said.

'Do you know who they are?'

'No, not a clue.' Jody paused, then added, 'As a matter of fact, they asked for Peter first, but when I said he didn't live here anymore, they said they'd speak to you.'

Two strange men! Mary thought. First asking for Peter then for me. Who could they be? An inner voice seemed to caution that this was no ordinary visit. She wondered what they could possibly want? It couldn't be business — not while 'the troubles' lasted. Thinking about 'the troubles' she was thankful to God that none of her family were involved.

'Will I bring them in, Mother?' Jody's voice jolted Mary back to reality.

'I suppose you'd better.'

Seconds later Jody ushered in the two men. They were both middle-aged, dressed in dust coats with soft hats. To Mary's mind, shady-looking characters; she couldn't decide whether it had to do with their rigid bearing or the way their shifty eyes avoided meeting hers. Her guard was up.

'Sorry to intrude on you like this, Mrs. O'Dwyer,' the taller of the two men said after doffing his hat. He had a distinct upper-class English accent, 'but we're trying to locate your son, Peter. We've something of mutual interest to discuss with him. Maybe you could put us in touch with him.'

Mary took a few seconds before answering. 'Have you tried his home?' she asked nonchalantly.

'We have,' the short man answered. Definitely Cockney. 'According to the neighbors the house has been empty for the past few days.'

'Well, my understanding is that he's on assignment in Cork,' Mary said. 'You know he works for The Independent Newspapers?'

'If you'll pardon my saying so, you've been misinformed, Mam,' the tall man said. 'According to the time sheets in his office he's presently in the city.'

Mary was fully aware of this fact, but with the kind of alarm bells that were going off in her head, she was damned if she was going to give these weird men any help. God! she worried, is Peter in some sort of trouble? Though fear gripped her heart, her face still remained a mask. The men waited for her answer, but she remained silent.

'Can you tell us when and where you last saw your son, Mam?' the small man asked. There was steel in his voice, which convinced Mary more than ever that the less she said the better. She hesitated gnawing on her lip as though racking her brain trying to remember.

Just then young Eileen, full of beans, bounded into the room. Mother,' she said, 'are there any biscuits left? We're starving.'

'There should be a tin of broken biscuits under the counter in the shop.'

'You know something, Mother,' Eileen prattled on, 'Theresa is here from next door. Would you believe they've hardly any food in the house.'

'Be sure and give her a bag of biscuits before she leaves.'

'Oh, goody!' Eileen looked up at the two men. 'Sorry for the intrusion.'

As Eileen was about to leave the tall man placed a hand on her arm and in an avuncular voice said, 'Maybe you could tell us when you last saw your brother?'

'Peter!' Eileen's eyes danced as she mentioned his name.

'Yes, Peter.'

'Oh he was here...' Eileen pursed her lips and thumped her head as if racking her brain trying to remember. Then she decided to be chatty. 'You know since Peter got married we see very little of him,' she sounded as though she was taking the men into her confidence. 'I miss him so terribly.'

Mary was holding her breath. She wished to God the child would leave.

'But have you seen him lately?' the small man persisted.

'Oh, yes,' Eileen had another think. Then she beamed as though she had made a great discovery. 'It was the day of the fire,' she said. 'I remember because didn't he bring the good news from the fire chief that we wouldn't have to leave.'

Mary, her voice cracking, swallowed hard and tried a diversionary tactic. 'Sometimes when his wife's on tour, we see a little more of him,' she said. 'She's an actress with the Abbey Players.

'Yeah,' Eileen added enthusiastically, 'those times he usually comes for tea.' Eileen sat down, she was so pleased to be discussing her favorite brother.

Mary, now on real tenterhooks, reminded the child, 'Love, don't forget your friend is waiting for her biscuit.'

'Oh sure!' Eileen jumped up and bounded out of the room.

After Eileen left the room, the small man said, 'As Peter's house is empty at the moment, I take it his wife is away?'

'More than likely.' Mary now decided to ask the blatant question. 'What exactly do you want to see my son about?'

'That's between him and us,' the tall man answered. He dug into an inside pocket and produced what looked like a scroll. 'I'm afraid, Mrs. O'Dwyer,' he said, 'we have to search your premises.' He placed the scroll in front of Mary. 'This document authorizes the search.'

It was an complete bombshell. However, despite the fear tightening her throat, Mary still maintained a cool, calm exterior. The two men stared hard at her as she unfurled the document and appeared to read it. The words were fuzzy, even with the glasses on, her vision was blurred. She knew it was nerves. The document looked officious enough, but the only words she could see clearly were, ISSUED BY THE GOVERNMENT OF GREAT BRITAIN AND IRELAND, because they were in large, bold letters. Giving the impression she'd read and understood the document, she handed it back to the tall man.

Then drawing on what little reserves of strength she'd left, she asked matter-of-factly, 'What exactly are you looking for?'

'We'll tell you that when we find it,' the short man answered brusquely. He sounded impatient.

'Who are you?' Mary now sounded just as impatient, 'And what gives you the right to come in here and demand to search my premises?'

'If you studied that document properly, Mam,' the tall man said, 'it's there in black and white what gives us the right.'

The small man intervened. 'As you can see, it clearly states that we represent His Majesty's Government and we have a duty to perform.' He cleared his throat and said politely, 'we're sorry about the inconvenience, but the job has to be done.'

The tall man said, 'If you like you can join us during the search.'

Mary decided to do just that. No way was she going to allow these strangers the run of her house without supervision. Dear God! she thought, how I wish some of the older members were here to lend me support.

They started in the basement. Beyond the area where the stocks of dry food were stored, the basement was chock-a-block with junk; old furniture, furnishings, children's toys — small, bulky, large – a rocking horse, some bicycles, tricycles and bits of both. Trunks filled with all sorts of clothes, ornaments, knickknacks, bric-a-brac, small toys (all of which Mary had been threatening to get rid of for years). The men ransacked the trunks, but found nothing.

It looked like the basement wasn't going to yield anything of interest until the small man moved further down the room and came across an obstruction in the form of large, empty packing cases stacked to the ceiling. Making his way around the obstruction, he found an opening. From the way his eyes lit up it was obvious he'd come across something of interest. Beckoning to the tall man, he pointed to a clearing behind the boxes. With Mary close on his heels, the tall man joined his colleague.

All Mary could see through the opening was a moist patch of black paint in the center of the clearing. The air of triumph with which the tall man bent down, blotted a sample of the paint on to some sort of special paper, put it into an envelope, then into his inside pocket, made Mary's heart turn over. She wondered, what on earth was in the black paint that made it so important? And in the name of God how did it get there?

The men now seemed satisfied with their prize and decided to continue the search of the rest of the house. If nothing else, it was thorough and methodical. In the reception rooms, cupboards, bureaus, drawers, were opened, contents lifted out and pitched back. Cushions on the chesterfield and armchairs were lifted and shaken. They even went so far as to kneel on the floor and look under the couch and armchairs. Next it was the bookshelves: every book was removed and vigorously shaken. Witnessing this outrage Mary's heart beat with a savage anger. What an indignity it was having to stand idly by and see these loathsome creatures ransacking her home, prying into matters that were private and none of their business.

In the bedrooms it was even worse. The contents of every cupboard, wardrobe, drawer from tall boys and dressing tables, were thrown on to the beds, then haphazardly thrown back when nothing of interest was unearthed. They even went so far as to lift the mattresses. Except for a bundle of letters under our Nancy's mattress, which they cursorily scanned and found amusing, they discovered nothing of interest. Until they reached Jane and Lily's bedroom. There on the bed mixed in with Lily's underwear was a sheet of green paper folded in two. The tall man hastily snatched it up and read it. From the way his shaggy eyebrows shot up it was evident he had found something important. Beaming triumphantly he handed the paper to his colleague.

As the colleague read, Mary could see his face too was sate with satisfaction. 'Just what we were looking for,' he remarked handing the sheet back to the tall man, who, once again put it into the safety of his inside pocket.

Now wild with anger, Mary shrieked, 'How dare you take that paper! Put it back this instant. Whatever it is, it belongs to my daughter. You've no right to remove it.'

'Sorry, Mam,' the tall man said, 'it's an important piece of evidence.'

'Evidence of what?'

'We're not at liberty to say,' the small man answered sharply.

'Surely I'm entitled to know what you've taken?'

'All we can tell you, Mam, is it's significant evidence,' the small man repeated, looking defiantly into Mary's eyes for the first time.

As they were leaving the tall man turned to Mary and said, 'You've been most cooperative, Mam. His face held the ghost of a smile, 'Thank you for your patience.'

§

On Friday afternoon the roof of the Post Office was hit by a petrol shell. Fire now gripped the building. There was an appeal for volunteers to help with putting out the flames on the roof where the fire was at its worst. Bud and Paddy volunteered. The roof was a scene of devastation and desolation. To the ping of relentless British snipers' bullets whizzing past their ears, ill-equipped volunteers courageously plied hoses to flames that beat pitilessly into their faces. Bud and Paddy emptied sacks that improvised as sandbags. Then flung them on the edge of the fire hoping to stamp out the flames. But it was the wrong tactic: it only served to make the flames spread in another directions. After all, it was petrol they were dealing with.

As the hours, that seemed like minutes, sped by the flames roared and leaped and the smoke curled in great black clouds. It now became clear that the fight against the flames was hopeless. The men were ordered below. A few obstinate ones stayed on, firing desperately into a void at British snipers. Bud and Paddy decided the roof was doomed and climbed down the only ladder not affected by the fire.

Now sheets of flame were gradually covering the ground floor as the concrete floors above began to crash in. Walls of flame moaned down the shafts to the cellars where panic-stricken volunteers carried cases of bombs, grenades, gelignite and other explosives trying to get them out of harm's way.

Plunkett marched down the line of the Kimmage Garrison calling the men to attention. In a voice filled with torment and eyes that glistened, he addressed the men, 'The fight against the flames will have to be abandoned,' he told them. 'We're going to have to evacuate the building.' Then in a lighter vein he said, 'Before we move out, we want you to come into the room where the hospital is, to secure rations.'

One by one the companies marched into the hospital where cheese and bread were served out and the men packed as much as possible into their haversacks and knapsacks. Pearse joined them amid the desolation and the flames. 'We're going to fight our way through Moore Street to another position and join forces with our comrades in the Four Courts,' he told the men. 'Be careful out there. Watch out for snipers. God go with you.'

Following instructions, the men filed off in retreat down a passage towards the only door that had access to Henry Street. The door — a very solid one — apparently hadn't been in use for a long time and the first men to reach it couldn't get a budge out of it.

The O'Rahilly, who was giving the orders, handed Ham and another tall, bulky volunteer each an axe. 'You and you,' he said, 'break down the door.' It took a while, but eventually the door was smashed and a passage cleared to allow the volunteers to stream into Henry Street. When the job was done, Ham reached for his rifle only to find it had disappeared. In its place was a German Mauser.

'Who does this Mauser belong to?' Ham shouted as loud as he could to those around him, trying by sheer volume to be heard above the din of the explosions. No one answered. Beside him, Bud whisked the Mauser out of his hand, put his head down and rammed his way through the crowd until he reached the front.

Facing the men and putting the Mauser high in the air for everyone to see, Bud shouted, 'Okay, lads, who the hell owns this Mauser? it was left against the wall over there?' The men stopped in their tracks but no one claimed the Mauser. 'Sorry,' Bud said to Ham, handing it back. 'I'm afraid you're stuck with it, boy.'

As instructed, Ham followed the volunteers into Henry Street across to the lane opposite.

The O'Rahilly was still in charge.

'Lads, we've orders to clear that British barricade in Moore Street,' he told the men, 'so fix bayonets and get ready for the charge.'

Automatically, Ham reached for his Holt bayonet. Then the reality dawned on him that he had a rifle without either ammunition or a bayonet. Conversely, a bayonet and ammunition without the related rifle.

Standing close by, the O'Rahilly saw his dilemma. 'You can't do much with that lot,' he said to Ham. 'Better fall out.'

'Load up,' came the order. Into the glare and turmoil the men dashed at the double. Ham's unit, as part of the sortie ordered to take out the British barricade in Moore Street, headed in that direction. Other volunteers dashed down lane ways, past alleyways into stables and outhouses.

Left alone, Ham listened in the somber light to the rattle and the flash of machine-gun fire, bullets patterning on cobblestones and on walls. Then for about five minutes there was silence. This was followed by more spluttering of gunfire. With nothing to defend himself, Ham felt naked, vulnerable and confused. A volunteer carrying an injured comrade staggered into the lane. It was Barney Mellows, the lad who informed Ham and Bud that the Rising was taking place.

Ham helped him to gently lay the comrade down, then felt his pulse. 'I'm afraid he's dead,' he told Barney who couldn't conceal his grief. Covering his face with his hands he wept unashamedly. Ham put a sympathetic arm around his shoulder and tried to distract him telling the story of his lost rifle.

'You're lucky!' Barney said, wiping the tears with the sleeve of his tunic. 'Your guardian angel musta been looking after ye.'

'It's bad out there?' Ham inquired.

'Absolute hell!' There were tears still in Barney's voice. 'Those poor bastards who lead the charge!' he said, 'They didn't stand a chance! That barricade was strewn right across Moore Street and had a battery of machine guns behind it.' Tears poured down Barney's face. 'Mowed down like sitting ducks they were, God help them!'

'What about The O'Rahilly?'

'The last I saw of him,' Barney said, 'he was being riddled with bullets as he charged towards the barricade with a grenade.'

Another volunteer limped into the lane. His name was Thomas. He was a stranger to Ham. He'd caught a bullet in his right leg. Thomas eased himself on to the ground. 'Jesus, Christ!' he said 'It's awful out there — so many corpses strewn all over the place.'

'Our lads?' Ham asked.

'Yeah, Tommies too. Some civilians.'

Thomas saw Barney cushioning his friend's head on his knees. He leaned towards him. 'How's he doing?' he asked.

'He's dead.' There was a sob in Barney's voice.

'Oh! I'm terribly sorry,' Thomas said, 'but ye know something, after the carnage I've just seen out there, we three are lucky to be alive.'

Once again Ham felt compelled to recount the story of his rifle. When he finished he said, 'I feel thoroughly guilty and ashamed.'

'What have you got to be ashamed of? You're alive, aren't you?' Thomas said.

'Did you hear any further word about joining up with the Four Courts garrison?' Ham asked Thomas.

'The only thing I can tell you is what I overheard The O'Rahilly saying to MacDermott before we left the Post Office.'

'What was that?'

'He told him there was a tight-armed cordon all around us, so the chances of breaking through were very remote.'

Behind them a muffled roar swelled to thunder; the explosives in the cellars of the General Post Office had been reached by the fire. A sea of flames shot higher and higher as the explosions resounded in the night. Great flames leaped to the sky from the building that had once been the Post Office. The place was an ocean of scarlet.

'There's little we can do now but hide till daylight,' Thomas said.

'Where do we hide?' Ham asked.

'Some of my comrades beckoned to me from a house in Moore Lane,' Thomas answered, 'but being so slow on the leg, I was afraid I'd be cut down crossing the street, so I didn't chance it.'

'Things seem to have quieted down a bit now,' Ham said. Suddenly he was conscious of the stillness; the gunfire had ceased leaving the crackle of the flames consuming the Post Office the only sound breaking the silence. 'Maybe we could make tracks to that house in Moore Lane?' Ham suggested.

'I'm game if you don't mind giving me a hand,' Thomas said struggling to his feet.

'Of course,' Ham said. He turned to Barney. 'Why don't you come with us?' he suggested.

'No,' Barney answered. He was beginning to feel ashamed of his weakness — crying so openly. 'I'll stay here with my friend.'

Ham assisted Thomas out of the lane way into Henry Street. As they approached Moore Street, he got his first glimpse of the carnage Thomas had referred to. Corpses were strewn all over the Street and on the pavements. My God! he thought, what a high price was paid to take out that barricade.

Tense and nervous, each expecting any moment to be the target of a sniper's bullet, the two men faltered across the top of Moore Street en route to Moore Lane. Progress was slow; along with

Thomas's handicap, there were so many corpses to be got around. They, Ham and Thomas, made fairly good progress and met no one. Ham thought, maybe after all my guardian angel is looking after me. Approaching Moore Lane, Ham saw a pile of bodies on the stones at the corner. As they got closer he could see a couple of gray-green uniforms among them. They lay face down, evidently they'd fallen on top of each other as they turned the corner and were mowed down by the death machines in Moore Street. Blood gushing from the pile of bodies ran in rivulets over the cobblestones. It was a sickening sight.

The muscles of Ham's stomach clenched and churned. He did his best not to show his distress in front of Thomas. 'The Lord have mercy on their souls,' Ham said passing by. Just beyond the pile of bodies was a solitary corpse. The face, streaked with black, lay upwards. It was Paddy — happy-go-lucky Paddy — the lad who kept everyone going with his funny yarns and anecdotes. It was too much for Ham; he was overcome with grief. His stomach now felt like a cauldron of fat acid.

Thomas noticed his distress. 'Know any of them?' he asked deferentially.

'Yes, the one with the black face — he was on the roof earlier fighting the fire.' Ham tried to sound unemotional but the tremor in his voice gave him away. 'He's one of our lads from the Kimmage garrison.'

'The poor divil!' Thomas said. 'Know any of the others?'

'I don't think so,' Ham bent down to have a closer look. 'Holy Jesus!' he cried out. A large Celtic cross was jutting out from the pile. Only one person wore that cross — Bud.

'Look,' Thomas said sympathetically, 'I can hop the rest of the way to the house if you want to tarry with your friend.'

Left alone, Ham picked two bodies off Bud. Reverently he stretched him out on the pavement beside Paddy, wiped the poor blackened face with his handkerchief. It was the only thing he could think to do. Suddenly the bile started to surge up his throat. He moved away and vomited in the corner. As long as he lived he would remember this terrible moment seeing his two friends ripped apart by British bullets. Such unbridled savagery. Staring at their blood-sodden bodies, Ham felt like he'd been catapulted into hell. Tears drenched his face. Sweet Jesus, he thought why couldn't I have been with Bud when this happened? On his knees cradling the head of his dead friend, Ham whispered the Act of Contrition into Bud's ear. Bud would appreciate that. Then picking up a Holt rifle belonging to one of the dead men, Ham left.

Chapter VI

Upstairs on the tram coming from Clontarf, Jane and Lily could see the distant red glow over the city. The tram stopped in Fairview. An inspector came on top. 'Okay, everybody off,' he said, 'the city's on fire, this tram can go no further.' Passengers circled him inundating him with questions. No, he didn't know which parts of the city were involved. He was sorry he couldn't be more specific. It meant a walk of about two miles for the girls.

Thankfully it was a fine night, with lots of people walking. Jane stopped a middle-aged couple coming from the opposite direction. 'Are you coming from the city by any chance?' she asked them.

'Yes,' the man answered.

'Is it as bad as it looks?' Jane asked.

'Yes, it's God awful! The whole of Sackville Street seems to be on fire. Wouldn't advise going near the place unless you have to.'

'We live there,' Lily chipped in.

'Oh! what part?'

'Parnell Street.'

'That's down from the Parnell Monument?'

'That's right.'

The girls' anxious faces prompted the man to say, 'Ach yis'll be all right if yis go through Ballybough.'

'Well, I got the impression the fire was at its worst at the Liffey's end,' the woman added in the hope of easing the girls' anxiety.

'Does that mean the fire isn't at the Parnell Street end?' Jane asked, her mouth dry with nerves.

'Hard to say,' the man said. 'There's a cordon around the whole of Sackville Street; no one's being allowed through.'

'We had to do a detour through the streets the back a Clerys,' the woman added.

'Every intersection we crossed, we could see the fire in the distance,' the man said, looking quite excited and animated. (Well, it wasn't every day in the week the city of Dublin went up in flames.)

'As far as we could see it's an absolute inferno,' the woman added for good measure.

'Not much help, were they?' Jane said to Lily as they as resumed walking.

'I suppose we'll have to find out for ourselves.'

As they got closer to the city the bitter, acrid smell of burning began to affect their throats, especially Lily, who, at the best of times was inclined to be chesty. She started having spasms of uncontrolled coughing. A lot of the people they met were coughing too. Some held shields, like handkerchiefs and scarves to their mouths and noses.

'Have you a handkerchief with you?' Jane asked Lily, dragging her handkerchief from her sleeve, holding it over her nose and mouth. It helped a bit.

Lily searched sleeves, pockets, handbag, but found no handkerchief. 'No,' she said, 'I don't seem to have one.'

'Here take this,' Jane proffered hers.

'No, it's okay.'

'It's not okay,' Jane insisted. 'Shut up arguing; just take the handkerchief.'

'But what'll you do?' Lily said taking it.

'I've a dirty one in here somewhere.' Jane rooted in her handbag and finally found the dirty handkerchief.

Now the smoke started to affect their eyes making them smart and stream. Suddenly Lily stopped dead in her tracks. Removing the handkerchief, she said, 'God almighty! We don't know what's facing us.' Her face was full of foreboding. 'Maybe we shouldn't be going home at all.'

'Where do you suggest we go?'

'Back to Clontarf.' Then seeing Jane's look of incredulity, Lily quickly added, 'It's only a suggestion.'

'Forget it! We're definitely going home,' Jane was adamant. 'Mother will be worried sick about us.'

'Supposing the shop is burnt down and they're not there when we get there?'

'We'll cross that bridge when we come to it.'

When they finally reached the Parnell Monument they were stopped by the British military manning the barricades separating Sackville Street from Parnell Street. Only then did they see the full fury of the fire. Thankfully, it looked as though it hadn't as yet reached the Parnell Street end.

'Sorry, ladies,' a good-looking, young British officer at the barricade challenged them. 'You cannot go into the city.'

'But we live just down there in Parnell Street,' Lily spluttered, pointing towards the street.

'I'm afraid you'll have to show me some identification.'

Jane remembered the funny Easter card (the one covered in pianos) she'd received from Sister Cecilia; luckily it was in her bag. 'Would this be any use?' she said producing the card.

The officer studied it. 'All right,' he said, 'but now I have to ask you to empty your handbags, your pockets and I'm afraid I have to frisk you.'

The handbags and the pockets produced nothing of any consequence. Lily was the first to be frisked by the young officer, then it was Jane's turn. As he patted down her sides to below her knees and back up again she had the oddest sensation.

'All right,' the officer said to Jane when he'd finished, 'you're clean.' He looked admiringly at her and thought, in the best Irish vernacular, it's many the heart that lassie will be after breakin.

Jane was thinking, I wonder does that man have any idea the affect those hands of his, running down and up my legs, are having on me?

'It's not a night for two lovely ladies to be abroad,' the officer cautioned. 'Get home as quickly as possible.'

They ran the last two hundred yards like the divil himself was on their heels. It was such a relief to see the buildings in their block still in tact with no fire or smoke coming from them.

'Oh, thanks be to God! The shop has been spared!' Jane cried out when they finally reached the hall door. She was tempted to fall on her knees at the doorstep and offer up a prayer of thanksgiving to God. They didn't notice the shadowy figure in the darkened doorway next door.

§

When there was no sign of Jane and Lily at eleven o'clock, the rest of the family — Mary, our Nancy, Jody and Eileen — went ahead with the family rosary. It was well past the youngsters' bedtime, so they couldn't wait any longer. With the rosary over and the children gone to bed, Mary now desperately needed to talk to someone. But who? Our Nancy? Not unless she'd undergone a complete transformation. Not in a million years would she want to have a serious conversation with her mother. Despite her skepticism, however, Mary, in desperation, decided to unburden herself to our Nancy. First she expressed her anxiety about Jane and Lily's safety being out so late on such a terrible night. As usual there was no response from our Nancy. Then tense as a strung wire, Mary asked the question about the men who'd paid her a visit that afternoon.

'Would you have any idea what was on that sheet of paper those men took from Lily's drawer?' she asked our Nancy.

'Not a notion,' our Nancy said caustically, adding peevishly, 'You know very well, Mother, I'm the last person on this earth Lily would confide in.' In any event, her expression of total disinterest said it all.

'I don't suppose you've a notion either about where the paint on the basement floor came from?' Mary asked, trying hard to control her irritation. God! It was like pulling teeth trying to get any information out of this child.

'Haven't a clue.' By now it was obvious that our Nancy couldn't wait to get away. At the door, she turned back and said loftily, 'If you ask me, those men were probably con merchants; next time you see them they'll be looking for money.' With that she was gone.

Mary asked herself why did I bother? Isn't it always the same with that child. Try having a conversation with our Nancy and the eyes glaze over. But sweet Mother of God! Wouldn't you think when she saw me out of my mind with worry she'd have made the effort and stayed awhile to keep me company. Course not. The subject was of no interest to her.

Now she had retired to her bedroom — the one she shared with Bridget. Tonight she'd have it all to herself. Mary felt utterly lost; like she was groping through a thick, murky fog, with no where to turn and no one to turn to. The rosary beads in a pile on the mantelpiece caught her eye. I'll say another rosary, she thought. Have to get strength from somewhere.

Mary had just finished the first Joyful mystery when Jane and Lily burst excitedly into the room, out of breath. Seeing them safe and sound Mary's relief was so immense it was all she could do not to burst into tears. Any ideas she had earlier about censuring them went out the window. Bristling with news, the girls rattled on and on about their day in Clontarf, the experience of walking home, the barricades, the intensity of the fire in Sackville Street, until Jane suddenly noticed her mother's nervous demeanor and her silence.

'Everything is all right here?' she asked her mother anxiously.

Mary took a deep breath, then told her daughters about the happenings of the afternoon. As she recounted the story she could see Lily becoming very agitated. 'In the name of God, Lily,' she asked, 'what was on that green paper the men took from your drawer?'

'It must have been one of Peter's hand-outs,' Lily said, trying to sound nonchalant.

'Hand-outs?' Mary repeated.

'Yeah. Leaflets he hands out to Mass-goers on Sundays.

The mention of Mass brought relief to Mary's face. 'Oh! Thank God!' she intoned solemnly. 'So that leaflet could have something to do with the Men's Sodality?' She smiled a watery smile. 'And there's me worried out of my mind about what those awful men had seized. Obviously, they were trying to pull a fast one.'

'Oh no, that particular leaflet wasn't about the men's sodality,' Lily said, in a low voice, the redness of her face doing little to mask her guilt.

'Well then, what was that leaflet about?' Mary inquired anxiously. Lily's cooked face was making her heart race again.

'It was more…or…less advertising for recruits for the volunteer movement,' Lily said, her voice barely audible.

'Jesus, Mary and Holy Saint Joseph!' Mary was aghast. 'If that's the case,' she said, 'I can understand why they looked so gratified; that *was* an important piece of evidence they'd got their hands on.'

'Why the hell didn't you destroy that pamphlet?' Jane screeched at Lily. 'I told you it would get us into trouble.'

'I just wanted to keep it as a souvenir,' Lily now cowered under the weight of her guilt.

Mary felt a stab of pity for Lily — after all, Peter's sins weren't Lily's. She moved on to the next question. 'The black paint on the basement floor?' she asked, 'how did it get there? What was so important about it that the men took a sample away?'

Jane looked at Lily. Well, she was the one with all the answers. By now Lily looked like she ready to burst through her face, she was so upset.

'Peter printed some pamphlets down there,' she said. Then seeing the look of horror on her mother's face, she rushed on reassuringly, 'Oh, but he only used the basement once in a while; he had to keep on the move.'

'And you knew about it all along and never said a word?' Mary accused her.

Lily flushed. 'I only found out about it myself last Thursday.' She was close to tears. 'And anyway, Peter swore me to secrecy.'

'That's right.' It was Peter's voice. He'd come through the back and was standing at the door. 'Don't blame Lily,' he said, 'the fault is entirely mine.'

Seeing her son in the flesh Mary's heart nearly failed her. 'Peter!' she screamed, her face suffused with a mixture of anger and fear.

'Where on earth have you been?'

'Hiding out,' Peter said. 'And now I need a bed for the night.'

'Oh, my God! You want to stay here!' Mary's voice was bleak. 'It's not safe — there are two men…'

'…looking for me?' Peter finished the sentence. 'They're G. Men; they've been nosing around my office for the past few days asking invasive questions.' He sounded cocky and very sure of himself.

Jane couldn't help feeling sorry for her mother; here was Peter — the apple of her eye — acting as if nothing unusual had happened, cavalier as you like, not a hint of remorse.

'Sweet Mother of God!' Mary said, now at her wit's end. 'What am I supposed to do?'

Just then there was a loud knock at the hall door. Shock waves ran through the room. Before anyone could say or do anything the patter of our Nancy's feet could be heard rushing to open the door.

The two men in dust coats brushed past her. Heading directly for the room showing a light under the door, they burst in. The tall man held a gun.

'Peter O'Dwyer,' he said, 'we're here to arrest you for crimes against His Majesty's Government.'

Mary jumped between the men and Peter. 'What crimes?' she screamed at them, her pent-up anguish now overpowering her.

'Distributing seditious literature among the populace,' the tall man replied, while the short man with a swift practiced motion cuffed Peter.

The tall man addressed Mary, 'I'm truly sorry, Mrs O'Dwyer,' he said, 'but we have to take your son into custody.'

Mary turned to Peter, appealing to him, 'Surely you've something to say in your defense?' she pleaded.

'Up the Republic!' Peter shouted, the venom coming in shafts from his eyes. 'And to hell with the British.'

As Peter was lead away at gunpoint, Mary decided this was a nightmare that would haunt her all her life. After Peter's departure, a stunned silence took possession of the room.

Jane eventually broke it, 'Don't worry, Mother,' she said gently, 'more than likely they only want to question him.' She could see her mother was shaken to the core.

'Yes,' Lily chipped in optimistically, 'I'm sure as soon as they're finished questioning him, they'll release him.'

Mary nodded her head gravely. She wasn't so sure. She'd seen the look of smug satisfaction on those men's faces when they studied that green paper. 'I wish to God they hadn't found that green paper,' she whispered, shaking her head sadly.

'I can't see what harm there was in it,' Lily remarked with more bravado than conviction.

'What are you talking about?' our Nancy couldn't keep her mouth clamped shut any longer. 'Wasn't there enough on that paper to get him arrested!' She couldn't hide her mounting contempt, 'And do you think Peter gives a damn about what happens to this family as a result of this scandal?' Our Nancy had no time for Peter; she thought it was absolutely sickening the way her mother fawned and drooled over him. God! The woman thought the sun shone out of his arse. 'Now because of Peter's crime we'll all be in disgrace; the family will be dragged down with him.'

'Don't you think Mother's upset enough,' Jane interrupted her tetchily, 'without you rubbing it in?'

'I'm calling a spade a spade!' Nancy was getting more and more nettled. She was thinking, all I ever get from this family is criticism and vitriol; except for Jody, nobody ever sees my point of view. Now she could tell by Lily's face that an attack on her was imminent. But before Lily could get the chance our Nancy was determined to get her spoke in. 'The rest of you can act like ostriches,' she said, 'but I'm telling you Peter will be lucky if he isn't put up against a wall and shot.' It was out before she could stop it. In a way, she would've taken the words back if she could; they were just the result of her irritation.

Profoundly shattered by our Nancy's vindictiveness, Mary put her hands over her face. A huge pit opened in front of her. For seconds Jane and Lily were so flabbergast, they were speechless. The silence engulfing the room was broken only by the tick-tock of the clock.

Then the blunder-bust Lily lashed out with a vengeance, 'Jesus, Christ! our Nancy!' she screamed. 'You're a right bloody bitch! That blasted tongue of yours would chastise the Pope himself!' By now Lily's face was purple with rage. 'If you can't say something pleasant,' she yelled, 'shut your bloody gob.'

'I'm only repeating what I heard.' Our Nancy retorted angrily. She was damned if she was going to take all that verbal abuse from Lily without hitting back. 'Besides,' she said, 'you're just as guilty, leaving that pamphlet around for the men to find.'

Before Lily could get another word in, Jane intervened. Keeping her voice calm and even, she asked our Nancy, 'What did you hear about captives being executed and who did you hear it from?'

'My friend (who everyone, but Mary, knew was Larry) told me the British never take prisoners during wartime.'

Beads of sweat broke out on Mary's forehead. 'You mean...they kill them?' she whispered.

'Yes,' our Nancy answered. But then when she saw the life sucked out of her mother's face, her spate of anger drained. (Or maybe she was having the slightest twinge of guilt?) 'Ach, it's probably just a rumor,' she said with a forced laugh. 'Sure isn't the city abounding with rumors at the moment.'

But the damage was done.

My God! Mary thought, maybe our Nancy is right. Maybe they will execute my only son. The nightmare had only begun.

Upstairs, blissfully unaware of the drama being enacted downstairs, Jody and Eileen were at their bedroom window at the back of the house, staring wide-eyed at the big fire in the distance. From time to time there were huge explosions. Their young minds, like thirsty sponges, soaked up the thrill of it all.

'Gosh! It's brilliant! I can't wait to get back to school and tell my friends about it,' Jody said. 'The fire, the explosions—sure it's better than a carnival.' Jody's eyes gleamed with pleasure at the thought of the exciting story she could now tell at school. 'You never know even Sister Theresa might enjoy hearing about it.'

'We're real lucky to be so close to it all,' Eileen said, totally fascinated. 'I bet none of the girls in my class got this close. They'll be so envious when I tell them after the holidays.'

A huge explosion shook the house.

'Wow!' Jody exclaimed. 'That was a big one! Did you see the flames shooting up into the sky?'

'Yeah. Just like those fireworks we saw at the Military Tattoo in Phoenix Park last summer.' Eileen's cheeks were flushed with excitement: this was surely the thrill of a lifetime.

Close by, snipers were still at work. Suddenly a bullet whizzed by the window.

'Maybe we shouldn't be standing here,' Jody said. She began to feel a bit nervous. 'Maybe it isn't safe.'

'I think you're right,' Eileen agreed. 'Perhaps we should get into bed. Anyway,' she said matter-of-factly, 'I've seen enough.'

Eileen was halfway to her bed and Jody was rearranging the lace curtains, when the window was shattered and the bullet struck Jody. 'Oh God!' she cried out holding her chest as she sank to the floor.

Quick as a flash Eileen was out of bed at her side. 'Are you all right, Jody?' she asked anxiously leaning over her.

Before Jody could answer, there was a rush of feet up the stairs. The door burst open. Lily dashed in, followed by Jane. 'In the name of God,' Lily spluttered, 'are you two mad? Do you want to get yourselves killed?'

Eileen was now on her knees hovering over Jody. 'I think Jody's not feeling well,' she said her eyes wide with terror.

'Jesus! Jesus! Jesus!' It was Jane screaming. She was seeing the blood seeping through Jody's nightdress. 'Sweet Mother of God! The child's been hit!'

When Mary finally arrived, Jane and Lily had lifted Jody on to the bed. Blood now saturated the child's nightdress. Mary let out a long, shuddering sob. She felt she was going to choke. She knew instinctively her child was dead. Falling on her knees beside the bed, Mary cradled Jody's hand in hers holding it tenderly against her face. Then as her body shook and trembled with sobbing, she placed the hand back on the coverlet. Lowering her face over it, she gave vent to her terrible grief.

Eileen started crying hysterically. 'Is she all right? She's going to be all right? She's got to be all right?' Her lamentable crying distracted Mary for an instant. She lifted her anguished face and said quietly to Jane, 'Get the child out of the room.'

Jane swept Eileen off her feet into her arms. Hugging her sister close to her breast, she stumbled from the room. 'There, there,' she said soothingly, forcing herself to sound normal. 'She's going to be fine. We'll get the doctor and he'll make her well.' She felt she had to be strong in front of young Eileen; at all costs she must not break down and cry.

'But I saw all the blood,' Eileen protested.

'I know,' Jane racked her brain trying to think of something to say that would put the child's mind at ease, 'but sure any cut will pump blood until it's patched up,' she said in a shaky voice. 'She may need stitches.' For the moment her reasoning seemed to appease the child.

On the landing they met our Nancy. She'd heard Eileen's hysterical crying and Jane too looked as if she'd seen a ghost. 'In the name of God, what's going on?' she asked anxiously.

'It's Jody,' Jane answered in a low voice. 'Better go in and give a hand.'

Lily, the tears spurting from her eyes, met our Nancy at the door. 'She's dead!' she sobbed. 'She's been hit by a bullet.'

It was now our Nancy's turn to lose control. At the sight of her little sister lying there in a nightgown soaked in blood, eyes closed, dark lashes lying on the little ashen face, her mother's head bent over her in prayer, something snapped in our Nancy's brain. Total desolation swept over her. She threw herself on the end of the bed over Jody's feet and wailed. 'Oh my God, Jody! you can't die! I love you so much! You mustn't...you can't leave us!' she sobbed uncontrollably into the bed.

Mary, her tears mixing with Jody's blood, was saying the Act of Contrition into Jody's ear. She was totally oblivious to everything around her, including our Nancy's demonstration of grief. The only thing registering in her mind, at that moment was the fact that God had taken her beloved thirteen-year-old child from her, up to heaven.

Though shocked to her foundations, Lily, the practical one, dragged our Nancy off the bed. 'For God's sake, our Nancy, pull your self together,' she sobbed quietly. 'Someone will have to go for help.' Her plea fell on deaf ears; our Nancy was too grief-stricken to hear. She sank over the bed weeping bitterly.

Jane came back into the room. 'I left Eileen in our bed,' she told Lily, her face now saturated with the tears she'd so resolutely held back for Eileen's sake. Lily put her arms around Jane. As they held each other their bodies shook with the force of their weeping. They were truly heartbroken. A lot of things that seemed so important a while ago now seemed inconsequential and trivial.

Lily was the first to regain self control. Pulling back from Jane, she said, 'Jane, somebody will have to go for the priest, the doctor and the police immediately.' Looking in her Mother's direction, she said, 'Mother's in no state to help — she's utterly devastated.' Then looking at our Nancy prostrate across the end of the bed crying her eyes out, 'And wouldn't you know it, she's a dead bloody loss! So it's up to us.'

Jane could see how this awful tragedy was affecting our Nancy. 'She can't help it,' she said to Lily. 'She was especially attached to her.' Jane leaned down and whispered through her sobs into our Nancy's ear. 'Our Nancy, you've got to be brave,' she said. 'Someone has to go for the doctor and the priest and the police. You've simply got to help.'

The word doctor seemed to bring a glimmer of hope to our Nancy. She stood up her tear-stained face showing the slightest animation. 'Yes, of course…that's right…we must get the doctor,' she said, 'maybe he can still save her.'

'Lily and I will see to it,' Jane told her.

Now more alert, our Nancy, at last, asked the crucial question, 'What can I do to help?'

'Go in and stay with Eileen in our bedroom,' Jane answered,

'She's absolutely distracted.' Jane wondered about our Nancy's notion that the doctor could save Jody. Surely, by now she realized Jody was dead. In her wisdom, however, Jane made no reference to it, deciding that her offer of help was too valuable. Keeping an even voice, Jane said, 'Our Nancy, I don't want Eileen to come back into this room again and see Jody's condition — it would be much too distressing for her.'

Our Nancy nodded her assent. 'All right, I'll look after Eileen. But get back quickly with the doctor.' With that she left the room.

Jane said to Lily, 'What about one of us knocking up some of the neighbors, get them to fetch the doctor and the police, while the other one goes for the priest. That way Mother won't be left abandoned; because there's no way we can depend on our Nancy.'

'If you'll knock up the neighbors, I'll go up to the priest's house, in Dominick Street,' Lily volunteered.

Not surprisingly, the Murphy family next door was very startled when they heard loud knocking on their hall door at half-past one in the morning. They wondered, was this someone come to tell them to evacuate the premises again? Or maybe it was someone seeking asylum?

'In the name of God,' Peadar Murphy shouted, his head shoved out the window, 'what do yis want at this hour a the night?'

Chapter VI

Ham stumbled the rest of the way to the first house in Moore Lane—entered at the corner of Moore Street. It appeared to be empty. The hall was dark.

Thomas' low voice reached him through the darkness. 'I'm over here sitting on the bottom of the stairs,' he said. 'Can't manage them without your help.'

'Anyone else here?' Ham whispered.

'No, looks like we have the place to ourselves. But I have the feeling it would be safer upstairs.' Thomas had a good idea what Ham was suffering. If he himself felt so nauseous after seeing the gruesome slaughter outside, it must have been hell for Ham seeing the butchered bodies of his comrades.

With Ham helping Thomas, they climbed the stairs and entered the front bedroom illuminated by the fire outside. Joy of joys, it had a big empty, double bed! Ham's exhausted body fell on it. 'After four sleepless nights,' he gasped, 'a decent bed has got to be a little bit of heaven!'

'My sentiments exactly,' Thomas said easing himself on to the other side of the bed.

Despite Ham's weariness, sleep did not come quickly. He couldn't cast out the image of his two dead friends, particularly Bud: there could never be another friend like Bud — so loyal, so sincere; theirs had been a unique friendship. And what about Alice? She would be heartbroken. Somehow he'd have to get word to her.

He must have dozed off because he was awakened suddenly by Thomas shaking him. 'For God's sake, get off the bed quickly,' he whispered. Thomas didn't need to elaborate: the racket outside

– gun fire, rifle fire and breaking glass — spoke for itself. Ham slid to the floor and curled up in a corner away from the windows. Shortly afterwards he fell into an uneasy sleep.

Suddenly Ham was conscious of someone entering the room. 'Don't disturb yourselves, lads,' the shadowy figure said, 'it's only me, Pearse.' He lay on his back on a table, allowing his legs to dangle. 'If the majority of the Dublin citizens could lay hands on us,' Pearse said, 'they'd tear us asunder.' Ham sensed he was a man with a very heavy cross. Ham dozed off again.

Next time he woke Pearse was gone. Now another sound was added to the din of the spluttering bullets from rifles and machine guns. Picks, spades, pokers, spiked and sharp-edged implements of every kind, were boring and smashing through the walls of the houses from the other end, carving out a tunnel. Volunteers had been working feverishly throughout the night converting this terrace of houses into a garrison — piling furniture against windows, placing obstructions on stairways, nailing planks against fragile doors.

Around five a.m. on Saturday morning six volunteers joined Ham and Thomas in the front bedroom. They had worked all night breaking through the walls. Too exhausted to talk, they dropped to the floor.

As the day wore on, from time to time there were sporadic bursts of gunfire outside.

Then around half-past two in the afternoon a volunteer doing a reconnaissance of the building, crept into the front bedroom. 'The officers have had a meeting at their new temporary Headquarters here in Moore Lane,' he told the occupants of the room. 'They want to talk to any volunteers I can round up. Yis are to follow me.'

'Do you want to make the journey?' Ham asked Thomas. He could see Thomas was in a lot of pain.

'If you don't mind helping me?'

'Course.'

Making allowances for the injured Thomas, the group moved slowly through the holes in the walls of the houses, then down a staircase, out into a warehouse yard at the end of Moore Street. Here they found companies of volunteers lined up.

'Thank God! At last!' Ham said to Thomas when he saw the assemblage. 'Now maybe we'll be apprised of what's happening.' He was impressed by the volunteers' orderliness and discipline, haggard and all as they were. And now that he had the proper rifle, he was hoping they'd be ordered to join forces with The Four Courts Garrison and he'd get the chance to have another crack at the enemy. After standing to attention for the best part of an hour, the volunteers were relieved to see Sean MacDermott, assisted by his friend, Mick Collins, coming towards them. He had evidently sustained an injury in his leg or foot.

In a voice that held a strong hint of tears, MacDermott addressed the volunteers. 'The following message was issued by Commandant General Pearse fifteen minutes ago.' He cleared his throat and read from a sheet that shook in his hands.

'In order to prevent the further slaughter of Dublin citizens and in the hope of saving the lives of our followers — now surrounded and hopelessly outnumbered — this afternoon the members of the **PROVISIONAL GOVERNMENT** present at a meeting at our new Headquarters here in Moore Lane, agreed to an unconditional surrender.'

He paused to allow the painful news to sink in. A wave of shock ran through the yard. MacDermott continued, 'The Commandants of the various garrisons and districts in the City and County, will order the men under their command to lay down their arms.'

Except for the odd sniffle, MacDermott's speech was greeted with silence.

MacDermott continued speaking, this time without a script.

'The only terms the British would listen to were an unconditional surrender.' His voice cracked, he bowed his head, cleared his throat, then continued. 'We're surrendering not to save our own skins, but to save the City and the people of the City. But no matter! I'm extremely proud of you. It's not your fault we haven't won a Republic. You put up a great fight…you were outclassed…that is all. The British, had the men, the munitions and the force. But this Easter will be remembered and your work will tell someday.'

The angle of MacDermott's bent head signaled his misery. Once again his statement was greeted with dead silence. Tears ran down the faces of many volunteers.

Finally marshaling a semblance of poise, MacDermott lifted his head and continued his address, 'Now our instructions are that all the people involved in the Rising are to march to Sackville Street and lay down their arms.'

With that MacDermott, abjectly blew his nose, turned and limped towards the building.

Ham and Thomas joined the lines of the couple of hundred volunteers who'd survived. With white flags fluttering at their front and rear, the defeated volunteers — sleepless, hungry and wounded — marched in pairs into Henry Street. (Ham helping Thomas.) The sight of the waxen corpses littering the street — many of them ordinary citizens — was horrifying. In the light of day the volunteers could now see the high cost of the Rising; the still smoldering ravaged and ruined City, sending up clouds of smoke to blot out the blue sky, the vast number of human dead littering the streets. A wave of revulsion ran through the lines. Once again Ham thought of Bud and Paddy lying back there on the cobblestones. How long, he wondered, would it be before they got a Christian burial?

The volunteers marched on into what remained of the burnt out Sackville Street, now lined with khaki uniforms. Two British officers covered each prisoner with revolvers and watched them closely as they dumped their arms, knapsacks and equipment in the street's center. Then after being frisked by ordinary British soldiers, the volunteers formed into lines.

Finally assembled, a British General, his chest bedecked in medals, strode down the lines. 'If there are any wounded among you,' he gave the order, 'please fall out.'

Thomas looked dubious. 'What do you think?' he asked Ham.

'Don't be daft!' Ham said. 'Of course you must fall out. You're injured, aren't you?'

Thomas fell out and was lead away by a khaki uniform.

Having finished his inspection, the general announced, 'You'll be fed and watered shortly.'

Junior Officers now started down the lines taking names and addresses. Standing in the center of the fourth line, Ham noticed a bit of a commotion in the lines ahead of him; heads were bobbing up and down. Soon the cause of the commotion arrived at his feet. It was Cairon, a Kimmage Garrison survivor: he had been crawling through the lines to get to Ham's side.

As he jerked the leg of Ham's trousers, he looked up and said in a low tone, 'Exercise caution, By! For Jaysus sake don't look down. Just tell me how to stand up beside you without being noticed?'

Ham looked around. 'Go behind me,' he instructed Ciaron, his hand hiding his mouth. 'And rise gradually; my height will cover you.' Ham was so pleased to see a familiar face. Since leaving the laneway in Henry Street, he hadn't laid eyes on another living member of the Kimmage Garrison. He was fast coming to the conclusion that he was the only survivor of that garrison.

A British Lieutenant finally arrived at their spot. Ciaron decided to give him a hard time giving his name as Gaeilge (in Irish) insisting that it be spelt correctly. 'That's O'Kallig,' the young lieutenant said spelling out O.K.A.L.L.I.G as he wrote.

'No, not at all, not at all!' Ciaron snapped looking very aggrieved. 'For God's sake! That isn't the way to spell it! It's O'C.E.A.L.L.A.I.G.' He spelt it out. Using an eraser the officer rubbed out what he'd written, and made the correction. Leaning over his shoulder, Ciaron pointed to the 'e' in O'Ceallaigh. 'There's a *sineadh* over that 'e,' ' he said.

'What's a *sheena?*' the lieutenant asked screwing up his face.

'A sloped line going uphill — gives it the blas.'

'*The blos?*' the Lieutenant queried; he was ready to scream at this idiot.

'Yes,' Ciaron said with much disdain. 'The blas, you know, the sweetness.'

Ham was finding it difficult to keep a straight face. When it came to his turn, he gave his name as Willie MacNamee. No more would he be known as Ham. The name died with Bud.

As promised the bedraggled volunteers were given chunks of bread and mugs of tea. As the afternoon dragged on they were made to stand in the middle of the street while more and more small parties of volunteers, who'd surrendered from the different garrisons, marched into Sackville Street and joined them. From the pavement citizens gaped at the volunteers.

'If looks could kill,' Ham remarked to Ciaron, 'we'd all be dead.' There was much sneering and jeering and some ugly incidents.

One involved a rasping middle-aged woman who came in front of the volunteers and spat. 'If yis wanted to fight, why didn't yis join yer brothers in France?' she shouted at them.

In another incident a drunk, weaving and waving on the pavement, swore offensively at the volunteers, 'Ye lot a cross-eyed bastards and sons of bitches!' he said, 'yis thought yis could get away with it, didn't yis? Now yis are getting yer just deserts.'

Hard as it was to swallow, it was very evident that the citizens of Dublin and the British had bonded in a terrible hatred against the volunteers and all they stood for.

It was evening before the next orders were issued. This time the prisoners — including the rank and file, Cumann na mBhan girls and the leaders — were ordered to form two lines and march up Sackville Street to the Rotunda Hospital. A sea of khaki lined the route from North Earl Street to the Parnell Monument. Arriving at the Rotunda Hospital, the volunteers, their limbs ready to fall off with weariness, were allowed to rest on a patch of grass in front of the hospital. All around them on roof tops snipers and machine gunners were in place keeping the vigil.

MacDermott addressed the men once again. 'Lads,' he said, 'I've nothing but the highest praise for you for holding out so long.' Then sounding completely bowed down with the weight of it all, he added, 'I anticipate that myself and the rest of the leaders will be executed, but I urge you most fervently to carry on the struggle.'

§

After the doctor and priest departed, and all the prayers were said, before retiring to her room rent with grief, Mary requested that Jody be moved to her bed. Peadar Murphy and his wife, Kathleen, insisted on doing whatever was necessary for Jody.

'It's bad enough that Jane and Lily have to cope with their sisters' hysteria and the mother's emotional condition,' Peadar said to Kathleen, 'without having to go through the torture of preparing their dead, little sister, all bandaged up, for her laying out.'

Overcome with grief Kathleen could only nod her head. The Murphys changed Jody into the, white nightie with the lace ruffles — her present from Bridget for her thirteenth birthday last month. Ministering to Jody, Peadar was hard pressed to hold back the tears. 'God!' he burst out, 'what a tragedy! Such a gorgeous child, cut down before she's had the chance to live. Heart wrenching, it is!' Kathleen couldn't answer, she could only cry.

When Jody was ready, Peadar carried her into Mary's room and laid her reverently on Mary's bed. Despite her paleness, Jody looked like she was sleeping — the sweet little face so peaceful. For the rest of the night Mary sat on a chair by the bedside. She was in a stupor, her mind and senses so dulled, she could barely think, act or feel. And despite the doctor's insistence that she needed medical assistance, she wouldn't take a sedative. She was determined that nothing would interfere with the vigil she intended keeping by the bedside of her beloved child. However, Jane saw to it that the doctor gave our Nancy and young Eileen strong sedatives: if only for their mother's sake, an end had to put to their hysterics. Mercifully, the sedatives acted quickly, sending them into a deep sleep, alleviating the pain for a little while.

Downstairs in the kitchen Kathleen busied herself making tea and buttering bread. But when she brought the hot, sweet tea and buttered bread to Mary, she wouldn't touch it. In fact, she was quite abrupt in her dismissal of Kathleen.

'The way Mary's acting,' Kathleen said when she joined the

others in the kitchen, 'I'd swear she's blaming herself for the child's death.' Kathleen wiped her tears in her apron. She was haunted by the sight of Mary sitting alone in the shadowy light of the candles surrounding the death bed, staring dry-eyed at the face of her dead child.

'I think we should take turns sitting with Mother,' Jane said to Lily as they sipped Kathleen's sweet tea — the best antidote for shock, according to Kathleen.

'I don't think I could bear to sit alone with Mother in that room. It's so eerie!' Lily said, feeling as though she'd burst apart the pain was so terrible. 'I wish to God, she'd come down. It must be crucifying for her sitting up there on her own staring at Jody.'

'Well, if it's what she wants,' Peadar interposed, 'we must respect her wishes.'

'I think Peadar's right,' Kathleen agreed.

'I'll go up and have another try,' Jane said standing up.

'Mother,' Jane pleaded to the back of Mary's head, 'don't you think t'would be better if you came downstairs for a while and had some company around you?' Mary didn't move a muscle. Moving round to face her mother, Jane went down on one knee and took hold of her hand. 'Or maybe you would think of lying down on Bridget's bed for a while?' she said.

But there was still no response from Mary.

Sitting up the rest of the night with their silent mother in the haunting presence of their dead sister was mental torture for Jane and Lily. Every time Jane looked at Jody she felt a knife twist in her heart. She tried to avert her eyes from her sister's face, but it was like a magnet compelling her gaze on it. Several times Jane noticed Lily nodding off and trying to jerk herself awake, but finally nature conquered will power, Lily dozed for about half an hour sitting bolt upright. Jane was happy for her.

Throughout the night Peadar and Kathleen — the angels from next door — made themselves indispensable. While Lily slept, Peadar stuck his head round the door. 'Anything I can do to help?' he asked Jane in a low voice.

Jane joined him at the door. 'I don't think so,' she whispered. 'Thanks all the same for offering. However, if it's not asking too much, I'm sure we could do with your help in the morning.'

'Of course,' Peadar said, 'just name it!' He nudged his head in Mary's direction his eyes burning with sympathy. 'How is she?' he asked.

'Just the same. Silent as the tomb. Not a move nor a motion.'

From time to time Kathleen arrived with more cups of tea. And though each time, Mary waved her away without even looking at her, Kathleen wasn't put off. 'Peadar and I are below in the kitchen if you need us,' she told Jane in a low voice.

By now Peadar and Kathleen had grasped the fact that Mary needed to grieve in private. So they kept their distance staying in the background. Nonetheless, they were a great comfort to Jane. At half-past six in the morning Peadar insisted on taking the workmen's tram out to Glasnevin to break the news to Bridget and to fetch her home. Though Bridget was rent asunder with shock on hearing the news, by the time herself and Michael arrived home, she seemed reasonably calm and composed. On the tram back, Peadar went to great lengths describing the family's ordeal the night before.

Strangely, the first question Bridget asked was, 'What about Peter? Has anyone been in touch with him?'

'Not so far,' Peadar said. 'It seems for the moment he can't be reached; he's somewhere an assignment.' Evidently Kathleen and himself were in the dark about Peter's arrest. Now the reality of the situation dawned on Bridget. In the absence of Peter, as the next eldest, the burden of helping her Mother with what needed to be done would fall on her shoulders. So, if only for her mother's sake, it was essential she portray a stoic front. She steeled herself for the ordeal that was to come.

Shortly after the travelers arrived home, Peadar and Kathleen left. The time had now come for Jane and Lily to break the awful news about Peter to Bridget. In hushed tones, Jane and Lily between them described what happened. As the story unfolded, Bridget appeared to be taking it calmly, until Lily blurted out, 'There's an awful chance he'll be executed.'

It was too much for Bridget. She reeled with the shock, the blood draining from her face.

Michael's alertness, putting his arms around her, prevented her from falling. 'Quick! We need brandy,' Michael shouted visibly shaking. 'Is there some in the house?'

'I'll fetch it,' Lily said rushing away. Michael made Bridget sit down and put her head between her knees.

Mercifully, Bridget's fainting spell was short-lived. 'My God!' she gasped looking up from her chair at Jane, her brown eyes larger than ever in her pretty, heart-shaped face, 'What a frightful time you've all been having!' Lily arrived back with a glass of brandy. It took a bit of coaxing but eventually Bridget, spluttering and slobbering, swallowed it. Seeing Bridget's natural color gradually return brought immense relief to everyone. Because Bridget still had to be told about their mother's emotional condition. Jane dreaded the telling. But then she remembered Bridget's amazing inner strength during many of the crises in the past when dependable, reliable Bridget shouldered more than her share. So it seemed like telepathy when Bridget asked, 'In the name of God, how is Mother coping with it all?'

'Well,' Jane stammered, 'to be honest with you I think it has affected her brain. It's like she's erected a brick wall around herself which none of us can penetrate.'

'Surely, the doctor gave her a sedative?' Bridget said, sagely.

'For God's sake, she wouldn't let the doctor near her,' Jane answered. 'She's acting so unlike herself.' Just thinking about it made Jane shake like a leaf. 'The whole night she wouldn't eat, drink, sleep or answer any of us when we spoke to her. She just sat there by the bedside like a stone image staring at Jody,' Jane's voice choked on her tears, 'even when I put my arms around her to comfort her,' she said. 'It was awful! Her body stiffened so much, I felt I was inflicting more pain.'

'I couldn't go near her,' Lily said, shaking her head sorrowfully. 'That cold, vacant stare of hers sent shivers down my spine. If you ask me, I think she's mentally deranged.'

'My God! What a terrible situation!' Bridget exclaimed. 'I'd better go up and see her.' She stood up. Then, true to her nature, had a twinge of optimism. 'You never know,' she said, 'I might be able to persuade her to see the doctor.'

'Would you like me to come with you?' Michael offered.

'No,' Bridget said quite adamantly. 'I think it would be best if I saw her on my own.' Then at the thought of seeing her dead, little sister for the first time, Bridget became unnerved. She turned to Jane. 'Maybe, you'd come with me?' she said meekly.

'Course,' Jane answered. On the stairs Jane filled Bridget in on how the shock had affected our Nancy and young Eileen; how hysterical they became and how they had to be sedated. 'Anyway,' Jane said looking at her watch, 'the doctor said they'd sleep for at least five hours. There're still a few hours to go.'

When they reached their mother's bedroom, Bridget braced herself for what was to come. With Jane's supportive arm around her, they entered the room.

Though Bridget had no illusions about what she was going to find on the other side of the door, she hadn't expected anything as distressing as this. Even from a distance it was obvious that her mother wasn't aware of her surroundings. She wasn't crying. She was frozen. Seeing little Jody laid out, Bridget's feet stuck to the floor; for seconds she couldn't move. She supposed it was shock. Notwithstanding her earlier determination to be strong for the family, at this moment, she was convulsed with grief; she had no control over tears that flowed like a waterfall.

Jane went ahead and paved the way speaking to their mother, who hadn't stirred since they entered the room. 'Mother,' Jane said quietly, 'Bridget is here at last.'

There was no response from Mary.

As Bridget advanced into the room on shaky legs, through her tears she could see the terrible transformation that had taken place in her mother; she looked twice her age, so dazed and stricken, she was hardly recognizable. Bridget felt a rush of terrible pain. Overcome with compassion, she couldn't stop herself putting her arms around her mother. But like Jane, she too experienced the same rebuff; the stiffening of the body, the face showing no emotion whatsoever. Seeing Bridget's distress, Jane gave her hand a sympathetic squeeze. It helped.

Nonetheless, Bridget now realized that the full responsibility for looking after the arrangements in relation to this bereavement, would unquestionably be hers. Summoning up her strength, she leaned over her mother and said softly, 'Mother, have you any ideas about the funeral and the burial? We have to make arrangements immediately.'

Still and silent, her gaze firmly fixed on Jody's face, Mary made no attempt to answer, no more than she'd acknowledged the presence of her two daughters in the room.

Bridget motioned to Jane to come outside. She'd set her mind to what she must do. Arriving back in the kitchen, though shaken in the extreme, Bridget appeared to be on top of things. She announced to those present—Jane, Lily, Michael and her Aunt Jude (just arrived)—'There isn't a moment to be lost. The funeral and burial arrangements must be made immediately.'

'Will you do it? Or do you want Lily and I to do it?' Jane asked.

'Of course, I'll do it,' Bridget responded. Distressing as the task was, Bridget realized she needed a distraction to occupy her mind. Making the funeral arrangements, though probably the saddest duty she'd ever be called upon to perform, would afford such a distraction. She needed time away from this house of sorrow to come to terms with the appalling happenings of the last twelve hours. Besides, Jane and Lily were in no condition to attend to the job. Exhaustion was written all over them.

Michael, tall, soft-spoken, very much the academic, insisted on accompanying her, saying, 'I'm coming with you whether you like it or not.'

Bridget graciously accepted his offer of help.

Lily butted in saying, 'We have another knotty problem.'

'What is it?' Bridget asked anxiously.

'It's Eileen! Somehow or other, we've got to get her out of the house.'

'Oh, my God! Eileen!' Bridget cried out. 'The poor, unfortunate child!' A thorn jabbed at her heart.

'Muscha,' Aunt Jude chipped in solicitously, 'and isn't that one of the reasons I'm here?' She shook her head dolefully. 'Eileen's too young to be asked to cope with a trauma the likes of this.' She was glad to see her words had a mollifying effect on the girls. 'As soon as she's awake, I'll whisk her over to my place,' she said tentatively. 'To all intents and purposes she's coming to play with our Peggy; no need for any fuss.'

'Jude, you're an angel!' Bridget's relief was profound. 'It would certainly solve the problem.' She was thinking, what would we do without Aunt Jude? So dependable! Always there in times of trouble.

'In the meantime,' Aunt Jude said somberly, 'I must look in on Mary and say wee a prayer at the bedside for...' her voice croaked as she tried to continue, '...the departed soul of that darlin, little girl.' Despite her resolve to be strong for the family's sake, she broke down and cried.

Just after Jude left the door opened and our Nancy, looking and acting like a zombie, entered. The family watched without a word as she moved mechanically around the kitchen, mooching between the gas cooker, the cupboards, and the sink, making her porridge, eventually sitting down at the table to eat it.

'Did you mention anything to Aunt Jude about Peter?' Bridget now asked Lily.

'No, I didn't. I was thinking it would be best to keep quiet about it for the moment.'

'Agreed,' Bridget said.

'Yes, Michael interjected, 'I think it would be most prudent if Peter's name wasn't mentioned.'

'Not even to relatives?' Jane inquired.

'Not even to relatives,' Bridget answered. 'In the event of anyone asking about him, we'll say he's on assignment and we're trying to contact him.'

'Am I correct,' Michael inquired, 'in assuming that at this moment the only people who know about Peter's arrest are the five of us here and your mother?'

'You are correct,' Jane answered.

'Well then,' Bridget was unequivocal, 'there's no need for anyone else to know, unless mother herself decides otherwise.'

'People aren't fools,' our Nancy, hunched over her porridge, interjected grouchily. She'd come alive at last and was being her usual negative self. 'What makes you think they'll accept that tall yarn about Peter? There's no way we can hush this scandal up.'

'Jesus, Christ! our Nancy!' Lily pounced on her, 'Why do you always have to be such a bloody shit-disturber.'

Bridget wished to God Lily would curb her tongue; she knew very well that Michael came from a family that boasted a brother a priest, another a Christian Brother and two sisters nuns? The last thing Bridget needed at this moment was Michael to be exposed to that sort of language. Though Lily had a heart of gold, she could be very volatile: you never knew what she'd come out with next, particularly when she was at loggerheads with our Nancy.

'Michael I think we'd better get going,' Bridget announced jumping up abruptly. It was one way of getting Michael away from Lily's coarse language.

'Certainly,' Michael was up like a shot. Evidently he wasn't impressed with Lily's language either. 'I'll get our coats from the hall stand,' he said heading for the door.

While Michael was out of the room Bridget whispered to Jane, giving the nod towards Nancy still hunched over her breakfast, 'When we're gone, do your best to persuade that wan to keep Peter's arrest a secret.'

With Bridget and Michael gone, Jane motioned to Lily to let her do the talking. 'Look it, our Nancy,' she reasoned, 'for pity sake! you've seen how devastated Mother is. Is it too much to ask that we keep quiet about Peter's arrest and spare her further suffering?'

'Well, I'm sorry, but I can't see how we can,' Nancy argued. 'Besides I don't like telling deliberate lies.'

It was too much for Lily. 'Jesus Christ! our Nancy!' she shrieked, 'you're such a fecken hypocrite!'

Lily's outburst, as usual, only managed to make things worse. Jane knew that stubborn, pigheaded look on our Nancy's face didn't bode well for any entreaties she might make. The acrimony between her sisters was making it more and more difficult to get our Nancy's cooperation.

As a last resort Jane appealed to Lily. Nodding towards the ceiling, she said, 'Lily, please try and keep your voice down.'

'I'm sorry,' Lily simmered down. Reminded about what was upstairs the terrible pain was back.

Jane tried another tack on our Nancy. 'Our Nancy, she said quietly and calmly, 'one has only to see mother's demeanor to realize how desperately she's trying to block this terrible suffering from her mind; there's just so much the human spirit can handle.' Jane used her most persuasive voice. 'For the love of God let's not mention the subject of Peter's arrest, unless Mother brings it up herself.'

'What am I supposed to say if people ask me where Peter is?'

'Just say you're not sure and change the subject.'

'That's stupid!' our Nancy burst out.

Lily's patience was exhausted. 'Oh, for Christ sake! Can't you say he's away on assignment in Timbuck-bloody-too!'

But our Nancy wouldn't let it go at that, certainly not with Lily attacking her. 'Mark my word,' she said mulishly, 'no matter how much we try to hush it up, it's bound to leak out.' She made for the door, leaving as she usually did, consternation behind.

Like a bolt out of the blue, Lily suddenly had a brain wave. 'Father Vincent!' she exclaimed. 'If anyone can reach our Mother, it's the saintly father.'

'That's it!' Jane said, her face filled with poignant relief.

'But how do we get in touch with him?' Lily asked.

'A telegram!' Jane answered. 'We'll send a telegram to Newbridge. If you'll hold the fort here, I'll go out and do it immediately.'

With Lily's concurrence, Jane grabbed her coat and hurried out the door. However, within half-an-hour she was back looking very discouraged. 'None of the post offices are open on account of the fighting,' she told Lily somberly.

'Eileen's gone,' Lily announced.

'With Aunt Jude?'

'Yes, they left shortly after you went out. Aunt Jude insisted on giving her breakfast at her place.'

'Was she upset?'

'Not really. Well, to tell you nothing but the truth, I got the impression she wasn't properly awake — the effects of the sedative, I suppose. I'd say she was more confused than upset.'

'Thank God for that.'

For the rest of the morning the house was invaded by callers — friends and relatives offering condolences. But Mary, would talk to none of them, nor would she stir from Jody's side. Even relatives, of whom she was very fond, met with the same stony stare and the same silence when they tried to talk to her.

So it seemed like a miracle that on this day of all days, the saintly Father Vincent should arrive on the doorstep. He was on one of his regular visits to the Priory House in Tallaght (outside Dublin) and as was his wont when visiting Dublin, was dropping in to see his sister, Mary. When he knocked on the door of the O'Dwyer home he had no idea he was entering a house of mourning. Father Vincent had been labeled 'the saintly Father' by the family because of the way Mary blessed herself every time she mentioned his name.

'He's not canonized yet,' the family would tease her. 'Hasn't he got to die first.'

The door was opened to Father Vincent by a flustered middle-aged lady (a stranger) who on seeing this tall, gaunt, imperious looking priest in his middle fifties, grabbed his arm fussily and said, 'Wait there, don't move, I'll fetch Bridget.' Then she dashed away to the back.

Father Vincent thought it was all very curious. Why had the lady said Bridget and not Mary? He couldn't help wondering too about the myriad of muffled voices coming from the back. Could it be there was something wrong with Mary? At last one of the nieces — the pretty one — appeared. Maybe now, he thought, I'll find out what's going on. But instead, our Nancy turned on her heel and fled. It came as no surprise to Father Vincent: sure since the nieces became teenagers he'd become accustomed to that sort of behavior. Hadn't they only to lay eyes on him and they were full of excuses to rush away. It was understandable really; why would they want to spend time with their boring old uncle? Finally Bridget, the level-headed niece, arrived. Strangely on this occasion his reception was altogether different; her strained, white face seemed to lighten up at the sight of him.

Bridget was thinking, maybe there is a God in heaven after all; if anyone can bring comfort and solace to Mother it's the saintly Father. But imagine him being in Dublin at this time? It was an absolute miracle! Bridget brought Father Vincent into Mary's small office at the back of the shop where they could have some privacy. She told him about Jody's tragedy. Then finished by saying, 'We're all totally shocked and grieved by the death, but now Mother has us worried sick. We fear this terrible tragedy has affected her brain. She just sits there at Jody's bedside staring at Jody, doing nothing, saying nothing. It's like she's hypnotized.'

'Did she see the doctor?'

'No. She adamantly refuses to see the doctor.' At this point Bridge broke down, the tears couldn't be held back any longer. Father Vincent waited patiently as she gradually regained her composure. 'We've done everything we can think of to get through to her,' Bridget continued, 'but, Oh dear God! Father! nothing works. We're at our wit's end.' Bridget's face was drenched with tears.

'There, there, child!' the good father said. Though totally shocked by the frightful news, he put on a brave front. Placing a comforting hand on Bridget's shoulder, he said, 'you'd like me to speak some words of comfort to your Mother?'

'Yes, please, Father! She can't go on like this. She needs help — spiritual and physical.'

'Bring me to her, child.'

Bridget lead the Father up the stairs to her Mother's bedroom. As he entered the room, as though by divine influence, Mary turned her head and gave the slightest sign of recognition. Closing the door behind her, Bridget gave a sigh of relief; she felt a ton weight had been lifted from her shoulders. Downstairs she told the family, 'Anyway, you'll be glad to know Mother at least registered Father Vincent's presence.' Then casting her eyes up to heaven she added, 'Please, please God! Let him be able to help her.'

'Did you mention anything to him about Peter?' Jane whispered.

'No. The poor man was shocked enough by Jody's tragedy without bogging him down with another one,' Bridget answered. 'Besides, I still think it's up to Mother if she wants to tell him.'

There was a huge turnout of the local people when Jody's body was brought to Dominick Street Church (around the corner from the Rotunda Hospital) for the 'removal of the remains' ceremony at six o'clock that Saturday evening. The funeral would take place on Monday. After the ceremony, Mary, looking dazed and bewildered sat with members of her family in the mourners' bench at the front of the church, allowing her limp hand to be grabbed in gestures of sympathy by sympathizers. Her eyes gave not a flicker of recognition to any of them. Some who tried to give her an affectionate hug were surprised at the way she shrugged them off. This was not the woman they knew: the woman who'd always been there for them in time of trouble. So fragile and withdrawn had she become, they hardly recognized her.

'The poor unfortunate creature! She's absolutely demented,' a customer remarked to a friend. 'Will she ever be the same again?'

Inside Mary was a great void, a dry, arid nothingness, no sap of life. She thought, this has got to be a bad dream. What am I doing sitting here in this church with all these people shaking my hand? Everything's so blurred. Then her eyes fell on the coffin covered in flowers at the foot of the alter and the memory of Jody's death came racing back. Sweet Mother of God! That coffin does contain the dead body of my beloved child—the child who should be playing the part of an angel in the Easter pageant this very evening at the school.

'Isn't little Jody now a real angel in Heaven,' Father Vincent had asserted earlier.

A few rows behind them a group of 'shawlies' were talking. Their conversation floated towards the mourners in front. 'Well, anyways, t'is all over now,' the first voice said. 'Didn't they surrender this afternoon.'

'Bloody fools, the lot of them!' a hard voice rejoined. They need their heads examined: fancy thinkin they could beat the blazes out of the British.'

'All the same, ye can't help feelin sorry for them,' a sympathetic voice joined in. 'Dirty eejits that they are, aren't they entitled to their beliefs.'

'Not if it means burning down our city.' It was the hard voice again.

Another voice joined in, 'The whole bang shoot of them are assembled down there in front of the Rotunda. T'is rumored they're all goin to be executed.'

Bridget, sitting next to her Mother, heard enough. 'Come on Mother,' she said, standing up abruptly. 'Better get home, there'll be people waiting.'

Mary dawdled. Her drawn face had gone a grainy white. The conversation behind her had just reminded her about Peter. *T'is rumored they're all going to be executed, that's what the woman said. 'T'is rumored they're all going to be executed.* The words kept going round and round in her brain. Sweet Jesus! she thought, am I to lose my only son too?

Father Vincent, a tower of strength all afternoon, sitting next to Mary, also overheard the conversation. He felt relieved that the fighting was over. But it was a wonder to him why Bridget, sitting on the other side of Mary, was frantically motioning to him that she wanted to get her mother out of the church; wasn't there still a long line of sympathizers waiting to shake Mary's hand. Sitting next to the Father on the other side, Jane who also picked up on the conversation behind, was grateful to Bridget for making the move to get their mother out of the church away from all that loose talk. But it seemed the Father was reluctant to go.

Leaning over she whispered in his ear, 'Bridget thinks Mother's feeling poorly and that she should go home.'

Father Vincent responded positively. 'Of course, of course,' he said putting his hand under Mary's arm helping her to rise to her feet.

On the way out of the church, the saintly priest was mobbed by relatives shaking his hand and having a word with him. Bridget, continued holding her Mother's arm in a steel like grip, propelling her towards the entrance. Though it meant leaving the Father behind, she was determined to get her mother through the milling crowd to the mourning coach that awaited them in the street.

Coming up the rear, Jane made a decision: she would talk to Father Vincent about Peter. As he'd made no reference to Peter when he rejoined the family after being with their Mother, it was evident he knew nothing. During the removal ceremony it suddenly occurred to Jane that maybe it was time the Father was put in the picture. After all, he was wiser than any of them. Surely, he'd be able to advise them about how to get information about their brother, his fate, his whereabouts? But then there was the complication about the family wanting to keep the arrest secret: would the saintly father understand? Anyway, there was only one way to find out: she'd have to talk to him. Jane hung around the periphery of the crowd surrounding the saintly priest in the church, awaiting the moment he would be free. Though he was the center of attention, the Father's great sensitivity directed his gaze to the spot where Jane now stood. Instinctively he knew the child badly needed to talk to him.

Politely excusing himself, he came to her side. 'What is it, my child?' he inquired.

'Oh Father, could I have a word with you in private?' Jane asked. There was a strong plea in her voice.

'Of course, child.' The father drew Jane into the recessed, ornate Grotto honoring the Mother of Perpetual Succor. 'Something is troubling you, child,' he said. 'What is it?'

'Did mother say anything to you about Peter?'

'No, we talked very little. In fact we spent most of the time praying,' he said. 'But I did notice Peter's absence. Does he know about his little sister's death?'

'No,' Jane said, her eyes filled with tears. She bent her head. Now that the moment had come, she wondered how to tell this holy man the awful news about Peter?

As she hesitated the Father could see her intense distress. 'What is it about Peter?' he asked, his voice now filled with great compassion. 'Please tell me. It doesn't matter how bad it is?'

'He's been arrested for seditious acts against the Government,' Jane blurted out. Then it became too much for her. She put her hands over her face and the grieving she'd so valiantly suppressed all day burst like a damn inside her. Her body shook with sobs. It wasn't easy for Father Vincent to stand and look at this grief stricken child, but he decided to give her time. Giving vent to pent up grief and sorrow was a lot healthier than holding it in the way Mary was: if she could just let go and give into her sorrow. Just weep. Eventually regaining her composure, wiping her eyes and blowing her nose, Jane said 'I'm sorry, Father.'

'You've nothing to be sorry about, child,' the Father said. 'But tell me when was Peter arrested?'

'About an hour before Jody's...her voice trailed off. 'Oh, Father!' she groaned, 'We don't know what's happened to him, whether he's dead or alive. There are rumors abroad in the city that all the rebels are being executed.'

'He was a rebel?'

'He was associated with them.'

Father Vincent looked really troubled now. 'Goodness, gracious, Child! Such a lot of trouble!'

'Father,' Jane rushed on. 'The family is trying to keep the arrest a secret. We feel it would be easier on Mother if we didn't talk about it to outsiders for the moment.'

'Of course, of course.' Father Vincent was very solicitous. He scratched his head, momentarily lost for words. Eventually he said, 'Dear oh, dear! What a terrible lot of suffering the good Lord in his wisdom is sending my poor sister Mary and her family.' His eyes misted over. 'Of course, it explains her terrible depression.'

He patted Jane's shoulder. 'You know child,' he said, 'the only way we can hope to alleviate suffering is through prayer; together we must pray to God to give your mother and her family the strength to carry this cross.' Father Vincent had a thought. 'Now about what you're telling me, am I to take it you'd prefer that I didn't mention the subject of Peter to your mother or anyone else?'

'Unless she brings it up herself, Father, I think it would be kinder not to mention it.'

'That's alright with me,' Father Vincent said. 'Let us wait and see.'

Back at the house throughout the evening, people came and went. They stood around talking in hushed tones, drinking tea and eating the sandwiches and cakes provided in abundance by the relatives from the country. Some of the people imbibed a dram or two of whiskey, while others filtered in and out, only staying long enough to convey sympathy and deliver flowers and Mass Cards.

Sitting in the parlor, practically on top of the fire, because she couldn't get warm, Mary's remoteness continued. She craved solitude. Mechanically she shook hands and accepted sympathy, speaking no words, her stare so vacant, one sympathizer remarked to a friend, 'The only place you'd see the likes of that stare is in an asylum.'

Throughout the evening Jane and Lily took turns standing close to their mother, from time to time endeavoring to get her to eat or drink something, but she just waved everything away; it seemed she was quite determined not to let food or drink pass her lips. Round eight o'clock, Maisy and Alecia, two Moore Street hawkers, arrived. They came loaded with baskets of fruit and vegetables for the house.

Bridget let them in. 'Oh, ladies, we're delighted to see you,' Bridget greeted them, 'but Mother would have my life if I were to accept that food.'

'Awe, come on now!' Maisy insisted, 'Don't you know there's a terrible shortage of food in the city?'

'How's the Mammie?' Alecia interjected.

'Not too good,' Bridget's voice held a sad note. 'But, I'm sure she'll be glad to see you. Nonetheless, I can't take that food from you. You see our cousins from the country brought enough food to feed an army.'

'Arrah, go on outa that!' Alecia said, 'With all the visitors you'll be having in the next few days, you're bound to have need of it.'

Bridget hadn't the strength to argue. She lead them into the parlor. Making a beeline for Mary, ahead of them, Bridget whispered into her ear about the hawker's generosity. As Mary listened, she jerked her head and looked surprised. Except for the sainted father's arrival in the bedroom, this was the only other time Mary showed awareness of anything.

After Alecia finished offering her condolences to Mary, Maisy took Mary's cold hands into her warm ones. 'Ah, Mrs. O'Dwyer, isn't it meself what knows exactly what you're goin through,' she said sadly 'Didn't I bury me own seven-year-old young fella last year. Died of the meningitis he did. To be sure, t'is a terrible heart scald.'

Listening to Maisy, Mary's dull, lusterless eyes seemed to come alive: evidently Maisy's words were having an affect on her. 'Oh! My dear!' Mary said, with genuine sympathy, 'I'm so terribly sorry, Maisy.' She shook her head despondently. 'I never knew.'

'Ah sure and why would ye? With all your responsibilities, aren't you the busy lady!'

'Busy or not!' Mary came on strong. Suddenly she was conscious of the world outside her own — a world where other people suffered. 'I should have done something to help you,' she said. She felt guilt-ridden. She was thinking, here's a woman who's gone through the same pain I'm going through now and I didn't lift a finger to help her.

It would seem Maisy had succeeded in doing what everyone else had failed to do — penetrate the impenetrable.

'Now, Mrs. O'Dwyer, you're not to go worrying yourself,' Maisy insisted, then leaned closer. 'You know something, Missus,' she said, 'the human spirit is a wondrous thing.' Her voice rang with great sincerity. 'Despite all the suffering and hardship the good Lord sends us, it seems He always provides us with the strength to pull through.' Her eyes were filled with tears. 'Believe me, no matter how sad and poorly ye feel this day, time *is* the great healer.'

Observing from afar, the family wondered what Maisy could possibly be saying that was having such a phenomenal effect on their Mother: she actually appeared quite spirited as they talked.

Mary then remembered about the food. 'Maisy,' she said, 'we can't accept the food you brought; it's taking it out of the mouths of your children.'

'Not at all, not at all, Missus!' Maisy gave a short laugh. 'As a matter a fact, you'd be doin them a favor. Sure aren't they fed up with the same auld diet day after day — nothin but fruit and vegetables. Even though I wasn't able to work the stall in Moore street this past week, didn't I keep goin to the market each mornin, hopin and prayin the fightin would soon be over. As a consequence, aren't we up to our eyeballs in fruit and vegetables.' She winked mischievously at Mary. 'Putting it crudely Missus, no one in our house suffers from the constipation, if ye get me drift.'

Mary's eyes held the vestige of a smile. She thought these people are salt of the earth. 'Well, all right,' she said. 'If you insist, but I must pay you for it.'

'Ach, all right, if it'll ease yer mind I'll accept the money, but not tonight. It can wait.'

'Now I want you to help yourselves to the food and drink on the tables there,' Mary told the two hawkers.

'Can I get ye somethin, Missus?' Alecia asked.

About to refuse, Mary had second thoughts. 'Well, maybe a sandwich or two,' she said.

'And a cuppa?' Maisy interjected.

'That would be nice,' Mary graciously accepted.

Mary had just received a cup of tea and a plate of sandwiches from Alecia, when the door burst open and this wild, crazed looking young woman dashed in. The heavy perfume that wafted in with her, plus her extraordinary dress made certain she got everyone's attention. The dress, comprised of copious veils in a variety of colors trailing down to her ankles, was in the style of a harem character. On her head a jewel-studded cap held a very elaborately embroidered shawl in place. Then there was an overload of jewelry jingling and jangling on her arms and legs. Completing the spectacle was a face that was a mask with dark make-up — a face that could only belong to an actress. Which was exactly what this eccentric creature was — Nancy Pete, Peter O'Dwyer's wife — the actress.

Seeing this exhibition, Jane couldn't help thinking, any minute now Nancy Pete will go into her Salome act and treat us too the 'dance of the seven veils.'

'A right sight for a house of mourning,' Lily whispered to Jane.

With arms flailing and hands clawing on the air, Nancy Pete let out a piercing scream followed by the words, 'Peter! My Peter! Why wasn't I told about my husband?'

Nobody answered. Nobody could. The room was in a state of shock.

Alecia, standing in front of Mary, blocked her from Nancy Pete's view for the moment. Until curiosity got the better of her and she turned round to see what the rumpus was all about, thus leaving Mary exposed to the daughter-in-law's verbal onslaught.

'Mother,' Nancy Pete shrilled rushing towards Mary, 'why was I kept in ignorance about the fate of my Peter? You knew. The family knew. Everyone knew but me, his wife?'

For seconds Mary's throat was paralyzed. Then her natural doggedness seemed to come to her assistance as she answered quietly, 'we didn't know where to contact you.'

'You could have found out from the Abbey Theater. Or someone could have placed a note in my letter box.'

People who didn't know her were impressed by Nancy Pete's beautiful body language, facial grimaces, perfect voice inflections. No question about it, she was a much talented actress, who, at this moment, was giving one of her best performances.

'Well, you see,' Mary stammered, 'because of Jody's tragedy, I'm afraid…' Mary was trying hard to find the right words to placate

Nancy Pete, 'it kind of slipped...'

'Do you think...what happened to my Peter is not...a tragedy?' Nancy Pete interjected in her flawless phrasing. Then in a voice that shrieked, 'Were it not for your Nancy telling me the facts, I'm quite sure your family's code of silence would've kept me in the dark indefinitely. '

Mary's face was a mirror of successive emotions, incredulity at first, then horror, then concern. At the best of times she didn't see eye to eye with her daughter-in-law. Well, they'd nothing in common. She did, however, appreciate the fact that Nancy Pete made her son happy. And wasn't that all that mattered?

Father Vincent, just back from reading his breviary, was shocked at what he was seeing and hearing: his niece-in-law, the actress, venting her rage on Mary, startled people — not a calm nerve among them — staring in amazement.

Someone said, '*What's she talking about? Nobody said anything about Peter and a tragedy?*'

If these people were filled with curiosity, who could blame them? Who would expect to encounter a spectacle the likes of this in a house of mourning? With practiced ease, Father Vincent took the situation in hand. After a quiet word in Nancy Pete's ear, he took her gently by the arm and lead her from the room. With the closing of the door, the room took a collective deep breath.

Now conscious of all the curious looks directed at her Mother, Jane felt that the situation needed to be explained in some way to the people. But no one was making a move to do anything about it and the silence was exceptionally embarrassing. I suppose I'd better do it myself, Jane decided. With much trepidation, she stood up. Inwardly quaking, she prayed, please God! Don't let me make a mess of this. She took a deep breath.

'In case you're all wondering what that commotion was all about,' she said, the words coming haltingly in the beginning, then as she gained confidence, coming in a rush, 'our brother, Peter, has been detained for questioning by the authorities.' Trying to keep her voice on an even keel, she continued, 'It's nothing very serious;

it's just that his wife, our sister-in-law, was away on tour with the Abbey players and has only just now found out.' She smiled whimsically, 'As you can see she's a bit upset.'

The hum of voices in the room resumed — picking up where they left off. People relaxed. Jane's explanation hit the mark.

Mary was grateful for Jane's intervention; proud of the way she'd handled things, the discretion she used.

'You did great!' Lily said speaking in a low tone squeezing Jane's shoulder. Then unable to conceal her aggravation she spluttered quietly, 'Jaysus! I'll bust our Nancy's face when I see her.' Looking around the room, she added, 'And have you noticed she's conveniently missing?'

Right enough, there was no sign of our Nancy.

'For God's sake, Lily!' Jane pleaded, 'Let's have some peace!'

The door opened to admit a supposedly more composed Nancy Pete. She was followed by Father Vincent who nodded benevolently, first to Mary, then to the other people present.

Overflowing with sympathy, Nancy Pete rushed towards Mary her arms outstretched, gushing and crying, 'Acone! Acone! Agus Acone! (Sorrow! Sorrow! And more sorrow!) Mary found herself drowning in an sea of georgette as Nancy Pete smothered her in an embrace. Then came the deluge of Nancy Pete's tears soaking her shoulder. Finally, Nancy Pete lifted her head. 'My god! Mother!' she wailed in a voice as plaintive as the banshee's. 'How can you bear the pain of it? Your darlin little Jody — that gorgeous, wonderful, child who reached out to life as a flower reaches out to the sun — her young life snuffed out like a candle! Lost to you forever!'

Mary cringed under the weight of her words. Once again the room was reduced to silence. This time Michael Barry intervened: placing his arm around Nancy's Pete's shoulder he whispered in her ear. Whatever words of wisdom were transmitted, Nancy Pete allowed Michael to usher her out of the room.

Jane was furious. 'God!' she whispered furtively to Lily. 'That damn woman! Wouldn't you think she could exercise a bit of tact.'

'Doesn't surprise me one bit,' Lily said bitingly. 'Even if it is a house of mourning, doesn't it provide Nancy Pete with an audience to strut her stuff.'

'Poor Mother!' Jane said. 'To be subjected to that kind of embarrassment and humiliation on such a sorrowful occasion. And just when she was beginning to look relaxed talking to Maisy. God! Nancy Pete's timing couldn't have been worse!' Jane was feeling acute pity for her Mother.

'Can you imagine Mother's state of mind now?' Lily said bristling with anger. 'Because things weren't bad enough, that exhibitionist bitch had to create a furor on top of it.'

Jane shook her head despairingly, 'It'll be all right if Mother doesn't collapse under the strain of it all.'

But Mary was far from collapsing. She astonished everyone standing up and cutting through the silence. Perhaps it was that, after a series of shocks, Mary's body acclimated itself, like being inoculated — each subsequent shock delivered less impact.

'In case you hadn't noticed,' Mary said deferentially, 'my daughter-in-law is an actress. If her husband, my son, Peter, was here, he'd explain the situation thus: 'Don't take it too seriously,' he'd say. 'It's just my dear wife, Nancy — the actress — getting carried away by the exuberance of her own verbosity!' '

The room erupted in laughter. An overwhelming sense of relief swept over the family as they listened to and laughed at their Mother. Surely now she was back to her normal, stable self again. If Nancy Pete had done nothing else, she'd given her mother-in-law a helping hand out of her terrible melancholia. Who would have guessed an hour ago that Mary would respond in such a frivolous fashion to Nancy Pete's foolishness? Now the family's burden would be lightened, because wasn't their Mother the ROCK from which they drew their strength?

§

In the Rotunda Gardens day passed into night. Earlier on, a sickening incident took place in front of the prisoners. They were witnesses to the insults of a British officer when he had Clarke and Willie Pearse (Padraig Pearse's brother) and others stripped and searched in front of them.

'You never know where the bastards have it hidden,' the officer remarked as he gave instructions to the khaki doing the job.

Totally outraged, Willie murmured to Ciaron, 'How low can human beings sink?' He was close to tears. 'It's God awful that we have to stand here helpless and witness this degradation.'

'Sure t'is common knowledge that the British Army look on us Irish Republicans as scum,' Ciaron answered angrily. 'They take a perverse pleasure in demeaning and degrading us.'

The night passed with the coatless mass of prisoners huddling together trying to keep warm, surrounded by a circle of bayonets keeping guard. Sleep came eventually to Willie, but only in tormented naps.

Dawn arrived. Throughout the morning the sky was plastered with white and black clouds. Later on when the sun broke through it brought a little warmth and comfort to the cold and weary prisoners. At midday the order was given to the prisoners to get into line and start marching. Heavily escorted, the prisoners marched down Sackville Street en route to Richmond Barracks. Passing the ruins of the Post Office and seeing the tricolor flags still flying over its portico, the volunteers couldn't suppress the urge to cheer wildly, while exacting abuse from their escorts. Through empty and smoldering streets the prisoners marched. En route some malcontents threw rotten food at them from upstairs windows, others yelled obscenities, while a few attempted to assault them. These times the prisoners were glad of the protection of their escorts.

Arriving at the Richmond Barracks there was a general halt in the yard, where known leaders were separated from the rest. After that, the Head of the Detective Branch spent his time peering closely into volunteer's faces, trying to identify lesser known leaders. A few compassionate Tommies with Irish accents held out water bottles to the thirsty prisoners only to have them ordered back by their officers. Obeying the order, an Irish Tommy spat on the ground. 'Men are human beings,' he muttered to his companion, 'even if they do pick you off from behind chimney pots.'

Willie wondered about all the winking and nodding being directed at the prisoners by Tommies with Irish accents. 'This sudden camaraderie fills me with suspicion,' he told Ciaron.

'Typical!' Ciaron remarked sounding very skeptical. 'The Irish Tommies and their so called friendliness! I wouldn't trust them as far as I'd throw them!' His face was filled with disdain. 'You can be sure those Irish Tommies have been well schooled in the art of soliciting information from the Irish prisoners.'

A sergeant arrived in serving out tins of bully beef and biscuits. 'Tuck in, lads,' he said, 'for yis might as well be shot on full bellies as on empty ones.'

After that, the men were ordered into a large gloomy barrack room to await their turn to be interrogated by detectives — G. men — In the smaller anterooms.

'Name?' the detective asked Willie.

'Willie MacNamee.'

'I see you have the rank of second lieutenant?'

'That's right.'

'So you'd know all the leaders associated with this rebellion?'

Willie didn't answer.

'Now, Willie,' a Tommy with an Irish accent standing close behind the detective, butted in, 'if you're prepared to cooperate with us and give us names — like if you'd point out any leaders among that crowd out there — we'd be only too happy to release you immediately and let you go back to your family.' His statement was followed by lots of winks and nods to Willie. Ciaron's words about the deviance of the Irish Tommies began to make sense. The Irish Tommy then leaned over the detective and said, 'Amn't I right, sir?'

The detective nodded affirmation. 'So, would you be prepared to give us that information?' the detective asked Willie.

Standing to attention, Willie said nothing. He was mindful of MacDermott, still at large, mingling with the prisoners outside: so far he had managed to stay unidentified. But even if it meant torture and death Willie was resolute; he would not betray the man. In his eyes, MacDermott was one of Ireland's greatest patriots.

'Who was your leader?' the detective asked.

'I'm not at liberty to say.'

'Which building?'

'Building?'

'Yes. The one you fought in?'

Willie remained silent. Behind the detective the Tommy continued his mime, indicating to Willie that he would get his freedom if he snitched.

'When did you join the volunteers?' the detective asked.

Again Willie was silent. Suddenly, something struck him as rather amusing. Imagine, he thought, what they'd say, if I told them I hadn't fired a single shot in the Rising. Wouldn't that be a big surprise. However, he'd no intention whatsoever of divulging this, or any other fact to these people. Amn't I feeling guilty enough, he thought, without adding to it by giving these shysters the satisfaction of knowing about my faulty rifle.

'All right, dismiss,' the detective ordered.

Willie left the room and joined his comrades. They all confirmed they'd had the exact same experience.

'They're really desperate to nab all the leaders,' Ciaron told Willie.

Collins, standing beside MacDermott, quietly commented on the volunteers' loyalty. 'T'would've been dead easy for them to point the finger at the leaders and gain their freedom,' he remarked, 'but thank the Lord our volunteers can't be bought. Betrayal is anathema to them.'

Late afternoon the volunteers found themselves back in the barrack yard with a forest of bayonets surrounding them. Once again they were ordered to line up for a march. As they set off on the march, Willie was glad to see MacDermott limping beside Collins. Thank God! he thought, he wasn't found out. He was remembering MacDermott's remarks about all the leaders being executed.

Suddenly there was panic.

'Stop!' cried a loud, angry voice. It was the voice of the Head of the Detective Branch. 'We want that man,' he said, pointing his finger at MacDermott. 'He was one of the signatories to the Proclamation of Independence.'

MacDermott was lead inside the barracks again. Watching his friend limp away, Collins looked sad and dejected. Obviously for a price, some rotter had ratted on MacDermott. It seemed Collins had been too optimistic about the volunteers' loyalty. Down the quay sides the prisoners marched, past smoking ruins and dismantled barricades.

As they neared the North Wall, a drunken woman reeled out of a side-lane waving a cabbage stalk. 'Fools, the lot a yis!' she shrilled. 'Yis might as well have tried to fight the bastards with pitchforks.'

Finally when the prisoners reached the boat, they were ordered down into the ship's hold, normally used for exporting cattle to Britain. Ready to die with fatigue, the first prisoners to arrive lay down on the stinking floor. Willie and Ciaron considered themselves lucky to get a place there. Then as more and more prisoners filed in and the floor area filled up with stretched out bodies, Willie suggested they tighten up by lying head to toe — like sardines in a tin. This made room for more prisoners to stretch out. Nonetheless, a lot of them had to stand throughout the journey.

After a long wait, the engine of the boat whirred and started up. It finally moved. It was pitch black when the boat reached the open sea. The swelling and dipping in the rough Irish Sea was the final assault on the prisoners' wracked and wretched bodies: along with the putrid stench of cattle dung, stinking body odors and sweaty socks, the prisoners now had to contend with sea-sickness. Lying on the floor in this fetid atmosphere, vomit spewing over him, Willie couldn't help feeling that the devil had opened the gates of hell and dragged him in.

Then suddenly out of the darkness a joker standing up, remarked, 'Wouldn't I give me soul now for a bottle a Guinness.'

'Course ye would,' came the reply from the floor, 'so that ye could drown us in it.'

Despite their agony, the prisoners roared laughing.

Willie dozed a while. In his dreams, when buildings weren't falling on him, he was swimming in a sea of sharks.

In the clear, cloudless dawn of the next day, Holyhead rose before them. Though the volunteers didn't know what was going to happen to them — if they were going to live or die or ever set foot on their native soil again — as they disembarked, amid the cry of the gulls that rose above the wind, it was evident that a great pride stirred in them. Maybe their dream had turned to dust, but they had the feeling that their deed would not be in vain.

COLLINS

Chapter VIII

Newbridge
Co. Kildare
5th May, 1916

Dear Mary:

At last my inquiries regarding Peter's fate have borne some fruit. I am pleased to be able to tell you that Peter is alive and well. Presently he is being detained in one of His Majesty's prisons in England. Unfortunately its location is unknown to me at this time.

I sincerely hope this modicum of news, acquired on good authority, will bring some ease to your mind. Though not very informative, it was the best intelligence I could glean from sources that must remain anonymous.

It goes without saying that I shall continue my efforts to uncover news of Peter. Be assured that should any fresh news come to hand, it will be promptly passed on to you.

Keep up the prayers as I do — remembering to offer a prayer for your special intention at the celebration of the Mass every day.

Try to take consolation from the words of Saint Augustine: 'Our hearts are restless until they're rested in the Lord.'

Yours in Jesus Christ
Vincent

§

Willie roved round and round, backwards and forwards in his small cell which kept him isolated from the outside world. Now in 'solitary' for two weeks in Stafford Prison, the only way he could tell the time of day was by the shadow of the sunlight on the high wall outside, seen through the bars of his tiny window. On dull or wet days he never knew the time until the roars of the sentries were heard at mealtimes. Otherwise there was an eternal silence, broken only by distant town noises. The first week Willie's mind was preoccupied with thoughts of Easter week and the Rising. He had lots of time to think. He wondered what had happened in Dublin since the surrender? What became of the leaders? Had the country beyond Dublin risen? Worst of all was the recurring nightmare that haunted him nightly — Bud lying in the middle of a heap of bodies, his blood flowing like a river over the cobblestones. In his dream Willie tried to reach him, but his feet were embedded in concrete. Invariably he woke with a jolt in a terrible sweat.

However, as time passed and the hunger Willie was feeling began to assert itself, these thoughts and dreams slowly faded. Food was an abstraction. Was there anything so real in life as food? His mind was continually consumed with thoughts of it. Even the crumbs that fell on the doorstep of his cell when the bread was handed in, became precious. And despite the food's tastelessness and meagerness, he couldn't remember when he had eaten with such savagery nor gulped cocoa with such gusto. He had stopped thinking.

An hour-and-a-half's exercise, in small groups, walking round and round the stone yard below, was the daily recreation at no fixed time. It was a joyless relaxation — keeping three paces apart, walking, doubling, trotting — while sentries kept watch outside the Guardroom beside the entrance. No talking.

This morning, for a few minutes, Willie doubled with a young man named O'Dwyer. He knew his name because Sergeant Power, the sentry on duty, obnoxious in the extreme, barked, 'O'Dwyer take that smirk off your face before I wipe it off.' Evidently O'Dwyer was the target of the sergeant's bad temper today. As Willie and O'Dwyer marched together round the yard, O'Dwyer held his hand open for Willie to read, 'Ten Leaders Executed.'

The shock made Willie stumble; his anger became so great he could feel the drum beat of his heart against his ribs. He stomach twisted in knots adding to his wretchedness. For seconds he was totally out of step with O'Dwyer.

Thankfully the exercise period was soon over. As the prisoners entered the building, O'Dwyer surreptitiously squeezed Willie's arm in sympathy. Back to the cell and the black iron door, Willie's mind was swallowed up with bitter thoughts about the brave men who had given their lives for Ireland. He wished to God he could find out more about the executions. Who were the ten? What else was happening in his country? But his solitude made it impossible.

At noon came food — a hash of beans, tinned meat threaded with lumps of fat which, despite its awfulness, he devoured with relish. During the afternoon, except for the odd shout or whistle at rare intervals from the bottom of the jail, there was silence everywhere. The sun's shadow a third of the way down on the wall out-side indicated four-thirty. Time for tea and chunks of bread — the last repast of the day. Silence again until evening. Then just before lights out, some Dublin lad would recite homespun poetry at the top of his voice:

'Oh, Kathleen Mavournine!
How Dublin aches for three,
Thy wounds will ever bleed,
Till thy soul be free.'

This would be followed by the song, 'I'll take you home again Kathleen.' God bless him, Willie thought. How he cheers us up. Trust a Dublin man to find fun in hell.

Through Peter's isolation mixed tidings broke once in a while when Walsh, an orderly who was sympathetic to the Cause, brought a whisper of news with the morning slop pail, or whenever he was on duty delivering chunks of bread, once in a while managing a few extra chunks for Peter. Taking necessities and luxuries for granted all his life, the problem of surviving hunger was not one Peter had ever contemplated, let alone had to deal with. With a stomach that was in a constant state of rumble and gurgle from hunger, Peter was mighty grateful for Walsh's munificence.

On the seventh of May, a week after Peter's arrival in Stafford Jail,

Walsh handed him a cutting from a newspaper. The cutting gave details of the executions, three days after the surrender of the three main leaders—Clarke, the old Fenian who had done so much to bring about the Rising, Thomas McDonagh, poet and rebel Commandant and Patrick Pearse, poet and Commandant General of Ireland's First Republican Army. Disbelief, anger and sadness roared through Peter in quick succession.

'That's British justice for you now!' Walsh said scathingly. 'Those poor bastards! It only took the British three days to court martial, sentence and shoot them, without even affording them proper legal aid.'

A few days later Walsh once again was the bearer of further bad news. Seven more leaders had been executed. The following Sunday at Mass—the one and only time the prisoners had any kind of human intercourse (heavily supervised, of course)—the priest called for prayers for the souls of the departed leaders, adding four more to the list, which now included Willie Pearse (Patrick Pearse's brother), all of whom were executed by firing squad.

Many of the prisoners were hearing the news of the executions for the first time. The congregation rocked with shock. Pain, contempt and disgust registered on faces that boldly tried to hold back the tears.

Sitting behind Willie, Collins couldn't contain his anger, 'Jesus Christ!' he roared at the top of his voice. 'Britain hasn't seen the last of this. Ireland will rise in a mighty revolt over these new graves.'

On the third Sunday, volunteer orderlies replaced the regular sentries at the Mass. This afforded the prisoners more freedom to communicate with each other. The world came nearer as notes and whispers passed among the prisoners in the makeshift chapel. Little attention was paid to the Mass. There were whispered questions about sentries hinting that changes would soon be taking place in Stafford Prison. Could anyone say what the changes were? Did it have anything to do with the prisoners' ultimate fate? Would they too be facing a firing squad like their leaders? Someone mentioned something about rumors of Asquith being in Dublin. It brought a glimmer of hope. Could it mean a provisional Government for Ireland? Release soon?

No one had any answers.

The following evening as Willie was dozing, the door opened and a Tommy, wearing a patch over his left eye, entered. 'Why the hell didn't you wait till the war was over. I'd have helped you then?' he said in a voice that sounded vaguely familiar. 'Nice mess you've gone and got yourselves into, with Pearse, Connolly and twelve of your best men shot. Dublin in ruins.'

The Tommy removed the patch revealing a black hole where the eye had once been. Then covered it up quickly, but not before Willie recognized that it was Frank Spenser from Liverpool — the same Frank, who, way back, had introduced Willie to Irish politics.

'Holy Smoke!' Willie roared and chuckled. 'What the hell are you doing here?' Despite his friend's grating remarks, Willie couldn't be more pleased to see him.

'Temporary duty. Even though I lost the eye and I'm having treatment for the other one, I insisted on doing some light work.'

'What happened to you?'

'Two days after reaching the Front a shell exploded about ten yards from the trench, killing ten of our men and blowing out my left eye.'

'What bad luck.'

'Not really. Didn't it get me away from the horrors of that dreadful war.' Frank looked heavenwards. 'The Lord's been good to me.'

'So, how is the sight in the right eye?'

'Twenty-twenty.' Frank took a fit of laughing. 'Of course, I'm playing up the blindness like mad. They won't be getting me back to that Front in a hurry. Anyway,' he continued, 'when I saw your name on the Prisoners' List as McNamee W., Irish Prisoner, Number 125F, I guessed t'was yourself and here I am to impart the glad tidings.'

'Glad tidings?'

'Yeah. The worse is over for you Irish prisoners. For the rest of your stay here you blokes are to be treated as political prisoners. Then, as soon as it can be arranged, you're going to be shoved up to a camp in Wales till the war is over.'

'Does that mean we can leave our cells?'

'Just that. From now on the only thing the cells will be used for is sleeping.'

'Well, thank God for that,' Willie answered with relief. 'But tell us, how did this miracle come about?'

'Do you know that fellow Mick Collins?'

'Yeah.'

'Ye can thank him for the change,' Frank said. 'Apparently since his arrival here he's been nagging for political status for you prisoners, insisting that none of you are criminals, which is the way you're being treated.' Frank gave a sudden fleeting smile. 'A very tenacious agitator you've got in that man Collins,' he said. 'Doesn't give up easily. Last week in my presence he had a blazing row with the sergeant major. Guess who came off worst?'

'The sergeant major?'

'The very man.'

'Well, God bless Mick!'

§

Mary's heart nearly burst with relief when she saw the English stamp and recognized Peter's scrawl on the envelope. On her way in from seven o'clock Mass she was, as usual, waylaying the postman.

'I hope it's the news you've been waiting for?' the postman remarked, handing her a bundle of letters with the English one prominently displayed on top. For the past few weeks he couldn't help noticing the way Mrs. O'Dwyer met him at the hall door every morning and grabbed the post from his hands before he had time to push it through the letterbox. Like so many Dublin mothers he encountered, Mrs. O'Dwyer had that look of expectancy when he arrived. But, with no letter there, the look became one of bleak disappointment which laid bare her blighted hopes. This morning, however, was different. Immediately her eyes fell on the English envelope, Mrs. O'Dwyer's face was transformed.

With the joy flowing from her, she said, 'The blessings a God on you, Tom. I think my prayers have been answered.'

> *North Internment Camp*
> *Frongoch*
> *WALES*
> *21st May, 1916*

Dear Mother:

No, this is not a figment of your imagination. Yes, it is a letter from your son, Peter, who, strangely enough, is not writing from the grave. Despite the diabolical hardship of prison life, where the mind is bound and the spirit shackled, I'm still in the land of the living, alive and kicking.

The point is, I would have written before now telling you where I was, but incarceration in solitary in the Stafford Jail didn't lend itself to the luxury of letter writing. Those three weeks in solitary, however, weren't entirely wasted. A lot of time was spent in reflection about the past when I took so much for granted, when I didn't appreciate how good life was and how important family and friends were. And yes, Mother, you'll be glad to know I'm working overtime on the rosary beads — doing lots of praying. Being allowed to write this letter is a sort of answer to prayer.

Another answer to prayer is the fact that we have now been moved to this camp in Wales and are at last being treated as political prisoners — termed 'internees' actually — which, among other things, gives us the freedom to write and receive one letter a month. Hence I'll have to ask you to communicate the news of my letter to my wife Nancy.

This Frongoch camp lies in the midst of the hills and valleys of North Wales — rough moorland country. Its wildness, background of mountains, scattered trees and rich growth of heather, remind some internees of their own homes in Ireland. It's agreeable country, suitable for the sport of shooting and fishing in which we internees are not allowed to participate. ('As yet' as my friend Mick Collins would say.) The camp is divided into two — a Northern one and a Southern one. As both camps seem to be quite full it's hard to say how many internees there are altogether.

The one bit of cheer in our lives is the big field that lies between the two camps. It's here that rude, violent contests, which courtesy demands we call football matches, take place. Up to recently we used a make shift paper ball. But yesterday we were the grateful recipients of a grand, solid football, donated by the Liverpool Gaelic League. What joy! The whole area, needless to say, is surrounded by barbed wire. Apparently German prisoners formally occupied this camp but were removed to make room for the Irish internees.

One of the many ironies is that at least a quarter of the men in my camp know little about the Rising. One man told me he was forced off the street, collected on sight in the Dublin round-up. His only crime was that he was walking the streets. Furthermore, the innocent men's protestations have been to no avail.

One consolation is that some of the mail-handlers have sympathy with the plight of the internees. So here's hoping when it comes to censoring this letter they won't obliterate too much of it with that blasted blue pencil of their's.

I sincerely hope that my Nancy and all the family are keeping well. For God's sake write soon and tell me all the news.

Love to you all,
Peter

Mary's eyes slowly misted over as she sat in silence staring at Peter's letter.

'I heard the news! A letter from Peter!' Bridget bounced excitedly into the room disturbing Mary's thoughts. Her mother raised her head. She looked anything but happy. 'My God!' Bridget gasped, 'He's all right, I hope?' Seeing her mother so downcast sent a shiver of dread through her.

'Yes, of course,' Mary said in a low voice: she had that faraway look that suggested woolgathering. 'Here' she said handing the letter to Bridget, 'read it for yourself.'

After reading the letter Bridget smiled reassuringly. 'Well, isn't that an almighty relief!' she said. 'At least we know he's alive and safe.'

'That he's alive and safe is about all we do know,' Mary said with an air of gloom. 'What I'd like to know is, how he is physically? Is he being properly fed? Is he sleeping properly? When will he be released?'

'Well, now, if he were to furnish the likes of that information, t'would surely be classified as loose talk by the censors and you'd probably end up with a letter full of blue blobs. Wouldn't that be much more frustrating?'

'I suppose you're right,' Mary said with a sigh. 'I should be grateful for small mercies.' She became pensive. 'Trouble is, I now have to pay a visit to that eccentric daughter-in-law of mine and show her the letter. And, to be sure,' she groaned, 'there'll be fire and brimstone over the fact that Peter wrote to me and not to her.'

'Look on the bright side,' Bridget said with a burst of laughter, 'won't you be assured of a grand performance.'

The mention of performance brought a smile to Mary's face. 'A performance I could well do without,' she said jocosely. Then she had an idea. 'Bridget, you wouldn't fancy doing the job, would you?'

'You mean visit Nancy Pete?'

'Yes.'

'And deprive you of all that wonderful theater.' Bridget went into paroxysms of laughter. 'Not to mention that the show will be free; won't cost you a penny.' Bridget's laughter was contagious enough to get Mary going.

Eventually simmering down and becoming more serious she said, 'As her mother-in-law, I suppose it is my duty to do the visiting and show her Peter's letter.' She sighed. 'Better take the bull by the horns and get the blooming interview over as quickly as possible.'

Mary set out that afternoon on foot to walk to the couple's Georgian Flat in Leeson Street; no sense in depending on the trams that were so erratic. Normally, the walk would be quite a pleasant one: about two miles, going through Sackville Street, Dame Street, round College Green, up Grafton Street (which would afford a glimpse at the high fashion in Switzer's windows), diagonally across Stephen's Green and on to Leeson Street. But since the Rising, traversing her beloved Sackville Street was no longer the pleasure it used to be. Seeing the burnt-out shells of buildings, the mountains of rubble, bricks and stones, was heart wrenching. It was a scene to be avoided. But today there was no alternative; it had to be faced. She was glad to see the workmen, however, making a start on cleaning up the mess in Sackville Street. Behind hoardings they were knocking down what remained of the buildings. The result was a cloud of floating dust which made the street look as if it was fog bound.

Notwithstanding the prevailing atmosphere, hawkers/shawlies were back trading around Nelson's Pillar. Their stalls were a riot of Spring flowers; daffodils, narcissus, tulips, azaleas, irises, hydrangea, mixed with potted geraniums in blazing shades of scarlet, puce and pink. If nothing else, the flowers brought color and cheer to the gloom of Sackville Street. Nelson's Pillar was a veritable oasis in a desert of dust and crumbling buildings. Seeing the shawlies reminded Mary of Alecia's words in the shop yesterday.

'And yet within a month,' Alecia whispered contemptuously, 'those selfsame 'shawlies' who spat at the volunteers, now, if you please, have pictures of the executed leaders on their walls with Sacred Heart lamps in front of them.'

Just thinking about those horrific executions of the leaders of the Sinn Fein Rebellion (the name now given to the Rising) brought a lump to Mary's throat. The executions had now gone on for three weeks. As recently as last week, Sean MacDermott was executed. Two days later it was James Connolly's turn. (He was quoted in the newspapers as being 'the father of the Rising.') Injured and unable to stand, Connolly faced the firing squad sitting in a chair.

Reading details of the executions Mary couldn't help feeling that this was a bad reflection on British justice. Later editions of the newspapers reported that masses of Irish people, who, like herself, had taken no part or no side in the Rising, shared her feelings about British injustice.

For instance, today one banner headline charged, EXECUTIONS SERVE TO LIGHT NEW FIRES OF HATRED WHERE NONE EXISTED BEFORE. Along with that, she noticed a lot of

Letters to the Editor protesting vehemently against the executions. Even hardliners, who were opposed to the Rising, went so far as to sing the praises of the very rebels they had hitherto condemned. Judging by the tone of today's paper, it was conceivable that the whole nation had banded together in one mighty voice denouncing the executions.

Allowing for Nancy Pete's melodramatic propensities, Mary was shocked at the girl's appearance when she opened the door. Ripely pregnant with her first child, Nancy Pete — who earlier in her pregnancy looked the picture of health — now looked more like a gravestone, her face bleached of color, her eyes dark-circled.

Striving to mask her shock, Mary blurted out, 'Nancy Pete, I hope I'm not disturbing you?' Then added hastily, 'But I've had a letter from Peter, which I thought...'

'Oh my God!' With a burst of joy, Nancy Pete suddenly threw her arms up to heaven, her bulk visibly shaking. 'He's alive! Oh my God! I can't believe it! He's alive!' she screeched. Then just as suddenly she calmed down. 'Mother,' she said, 'you'd better come in.' With a lavish flourish, Nancy Pete ushered Mary into her beautiful Georgian drawing room with its high ceiling painted a sunburst yellow and its carved moldings painted a gloss white. 'It's a great treat for me to unexpectedly entertain any member of the O'Dwyer family,' Nancy Pete remarked, pursing and tightening her lips provocatively as she pumped the cushions on the chesterfield. Then, with a tinge of sarcasm, she added, 'particularly at a time like this when I feel so abandoned, forsaken and alone.'

The theatricals had commenced.

Consciously Mary forced herself to relax as she eased herself on to the comfortable chesterfield in this lavish drawing room with its showy furniture and furnishings. Trusting her hand into her purse Mary produced Peter's letter.

Contrary to expectations, when Nancy Pete laid her eyes on the letter she burst into bitter tears. 'Why! why! why is it always this way?' she cried resentfully tearing wildly at her hair as her tears flowed.

'Which way?'

'Which way do you think?' Nancy Pete's voice was shrill and contemptuous. 'Do I have to spell it out for you, Mother?'

Uncertain, Mary shook her head. 'I don't know what you're talking about?'

'For God's sake, Mother,' Nancy Pete said stiffly, 'can't you see I'm always the last person to hear news of my husband.'

'Nancy Pete,' Mary quietly explained. 'I only received this letter this morning.'

'Why you and not me?'

'Peter explains all that in his letter,' Mary said trusting the letter into Nancy's Pete's soft, manicured hand which contrasted so greatly with her own coarse one. Wiping the tears dramatically with the back of her hand, Nancy Pete read the letter.

Finished reading, she asked in her beautifully articulated voice, 'Am I supposed to leap in with words of gratitude because you took the trouble to let me see this letter?'

'Oh, Nancy!' Mary protested, 'don't be like that.' She was finding it hard to keep up this forced politeness. 'I came as quickly as I could. It was Peter's decision, not mine, to write to me rather than you. As to why? Well, I'm in as much a quandary as you are.' Mary could see her explanation didn't make a blind bit of difference.

'The O'Dwyers are such a spider-web of a family,' Nancy Pete, said spitefully, her face darkening.

Mary was thinking, is it any wonder I dread these interviews with my daughter-in-law. She decided to ignore the remark: in her world grace and dignity were more important. 'Nancy,' Mary said desultorily, 'any chance of a cup of tea? I've just walked the whole way from Parnell Street, I could really do with one.'

'Yes, of course.' Nancy hoisted her huge frame from the chair. 'What am I thinking about,' she said, making for the kitchen.

What was she thinking about? A good question Mary thought after she left. Wasn't it obvious? She was taking full advantage of this occasion to vent her grievances against the O'Dwyer family. The Lord only knows why. While Nancy Pete prepared the tea in the kitchen, Mary sat at the window watching the evening invade Leeson Street. Now jammed with traffic, the impatient ding-dong of a tram could be heard obviously grousing at the traffic on the tram lines — a lovely *normal* sound.

When Nancy Pete appeared with the tea tray, Mary could see her peevishness had moderated somewhat.

'I'm sorry I've nothing better to offer you but plain biscuits,' Nancy Pete apologized as she poured the tea from the silver plated teapot into an expensive china tea cup.

'Don't worry about it,' Mary said. 'It's the tea I want, not the biscuits.' During Nancy Pete's absence, Mary had made a decision. Picking up Peter's letter from the occasional table, Mary handed it to Nancy Pete, saying, 'As Peter is only allowed the one letter per month, you answer this.'

Nancy Pete gave a watery smile. Then bristled with self-importance. 'Naturally, as his wife, I'm the obvious person to do so.'

'Well, that's fine with me,' Mary said. 'Except that I'll have to ask you to break the news of Jody's death to him.'

'My God! He still doesn't know?'

'Who would tell him?'

As could only happen in a Nancy Pete imbroglio, suddenly she became all penitent. 'Gosh, Mother!' she said with tears in her eyes. 'I'm in such suffering over Peter, I think I'm going insane. Excuse me if I was rude to you.'

'There's no need to explain to me,' Mary answered. 'When Jody died I nearly went insane myself: it was having to put on a face for the rest of the family that helped me to hold on to my sanity.'

Nancy Pete handed the letter back to Mary. 'You answer it, Mother,' she said quite unequivocally. 'Such agonizing news should be broken to him by his mother.' Her hand stroked her large belly lovingly. 'God! He'll be absolutely shattered.'

§

Peter was glad he chose to read the letter from home in the privacy of his hut. As anticipated he found the place empty—most of the men were away having breakfast. The news of Jody's death shook him to the core; it was difficult to grasp the fact that he would never see his darling little sister again. He sat on his bunk for at least five minutes holding the letter in his hand, staring blankly into space while the tears flowed freely down his face. And to think that it happened all those weeks ago and he didn't know a thing about it.

'Bad news?' a quiet voice asked at his elbow. Startled, Peter looked up. The voice belonged to that fellow, Willie, whom he originally met in the Stafford Jail. He seemed genuinely concerned. Quickly, Peter mopped his tears with his rag of a handkerchief.

'You could say that,' he answered. 'On top of everything else, my thirteen-year-old little sister was accidentally shot and killed the night of the surrender.'

'Another terrible, terrible tragedy!' Willie sighed heavily. 'God! I'm really sorry!' Then he inquired, 'how is the mother holding up?'

'My mother is very spiritual,' Peter said. 'As a result, she's very accepting of the Lord's will.'

'Accepting the Lord's will is about the only thing any of us can do,' Willie said bitterly. 'What alternative do we have?'

'According to Collins, there's always an alternative.'

'Speaking of Mick,' Willie remembered, 'that's the reason I'm here. Mick sent me.' Willie winked. 'That *special meeting* is scheduled for ten o'clock this morning in hut number ten. But maybe,' he suggested realistically, 'you don't feel up to attending it?'

Peter stood up. 'Yes, I do feel up to attending it,' he said resolutely. 'It will serve as a badly needed distraction. Besides,' he went on, tucking the letter into his back pocket, 'Mick is one man who makes a lot of sense.'

'Lads, we're all getting lazy and slothful, we've got to do something about getting some exercise.' Collins, a fine figure of a man in his mid-twenties with a handsome, genial face, addressed the large gathering squashed into fifty bunks in hut number ten. 'I'm thinking of organizing regular route marches, but before doing so, I'd like to get your views.'

Most of the attendance nodded assent. 'T''would be fantastic!' Willie said. 'But are you sure the powers that be will give the necessary permission?'

'A dogged persistence will force them to give permission,' Collins remarked with a gleam in his eye. 'It may or may not have come to you attention that I'm a person who will not take No for an answer.'

'Yeah!' a Cork man replied. 'You're great at getting up their noses.'

'Hear! Hear!' the chorus echoed around the hut.

'Thanks for the vote of confidence,' Collins said. It had now become evident that Collins was a born leader; self-assured and daring where the authorities were concerned. 'Right,' Collins declared. 'So are we all in agreement that we want to participate in daily route marches?'

'Yeah!' The roar nearly lifted the roof.

'Right then,' Collins said, impressed with the response. 'So starting tomorrow morning after breakfast, we'll assemble in front of this hut — number ten — geared up, bright eyed and bushy-tailed, ready for an energetic march. Everyone is welcome. Well, that's about it, unless,' Collins looked inquiringly at his audience, 'there are questions?'

No one answered because, at this moment, his audience, were stampeding towards the entrance, eager to get out into the fresh air away from the terrible heat, the stuffiness and the stench in hut number ten. It was an unusually hot day for early June.

Undaunted by the mass exodus, Collins called after them, 'Be sure and bring lots of bottled drinking water; route marches can be thirsty work.'

Outside Willie caught up with Peter O'Dwyer. 'He seems pretty confident about getting permission for the marches?' he said.

'If anyone can do it, Collins can,' Peter replied.

'To be sure,' Willie concurred. 'What an extraordinary man he is.' He smiled a slow smile. 'He can almost achieve the impossible.'

'We could do with more men like him,' Peter said with conviction. 'He's a consummate organizer who won't let anyone or anything stand in his way. Rarely have I met the likes of him. Moreover, he seems to have the energy of a dozen men.'

Since Collins had succeeded in getting political status for the prisoners, which allowed them to mix freely, it was hardly surprising that once again he wangled permission for the route marches.

The next day was another very hot one. Even so, there was quite a big turnout for the first march. Bristling with energy, Collins lead the march at a brisk pace. So brisk that after the fifth time around the field, Willie began to lag behind; the going was much too fast for him. He was glad to see that he wasn't alone; a number of his comrades lagged with him, among them Peter O'Dwyer. Panting and sweating bullets (as Collins would put it) the marchers eventually arrived back to base (hut number ten).

Peter, who like everyone else was gasping for breath, motioned to Willie that he wanted to have a word with him. When he ultimately got his breath, he asked Willie, 'Have you played in any of the football matches at all?'

Willie took seconds to answer. 'A few,' he panted. 'To tell you nothing but the truth,' he said, 'I'm terribly out of condition.' The beads of perspiration stood out on his forehead. He stopped to take a couple of breaths. 'I suppose it's the effects of the starvation in that Stafford Jail.' Right enough Willie, who was naturally on the thin side, was now close to skin and bone.

'It's just I was wondering if we could try to organize two teams to play football on a regular basis?' Peter suggested.

'Let's have a word with the *big fella*,' Willie said, nodding in Collins' direction.

'As long as I can have this big, long, lanky streak,' Collins said jocosely, referring to Willie, 'as my goalie, I'm game.' Then he asked Willie, 'What part of Ireland do you come from?'

'Mayo.'

'Mayo! God help us!' Collins repeated with a ragged laugh. 'Do ye think, Willie, you could tolerate being goalie for a bunch of thick Cork men?'

'Speak for yerself,' a jocular Cork man threw in as he passed by.

They all laughed.

'You have yourself a goalie without prejudice,' Willie said, grinning broadly. He was thinking t'would be bloody marvelous to play football provided it didn't make too many demands on his energy. Wouldn't goalie be the ideal position.

'Right then,' Peter said enthusiastically. 'I'll get to work on putting an opposing team together.'

'No matter how good your team is,' Collins said playfully digging Willie in the ribs, 'we Cork men, together with our champion goalie from Mayo, will beat the lard out of yis.'

Considering Willie had had no formal training, except for kicking a football about with the lads in his native Mayo, he was surprised at his ability to stop goals; his height it seemed had a lot to do with it. Collins seemed impressed with Willie's performance and made a point of congratulating him every time he stopped a goal. Then after each match, Collins invariably engaged Willie in animated conversation about the match, discussing how the players had performed, suggesting how they could improve their game.

Willie got the distinct impression that Collins thought he was an expert on football and he'd no intention of enlightening him to the contrary. He enjoyed the attention he got from this extraordinary man who tackled everything — including football — with so much zeal.

One day when their team had had a convincing win, Collins joined Willie afterwards. 'Begorra By!' Collins said, slapping Willie on the back, 'But weren't you the real Aly Daly today saving all those goals.'

'Thanks,' Willie answered.

Collins paused for a moment as if collecting his thoughts. 'Willie,' he said tentatively, 'how would you feel about being on the executive?'

'What executive?'

'The Prisoner of War executive.'

'Oh! There is such a thing?' Willie said. 'I thought it was all hearsay.'

'The Executive is no longer hearsay; it's now a fact of life,' Collins said proudly. 'At last, our Prisoner of War status is being recognized by the camp authorities: we've been given the 'go ahead' to run the camp under our own executive. We're presently in the process of forming it. So far we have M.J. O'Reilly as our first commandant. And he's chosen me to be his assistant.'

Willie could tell by Collins' engaging smile that he felt very proud to be holding that position. M.J. O'Reilly had been a former Plunkett aide-de-camp. 'Do you think I'd be up to it?' Willie asked warily.

'Course you would,' Collins laughed. 'Anyone who can stop goals the way you do, shouldn't have any trouble doing the job.'

'The job? Meaning what?' Willie asked.

'Well, basically you'd be asked to help out with the administration and the running of the camp.'

'In what capacity?'

'You'd have a choice,' Collins answered. 'The Executive's first goal, however, would be to establish some sort of discipline.'

'How would you go about doing that?'

'Well, given the necessary volunteers, the executive would delegate jobs that badly need doing. T'would motivate the men to become more active. Because there's nothing worse than idleness to create boredom, laziness and discontent.'

'So what kind of jobs would the volunteers be asked to do?'

'As you can see,' Collins said, 'conditions in the camp are far from ideal; hundreds of jobs are crying out to be done.'

'Such as?'

'Well, to begin with,' Collins said, 'there are those leaky roofs in some of the huts; there must be some skilled workers among us who could fix them?'

'That's one job I could do myself,' Willie said.

'Great! T'would be a start anyways,' Collins said, much encouraged. 'Then, there's our living quarters,' he went on, 'they could be made more comfortable.'

'Like getting our sheets changed every day,' Willie said, his face a riot of laughter.

'Now wouldn't that be something!' Collins joined him in the laughter. 'To be greeted each morning by a strappin, young Welsh chambermaid saying, 'I've come to change your sheets.' ' Collins then became serious. 'No,' he said, 'just because we succeeded in getting relative political status is no reason to become complacent. There are still entitlements we're being denied.'

'Entitlements, such as?'

'The mail situation!' Collins declared disdainfully.

'One measly letter a month!' he said. 'Sure it's nothing short of an insult.'

'Couldn't agree more.'

'It's one situation I intend to tackle immediately.' Collins said, full of resolve. As usual, he was getting to the core of things. 'However,' he continued, 'when the executive is finally set up, someone will have to be appointed as a Personal Relations officer.' Willie raised a quizzical eyebrow. 'Don't you know, Willie, where so many men are banded together there's bound to be lots of disagreements, either between the men themselves or between the men and the authorities.' Collins now looked quite grim. 'Hopefully the P.R. person would be able to resolve some of those disagreements. In some cases he might be required to liaise between the men and the authorities. Whoever volunteers for the job would need to be a special kind of person; a compassionate person with tons of patience.'

'Rule me out,' Willie said with a watery smile. 'I'm not big on patience.'

'No more than meself,' Collins gave a roguish grin. 'To tell ye nothing but the truth, Willie,' he said in a hushed voice, 'the true aim of the executive is to get to know as many prisoners as possible, their backgrounds, their politics, et cetera. So, William,' Collins said with forced lightness, 'what do you think? Would you like to be part of the Board of the Executive?'

Willie's green eyes sparkled with pleasure. 'But of course, I would,' he said. 'I'd be honored.'

'Right then, come to the back of hut number ten after supper this evening for your induction,' Collins said.

When Collins left, Willie smiled quietly to himself. He felt extremely proud to be asked to be a member of the executive, not only because Collins trusted him, but because he would be in a position to make the acquaintance of a lot of prisoners who were, as yet, strangers to him. Hadn't he learnt from experience that inspired ideas can come out of lighthearted conversations and discussions?

Chapter IX

At lunchtime Mary discussed with our Nancy and Jane the letter she received that morning from Peter. 'Apparently the prisoners are now allowed to have visitors,' she told them. 'And Peter is really impatient to see someone from home.' She read aloud the part where he pleaded, 'For God's sake, will some member or members of the family show mercy and pay me a visit in this awful dump? I need something to look forward to.'

'So when are you going to go?' our Nancy inquired.

'I'm not,' Mary said without hesitation. 'In the name of God how can I?'

'The shop?' Jane said.

'Of course the shop!' Mary answered. 'Well, with Bridget and Sheila away on holidays for the next couple of weeks, I can't be spared. So I couldn't possibly make the journey.'

It was the second week in July. Staff holidays in the dairy had commenced. In the absence of the two assistants, Mary now had to rely on our Nancy and Jane to help out. Lily, the cute one, made it her business to commit herself to working on Uncle Tom's farm for the rest of the summer. Thus dodging the drudgery of working in the dairy.

'Surely, it's up to Nancy Pete to go?' our Nancy remarked, casually. 'He is her husband after all!'

'Our Nancy!' Mary burst out aghast. 'What can you be thinking? Imagine it! Nancy Pete going on that long journey with the birth only a few weeks away.'

'Sorry I opened my mouth,' our Nancy said huffily.

'I bet Nancy Pete hasn't given a thought to her pregnancy and is all set to go,' Jane said, looking amused. She had visions of Nancy Pete creating pandemonium giving birth on the Mail boat or on the train between Hollyhead and Frongoch.

'You couldn't be more right, Jane,' Mary said tartly. 'Nancy Pete has decided that her pregnancy will not stand in the way of her being reunited with her darling husband.'

'Oh! You've spoken to her already?' our Nancy said.

'I had to,' Mary frowned. 'After the hullabaloo she kicked up last time over Peter's letter — accusing me of all sorts of things — I'd no option but to rush over there first thing this morning.'

'So what happened?' Jane asked.

'Well, we had the usual theatricals,' Mary said, 'followed by her insistence that she had to be the one to go.' Mary's mouth twitched with annoyance. 'I did everything in my power to talk her out of it. Made the case that as you two girls were on holidays, wouldn't it be more sensible for one of you to make the trip?'

'What did she say to that?' Jane asked.

'Oh, she argued till she was blue in the face that you two were only sisters, wasn't she his adoring wife?'

Jane said, 'I can just imagine the drama! The labored talk about being the loving and dutiful wife.' She gave a good imitation of Nancy Pete stroking her large belly, mimicking her eloquent voice and facial grimaces, saying, 'Course I must go! He'll be frantic to see me! It's a cry for help!'

Mary laughed heartily at Jane's perfect imitation of her sister-in-law; it was so close to what had actually happened.

'You could be a stand-in for her anytime,' our Nancy said, snickering.

Mary stopped laughing. 'I don't know why I'm laughing,' she said. 'The situation is very serious.'

'Hard to be serious talking about Nancy Pete,' Jane said.

'Well, this is different,' Mary said. 'There is a baby involved.'

'You're absolutely right,' Jane now became serious. 'Does she have any idea the risk she'd be taking going on such a long journey at this particular time?'

'That's just the point,' Mary answered. 'Even when I mentioned the fact that she could risk losing the baby, she refused to budge.' Mary shook her head, bewildered. 'As a last resort, I said, as you're in the final stages of pregnancy, I'm sure the last person Peter expects to see is you.'

'To which she replied…?' Jane eyes bulged with curiosity.

Mary said, 'She hesitated for seconds, appeared to be considering what I said, then the face lights up and, if you please, she comes up with this bright idea about one of his sisters accompanying her? 'It wouldn't be such a risk then,' she says.' Mary looked from one daughter to the other. 'So, which one of you girls would like to volunteer for the job?' she asked with forced seriousness. 'Nancy?' she stared at our Nancy. 'As the next eldest and the one most likely to be doing the traveling, it would be up to you?'

'Oh, no! Count me out!' Even thinking about it, our Nancy was ready to have a panic attack. 'There's no way I'll get involved in the birth of that baby,' she said adamantly.

'Jane?' Mary looked inquiringly at Jane.

'What the hell do I know about birthing babies?' Jane wrinkled her nose in distaste. 'That woman is a head case!'

'She has certainly presented us with a big dilemma,' Mary said. 'How can the family possibly make travel plans if she insists on going and you girls refuse to accompany her.'

'Could we go without telling her?' our Nancy suggested.

'Imagine the hell she'd raise when she found out,' Mary answered.

Our Nancy said, 'She needn't find out.'

'But of course she'll find out,' Jane butted in. 'How the hell could we keep it from her. Wouldn't there be letters from Peter talking about the visit.'

'Besides,' Mary added, 'it would be most unnatural for a member of Peter's family to visit him and not bring at least a letter from his wife.'

Jane said, 'So, it looks like we'll just have to sit tight until the baby arrives and she's ensconced in the nursing home before plans can be made to visit Peter.'

'It seems awful,' Mary said dolefully, 'He's so anxious to see a member of the family immediately.'

'And all because of that bloody witch he's married to,' our Nancy said venomously. 'She's preventing everyone from going.'

'Less of the bad language,' Mary rebuked our Nancy.

Jane's mind was wandering. God! She was thinking, wouldn't it be marvelous if she could make the trip to Wales and have a break from slaving in that damn shop! With Lily away in County Meath it now fell to her lot to do the lion's share of filling in in the shop for the next four weeks. True to form, our Nancy, who was supposed to share the burden with her, did the minimum; always finding an excuse to dodge the work, like she was having an interview for a job, or a friend was in trouble and needed her help, or, if the worst came to the worst, taking to the bed with influenza. Anyway, even if Nancy Pete didn't go to Wales, it wouldn't make a scintilla of difference to her. The irony was, that as the next eldest, our Nancy — the one sister with no great love for her brother — would be the lucky one.

Imagine! she thought. The only way I could possibly make the trip to Wales would be to act as a midwife to Nancy Pete. What a proposition! Life could be so unfair.

§

Jane wiped the spray from her face as she stood leaning on the rail of the ship that was carrying herself and our Nancy to Holyhead. As the ship nuzzled its coarse, amid screeching wind and mountainous waves, Jane was determined not to yield to the queasiness nagging at her stomach. Unlike petulant Nancy, who had retired to their cabin because of the sea sickness, Jane decided the sensible thing would be to stay outside. Surely the bracing sea air would help to stave off the sea sickness.

Not for the first time Jane marveled at the extraordinary series of events that lead to her being there. First, there was Nancy Pete's baby — a boy — arriving two weeks early; it definitely ruled out any notion Nancy Pete had of traveling to Frongoch. So automatically our Nancy was designated to represent the family on the visit. Then fate intervened. The day after the baby's arrival, Mary received an unexpected letter from Peter. (It seemed that the rule, apropos one letter per month, had been relaxed.) In this letter, Peter asked would whoever was coming over, be kind enough to bring parcels and letters for the prisoners from their families. He gave the address of the place where these could be collected, as a huckster shop in Strand Street.

'You're surely not expecting me to carry that load to Frongoch?' our Nancy nearly had apoplexy when Mary showed her the box full of parcels and letters for the prisoners.

'Well, I carried the box on my own from the shop in Strand Street,' Mary asserted. 'And I'm a lot older then you.'

'No,' our Nancy was most emphatic in her refusal. 'I will not be weighed down with that load.' She took a bundle of letters and six small parcels from the box. 'That's it,' she said. 'That's as much as I'll carry.'

Mary looked ready to kill her. 'Those unfortunate prisoners!' she said bitterly. 'It would be just too bad if they were depending on a heartless creature the likes of you to bring them any kind of comfort.'

Our Nancy was as usual sullen and silent. Mary knew she was wasting her breath arguing with her. It would only end up the same as it always did; done her way or not at all. At this point, Jane, taking her break from the shop, popped into her mother's office carrying two mugs of tea, one for Mary and one for herself.

It was then that Mary spontaneously propositioned her. 'Jane,' she said, 'how would you feel about going to Frongoch with your sister, Nancy?' Jane couldn't believe her ears. 'What's the catch?' she asked immediately.

Mary indicated the box of parcels for the prisoners. 'Well, if you call carrying parcels and letters to unfortunate prisoners a catch,' she said, 'then that's the catch.'

'You're serious?'

'I was never more serious in my life,' Mary answered. 'Our Nancy refuses to take more than six parcels — small ones at that.'

Jane picked the rest of the parcels out of the box. There were fifteen. 'Wouldn't they easily fit into a suitcase?' she suggested.

'Of course they'd fit into a suitcase,' our Nancy said aggressively. 'But I have my own suitcase to carry and I've no intention of carrying another one.'

'Well, if you're serious about me going,' Jane addressed her mother, 'I'd be quite happy to take care of the suitcase carrying those parcels.'

So against all odds, here she was making the trip to Frongoch. Jane thought, it's an ill-wind that blows somebody good! But then she wondered.

§

'O'Dwyer, Peter—you have visitors.' The call came over the camp Tannoy.

'That's you,' Willie said, with a happy chuckle, playfully slapping Peter on his bare rump. After the route march, they were having a wash down under the hose rigged up in the makeshift shelter outside the huts. This was one of the first projects undertaken by the Executive and one in which Willie, with his laboring experience, had a hand in.

'Good timing,' Peter said as he toweled himself. 'At least now I'll smell more like a human being than an animal.' Peter smiled with anticipation as he dressed. 'I can't wait to see them.' Then after thinking for a second, he said, 'Why don't you come with me and meet them? T'would do you good to hear all the news first hand.'

Willie hesitated. 'I'd certainly like to meet them and hear all the news, but I'd be intruding surely?'

'Not at all,' Peter assured him.

'Tell you what,' Willie said, 'you fire ahead and have some private time with your visitors. I'll join you later.'

'Right,' Peter said and went out.

'Sweet Jesus!' Our Nancy sullenly surveyed the dark, dreary Visitors' Hut full of hard wooden benches and worm-eaten tables. 'I sincerely hope he comes soon. This has got to be the most depressing place on earth. I can't wait to get out of it.'

Jane remained silent. She was sick and tired of our Nancy's perpetual complaints. They were barely on the boat when they started. When she wasn't moaning about missing Larry this weekend, it was how cold the boat was and how she should have brought her cardigan. The latter, of course, was for Jane's benefit; she obviously wanted Jane to lend her hers. But Jane was feeling the cold too and had no intention of parting with her cardigan. Then there were our Nancy's new shoes, pinching her so much they were killing her. After that came the sea-sickness.

When Jane eventually returned to the cabin, not feeling well herself, aching to lie down, Our Nancy treated her like her personal slave: 'Empty that kidney tray; get me another blanket; get handkerchiefs out of my case. No, not those — they're just for show — the bigger ones.' The orders were non-stop.

But worst of all was the scene our Nancy created in the Station Restaurant when they were waiting for the train to Frongoch. The outrageous way she verbally attacked the elderly waitress. 'Call this tea?' she stood up and shouted across the room at the unfortunate woman now attending customers on the other side. If a bomb had rocked the place, the diners couldn't have looked more shocked. 'It's poisonous!' our Nancy shouted as the embarrassed waitress hurried back to their table. Jane could see that every eye in the room was on our Nancy. With all her heart she wished the ground would open and swallow her. 'Do I look stupid enough to drink poison?' our Nancy continued her vitriolic attach on the waitress.

'I'm so terribly sorry,' the flustered waitress apologized. 'I'll bring you another cup.'

'Don't bother your arse!' our Nancy shouted shoving the full cup of tea at her, slobbering it into the saucer and on to the waitress' clothes.

To say Jane was mortified would be putting it mildly. Granted the tea was a little on the cool side, but considering it was war time, it wasn't all that bad; it was certainly as good as the tea they got at home if they were lucky.

Meantime, Jane was having great difficulty with the weight of the big case — lifting and lugging it on and off the boat and the train. Too late she realized she'd bitten off more than she could chew. When she volunteered to do the job, she'd no idea the case would be so heavy. Of course, Mother being Mother, had put in a load of extra tinned food for Peter, which added to the weight. And needless to say, no help was forthcoming from our Nancy. As far as she was concerned, it was strictly Jane's problem. Hadn't she made it clear from the outset that she wanted nothing to do with the transportation of those parcels?

So by the time they reached Frongoch, Jane was ready to die with exhaustion. So many times she wishes to God, it was Lily and not our Nancy she was traveling with. In the first instance, Lily would've insisted on sharing the load. With Lily as her companion too the trip could have been a great adventure. She consoled herself with the thoughts of seeing Peter and the bit of cheer the letters and parcels would bring to the wretched prisoners.

Peter eventually arrived. For someone who looked so emaciated, he was very cheerful. Warmly hugging his sisters, he said, 'God! You're a sight for sore eyes!' After which he escorted them to a table.

'You have a son,' Jane blurted out as soon she sat down. She couldn't hold it in any longer.

'Jesus! Are you serious?' Peter's gaunt face lit up with elation. 'Since when?' he asked.

'Day before yesterday,' Jane answered. 'Baby weighs seven and a half pounds, Mother and son are doing fine. They send their love.' She handed Peter a letter from Nancy Pete.

'I wasn't expecting news for at least a month,' Peter said, taking the letter. 'It must have arrived early?'

'Two weeks to be exact,' Jane answered.

Indicating the letter, Peter said, 'I'll read it later.'

Our Nancy's head was turned concentrating on other prisoners with visitors. She appeared to be totally disinterested in chatting with Peter. Jane thought, I shudder to think what would have happened if I hadn't come: the bitch would probably have dumped the parcels, said the minimum and made a quick getaway.

Eventually Peter tapped our Nancy on the shoulder and got her attention. 'So how does it feel being an aunt?' he asked.

'Oh! Okay, I suppose.' With an effort our Nancy dragged her eyes back to her brother. Looking hard at him, she said, 'You don't look great. Do they not feed you here?' Then she nodded her head in the direction of the big case standing between herself and Jane. 'For God's sake, Jane,' she said, 'give him his food parcel before he fades away before our eyes.'

Placing the case flat on the floor, Jane opened it, found Peter's big parcel sitting on top and handed it to him. Peter shook the parcel the way a child would a wrapped toy. 'Food, I hope?' he said optimistically.

'Lots!' our Nancy answered with great aplomb, giving the impression she had a lot to do with the making up of the parcel.

'Soap too, I hope?' Peter asked.

'Oodles of it,' Nancy replied confidently.

'Excuse me,' Jane butted in. 'Our Nancy, you've got it wrong: due to the war there's a great shortage of soap.' Nancy's slyness in taking credit for the parcels made Jane furious; she felt like belting her one, but realized it was neither the time nor the place to start a row. She turned to Peter. 'Mother said to tell you that she could only manage a couple of bars of soap.' Once again, our Nancy lost interest: her eyes wandered round the visitors' hut. Suddenly, Jane remembered her list. She delved into her purse and produced an envelope. Handing it to Peter she said, 'Here's a list of the names on the packages.' The night before, on her mother's advice, she had stayed up late making out the list in alphabetical order.

'What a great idea!' Peter said when he drew the list out of the envelope and scrutinized it. 'Oh! I see you have a parcel for Willie

MacNamee?' he said. 'He's a good friend of mine. As a matter of fact, I asked him to —' He stopped mid-sentence as he saw Willie entering the building. 'Oh! Here he comes,' he said, his eyes beaming a welcome at Willie.

Jane was in the middle of taking the parcels out of the case and stacking them on the table. When she looked up she saw this vision of a man — a giant with ash blond hair, straight, a forelock falling across his forehead — striding across the boards towards them. She thought, God! Even if he is thin as a whippet, he's the most attractive man I've ever laid eyes on. Willie's engaging, boyish smile at Jane sent a welter of sensations bumping in her head. With much disinclination she forced her gaze from his face. How often had the Sisters told them it was bad manners to stare?

Peter said, 'Willie meet my two sisters, Jane and Nancy.'

Needless to say, the fact of another man joining them got our Nancy's immediate attention. Her wandering eyes came swiftly back to the table. Willie shook both their hands giving Jane a most disarming grin as he shook hers.

'We have a parcel for you, Willie,' our Nancy said without preamble. She was suddenly full of sauciness, focusing her attention on Willie and doing what she did best — batting her long eyelashes flirtatiously at him. Keeping her head down Jane continued to take more parcels from the case adding them to the pile on the table. Nancy meantime, self-important as be damned, busied herself looking for Willie's parcel among the ones on the table. Failing to find it, she importuned impatiently, 'Jane, where the hell is Willie's parcel?'

'I'm doing my best to find it,' Jane said, giving the impression she was searching feverishly among the parcels left in the case. In view of the mixed emotions she was feeling at this moment — between the effect this Adonis, Willie, was having on her and the fury she felt at our Nancy's calculated artfulness — she was glad to have this distraction. And until she could portray a calm facade she intended to drag out searching for Willie's parcel as long as she could. Keeping her head down helped her to avoid Willie's penetrating gaze.

'Believe it or not, Willie,' Peter interjected jubilantly, 'I'm a father! It's a boy!'

'That's wonderful news!' Willie sounded extraordinarily pleased for him. 'Congratulations! We'll have to celebrate the occasion somehow.'

'I sincerely hope the Mother had the good sense to include a bottle of 'cheer' in my lot,' Peter said, probing the outside of the parcel with his hands, 'so that we can celebrate properly.'

'Yeah. She did just that,' Jane's voice came from under the table. 'She included a bottle of port wine.'

'Fantastic!' Peter grinned with satisfaction. 'One can always rely on good, old, dependable Mother to do the right thing.' Peter then became conscious of Jane's invisibleness. 'Jane,' he inquired, 'what the hell are you doing down there?'

'Looking for Willie's parcel,' Jane answered. Then suddenly she gave a whoop of triumph. 'Oh! There it is!' she said. 'At last!' Jane popped up from the depths bearing a medium-sized parcel. 'It was right at the bottom,' she said, handing the parcel to Willie. She smiled softly at him; he smiled back. Their eyes locked for several silent seconds. Willie saw a girl in her teens with a lovely smiling face, framed by dark wavy hair, big brown eyes and a wide generous mouth. Not the type of girl you'd ever forget meeting.

'Thanks ever so much,' Willie said as he took the parcel. 'You've no idea how much I appreciate this.' Looking into Jane's eyes, for some reason his heart did a leap against his ribs. Surely she was gorgeous.

'Well, aren't you going to open it?' our Nancy disturbed Willie's musings, looking deliberately at the parcel.

Willie hesitated. 'You mean...open it here?' He screwed up his face to cover his surprise. Then looked at Peter.

'Don't be ridiculous!' Peter gave our Nancy a withering look. 'Of course he isn't opening it here.'

'What's ridiculous about it?' our Nancy asked. 'We girls would like to see what we've just lugged across the Irish Sea?'

For seconds Willie tried not to show his irritation. 'Well, if you insist,' he said passively as he began to undo the knots in the twine. No matter how unpleasant it was, he couldn't resist a challenge. Particularly when it came from someone as self-assured as this young woman.

Jane gritted her teeth, she was dumbfounded at our Nancy's audacity. She thought, the bloody cheek of her! Not an ounce of help did she give me with the lugging of that case. Instinctively, Jane put her hand over Willie's hand, holding on to it, preventing him from going any further with the untying of the knots. 'What's in that parcel is strictly your business and no one else's,' she said, looking defiantly at our Nancy.

'Well,' Willie said politely, 'if your sister is so intrigued to see what's in the parcel, I don't mind...'

'But I do,' Jane insisted. 'That parcel is to be opened in private.' Then in an effort to bring levity to the situation, she smiled a lightening smile, and in her best common Dublin accent, said, 'As the person who transported that parcel from Ireland, I insist dat dem's deh rules.'

Willie roared laughing.

'Well put, sis,' Peter joined in the laughter. 'Now, tell us the latest news from the auld sod?'

'Well, first and foremost, Sackville Street has been leveled and is being cleaned up,' Jane told them. 'The dust'd only eat ye.' Once again she used the common Dublin accent.

Willie's laughter was so hysterical, you'd think he was on a joyride at a carnival.

'What a perfectly, wonderful description!' he said. 'I can nearly taste the dust.' Not only was this girl beautiful, but she had a dazzling wit.

Our Nancy didn't like being left out. 'I've been having interviews for jobs since I finished school,' she said to nobody in particular.

'What kind of jobs?' Peter asked.

'Trainee hairdressing.'

'Any success?'

'No. Not so far.'

'What about the dairy?' Peter said, 'I'm sure the Mother could do with your help.'

'Forget it! It's the last place on earth I'd want to work.'

'So what about you?' Willie asked Jane warmly. 'What are you doing?'

'Oh, I've another year to go at school,' Jane answered. 'Mind you, at the moment I'm stuck in the shop filling in for the holidays. Like our Nancy,' she said dispassionately, 'I detest the work. But sure somebody has to do it.'

Our Nancy said to Willie, 'You're not from Dublin?'

'How did you guess?'

'Your accent.'

'Not as colorful as the Dublin one?'

'Depends on which part of Dublin you come from,' our Nancy prided herself on having a cultured Dublin accent rather than the common one used by the shawlies and now by her sister trying to be smart.

'From where I'm sitting, I'm thinking all you O'Dwyers have very nice accents,' Willie asserted. 'Mine is nondescript; it's a Mayo one.'

'On the contrary, I think it's quite a pleasant one,' Our Nancy said condescendingly. Then seeing that she had Willie's attention, pressed her advantage. 'So what part did you play in the Rising?' she asked, staring first into his eyes, then at his chest, then back to his eyes again.

The question seemed to have a remarkable effect on Willie. For seconds his face lit up, then he proceeded to talk earnestly about the Rising. It was unfortunate that just as Willie began to describe this experiences in the Rising, Peter picked that moment to engage Jane in a private conversation. Looking quite solemn, unusual for him, he asked her quietly about Nancy Pete (her demeanor during and after the birth) and about Jody's death — he never heard the full story. Finally, about the political climate presently in Ireland.

As Jane answered all Peter's questions, she was conscious of the cunning way our Nancy was manipulating Willie; skillfully holding him captive to her questions. The phony bitch! she thought. Our Nancy had as much interest in the Rising as she had in the back of her hand. Jane longed to hear what Willie had to say, but seeing how anxious Peter was to talk about family matters, she couldn't very well not answer his questions. Anyway, apart from delivering the prisoners' parcels and letters, wasn't the prime purpose of this visit to bring Peter tidings of home? The sight of Willie talking animatedly about the Rising while Nancy stared seductively into his eyes, sent a surge of deep resentment through Jane. Suddenly she realized that, for the first time in her life, she was intensely jealous. The situation continued thus until the girls took their leave of the two prisoners. Jane's only consolation was the way Willie squeezed her hand and gave her such a friendly smile when he said good-bye.

Chapter X

Throughout July and August, some internees, who insisted they were innocent bystanders, were taken in batches to London for interrogation; afterwards many of them were released. Gradually, there was a general exodus of internees from Frongoch. By the end of August 1916, only six hundred and fifty men remained. As a consequence, the North Camp was closed down and its internees moved to the South Camp.

Shortly after the newcomers settled in the South camp it became evident that life there was not going to be as free and easy as it had been in the North Camp. In charge was a Colonel Braithwaite, a Brit, cold and conscientious, who took duty beyond the bounds of reason and, into the bargain, disliked the Irish. He decided that these internees from the North Camp, who had been living the life of Reilly, needed to be disciplined and brought down to earth. There was more to an internment camp than 'an internees' executive' determining at meetings how the camp should be run. Or internees having daily route marches and regular football matches. It was time these lazy Irish bastards were denied the privilege of being selective about the jobs they would do. From now on they would take orders from the camp authorities, that meant pulling their weight with all the work in the camp.

One of Braithwaite's first moves in his campaign was to have W.J. O'Reilly removed from Frongoch and sent to Reading Jail. O'Reilly was Commandant and P.R. man of the executive. His strength lay in his determination not to yield on any protestations he made on behalf of the internees. So Braithwaite decided he had to go. The first new order issued to the new arrivals concerned the emptying of the ash bins around the soldiers' quarters. They refused to obey. Spurred on by Collins and their annoyance at O'Reilly's removal, a spirit of stubbornness asserted itself in the camp. For this refusal the internees were punished: in batches of eight they were removed to the empty loneliness of the former North Camp and all privileges were stopped. Willie was in the second batch. Deprived of letters, magazines and cigarettes, they still wouldn't accept what they considered an injustice.

In Willie's isolation, he let his mind journey back to that memorable day when he met Jane. He was remembering her lovely, smiling face, her delightful naturalness and her marvelous wit. She was so different from other girls he had met. Despite her youth, there was that something about her that stirred a tenderness in him that he thought had long gone — what with the violence and the vengeance that had become part of his life. He regretted that their time together had been so brief. It was here, alone and isolated in the North Camp, that Willie made a resolution: if and when he was released he would do everything in his power to meet the lovely Jane again.

During this period another side of Collins was revealed; he became one of the leaders in a system of smuggling the forbidden things to the men in the North camp. Daily the Brits grew weary of attempting counteraction to this smuggling. On one occasion one of them remarked to Willie, 'If you were bloody Gerries, we'd know what to do. But you're not. You're Irish!'

Later, at a covert meeting between Collins and the men, the silver-tongued Collins advocated a dogged persistence. 'If you take my tip,' he said, 'you'll just sit down, refuse to budge and you have the British beaten. For a time they'll raise Cain, but in the end they'll despair. Our unorthodox methods will always beat them. Besides,' Collins added cheerfully, 'doesn't it add a bit of spice to our monotonous lives?'

Willie noticed that it was in this atmosphere of struggle and conspiracy the real Collins emerged. He was a realist and a clear thinker whom the men found pleasant to listen to. He explained himself easily without condescending. The smuggling and the methods used to beat the ban appealed to his nature. But what was more in tone with his character was making contact man-to-man, as opposed to the kind of leader who organized from a distance, unseen and unknown. Even as Collins forecast, the struggle was soon over.

By October, no more bins had to be emptied. Willie was back just in time for the next event of importance—the daily roll call being introduced for the first time. On Collins' instructions a number of men refused to answer the roll calls. 'That way,' Collins contended, 'we internees can be sure of keeping our identities anonymous.'

Once again the British were extremely cautious with these slick, cunning Irishmen. Past mistakes haunted them. Forthwith, they confined the 'unidentified internees' (which included Collins, Peter and Willie), separating them from the rest and all privileges were stopped. Even so, they were unsuccessful: the system of smuggling and communication began all over again. With the exodus of the bystanders in late August, a core of sound nationalism was left behind. Collins was proving to be one of the shrewdest of this core; a man certain of his every action.

Then to everyone's surprise Collins suddenly decided to cooperate with the authorities - doing domestic chores. 'Of course,' he explained to his comrades, 'there's method in my madness. Doing those chores, won't I have access to places that would normally be beyond the pale to the likes of me.' Shortly afterwards, during a nocturnal discussion after lights out, under the pilot light, Collins told his comrades in a solemn tone, 'This whole situation is becoming more and more complex for the British. I found this out today when I was cleaning their lavatory.'

There was a roar of laughter and comments like, 'You're joking of course!' and 'You never cleaned a lavatory in your life!'

'Keep it down, lads,' Collins cautioned. 'Well now, I'm going to tell you something,' he said pertly. 'I've been cleaning their lavs for the past week.' He sounded quite proud of it. 'Sometimes cleaning lavs can be a very worthwhile exercise. Take today for instance.

Didn't I hit the jackpot: someone got careless and left a newspaper on the floor which was definitely not intended for the eyes of the internees.'

Peter interjected jokingly, 'Full of naked women?'

'Wishful thinking, By!' Collins said with a broad smile. 'No, seriously lads,' he continued, 'the paper gave full details about the way America has continued to protest about the executions.'

'Sure we already knew about that,' a Cork man retorted in a bored voice.

'Maybe you did,' Collins said. 'But it's the next bit you don't know about.' He seemed to be getting real pleasure recounting it.

'Which is?' the chorus asked.

'America is now asking why men, against whom no definite charges have been laid, are compelled to suffer prolonged imprisonment at camps such as Frongoch? They even went as far as to name this place.'

'Jesus! That's great!' the statement came from the back.

'Maybe as a result, we'll be released soon?' someone else said through the darkness.

'Maybe, but I rather doubt it,' Collins answered gloomily.

As summer drifted into autumn and the countryside was looking its best, though physical activity was reduced to one football match and one route march per week, the internees found something of greater interest to occupy their minds. Once again Collins was the great innovator. During another nocturnal session he disclosed to those, who didn't already know, that for the past couple of months he had been busy secretly setting up an Irish Republican Brotherhood network within the camp. Seeing to it that those in charge of the huts and holding key camp administrative positions were all I.R.B. men. After which he badgered the bellicose Braithwaite into agreeing to let him organize language classes for the men — classes such as French, Spanish and Irish. They had the necessary teachers in the camp. What he didn't tell Braithwaite was that the classes would be mostly concerned with teaching Gaelic (Irish.)

In a letter to Collins a good friend had pointed out that the Irish language was being rapidly fostered in other places of internment and imprisonment. 'In such places,' the friend wrote, 'a tremendous surge of nationalism is beginning.' So Collins recognized that the idea of a native language was a means of stimulation towards freedom. Willie was pleased that once again he was been given the chance to learn his native tongue. But at time passed, the language classes began to take second place to discussions about military matters — particularly guerrilla warfare.

When one Irish language session was taken over completely by these military matters, Collins apologized to Willie, 'Sorry about not having the Irish class, Willie,' he said. 'I know how keen you are to learn Irish.'

Willie chortled, 'This is much more interesting.'

'Anyway,' Collins continued addressing the group, 'the fact that we have people who are nationalists from all parts of Ireland here in the camp at this time, is a golden opportunity to build up contacts all over the country for when we're released. With these contacts already established we can at least think about waging some kind of guerrilla warfare against the bloody British. Now, in case you don't know it, guerrilla warfare means living rough. But it's the only way that I can see of achieving our goal. If nothing else, the Easter Week debacle taught us one thing, and that is that taking over buildings is not the way to go. No! In a nutshell, what is needed is quick, slick, surprise attacks on Government buildings and Police barracks. If necessary, plundering, burning and shooting. Then disappearing like flies into the backwoods, the mountains where possible.'

'Like you advocated all along,' Willie interjected, 'it's only through more violent action that Ireland will get its freedom.'

'True for you, By!' Collins acknowledged. 'But the next time, t'will be a very different kind of action.'

Someone wanted to know, would they have the ghost of a chance of succeeding?

'I can't see why not,' Collins answered. 'Secretly I've been given to understand that a lot of the volunteers who escaped arrest after the Rising, have kept a skeleton network going in Ireland through bogus branches of the Gaelic League — one of the few organizations that hasn't been suppressed by the British.'

'Fantastic!' Someone in the back applauded.

Collins continued, 'I'm quite sure that when we get out of here, that network would be more than pleased to have our crop of nationalists swell their numbers.'

Peter said, 'When my sister, Jane, was visiting, she told me that the executions stirred up very powerful feelings against the British. As a consequence there's been a big turnabout in the Irish people's attitude.'

'Those executions transcend decency,' Collins said. 'Thank the Lord the Irish people are at last recognizing the fact and might even be prepared to support us. By the same token, the nationalists on the outside have something of an ace up their sleeves, known to but a few.'

'Mother a God, what could that be?' someone burst out.

'Hopefully, it's support from a section of the Royal Irish Constabulary,' Collins said.

'You can't be serious!' someone cried out contemptuously. 'The R.I.C.! Them murderin policemen!'

'I'm very serious!' Collins said. 'The way I heard it was that some Irish R.I.C. members helped our people in trouble after the Rising. This was interpreted as showing support for the Cause. Needless to say, that kind of support could be invaluable in the future.' Collins paused, then continued, 'The Irish network outside is presently trying to establish a rapport with those particular R.I.C. members.'

A Cork man remarked, 'The R.I.C have so much blood on their hands, they're the last people I'd expect to give our crowd the time a day, don't mind support.'

'Well now it seems they're not all tarred with the same brush,' Collins said. 'Time will tell.'

Though the men continued to attend the bogus language classes — learning more about guerrilla warfare than a language — snippets of news about America's attitude to the continued internment of Irish prisoners, created a never-ending agitation in the camp against imprisonment. During this time, Peter and Willie talked a lot about the prevailing atmosphere.

Peter pointed out in one of their conversations, 'The British badly miscalculated things; they thought that following the failure of the Rising, the men who took part in it would be a broken force. But as we can see, the men are far from crushed in spirit.'

'Instead, the flame that nearly died in the ruins of Dublin, was rekindled here in Frongoch,' Willie added.

'I couldn't have put it better myself,' Peter complimented Willie. 'I take it you're committed to Mick's network if and when we're released?'

'Yeah,' Willie answered enthusiastically. Then inquired, 'Do you think you could be a participant now that you're a father?'

'I'd certainly like to,' Peter said. 'But I suppose fatherhood will make a difference.'

Winter came drab and desolate. The remoteness and the wildness of this part of Wales contributed to the loneliness in the hearts of the internees. Their only compensation was covert meetings and sleep. The thought of spending Christmas in this desolate camp, away from their homes, was so depressing. So it was with joy and jubilation that the internees received word from the Adjutant of the camp on the morning of the 22nd December, that they were being released. He requested the names and addresses of the released men. At once the internees were filled with suspicion: convinced that the bait of freedom was being dangled in an attempt to identify 'wanted men.'

Collins condemned the whole business as a trap. There followed an uneasy silence. Until wearily the Adjutant explained it was not a trap. 'It's a goodwill gesture on the part of the British Government,' he told the men.

The silence continued, until the Adjutant, in desperation, decided to allow the internees to write out their own lists.

Collins agreed.

There was nothing more to it. Thanks be to God, all the internees were leaving Frongoch. Saying good-bye to his friends, Collins winked with intent and said, 'We'll live to fight another day. I'll be in touch.'

With his own personal intelligence service now in place, Collins left Frongoch with the knowledge that a basic underground structure awaited him in Ireland which he would take over and expand.

Chapter XI

'When is the Christmas tree going to arrive?' Eileen asked Jane and Lily anxiously. Their mother had just left the kitchen after a rushed lunch because the shop was so busy. Eileen couldn't help noticing that during lunch they discussed everything and anything but their own plans for Christmas. Lily looked hard at Jane. Neither sister had the heart to tell Eileen the truth. On her first day home from school, when Jane broached the subject of Christmas to the mother, Mary made it clear that as they were still in mourning, there would be no Christmas celebrations in the O'Dwyer home this year. What's more, she didn't want to hear another word about it. Since then, except that each member got the usual Christmas bonus with their pocket money, the only thing their mother had any interest in was the shop. She wouldn't countenance any talk about Christmas trees, decorations or presents.

'Don't worry, lovey,' Lily said reassuringly to Eileen. 'Alecia's bound to keep a tree for us as usual; she never lets us down.'

'But it's three days to Christmas,' Eileen countered, her innocent eyes wide and uncertain. 'If we don't get the tree soon, there won't be time to decorate it.'

Jane ruffled Eileen's hair and asked her, 'Have you finished your Christmas shopping yet?' It was one way to change the subject.

'It's all done except for Mother's present.'

Lily said, 'Well then, hadn't you better hurry up and buy it; only two more shopping days to Christmas.'

'Trouble is,' Eileen muttered despondently, 'I haven't enough money.' She waved her hand in the direction of the shop, 'And Mother's in such a strange mood these days, I'm afraid to ask for it.'

'How much do you need?' Jane asked.

'Five and eleven pence. That's what the scarf I want to buy Mother costs in the Henry Street Department Store.'

'Right,' Jane said. 'Don't go near Mother. I'll give it to you. And I'll get it for you right away.' She left the room.

'Do you think Mother is sick or something?' Eileen asked Lily after Jane left.

Lily deliberated for seconds before she answered. 'I doubt it,' she said. 'She wouldn't be habitually in that shop if she was sick.' With the approach of the Christmas season, Lily hoped against hope that the excitement it generated would be a healthy diversion for Eileen; keeping her mind off Jody. Instead of which there was this terrible pall of gloom over the house. She wanted to scream at her mother: for crying out loud! Doesn't every child in the world adore Christmas! How can you deny Eileen this pleasure? She couldn't imagine anything crueler than saying to the child, 'We're not celebrating Christmas this year because we're still in mourning.' Lily thought, instead of Christmas being a happy, joyous occasion for Eileen and everyone else, Mother seems determined to make it a miserable reminder of Jody's tragic death.

Thankfully Jane arrived back with the money. 'Now, I'm giving you ten shillings,' she said to Eileen handing her a ten shilling note.

'But I only need...'

'Never mind about that,' Jane interjected, 'there could be some other knickknacks you might want to buy.'

'Oh! Thanks a million! You're an angel!' Eileen looked a mite more cheerful as she left the room.

After she had gone, Lily burst out, 'That poor child who looks forward so much to Christmas. How can we tell her that this year Christmas will be a non-event,' she said dolefully. 'You'd think for the child's sake Mother'd make an effort.'

Jane shook her head dismally. Tears were in her eyes. 'Well, I suppose,' she said, 'between Jody's death and Peter's imprisonment, it's probably hard for Mother to contemplate celebrating Christmas the usual way.'

'Do you think we'll even have a turkey?' Lily asked.

'Of course,' Jane grinned. 'Mother can't very well say no to the turkey she gets as a present from the wholesalers.'

Lily said, 'Knowing our mother, t'wouldn't surprise me one bit if she gave the damn turkey away to the poor.'

An air of despondency pervaded the kitchen. 'We'll just have to wait and see,' Jane said. Then suddenly she brightened up. 'Enough of this gloom,' she said. 'Maybe Mother will have a change of heart when she sees everyone else celebrating.'

'She'll want to have it soon,' Lily said, then added with a rush of annoyance, 'Anyway, whether she likes it or not, I intend to give her and every member of this family a Christmas present.'

'Me too,' Jane rejoined. 'And there's little she can do about that.'

Just then Bridget came tearing into the kitchen waving the newspaper. 'Look! Look at this!' she said, her face luminous. Before the sisters could say anything, Bridget read out the headline: 'Frongoch internees being released for Christmas.'

'Sacred Heart a God!' Lily exploded. 'Does Mother know?'

'She was the first to hear,' Bridget said. 'A customer brought the paper into the shop to show it to her.'

'Surely this will change her mind about Christmas?' Jane said, ever the optimist.

'Yes,' Bridget answered sounding really excited. 'If you ask me, I think Mother's had an epiphany: she wants you two girls to go round to Moore Street immediately and get the biggest and the best Christmas tree you can lay your hands on, and extra ornaments.' She handed Jane a five-pound note.

'But sure we have masses of ornaments already,' Lily said. (Every year after Christmas, it was Lily's job to pack the Christmas ornaments in the big box and put them safely away in the basement.)

'Even so,' Bridget threw in, 'she still wants more ornaments — the bigger the better.' The girls couldn't help noticing how happy and relaxed Bridget was; she too had been down in the dumps about not celebrating Christmas. 'So off you go, the pair of you and get all the stuff.' Bridget now sounded unusually assertive. 'Don't argue, just do it!'

After pushing and shoving their way through the multitudes of Christmas shoppers that thronged Moore Street, amid hawkers cries of, 'Three for a shillin the jumpin jacks. Are ye buyin, missus? I have a bag. Ah! No Missus, I couldn't make it any cheaper; that's a real bargain!'

Jane and Lily eventually arrived at Alecia's stall.

'Ah! There yis are at last,' Alecia hailed them. I'm havin the divil's own job trying to hold on to your Christmas tree; it musta been inquired about a dozen times.' Alecia waved her hand in the direction of her twelve-year-old son who stood among the Christmas trees. 'My young fella, Christy, over there, has been standing guard over it, makin sure that nobody swipes it.'

'Alecia, you're a gem!' Jane said. 'We really appreciate it.'

'I wasn't sure if yis'd be wantin the tree this year on account of...' Alecia broke off mid-sentence to address a customer. 'Yes, Missus, that tree is definitely sold.' She turned back to Jane and Lily. 'See what I mean?' she said, winking at the girls. 'That lady has been back three times in the past hour wantin to buy your tree.' Alecia changed the subject. 'I'm glad yis are celebrating Christmas despite being in mourning. Sure life has to go on, doesn't it?'

'True for you, Alecia,' Lily said, giving her a bright smile.

Alecia shouted across to her bored looking son. 'They're here for their tree, Christy,' she said, pointing out Jane and Lily. 'Ye can parcel it up now.'

Christy rolled his eyes and mumbled under his breath, 'And about bloody time too!'

Lily studied the Christmas ornaments on Alecia's stall. They weren't great; sure what they had at home were just as good, if not better. 'Is this you full range of ornaments?' she asked Alecia.

'I'm afraid they are, love,' Alecia answered. 'But now, I won't be insulted if you find better ones at the other stalls. As a matter a fact, Maisy over there has...' Alecia's flow of words was once again interrupted as she beheld an elderly lady customer dismantling a pyramid of oranges on her stall. 'In the name a God, Missus!' Alecia shouted at her, 'What do ye think yer doin?'

'I've just dropped a sixpence into that pyramid,' the lady said sounding very precise. 'Amn't I trying to find it.'

'Ah now, Missus,' Alecia said persuasively, 'You've as much chance of finding that sixpence as you have finding a needle in a haystack.' She suppressed a smile. 'Tell ye what I'll do,' she added. 'If I find the sixpence, I'll light six candles for ye. How'd that be?'

'This place is as good as the pantomime,' Jane spluttered with laughter as herself and Lily stumbled under the weight of the Christmas tree towards Maisy's stand for the ornaments.

With the news of Peter's release the rush was on to tackle the Christmas chores. Cleaning the house took priority. Before any decorative ornaments could be put in place, the house had to undergo the usual special Christmas cleaning. Though Charmaine, the daily cleaning woman, was an absolute treasure, there were jobs she couldn't get round to doing on ordinary week days. Jobs such as cleaning the windows, laundering net curtains, washing paintwork on doors, skirtings and kitchen walls, washing and polishing the globes covering the gas lamps, getting rid of colonies of cobwebs in the corners and crevices of the ceilings. Normally these jobs required Charmaine to work overtime. (And she was glad of the money.) But this Christmas, mysteriously, the missus didn't seem to want any of them done. Because every time Charmaine brought up the subject of the special Christmas cleaning, she was confronted by the missus' vacant stare as you'd want to be thick in the head not to take the hint. So now it fell to the lot of Jane, Lily and Charmaine to do the cleaning in a hurry. Our Nancy, just started in her job as a trainee hairdresser, was, of course not available. Not that she'd be worth a damn anyway. So for the next few hours the O'Dwyer home was taken over by an orgy of house cleaning.

Later that evening when the house was spanking clean, Jane, Lily, Charmaine and Eileen (now over the moon with joy about the news of Peter's return) tackled the tree. It took all four of them to ballast it in its special tub of rocks and clay. Then came the nice part; decorating the tree with hundreds of candles in clip on holders, colored silver balls, trinkets, knickknacks, yards of silver streamers, chains and tinsel. Finally, came the placing of the largest angel imaginable on top.

As all four of them dressed the tree, Eileen's face glowed with happiness. 'Oh God!' she exclaimed, 'How I love Christmas. It's my most favorite time of the whole year.'

As soon as the tree was finished, Eileen insisted on lighting a few of the high-up candles. Then she lead the others—Jane, Lily and Charmaine—in a chain dance around the tree, singing, 'Peter's coming home for Christmas, home for Christmas, home for Christmas. Peter's coming home for Christmas on a cold and frosty morning.'

The others joined in the song. It was pure delight to see Eileen so happy.

When the dance was over they all stood back from the tree and studied it. 'It's probably the best dressed tree we've ever had,' Lily said.

'Yeah,' Jane said fixing her eye on the huge angel on top. 'Even the angel—big and all as it is—fits in beautifully. And you know something?' she added, 'The only reason I bought that angel was because I didn't want to hurt Maisy's feelings.' With her head held sideways she now studied it further. 'It's so darn big and awkward looking, I was sure it would look absolutely ridiculous. But it doesn't.'

'It's perfectly proportioned to the tree,' Lily said.

'Oh! It's oney beautiful,' Charmaine enthused. She was wishing to God she had an angel like that for her own tree.

'Holy smoke!' Eileen exclaimed, sounding very self-important, 'I'd better get started on my job.'

Her job was to look after the holly (sent by the country cousins), which up to now lay in a heap on the floor in the hall. It was traditional to place a sprig of holly behind each picture in the hall and parlor. Fixing the holly in the hall, Eileen made a bizarre discovery: behind one of the big pictures, swatches of the red wallpaper had been torn away. It didn't take her long to put two and two together:

Jane and Lily's lovely pink complexions were now explained.

With the ceiling cleared of cobwebs, Jane and Lily could now start hanging the colored paper chains in the parlor.

Jane was up the ladder fixing the end of the chain to the ceiling's Georgian centerpiece, when out of the blue, Lily, who stood holding the end of the chain, said, 'I wonder will your Willie be released with our Peter?' The ladder shook so violently Lily had visions of Jane landing on her arse in the middle of the floor. But thankfully, she had the presence of mind to grab the ladder and prevent what could have been a nasty accident.

'Jesus!' Jane said, staring down at her, 'What a time you pick to mention such a thing.'

'It just occurred to me this minute,' Lily giggled.

Descending the ladder, Jane panted, 'Well, the least you could have done was wait till I had my feet on solid ground before mentioning it.'

'So what do you think?' Lily asked, full of curiosity.

'We've been so busy with the Christmas chores, I didn't give it a thought.' Despite her galloping heart beat, Jane was surprised to hear her voice sound so normal.

'Well, you can start thinking about it now,' Lily pronounced. 'You never know; you may be seeing him sooner than you think.'

'What odds?' Jane said, her brow furrowed. 'Sure if he's interested in anyone, it's our Nancy.'

'Don't be such a pessimist.'

'I'm being a realist,' Jane said. 'No sense in getting all het up when I know there's no hope.'

Eileen, full of beans, picked this moment to dash into the room. 'Come on you two, come and see my handiwork.'

Jane and Lily followed her into the hall. 'Look,' Eileen said pointing to the crib. 'See what I've done with it.'

Eileen's artistry amazed her sisters. It showed great imagination and ingenuity. She'd arranged the holly beautifully around the crib. Along with that she had a glittering star, of her own making, hanging by a thread over it.

'That's fantastic,' Lily exclaimed, giving Eileen a hug.

'Imagine! We have an artist in the family we didn't know about.'

'Gosh!' Jane said, 'Mother'll be thrilled. The crib never looked so good.' She kissed Eileen on the cheek. 'All that glitter!' she said, 'It's so effective. Where did you get the idea?'

'My secret,' Eileen said, trying to sound mysterious. 'Incidentally,' she added with a knowing smile, 'I discovered *your* big secret.' Jerking her thumb in the direction of the big picture, she precociously mimed applying rouge to her cheeks. 'All those bald spots behind that picture!' She took a fit of laughing. Then stopped to put her fingers to her lips. 'Don't worry,' she said, 'your secret is safe with me.'

Jane and Lily started giggling. 'You're a right little ferret!' Lily exclaimed. Eileen left her sisters to finish off placing the holly behind the pictures in the parlor. When she was gone Lily smiled a happy smile. 'God!' she said to Jane, 'It's hard to believe that in such a short space of time the atmosphere could change so dramatically.'

But the best was yet to come - the biggest surprise of all. Mary pronounced that this Christmas Day the dairy would be closed all day. For the first time in its history notices were displayed around the shop and in the windows, declaring, 'The O'Dwyer Family Dairy will be closed on Christmas Day.'

'My God!' Jane burst out when she saw the notices, 'Mother must indeed have had an epiphany!'

§

Dropping in to see his mother for a short, hurried visit on Christmas Eve, Peter got an exultant welcome from everyone present. It was more or less taken for granted that himself, Nancy Pete and Baby Colbert would be having Christmas dinner with the family. Until he explained that Nancy Pete had already made arrangements for them to spend Christmas Day with her family. So any plans Mary may have had of a 'welcome home' party for Peter on Christmas

Day were well and truly quashed. And because that wasn't enough of a set back, Peter went on to explain that his diary for the following week was already full of engagements made by Nancy Pete. Though Mary was disappointed, she couldn't really blame anyone. After all, Peter was now married and his first duty was to his wife. Consequently, there was a great sense of anti-climax when the O'Dwyer family sat down to eat their Christmas dinner. Though nobody would voice it, the family felt that all the hard work getting the house ready for Peter's return had been something of a wasted effort. Suddenly Eileen mooted the idea of having a Party for Peter on New Year's Eve.

'You can be sure that he's tied up that night too,' Mary said despondently.

'No, he isn't,' Bridget chipped in.

'How do you know?' Mary asked.

'Because he said quietly to me that it would be nice if the family could at least get together on New Year's Eve.'

'That's it!' Lily said with a rush of excitement. 'Why don't we have our surprise party for him on that night? We could make out it's just an ordinary party to ring in the New Year.

At first Mary concurred with the idea, but then when she thought about the practicalities, she began to have doubts. 'Do you think for one minute we could keep the surprise part, a surprise?' she asked.

'Can't see why not,' Jane said. 'Couldn't we swear everyone to secrecy?'

'What would you think about enlisting Nancy Pete's help?' Bridget asked.

'I'd agree wholeheartedly,' Jane was very positive.

'Personally,' Lily put in, 'I can't see how we could possibly pull it off without Nancy Pete's help. Well, first of all, she'd have to agree to it. Hopefully, that could be achieved without too much acrimony.' Lily rolled her eyes. 'Then presuming she does agree, apart from organizing Peter, she'd need to give us the names and addresses of the friends she thinks Peter would like to see here.'

'Oh! Let's do it!' Jane's face glowed with excitement. She turned to Mary. 'Mother,' she said, 'you wouldn't have to worry about a thing.' She winked at Lily. 'Lily and I will attend to all the preparations and arrangements.'

'So who'll approach Nancy Pete?' Laughing, Bridget brought the conversation back down to earth.

'Seeing as how you two will be looking after all the arrangements,' our Nancy put in truculently, looking at Jane and Lily, 'Why don't you toss a coin between you to see who'll do it?' This was our Nancy's sole contribution to the conversation.

'Okay, I'm game to toss for it,' Jane said amicably.

'Me too,' Lily said looking amused. Then a thought struck her. 'What about yourself?' she asked our Nancy. 'You're so pally with her, wouldn't you be the ideal person to approach her?'

'Oh! No! No way! Count me out!' our Nancy said churlishly. Then stood up and left the room.

Mary was worried. If her fiery, volatile daughter, Lily, were to win the toss, making her the person to deal with Nancy Pete, there was no guarantee she wouldn't blow up and cause an almighty row if Nancy Pete disagreed. Mary intervened diplomatically. 'Jane,' she said, 'as the eldest of the two, I think it would be more appropriate if you did the talking to Nancy Pete.'

As luck would have it, Peter and the family dropped in again for a short visit on Saint Stephen' Day. When Nancy Pete was changing baby Colbert's nappy in Mary's bedroom, Jane collared her and explained about the welcome home party the family had in mind for Peter. Surprisingly, Nancy Pete found the whole idea *fascinating*. (Her words.) There and then she gave Jane the names and addresses of Peter's close friends. Not only that, she took the trouble to give Jane lots of useful tips about the catering; explaining that it was the way she catered for, what she termed, 'soirées.'

Chapter XII

On whirring wheels through uneventful landscape the train carried Willie eastward after he had spent Christmas with his family in Mayo. The visit had been most disappointing. Soon after his arrival it became clear that his parents were totally opposed to any discussions about 'the troubles.' As far as they were concerned the subject was taboo. He got his first hint of this when he was barely in the door. As soon as his brother, Martin, full of curiosity, started asking questions about the Rising, their domineering mother, Ellen, put an end to it, butting in and saying to Martin, 'time you saw to the cows, Martin.'

Afterwards, when his mother was absent, at the sound of a knock on the door, his mild-mannered father, Patrick, became nervous and upset. 'Say nothing about the 'troubles,' he cautioned Willie excitedly. 'To all intents and purposes you're still working in Liverpool.'

Following these incidents, except for answering the odd whispered surreptitious question from Martin when they were alone, it was as if the Rising and Willie's imprisonment never happened. Instead of the hero's welcome Willie had anticipated, his parents gave him the impression that they were ashamed of the part he played in fighting for the Cause. Willie thought, the people in this part of Mayo seem to be cocooned from the rest of the world. It could well be that the barren soil from which they scratched an existence was responsible; the hardship of battling to keep body and soul together was enough of a challenge without getting bogged down in Irish politics. They were people who were proficient in ignorance, who automatically accepted that poverty and deprivation was their lot. It should have come as no surprise to Willie. Wasn't it this backwoods lifestyle that sent him scrambling out of the country in the first place?

Nonetheless he felt very frustrated. He badly wanted to have a dialogue with his parents and his people about the Rising. Open their eyes and their minds to what was happening in the rest of the country, tell them a little bit about his own hair-raising experiences. But their total disinterest in hearing about killings and strife couldn't be clearer. Into the bargain the only bit of excitement in his parents' lives seemed to be the Christmas cards and letters, carrying the almighty dollars, from the two brothers and the sister in the States. (Who, by the same token, the mother boasted, were making great names for themselves and lots of money.) Otherwise, the sole topic of conversation was about the new bull borrowed from a neighbor; his background, his pedigree, more important, would he be up to the job?

Despite the frustration Willie felt having to keep his mouth clamped shut about the Rising and his experiences, he enjoyed the goose and the home cured bacon on Christmas Day and the odd drinks with the local people who dropped in. At which times he was very much the listener. He was remembering past Christmases before he emigrated, when, despite their impoverishment, food would be plentiful. After Christmas, however, it was back to a stable diet of potatoes and turnips on weekdays and bacon and cabbage on Sundays. As far as Willie was concerned, the best moment of the visit was after he'd said good-bye to the parents before setting out on Martin's bicycle for the railway station. Martin, a man of few words, came to the door to see him off.

Resolutely he stuck a five-pound note into Willie's breast pocket and said, 'I think you did great!' Then nodding in the direction of the kitchen where the mother was spinning raw wool on the spinning wheel and the father was cobbling his boot, he added, 'Never mind what *they're* thinking.' He hugged Willie affectionately. 'Don't leave it too long till your next visit.'

So Willie's Christmas visit was shorter than anticipated. Now on

New Year's Eve, he was making his way back to Dublin to where he hoped the action was. In contrast to the westward journey From Dublin to Mayo on Christmas Eve, when the train was heaving with passengers and Willie had to stand most of the way, today — New Year's Eve — the train was relatively empty. Besides himself, only one other passenger — an elderly gentleman — occupied the carriage. His name was Diarmuid. Toothless, eyes pale blue and red-veined, Diarmuid was about the last person Willie would have expected to have any interest in Irish politics. Nonetheless, Diarmuid immediately struck up a conversation which lead to a discussion about that very subject. He encouraged Willie to talk freely about his experiences in the G.P.O during the Rebellion and afterwards in Frongoch. And despite the fact that he seemed well versed in most of the events that took place during that period, he asked highly intelligent questions and listened attentively to Willie's answers. It was like a new lease of life to Willie.

'I've the greatest admiration for you volunteers,' Diarmuid remarked. 'Surely you've done more than her share for your country. And what thanks did ye get?' The words were music to Willie's ears. After six days of forced silence, it was so refreshing to talk frankly and openly about his part in the Rising to someone who was genuinely interested.

'You surprise me!' he told Diarmuid. 'Showing so much interest and sympathy. I was beginning to think the people in Mayo were cut off from the rest of the country.'

Diarmuid said, 'You'll have to forgive the people living in these parts; sure they haven't the foggiest notion about what's going on in the country, never mind the world. To be honest with you, were it not for the fact that I commute regularly to Dublin to see my daughter, I'd probably be just as ignorant. Talking to other commuters, arguing the toss with my son-in-law in Dublin and reading the Dublin newspapers, has kept me pretty well informed.'

Making the connection from Galway to Dublin at Ballinasloe, was a young man, thin and earnest, probably in his late twenties, named Fiocra. He joined Willie and Diarmuid in their carriage. In conversation with them, Fiocra made the disclosure that he was a freelance journalist and a true nationalist. During their conversation Diarmuid prevailed on Willie to tell Fiocra his story — particularly the bit about losing his rifle in the G.P.O.

Fiocra found Willie's story very impressive. 'Goodness, Willie,' he said, 'you've really been through the mill. But what a miraculous escape you had after the surrender.' He was thinking Willie's story would be well worth publishing when the troubles were over. Smiling he said, 'You know something, I think my guardian angel was working overtime that week too. Wasn't I one of the lucky ones who escaped by the skin of my teeth through a lavatory window in a pub in Galway where a number of our lads were rounded up.' He scratched his head. 'Most of the lads they nabbed that night ended up in British prisons and prisoner of war camps. You may have run into some of them in Frongoch? But think about this,' he went on grimly, 'didn't the British make a terrible mistake by rounding up thousands of lukewarm, mild nationalists, clamping them in jails. Those lads went in tepid and came out roaring revolutionaries.'

'It's not surprising!' Willie laughed heartily, then said, 'I shouldn't be laughing. God help them! I actually met some of those innocent bystanders in Frongoch.' Then he changed the subject to one that was near to his heart. 'Tell us,' he asked, 'how do you think the country is faring now?' Having come up against a stone wall of silence in his hometown, he was keen to get the viewpoint of someone else from that part of the country.

For seconds Fiocra was silent. Eventually, as if laboring under a very heavy burden, he uttered the words, 'The aftermath of the Rising has proved to be a challenge from the dead!' Then seeing the effect his profound words had on the two men — their silence and their looks of puzzlement — Fiocra hastily added, 'The reason I say this is because of the horror of the executions; those executions seem to have had a terrible emotional effect on most of the population.'

Willie nodded his head. 'In the short time I've been back, I got the same impression,' he said. 'But what I'm really interested in, is, what the population's feelings are now with regard to the Irish Parliamentary Party presently representing Ireland in Westminster?' This was another subject close to Willie's heart. Fiocra's answer could be most important.

Again Fiocra took a while to answer. 'Not good!' he said abruptly. Then sounding very earnest, added, 'The nation has, once and for all, lost all faith in that party. Consequently, the IPP's hold on the country has loosened considerably. In fact, I'd go so far as to say that presently anything with the slightest tinge of British about it, now stinks with most of the Irish population.'

'As bad as that?'

'Yes. As bad as that,' Fiocra declared. 'Even in rural Ireland.' His mouth twitched in agitation. 'From what I've been hearing,' he went on, 'politically, the country seems to be in a wilderness. The people are muddled and restless, but keen in their hatred of the British. There's been talk recently in Galway and other parts of the West about turning away from the authority of the IPP and forming our own parliamentary party here in Ireland. But how do we start such a party? Where do the people anchor their political psyche?'

Willie smiled a slow smile. 'I think I may know the very person who might be able to answer those questions,' he said. 'His name is Collins. He was a prisoner in Frongoch when I was there. There was a saying among the internees —"if anyone can do it Collins can."'

'That's the man that the Dublin crowd were cheering so wildly two days before Christmas,' Diarmuid threw in laughing heartily. 'And him leading the march, brazen as you like in broad daylight with his deportee comrades in their banned military uniforms.'

'I was part of that march,' Willie acknowledged proudly. 'Yeah,' he continued, 'we marched from the ship right along the Docks, up the Quays and into Sackville Street. I couldn't believe the reception the Dubliners were giving us.'

'And why wouldn't they?' Diarmuid said sagely. 'After what you lads had done trying to win the freedom.'

Willie had to smile at the incongruity of it all. 'Well, we volunteers did help to reduce their lovely city to ruins,' he said sounding quite solemn.

'But remember the British had a bigger hand in destroying the city than you lads did,' Diarmuid retorted. 'Among other things, didn't they bring one of their battle ships up the Liffey to shell the city?'

'That's as maybe,' Willie rejoined, 'still, we started it.'

Fiocra butted in. He seemed anxious to get his bit in. 'I believe on the day the deportees marched through the city, the G-Men from the Castle had to stand idly by and look on meekly at their defiance. They couldn't lift a finger to stop them for fear the Dubliners would lynch them.'

They all laughed.

'To be sure there were no flies on those deportees,' Diarmuid's eyes sparkled with merriment. 'When they saw the crowd was with them, they took full advantage of the situation. Wasn't I the lucky one to be crossing O'Connell Bridge on my way to the Broadstone railway station at the time they were passing and witnessed it all with my very own eyes. Proud of yis I was,' Diarmuid declared. 'I says under me breath...*and the best of good luck to yis lads; yis deserve it.*'

'Thanks,' Willie clapped his hand on the old man's shoulder. He could feel a prickle of tears of appreciation. He turned to Fiocra. 'It might be to our mutual advantage,' he said, 'to stay in touch.' He had the feeling that his meeting with Fiocra was fortuitous; Fiocra might turn out to be a very good contact in Galway in the future.

'You're dead right,' Fiocra said. 'The exact same thought occurred to me. Do you have an address in Dublin where I could reach you?' he asked.

'Not as yet, I haven't,' Willie answered. 'As a matter of fact, one of the first things I have to do when I get to Dublin is find digs.'

'In the meantime,' Fiocra threw in, 'is there a watering hole you'd frequent where I might run into you sometime? I make the trip to Dublin quite frequently.'

'Yes, of course. I should have thought of that myself,' Willie pounced on the idea. 'There's a pub called Flanagans in Lower Leeson Street. I'll probably end up there myself tonight sometime: I believe it's a favorite haunt of some of my comrades. But to be on the safe side, maybe I should get your address in Galway now.'

'Sure,' Fiocra said. He produced a small pad from his inside pocket. 'There,' he said tearing a sheet off the pad, handing it to Willie. 'That's my name and address written on top.'

§

On his way through Flanagan's pub, Willie heard a burst of applause coming from the back, then when the noise died down, came the familiar tone of Collins' West Cork accent.

'Great stuff, Sean,' he said, 'it calls for an encore.'

'Are you with Mick's party?' the barman leaned over the counter and asked Willie as he was passing.

'Yes,' Willie said confidently. He nodded his head in the direction of the snug. 'Is it all right to go in?'

'Sure,' the barman said, 'any friend of Mick's is a friend of ours.'

Inside the snug Collins and a party of young men were gathered. The group included Peter O'Dwyer and Ciaron, Willie's friend from the Kimmage Garrison.

When Collins saw Willie coming through the door, he greeted him cordially. 'Ah! Willie!' he said. 'Come on in. T'is fit and well you're lookin. I hope you're in good vice tonight.' Roars of laughter filled the snug. Collins addressed the gathering. 'Tighten up there lads,' he said. 'Make room for a champion goalie from Mayo.'

There was screeching and scratching of chairs as the group made room for Willie at the table. Some of the lads were ex-Frongoch, some strangers. Willie found a seat next to Peter O'Dwyer who welcomed him warmly.

Collins opened the hatch into the pub. 'Give us another pint a Guinness there, Dan,' he shouted to the barman through the opening.

'Okay, Mick!' Peter now called on Collins. 'This time you're not going to weasel out of it. We want to hear your rendition of 'Kelly, Burke and Shea.''

'Right, lads!' Collins rose abruptly, looking very self-assured and with his hands in his pockets, scanned the ceiling and the floor before starting to recite 'Kelly Burke and Shea' with great feeling:

Oh the fighting races don't die out
If they seldom die in bed
For love is first in their hearts, no doubt

Said Burke; then Kelly said
'When Michael, the Irish Arch angel, stands
The angel with the sword
And the battle dead from a hundred lands
Are ranged in one big hoarde
Our line that for Gabriel's trumpet waits
Will stretch three deep that day
From Jehosaphat to the Golden Gates -
Kelly, Burke and Shea.
Well, here's thank God
For the race and the sod'
Said Kelly, Burke and Shea.

'Arrah! That's as much as I can remember,' Collins said disconsolately stopping abruptly. Then taking a bow, with the applause ringing in his ears, he sat down. Turning to Willie, he asked, 'Do have a party piece at all?'

Willie looked hard at his untouched pint sitting on the table in front of him. 'Maybe when I get this pint inside me, I might,' he said.

Liam Curtin, a Dubliner with a great gift for storytelling — not a Frongoch man — began to recount his favorite stories of the quaint characters who drifted in and out of his family grocery and the long procession of crooks, twisters, humbugs and rogues he'd had to deal with in his business. When he finished with all the yarns, he appealed to the group to give Home Rule a chance.

'Dry up, you old twister!' Collins said. Home Rule is all bloody bunk! We want a Republic!'

'All right, Mick,' said Curtain. 'As you will, but consider at least—'

"Constitutional balderdash!' Collins shouted. Clearly Collins had had a few too many. It was the first time Willie ever saw him like this. Collins turned to the company and said, 'Okay, lads, this is a night for celebrating, how about a few bars of 'The Holy Ground.'?'

Whereupon the Cork men present raised their voices in unison, singing a rousing version of the song.

Adieu, my fair young maiden.
A thousand times adieu
We must bid farewell to the Holy Ground
And the girls that we love true.
We will sail the salt sea over
and return again for sure
to seek the girls who wait for us
in the Holy Ground once more.
FINE GIRREL YOU ARE.
You're the girl that I adore
And still I live in hopes to see
the Holy Ground once more
FINE GIRREL YOU ARE.

The barman came to collect the debris and take orders. 'Keep it down, lads,' he pleaded when they finished. 'You're drawing attention to yourselves.' He spoke in low tones to Collins. 'There are a couple of G-men out there,' he said, nodding his head in the direction of the bar. 'Yis'd want to watch it.'

'Never mind the lousers!' Collins roared. 'There's too much bloody G-manitis in this bloody city for my taste. Half the bloody jails are filled by fellows sprinting across the road when they see a policeman.'

There was laughter all round.

'True for ye, Mick,' A Cork man affirmed.

'Okay, lads,' the barman intervened, 'I'm still here waiting to take your orders.' He had his pad at the ready.

'Make it the same again,' Collins answered.

Peter O'Dwyer turned to Willie. 'Have you any plans to celebrate the New Year?' he asked him

'No,' Willie said, 'the train from the West didn't get in till after seven. So I only had time to organize a room for the night. Then I came straight here.'

Peter said, 'There's a bit of a party in my mother's house tonight to ring in the New Year. Would you be interested in coming?'

'Sounds good!' Willie tried not to sound overly enthusiastic, but the twinkle in his eyes gave him away. 'Does that mean I might get to meet your sisters again?'

'Could well be,' Peter answered. His eyes crinkled in amusement. He wondered which sister Willie was interested in because God help him if it was our Nancy. 'By the way,' he changed the subject, 'where are you dossing tonight?'

'In a place down the Quays called Phelan's Hostel. Tomorrow I'll be looking for something more permanent.'

Peter stood up. 'I have to go now,' he said. 'Should've been home an hour ago; the ball and chain will be on the warpath. But you know the way it is when you meet up with Mick?'

'Only too well.'

'Anyway,' Peter went on, 'when you finish your pint come to my place: it's just up the street, number a hundred and nineteen. Ring the bell. Then we can all go together to the party. All, being my wife, Nancy and my new son, Colbert.' There was no denying the pride in Peter's voice mentioning his son's name.

'Called after Cornelius Colbert, no doubt,' Willie interjected.

Peter nodded his head. 'The Lord have mercy on his soul!' he said grimly. Cornelius Colbert was one of the executed leaders.

After Peter left, Ciaron leaned over to Willie. 'Did I hear you say you were looking for digs?' he asked.

'Yeah, you did.'

'Well, if you're interested, the place where I've got digs has a vacancy. It's in Drumcondra.'

'That's the North Side?'

'Yeah, it's close to the city, very reasonable, (just seven-and-six a week all told.) It's really comfortable and the landlady feeds us like fighting cocks.'

'Sounds perfect,' Willie said. 'Give us the address.'

As Ciaron wrote down the address he remarked, 'I tell ye something, the way our landlady stuffs food into us, she'll have flesh on those bones of your's in no time.'

When Willie arrived at the O'Dwyer flat, Nancy Pete practically fell over herself with politeness; a bit too much for Willie's taste. In Frongoch Peter mentioned in passing that his wife was an actress and Willie was intrigued to meet her. But he was barely ensconced in the beautiful Georgian drawing room, when the fuss started.

'Peter, for God's sake give Willie a drink,' Nancy Pete demanded of her husband. 'No! Not that awful glass,' she shrieked. 'Don't make a show of us! Use one of the cut glasses from the china cabinet there.' (As if Willie was used to cut glass.)

Without demurring, Peter dutifully carried out all her orders. He poured a whiskey for Willie, which Willie didn't really want, but rather than aggravate the situation said nothing. Peter held the glass up for Willie's comment. 'Enough? More? Too much?' he asked.

'About half of that,' Willie answered.

'Sure that's not a drink at all!' Nancy Pete remarked in her beautiful, articulated voice.

Willie said, 'Mrs. O'Dwyer, I've already had two pints. To be honest with you, I'm quite abstemious; I only drink once in a while.'

'But surely you can break out on New Year's Eve?' Nancy Pete sounded sardonic. The way she said it made Willie feel a right weakling. He tried to conceal his annoyance. But Peter saw it in his face.

'Nancy,' he reproached her, 'For Christ sake! Will you stop pestering the man, pushing drink on him that he doesn't want.' He reduced the whiskey in the glass, diluted it with water and handed it to Willie.

Nancy looked hurt and baffled. 'I'm just trying to be hospitable,' she said, her voice a pathetic whine.

'Okay,' Peter came across and gave Nancy a hug. 'Despite all her fussiness,' he said to Willie, 'my wife has a heart of gold.'

'What fussiness?' Nancy Pete said aggressively. Once again she was on the attack. Willie could see that Peter had his hands full with a wife that was both demanding and controlling.

Looking at his watch, Peter ignored the question. 'It's after half-past nine,' he said. 'I wonder what's happened to our cab?'

'It's New Years Eve, remember,' Nancy Pete said derisively. 'What can you expect?'

'Have you all the bits and pieces packed for the little fellow?' Peter asked her.

'Not much to pack,' Nancy Pete languidly stroked her large bosom. 'Isn't his food always ready for him in here.'

Willie felt most uncomfortable.

§

The New Year's Eve surprise Welcome Home Party for Peter turned into a great affair altogether. Before Peter's arrival, everyone invited — relatives, friends of Peters and family friends, together with wives and girl friends — turned up in good time. In all about sixty guests.

To make room for such a large number of people, the parlor was cleared of all its furniture except for the seating: couches, armchairs and easy chairs were placed around the walls. The sole remaining piece of furniture was the piano which occupied a corner. As far as the food was concerned, the family adhered to the tradition of having it in the kitchen where the large kitchen table and side tables were covered with what Nancy Pete termed, a running buffet: a veritable feast consisting of turkey and ham sandwiches, shellfish and mushroom savories, cocktail sausages and multiple cheeses. For dessert, there was trifle smothered in whipped cream, and mince pies.

Drinks too were also be had in the kitchen. Taigh Murphy having taken care of the supplies which included an iron lung of Guinness, crates of beer, bottles of wines and spirits and non-alcoholic beverages, along with a supply of glasses. There was punch too — hot, strong and sweet — and cups of tea for anyone who wanted them. Acting as hostesses, the daughters of the house directed the guests to where the food and drink was. It was noticeable that, after imbibing a few drinks, the guests lightened up considerably and the atmosphere was charged with much laughter as yarns and anecdotes were exchanged.

But by ten o'clock when Peter still hadn't put in an appearance, Daniel, one of his newspaper friends (pointing to the banner over the fireplace, which announced WELCOME HOME, PETER AND HAPPY NEW YEAR EVERYONE) asked Bridget, 'when are we going to see the guest of honor?'

'Well, you know there's a new baby,' Bridget explained. Needless to say, Peter's life is not as free and easy as it used to be.' When Peter still hadn't arrived by quarter past ten, however, Bridget decided the time had come for some musical entertainment. She sought Jane out. 'Be an angel and give us a few bars on the piano,' she said to her. 'Peter or no Peter, I get the feeling our guests wouldn't mind a bit of entertainment.'

'Just thinking the same thing,' Jane said. At former parties normally around this time, the entertainment would be in full swing. Of course, Peter himself contributed a lot performing Gilbert and Sullivan arias as guests joined in the choruses. 'Okay,' Jane said, 'let's ask Aunt Jude to do her party piece; pierce our ears with the screeching high notes.'

'You mean...?' Bridget cast her eyes up to heaven.

'Yeah,' Jane interjected with an indulgent smile. 'Well, look at her; isn't she only itching to be asked. So let's get it over with.'

'Right, you get to the piano,' Bridget said compliantly, 'and I'll organize Jude.'

In her high, quivering voice with Jane accompanying her on the piano, Jude was halfway through the song 'The Kerry Dances' when Peter's entourage arrived and created a hubbub in the hall. It was an awkward moment for the musicians: they didn't know whether to go on or to stop. If Jane had her way they would definitely have stopped. Because when Aunt Jude wasn't slithering off the high notes she was screeching them.

Mary, however, made the decision. Jumping up she said to Jude, 'No, don't stop. Go on, continue singing. By the time they have their coats off and the baby is settled upstairs, you'll be well and truly finished.'

Jude had barely finished the song and was acknowledging the

applause, when Bridget rushed over to Jane at the piano and gave her the beck. 'He's on his way in, Jane.'

As Peter entered the room, Jane broke into 'For he's a jolly good fellow' and the crowd joined in singing.

As soon as they finished, Daniel, Peter's newspaper friend, started a chorus of 'Why was he born so beautiful, why was he born at all? He's no bloody use to anyone, he's no bloody use at all.'

The people who knew the words joined in. Peter's face was aglow with joy and surprise at this incredible welcome home party.

From the door Willie found it difficult to see even one familiar face the way the crowd surrounded Peter — clapping, cheering and singing. With no one taking the slightest bit of notice of him, he felt unaccountably ill as ease; like an interloper who had crashed a party. Some relative had opened the door to them when they arrived. Nancy Pete swept up the stairs to attend to the baby, while Peter was rushed into the parlor for the welcome home ceremonies. There was no time for introductions. As Willie surveyed the scene in the parlor, he couldn't help comparing this jubilant welcome home for Peter with the one he received from his own family in Mayo.

Suddenly Willie heard a surprised, vaguely familiar voice behind him saying, 'Well, will you look who's here!' Turning he saw our Nancy, looking as beautiful as ever and apparently quite pleased to see him. He couldn't decide whether it was a good thing or not, because at that particular moment he'd made up his mind to slip away unnoticed.

When the singing ended and after Mary had ushered Peter through to the kitchen to be fed, Bridget spoke to Jane at the Piano.

'While they're all on their feet, Jane, she said, 'play them a waltz or something.'

'Right,' Jane acquiesced. 'I suppose I'd better keep the momentum going.' Jane broke into 'The Merry Widow Waltz' and the guests took their partners and danced.

'Would you like to have this dance with me?' Nancy asked Willie. Willie was embarrassed. Though he had a few dancing lessons in Liverpool, he still felt bloody awkward on the dance floor. Still, he decided that with the room so crammed with dancers, even if he was a good dancer, the best they could hope to do was shuffle around the room.

'Well, if you can stand a dancer who has two left feet,' he answered our Nancy, 'I'm game.'

'I'll take my chances,' Nancy laughed. 'Besides,' she added, indicating the crowded floor, 'if you do trip me up there are enough people around to cushion my fall.'

At first Willie tried to play it safe keeping near the door. But our Nancy had other ideas. Suddenly she propelled him right into the middle of the dancers.

Halfway through the waltz, Jane looked up from the piano. Holy Mother of God! Am I seeing right? she groaned, as her heart sank like a stone.

There they were: Willie and our Nancy, not only dancing, but laughing and joking like longtime lovers. The shock of it made her stumble on the notes. But then, thank God, reality sustained her. The most important thing now was to concentrate on the music and keep the dance going. But, dear God! she thought, plodding on, how I wish I wasn't a pianist. Stuck at this bloody piano! Helpless!

Trying desperately to bottle up her resentment, she banged out the tune louder than ever. Meanwhile Willie was so preoccupied with looking down at his feet, making sure they didn't trample all over our Nancy's, he didn't catch sight of Jane at the piano.

Our Nancy chatted away, asking him questions, which he answered in monosyllables. Questions like: Where he spent Christmas? Future plans? Did he intend staying on in Dublin? From time to time he lifted his head long enough to search for Jane among the dancers.

When the dance ended, Lily rushed over to the piano. 'Please, Jane,' she urged, 'play us another waltz.' Rolling her eyes in sign language, she added, 'I've actually got myself a real, live male partner.' But then when Jane grabbed her arm and looked like she was falling apart, she realized something was seriously wrong. 'What's up?' she asked apprehensively.

'He's here!' Jane whispered, her eyes big as saucers

'Who's here?' Lily's tone matched Jane's.

'Willie!'

'Jesus! Where is he?'

'He's over there dancing with our Nancy.' Lily followed the direction of Jane's eyes and saw Willie and our Nancy standing beside the door chatting.

'Oh my God!' Lily said. 'When did he arrive?''

'Haven't a notion.'

'Look,' Lily made a quick decision. 'Just go ahead and play another waltz while I put the skids under that Nancy wan.'

'For God's sake, Lily, don't make a scene.'

'I've no intentions of making a scene,' Lily assured her. Jane played 'Alice Blue Gown' and the dancers, standing in wait, resumed dancing. After a word with her gorgeous male partner, Lily approached Willie and our Nancy, about to start dancing.

Tapping our Nancy on the shoulder she said, 'Pardon me! But I'm cutting in.' Though she sounded polite and courteous, our Nancy could tell it was only on the surface. Reluctantly, our Nancy introduced Willie to Lily. Then Lily put her hands up appropriately in front of Willie, indicating she wanted to dance with him. 'Dance, Willie?' she said.

'You could be taking your life in your hands dancing with me,' Willie said jocosely as he put his arm round her.

'Don't you worry about that,' Lily laughed. 'Like the proverbial cat, I've nine lives.' As they started dancing, or more to the point, shuffling, Lily asked Willie, 'What time did you arrive?'

'Oh, just a while ago. I came with Peter and the missus and the baby.'

'So you haven't had any supper yet?' Lily asked the practical question.

'Oh! No need to worry about that.'

'Excuse me, but I do need to worry about it!' Lily said, looking quite solemn. 'I happen to be one of the proud caterers. Come on,' she said, pulling Willie by the arm towards the kitchen, 'there's loads of food left and it's got to be consumed tonight, otherwise it'll go to waste.

The kitchen was empty except for Charmaine who was busy at the corner table replenishing plates of food for the late comers. The first thing Lily did was pour Willie a glass of beer. 'Sit down there at the table and make yourself at home,' she told him. Then taking the full plates from Charmaine, she put such scrumptious food in front of him as would make any hungry person's mouth water.

Mother of God! Willie thought, what a meal! It's truly fit for a king! He was certainly ready for it and attacked it with gusto. 'Sorry, Lily, if I appear greedy,' he said between mouthfuls, 'but it must be twelve hours since I've eaten, and then it was just a biscuit and cup of tea on the train.'

'No need to apologize,' Lily said. 'After such a long fast, is it any wonder you're hungry. But what is a wonder,' she added, 'is why no member of the family took the trouble to look after you. What the bloody hell was Peter thinking about?' Lily looked fit to be tied. 'Jesus! All he had to do was introduce you to a member of the family.'

'Now don't go blaming Peter,' Willie said with a wry smile. 'This is an extraordinary night for him. What with a surprise party and a new son and heir to show off, who could blame him if he was distracted. Anyway,' he added deferentially, 'didn't your sister Nancy come to the rescue.'

'Huh! Some rescue!' Lily snorted. 'I bet she didn't ask if you had a mouth on ye?'

Willie had to laugh at her expression. He decided, if nothing else, this sister was just as down-to-earth as Jane; making him feel so relaxed and at home. As he pondered on how to bring up the subject of Jane without making it too obvious, Lily herself introduced it.

'You know, if it wasn't for Jane, you'd've been allowed to starve,' she said.

'Oh, Jane is here?' Willie sounded surprised. At the same time he could feel the blood thumping in his pulse.

'Yes. She's playing the piano. Did you not see her?'

'Good God! That's her playing the piano?' Willie looked astonished.

'Yes, of course.'

'Well, Lily, to be honest with you, I was so busy watching my feet when I was dancing, I didn't even glance in the direction of the piano.' Willie was silent for a few seconds, then his face lit up. 'Goodness!' he said, 'Isn't she very talented.'

'We think so.'

The music could be heard clearly in the kitchen. It stopped for a few seconds, then started again. This time it was a rhythmic fox-trot 'Happy days are here again.'

'Gosh!' Willie exclaimed, fascinated as he listened, 'She plays like a professional. It's amazing!'

'So amazing,' Lily said caustically, 'that if that crowd have their way they'll have her stuck at that piano all night!' Suddenly it struck her that she should be doing something about it. 'Look,' she said to Willie, 'you carry on eating. I'll be back in a minute.' She left the room. In the hall Lily ran into Bridget. 'Where the hell is Peter?' she asked her.

It was obvious to Bridget that she had a bee in her bonnet. 'The last time I saw him, he was having a chat with that newspaper friend of his, Daniel, in Mother's office.'

'I'll soon put an end to that,' Lily said matter-of-factly. Bridget raised her eyes to heaven. She hoped to God Lily wasn't going to start a row.

Lily found Peter and Daniel deep in conversation in the mother's office. 'For Christ sakes!' she said, rushing in, glaring at Peter and rudely interrupting his conversation, 'Will you take over playing that bloody piano from Jane and start a sing-song?'

'But Jane is doing a super job,' Peter asserted. 'I can't believe how good she is. Gracious! She's come on by leaps and—'

'Which is all jolly fine,' Lily interjected, 'but at this particular moment she could do with a break.' Lily turned to Daniel. 'Sorry!' she apologized, 'but this party was given in honor of this fella and we've seen nothing of him, nor heard nothing from him all evening.'

'I quite understand,' Daniel responded.

'Now, Lily, hold on to your horses!' Peter threw in. 'Don't get excited!' He knew of old that Lily's red face bespoke a frenzy of impatience. 'Leave us for a minute or so,' he said soothingly. 'Daniel and I are discussing something which could be immensely important to my future.'

'Okay,' Lily relented. Then casually looked up at the clock on the wall. 'Christ!' she exclaimed horrified, 'Will you look at the time! It's a quarter to twelve already! Peter,' she said, jocularly poking his chest with her index finger, 'I want you at that fecken piano by five to twelve and not a minute later.'

'Yes, Mam! Certainly, Mam! At your service, Mam!' Peter clicked his heels.

On her way through the hall Lily bumped into our Nancy looking like her nose was very much out of joint. 'What the hell did you do with Willie?' she barked at Lily.

'I did what you neglected to do. I fed him.'

'I'd every intention of doing just that when you butted in.' Our Nancy's voice dripped with contempt.

'Oh, go and shite!' Lily said, 'You're full of good intentions, but you never bloody do anything about them.'

Before returning to the kitchen, Lily decided she'd better put Jane's mind at rest. Poor Jane! she thought. Stuck at that damn piano, forced to leave the field wide open for that bitch to take advantage. When she saw how fraught with agitation Jane was as she continued playing the piano, she was glad to be able to reassure her. 'He's in the kitchen, eating all before him,' she said softly into Jane's ear. 'Peter has promised to relieve you shortly. Could you stick it out for a few more minutes?'

'Where's our Nancy?' Jane whispered back.

'Last time I saw her, she was in the hall. Never mind, *he's* in the kitchen, so you've nothing to worry about.' Jane's face registered enormous relief. But when Lily finally reached the kitchen she realized there was much to worry about: our Nancy was there flirting like mad with Willie. 'Sorry, I took so long,' Lily said to Willie barging in on their conversation. 'I was trying to find Peter. It's traditional for him to play Auld Lang Syne when we're ringing in the new year.'

'Since when?' our Nancy spat the words at her. 'I can't remember when Peter was last with us on a New Year's Eve.'

Bitch! Lily thought. *She'll pay for this!* Quickly she changed the subject. 'Have some more trifle,' she said to Willie pushing the bowl under his nose.

'Good God, no!' Willie burst out. 'I can't remember when I eat so much. The food is absolutely delicious!'

Lily poured another beer for Willie. 'Well, you'll be wanting this,' she said handing it to him. 'We're about to ring in the New Year.'

Willie looked at the clock on the kitchen wall. 'Gracious!' he said. 'It's that time already!'

Thankfully at that moment Eileen, eyes aglitter with excitement, stuck her head into the kitchen and shouted, 'Come on everybody, to the parlor. It's three minutes to twelve. Time to get ready to ring in the New Year.'

To Lily's chagrin, our Nancy linked Willie into the parlor. The music had stopped, the lights were dimmed and Peter was, at last, at the piano with Nancy Pete hovering around him. Jane was nowhere to be seen.

Peter stood up. 'Okay, everybody,' he announced, 'we've come to the most important part of the evening. I hope everyone is holding a glass — preferably a full one.' He looked at his watch, 'Right, twelve seconds to go. We'll start counting when I give the beck.' A second later he stroked the air with his hand. 'Now!' he said.

The countdown started: 'Ten, nine, eight, seven, six, five, four, three, two, one.' When 'one' was reached, the sound of a gong resounded through the room; standing at the door, the keeper was Jane. The words *Happy New Year* reverberated throughout the room as each person embraced their nearest and dearest. After hugging Michael, Bridget opened the window allowing the sound of the bells of Christ Church Cathedral and other bells ringing over the city to enter the room.

Our Nancy, about to throw her arms around Willie was restrained by his hand catching hers in a friendly handshake. 'Happy New Year, Nancy,' he said formally. Following which he excused himself, left her side and made his way across the room to join Jane at the door. 'Happy New Year, Jane,' he said breathlessly as he took her hand and it was as if someone had turned a light on inside.

'Happy New Year, Willie,' Jane responded, her heart soaring with her own happiness.

Peter struck up 'Old Lang Syne' on the piano and all present made a circle of entwined hands as they sang,

Should old acquaintance be forgot
And never brought to mind,
Should old acquaintance be forgot
For the sake of old Auld Lang Syne.
For Auld Lang Syne my dear
For Auld Lang syne,
We'll drink a cup of kindness yet
For the sake of Auld lang Syne!

As the singing finished, once again there were lots of hand shakes, hugs and kisses all around the room. Suddenly, Willie's arms were around Jane and she found herself in a big bear hug. My God! She felt such happiness! It was as if it was growing out of her like wings.

Chapter XIII

Willie rang the bell of Sadie Walsh's house in Drumcondra. It was a plain, red-brick, two-story building with steps running up to the hall door and a basement. A young man in a soft hat and a trench coat opened the door, obviously on his way out.

'Is Mrs. Walsh at home?' Willie asked him.

'Sadie!' the young man shouted over his shoulder. 'There's a fella here to see you.' He smiled a guileful smile. 'I suppose you're here about the digs.'

Sadie, a woman in her fifties, with twinkling brown eyes and the sure movements of a bird, scurried from the kitchen at the end of the hall, wiping her hands in her apron. She spoke with a refined Dublin accent. 'You'll have to excuse the cut of me,' she said. 'I'm in the throes of baking cakes.' In the sitting room into which Sadie lead Willie, the upholstery was shabby, the old pieces of furniture dark and dowdy. Strewn around the room newspapers and magazines made quite a mess. However, despite all this, there was a great sense of homeliness about the room. 'You're the young man Ciaron was telling me about?' Sadie said as she busied herself picking newspapers up off the linoleum.

'That's right, Mrs. Walsh.'

'Call me Sadie; everyone does.'

'If you insist,' Willie laughed.'

'I do,' Sadie's smile was ingratiating. 'Now about the terms,' she went on, 'they're the same as those for Ciaron. That suit you?'

'Oh absolutely! They're very reasonable.'

Sadie said, 'Well, I don't know whether Ciaron told you or not, but I give a special discount to you lads who fought for the freedom.'

'You're a Nationalist?'

'I'm more than a Nationalist, I'm an out and out Republican.' Willie decided he liked this woman; she was warm, chirpy and maternal. 'Come on now, I'll show you the room.' Sadie lead Willie up the stairs, stopping on the return landing which held the bathroom, the lavatory and the bedroom Willie would occupy. 'Sorry it's a bit on the small side,' Sadie said ushering Willie into the bedroom. 'But,' she reasoned, 'you have the advantage of being near all the conveniences. Maybe that'll compensate for the smallness of the room.'

The room was certainly small and poky, with a single bed, small wardrobe and a bedside table. A window looked out on the back garden which was a jungle. Willie decided the room was more than adequate for his requirements. Anyway, he thought, what can you expect for that kind of money? 'It's absolutely perfect,' he told Sadie.

Willie paid Sadie a week's rent in advance and arranged to take up residence the following morning. This evening Willie had a heavy date with Jane. He was taking her to the Symphony Concert in the Metropolitan Hall. As he sat on the tram bringing him back to the city, his mind wandered back to the wonder of this miracle. If anyone told him this time last week, when he was so miserable in Mayo, that tonight, the first night of the year nineteen-seventeen, he would be in the company of his beloved Jane, he would have said they needed their heads examined.

It wasn't easy either getting Jane on her own last night to ask her out. What with the way the sister, Nancy, had carried on. She acted as if she owned him, clinging to him all evening like some grotesque limpet. Were it not for Lily's timely intervention, manipulating the pushy sister out of the room on some pretext of other, the opportunity to speak to Jane would never have presented itself. When he eventually asked her if she would come to the Concert, he noticed that she was as flushed as he was. His heart was banging in his chest as he waited for her answer.

Peering up at him through half closed eyes, she smiled softly and said, 'Why, I'd love to come!' Then seeing sister Nancy making a beeline back to them, she hastily inquired, 'Quickly, what time and where will I meet you?'

Willie leaned down and whispered, 'Half seven, outside the Metropolitan Hall in Abbey Street.' Then after thanking Jane and our Nancy for their hospitality, he said 'goodnight' and left in a hurry. At this moment sitting on the tram, Willie could hardly contain his excitement at the prospect of seeing this wonderful girl again.

§

'Do you think I could borrow your new green hat to wear tonight?' Jane asked Lily as they were getting ready to go to Mass on New Year's morning.

'Course,' Lily said. 'Would you like the green scarf to go with it?'

'That'd be marvelous.'

'So you've made the decision about what you're going to wear?'

'With a wardrobe like mine, it wasn't difficult,' Jane said.

'I wish to God I was nearer your size,' Lily offered. 'Then you could have the pick of my wardrobe.'

'Gosh! If only I could borrow our Nancy's new midnight blue skirt and top,' Jane said wistfully, 'wouldn't I look the bees knees. Ach!' she said despondently, 'I suppose t'will have to be what I wore last night — the old gray dress with a clean lace collar.'

'Maybe Bridget would lend you her fur jacket,' Lily suggested.

'I'm sure she would, but now wouldn't I look funny wearing a fur jacket visiting the tenements?' Jane's eyes twinkled with merriment. The two girls then went into kinks of laughter.

In bed last night, they spent hours trying to think up a good white lie for the mother explaining Jane's absence on New Year's night. Finally, they came up with the solution: the mother and the family would be told that Jane and Lily were making a special New Year's visit to the tenements on behalf of the Legion of Mary. Once in a while during the holidays Jane and Lily did make such visits — not that they were particularly keen on doing them. But their mother would be thrilled thinking the girls were starting off the new year doing such charitable work (visiting and counseling the poor and the needy). It would mean no awkward questions. The plan was that Lily and Jane would leave the house together and arrive home together. While Jane was on her date with Willie, Lily would spend the evening as planned with Elizabeth Crowley—her friend from the National school—in her house in Capel Street.

'Why don't you take Bridget into your confidence about the date and borrow the jacket?' Lily asked. 'T'would be lovely on you. Couldn't you put it in a bag, come with me to Crowleys and change there?'

'I think the lie would burden Bridget too much,' Jane said. 'Since her engagement she's become very conscience-stricken about deceiving Mother.'

'Probably Michael's influence,' Lily said. 'All those priests and nuns in his family—he's a real square.'

'He's mad about Bridget and that's all that matters.'

'I suppose you're right,' Lily concurred. 'In any event,' she went on, 'we're sticking to the story about doing the Legion's work tonight?' She grinned at Jane like an errant child.

'Oh, absolutely!' Jane said emphatically. Then giving Lily a sisterly hug, she added, 'you're an absolute angel! Only for you getting rid of that Nancy wan last night, I'm quite sure I wouldn't have this date tonight. Goodness! But didn't she have her hooks into him!'

'She was like bloody gum stuck to his shoe,' Lily laughed.

It occurred to Jane that she didn't know the whole story. 'How did you manage it?' she asked.

'Manage what?'

'To get her to leave the room?'

Lily gave a ragged laugh. 'I told her her shift was showing.'

'And was it?'

'Course not!' Lily laughed wickedly. 'But you know our Nancy—vanity, thy name is Nancy!'

The two girls howled with laughter.

'In any event,' Jane said, 'it did the trick; you really did me a favor.'

'Believe you me, it gave me the greatest of pleasure!' Lily said, with a beaming smile. 'You know something, if that bitch knew you were walking out with Willie tonight, she'd find some way to sabotage it.'

'I'm quite sure she would,' Jane answered. 'But do you think she's really keen on him, or is it just that she's trying to outsmart me?'

'Keen on him!' Lily repeated with much surprise. 'Isn't she only bloody crazy about him!'

'What about Larry?'

'She'd dump that poor fella at the drop of a hat if she thought she could get something going with Willie.'

'T'was a pity about Larry getting the flu and not being able to come to the party.'

'T'wouldn't surprise me one bit if Larry was cooling off,' Lily said bluntly. 'And just invented the flu as an excuse not to come.'

'Good God!' Jane exclaimed, 'if it's broken off with Larry, the field will be clear for her to go after Willie and I can watch out for squalls.'

'Now, Jane, haven't you very little faith in yourself?' Lily lectured. 'Remember, t'was you and not our Nancy Willie invited out. And another thing; it wasn't our Nancy he hugged at midnight last night either, was it? Doesn't that tell you something?'

'But the fact that he hugged me still didn't stop our Nancy from flinging herself at him afterwards,' Jane lamented.

'That's because she thinks she can have any man she puts her eye on,' Lily said contemptuously.

'She probably could too,' Jane said. 'She's so beautiful.'

'You're just as beautiful.' Lily became impatient. 'For God's sake get it into that crazy head of yours that it's you and only you Willie fancies.'

'If only I could be sure.'

'Hey, stop looking on the dark side,' Lily chided. 'Go out and enjoy yourself and forget about the bitch.'

§

Willie was grateful that the rain and the sleet had cleared as he waited for Jane outside the Metropolitan Hall. For the umpteenth time he glanced up at the clock over Mooney's Bar and Grill. It showed ten to eight. People were pouring into the hall. As the tickets weren't numbered, he hoped to God Jane would come soon. Otherwise they could be stuck with really bad seats. Then he saw her dashing down Abbey Street towards him — a vision in a light colored tweed coat, topped with an emerald green hat, matching scarf and gloves. He thought, everything about this girl is colorful and vibrant.

'Gosh! I'm so sorry for being late,' Jane gasped out the apology when she reached him. She was very out of breath. 'But there was... a bit of a problem at home...just as I was leaving.'

'No need to apologize,' Willie smiled reassuringly as he ushered her quickly through the door of the Metropolitan Hall. 'The important thing is you're here.' He helped out of her coat and checked it in at the cloakroom. Having disposed of his own earlier accounted for the fact that he was frozen to the marrow standing outside. Jane kept her green hat on and the scarf draped across her shoulders. Willie looked at her admiringly. 'You look wonderful,' he said.

'Thanks,' Jane tried to sound normal. If he only knew how much my insides are churning at this moment, she thought. The forced calmness is just a front. When they got inside the hall, the only seats that were available were single ones on the sides, near the back. 'God! I'm so terribly sorry.' Once again Jane apologized, profusely. 'It's all my fault being late.' She felt guilty as hell.

Willie answered, 'For goodness sake, stop worrying about it. It's an orchestra we'll be listening to, so it doesn't matter which part of the hall we're in.' He was remembering the time he spent in the Gods of the Liverpool Opera House. Luckily they found two single seats situated behind one another. Willie sat behind Jane, so they weren't completely cut off from each other. The orchestra was already tuning up. The conductor arrived. After taking his bow, he tapped his baton and the music commenced. It was Bach — not really Jane's favorite music. It was what she called 'serious music'; the sort she studied for exams and the sort that constantly filtered out of Music Rooms at school.

For the moment it didn't matter that herself and Willie were sitting apart. She owed Willie an explanation about why she was late. It meant a rational story; a story giving little or no details. Uppermost in Jane's mind as she listened to the music was the mischief our Nancy had created that day.

It started at lunchtime, when, confident there would be no complications, Jane and Lily told the whopping lie about going to visit the tenements that evening. Of all things to happen our Nancy volunteered to go with them! Then just to make things worse, on hearing her wayward daughter make the offer, Mary was wholly in favor of it. She jumped in exclaiming, 'What a marvelous idea! It would be so good for you, Nancy, to see how these people live; in squalor and poverty.'

Jane was convinced our Nancy suspected the truth and was determined to sabotage her meeting with Willie. Dammit! she thought, Why should she suddenly show an interest in doing charitable work when she hasn't a charitable bone in her body? It certainly presented herself and Lily with a big problem.

'What did I tell you,' Lily said to Jane when they were alone, 'that wan is fecken psychic.'

'What on earth are we going to do?' Jane sounded desperate.

'Only one thing we can do,' Lily said with purpose.

'And that is?'

'Well, even if she is going to the tenements, won't she have to titivate herself and put on the war paint before she goes. That means a trip to the bedroom. While she's busy at it, you and I will bolt out that front door and run like hell.'

Jane took a fit of laughing. 'Trust you to come up with the solution,' she said.

The trouble was our Nancy was not a bit accommodating.

Up to half-past seven she dithered and dawdled, killing time, until Lily eventually let fly. 'Well, are you coming or not?' she shouted at her. 'We can't wait all night.'

As Lily predicted, our Nancy had to go to her bedroom. 'I'll only be a minute,' she said making for the door. 'Wait for me.'

Only then could Jane and Lily do a bunk. Hence, Jane had to run the whole way from Parnell Street to Abbey Street.

'So what was the big problem at home that delayed you?' Willie asked Jane as they sipped cups of tea in the lobby during the interval.

Jane took a deep breath. She thought, here I go again telling more lies. 'It's just that I thought Mother was going to be out visiting tonight, which meant I wouldn't have to tell her a white lie about where I was going. But instead she was staying home.'

Willie looked surprised. 'You mean she would have objected to you coming out with me?'

'Not necessarily you!' Jane said. 'She would have objected to me going out with any man.' Jane managed a small smile. 'I'm not yet eighteen. Mother is very old-fashioned, very Victorian. According to her, girls my age should be chaperoned.'

'So what white lie did you tell your mother about where you were going tonight?' Willie asked.

'Oh, thank God! Lily came up with a really good one. Just at the last minute she spun the yarn that I was accompanying her on visit her friend's house in Capel Street.' Jane decided to keep the story simple. Wouldn't it be enough to put any man off were she to go into reams of explanations about the tenements and the complications created by our Nancy. The last thing she needed was for this adorable man to think she was a pathological liar.

'So you're supposed to be visiting Lily's friend in Capel Street — is that the story tonight?' Willie asked, grinning from ear to ear.

'Yes,' Jane said. She laughed when she saw how amused he was. And thought, I wonder would he find the truth so funny? 'It's all jolly fine for you,' she said. 'You're a free agent, free to do what you like. You don't have to answer to anyone.'

'Sometimes I wish I did.' Strangely, Willie sounded heavy laden.

'Oh that's a surprise!'

'There's another way of looking at it,' Willie said. 'I think it helps a lot to know that somebody cares about your welfare. Did you ever think about it that way?'

'No, I'm usually too busy trying to think up a big, fat fib when it's needed.'

'And how often do you need it?' Willie asked.

'Not very often,' Jane said. 'Only when I want to do something that I know Mother won't approve of.'

Jane hardly heard the music during the second half of the concert, she was so busy trying to think up an appropriate white lie to explain to the mother why Lily and herself had left our Nancy in the lurch. She wavered between thoughts of that and the words Willie uttered about having someone to care for him. The poignant way he said it suggested that he might be lonely. There was still a lot she had to learn about Willie.

'Do you have to rush home immediately, or would you have time to have a cup of tea or cocoa or something?' Willie asked Jane as they were leaving the Metropolitan Hall.

Jane looked at her watch. 'Just gone half-past nine,' she announced. Then more positive, 'Yes,' she said, giving him a radiant smile, 'I would have time and I'd like it. As long as I'm home by eleven, everything will be fine. But remember, I still have to pick Lily up in Capel Street en route.'

'The big fib!' Willie burst out laughing.

His laughter was so infectious, it got Jane going. 'See what I mean about being free,' she said. 'You don't have to tell fibs to anyone.' She thought, little does he know that I've still to face the music at home with Mother and our Nancy, explaining why Lily and I disappeared so suddenly. I hope to God Lily can come up with some practical explanation because I've drawn a blank; I can't think of anything.

They found a quaint little café at the corner of Liffey Street; small and intimate with red check tablecloths and candle light, it was simple but charming.

'This is delightful,' Willie remarked as he pulled out the chair from the table for Jane.

'Very soothing on the nerves,' Jane blurted out. Then suddenly realized she would have to watch what she said. Willie didn't know, nor was he going to know, the ordeal she still had to face at home. Determined to enjoy what was left of the evening, she relegated these thoughts to the back of her mind.

'I hope the music didn't unnerve you?' Willie said, concerned. 'Normally, I like classical music, but maybe you found it a bit on the heavy side.'

'Oh no! Not at all,' Jane hastened to assure him. 'The music was very pleasant. It was quite familiar actually; we hear it all the time at school.'

'But it was definitely not your kind of music?'

'What do you think is my kind of music?'

'Well, I suppose it's the kind you played last night,' Willie said. 'Very modern and rhythmic. By the way,' he added, 'I think you're a marvelous pianist.'

'Thanks.'

'I really mean it!' Willie said convincingly. 'You had all those people dancing; it made such a difference to the party.'

'Well, thanks again: it's good to know I have at least one fan.'

'A fan and an admirer,' Willie added touching Jane's hand across the table. It had an electrifying effect on her. Thankfully, the moment was interrupted by the waitress arriving and handing them menus. They ordered cups of cocoa and pastries.

'I'd love to hear details about the part you played in the Rising,' Jane said as soon as the waitress was out of earshot.

'I thought by now people would be sick and tired of hearing about it,' Willie protested.

'Well, I'm not one of them.' Jane felt she had to convince him.

For the next half hour Willie described his experiences in the G.P.O. during the Rising and in Frongoch. His narrative was very expressive. She was very touched when she saw tears in his eyes as he talked about his friend Bud. She found herself unable to keep from watching him; the wonderful face as it went through the motions of looking serious, of contemplating a question, of smiling suddenly. Noticing too, how beautiful his hands were and how restless.

When he finished, Jane made the comment, 'Truly, you're a real hero.'

'Or a real fool,' Willie said bitterly. 'What did we achieve eventually but death and destruction. We're no closer to having a Republic than we were before the Rising.'

'Don't be such a pessimist,' Jane said. 'Rome wasn't built in a day.'

Willie was thinking, not only is this girl beautiful, but for her age, she's startlingly intelligent. So unlike every other girl I've ever met. Such a good listener.

'So are you going to return to Liverpool?' Jane asked.

'Definitely not,' Willie was adamant. 'There's no way I could avoid conscription if I went back.'

'You mean you'd have to fight in the Great War?'

'Absolutely!' Willie said. 'Needless to say fighting for the enemy is the last thing I want to do.' He said it with loathing. 'No,' he continued, 'I've a few good contacts in Dublin; through them, I'm hoping to get some sort of job.'

'What about the Cause?' Jane asked. 'Do you think you'll go on fighting for it?'

'At this moment, I'm not sure.'

Jane checked her watch. 'And at this moment,' she said, 'we're going to have to move. It's half-past ten.'

When they left the café Willie said, 'I'll walk you as far as your friend's house in Capel Street.'

'Oh, you're an absolute angel!' Jane sounded very relieved. 'I'm a bit nervous walking through these back streets on my own at night.'

'You didn't think I'd allow you to walk on you own, now did you?' Willie said taking Jane's hand. Again at his touch Jane could feel such tender, racing feelings in her blood and in her skin.

'Well, I wasn't sure,' she said timidly.

'What kind of bloke do you take me for?' Willie looked puzzled.

'After all those stories — daring, heroic, chivalrous.'

'So when am I going to see you again?' Willie asked.

"Well, I'm not going back to school till the ninth of January,' Jane said, then held her breath.

'I'm not too sure about my own movements for the next few days,' Willie said. 'Could I write to you?'

'That's a good idea.'

'Just in case,' Willie asked, 'when will you be back in Dublin again?'

'Easter, for the holidays.'

'As long as that?'

'Afraid so.'

'Well then, its imperative that I see you before you return to school.' Willie hesitated. 'That is, of course, if you'd like to see me?'

Did she want to see him again? God, she would trek to the other side of the world to see him. 'Of course, I'd like to see you again,' she assured him. Then she became embarrassed. Gosh, she thought, I mustn't gush to much and appear to eager. 'I really enjoyed the music this evening, and, of course, your company,' she said modestly.

By now they had reached the house in Capel Street.

'Here we are,' Jane said, stopping.

'I'd better make myself scarce,' Willie laughed. 'Your life is complicated enough without having to explain me to your friends.'

'Do you mind?' Jane said apologetically. 'I'd like to ask you to meet them, but you know the way it is; word just might get back to Mother.'

'Don't say another word. I'll be in touch.' Willie said putting his arms around her, giving her a huge hug. Then he was gone.

'So what story are we going to tell Mother about tonight?' Jane, still starry-eyed from her date, asked Lily as they wended their way back to Parnell Street.

'God! I was hoping you'd worked something out yourself.'

'Lily, you've got to be joking!' Jane said. 'And I out on a date with that gorgeous, wonderful man, trying to make an indelible impression on him.'

Lily laughed heartily. 'I'm only joking,' she said.

'What would you think about saying that just after our Nancy went to her bedroom, a child from the tenements called to the door and said there was an emergency in their room in the tenements?'

'What kind of an emergency?'

'The father beating up the mother,' Lily said, with a wily grin. 'So, of course we'd no option but to dash over there.'

'Jesus, Lily! Where do you get them?' Jane was in fits of laughter. 'I can just see the two of us intervening in such a situation.'

'Well, that sort of thing goes on all the time in those tenements,' Lily said, matter-of-factly, 'particularly around Christmas time. It could easily have happened tonight; after all, it is New Year's Night.'

'Ach, I suppose it's conceivable,' Jane said. 'We'll make it the story. But to be on the safe side, let's coordinate the details so that we don't make eegits of ourselves contradicting each other.'

'Okay, the story is,' Lily was emphatic, 'when we arrived at the room in question the row was over, the father had left and we stayed a long time with the unfortunate mother, trying to pacify her. How does that sound?'

'You're a genius.'

Thank God, their Mother swallowed the story hook, line and sinker. 'Maybe next time when you're visiting the tenements, you'll invite our Nancy to go with you,' she said. 'I'm really disappointed she missed the opportunity tonight; although it couldn't be helped.'

Chapter XIV

The Ireland to which Willie returned already showed a marked difference from the country from which he had departed as a British prisoner. Collins put his finger on it very succinctly on the night of the third of January, when he addressed an official meeting, which included some of his fellow internees and members of the phony Gaelic League, at the League's Dublin Headquarters.

'Consider the present situation,' Collins began. 'Both the British authorities and the Irish Parliamentary Party are in a corner, driven there by their own actions and by the will of the Irish people. The situation is now ripe for an advancement along the road to salvation. Will any Irishman want to let this opportunity pass?'

Peter O'Dwyer said from the floor, 'Wouldn't we want to have the kind of minds that grow mushrooms, not to take advantage of the situation as it now stands.' The room responded with laughter. 'Nonetheless, Peter went on, 'from what I've been hearing the general consensus seems to be that we need good, strong leadership.'

'Hear! Hear!'

'Well, now lads,' Collins said animatedly, 'I think I can say with impunity that in the near future I'll be able to devote a lot of time and energy working on that.' He grinned mischievously. 'I'm going to let you into a little secret: haven't I just landed the job of Secretary to the National Aid Association — that's the body that was set up to alleviate the distress caused by the Rising. My salary will be two pounds, ten shillings a week — not to be sneezed at. Anyway, this position should afford me ample opportunity to make contact with the right people.'

'Like the men of the Irish Republican Brotherhood and Sinn

Fein?' Willie suggested.

'The very ones,' Collins said. 'In a week or two when I'm settled in the job, I should have a good idea about what's what. So hopefully I'll have something useful to report at our next meeting.'

'Which is when and where?' a voice from the floor inquired.

'Here, this day week, time to be determined.' Then with a roguish wink, he went on. 'Notices about the Irish classes you'll be attending in this building will be posted in the usual place.' Collins checked his watch. 'Now, as this room is due to be taken over by the Irish Dancing class, I'll be in room number three down the corridor hearing confessions for the next half hour. And answering questions about such things as the text books you'll be needing for the Irish classes.' (He winked.) With that Collins stood up and headed for room number three. Willie was first in line following on his heels. After Collins settled himself at the small table, he looked up at Willie. He could tell by his countenance that something was bothering him. 'The bauld Willie!' Collins greeted him smiling while he raised inquiring eyebrows. 'What can I do for you?'

'Well, I don't know if you can do anything. But sure it's worth a try anyway,' Willie said. 'I need to have an income; that means getting a job.'

'But, of course!' Collins began taking notes. 'Not an easy task for an ex-con, eh?' A burst of laughter. 'I'll tell you something, Willie,' he said, becoming more serious. 'Were it not for the help I got from Joe McGrath, I'm thinking the job of secretary to the Aid Association would never have been mine. We help each other eh?' Collins then spoke decisively. 'Leave it with me, by: gimme a few days.' He looked hard at Willie's thinness. 'You're so bloody skinny and frail looking, I'd say a laboring job'd be out of the question.'

'No. It's by no means out of the question,' Willie declared. 'I'm quite prepared to do a laboring job if I can get nothing else.'

'You've tried yerself, I take it?'

'Yeah. But there's nothing doing anywhere,' Willie said.

'Ach, never mind, we'll find you some sorta job,' Collins sounded optimistic. 'Preferably something not too strenuous. Meantime if you're strapped for money, drop in and see me during the day at the Aid Association Center: I'll see to it that you get some of that financial aid we're doling out to victims of the Rising.' He laughed boisterously. 'Mind you, I have the feeling the Association didn't have us convicts in mind when they set up their aid center. But sure we can always bend the rules a bit.'

'Personally, I'd rather have the job than the charity,' Willie smiled trying to make light of it.

'But, of course,' Collins agreed. 'Now do you think you can make the meeting tomorrow night at O'Dea's pub on the Quays?'

'I've the best intentions of doing so.'

'Well, I'm expecting a few good contacts to be in attendance,' Collins said. 'Maybe we could sound them out about a job for you.'

It was ironical that at the meeting the following night, it should be Peter O'Dwyer who informed Willie about the jobs being advertised for the newly opened Tivoli Cinema.

'What the hell do I know about moving pictures?' Willie laughed asking Peter the question.

'No more than myself! But, like the rest of us, you can always chance your arm.'

'That's exactly what I would be doing.'

'Go for it, Willie,' Collins, listening to the conversation, encouraged him. Then he stopped to have a little think. 'Ye know something, Dan Keating, over there,' he pointed to Dan on the other side of the table, 'is a good friend of Finbar Clancy, who's owns the new Tivoli. I'm sure if I asked him, he'd put in a good word for you.' With that Collins stood up, went round the table to where Dan was sitting, bent down and had a word in his ear. Willie could see Dan nodding his head affirmatively. He looked hard at Willie and indicated he'd have a word with him after the meeting.

§

> 39, Carlingford Avenue
> Drumcondra
> 5th January, 1917

Dear Jane,

Apologies for not writing sooner, but I had so many things to attend to; what with settling into my new digs in Drumcondra and getting fixed up in a new job. Believe it or not, the job has the fancy title of Assistant to the Chief Projectionist of the new Tivoli Cinema. Finbar, probably in his forties, is the owner and chief projectionist. He's a man who's helpful and warm hearted and certainly seems to know his stuff.

You'll probably wonder what I know about the operation of these moving pictures. The answer is a big zero. But I'm optimistic. (One has to be these days if one is to survive.) The hours aren't great. I don't start work until half-past five each evening. Then there's the extra matinee show on Saturday afternoons which makes it a very long day. Sunday I'm off, the cinema is closed.

Which brings me to the question, when am I going to see you again? How about this Sunday? Do you think you could meet me after ten o'clock Mass in the Pro Cathedral. We could decide what to do when we meet.

I realize it's very short notice and if you don't turn up I'll understand. But I'll be there anyway, standing under the clock over the main door of the Pro Cathedral, at half-past ten.

I sincerely hope you can make it.

> *Yours truly,*
> *Willie.*

§

'So it is from Willie?' Lily sounded full of spirited curiosity.

'Who else?' Jane said, her face aglow. She had just finished reading the letter in the privacy of her bedroom when Lily burst in the door.

'What does he say?' Lily asked excitedly. 'Quick! Tell us!'

'He wants me to meet him outside the Pro Cathedral after ten o'clock Mass on Sunday.'

'That's fantastic!' Lily couldn't hide her delight at Jane's good news. Though Jane hadn't mentioned the subject all week, Lily could see how disappointed and deflated she was as each day passed without a letter from Willie.

'Once again I'm going to have a problem explaining my absence to Mother,' Jane said gloomily. 'Well, with the shops closed I can't very well say I'm going shopping.' Stumped, Jane went on, 'You're the genius at making up stories. Could you suggest a convincing fib I could use?'

'It's obvious,' Lily said without hesitation. 'You're visiting your school friend, Doreen, in Clontarf.'

Jane thought about it for a second. 'No,' she said, her brow furrowing. 'Definitely wouldn't wash. Why would I be seeing Doreen in Dublin on Sunday, when I'll be seeing her at school the next day?' Jane continued. 'Along with that, as this is our last Sunday of the holidays, Mother will expect us to stay around. I'm sure my disappearing out to Clontarf wouldn't sit well with her.'

'You have a point.'

Jane had another think, then said, 'Whenever we go out together, Mother never queries where we're going.'

'True,' Lily said easily. Then suddenly looked shocked. 'My God! You're not suggesting that I accompany you on your date?'

'No, no, not at all!' Jane laughed hysterically. She could just imagine Willie's reaction if she turned up with her sister in tow.

Lily said, 'If it wasn't Sunday, I could do what I did the other night; wait for you at Elizabeth's house. Only I know for a fact that Elizabeth visits her grandparents every Sunday.'

They mulled over the question for a while. Then the solution came to Jane. 'I think, I've got it,' she said excitedly, 'that is, if you're agreeable?'

'What is it?' Lily asked her cheeks flushed.

'How would you feel about paying your nephew, baby Colbert, a visit after Mass on Sunday?'

Lily spluttered, 'You mean you want me to wait at Peter's place while you're on your date?'

'That's right,' Jane said, holding her head sideways with the look of a pleading dog that rarely failed to get its way. 'Would you do that for me?' Rushing on, she added, 'You know that no questions will be asked if we leave together as though we're going to Mass as usual. Then just as we're leaving we could mention casually that we'll be dropping in to see baby Colbert afterwards.'

Lily's mind raced, this request of Jane's was trickier than usual. 'If I was sure Peter would be there, I wouldn't mind paying a visit,' she said. 'But if he's not there...well, I don't think I could contend with his wife's nonsense. I might end up pushing her face in.'

'Peter's bound to be at home,' Jane said. 'After all, it is Sunday — family day.'

'Right, if I take a chance and Peter is there,' Lily said, 'am I to take him into my confidence about yourself and Willie?'

Jane thought about the question, then said slowly, 'If we tell Peter he's bound to tell Nancy Pete. And you know what'll happen then.'

'The world and his wife will be told,' Lily burst out.

'No,' Jane was decisive. 'I think t'would be best if you say nothing about me to Peter. Just drop in casually. Say you were in the area.' Jane's' eyes danced with merriment. 'You could rave about how much you love babies. How gorgeous they are at that age.'

'Me? Rave about babies!' Lily spluttered. 'That's a good one! For God's sake, the only thing I know about babies is what I see coming into the shop; and they're usually bawling and snotty-nosed.'

'I wouldn't be too long,' Jane said appealingly.

'Ach! I'll do it,' Lily said amiably. 'As I see it, the only alternative would be for me to spend hours in a church praying myself to death, lighting candles by the dozen and giving people the impression I'm a religious maniac.'

Jane roared laughing. Lily could be so funny at times. Then she became serious. 'Later, when I eventually arrive at Peter's place,' she said, 'you would, of course, be suitably surprised.'

'How long do you think you'll be?' Lily asked.

'Probably a couple of hours; the length it takes to have a cup of tea somewhere.' A lightheartedness enveloped Jane. She could now look forward to seeing Willie without having to worry about it. Once again Lily had come to her rescue. She owed her sister a monumental debt of gratitude. 'Gosh Lily!' she said giving her sister a hug, 'you're an absolute gem! What would I do without you?'

'When my times comes,' Lily said, her face covered in smiles, 'I'll expect you to do the same for me.'

'And I will, with knobs on.'

For the next twenty-four hours Jane was in a state of euphoric suspension at the thought of seeing Willie again. Being with him on the night of the concert was akin to being with a soul mate; she felt so comfortable. Thank God, she thought, he succeeded in getting a job. Surely now he'll stay on in Dublin? But, how she wished she didn't have to go back to school on Monday.

§

Willie tucked his arm inside Jane's as they walked towards the Quays. His touch gave Jane such a warm glow inside. Though it was January, it was an exceptionally fine day — cold and crisp with the sun shining in a clear blue sky.

'It's such a nice day,' Willie said, 'what would you think about taking the tram to Chapelizod and having a bit of a stroll along the Liffey? I know of a lovely track.'

A shocked silence followed the question. Jesus! Jane thought, what do I say? She was thinking about Lily waiting at Peter's place, expecting her to arrive by one o'clock at the latest. Now if they were to go to Chapelizod, with the slowness of the tram, they'd probably get there just about the time she should be picking up Lily. Dear God! she thought, why does life have to be so complicated?

'It doesn't appeal to you?' Willie broke into her thoughts, looking vaguely disappointed.

'Yes, of course it does,' Jane said in a fake cheery voice. 'It's just that the days are so short for that type of a walk.'

'We needn't make it a long walk,' Willie said. He seemed very keen on the idea. 'Wouldn't it be nice to get away from the crowded city and the traffic for a little while?' Then cheerfully he threw in, 'There's a quaint Country Inn in Chapelizod where they serve bacon, eggs and sausages, homemade scones, hot tea. We could have lunch there.'

'Say no more; it sounds marvelous!' Jane said with forced lightness. 'Let's do it!' She was thinking, sure it doesn't matter where we go as long as we're together. Somehow or other she'd make it up to Lily in the future. Now if she was to enjoy herself for the rest of the day, she must try to banish from her mind all thoughts of Lily and her good deed.

Having crossed O'Connell Bridge to get the tram at Eden Quay, they waited twenty minutes for it to arrive. 'So when do you start your new job?' Jane asked Willie as they sat on the top deck of the tram that jolted along the Quays.

'I already started last night,' Willie said, his eyes brimming with amusement. 'Let me say, it wasn't a spectacular start.'

'Don't tell me you've lost the job already?' Jane said lightheartedly. She could see Willie wasn't too put out about the situation.

'No, not yet,' Willie laughed. 'Thank God the boss is kind and understanding and he makes allowances for human error.'

'Assistant to the Chief Projectionist,' Jane said. 'What exactly do you do?'

'In a nutshell, apart from looking after the two cameras, feeding them with the proper reels of film throughout the evening, the function that takes up most time is the rewinding of the film after each showing. That done the reel is restored to its rightful container. Believe it or not, some movies can take as many as five reels of film. Of course the reels are all numbered and labeled.'

'So what went wrong last night?'

'As I was about to rewind a reel, didn't I let the damn thing drop on to the floor sending reams of film swirling all over the place,' Willie laughed. 'Was my face red!'

'Well, you're a learner,' Jane pointed out sympathetically. 'They can't expect perfection the first night.'

'They wouldn't want to if they're going to employ somebody with sloppy fingers the likes of mine,' Willie grinned sheepishly. 'I felt such an eejit; to think I couldn't even do that much right. Needless to say, I was in the projection room for hours after we finished, trying to remedy the damage. Those films are very delicate. Sometimes there can be problems with the sprockets on the sides — they're the holes that propel the film through the projector. The slightest crease or pucker can make the film stick. With the result that I had to go at a snail's pace rewinding that reel,' Willie chuckled. 'Throughout the evening, even with everything running smoothly, if there was a delay of more than five minutes changing over the reels, the audience became thoroughly impatient and obstreperous; banging mineral bottles on the benches, shouting, 'show the pictures! We paid to see the pictures!' Now can you imagine what it would be like tomorrow night, if, because of my stupidity, there was a major breakdown and the audience had to wait twenty minutes or so for it to be fixed? There'd be a riot surely.' Willie laughed heartily, 'And that'd be the end of MacNamee's career as an assistant projectionist.'

Jane laughed with him. 'I'll keep my fingers crossed for you,' she said.

'Of course, you'll be back at school then?'

'Yeah. Back to the grind,' Jane said glumly. 'Thank God, I finish in June.'

The tram was now running alongside the Phoenix Park getting close to Chapelizod. Surreptitiously Jane checked her watch. It was five-past twelve. She wondered how Lily was faring?

'We get off at the next stop,' Willie said standing up.

The copper grass dead from frost crackled under their feet as they trekked along the track that ran parallel with a metallic colored Liffey. Prisms of sunlight twinkled through bare, twiggy trees. They met a lot of people; couples holding hands, sauntering elderly couples, people walking dogs. Obviously, like themselves, they were lured out by the sunshine. Benches along the route held people who stared in reflection at the water.. All around was peace and serenity.

Jane found Willie a very good conversationalist; at the same time he didn't monopolize the conversation. No, in fact he encouraged her to talk a lot about her life. He seemed particularly interested in her experiences during Easter week, laughed heartily at her description of the tramp to the G.P.O on Easter Monday carrying the money. Then during the big fire when the girls had to carry the money around necks; how they looked like great, bit fat matrons. He was discovering that Jane had the gift of making an ordinary story sound hysterically funny.

'You know something,' he told her, 'you're a marvelous storyteller. Your sense of humor is so wonderful; it makes even the most horrific occurrences sound lighthearted. I could listen to you for hours.'

'Well, thank you very much.'

'I mean it.'

However, Jane was now getting very uneasy. For the umpteenth time she surreptitiously checked her watch: it was ten to two and they still had to eat lunch and get back on that agonizingly slow tram. She kept wondering how she could introduce the subject of lunch without appearing too pushy. It was evident that Willie was not only enjoying her company, but he seemed to love the out-of-doors. She too loved the out-of-doors, but not when she was supposed to be somewhere else.

She decided to be brazen. 'How far away is the inn you talked about?' she inquired.

'Oh, we can branch off to the right a little ways up here,' Willie said. 'After that we should reach the village in a matter of minutes.' As an afterthought, he asked, 'Are you hungry?'

'Starving,' Jane fibbed. Truth to tell, she had no appetite at all worrying about the time and Lily waiting patiently at Peter's place, expecting her to arrive any minute.

'Oh! you should have said something!' Willie sounded quite concerned. 'What time is it anyway?'

This time Jane openly looked at her watch. 'Five to two.'

'Gracious! How the time has flown!' Willie exclaimed. 'Any

wonder you're hungry.'

The village consisted of a string of low cottage-style houses straddling the main street. Thankfully, the Inn was at the end close to where they emerged from the track. While they were eating their fry, Willie talked about Liverpool and how he came to join the volunteers.

Last of all, he talked about Bud and the many interesting things they did together. The tears in his eyes told Jane that he still grieved for his dead friend. Caught up in Willie's reminiscences, for a while Jane forgot the time and Lily at Peter's place awaiting her arrival. Willie ended saying, 'Today I laid a ghost to rest!'

'How so?'

'Myself and Bud did that walk quite frequently before the Rising. But after Bud died I swore I'd never do it again.' He smiled warmly at Jane. 'It took someone like you to change my mind.'

§

'Good heavens!' Nancy Pete shrilled when she opened the door to Lily. 'This is an incredible surprise!'

'I thought I'd pay my nephew a visit,' Lily said, thrusting a fancy bag into Nancy Pete's hand. 'It's just a little present for him,' she explained.

'Oh, do come in,' Nancy Pete fussed and blustered. 'Peter!' she shouted. 'Come and see who's come to visit us.'

Peter raced from the kitchen rattling the newspaper. 'Great to see you, Lil,' he said, effusive in his greeting. Then it struck him as sort of peculiar that, out of the blue, Lily should be visiting them. 'There's nothing the matter at home, I hope?' he asked apprehensively.

'No. 'Course not,' Lily declared, a characteristic smile spreading across her face. 'I was in the neighborhood and I thought, wouldn't it be nice to pop in and see Baby Colbert.'

'That was a very nice thought!' Nancy Pete was undeniably impressed. 'It's most unusual for girls your age to be interested in babies.'

'Here, let me take your coat,' Peter interjected, being practical.

Lily took the coat off and handed it to him. 'Oh, I've always loved babies,' she said, adding cheerlessly, 'being away at school I'm going to be denied the pleasure of seeing baby's Colbert's development.' Then feeling a right hypocrite she added, 'and they say babies develop more in their first year than they do the rest of their lives.'

'Come into the kitchen where the heat is,' Peter said.

Right enough, the kitchen was beautifully warm and cozy. With the front shutter of the range down, the glowing coals gave off a massive heat.

'Yes, indeed,' Nancy Pete sat comfortably at the table allowing Peter to attend to the tea making. 'Quite possibly, baby Colbert will be walking by the next time you see him; that'll be Easter?'

'That's what I mean,' Lily said, trying hard to sound sincere. 'They grow so fast.'

Peter started laying the table, putting out the ordinary kitchen cups and saucers.

'Not those Peter!' Nancy Pete rebuked him. 'That crockery is strictly for our own use; it's definitely not for visitors.'

'Sorry,' Peter took the crockery back. Then asked warily, 'So which cups and saucers are we using this time?'

'The ones in the china cabinet in the drawing room,' Nancy Pete answered.

'Oh, for goodness sake!' Lily protested. 'You don't have to put out the best china for me.'

'Lily, there's something you must understand about Nancy,' Peter said mockingly, 'every opportunity that presents itself she trots out the best china.'

'Now, Peter, that's not true!' As only she could, Nancy Pete started pouting. 'Amn't I paying your sister a compliment using the best china,' she said. Peter left the room. Shortly afterwards he arrived back with a tray full of the best china. After he arranged the china on the table, Nancy Pete picked up a cup and swiped a speck of dust from the inside with her finger. 'I'm afraid, love,' she told Peter, 'you're going to have to wash and polish all that china.' Once again Peter meekly retrieved the cups, saucers and plates, washed, dried and polished them at the sink and eventually returned them to the table. Then as the kettle was on the boil, he proceeded to make the tea. All of a sudden Nancy Pete jumped up from the table and made a point of interfering with him. 'For God's sake, Peter!' she said, her mouth twisting contemptuously. 'You know damn well I like my tea weak — two spoonfuls of tea is one spoonful too many. I can't stand when the tea tastes like tar.'

'You can have the first cup,' Peter said in appeasement.

Lily thought, what a commotion about a bloody cup of tea. She was finding it difficult to exercise self-control and not to scream at her sister-in-law, the stupid way she was carrying on. But for Peter's sake, she kept her mouth shut. Then trying to distract Nancy Pete from the tea situation, she asked, 'Is baby Colbert sleeping?'

'Yes, he's having his morning nap,' Nancy Pete said off-handedly. Her eyes were glued to the teapot; it seemed at this moment the most important thing in her life was the color of the tea coming out of it. Finally, she dragged her eyes away from the teapot to check the clock on the wall. It showed twenty-past twelve. 'I'll be lifting baby Colbert at one o'clock for his lunch,' she told Lily. No sooner had Peter finished pouring the tea, then Nancy Pete pointed to a cupboard. 'The biscuits, Peter,' she demanded, 'they're in there.'

'Yes, Mam! certainly Mam!' Peter said humorously, as once again he jumped up and got the biscuits.

Nancy Pete tasted her tea, then shot over to the sink and spurted the mouthful of tea into it. 'It's ghastly!' she screamed. She wiped her mouth exaggeratedly as she came back to the table. 'I warned you, Peter, it would be too strong,' she said accusingly, 'but would you listen!'

Once again, Peter was on his feet. 'I'll throw half of it out and top it up with boiling water,' he said hastily grabbing the cup. Horror of horrors! The cup slipped through his fingers and crashed on to the floor.

Looking at Nancy Pete's expression, Lily thought, any minute now she's going to have a seizure.

'Sweet Mother of God!' Nancy Pete held her hand over her mouth, horrified, as she stared at her beautiful china cup in pieces on the floor. 'My best Hampton china!' she said. By now she looked like she was ready to burst into tears.

Like a shot Peter was down on his knees collecting the pieces. 'God! I'm terribly sorry!' He too looked like he was about to burst into tears.

At that moment Lily had the greatest urge to give Nancy Pete a good root up the arse. Isn't it all her own bloody fault making such a fuss, she thought.

Luckily, Baby Colbert chose this moment to roar his head off and draw attention to himself in the bedroom.

For Peter, his intervention couldn't be more timely. 'I'll get him,' he said hurriedly rising to his feet.

'You'll do no such thing!' Nancy Pete sniped at him. 'You're so stupid, you'd probably drop him too.' Going towards the door, she turned and snapped. 'Better clean up the mess, Peter; it's about the only thing you're good for.'

After her departure there was a short silence. Then with an effort Peter grinned at Lily. 'You'll have to excuse her outburst,' he said, casting his eyes up to heaven. 'It goes with the artistic temperament.'

Suddenly, they both started laughing. And although the tension eased, it was obvious that Peter was masking his feelings with a show of nonchalance. As she sipped her tea, Lily thought, My God! When you compare the treatment that woman dishes out to Peter with the way he was treated at home. The white-haired boy — whom everyone danced attendance on and envied so much — has now become a doormat. It's unbelievable!

Peter cleaned up the mess on the floor. Then holding up the three pieces of broken cup in his hand, he asked Lily, 'What the hell should I do with these?' He looked so lost, her heart went out to him. 'No matter what I do, it's bound to be the wrong thing,' he said. 'But do you think I should throw them out?'

'I'd hold on to them,' Lily said decisively. 'You may be able to get the cup repaired.'

'I doubt it very much,' Peter said throwing the pieces into the dust bin beside the sink.

Nancy Pete arrived back carrying baby Colbert, now six months old and quite big for his age. Thankfully the distraction of her baby seemed to have mollified Nancy Pete somewhat.

'Look who's here,' she chirped at Colbert. 'Your Auntie Lily.' She turned to Lily, 'Would you like to hold him while I get myself ready?'

'Of course,' Lily took him in her arms. She wouldn't dare say no. For the next few seconds Lily's attention was centered on Baby Colbert, billing and cooing at him, trying to make him smile. Next time she looked up, she was horrified to see Nancy Pete sitting in the chair opposite, the front of her dress and the bust bodice down round her waist, her heavy bosoms totally exposed. They put her in mind of the cows on her cousins' farm with their bursting udders before they were milked. Overwhelmed with embarrassment Lily didn't know where to look.

'Okay, I'll take him now,' Nancy Pete, totally unabashed, held up her arms. Looking everywhere and anywhere but at those awful bosoms, Lily placed Baby Colbert on Nancy Pete's lap. It was the first time she ever saw a baby openly suckled. She felt mortified and embarrassment in front of Peter.

Sensing her discomfort Peter jumped up and said, 'Come on, Lil, to the drawing room. I want to show you some sketches I did when I was in Frongoch.'

'That should be interesting,' Lily said, breathing a sigh of relief as she followed him into the freezing drawing room. She wondered which was worse: freezing to death in this big room or being in the warmth of the kitchen listening to her sister-in-law hurling insults at her brother. Not to mention looking at those big, fat bosoms. Please God, let Jane come soon, she prayed. I can't wait to get to hell out of here. If plenary indulgences were granted for doing good works, she thought, I should be stacking them up in their hundreds doing this favor for Jane.

Peter produced a bundle of landscape sketches surrounding the Frongoch camp. They showed remarkable aptitude.

Lily poured over them, then exclaimed, 'Gosh! I didn't realize you were so good at art.'

'Neither did I,' Peter laughed, 'but needs must when the divil drives.'

'What about your writing?'

'I did lots of that too,' Peter said, 'ostensibly in the early days. But towards the end of my stay in Frongoch, the days were so endless, I needed something more challenging if I wasn't to go bonkers.' Peter now saw that Lily was freezing with the cold. 'I'm sorry about the room being so cold,' he said. 'I'd light the fire only we're visiting the in-laws in the afternoon. Anyway,' he went on, 'you came to see the little man. He should be finished feeding by now and he's always at his best after his feed.'

They returned to the warmth of the kitchen. Right enough, Baby Colbert was in great form, lying on a rug on the floor, kicking his heels in the air and looking absolutely adorable. Lily went down on her knees beside him to play with him.

Suddenly, Nancy Pete remembered the fancy paper bag Lily had handed her, which she carelessly threw on the hall table. 'Oh!' she said, melodramatically stroking her big, fat bosom (now thankfully covered), 'his new present! We nearly forgot it.' She left the room.

When she was gone, Peter rolled up his sleeves. 'You'll stay to lunch, Lil?' he said.

'Only if it's convenient,' Lily answered with a wry smile. She was wishing to God she didn't have to.

'Of course it's convenient.'

Nancy Pete arrived back with the fancy bag. 'Oh! Baby!' she shrilled with delight as she went down on her knees and put the rattle into Baby Colbert's hand. 'Look at what your Auntie Lily brought you — a lovely rattle.'

'Sorry,' Lily apologized, 'it's not much of a present. But with all the shops closed, I was lucky to be able to get anything in the way of a toy: that was purchased in the shop attached to Saint Vincent's Hospital.'

'Saint Vincent's Hospital! That's a new one!' Nancy Pete said, her eyes now dancing with pleasure as she watched baby Colbert gleefully shake his new rattle. Meantime, Peter was like a hen on a hot griddle, running in and out of the pantry.

Finally he said to Nancy Pete, 'I'm going to make lunch, do we have any bread?'

'Oh God!' Nancy Pete put her hand over her heart dramatically. 'I forgot to get it!'

'Okay, no panic!' Peter said. 'I'll nip down to the huckster shop on the corner and get some.'

'Could I do it for you?' Lily offered, trying not to sound too eager, because by now she desperately needed to get away from this awful domestic scene.

'God, that'd be marvelous!' Peter seemed really glad of her offer. He addressed Nancy Pete. 'I was planning to cook rashers and eggs,' he said. Then a thought struck him. 'Before Lily leaves, do we have enough supplies?' he asked her.

Nancy Pete looked at Lily. 'You're staying to lunch I take it?' she blurted out bluntly.

'Course she is,' Peter answered before Lily could speak.

'In that case,' Nancy Pete addressed Lily, 'maybe you'd get some eggs. If I remember correctly we only have two.'

Peter walked Lily to the door explaining where the shop was and giving her the money. When Lily got outside, she let out a long sigh of relief and filled her lungs with great big globs of fresh air. Oh! The joy of getting away from that house! She thought, that woman would drive anyone insane. How the hell does Peter put up with it? She looked at her watch. It showed twenty to two. Please, please God! she prayed, let Jane be there when I get back.

But Jane wasn't there when she got back. Nor did she appear during the turbulent lunch that followed when Baby Colbert decided to exercise his powerful lungs and it seemed impossible to placate him. Naturally, it then became Peter's duty to attend to the bawling child. For a solid twenty minutes Peter strode up and down the kitchen, rocking the child while trying to eat his lunch with one hand. Meanwhile, Nancy Pete, looking like Lady Muck, sat at the table unruffled, eating her lunch.

No sooner had she finished than the harangue started again: torrents of fault-finding and non-stop orders were flung at her unfortunate husband: 'You're not holding him correctly. Give him some gripe water in his bottle. Pat him on the back. His nappy needs changing.' It now suited her to let her stupid husband take over caring for their cranky child.

Lily was astonished at Peter's infinite patience with both his wife and his child. Today she was seeing another side of her brother. It was an eye-opener. Imagine, she thought, what Mother's reaction would be if she ever found out that her son—her pride and joy—was now a mat on which Nancy Pete wiped her feet.

When it came to three o'clock—time for Peter and his family to set out for their visit - with no sign of Jane, Lily put her coat on and left.

§

'In the name of God, where have you been?' Bridget met Lily at the door wearing an expression of intense anxiety. 'And where the hell is Jane?' she barked. Bridget barking was totally alien to her character; something was radically wrong.

Gulping with fear, Lily asked, 'What's the panic about?' As yet she hadn't thought up a good lie to explain Jane's absence. The whole way home she was preoccupied with thoughts of her brother; the way he humbly accepted the awful treatment meted out by his bitch of a wife. God! He did everything but apologize for being alive!

'Eileen's in the hospital,' Bridget blurted out.

'Oh my God!' Lily had a sense of blind panic 'For God's sake what happened to her?'

'She fell off the ladder and injured herself when she was removing the Christmas chains,' Bridget said accusingly. 'Mother raced her up to the Richmond Hospital.'

Lily felt a hard knot of guilt forming in her chest. Looking after the Christmas chains was her and Jane's responsibility; that included removing them. 'When did this happen?' she inquired with a tremble in her voice.

'Just after lunch,' Bridget was very distressed. 'The poor child was writhing around the floor in agony. Of course, we were expecting the pair of you back any minute to give a hand,' she said. 'All we knew was that the two of you were dropping into see baby Colbert after Mass; that was hours ago. Sure, look at it now — it's practically dark.' Bridget looked really troubled. 'To make matters worse, Marie in the shop had already gone home sick with the flu. That left me on my own.' Again Bridget asked impatiently, 'Where on earth is Jane?'

'Had I better run up to the Richmond hospital and see how Eileen is?' Lily once again evaded the question. Now with the extra worry of Eileen, butterflies were flitting round her stomach.

'Yes, that'd be a good idea,' Bridget agreed. 'Mother could do with your support.' Then once again she burst out in exasperation, 'Why the hell isn't Jane with you? I could really do with her help in the shop.'

Lily decided the moment of truth had arrived. There was no avoiding it; she would have to make a clean breast of it to Bridget. The words *what a tangled web we weave, when at first we do deceive* were spinning around in her head. 'Bridget!' Lily laughed nervously. 'I'll have to ask you to keep a secret — it's about Jane.'

Bridget's eyes widened. 'What about Jane?' she whispered. A tremulous chill flew round her heart. Sacred heart of Jesus! she thought, why is it that trouble never comes alone!

'She's walking out with Willie,' Lily blustered. 'You know that friend of Peter's.' What a relief it was to get it off her chest and tell Bridget; all day long she'd felt like a pawn in some sinister plot, being pushed around from Billy to Jack. Bridget saw the tension drain from Lily's face after she finished explaining.

'But, my goodness!' she exclaimed, her mood lightening, 'why didn't she tell me?'

'Lily said, 'Oh, the usual reasons: we couldn't tell Mother and she didn't want to put you in an awkward position with Mother by telling you. What you didn't know you couldn't tell lies about.'

Bridget said, 'For goodness sake, wasn't I through the mill myself in the early days with Michael.' She laughed. 'Of all people she should've known I'd understand.' Bridget stopped to think.

'So she's still with him, is she?'

'As far as I know, she is,' Lily said, 'But don't ask me where they are. I only know I spent one of the most miserable days of my life waiting for her at Peter's place. Then they had to go to visit Nancy Pete's parents.'

'Look,' Bridget said, 'you can tell me about all that later. The most important thing now is for you to get to the hospital as quickly as possible.'

'What do I tell Mother about Jane?' Lily asked concerned. 'I'm flat out of lies.'

Bridget thought for a moment, then said, 'We'll tell Mother that when the two of you were on your way home you ran into a friend of Jane's who coaxed her into having a cup of tea with her in one of the hotels. How's that?'

'You'e a real pal!' Lily felt such relief she threw her arms around Bridget's neck.'

'Okay, off you go as quick as you can,' Bridget said. 'In the meantime, if Jane turns up, I'll tell her what the story is.' Once again Bridget became very anxious, 'I hope to God Eileen is all right.'

As she made her way towards the Richmond Hospital, Lily thought, all the trouble we could have saved ourselves if only we'd taken Bridget into our confidence in the first place. Arriving at the hospital she met Mary and Eileen coming through the Exit door. Eileen's left arm was covered in plaster of Paris and in a sling.

Seeing Lily's worried expression, Mary hastened to reassure her. 'It's not too serious,' she said. 'It's just broken.'

'No complications?' Lily asked earnestly.

'No thank God!' Mary said. 'She should be out of the cast in about six weeks.'

Eileen, though a little white and pinched in the face, didn't look too concerned. Mary motioned towards her. 'She feels quite important,' she said. 'Well, with an arm in plaster won't she get lots of attention and sympathy at school.'

'Yeah,' Eileen put in, 'and lots of signatures too.'

Lily murmured a prayer of thanks to the good Lord. Though she was really sorry about Eileen's arm, she was grateful that the diversion had taken the heat off her.

When they got home Jane had arrived.

Chapter XV

February 1917

'And pull it off we did,' Collins said gleefully to Willie who was paying him a visit in his National Aid Association Office. Collins was referring to the recent election in North Roscommon which was easily won by the Sinn Fein candidate, Count Plunkett. (Father of the executed Joseph Plunkett.) Plunkett was chosen and supported by cooperative elements of Sinn Fein, The Irish Republican Brotherhood, the Nation League and the Irish Volunteers. Between these elements there was, as yet, only a loose cohesion. They had no formal or unified policy except opposition to England and the IPP (the Irish Parliamentary Party), which they regarded a subservient to the British Government. They were, of course, united by a devotion to the memory of Joseph Plunkett. So the election was fought mainly on an emotional issue. And no one worked more ably and more willingly than Collins to ensure victory in North Roscommon. 'And to think the bauld Count got nearly twice as many votes as his parliamentary opponent,' Collins said, making no attempt to hide the irony in his voice.

'It's amazing!' Willie said. 'But don't forget a lot of the credit goes to yourself and Griffin. (Arthur Griffin — political rather than republican — was the leader of the non-violent, pre-war Sinn Fein. Notwithstanding, he served a term of imprisonment in Wandsworth and Reading jails and was only recently released.)

'Not only is it a victory for our candidate,' Collins crowed, 'But a vote of sympathy for the republican rebels.'

'And the executions. Don't forget those,' Willie added. 'Not to mention the continued failure of the damn British to implement Home Rule.' Willie gave voice to his rage.

'Now all we have to do is convince Plunkett to abstain from attending the Westminster parliament,' Collins said vehemently.

'Will it be difficult?'

'Hard to say. So far he's holding the cards close to the chest,' Collins checked his watch. We should know his decision by this evening.'

'We're having a meeting. Griffin will be there. If anyone can talk Plunkett into turning his back on Westminster, it's Griffin.'

Later that evening, without any pressure being brought to bear on him, Plunkett announced, 'I fully intend to abstain from attending the Westminster parliament.' It was said without a hint of fluster.

And everyone was happy.

§

Willie meantime was making great progress learning the tricks of the 'picture' trade. 'I'm getting so good at the job,' he wrote Jane, 'Finbar, the boss, frequently leaves me in charge. Not bad for a lad who made such a mess of the reel of film on his first night.' Since Jane's return to school, Willie wrote regularly each week. His letters talked mostly about his work and about how much he missed her. He usually ended saying, 'Roll on Easter! I can't wait to see you.'

Lily always knew when Jane received a letter from Willie. The radiance in her face said it all. 'Don't have to ask why you're looking so happy,' Lily said to Jane when they met in the corridor during a break between classes. 'I take it there was another letter from himself this morning?'

'Is it that obvious?'

'It's lovely to see you so happy,' Lily remarked. 'But what the hell do you find to talk about in your letters?'

'You'd be surprised.' A luminous smile lit up Jane's face. 'Apart from telling me that he loves me, this morning's letter was full of news about the bye-election in North Roscommon. It seems their

Sinn Fein candidate won by a huge majority. Willie's over the moon with delight.'

'Was he involved in the campaign?' Lily asked.

'Not much. It's the one thing he's disappointed about. He would love to have been more involved, but his job wouldn't allow it. However, he did make a contribution in his spare time, stuffing thousands of leaflets into envelopes.'

'Still very much the patriot,' Lily said. Then added, 'Okay, so his letters are very interesting; he's on the outside. But what exciting news do you have to impart to a patriot? Could it possibly be about the bitchy nuns?'

'That's an awful thing to say.' Jane was full of mock indignation.

'Oh! It's all right for you,' Lily's voice sounded wistful. 'You're teacher's pet. You play the piano and keep getting first class honors in your exams.'

Jane didn't answer that. Obviously her sister was having an 'off' day. Not surprising. She really put her foot in it yesterday letting Sister Agnes overhear her curse and swear which resulted in her being kept back after school to fill a notebook with the words *I must not be profane*. Unfortunately, it meant missing the hockey game — her one and only interest in the school.

'Ach, I'm sorry, Jane,' Lily apologized giving Jane a hug. 'Though at times I'm green with envy about your popularity, I'm delighted things are working out with Willie and yourself.'

Lily adjusted the loose slide that was threatening to fall out of her hair; the hair that had now become the bane of her life. It started when she got back to school after Christmas and discovered her friend, Mairead, had allowed her hair to grow long. It was so marvelous and adaptable. The way she could arrange it in so many different styles; as a chignon at the nape of her neck, piled in curls on the top of her head or hanging loose. Lily thought, well, my hair is just as straight as Mairead's, why don't I let mine grow too? By now Mairead's hair was down to her waist. Not so Lily's. It had reached her shoulders, but instead of growing down it was growing out. It was now so thick and bushy it was totally unmanageable. Worse still, whenever she looked in the mirror her moon face looked moonier than ever.

As Lily fixed the slide back into her hair, Jane looked critically at it. 'If you don't mind me saying so, it's much nicer short,' she said indulgently.

'Tell me about it,' Lily said with disgust. 'If it's possible for hair the likes a mine to ever look decent, it's got to be short. I'll be paying the hairdresser a visit this coming Saturday.'

The Easter break from school commenced on Ash Wednesday morning after the students received their 'ashes' and had breakfast. Except for the foreign students who were staying put, the rest couldn't wait to get away. The school rang with the voices of girls saying their good-byes. The non-arrival of Willie's weekly letter didn't unduly upset Jane. After all, it was Holy Week; a short week. It would surely be waiting for her at home. So far no concrete arrangements had been made about their next meeting. Arriving home, Jane's first act was to look for Willie's letter. It didn't exist; the family post box in the kitchen was empty. Ah well, she thought, there's always tomorrow, Thursday's and Saturday's posts.

But Jane was in for a disappointment. Neither of the two posts on Thursday carried a letter from Willie. That left only Saturday's posts before Easter. After that, with the Bank Holiday intervening, there would be no further post until Tuesday. But the Saturday posts too failed to bring the longed for letter from Willie.

With disappointment written all over her, Jane said to Lily, 'I can't understand it. He must be sick or something? It doesn't make a bit of sense.'

'It certainly doesn't,' Lily said sympathetically, 'unless he intends to call.'

'No, he'll never do that,' Jane said decisively. 'He knows how strongly Mother feels about girls my age walking out without being chaperoned.'

'Would you think of dropping around to the Tivoli Cinema this afternoon to see him?' Lily suggested.

'No. I've a better idea,' Jane became suddenly animated. 'What would you think about you and I going to the pictures tonight? Apart from seeing him, wouldn't it be a nice break.'

'It's Easter Saturday! The night we attend the Easter Vigil Ceremonies,' Lily reminded her. 'Mother'd have a fit if we weren't there.' She laughed, 'And I certainly couldn't think up a suitable lie to explain why.'

'Oh God! I forgot about the ceremonies.'

'He has a matinee on Saturdays?' Lily said.

'As far as I know.'

'Okay, then, let's just drop around now and see him,' Lily said very positively.

'You'd come with me?'

'Yes, of course.' It came natural to Lily to be supportive. 'That is,' she had a doubt, 'unless you'd prefer I didn't come?'

'Course, I want you to come'

So on the pretext of going to the church to pray, the girls left for the Tivoli cinema. To their disappointment they found the place locked, barred and bolted with a sign on the main door reading, 'The Tivoli Cinema will be closed from Ash Wednesday until Easter Monday, when it will open for the matinee at 2.30 p.m.'

'Come with me to Clontarf,' Lily suggested to Jane as they walked home from Mass on Easter Sunday. She could see Jane was very distressed about not hearing from Willie. Were she to wait in all day and there was no word from him, she'd be more depressed than ever. It was Easter, after all; a time to celebrate.

'No,' Jane broke into Lily's thoughts, 'thanks for the offer all the same. But I think t'would be best if I stayed put in case he tries to get a message to me.'

By three o'clock when there was no message from Willie, Jane felt utterly miserable. Her heart ached. With all her being she longed to see him. Throughout last term he hadn't been out of her thoughts for one minute. Now her only consolation was thinking about the lovely words he used ending each letter: 'I can't wait to see you.'

Suddenly, the clutter in her head cleared: she decided there was only one logical explanation for Willie's silence. He was sick; too sick to write a letter. She thought, I can't stand this uncertainty another minute and made the decision. I'll call up to the house in Drumcondra. It'll have to be today, because tomorrow —blast it! - I'll be stuck in that damn shop doing my Bank Holiday stint! Which reminded her that her mother hadn't as yet given Lily and herself the times of their shifts. With our Nancy working full time at the hairdressing, there was no question of her helping out.

It was bad enough that the Whitehall tram, running through Drumcondra, took an hour to come, but finding no one home at 39, Carlingford Avenue was the last straw. What to do? Inspiration. Write a note and drop it in the letterbox.

Dear Willie,

As I didn't hear from you, I called to the house but no one was home. Just to say I have to work as usual in the shop tomorrow, the Bank holiday Monday. But I'll be on holidays till Monday Week. Maybe you'd drop me a line.

Hope you're not sick or anything?

Regards, J.

'There's going to be another bye-election in Longford in May,' Collins excitedly informed Willie and Peter over a pint in Flanagan's pub on Palm Sunday morning (the Sunday before Easter). 'And once again, we're putting up a Sinn Fein candidate.'

'Who is it going to be this time?' Peter inquired.

'A sentenced prisoner by the name of McGuinness, who's still in Lewes Jail in Britain. We've made his particular circumstance the theme.'

'Do you think he has a chance?' Willie asked.

'Well, for starters we have posters displayed all over Longford showing a man in convict's garb, carrying the inscription: 'Put him in to get him out,' Collins said looking ferociously determined. Willie and Peter laughed boisterously. No one but Collins could think that one up.

'Your idea, Mick, no doubt?' Peter exclaimed when he got his breath back.

Collins smiled wickedly. 'The poster idea was my idea all right but—'

Willie intervened, 'Are the same people who sponsored Plunkett sponsoring McGuinness?' he asked.

'Yeah. Just the same,' Collins said. 'After Plunkett's great victory, we've become much more cohesive.'

'That's marvelous,' Willie enthused.

'However,' Collins continued, 'by all accounts they have a problem. I won't bore you with interminable details, but it seems that despite the fact that there are hundreds of eager helpers involved in the Longford campaign, there's a dearth of experienced people.' Collins looked hard at Willie. 'Any way you could manage to go to Longford and give them a hand, Willie?' he asked.

After weighing up the pros and cons, Willie said, 'I'd like to but there's the job.'

'I'll have a word with Finbar.'

'As it happens,' Willie continued. 'This week being Holy Week, the cinema is closed from Ash Wednesday till the Matinee on Easter Monday. I'd definitely be available to go to Longford from Wednesday to Sunday. After that I'd have a problem.'

Collins said, 'I'm sure something could be arranged.'

'If it's any help, Willie,' Peter chipped in, 'shown the ropes, I could possibly act as a stand-in for you a couple of nights a week. I'd rather enjoy it, in fact.' Peter was thinking how nice it would be to get away from the 'ball and chain' for a few hours.

'Darling, it's so lovely to have you home,' she effused each evening when he arrived home. But unless he agreed with everything she said, her charm disappeared and her voice rose to almost yelling. The pity was when she was in a normal mood there couldn't be a nicer person. But the trouble was one didn't know when she was going to be in a normal mood. A wrong word or a fancied slight could trigger her sulks and her moodiness.

'Good suggestion Peter,' Collins vociferated heartily. 'Don't be surprised if we take you up on it.' Collins then inclined his head and smiled at Peter. 'Any chance you could go to Longford yourself?'

'No, definitely not! I'm only just getting settled in the job in the

Independent again. If I took time off at this stage, I'd say I could wave good-bye to it,' Peter grimaced. 'Not to mention the ball and chain. If I disappeared for any length of time, my life wouldn't be worth a quenched match.'

'Quite understandable,' Collins said. 'Of course, you have a wife and child to think about.' After a few seconds, Collins said, 'Tell you what, the pair of you meet me here at lunchtime tomorrow. By then I should have things sorted out.'

When Peter and Willie arrived in Flanagans pub on Monday, to their surprise, not only was Collins there, but Finbar Clancy was with him.

'Now,' Collins greeted them cordially, 'it's all arranged.' He clapped Finbar on the back. 'Finbar here says that you Willie, can have the time off until after the elections, if you, Peter, could show the pictures for even two nights a week: the other nights and the matinees he'll do himself.'

Looking pleased, Finbar threw in, 'Anything for the Cause!'

'Great!' Peter enthused. 'But the only nights I could do would be Tuesdays and Thursdays, if that's any use.'

'Fine!' Finbar said, 'Any help you can give would be really appreciated.' He then looked hard at Willie who was dumbfounded. 'Well, Willie?' he said. 'Is that all right with you?' Willie was totally unprepared for this all embracing commitment. Granted he was ready to go to Longford from Ash Wednesday till the following Easter Sunday. But he hadn't reckoned on Collins pledging his services for the duration of the campaign, without consulting him. His head ran riot with thoughts of Jane. What to do about her? The uncertainty about his movements between Ash Wednesday and Easter Sunday delayed the writing of the weekly letter to her. Of course, he should have borne in mind Collins' knack of 'fixing' things; he wasn't one to allow the grass to grow under his feet. 'Well, Willie?' Finbar looked quizzically at him.

For seconds Willie was hesitant, then said, 'About money?'

'All taken care of,' Collins interjected. 'You'll be paid out of campaign funds.'

'Right, that's fine,' Willie feigned a cheerfulness he was far from feeling. At this moment all he could think about was getting an explanatory letter to Jane as quickly as possible.

'I take it you'll be able to leave on Wednesday morning?' Collins interrupted his thoughts.

'Yeah,' Willie said with forced cheerfulness. 'What time is the train?'

'Seven in the morning from Broadstone,' Collins told him. He then produced a bulky package from his inside pocket. 'Here,' he said, 'your fare and one month's salary. There's also a letter to Frank O'Meara who's in charge of the operation in Longford. His address is on the envelope. Give it to him on your arrival.' Collins grabbed Willie's shoulder affectionately. 'Thanks, Willie,' he said, 'for doing the needful. I know you'll be a great help to O'Meara.' He then added. 'I hope to be in Longford myself next week. But until I know how things stand in the office, I can't say which day.'

Willie took the envelope. As usual Collins had thought of everything.

§

When there was no word from Willie for the rest of the Easter break, Jane felt as if a vital part of her had died, leaving an aching emptiness that nothing could fill. Her hapless feelings showed only too clearly on her face.

And Mary noticed it. 'Jane's acting very pique,' Mary remarked to Lily on the Wednesday after Easter. 'And come to think of it, she's not looking at all well either. It there something wrong at school?'

'No, everything's fine.'

'Maybe she's coming down with something?' Mary seemed quite concerned. 'Do you know are her bowel movements regular?'

'As far as I know they are.'

'What she probably needs is a couple of spoonfuls of caster oil?' Mary suggested. (Throughout Mary's life, caster oil was the cure for everything that ailed you.)

'No, I'd say, she definitely doesn't need caster oil.'

'That night going to bed, Lily gave Jane a laugh repeating the conversation she had with her mother.

'Gosh!' That's all I need,' Jane said, 'a dose of the runs.'

'Wouldn't that be the ideal time for Willie to show up?' Lily quipped. 'With you stuck in the lavatory.'

'There's no fear of that. Whatever about sending a letter,' Jane said disconsolately, 'Willie will definitely not show up.'

'Look,' Lily said in a gust of sudden rage, 'If that fella, Willie, is getting you down so much, why don't we go to the pictures tomorrow night and confront him afterwards?'

'No, I'm not going to run after him,' Jane was righteously adamant. 'After all, I did leave a note for him at his house. The least he could do is drop me a line letting me know where I stand.'

The one bright spot of the Easter break happened on Thursday morning when Bridget announced at breakfast that Michael and herself were buying the engagement ring the following Saturday. Bridget went on to say, 'Michael has been told unofficially that he's got his final exam.' Her eyes danced with joy. 'So now we can start planning our wedding.'

Jane jumped up from the breakfast table and threw her arms around Bridget's neck.

'That's fantastic news,' she enthused. It was the first time this holiday she'd shown the slightest interest in anything other than what the postman brought each day.

Lily followed suit, giving Bridget a great, big hug. 'When is it going to be?' she asked.

'We're thinking about a September wedding.'

'Wonderful! Wonderful!' Lily called out excitedly and straightaway blurted out, 'Can Jane and I be your bridesmaids?'

Bridget hesitated, then said, 'That will have to be decided at a later date.'

'Oh, I forgot! The Nancy wan!' Lily said dejectedly. 'As the next eldest, of course, she'll have to get first preference.'

'Maybe I could have three bridesmaids,' Bridget said in appeasement. Then stopped as suddenly something struck her. 'Gosh! There's Eileen too,' she gasped. 'She's bound to want to be a flower girl. Bridget was getting a taste of some of the knotty problems that were about to crop up as she planned her wedding. 'Anyway,' she continued, getting away from the subject of bridesmaids and flower girls, 'Michael and I thought we'd have a bit of a celebration — a sort of engagement party — this coming Sunday to let the families meet. Can I take it that you two will be around?'

'Of course,' Jane and Lily said in unison.

'Can we do anything to help?' Jane asked. God knows she desperately needed a distraction of some sort.

'No, everything is arranged,' Bridget said, giving a closed-mouth smile. 'It's going to be a very sober affair, anyway. Well, with a priest, a Christian brother and two nuns present, what can you expect? Just cups of tea, sandwiches, cakes, and hopefully, some scintillating conversation.'

Lily burst out, 'Are Peter and Nancy Pete coming?'

'They got an invitation. So far I haven't heard from them?'

Lily said, 'I bet you'd be pleased if they didn't come? Well, Nancy Pete anyway.'

'As it's going to be from three to five in the afternoon to facilitate the people in religious orders who, thankfully need to get away, I think we could just about tolerate Nancy Pete's eccentricities for that length of time.' Bridget's hand was on her breast breathing deeply; she was consoling herself with thoughts of when the ordeal would be over.

'As long as she doesn't produce the bare bosoms and feed the child in front of them,' Lily threw in, laughing heartily.

'Goodness! Don't even mention such a thing!' Bridget shuddered.

As it turned out the engagement party wasn't quite as somber as anticipated. When the introductions and the congratulations were done with, Peter and Nancy Pete not having arrived, the party settled down to drinking tea, eating sandwiches and cakes as they indulged in small talk.

As was only natural, the conversation eventually centered around the wedding plans. Michael and Bridget did most of the talking, telling the company that they hoped the wedding could take place in September. They then went on to explain that a lot depended on whether or not they could get the house they liked so much in Clontarf; they'd set their hearts on it. But price-wise it was a lot higher than they could afford. However, the price was still being negotiated.

Mrs. Barry, Michael's mother, who was very deaf and very curious, interrupted the conversation asking Sister Oonagh, sitting beside her, 'What are they saying?'

'They're talking about a house they'd like to buy,' Sister Oonagh roared into her mother's ear.

'Where?' Mrs. Barry wanted to know.

'In Clontarf,' Sister Oonagh told her.

Mrs. Barry nodded her approval, 'Very good.'

'I've told them to go ahead and buy the house,' Mary threw in insouciantly. 'I'll help them out financially.'

Bridget jumped in, 'Mother, you've already done more than your share, giving us the down payment,' she sounded very dogmatic.

Sister Angela, Michael's older, tall, wiry sister, interjected laughing, 'Bridget, did you ever hear the saying *never look a gift horse in the mouth?*'

Sister Angela's remark brought smiles to the faces of her family. As a confraternity member of the Little Sisters of the Poor, they knew only too well about Angela's perpetual begging.

'Thank you, Sister,' Mary said appreciatively. Bridget twitched with discomfort. Michael was silent. There was an awkward pause in the room.

Sitting on the sofa between Anthony, the Christian Brother, bony and round shouldered and Sister Angela, Father Sebastian, Michael's oldest brother, bald, with an overflowing waistline, threw in jovially, 'Right, that's settled then. It'll be September.' He clasped his hands in gratification then produced his diary. 'Now I'll need to get a definite date so that I'll be available to perform the ceremony.'

Mary now looked uncomfortable. Nonetheless, she butted in. 'But I've already asked Bridget's Uncle, the Reverend Father Vincent, to perform the ceremony,' she said.

It was the nearest thing to a bombshell. For seconds the room was in total silence. Bridget wished the floor would open and swallow her.

Mrs. Barry intervened keeping the conversation going. 'What are they saying?' she asked Sister Oonagh.

'They're discussing who is going to be the celebrant of the wedding,' Sister Oonagh roared into her mother's ear.

'Sebastian, of course,' Mrs. Barry affirmed positively.

Bridget at last found her voice. 'But Mother!' she gasped. 'You never mentioned a word of this to me.'

'Oh, between one thing and another,' Mary said. 'I didn't get round to it.' Bridget felt she hadn't a leg to stand on. After all, her mother was helping to buy the house.

Michael quietly interjected. 'Look,' he said, 'everything is very much up in the air at the moment; these details will be ironed out later.'

While this was all going on, Jane kept busy with the catering; back and forth to the kitchen, refilling the teapot, replenishing sandwiches and cakes. Having missed Mary's gaffe, she arrived back to a room so thick with tension you could slice it. And poor Bridget—God help her!—looked absolutely shattered.

To everyone's relief, Sister Angela changed the subject to inquire about the school Lily was attending.

'Sienna Convent in Drogheda,' Lily told her.

Sister Angela expressed surprise, 'Oh! They're still teaching? I heard they had become a silent Order.'

Sister Oonagh interjected, 'Just a rumor, Angela.'

'Well now, I got it on good authority, months ago, that they were about to become silent.'

'I'm the one who's in the teaching profession,' Sister Oonagh said haughtily. 'You're…well you're…'

'Go on, say it,' Sister Angela said bluntly, 'I'm the one who goes from door to door begging.'

Lily butted in. 'Does that mean Sienna Convent won't be a teaching order any longer?' she asked nonchalantly. Two feats to be accomplished here, Lily thought, as she asked the question. First, break up the bickering sisters and second, find out if she would have to return to that awful school next year.

'Probably,' Sister Oonagh asserted. 'But it could be years before the changeover becomes effective.' Sister Oonagh's answer was a blight on Lily's hopes.

Laughing, Mary drew attention to Lily's disappointed face, 'Could it be more obvious to everyone that our Lily does not regard school with much bliss?' she asked the two nuns.

Lily shrugged her shoulders and blushed faintly.

'Which of us didn't have the same feelings at her age?' Sister Oonagh haw-hawed artificially. Sister Oonagh then turned her attention to our Nancy who sat looking bored to distraction. 'You've gone into hairdressing, I believe?' she said.

Our Nancy allowed a smile to crack her face. 'Yes, I started before Christmas.'

'How do you like it?' Sister Oonagh asked.

'Oh, it's a job. I suppose it's all right.'

The conversation was now interrupted by Peter's arrival. Thankfully, on his own. (Bridget stifled a sigh of relief.) She prayed to God his presence would introduce topics of interest to the men. Because up to now all she could hear was the cackle of women's voices, with her mother-law-to-be continually interrupting the flow, asking *What did she say? What did he say? What did they say?*

And ne'er a word issuing from Anthony, the Christian brother!

The men were particularly interested in hearing about Peter's experiences during the Rising and as a Prisoner of War. As he recounted them, Peter, the great raconteur, held everyone's attention. Even Mrs. Barry kept quiet. Bridget now began to relax. The party was at last going well.

Until an explosion of farts came from behind the sofa, followed by the awful stench.

Bridget's hand flew to her mouth in horror. Lily dashed out the door heading for the kitchen. The room was stunned into silence.

Seeing the consternation caused by the incident, Eileen, wide-eyed and innocent, piped up, 'It's Fluffy. He has diarrhea. He ate the whole of the Easter Egg I was saving for school.'

The cat shot out from behind the sofa and made a beeline for the door.

In an effort to force a light-hearted moment, Father Sebastion, laughing heartily, quipped, 'What's natural is not to be wondered at.'

Thankfully his remark eased the shock and tension in the room. Even Bridget smiled and began to see the funny side. Lily arrived back with a bucket filled with a mixture of water and washing powder, together with a mop and floor cloths, to clean up the mess. To get to it, the sofa had to be pushed out from the wall, which meant the clergy had to remove themselves and stand in wait for Lily to complete the job.

Midst all the confusion, Mrs. Barry was heard to say, 'What's all the fuss about? Why are they all standing?'

Bridget thought, not only has she lost her hearing, but she's lost her sense of smell.

§

Dear Jane,

By the time you receive this letter I will be in Longford campaigning for the Sinn Fein candidate contesting the upcoming bye-election due to be held here in May.

Unfortunately, it means that all the lovely plans I had in mind for us over the Easter holiday will have to be put on hold. I feel wretched about it. But when Collins asked me to help out, I couldn't very well refuse. (You know Collins; when he makes up his mind about anything there's no dissuading him.) It would have been fine had I been able to stall starting the job in Longford until after your return to school. But Collins wanted me there on Ash Wednesday. Holy Week is the ideal time to campaign outside churches. What with all the ceremonies: Ash Wednesday (The Ashes), Holy Thursday (The Seven churches), Good Friday (The Stations of the Cross), Holy Saturday (The Easter Ceremonies) and Easter Sunday (Mass). So it looks like most of my time will be spent outside a church for the duration of the first week anyway.

As it happens, I'm just one of a body of campaign workers supplied by Collins, who's trying his best to rival the traditionally efficient machine of the Irish Parliamentary Party.

Jane, I'm profoundly disappointed that I won't be able to see you during the Easter break: I was so looking forward to it. Please God we'll make up for it at a later date. I want to get this letter to you before you break up at school, so I'll bring this chatter to a close.

As soon as I'm settled in Longford, I'll write a long letter telling you all my news.

God bless and keep you safe.
Love Willie.

Willie's letter was waiting for Jane in the convent post box when she arrived back to school.

§

Frank O'Meara of the gray whiskers, bright eyes and high color (tonight, higher than ever) approached Collins standing at the back of the Longford National School Hall used for polling that day. Presently, as the assemblage awaited the results of the election, Collins entertained them with yarns and anecdotes.

'We have the result at last, Mick,' Frank said, indicating the sheet he was carrying. 'Would you do the honors?'

Collins could tell from the collusive wink and the glow in Frank's eyes, that the news was good. 'With pleasure,' he said, taking the paper from Frank.

He then proceeded to push his way through the masses thronging the hall, finally climbing on to the dais at its end.

'Can I have your attention, everyone? Please!' Collins bellowed from the dais, in the tones of a scoutmaster.

Gradually a hush came over the room.

Collins began writing on the blackboard. As he wrote he spoke the words. 'Now, the result of the Longford County Bye-election held this day, the 9th May 1917, is as follows: Matthew Carolan (Irish Parliamentary Party) l,461 votes. Joseph McGuinness (Sinn Fein) l,498 votes.'

Whoops of delight greeted this announcement. Up front Willie, standing among the other campaign workers, threw his hat into the air with theirs. The joy and acclamation in the room was the most fervent anyone could ever imagine. Collins stretched his hands towards the noisy hordes, indicating his desire to say a few words. The noise died down.

'Now,' Collins shouted, 'it's been a very, long hard day for all of us. So I won't take up any more of your time talking the talk. But I would like to say, first, a big thanks to our campaign workers for making this victory possible. The martyrs of 1916, who have carried the day, would be proud of you.'

The hall erupted in ferocious cheering. Then simmered down.

'Second,' Collins went on, 'combined with Plunkett's victory in Roscommon, the result of this election is a sign of coming change.' He hesitated a second for effect, then continued, 'These victories,' he said, 'are like a small stream that will get deeper and broader with each bye-election and will eventually be a great river by the time it reaches the sea.'

Again cheering and clapping from the audience. Willie, exuberant, poked Thomas Ashe, standing beside him. Ashe was a prominent colleague of Collins' in the I.R.B. He fought in the Rising and was now part of Collins' machine. Like Willie, he had been helping out in the campaign.

'The old 'hut' paid off,' Willie said to Ashe under his hand, his eyes brimming with merriment.

'You can say that again,' Ashe responded, grinning.

The *hut* in question had been set up by Sinn Fein supporters in an effort to rig the election. It provided a selection of men's and women's clothing in which Sinn Fein supporters could disguise themselves and go to the polls several times to vote in the names of people who were dead, ill or away. Before the election, the polling list had been thoroughly studied for this purpose. Willie and Ashe now realized that the small majority of thirty-seven votes could well be the result of the impostors' votes.

During the election campaign Willie and Ashe became good friends. Mostly they talked politics and about the excitement Collins brought to their lives. In one of their conversations Ashe let Willie into a secret he was privy to regarding the state of play among the leaders. It would appear that a movement was afoot, headed by Catha Brugha, a former stalwart, to do away with the old established I.R.B. and replace it with the comparatively new, but nonetheless, considerable force of Sinn Fein. Collins wanted to reorganize the I.R.B., but Brugha thought it was a waste of time.

'So at the moment there's this clash between Collins and Brugha,' Ashe said. 'If you ask me, it's jealousy on Brugha's part towards what he considers his younger rival.' Ashe scratched his head. Well, as I see it, what it boils down to is the opinion of the idealist, Brugha, against the opinion of the realist Collins.' Ashe stopped to think for a moment before he continued, 'This sort of disunity doesn't help the Cause. I wish Brugha would be more collaborative.'

§

*39, Carlingford Avenue,
Dublin.
12th May, 1917*

Dear Jane,

Sorry my letters were so infrequent while I was in Longford. Towards the end of the campaign things became so hectic and I was so utterly tired and fatigued every night, I couldn't put two sentences together, no more than I could put pen to paper. Anyway, now that I'm back in Dublin and things are back to normal, I'll have more time to write. So I'll try to make it up to you.

Just in case you don't already know, we won the Longford bye-election. It was a slim majority. But nonetheless we won. Need I say how elated I was about the result. It means we now have two elected members to Parliament, both of whom will refrain from sitting in Westminster. Also it's been announced that McGuinness, the elected member for Longford, is about to be released from jail. Yahoo!

Oh, another bit of good news I've just heard, is that a sitting member of parliament, named Ginnell, is also going to refrain from sitting in Westminster. Which means Westminster is going to be three members short. Collins is full of talk about setting up our own Irish Parliament. I think it's wishful thinking. I can't see it happening for a long time. But then with Collins' doggedness and perseverance, you never know? All we can do is hope and pray that someday it will come to pass.

Hope your exams are going well. This is a trying time for students. It was great you received first class honors in the music. I'm very proud of you.

Your story about the engagement party was hysterically funny. I can just imagine the effect Fluffy's indiscretion had on the company. She certainly picked the time to let off steam and make an impression. Poor Bridget! She must have been mortified.

By the way, did you know that your brother, Peter, stood in for me two nights a week showing the pictures while I was in Longford? It seems he enjoyed it immensely. So much so he seemed loath to relinquish the job on my return. Now he talks about giving up journalism and going into the picture business. According to your brother, moving pictures will take over the world in the not too distant future. As far as I know, Peter is still unaware of our relationship. Now, as you're going to be coming home from school for good at the end of June, would you think of putting him in the picture soon? Don't you think that things would be less complicated if he knew about us?

Think about it anyway. Write soon.

Love you. Dying to see you.
Willie

Chapter XVI

As Jane danced the old-time waltz with Willie, she could hardly contain her excitement. Here she was, at last, in Willie's arms. No, it wasn't fantasy. She could feel the blood thundering through her veins.

When she first read Willie's letter with the gorgeous invitation to the Ceilidhe in the Mayo Men's Club on Parnell Square (which included old-time waltzes,) after her initial excitement, she went through agonies of doubt about being able to accept it. Once again the obstacle was her mother. What tall yarn could she invent by way of explanation to her? She consulted Bridget and Lily. Between them they eventually worked out a solution. In the beginning it wasn't easy.

First Bridget, the voice of reason, while fully supportive of her going to the ceilidhe, was dead against telling the mother. 'You've only just turned eighteen,' she reminded Jane. 'There's no way Mother would countenance you stopping out that late. Besides, if she knew yourself and Willie were walking out, she'd be bound to put on end to it, on the grounds that you're much too young to be going steady with anyone.'

Of course Bridget was absolutely right.

Lily piped up optimistically, 'Couldn't you climb down from our bedroom on the night? That way Mother wouldn't know.'

'You mean climb down the drain pipe?' Jane asked.

'Either that or we tie sheets together to make a rope.'

Bridget was horror-stricken. 'For God's sake, Lily!' she exclaimed. 'Do you want her to break her blooming neck?'

Lily turned aggressively to Bridget. 'Well, do you have a better idea? The heroine in the book I'm reading presently does it all the time. It's the only way she can get to see her lover.'

Bridget smiled whimsically at Lily's innocence. 'Look, Jane,' she said, 'if you can get out of the house without Mother knowing you can certainly have my key to get back in.'

'I think that Lily's idea of climbing down from the bedroom is a good one,' Jane said laughing. 'But I wouldn't need to use sheets, sure there are ropes galore in the stables. I could get one of them.'

'Good!' Lily said, her eyes bright and eager. This had all the elements of a fantastic adventure.

So with one of Bridget's old shop coats covering her street clothes, Jane slithered, at breakneck speed down a strong, fiber rope, plopping heavily at the bottom.

Meanwhile Lily, with head stuck out the window, held her breath. When she heard the plopping sound from below, she whispered, 'Are you all right, Jane?'

'Fine,' Jane answered picking herself up. After depositing the rope and the shop coat in the stables, Jane let herself out through the back gate.

Over the past months, millions of times Jane thought about her next meeting with Willie: probably drinking cups of tea or cocoa in some small café, going for a walk. Better still, going to a theater or concert. Not in her wildest dreams did she envision anything as romantic as this reunion. Imagine ending up in Willie's arms waltzing. And he, of the two left feet (as he called it) dancing in perfect step.

'I took a few dance lessons over the winter in preparation for this,' Willie beamed down at Jane's happy face.'

'I sensed it,' Jane responded. 'Your timing is perfect.' Ballroom dancing being part of the school curriculum, Jane was an accomplished dancer.

When the dance ended, Willie escorted Jane back to their table, holding her hand like he would never let it go. Tonight it seemed he couldn't lavish enough love and tenderness on her; touching, laughing, dancing, including her in every conversation he had with his friends. Bringing her tea and sandwiches at the interval. Jane's heart beat so rapidly with happiness she had visions of it setting the ruffles of her blouse a flutter.

Holding hands sauntering down Parnell Square on the way home Willie, said, an impish glint in his eye, 'Am I going to have to help you climb up that rope to your bedroom tonight?'

'No, thank God, I have Bridget's latch key to let me in,' Jane answered. Then added staunchly, 'And even if I did have to climb that rope tonight, t'would be well worth it. I've had such a lovely time.' She gave a good natured laugh.

'Me too,' Willie gave her an engaging, boyish smile.

'Thank you for inviting me.'

'My pleasure.' When they reached the hall door, Willie touched Jane's face with anxious fingers. 'You're so lovely, Jane,' he said. 'You've no idea how much you're in my thoughts; the beauty of your smile, your presence, the warmth of your soul…'

Jane interjected. 'Gosh! You're making me sound like a saint,' she said flippantly. Somehow or other she had to hide the ecstasy she was feeling. 'But a saint doesn't furtively slither down a rope from her bedroom — defying her mother — to taste of the forbidden fruit.'

'I like that,' Willie chuckled.

'What?'

'A simple ceilidhe — the forbidden fruit.'

'That's how she'd see it, anyway.'

Willie then became serious. Staring into Jane's wonderful brown eyes, he asked, 'Would you mind if I kissed you, or would that be forbidden fruit?'

'Course not. And I'd like it.'

The kiss was long and hard. At what stage of it Jane's arms went round his neck, she wasn't aware, but he held her all the closer. Jane could feel his heart banging against her chest. It was electric. They both felt it was from this moment that their life together began.

When he released her, Willie impulsively uttered the words, 'I love you, Jane!'

Jane couldn't hold back any longer. With eyes that glittered with tears, she told him, 'I love you too, Willie. You're never out of my thoughts.'

Once again Willie crushed her to his breast and kissed her with increased urgency; her neck, her cheeks her forehead, her lips. 'God, how I love you!' he kept saying. 'You're the most wonderful girl in the world. And you're constantly in my thoughts.'

Jane couldn't believe the rush of desire she was experiencing at this moment. God! how she loved him too! With all her heart she wished she could stay with him forever.

Suddenly Willie pulled back abruptly. For an instant he seemed troubled. After a while he gave voice to it. 'Jane,' he said, 'we can't go on meeting stealthily like this. Surely there's some way or other of introducing me to your mother? As a friend of Peter's for instance?'

'I know the situation is b…awful!' Jane agreed. 'I'm a bag of nerves every time I have to sneak out to see you.'

'So what are we going to do about it?'

Jane paused to think for a moment. 'Well, Bridget is getting married in September,' she said. 'She suggested that maybe she could invite you to the wedding as Peter's friend. Then to all intents and purposes, as far as Mother is concerned, you and I are meeting for the first time and…'

'Falling in love,' Willie interjected.

'Yes.' Once again Jane threw her arms affectionately around Willie. 'Well,' she explained, 'the family would be present and I'd have their support. After that maybe things would be easier for us.'

'In the meantime?' Willie asked.

'I'll clamber out the bedroom window and do what I did tonight.'

'Climb down the rope?'

'Yes.'

'The idea of you climbing down that rope sends chills down my spine,' Willie said. 'What if you fell?'

'Well, maybe we could arrange for you to be at the bottom of the rope to catch me,' Jane said flippantly.

'You're a holy terror!' Willie planted another kiss on her lips.

§

On the following Wednesday night, when Willie was rewinding the film after the show, Finbar stuck his head in the door. 'Mick wants you to attend an important meeting tomorrow night in the Gaelic League Headquarters,' he told Willie.

'How will I managed to be in two places at the same time?' Willie asked facetiously.

'Oh, never mind that,' Finbar indicated the film Willie was rewinding. 'I'll take over while you're away.'

'Sounds intriguing,' Willie said. 'Any idea what it's all about?'

'A vague one,' Finbar said. 'But it goes without saying that Mick will do a better job explaining it.'

'Now here's the good news,' Collins, his eyes sparkling, addressed the large meeting in the Gaelic League Headquarters. 'By now t'is probably known to all of you that, once again the British Government, as a gesture of goodwill, has released the remaining prisoners of the Rising. Among them is our own Eamonn DeValera.' Collins motioned towards DeValera—lean and haggard looking—sitting beside him at the table. 'Dev as he's known to all, was a Senior Commander in the 1916 Rising. The fact that he had American citizenship saved him from execution: it was commuted to penal servitude for life.'

Somebody at the back shouted, 'Good old Dev! Let's give him three cheers. Hip, Hip!' The room exploded with resounding 'hip, hip, hoorays' three times.

'Now,' Collins went on, 'this week we had word that Major William Redmond MP—brother of John Redmond (leader of the IPP)—has been killed in the Battle of Messines. This creates a vacancy in East Clare. So, to get to the point, it has been decided to make Dev our candidate for the upcoming bye-election in East Clare this July.'

Sitting on the other side of Collins, Cathal Brugha, middle-aged, with a dour expression and a manner that was rigidly precise, stood up and spoke in glowing terms about DeValera.

He started by saying, 'DeValera's conduct during the Easter Rising gave some indication of his great possibilities as a leader.' Nodding cordially at Dev, 'And,' he continued, 'by all accounts from the time he was imprisoned after the Rising, the qualities he showed during the Rising became even more evident. This is not hearsay; this information comes from fellow prisoners. According to them the standard of character DeValera set was beyond reproach. He was described as a character of strength which allowed of no weakness, who set an impeccable example for other prisoners to follow. Small wonder then, when he was released recently, he was greeted by many of the populace as the hero-in-chief.'

Finished speaking, looking extraordinarily self-satisfied, Brugha sat down. His speech brought forth murmurs of acclamation and lots of clapping. There seemed to be general agreement among the audience that DeValera was the candidate of choice for the upcoming bye-election in East Clare.

Collins turned to DeValera. 'Say a few words to them, Dev,' he said.

DeValera stood up — all six-foot, six inches of lankiness, thin as a rail and pale as a ghost.

'A cairde gael,' he addressed the meeting as gaelidge (Irish). 'Thank you for your vote of confidence.' He turned to Cathal Brugha and said, 'and thank you, Cathal, for those kind remarks.' Then he continued, 'Although I have my doubts as to whether I would be a suitable candidate, I've decided to stand.' Once again he indicated Brugha and Collins, 'My good friends, Cathal and Mick there, have me convinced that I'd be the right candidate.'

'They're right,' someone shouted from the back. I was in prison with you and saw how you frustrated the British authorities, arguing the toss with them about our status; insisting we be treated as prisoners of war.'

'Yes,' another voice added, 'in prison, we couldn't've had a better leader.'

'Gura mila mhait agaibh,' (a million thanks) DeValera said. Then looking quite touched, he sat down.

Collins once again stood up. 'Well, that's marvelous!' he said. 'We're all in agreement.' He took a second to think. 'Now for the serious bit,' he said. 'We want all the campaigners we can get to assemble in East Clare as soon as possible. So, I'm hoping that all you lads and lassies, who gave so generously of your time in the last two bye-elections, will agree to assist in this one.'

'To be sure.'

'Most assuredly.'

The responses were very positive.

'You know the drill,' Collins said holding up a sheet of paper. 'Just put your names and addresses on this list here on the table and get your arses, down to the Limerick headquarters, on the double, by Monday next.'

As the meeting was breaking up, Collins collared Willie. 'I've had a word with Finbar,' he said. 'He's agreed to let you have the time off to help out in Clare. He gave Willie a collusive grin. 'That all right with you, Willie?'

'I suppose if it's all right with Finbar,' Willie said, 'It's all right with me.'

§

As arranged, Willie met Jane on Thursday for lunch in their cozy, little café on the corner of Liffey Street. Jane couldn't help noticing the strain on Willie's face when she arrived.

Without putting a tooth in it, she said straight out, 'Something's wrong?'

Willie answered, looking particularly guilty, 'I'm afraid I haven't the best news for you.' He hesitated.

'What is it?' Jane asked, panic gripping her.

'It seems once again circumstances have conspired to keep us apart.'

'You're going away again?' Jane tried to calm the dull knot of alarm inside her.

'Yes,' Willie's tone was contrite.

'When, where and for how long?' Jane asked in a small voice looking down at the check tablecloth lest he see the pain in her eyes.

'When? Monday next,' Willie answered. 'Where, East Clare. How long, until the bye-election there in July is over. DeValera is our candidate.' He took Jane's hand in his. 'It seems I've now become part and parcel of Collins machine.'

'Which means you have to fall in with any plans he makes for you?'

'Precisely.'

'What about your job?' Jane asked in a flat voice.

'Once again Collins has prevailed on Finbar to let me have time off for the duration of the campaign.' For seconds there was a telling silence. Willie eventually broke it. 'Jane,' he said gently, 'if we win this East Clare bye-election, we may be able to think about setting up our own parliament.' Willie paused for a second. 'In DeValera—the one and only leader of the sixteen rising not to be executed—we have a very strong candidate. Mark my word, he's going to win this bye-election.'

'You seem very confident?'

'Yes, we are confident,' Willie said. 'But despite this confidence we still need to devote lots of energy to his campaign. Dev'll need all the help he can get.' Willie grinned that boyish grin, the one that reduced Jane to putty. 'So you see,' he continued, 'it's up to the 'Collins Machine' to make sure Dev is victorious.'

'Of course you're right, Willie,' Jane said, her dark eyes glowing with intensity. 'It's one thing to talk about freedom and a united Ireland, another, to do something about it; you're definitely in that league.'

Willie was happy that Jane was at last beginning to understand something of his nationalist feelings.

'It's Collins,' he said. 'He just won't let us forget the martyrs of 1916 and what they set out to accomplish.' Breaking into a robust laugh, Willie said, 'As a result he has the lot of us—his supporters—jumping through hoops.'

'From what you tell me,' Jane said, 'he sounds like an extraordinarily determined man.'

Willie said, 'Determined is an understatement.' Then added gently, 'Jane, I really hate this separation from you.'

'I hate it too,' Jane said passionately, 'but apparently you have no choice.' Then gently stroking Willie's arm, she added, 'Willie, I know you love me as much as I love you. And I completely understand that you have to do what you think is right.' She tried to sound chirpy. 'You mustn't think you have to put me before your country.'

Willie looked at her in amazement. She really did understand his position. Overwhelmed with relief, he said with a deep, warm glow in his eyes, 'Darling Jane, you're so understanding; you're like sunlight pouring into my heart.'

'What a lovely expression!' Jane exclaimed ardently.

'That's how I feel when I'm with you,' Willie asserted.

'And do you think for one minute I want to shut out that sunshine?'

§

Willie was glad to see his old friend Thomas Ashe was part of the team campaigning for DeValera in East Clare. During one of their many conversations, Ashe confided in him that, in the midst of this apparent political clover, the clash between Collins and Brugha had widened considerably.

'Putting it bluntly,' he said, 'Brugha now insists that the I.R.B. has outlived its usefulness and wants it disbanded.'

'So all Collins' ideas about reorganizing go out the window?'

'Exactly,' Ashe said.

'That's ridiculous!' Willie was angry. 'Without the I.R.B. where would we be today? Isn't it the backbone of the whole movement?'

Ashe nodded his agreement. 'I'm sorry to say Brugha's opinion has considerable backing,' he said solemnly, 'including Dev's.'

'But Dev himself was a former member of the pre-1916 I.R.B?'

'Yes, he was, of course,' Ashe affirmed. 'But it seems that now he's declined to have anything to do with the reorganization of the

Brotherhood on the grounds that it's a secret society, and as such condemned by the Catholic Hierarchy.' Ashe had difficulty keeping the disdain out of his voice. 'It appears he's now taken sides with Cathal Brugha on that score.'

'How is Collins reacting to all this?' Willie asked.

'Not saying much.' Ashe shook his head. 'However, at one of the political meetings he did refer briefly to the matter. He pointed out that Sinn Fein's ideals are but the re-weighed ideals of the I.R.B. Nor,' he stated, 'does Sinn Fein outweigh the uses of the I.R.B. which has more than proved itself in the past and is respected by many. People should think seriously about the prospects of Sinn Fein.'

'Considering he fought in the 1916 rebellion, I'm very surprised that Dev isn't supporting Collins,' Willie said.

'Me too,' Ashe agreed. 'Surely this is a time when to be united is to have the strongest asset. Instead of which there is a growing undercurrent of mistrust.' Ashe stopped to think. Then with a sudden sprint, he asked, 'Have we reached the state of power when we can afford to cast aside a proven ideal for a barely proven one? Are we so great that we can afford to quarrel among ourselves oblivious to the common enemy?'

Willie could see Ashe was deeply affected by the situation. Ashe went on, 'Men and movements should be as nothing in this time of great test. Ireland, our country, should be our main thought.'

Willie now began to understand why such a strong bond existed between Collins and Ashe. Listening to Ashe was like listening to Collins. He had yet to meet anyone who could give voice to Collins' ideals as concisely as Ashe.

Meanwhile, the campaign to elect DeValera was gathering momentum. To everyone's surprise Dev was proving to be unusually popular among the populace of East Clare. Thousands of people rallied to his meetings to hear his speeches. Along with that, an important source of support was beginning to come from the clergy, who were formerly solidly behind the I.P.P. — Redmond's Parliamentary Party. This was significant in its implications.

One East Clare parish priest at a campaign meeting suddenly asked DeValera to give him his hand. Then raising Dev's hand in the air, he declared to the audience, 'DeValera, you have given me your hand, in return I give you the hearts of our people.'

Collins and some of Dev's supporters preached the classical Sinn Fein doctrine that elected members should stay away from Westminster and form their own Parliament in Dublin. Though how exactly they would get the British Government to recognize that parliament was not clear. In his speeches, Dev talked about appealing over the heads of the British Government to the International Peace Conference, which would sit at the end of the Great War. Other speakers spoke of appealing to the American people. But, as far as Willie could gather from Ashe, Collins had different ideas for both organizations — the I.R.B and Sinn Fein.

Once, when Willie had the chance to talk to Collins — now resigned from the National Aid Association and working full time on Dev's campaign—Collins told him, 'Dev has a mind of his own.' Then with furrowed brow, added, 'However, I wish to God he would accept that there's room for both organizations — the I.R.B. and Sinn Fein.'

The result of the election was a resounding victory for DeValera who got twice as many votes as his IPP opponent. It left no doubt as to the popularity of DeValera.

Chapter XVII

Jane raced down Abbey Street. She was meeting Willie for lunch in what was now designated 'their retreat.' Willie's letter arranging the rendezvous — the little café in Liffey Street away from prying eyes, as he put it — arrived this morning. And now she was about to see him for the first time in three weeks. A welter of sensations bumped around inside her at the prospect of seeing him: her heart raced and her pulse quickened.

He was there when she arrived, her wonderful, brave warrior. He looked handsomer than ever with the tan he acquired out of doors in the recent fine weather, not to mention his overly bleached, flaxen hair. Before he stood up, Jane couldn't resist the urge to plant a light, fleeting kiss on his lips. Then when he did stand up, she hugged him like she never wanted to let him go. He hugged her back and stroked her hair lovingly.

'And I missed you too,' he said, forestalling her. 'You're a sight for sore eyes.' After ordering the soup and sandwiches, Willie said, 'I got the Invitation to Bridge's wedding.'

'You're coming, I hope?' Jane asked spiritedly.

'Wouldn't miss it for words,' Willie answered. Willie could see that Jane was bubbling over with excitement about something. By now he could practically read her like a book. 'All right! Out with it,' he said. 'Apart from the fact that you're to be a bridesmaid, what's your good news?'

Jane laughed with rich delight. 'You won't believe it.'

'Try me.'

'I've got a job,' Jane burst out joyously.

Her ferment was so great Willie deduced that the job couldn't possibly be in her mother's dairy. 'Congratulations,' he said earnestly. 'I take it, the job is not in your mother's shop?'

'No, no. I mean, yes,' Jane was confused. 'It's not in Mother's shop,' she said excitedly. 'It's in the Henry Street Department Store. I start as an apprentice assistant there on Monday.' She gulped to catch her breath. 'Then after a year,' she continued, 'given that my work is satisfactory, I'll be promoted to a fully fledged assistant. Isn't that absolutely marvelous?'

'It's fantastic!' Willie said with sincerity. Then remembering her mother's strictness, he asked, 'How did your mother take the news?'

'She doesn't know yet,' Jane pulled an anxious face. 'It's going to be a bit of a bombshell. There could be 'a strange face in heaven' when I tell her. Though she hasn't said anything yet, I know she expects me to take over from Bridget after she's married.'

Willie, smiling at her funny expression, asked, 'when did you get the job?'

'A week ago,' Jane answered. 'It was like a miracle. I was walking past the Store and there it was — a notice in the window saying, *Trainee Assistants Wanted. Apply Personnel Officer.*

Willie looked bewildered. 'So you wandered in from the street,' he said, 'and landed the job there and then, just like that?'

Jane was suddenly on edge. 'It wasn't as easy as that,' she said. 'I had to be interviewed by their Personnel Officer who asked me to bring my School Report in the next day. Thank God, she was impressed enough by it. Anyway I got the job.'

'And she liked the look of you,' Willie said looking admiringly at her. 'Who wouldn't?'

'Don't talk like that, Willie.' Jane seemed to take offense; she perceived he was insinuating that her looks, rather than her intelligence, got her the job. 'I do have a brain you know.'

Willie took Jane's hand gently in his. 'Darling, Jane,' he said. 'I was only joking. You don't have to tell me you have a brain,' he grinned. 'It was that brain of yours, along with all those other adorable traits, that attracted me to you in the first place.'

Jane had to smile. 'You have a marvelous knack of wangling out of things, Willie,' she said lightheartedly. Then she apologized, 'I'm sorry, I'm a bit tense thinking about how I'm going to break the news to Mother.'

'When do you intend telling her?'

'It'll have to be immediately; I start on Monday next.' Jane's brow furrowed. 'She'll probably have my guts for garters, but I don't care. I'm determined I want to work in that Department Store, not in her blooming shop.'

'That's the spirit,' Willie egged her on. As they were parting Willie said, 'Let's meet here on Friday for lunch and you can tell me all about how it went with your mother.'

On arriving home, Jane spent a quarter of an hour looking for Lily inside and outside the house without success. She needed back-up support when she confronted her mother. Eventually in desperation, she accosted Bridget in the shop. 'Where the hell is Lily?' she barked at her.

'As far as I know she's around in Moore Street doing the vegetable shopping.' Bridget could see that Jane was in a right sweat. 'Is something wrong?' she asked anxiously.

'Where's Mother?' Jane asked, looking furtively behind her.

'In the office doing the accounts.' Bridget screwed up her face quizzically. 'Why all the hysteria?'

'Could you come to the parlor for a few seconds, Bridget?' Jane decided to take Bridget into her confidence. 'I've something to tell you.'

'It won't take long, will it?' Bridget said. 'I've only Marie helping me in the shop today.'

'No,' Jane said sharply. 'It shouldn't take long. But it's important.'

Following Jane into the parlor, Bridget couldn't help wondering what was worrying her? Surely it wasn't Willie again? When they got to the parlor, Jane was silent for a few seconds.

'Well, what have you to tell me that's so important?' Bridget asked.

'I've got a job! Starting next Monday,' Jane blurted out.

'What kind of job?' Bridget asked, somewhat relieved.

'As an apprentice assistant in the Henry Street Department Store.'

'But that's marvelous,' Bridget said spiritedly.

'How am I going to tell Mother?'

'Good question!' Bridget said. 'Now I can see your dilemma.' Bridget stroked her forehead contemplating. 'Mother's going to be very disappointed if a member of the family doesn't continue to uphold the tradition of working alongside her in the shop.'

'I know Mother has her heart set on me doing the job when you leave,' Jane said. 'But, Bridget,' she nodded her head defensively, 'I just detest that bloody shop.'

'You don't have to explain about that shop to me,' Bridget said bitterly. 'I'm now counting the hours.'

'When would be the best time to break the news to Mother, do you think?' Jane asked.

Without stopping to think, Bridget said very positively, 'Breakfast-time tomorrow morning. The family's usually all there. Between us we could give you some support. Except, of course, our contrary sister, Nancy.' Bridget took a little time to think. Then said, 'Yes, definitely. In the morning Mother is usually in a great hurry to get to the shop, so she won't have much time to give vent to her vexation.'

'Good psychology, that,' Jane said. 'Thanks a million for the advice. I really appreciate it.'

'I can't believe it, Jane!' Mary nearly choked on her tea. 'You of all people!' Going on Bridget's advice Jane made the announcement about the job at the breakfast table the next morning. Lily was missing; at the church doing the Tridium to Saint Jude (the worker of miracles) praying for her own and Jane's intentions. 'What on earth am I going to do when Bridget leaves?' Mary said, overwrought with the shock of it all.

'I'm sure there are lots of girls who would be glad of the job,' Bridget put in.

'But they're not family.' Mary's voice was rough with emotion.

'O'Dwyer's Family Dairy is supposed to be a family enterprise. How can we justify the name when there isn't one member of the family assisting in the shop?'

'I'm sorry, Mother,' Jane said defensively. 'But I just can't work in that dairy; the work is just too exhausting and the hours much too long.'

'I know the work is hard,' Mary agreed, 'but the pay is good and when I die it'll be your inheritance.' It seemed Mary was now resorting to bribery. 'Naturally, the members of the family who contributed to working in the dairy will fare better than the ones who didn't.'

To everyone's surprise, our Nancy put in morosely, 'Those members who gave their services to the shop may not live long enough to enjoy their inheritance. We're not all work horses like you, Mother.'

Mary's look of incredulity was wasted on our Nancy; it rolled off her like water off a duck. Jane, too, was astonished at our Nancy sticking her neck out. This was definitely a first. She couldn't remember her sister ever supporting anything family related, unless it was in her own interests.

Marie, from the shop stuck her head round the door. 'I'm sorry, Mrs. O'Dwyer,' she said. 'But the sales rep. from Willwoods is here; you have an appointment with him this morning, remember?'

'I'll be there presently, Marie.' Mary said brusquely, sounding unusually dismissive. She then turned to Jane. 'Is there any way I can talk you out of this job?' she asked her. 'Maybe if I were to shorten your hours and up your salary, you'd reconsider?' She sounded so desperate and so lost, Jane felt a surge of compassion for her. She hadn't the heart to come straight out with a blunt refusal.

'All right, I'll think about it,' she said unenthusiastically, 'but don't bank on it, Mother.'

Mary left the room looking disoriented. She closed the door. It clicked neatly letting silence fill the room.

The silence was broken by our Nancy, remarking, with a whirl of excitement, 'That's great, Jane! You'll be able to get five-percent discount off all purchases made by yourself and the family.'

Jane now began to understand why our Nancy had been so generous with her support. She hadn't even started in the job and here was her opportunist sister, talking about discount already. Jane concluded that if our Nancy had a heart at all, it was the size of a thimble.

§

Bridget, meantime, was having more than her share of problems planning the wedding. Chief among them was the disagreement between herself and her mother about who the celebrant of the ceremony would be. Now six weeks away from the wedding, between Mary insisting that Father Vincent had to be the celebrant and Michael taking it for granted that his brother, Father Sebastian, was the celebrant, Bridget felt she was being pulled apart. For the past two weeks she decided to let things slide with her mother, hoping to God she would come to her senses and realize how unreasonable she was being. But no such luck. According to Mary, it had to be the saintly Father Vincent. They couldn't get anyone holier. What's more, the last time they discussed the matter she made it abundantly clear she didn't want to hear another word about it. On her own with her mother at the tea break this morning Bridget resolved to solve the problem.

'Mother,' she said in an unusually domineering tone, 'once and for all we've got to sort out the question of who the celebrant of our marriage is going to be.' Forcing herself to sound casual, she continued, 'Father Sebastian, Michael's brother, is the obvious person to perform the ceremony.' Mary could see Bridget was upset but tactfully pretended not to notice.

Exasperated, she answered, 'Surely at this stage you don't expect me to turn round and tell Father Vincent that he's not to be the celebrant after all.' Then really agitated, she continued, 'He's gone to a terrible lot of trouble arranging everything in his life to fit in with your wedding.'

'Of course he can come to the wedding,' Bridget said, having difficulty fighting down her impatience. 'But he doesn't necessarily have to be the celebrant.'

'Do you realize who you're talking about?' Her mother appeared to be incensed. 'How privileged yourself and Michael should feel having such a saintly man perform the ceremony.'

'Yes, Mother,' Bridget gritted her teeth. 'I realize all that.' She felt like screaming. 'But have you any idea the impossible situation you're placing me in? On the one hand, I have you insisting that Father Vincent is the celebrant, on the other hand, Michael is taking it for granted that his brother, Father Sebastian, will be doing the honors.'

'Father Vincent is the right person to do it,' Mary said with sickening clarity. 'He's older, wiser and more experienced.' Mary shuffled to her feet. She indicated the clock on the wall. 'We've taken more than fifteen minutes for our tea break,' she said, then left the room.

Once again Bridget felt as if she'd been battering her head against a stone wall. There was no give whatsoever in her mother. Now she'd have to tell Michael tonight that because her mother said so, the ceremony would not be conducted by his brother. The great Father Vincent would supplant him. What an insult to Father Sebastian. Oh! To be able to just slip away to Rome and have a quiet, simple wedding.

At teatime Bridget took a late tea. When she arrived in the kitchen she found Jane and Lily at the table having theirs. Noticing her despondency, Jane touched her hand sympathetically. 'A problem shared can be a problem solved sometimes,' she said. 'What's the matter, Bridget?' Bridget was slow to answer.

Lily butted in. 'It's about Mother and her grand ideas about your wedding, isn't it?' she said looking rattled. 'The damn cheek of her dictating to you and Michael who the celebrant should be.'

Bridget looked at Lily incredulously. 'How did you know?' she asked.

'Oh, I eavesdropped at the door this morning when you were having your discussion,' she said. Then added indignantly, 'I can't believe she's being so fecking unreasonable about it.'

'Tonight I have to break the news to Michael that his own brother is not going to be the celebrant,' Bridget said unhappily. 'I can't leave it any longer to tell him.'

Jane said, 'You mean she's still sticking to her guns about Father Vincent performing the ceremony?'

'Precisely,' Bridget said her eyes full of misery.

Jane thought for a second. 'If I wasn't already in her bad books, I'd try and talk sense to her,' she said.

Lily suddenly exploded, 'Peter!' she whooped. 'He'd be the one to sort her out.'

Bridget brightened up. 'You know, Lily you might be right.'

'Of course I'm right,' Lily said positively. 'Now, Bridget, you're to sit tight. Under no circumstances are you to mention the subject to Michael tonight. Because, first thing tomorrow morning I intend to charge round to Peter's office and give him the lowdown on the way Mother is interfering in your marriage arrangements.' Lily's face showed the annoyance she was feeling. 'The stupidity of that woman insisting that Father Vincent be the celebrant and the groom with a brother a priest! It's ridiculous! And it's time someone put an end to it.' Her eyes brimmed with mirth. 'Unfortunately for Peter that someone has be him. Because he's the only one Mother ever listens to.'

The following Friday two letters of equal significance arrived by post to the O'Dwyer residence. The one, marked 'personal,' addressed to Mary, was in Peter's handwriting. The other addressed to Jane was in Willie's.

Jane sought the sanctuary of her bedroom to read hers.

Dearest Jane,

I have to make this a quick scribble because I'm in Westland Row Railway Station about to board the train to Kilkenny where they're holding another bye-election in August. This time the Sinn Fein candidate is Liam Cosgrave. I was commissioned to help out in this campaign on very short notice. Hence, I won't be able to see you for lunch at our retreat on Friday. Once again it means separation. I'm truly sorry. But I'm sure you realize it's all in a good cause. Please God, I shall be back in Dublin soon after the election.

Need I say I would be delighted to have a letter from you giving me all your news, particularly about the job. I do hope you decided to take it. If so, I'll be dying to hear how you got on? My address in Kilkenny is,

The Sinn Fein Headquarters,
Castle Street,
Kilkenny.

Be sure and mark the envelope 'private and personal.' I wish this note wasn't so short and so blunt. Be assured when I get to Kilkenny and get sorted out, I'll write you a long letter giving you all my news.
Love you.
Willie

That evening, when Bridget, Jane and Lily were on their own at teatime, looking very dejected, Bridget, told the others, 'Though the letter from Peter arrived by first post this morning, not a single word has passed her lips about it.'

Lily nearly had a fit. 'Christ, Almighty!' she exploded, 'It's like climbing bloody Mount Everest backwards to get our mother to back down.'

'Particularly when it concerns Father Vincent,' Bridget added bitterly. 'Isn't he blessed in her eyes.'

'Maybe she needs a little time to mull over the contents of Peter's letter,' Jane suggested, trying to be helpful.

Lily looked at her watch. 'It's now half six,' she said. 'The letter arrived at seven this morning.' Her eyes sparked with fury. 'How much more time does she need?'

Just then our Nancy arrived. The room went silent. Detecting an atmosphere, our Nancy asked, 'So what's the story?'

Furtive looks passed between the three sisters. The last thing they needed was to have our Nancy involved in this conspiracy. Before anyone could answer, Mary arrived.

She addressed Bridget. 'About the celebrant of your marriage,' she said in a sharp-edged tone, 'I've decided to write to Father Vincent and tell him that, as your brother-in-law, Father Sebastian, will be performing the ceremony, his services won't be required. However,' she added, more conciliatory, 'I thought I'd suggest he might like to assist at the Mass.' There was a moment's silence. Bridget wasn't sure how to answer her. 'Well, Bridget,' Mary expostulated, 'you've got your way; what have you got to say?'

Bridget said, 'Thanks, Mother. I do appreciate it.' Her expression was one of intense relief. Mary then turned to Jane and addressed her.

'As for you, young woman,' she said deprecatingly, 'reluctantly I've come to terms with your treachery and renunciation. So go ahead and take that job.' With that, Mary turned on her heel and left the room with her head held high.

'Jesus! I can't believe it!' Lily spluttered. 'Peter must have given her one helluva dressing down in that letter. He actually managed to kill two birds with the one stone.' She turned to Jane. 'While I was at it with Peter, I happened to mention about Mother's stubborn mind-set with regard to the job you wanted to take in the Department Store; the pressure she was putting on you not to take it.'

'Oh! Thanks a million, Lily,' Jane said. 'You've saved me an awful lot of heartache.'

'Me too,' Bridget said jubilantly. 'What a relief! Thank God I didn't mention a word to Michael last night. I can't thank you enough, Lily.'

Jane said to Bridget, 'We're both very indebted to Peter for intervening. Maybe we should buy him something?'

Before Bridget could answer, our Nancy butted in. 'Have I got the gist?' she asked. 'Has Peter actually succeeded in making the auld cow pull in her horns?'

The three sisters burst out laughing.

§

Dublin,
6th August, 1917.

Dear Willie,
It's the August Bank Holiday Monday and for a change I'm not

doing my usual stint in Mother's shop. No. Now that I'm working full time in the Henry Street Department Store, (says she with a breast full of pride,) I'm spared that chore.

About the job: I've been placed in the Women's Millinery Department (in case you don't know what that is, we sell women's hats.) I have to tell you, I blundered pretty badly my first hour on the job. Determined to demonstrate what a smart girl I was, I did the unmentionable — tried to serve a customer. A definite no-no for apprentices.

Apparently there's a pecking order in all the departments, which was unknown to me. Topping the pecking order, is The Buyer. In our case it's a Miss Bullingsworth; fiftyish, big, corpulent and indubitably English. In the store she's commonly known as 'the bull.' Lucky for me, it was her week to be buying in England, so she wasn't around, thank God, when I made my faux pas. According to Kathleen — the Supervisor, and second in the pecking order — had 'the bull' been present I would have been bawled out. She told me, the bull has a tongue in her that shoots in and out like a snakes when she's delivering harsh criticism. Kathleen, probably in her middle thirties, is warm and witty, someone you couldn't help liking. Well, she was the only one who took the trouble to explain about the pecking order and what exactly my duties were.

First, I'm not supposed to serve a customer until I've served my apprenticeship. At this stage, my duties appear extremely dull: they're mainly concerned with looking after stock. When I'm not chasing between the stockroom and the millinery department carrying hats, replenishing stocks behind the counter, I'm busy checking Inventories in the stockroom. This has to be done on a daily basis so that the Buyer, when she goes on her buying trips abroad, will know exactly what to buy. Usually she makes the trip the first week of every month.

You wouldn't believe the number of hats I have to look after. Hundreds. All different styles, shapes, colors and sizes; tall, flat, wide-brimmed, narrow brimmed, non-brimmed. Some adorned with ribbons, some with artificial flowers, some draped in veils. And some, the most expensive, festooned in everything — flowers, ribbons and veils. Each with its own box. To cope with this responsibility I spend most of my days in the stockroom, checking, counting and filling out forms.

Third in the pecking order is Philomena; she's just finished her apprenticeship and, as a fully fledged assistant now, is entitled to serve customers. I'm her replacement. Philomena is tall, thin and comely. Her pleasant appearance is a great asset selling hats; they look so nice when she models them. She shows me a lot of sympathy. Says, 'As an apprentice you're nothing more than a skivvy doing all the running and fetching for everyone in the department. Nonetheless,' she adds consolingly, 'if you can stick the drudgery for the twelve months, it's well worth the effort.' Easy for her to say now that she has it all behind her.

A nice part of the job is when I'm asked to replace a hat on a mannequin's bare head in the department. I really enjoy arranging it. Makes me feel important. Gives me a taste of what it's like to be behind the counter of a Millinery Department. The only other time I appear behind that counter is in my capacity as tea maker at ten in the morning and four in the afternoon. Once in a while, if 'the bull' is absent and the department isn't busy, I loiter for as long as it takes to drink the tea. This helps to get better acquainted with my colleagues. Afterwards, needless to say, I'm the one who clears away the tea things, does the washing up and putting away. In other words, I do the skivvying.

On the home front, despite many problems, Bridget is blazing ahead with plans for the wedding. Remember I told you about the dispute over who would be the celebrant. Well, thank God! It's settled at last. Peter wrote a letter to Mother intervening on Bridget's behalf and, strangely enough, on my behalf. With the result that Mother now accepts that Michael's brother, Father Sebastian, should perform the ceremony. (Which only makes sense.) And that I should be allowed to work in the place of my choice. God bless Peter!

By the way I'm to be a bridesmaid. Choosing her bridesmaids too, presented Bridget with another big problem. Because Lily, who was mad keen to be one, had to be disappointed. Well, Bridget reckoned two bridesmaids, myself and our Nancy, were enough. It's hard on

Lily. As you know, there's no love lost between herself and our Nancy and the fact that our Nancy is to be a bridesmaid is going between Lily and her rest. Today she's doing her stint in the shop. Not her favorite past time either.

No, this definitely isn't Lily's best time. Along with everything else, she doesn't want to return to Sienna Convent by herself next term. Consequently, a battle royal rages between herself and Mother, who's adamant about her finishing her education there. Lily tells me she hollering at Saint Jude asking him to work a miracle whereby she'll be saved from returning to that awful school. Unlike me, she hates the convent, the school and the nuns. Mind you, she's not all that popular with them; her cursing and swearing sees to it. Well, that's more or less my news. Except to say that I miss you like hell and long for your return.

Please write soon. Your letters bring you close to me.
God Bless
Jane

Willie smiled as he read Jane's letter. From it he deduced that Jane's job in the Department Store was not unlike his own here in the Kilkenny Sinn Fein Headquarters Office. Only, whereas Jane checked lists of hats, he was involved in checking lists of names and addresses of voters living in the Kilkenny constituency. And though the work was tedious and boring, it was extremely important. To add to his burden, Dan, his helper, sent word this morning that he had influenza and wouldn't be coming in. So Willie was obliged to do double duty: to make sure the lists of non-canvassed voters were up-to-date, ready for the three young volunteers working in the field today. Presently, he was grappling with a mountain of paper; a jumble of lists that contained names and addresses of canvassed voters mixed in with the non-canvassed ones.

Willie looked at the clock. He hadn't much time. Any minute now the field workers would be in looking for their new lists. On weekdays volunteers were in short supply. At the weekends, however, they were there in greater numbers. And though most of the donkey work was already done by Willie, he was glad to be able to slow down and take things easy. Willie noticed a lot of the voters who hadn't been canvassed, lived in the rural areas of Kilkenny. That meant bicycles. No problem there. Apart from horse-drawn carts, bicycles were the commonest form of transport in Kilkenny. If the lads didn't own one, they could always borrow the neighbors.

Suddenly the door burst open and Thomas Ashe dashed in. His face was highly flushed, his demeanor panic-stricken. 'Is Collins around?' he asked, his wild eyes darting around the office.

'No, I haven't seen Collins for a few days,' Willie answered. 'But you know Collins, he's the mercurial Pimpernel.' Then seeing this normally well-composed man looking so terror-struck, Willie suddenly felt a stinging sense of alarm. 'Something is wrong?' he said anxiously.

'They're after me,' Ashe said, his face taking on a very grave expression.

'Who are they?' Willie asked fearfully.

'The constabulary,' Ashe said. 'There's a warrant out for my arrest.'

'For God's sake! on what grounds?' Willie was astounded.

'Oh, something to do with a speech I made at one of the meetings; they contend it was seditious and inflammatory.'

'You can't be serious?' Willie gasped.

'I am serious,' Ashe said. 'Of course, it's obvious they're making me a scapegoat.'

'How did you find out?' Willie asked.

'A young lad I befriended in the barracks overheard a couple of the constabulary discussing the matter and came tearing over to my digs to warn me.'

'God's truth! That's terrible!'

Ashe looked around the office. 'I'd better get out of here,' he said. 'After my digs, this place is obviously the next one to be raided.'

'Where will you go?' Willie said, his eyes really troubled. Ashe's safety was vital.

'Oh, I'll find a spot under a hedge somewhere.'

'You'll do nothing of the sort.' Willie said, putting his hand into his pocket and digging out his latch key. 'Here, take this. It's the key to my digs.'

Ashe grabbed the key. 'Address?' he said with great urgency.

'Twenty Leonard Place,' Willie said. 'It's one of those artisan houses behind the church. A few of us are renting it. The owner is Mrs. Mulloy. Tell her I sent you.' Willie gave Ashe a collusive wink, 'She's one of us.'

'Gura mile mhait agat, Willie,' (thanks a million) Ashe said. Then pulled his cap well down over his eyes and headed for the street.

Willie called after him, 'I'll try to find Collins, but it could be like looking for a needle in a haystack. Meanwhile you lie low in my digs. Help yourself to anything in the way of food and drink. I'll drop in at lunch time. Hopefully by then I'll have run Collins to earth.'

When the three field workers arrived to collect their lists, Willie announced, 'You've a different job this morning.'

'Oh! We're not canvassing?' Tim a sixteen year old, asked, surprised.

'No, we have to find Collins in a hurry,' Willie tried not to make it sound too urgent. 'I'm stuck here on my own, so I'll have to ask you lads to do the needful and report back to me. You know all his haunts?'

'I only know one,' Dessie, the smartest of the group, said, gurgling at his own joke. 'Back room, Maguire's Pub.'

'One of you try Maguire's,' Willie said. 'If he's not there, maybe Maguire might know his movements. The rest of you scour the district.'

From the moment the three volunteers left, Willie couldn't concentrate on his work. His mind swirled with thoughts of Ashe. Here was a man who was leader of the North County Dublin volunteers during the Rising. He lead his command in an engagement with The Royal Irish Constabulary at Ashbourne, County Dublin, capturing four barracks and large quantities of arms and ammunition. After the surrender he was sentenced to death, but, like Dev, his sentence was commuted to penal servitude for life. He was released early 1917. Ashe was a powerful orator who at times got carried away in his speeches; these times the speeches were filled with venom and passion and invariably gave harrowing details of atrocities perpetrated by the British against the Irish over the centuries.

When it came to noon and none of the field volunteers had returned, Willie decided to take an early lunch. His first stop was Maguire's Pub. He decided by now the pub would have come alive with lunchtime customers. If Maguire had no knowledge of Collins, maybe a customer might.

'The very man!' Maguire, a tall, stooped-shouldered man in his sixties, hailed Willie from behind the counter.

'Oh!' Willie expressed surprise. Maguire beckoned to Willie to come to the far end of the counter where they could talk in private. After pushing his way through the dozen or so customers at the counter, Willie eventually came face to face with Maguire who wore a doleful expression.

'It's bad news, I'm afraid,' Maguire said in a low tone.

'Bad! How bad?'

'Word is that Thomas Ashe has been arrested,' Maguire said quietly, though the anger poured out of him.

'Where and when?' Willie asked mechanically. Though he had received a forewarning, it was still like a punch in the solar plexus.

'As far as I know,' Maguire said, 'he was picked up by the Constabulary a few hours ago near those artisan houses behind the church.'

'How did you find out?'

'Uh! The grapevine.'

'Any idea where Collins could possibly be?'

'He's not in town. That's for sure,' Maguire said. 'If he was, somehow or other he would have spirited Ashe out of harm's way.'

'Is Ashe at the local barracks, do you know?'

'No, apparently not; they've taken him to Dublin. They're wasting no time.' A customer called for a pint, bringing the conversation to an end. Before he left, Maguire asked Willie, 'Can I get you anthin?'

'Yes, a pint.' After serving the customer, Maguire arrived back with Willie's pint.

'You know something,' Maguire said, 'as the saying goes *It's many a time a man's mouth broke his nose*. Listening to Ashe's speeches, at times it seemed he went out of his way to antagonize the British, rubbing their noses in Republican shite.'

Willie had to laugh at Maguire's description. But then became serious, he said, 'Like Collins, Ashe feels very passionate about seeing Ireland as a republic. But unlike Collins he wears his heart on his sleeve.'

'Ach, I suppose, the most they can do is fine him.'

'I hope you're right,' Willie sighed.

There was a call for another drink which Maguire acknowledged saying, 'I'll be right with ye, sir.' Preparing to leave, Maguire put his finger to his lips and chose his words carefully, 'At times the likes of these, it's best to say nothing.' Then giving Willie a wink, 'No doubt Collins will sort it out.'

The following day, Collins arrived in a very black mood to see Willie. More than usual his language was laced with lots of *damns, bloodies and buggars,* which came as natural to him as saying 'God bless you.'

'I'll never bloody forgive myself for not being here yesterday to help Ashe,' he said to Willie. 'But after arguing for hours with that bugger, Cathal Brugha, above in Dublin, trying to establish the IRB's status and getting nowhere (I swear t'was like talking to a brick wall), I decided I needed a healthy distraction. So on my way to Kilkenny,' he grinned, mischievously, 'I did a bit of a detour as far as Roscommon and spent the night at my fiancée's place.'

Willie laughed. 'A bit of a detour!' he said, 'More like a round trip of Ireland.'

Collins laughed with him. 'I suppose you're right,' he said. 'But believe me, Willie, I needed the break.'

'Ashe seemed to think he was being made a scapegoat,' Willie said.

'Could well be,' Collins answered. Then with a momentary thwarted frown, added, 'It's me they're after, you know. God damn them!'

'But sure what can they charge him with?' Willie asked.

'That's just it,' Collins declared. 'They're just holding him without charging him. Willie, the fact that Sinn Fein is doing so well in these bye-elections has put the wind up them crosswise; they'd arrest a donkey if they thought he was baying in Irish. The curse of the seven blind bastards on them!'

Collins' language brought a smile to Willie's face. It was said about Collins that he swore so artistically people immediately forgot about the swearing and merely remembered the skill by which he did it. Willie was getting a taste of it now. Collins looked around the office, then asked Willie earnestly, 'How are you coping here, Willie? There doesn't seem to be anyone around but yourself?'

'I'm running a bit behind,' Willie said. 'And yes, I am short-handed; my assistant has influenza and will probably be out for the rest of the week. Thankfully, the weekend should bring reinforcements from Dublin and the provinces.'

'I'll organize some extra help for you now before I leave,' Collins said.

'Oh! You're leaving!'

'Yes, I'm going back to Dublin to see what I can do about Ashe,' Collins said.

'Be careful!' Willie said looking worried. 'For God's sake, don't you get yourself arrested.'

'Little fear of that,' Collins said. 'As you know, I don't flaunt politics in their faces. In fact, I don't think they've any idea what I look like.'

'Yeah. I've noticed you're very camera shy.'

'With a purpose,' Collins winked slyly. 'Maybe that's where Ashe and I differ. He makes no secret about his passion to see Ireland a republic.'

Right enough, an hour later help arrived for Willie in the form of Colm; a man in his forties, very much the patriot who was ready to roll up his sleeves and get on with the work.

Chapter XVIII

This morning, on her way to the Stock Room, Jane was feeling anything but secure. Since she started in the job she considered the Millinery Stock Room her private domain. But yesterday this all changed when two people, both males, invaded her privacy.

First there was the man in the morning. He was elderly. He seemed harmless. In fact, as he shuffled around opening and shutting hat boxes and tut-tutting to himself in frustration, Jane got the distinct impression he suffered from some form of dementia. Jane asked if she could help, but he ignored her and just slunk away muttering aspirations to the Sacred Heart and the Blessed Virgin to assist him in whatever duty he was trying to perform. Obviously, he was in the wrong sector of that vast store area and was totally muddled.

In the afternoon Percy arrived. She had seen Percy a couple of times strutting around the store like a peacock. He was a fellow in his late twenties, handsome in a sinewy sort of way, square, heavy shoulders, thick, muscular neck. Once, when she was on an afternoon tea break behind the counter, he passed by and looked at her with undisguised admiration.

'Who is he?' Jane asked Philomena.

'He's Percy, the Managing Director's son. Thinks he's cock of the walk; coasts through life on his charm and the family's name.'

'You seem to know a lot about him?'

'Like most of the young girls working in the store—particularly the new ones—he tried his charm on me. But there was nothing doing. I recognize a jerk when I see one. He's conceited and egotistical and a pain in the arse.'

So here he was, this pain in the arse, Percy, mooching around Jane's stock room, opening boxes, taking out hats, putting them back. Finally, he took one of the gaudiest hats imaginable out of one of the boxes then turned to Jane, who had her head firmly buried in her forms.

'Miss,' he said in a posh English accent, his eyes boring into Jane, 'would you mind trying on this hat?'

Anger at his presumption seethed behind the mask on Jane's face. 'Sorry,' she said, compressing her lips for an instant to swallow her anger. 'It's not my job to model hats.'

'Oh!' his eyes widened in mock surprise. 'Have you any idea who I am?'

'Yes, sir,' Jane answered sounding indifferent. 'You're the Managing Director's son. But I still don't model hats.'

He was thoughtful for a moment. 'Right,' he began tentatively, 'I suppose I shouldn't have asked, but you're so pretty, I thought you could do justice to this particular hat.'

'Sorry,' Jane said, mustering her best Sienna Convent accent, 'but your *plamass* won't work either.' She then added, 'If you don't mind me saying so, sir, you've no right to be down here in the first place.' She could see from his dark looks that her statement had ruffled his feathers.

'Excuse me, madam,' he said self righteously, 'but as the Managing Director's son, I've the right to go any place I choose in this building.'

'Sir,' Jane asserted indignantly, pulling herself up to her full height of five feet, six inches, 'I'm responsible for these hats. If anything is missing, I'm the one who must account for it.' She went on. 'That door is only open when I'm here. So except for the staff of the millinery department and myself, it's locked to everyone, including the Managing Director's son.'

'Point taken,' Percy said. Then added mockingly, 'Imagine it! The lady has brains as well as beauty.' He skulked towards the door. Then turned back, and as arrogant as you like, says, 'Would you fancy having dinner in with me in the Shelbourne some night?'

'My boyfriend would take a dim view.'

Percy slammed the door after him on his way out.

§

'What!' our Nancy spluttered at Jane. 'You actually turned down an invitation to dine in the Shelbourne?' Then brimming with bewilderment, she added, 'You need to have your head examined.'

Jane, Lily and our Nancy were as usual having breakfast together and Jane had just told them about yesterday's experience with Percy. 'Of course I turned him down,' Jane said. 'He's a jerk who's tried it on with every young girl in the store. He thinks he's God's gift to the full female staff.'

'The nerve of him asking you to model a hat for him,' Lily said indignantly. 'You did the right thing refusing, Jane. Smart Alexs like him need to be put in their place.'

'He is the Managing Director's son!' our Nancy painstakingly pointed out. 'If I thought he'd take me to the Shelbourne for dinner, I'd model anything for him.'

'Including underwear, I suppose,' Lily said with a sneer.

'If necessary.' Our Nancy tossed her beautifully coiffured head, scooped up the last of her porridge and stood up to leave. When she reached the door, she turned back. 'Did I tell you I ran into that fellow, Willie, yesterday on O'Connell Bridge?'

With that she was gone. Jane and Lily looked at each other through a telling silence. Eventually Lily broke the silence. 'Did you know he was in town?' she inquired of Jane.

'That's the first I heard of it.' Jane felt like she'd been hit by a thunderbolt. 'Of all people to meet him, it had to be her!' Jane said her eyes focused on the back of the door.

Lily pondered the question, then said with certainty, 'Ach, he's bound to drop into the store to see you sometime today.'

'I hope you're right,' Jane said. 'It just drives me crazy the way that Nancy wan can drop a bombshell like that and no one can challenge it or even ask a blooming question.'

For the rest of the day Jane was on tenterhooks. Arriving at the store that morning, the first thing she did was put Philomena in the picture and on alert. 'If anyone resembling a blond Viking should appear in the store today,' Jane told her, 'whether he asks for me or not, would you be an angel and come to the stockroom to appraise me?'

'Sure,' Philomena said, the mischief glinting in her eyes. 'A blond Viking! Now how could anyone miss that! My eyes will be scouring the store all day.'

As it turned out Willie didn't appear, so there was no need for Philomena to make the trip to the stockroom. When it came to six o'clock closing and there was no sign of Willie, Jane was quite depressed: she felt like a dark cloud was hovering over her.

At home, Lily, in the bedroom reluctantly trying on her new school uniform, was agog with curiosity when Jane arrived. 'Well, don't keep me in suspense,' she said. 'What transpired with Willie?'

'Nothing, absolutely nothing!' Jane said despondently. He didn't appear.

'Why don't you ask the Nancy wan straight out what he said to her yesterday,' Lily suggested.

'God no!' Jane said. 'You know exactly what would happen if that wan got wind of our relationship.'

'Of course,' Lily agreed. 'T'would become her business to sabotage it.' Lily was silent for a second. Then suddenly the answer came to her. 'Let me have a go at her,' she said.

At teatime that evening when the mother left Jane, Lily, Bridget and our Nancy behind in the kitchen, Lily brought up the subject of Willie. 'Did Willie mention anything about coming to Bridget's wedding when you met him yesterday?' she asked our Nancy offhandedly.

'No!' Our Nancy sounded quite shocked. 'Is he invited?'

Lily looked hard at Bridget. 'Did I hear you say something about Willie being on the wedding list?' she asked.

'Yes, he's been invited all right,' Bridget said in a voice that sounded a little shaky.

'Huh!' said our Nancy with smoldering eyes. 'Will someone please tell me why Willie's being invited and he's not even a relative?' Lily looked hard at Bridget.

'Oh! T'was Peter's idea,' Bridget said impatiently; then she stood up abruptly and made for the door. As far as she was concerned, this conversation was at an end.

As soon as Bridget left our Nancy got all fired up. 'I can't believe it!' she said. 'Despite the fact that a lot of our relatives were not invited because of the numbers, that Willie fella,' she accentuated his name, 'gets an invitation. What's so special about…?'

'He's only one person,' Lily interrupted her. 'If Bridget were to ask all the relatives, there wouldn't be a church big enough to hold them.'

Our Nancy thought for a second, then said, 'Does Mother know about Willie coming to the wedding?' Our Nancy was facing Lily and didn't see the look of horror spread over Jane's face as she wondered how Lily would answer this question.

Thankfully Lily had her wits about her. She realized that not only would she not get a word out of our Nancy about Willie, but she could be about to open a can of worms. There was only one way out and that was to change the subject. 'What do they charge for a 'permanent' at your hairdressing salon?' she asked our Nancy, threading her fingers through her short, stringy hair.

Now all ears, our Nancy asked, 'Why? Are you thinking of getting one?'

'I wouldn't be asking, if I wasn't.'

For a change, our Nancy seemed more than disposed to discuss the matter. 'Well,' she said, 'we have a cheap one and an expensive one.'

'How much?' Lily asked.

'The cheap one works out at half a crown, the expensive one, five shillings.

For once our Nancy's eyes reflected lively interest. 'Personally, I'd recommend the expensive one; it's not quite so frizzy. It takes two hours. Do you want me to book you in?'

'Yes,' Lily said, doing her best to sound enthusiastic. 'I suppose so.' She looked inquiringly at Jane.

At that moment, our Nancy's eyes were critically trained on Lily's hair, so Jane was able to furtively throw her eyes up to heaven and indicate to Lily, 'For God's sake! No!'

Lily then asked Jane straight out, 'What do you think, Jane?'

Jane studied Lily's hair thoughtfully. 'I don't know,' she said screwing up her face. 'I can't see you with frizzy hair.'

'Be honest, Jane, do you think my hair would be improved by a permanent?' Lily pretended to plead with Jane. It was ploy to play for time.

'I'd say better leave well alone,' Jane said positively. She had visions of Lily looking like a golliwog doll. In all seriousness she couldn't ask her sister to make such a sacrifice.

'You definitely think it wouldn't suit me, Jane?' Lily persisted, giving the impression that Jane's view was of the utmost importance.

Our Nancy butted in angrily. 'Oh, for God's sake! I wouldn't copy her!' she said stroking her own hair dotingly. 'Where her hair is concerned, she's stuck in a groove; same old mop, same old style.'

'I happen to like my hair the way it is,' Jane said passively.

'I'll think about it,' Lily said, knowing full well she'd no intention whatsoever of having it done. 'And let ye know by the weekend.'

'Well, if you want a Saturday appointment, you'd better make you mind up soon,' our Nancy said. 'Saturdays are extremely busy.'

§

As the train clickety-clacked southwards from Dublin to Kilkenny, Willie pondered on the last twelve hours. To say the least, those hours were the most frenzied and upsetting since joining the campaign machine in the Kilkenny bye-election. It all started early this morning when Collins breezed into the office and without as much as a by your leave, pitched Willie into sudden action.

'Willie,' he announced straight forwardly, 'You can forget about the work here, you're going to Dublin.'

'I am,' Willie said, his eyes jolting in his head with surprise. He wondered why he was surprised. Weren't quick, sudden, decisions standard practice for Collins? With tongue very much in cheek, he asked, 'When am I making this trip?'

'Now, immediately,' Collins said. 'It's all arranged. You're getting a lift in Eoin O'Brien's van.' Collins checked his watch. 'He'll call for you in an hour.'

Dubious, Willie asked, 'Why exactly am I going to Dublin?'

'You're going to visit Thomas Ashe in Mountjoy Prison,' Collins said. 'He asked to see you.' Then looking very grave, he continued. 'About this mission,' he said. 'It's very hush hush. So don't breathe a word to anyone in Dublin or anywhere else.'

'Why all the secrecy?' Willie asked.

'Because you could well be in danger,' Collins said. 'They've also arrested Austin Stack and Fionan Lynch.'

'Any idea why they're making these arrests?' Willie asked.

'Intimidation, I'd say,' Collins answered. 'They're obviously not happy about what's happening in the bye-elections.'

Willie looked at the mass of paper on his desk. 'What about the work I'm doing here?' he asked.

'I'll take over here for the day,' Collins said. 'We'll expect you back on the evening train.'

'It's just a flying visit then?' Willie said.

'Precisely.'

'Have you visited Ashe yourself lately?' Willie asked.

'Yesterday, very briefly,' Collins said. 'That's when he made the request to see you.'

'How is he?'

'Frustrated,' Collins made no effort to hide his exasperation. 'The bloody fools still haven't charged him. Worse still, he's being treated like a common criminal.' Collins stroked his brow in perturbation. 'Of course somebody may have leaked to the British authorities the fact that Ashe is very much involved with revising the Constitution of the IRB.'

'I thought that was strictly your territory,' Willie said.

'Well, secretly I'm doing most of the work, but because of the clash with Sinn Fein, Ashe and Dermot Lynch are giving me a hand, plus providing me with a front. Anyway,' Collins went on, 'about your visit. An arrangement has been made with Warden Styles in Mountjoy for Ashe's cousin,' he pointed a finger at Willie, 'that's you, Willie, to visit Ashe this afternoon.'

It was a fine morning except for the white and black clouds burdening the sky. Conscious of the secrecy of his mission, Willie elected to keep the conversation with Eoin O'Brien away from politics. But Eoin, a great chatterbox, talked incessantly about that very subject, with the result that Willie found himself telling him about his experiences in the G.P.O. during the sixteen rising.

Arriving in Dublin, Willie went straight to Mountjoy Prison. Unfortunately, Warden Styles was at lunch; it meant Willie had to come back later. What to do in the interim? One idea was to go into the city and see Jane. But then Willie remembered Collins warnings: 'Don't breathe a word to a soul; you could put yourself in danger.' Much as he'd relish seeing Jane, he decided it would be too risky. Collins' warning still rang in his ears. 'Your safety is all important, Willie. When you leave the prison, take every precaution against being followed by a G. Man, because spying around prisons, is their preferred territory. It's where they keep tabs on prisoners' visitors.' Then, as only he could put it, Collins added, 'Even if it means hopping on and off trams going in different directions, baffle the buggers any way you can.'

Willie found a small café round the corner from the prison. As he hungrily ate the thick vegetable soup and the hunks of brown soda bread and butter, he toyed with the idea of writing to Jane. But once again decided against it: inevitably she would expect an explanation about why he was in Dublin. He hated the subterfuge. But it couldn't be helped. Deviating from the rules could be the difference between being free and being locked up. Best do as Collins advised and contact no one. What she didn't know wouldn't worry her. But a nagging doubt twisted away at him all the same.

When he returned later to the prison, Warden Styles was back from lunch and available to escort him to Ashe's cell. Walking through Mountjoy prison brought back memories of the Stafford Prison. Except that this prison was like a tomb that had no knowledge of the brightness outside.

On seeing Willie, Ashe let out an exclamation of surprise. 'Goodness you're here already!' he said. Then with eyes that crinkled a welcome, he shook Willie's hand. As soon as Styles left them alone, Ashe asked, 'How did you get here so fast? T'was only yesterday I asked Collins if you could come to see me. I take it you're still working in Kilkenny?'

'Yeah, I am still working in Kilkenny. But you know Collins,' Willie chortled, 'he isn't one to waste time. First thing this morning he arranged a lift for me to Dublin. So here I am.'

'No sooner said than done,' Ashe added. 'The man never ceases to amaze me.'

Willie was shocked by Ashe's appearance. Never very robust, his face was horribly thin and gaunt and he looked so frail you could nearly blow him away. Willie asked, 'so what did you want to see me about?' Then before Ashe could answer, he added, 'First of all, let me say how terribly upset I was to hear about your incarceration.' Looking around the bareness and bleakness of the cell, he asked, sounding outraged, 'Have the authorities come up with any reason for this?'

'Only what they originally said, 'that my speeches were calculated to cause disaffection.'

'And you still haven't been officially charged?' Willie said.

For a while Ashe hesitated, then as if a switch went on, he said, 'No, and it doesn't look like they're going to charge me.' His voice sounded bitter. Looking Willie straight in the eye, he said, 'Willie, the reason I asked to see you was to tell you that I'm not going to put up with being treated like a common criminal any longer. If they won't give me and my comrades, Stack and Lynch, Prisoner of War status, we intend to go on hunger strike.' He hesitated, then continued. 'I didn't tell Collins yesterday because I knew he would try to talk me out of it.' Ashe held out his hands in a curiously supplicating gesture. 'Willie,' he said, 'I want you to break the news to Collins.'

'My God! You can't be serious?' Willie entreated. 'Look at the cut of you; you'd last no length on hunger strike.'

'Oh, I may not look it, but I'm really as fit as a fiddle.'

'Is there no way I can talk you out of this?' Willie importuned.

"Fraid not.' There was a tremble in Ashe's voice. 'I'm adamant.'

Willie pleaded, 'If you won't think about yourself, what about Collins and your comrades? Don't you realize how important you are to them? How much they depend on you? If anything happens to you, they'll be devastated.'

Ashe smiled and shook his head. 'There's a principal involved here, Willie,' he said, his face resolute and unflinching. 'It's just like Lewes Prison all over again. No,' he added, 'I'm adamant. I won't be talked out of it.' He then seemed to wander off in his mind. 'Collins once said to me, 'have you ever noticed, Tom, how much of the world's work can get accomplished by two fellows sitting quietly down in a quiet room having a quiet chat. But look at us; here we are being eaten alive by committees, interim reports and fact-finding missions and the rest of it, and we're getting no place fast." Ashe smiled languidly. 'There's a lot of logic in Collins' words, don't you think?'

'God!' Willie exploded, 'How I hate the bloody British!'

'Feelings of hate only succeed in clouding your judgment and dimming your resolve,' Ashe said with surprising mildness. 'Such feelings are a terrible waste of energy.'

Somebody rattled keys impatiently outside the cell door. It was Willie's cue to end the visit. Willie put his arms around Ashe. He was close to tears. 'God, Tom,' he said, 'don't go on hunger strike for the moment. I know Collins will move heaven and earth on the outside to get you out of here. Can you imagine his reaction when I tell him you intend to go on hunger strike?'

Ashe grinned broadly. 'I know he'll be breathing fire and spitting bullets,' he said, 'but it won't stop me doing what I think is right.'

Willie left the prison very much in a stupor. He hopped on to the first tram going into the city. His mind was in such turmoil over Ashe, he didn't give a single thought to his own safety, as directed by Collins, 'Make sure you're not being followed.'

When he alighted from the tram in Sackville Street, the sky was fifteen shades of gray and a light drizzle was coming down. To get to Westland Row Station, he had to cross over O'Connell Bridge and walk down D'Olier Street. As he stood in a queue waiting for the policeman on point duty to give the pedestrians the beck to cross, he was suddenly plunged into reality by the rough thrust of a hand on his shoulder. His immediate reaction was to think, God! It's a G. Man! I've been followed! Only when he heard the bark of delight and the rasp of female laughter did he relax and begin to turn round.

'As I live and breathe, if it isn't Willie McNamee!' The voice and the face belonged to Nancy O'Dwyer. Who, in turn was amazed by Willie's warm greeting. He actually shook her hand. Little did she realize his immense relief at finding that the heavy hand on his shoulder didn't belong to a G. Man.

Flirtation was written all over Nancy. 'We haven't seen you in months,' she said coquettishly. 'Where have you been hiding?'

'Oh!' Willie said, his breath expelling loudly with relief. 'At the moment I'm based down the country.' He realized if he were to get away quickly, he had to sound plausible. 'I'm in a terrible rush to catch the train at Westland Row Railway Station,' he apologized. He checked his watch. 'And I'm afraid I'm on the last minute.' Just then the policeman directed the pedestrians to cross. 'Forgive me if I don't dally,' he said, as he began to rush away, 'but trains don't wait for latecomers.' With that he tipped his hat to her and hurriedly disappeared into the crowd crossing the street.

Walking down D'Olier Street Willie shuddered thinking about the probing questions Nancy could have asked. After his traumatic experience at the prison he was in no condition to invent falsehoods to put her off. Now he'd have to think up an explanation for Jane.

As the train drew nearer to Limerick, Willie felt the weight of of the world on his shoulders at the thought of breaking the news about Ashe to Collins. How would Collins react? Meekly or like a volcano? How would he go about trying to resolve the problem? One way or the other, Collins would be desolate. Trouble was, the Kilkenny bye-election campaign was monopolizing an awful lot of his time presently, because Cosgrave in Kilkenny, was not proving as popular as DeValera in Clare.

Willie found himself thinking about Collins, the man. Collins knew himself—and he frequently mentioned it to his comrades—that he was a hard and exacting task master. Yes, a difficult man to work with in some moods. Ranting like a fishmonger's wife one minute, with outstretched hand and an apology five minutes later when his sense of justice erupted to reproach his outburst. A gallery of portraits of Collins, reconstructed from chance phrases and glimpses, presented themselves to Willie. Collins, the young schoolboy racing barefoot over road, hill and stream in Clonakilty. Collins, an alert and dashing figure on the hurling or football field. Collins, orating in the political clubs in London. Collins' experiences in the Counting Houses of London. The wanderer of sixteen years, athirst with an exile's dreams, plans, longings. Stirred to the depths by the dream of Ireland free; which, Collins himself contended, was never so dear to the Irish as when they were living in a foreign country.

Then after Frongoch came the restlessness: a curious power seemed to emanate from him. By some inborn genius he had gone onward to form his electioneering machine, which proved so successful in the past three bye-elections and promised to do the same in the next. Where would Ireland be without him? Cosgrave went on to win the election by 722 votes against his opponents 392, gaining another foothold for Sinn Fein in the fortunes of the country. Coupled with this victory was the decision of Laurence Ginnell, an Irish Parliamentary Party MP, to refrain from attending Westminster. His decision was of supreme importance. It was almost unthinkable that a member of the supposedly powerful IPP should refuse—along with the newly elected *rebels*—to attend Westminster. But it seemed that Ginell's voice was the only dissenting one raised in the Westminster Parliament against the executions of the Easter Rising leaders. It now seemed that the days of the IPP were numbered.

§

'The Catering people in the Gresham Hotel are pressing me to let them have the final numbers for the wedding reception,' Bridget told Jane when they were on their own at teatime one evening in August. 'Are you sure Willie's coming?'

'The last I heard he was coming,' Jane said in a flat voice. 'According to his letters he should be back in Dublin by the end of the month.'

'Did you ever find out what he was doing in Dublin last week?'

'No,' Jane said. She had that worried look she'd been carrying around all week. Bridget traced it back to the day when our Nancy announced she'd met Willie on O'Connell Bridge.

'Have you had a letter from him recently?' Bridget inquired.

'Yes, I had one the other day in which he said that due to pressure of work, it had to be brief.' Jane looked particularly agitated. 'Oh, he's in good form, but there wasn't a mention about his latest trip to Dublin. I can't understand it; normally Willie is open and frank about things like that.'

Bridget could see that Jane was uncomfortable discussing the matter so she changed the subject. 'Did you have the second fitting for your bridesmaid's dress?' she asked.

'I did,' Jane answered. 'But our Nancy hasn't even had her first fitting. And the dressmaker is worried that the dress won't be ready in time.'

Bridget made a distasteful face. Ruffled, she said, 'I'm sick and tired of reminding that wan about going to the dressmaker.'

Just then the person in question entered the kitchen.

'Our Nancy!' Bridget assailed her, 'if you want to be my bridesmaid you'd better get yourself to the dressmaker as quickly as possible.'

'Ach, I've tried on numerous occasions to make it, but there's always something cropping up to stop me,' Our Nancy said indifferently as she filled a plate from the pots on the stove.

'Where there's a will there's a way,' Bridget barked at her.

As she said these words, Mary arrived. 'Are you two having a row?' she asked.

'No, not a row,' Bridget answered. 'I'm just trying to drive home to our Nancy that if she wants to be my bridesmaid she'd better get herself to the dressmaker immediately. She's missed all her appointments.'

'Talking about the wedding,' Mary interjected. 'I know you've invited only Sean and Siobain from that family, but I'm having second thoughts about inviting the parents—Aunt Maggie and Uncle Tom.' When she saw Bridget's look of disinclination, she hurriedly added, 'After all, the O'Dwyer Family Dairy might not be enjoying the success it is were it not for their champion milk.'

'Mother!' Bridget exclaimed, 'I thought we were in agreement about inviting only two members from each of the relatives' families. If we make an exception in their case, there could be ructions with the other aunts and uncles who weren't invited.'

'What about Willie McNamee?' our Nancy interrupted, sounding particularly churlish. 'He's not even a relative and he's been invited?'

The question seemed to shatter Bridget; it was like being caught with her hand in the till.

Before she had time to answer, Mary butted in. 'Who is this Willie person anyway?' she asked, with eyebrows raised inquisitively.

'Oh, he's a friend of Peter's,' Bridget tried nonchalance.

Now feeling extremely self-conscious, Jane left the room.

'Why this Willie person?' Mary asked. 'After all, it's your wedding, not Peter's.'

'Yes, I know, it's mine and Michael's!' Bridget hissed with unexpected rancor. 'So it should be our decision.' She paused, misgiving flooded her face; she realized she may have gone too far, but then decided to brazen it out, 'Anyway Willie's been invited, so we can't un-invite him.'

'I wish you had consulted me first,' Mary said impatiently. 'For days now I've been asking to see that final list.'

'Mother we went over that list a dozen times before I sent the invitations out. And you were in total agreement with it.'

'Yes,' Mary said, 'but now I find out you're inviting people we didn't even discuss.'

'I know,' Bridget said, getting even more edgy. 'But surely as it's Michael's and my wedding, it's our prerogative to invite a few of our own young friends.' Bridget stood up and started to leave. She felt she'd explode if she had to listen to any more of this nonsense.

As she reached the door, Mary said irately, 'It may be your wedding, but just remember who's picking up the bill.'

Mary's parting shot really stung Bridget. She thought, will I ever be allowed to forget it? And anyway, t'was Mother's idea, not mine, to have a big, swanky wedding. It's pride on her part, of course, (though she'd be the last one to admit it.) She's determined to demonstrate that she can put on as good a show for my wedding as Nancy Pete's parents did for hers. As far as Michael and I are concerned, we'd settle for a small wedding with just the two families, followed by a breakfast in a small hotel. Instead, here I am saddled with this big, splashy, white wedding, complete with bridesmaids, Eileen, a flower girl, men in tails, a three-tier wedding cake and, for good measure, a big reception in the Gresham Hotel after the ceremony.

During the early days of preparation there were so many arguments with her mother about who should and should not be invited; her mother constantly arguing that they didn't want to hurt anyone's feelings. Such a lot of twaddle! There were times when Bridget felt like screaming. Now she was counting the hours 'till it was all over.

On her way back to the shop she ran into Jane who looked at her with anxious eyes. 'Gosh! I'm so sorry, Bridget!' she said. 'I seem to have dropped you in it with a vengeance.'

'Don't worry about it, Jane,' Bridget said soothingly, 'it's just that Nancy wan rattling my cage, trying to get her own back because I refused to invite her latest beau, Claude, the hairdresser — who'll probably last a month because she changes boyfriends as regularly as she changes her stockings.'

'I sincerely hope Mother and Peter don't come into contact between this and the wedding,' Jane said, sounding overwrought. 'If they meet and Mother brings up the subject of Willie coming to the wedding the cat could be well and truly out of the bag.'

Bridget dropped her voice to a whisper. 'Jane,' she said sounding unusually solemn, 'I have a confession. I've already told Peter that you and Willie are secretly walking out. And, the story is that I've invited Willie to the wedding as *his* friend.'

'Good Lord!' Jane expostulated, 'Why did you do that?' she said, with big, anxious eyes.

'Ach,' Bridget uttered impatiently, 'last week after Lily blew the gaff to our Nancy about Willie's invitation, I had to do something about it.'

Jane felt like a bucket of water had been thrown over her. 'Peter's bound to tell Nancy Pete,' she said sounding desperate. 'Then it'll all come out.'

'I swore him to secrecy,' Bridget said. 'I'm sure he won't breathe a word of it to Nancy Pete or anyone else.' Then smiling a stalwart and supportive smile, she added, 'strange as it seems, Peter has been known to do the right thing and use discretion when necessary.'

'Did you speak to him personally?'

'No, unfortunately when I called to the Independent Office, he was out,' Bridget said. 'I just left a note, marked private and confidential, in a sealed envelope addressed to him. I purposely delivered the note to his office to make sure that Nancy Pete wouldn't know of its existence. So now you can put your mind at rest.'

Jane crossed her fingers. 'Please God, he'll do the right thing and keep it to himself,?' she bleated. 'I don't want Mother to hear about Willie and my relationship from the wrong source.'

'Stop bidding the devil good morrow,' Bridget said. 'It may never happen.'

Chapter XIX

The news of Ashe's sudden death in September rocked the nation. Reports in the newspapers said he died in circumstances of extreme cruelty and misery: having gone on full hunger strike, on the fifth day he was removed to the Mater Hospital and died a few hours later. At the inquest the coroner's jury came out with a direct verdict laying the whole of the blame on the Dublin Castle authority. The bed, bedding and the boots belonging to the prisoner had been taken away from him. He had been left lying on the cold floor of his cell for more than fifty hours. Following which cruelty, an assistant doctor, without previous experience, had attempted forcible feeding. The jury went on to say, 'We censure the Castle authorities for not acting more promptly, especially when the grave condition of the deceased was brought to their attention the previous Saturday by the Lord Mayor of Dublin and Sir John Irwin (whose visits were arranged by Collins).

Many thousands of people visited the Mater Hospital where Ashe's body, clad in the volunteer uniform, lay in state. His funeral was a demonstration of public mourning. At the funeral mass, among the speakers a devastated Collins spoke this eulogy:

'The character of Ashe was one of faith and endeavor and a will to do things in a quiet and unassuming way. He was a former National School teacher, a poet and a singer of ballads and a fine speaker of his native tongue. In the Easter Rising he commanded a detachment at Ashbourne and personally distinguished himself in the fighting there. With DeValera and others, he was a prisoner in Lewes Jail. Ashe later often clashed on points of opinion with his former leader, especially in regard to the IRB, on whose councils he was a force of some consequence. He will be sadly missed.'

Collins turned Ashe's funeral into a great national demonstration with volunteers in uniform and rifles reversed flanking the coffin, among them was a very sad Willie, clad also in uniform. Later Willie was privileged to be a pallbearer. Another 9,000 volunteers followed the funeral procession through the crowded streets of Dublin, together with more than 30,000 mourners. A volley was fired over Ashe' grave in the cemetery and Collins, standing by in uniform, delivered a very brief graveside oration.

'That volley which we have just heard is the only speech which it is proper to make over the grave of a dead Fenian.'

The night before Ashe's funeral, distracted about the circumstances of his death, Willie insisted on keeping the vigil flanking Ashe's casket throughout the night. Though a rota was arranged with replacement soldiers arriving on the hour, he was determined not to be relieved. Having failed to talk Ashe out of going on hunger strike, Willie felt the least he could do was pay his friend this last tribute and be there for him. In anticipation of the vigil and the pall bearing, he told Jane at their brief meeting yesterday that it was very doubtful he would be able to get to the wedding. Having to dash over to see Collins to receive his final orders about the funeral and be outfitted in a uniform, he had no option but to leave her in a hurry. When he arrived in Collins' office he was amazed to see the toll Ashe's death had taken on him.

Despite his grief, however, Collins had all the arrangements made and as he said himself, 'Everything's under control.'

During the night as Willie stood to attention beside the casket he could still see Jane's face; her disappointment about him not attending the wedding was so huge she couldn't hide it.

'Not even after the funeral?' she asked in a small voice.

'Well, being up all night,' Willie said, 'I doubt I'd be fit company for anyone or anything, much less a wedding.' He took her hand in his. 'Jane,' he said mournfully, 'Ashe was my good friend; I have to do this.'

Willie's face was so sad, Jane longed to put her arms around him, to soothe him and to kiss him. She wanted to blurt out her love and her longing for him and to hell with the consequences. But being in a public place — their retreat — forced her to curb those feelings.

Instead, she smiled bravely, squeezed his hand and said, 'Dear Willie, I'm so terribly sorry your friend died in such a sickening manner. It's horrible for you.'

After his return from Kilkenny when Ashe's hunger strike was public news, Willie was free to tell Jane the details of his mysterious visit to Dublin in August. Afterwards, Jane admitted to Lily and Bridget that she felt a right eejit being so worried at the time. Still, the way the whole business was shrouded in mystery, could anyone blame her? Meanwhile, she felt drained and empty at the thought of Willie not being at the wedding. Now those marvelous plans to introduce him to her mother would have to be shelved indefinitely.

§

It was ironical that Bridget's wedding should be the same day as Thomas Ashe's funeral. Around the time that half the city of Dublin was attending this funeral, Bridget and Michael were above in Dominick Street Church exchanging marriage vows. Uppermost in Bridget's mind were offerings of thanksgiving to the Lord that through His mercy she had somehow managed to overcome the many obstacles encountered in the run-up to this special day. Particularly the last minute one, yesterday, when Peter sent word that, due to Ashe's funeral he wouldn't be able to walk her down the aisle, nor would he be present for the ceremony. However, he pledged to be at the reception later on. For Bridget, this was just about the last straw. The girls (Bridget, Jane and Lily) deliberated for hours trying to think of someone who could stand in for Peter. Until lunchtime, when Mary joined them and automatically came up with the solution.

'Why don't we ask Uncle Tom?' she said. 'Himself and Aunt Maggie are guests in the Gresham Hotel for the two nights — tonight and tomorrow night.'

This then was how Uncle Tom came to be giving Bridget away. He stepped into the breach at the last minute. Bridge now realized how grateful she should be to her mother for sticking to her guns about inviting the aunt and the uncle. Short of asking Taigh, the Publican down the street, to come to the rescue, Uncle Tom was their best bet.

Peter's absence, however, presented the O'Dwyer family with another problem; namely, Nancy Pete. Left without an escort, she took the only way out she knew; it would now be the responsibility of the O'Dwyer family to escort her to the wedding. On the morning of the wedding, when prenuptial pandemonium reigned in the O'Dwyer household, Nancy Pete, ripely pregnant with her second baby, arrived by cab at their door.

Every bedroom in the house was alive with activity as the O'Dwyer family dressed in their special clothes. Bridget was in Mary's bedroom about to get into her white satin wedding dress. Our Nancy—with Bridget's room all to herself—was about to don her blue taffeta bridesmaid's dress and coronet of forget-me-nots. Jane, already dressed in matching bridesmaid's dress, was in Eileen's bedroom along with Lily, both lending Eileen a hand with her dressing as a flower girl. Eileen's dress was also white satin, layered and frilly. On her head she wore a coronet made from the same material. Last, but not least, Mary, helping Bridget with her dressing, was in her housecoat ready to slip into her smart navy suit and fashionable cloche hat with the cluster of artificial flowers and ribbons at its side.

On Nancy Pete's heels came Uncle Tom and Aunt Maggie. Charmaine, totally confused, put them all in the parlor. She thought, wasn't it very peculiar that visitors would intrude on the family and they trying to get dressed for the wedding. Besides no one told her about visitors coming at this hour of the day. Maybe later, but not now. In a panic she rushed upstairs and knocked on Mary's bedroom door. Mary opened the door giving her a chance to glimpse the bride in all her glory.

'We have visitors downstairs, Mam,' Chaimaine announced.

'Who are they?'

'Mrs. Peter O'Dwyer and an elderly couple who said they were your aunt and uncle.'

Mary checked her watch. 'Goodness!' she exclaimed. 'They're here much too early; they're not expected for at least another three-quarters of a hour.'

'I put them in the parlor, Mam,' Charmaine said. Then went into raptures about how gorgeous Bridget looked in her bridal dress. 'You look a dream!' she said to Bridget through the door. 'Wonderful, beautiful, fantastic.' She ran out of superlatives.

'Thanks, Charmaine,' Bridget accepted the compliments graciously.

Mary said to Charmaine, 'While I'm finding a member of the family to go down and entertain our guests, would you be good enough to make a cup of tea for them?'

'Certainly, Mam.'

As Lily was the only one not wearing dressy clothes, Mary decided she would be the right person to entertain the guests.

She found Lily with Jane in Eileen's bedroom helping to put the finishing touches to Eileen's dressing. Lucky for them she didn't arrive minutes earlier; she'd have witnessed the girls rouging their cheeks and lips with strips of red wallpaper.

Mary addressed Lily, 'Lily, for God's sake, will you go downstairs and entertain Nancy Pete, Uncle Tom and Aunt Maggie. Though they're here much too early, we can't very well ignore them. Particularly as Uncle Tom is doing the needful.'

'Why me?' Lily asked.

'You're the only one who's ready. Also, you're the only one, apart from myself, who's not wearing dressy clothes.'

Right enough, like her mother, Lily wore a simple, tailored beige suit. Her hat, however, made up for the plainness of the suit. Made of ostrich feathers, it couldn't be more flattering, highlighting as it did the gold specks in her eyes. Mary looked approvingly at Lily; she couldn't remember when she last saw her looking so smart. 'Oh, your outfit is really elegant,' she said effusively.

'Coming from you that's high praise indeed,' Lily said, appreciatively, 'but it doesn't take the sting out of having to contend with those difficult guests downstairs.'

'Stop making a fuss,' Mary sounded aggravated. 'I'd do it myself only I'm the mother of the bride. As such I'd like to spend these last minutes with Bridget.' She paused. 'Is that asking too much?'

'All right, all right, I'll do it!'

Sitting in the parlor drinking tea supplied by Charmaine, Uncle Tom, Aunt Maggie and Nancy Pete made small talk.

'Let me guess,' Nancy Pete said in her precisely modulated voice, looking pointedly at Uncle Tom and Aunt Maggie, 'you're from the country?'

'How'd ye guess?' Uncle Tom asked.

'Your clothes,' Nancy Pete said.

'What's wrong with our clothes?' Aunt Maggie sounded off aggressively.

'Oh, nothing!' Nancy Pete said, putting a cigarette into a long cigarette holder and lighting up. 'It's just that country clothes are never as smart as city ones; they stand out like sore thumbs in most gatherings.' Taking a puff of the cigarette, she indicated her own outfit — shapeless layers of purple georgette. 'I bought this outfit in Switzers of Grafton Street,' she said pompously.

'Well, unfortunately we don't have a Switzers in the County Meath,' Maggie said robustly. Whereupon, as Nancy Pete puffed rings of smoke in the air, Maggie scowled at her. Pointing to her distended stomach, she barked, 'In the name of God, how do you think that baby can survive and you smoking that cigarette?'

'Oh, I only smoke when I'm stressed.'

'And what, may I ask, have you to be stressed about?'

'My husband!' Nancy Pete indulged in some bosom stroking. 'He abandoned me for some patriot's funeral. Left me to fend for myself. And I in this condition.'

Lily arrived. She detected tension in the room. Well, she thought, put two ratty people like Nancy Pete and Aunt Maggie in close proximity, what can you expect?

Clapping her hands gleefully and saying, 'Well, here we are at last all set for the big day!' She was endeavoring to bring lightness to the room. But the statement was met with silence. Noticing the cups and saucers in their hands, Lily continued the liveliness. 'I see Charmaine has been looking after you?'

Responses were wry smiles and nodding heads. Then as an afterthought, Lily asked, 'Would any of you like something to eat?'

'Oh, no! Not at all!' Uncle Tom hastened to say. 'We had a huge breakfast in the Gresham Hotel this morning.'

'Isn't it well for some people!' Nancy Pete said derisively. Up to this Nancy Pete had been scrutinizing Lily from head to toe. 'Nice hat!' she said.

'Thanks,' Lily muttered.

Nancy Pete's critical study of Lily continued. 'But I'm not sure about the suit,' she said.

'Jesus, Christ!' Lily exclaimed. (At which Aunt Maggie crossed herself.) 'It cost enough! What the hell is wrong with it?'

'Not your color.'

'But of course,' Lily said, peeved. 'I forgot. When it comes to fashion, you're a bloody expert.'

'Well,' Nancy Pete said after more breast stroking, 'I'm in the theater business, remember. If I can't recognize bad taste, who can?'

'You mean to say all those awful Salome style layers you drape yourself in are considered high fashion?'

'Yes, anyone in the Abbey Theater will tell you that I'm considered one of their best dressers.'

'Well, if that's the case,' Lily spat the words at Nancy Pete, 'their taste, like yours, is in their bloody mouths.' With that she left the room abruptly.

For a change, Nancy Pete looked stunned. Outside the door, Lily ran into Charmaine coming in with a plateful of sandwiches. Charmaine had obviously heard part of the conversation.

'Don't mind her,' she said to Lily as loud as she could, 'you look gorgeous.'

Aunt Maggie, smiled slyly at her husband, showing her appreciation of Charmaine's comments.

§

After Ashe's casket was lowered into the grave, despite the sunshine, a heavy cloud of sadness hung over the vast gathering. People talked in hushed tones. It was clear that powerful feelings were stirring. Willie, his face contorted with the pain of his loss and tears scalding his eyes, decided he needed to be alone with his grief. He broke away from the group surrounding him, which included Collins, Dev, Brugha and some other well-known patriots, along with the pallbearers. As he pushed his way through the throngs of mourners, heading for the entrance, Peter O'Dwyer caught up with him. He was wearing a long trench coat over his morning suit.

'You seem to be in a desperate hurry to get away?' he panted. 'I suppose you're heading home to get into your glad rags?'

Willie hastily dashed the tears away. 'What do you mean get into my *glad rags?*' he asked, incomprehension glazing his eyes.

'You know, for the wedding?' Peter answered.

'What wedding?'

'Bridget's, of course; it's on today,' Peter said. 'I believe you were invited.'

'Who told you?' Willie asked brusquely.

'Bridget. She told me the whole yarn about the big secret,' Peter smiled conspiratorially. 'You know about you being invited to the wedding as my friend so as to pull the wool over the mother's eyes.'

Willie looked nonplussed. 'Does Jane know that your know?' he asked. 'She was so insistent on—'

'Yes,' Peter interjected, 'she knows. My understanding is your presence at Bridget's wedding is to hoodwink the mother into thinking that it was on this occasion that you and Jane first became attracted to each other.' Peter laughed. But when he saw Willie wasn't joining him in the laughter, he began to have doubts. 'Do I have it right?' he asked, puzzled. 'Or is this cockeyed story something you're hearing for the first time?'

Willie's face split into a grin. 'As it happens, you do have it right,' he said. 'But I told Jane that due to Ashe's funeral arrangements, I wouldn't be coming to the wedding.'

'Ach, never mind that. Come on!' Peter said. 'We both need cheering up; why don't we make tracks to the Gresham Hotel and partake of some of that hearty cheer?'

'I don't know that I can do that,' Willie said reluctantly. 'After that all-night vigil, the only thing I'm fit for is bed.'

'Where you'll toss and turn thinking about Ashe and all the things that might have been done to prevent his tragedy.' Willie was silent. 'Come on, Willie, more than ever now you need a distraction,' Peter pressured him. 'Don't you realize that a certain party would be thrilled to see you?' He grinned waggishly.

Willie wavered. 'But I'm not dressed properly,' he demurred. 'I'd be very conspicuous in this uniform.'

'That uniform could serve as a reminder about what went down today to all those smug, fence-sitters at the wedding.' Peter said sagely. 'All the more reason to wear it.'

Willie was still indecisive. He opened his mouth to speak, changed his mind, swallowed hard and then said, 'I just don't know.'

§

Sitting between Father Sebastian, who never stopped talking and Brother Anthony, who never opened his mouth, Jane found it difficult to appear interested in what the priest was telling her about his experiences as a missionary in Africa. Her mind was a mile away thinking about Willie. How distraught he was telling her the details of Ashe's tragedy! His shoulders seemed to sag with the weight of it. He was full of guilt, taking a lot of the blame for not doing more to save his friend. Though she was convinced the day would be more enjoyable with him there, since Jody's tragic death, Jane had come to accept that one should never take things for granted; what seemed safe and permanent could be taken away in an instant. Fate could be so cruel at times. Father Sebastian prattled away as he eat. Once in a while Jane caught bits of his conversation.

'Of course there was only one solution,' he was saying at the moment, 'my mosquito net would have to serve as the child's communion veil. Which meant I was left without a mosquito net for weeks.' A trickle of laughter from him, which Jane was hard pressed to join in. 'Well,' he continued, 'it took such a long time to get my new net, the mosquitoes had a whale of a time making a meal of me at nighttime.' He guffawed loudly.

Mary on the other side, listening intently, laughed with him. Jane was glad that someone appreciated this man's brilliant mind. In her case, she was thankful to be sitting at his side rather than in front of him. That way he couldn't see her glazed, apathetic eyes that showed a mind that was decidedly not in synch with what he was saying. Her mind now drifted back to the bad experience she had in the store last week when she approached 'the bull' to get the day off for the wedding. To her astonishment, the bull refused to let her off.

'As you well know,' she said, looking furious, 'Saturdays are our busiest days. We can't possibly spare you.'

Philomena, bless her heart! piped up supporting her. 'But Miss Bullingsworth,' she said brightly, 'I could easily do double duty.'

Nonetheless, the bull would have none of it. 'She's here barely two months,' she said flatly, 'and already she's looking for days off. It's completely out of the question.'

'But it's my sister's wedding,' Jane protested.

'I don't care who's wedding it is,' the bull said now in a flurry of agitation. 'You can't have the day off.'

Later during the tea break, when the bull was away at a meeting, Kathleen said to Jane, 'You shouldn't have said a word about the wedding.'

'What else could I say?' Jane asked.

'Just call in sick,' Kathleen said.

'But that would've been dishonest.'

'Well,' Kathleen laughed, 'it now looks like the only way you'll get to your sister's wedding is by being dishonest.'

'You mean, take sick leave?'

'Just that,' Kathleen answered. 'The bull won't be able to do anything about it; she'll just have to accept it. Of course,' she added, 'you'll be docked a day's pay.'

So that was how Jane managed to get to the wedding. That morning she sent Eileen around to the store to say that her sister, Jane, was sick and wouldn't be able to come in today. More lies. Would they ever stop? Now she would have to face the blazing bull's wrath on Monday morning. She certainly wasn't looking forward to that. Ach, she thought, no use brooding on it. Best put it aside for now. This is a day to celebrate.

Suddenly Brother Anthony, on the other side, touched Jane's arm, jerking her back to reality. 'Could I trouble you to pass me the salt?' he asked timidly. They were having the soup course.

'Certainly,' Jane said, passing the salt. Then she began to feel guilty about not making an effort to talk to him. He appeared so shy and diffident. But, try as she might, conversation with him was so stilted, it was like pulling teeth.

Meanwhile, Father Sebastian thankfully turned his full attention to Mary, on his other side. This relieved Jane of the burden of trying to concentrate on what he was saying. Jane saw Peter coming through the entrance at the other end of the Banqueting Hall. He was followed by a soldier in uniform, too far away for Jane to recognize. Nancy Pete, very visible in her purple, sitting at the long table the furthermost end of the room beckoned furiously to Peter to come and sit in the place she'd reserved for him beside her. Peter indicated he had to do something about finding a place for his soldier friend. He left the room. In his absence Nancy Pete greeted the soldier cordially and appeared to talk to him like they were old friends. After a while Peter arrived back with the Head Waiter. After shuffling chairs around and asking guests to tighten up their seats, the Head Waiter finally succeeded in making a place at the table , for the soldier between Peter and Nancy Pete.

The next thing Jane saw was Lily, seated further down the table, among the country cousins, jump up and dash towards the top table. Excitement was written all over her. Scrambling on to the dais which held the top table, she wended her way to where Jane was sitting.

'Jaysus!' she exploded excitedly behind Jane. Then stopped dead when she saw Father Sebastian bless himself and say, 'blessed be His holy name!' Turning to the Father with a face that was brick color, she apologized, saying, 'savin your presence Father. ' Then leaning over Jane she whispered, 'Did you see who came in with Peter?'

'Not Willie?' Jane whispered back. It was beyond belief.

'Yes, Willie!' Lily said. 'He's in the uniform.'

'Oh, my God!' Jane put her hand to her mouth to stifle the exclamation. She tried to calm her racing heart. 'What should I do?' she whispered.

'Well, when the meal and the speeches are over,' Lily said with practicality, 'you'll be expected to socialize among the guests.' Lily then turned on her heel and made tracks back to her own table.

After Lily left Jane forgot about her frustrations. She felt alive again. Father Sebastian couldn't help noticing a big change in Jane after the blasphemous sister left. Suddenly, she was full of exuberant conversation: she sounded silly and lighthearted, laughing heartily at his anecdotes, which to his mind, weren't all that funny. He decided it must've been some very good news the sister imparted to bring about such a change in the child.

The full length of the long banqueting room stood between Jane and Willie. So Willie couldn't see Jane's face clearly. As soon as he was seated, Peter passed a bottle of wine to him. 'Drink up, Willie,' he said. 'T'will help to dull the pain.'

From then onwards, Nancy Pete saw to it that Willie's glass was never empty. Every few minutes she topped it up till eventually he lost count of the number of glasses of wine he'd imbibed. Gradually the feelings of exhaustion and guilt that he came in with, dissipated. Much to his surprise he was enjoying himself. In fact, he was glad that Peter had ignored his expostulations at the cemetery and insisted on him accompanying him to the wedding.

With the wine flowing so freely, Willie became cautiously confident and began answering questions about his uniform. 'No,' he informed people who inquired, 'I'm not in the British Army.' And went on to explain that he was with the Irish Volunteers and had been a pallbearer that day for Thomas Ashe, the patriot who died so tragically last week in Mountjoy prison. Some guests found Willie quite interesting; his charm lay partly in a hesitant smile that was both shy and slightly melancholy. Other guests shrugged him off as a subversive.

After the cutting of the cake and the serving of a portion to each guest, the speeches commenced. The best man got the ball rolling by standing up and ringing a little bell to get everyone's attention. As soon as there was silence, he said, 'Ladies and gentlemen, it's now my very pleasant duty to propose a toast to the newlyweds. But first I'd like to say a few words about the groom who's been my friend since the first class.' He then went on to sing Michael's praises; artfully describing funny incidents he shared with Michael when they were schoolboys and later as young men. Nothing very egregious; just lots of amusing, boyish pranks which evoked lots of laughter. His speech was short and complimentary, his point being that, in marrying Michael, Bridget was getting herself a treasure. He ended by saying, 'I'll ask you all now to stand and raise your glasses (filled with champagne, I hope) and toast the newlyweds.'

All, except the couple stood and raised their glasses saying, 'To the newlyweds.'

After everyone resumed their seats, the best man turned to Father Sebastian and said, 'Now, I'd like to ask Michael's brother, Father Sebastian, to say a few words.'

Father Sebastian stood up. After raising his glass in another toast to the couple, he said, 'I pray that God will shower every grace and blessing on this union.' After this the good Father got carried away telling stories about his life as a missionary in Africa.

Peter whispered to Willie across Nancy Pete's chest, 'He's trying to proselytize all the non-Catholics present to the faith.' Willie nodded. He wondered how much longer he'd have to wait till he could lay eyes on his lovely Jane. Father's Sebastian's speech lasted a good thirty minutes. As soon as he finished, the best man called on the reverend Father Vincent — uncle of the bride — to say a few words.

Father Vincent stood up. He too seemed to think he was in the pulpit. He opened his speech by reminding everyone in the room that this was the Feast Day of Saint Francis. Then went on to extol the virtues of the saint.

'Saint Francis,' he said, 'was a holy man. He had no interest in riches. He lived in grinding poverty. When he could, he helped the poor. His life was dedicated to doing good works. He was probably one of the most unselfish saints that ever lived.'

Jane thought, with all this religion we might as well be in a church and not at a wedding reception. Of course, this was why her mother revered Father Vincent: at this moment the poor man could think of nothing else but to hold Saint Francis up as a model of how people should live their lives.

Last year during the time they had all that trouble with Jody dying and Peter arrested, Jane overheard the father say to her mother, *'Always remember, Mary, whom God loves, he persecutes.'*

At the time, Jane was sorely tempted to answer, 'I wish to God he didn't love our family so much.'

As Father Vincent rambled on and on about Saint Francis, Sister Oonagh, sitting between him and her mother — keeping her informed about what the good father was saying — finally pulled on his sleeve and got his attention. She nodded her head in the direction of the newlyweds, which reminded him that his speech should be about them and not about Saint Francis.

Father Vincent was quick on the uptake. After hemming and hawing and clearing his throat, he said, 'Of course, this day belongs to Michael and Bridget. I want to wish them every happiness.' Then he added, 'At the same time, I hope they will remember that their blessed union took place on the feast day of Saint Francis. If they model their lives on his, their happiness will be assured.'

Jane thought, thank God for Sister Oonagh's pragmatism. Were it not for her, father Vincent could have gone on for days. These speeches were much too long. How she wished she was sitting beside Willie. It was so frustrating looking at him from such a distance.

Father Vincent sat down. Except for Mary, who preened with pride listening to the mellifluous tones of her saintly brother, the room gave a collective sigh of relief when he finished. Gradually the stilled voices of the guests found themselves and the room erupted into a strident buzz.

Leaning across Nancy Pete, Peter said to Willie, 'These long-winded speeches should excuse us all from going to Mass tomorrow.'

'I thought the speeches were very interesting,' Nancy Pete patronizingly put in. 'But then, Peter, you have no soul.'

'I do have a soul,' Peter said, 'but if I were to say their speeches were great, you'd say they were terrible just to be contrary.'

'You know very well, Peter, I admire intelligence,' Nancy Pete said pompously. She pointed to her heart. 'The trouble with you is, you have no feelings in here.'

'God!' Peter retorted angrily. 'You have the audacity to talk about feelings when all you ever do is hurt peoples' feelings.'

Willie was glad when the best man stood up again and rang his little bell. It interrupted the row now taking place between Peter and his wife, across his chest. Both were obviously the worst for wear from imbibing too much wine which was undoubtedly due to all the long-winded speeches.

As soon as there was silence, the best man said, 'I'm now going to call on the groom to say a few words.'

Michael stood up.

Well-versed in the protocol, he opened by saying, 'Reverend Fathers, Brother Anthony, Sister Oonagh and Sister Angela, Ladies and Gentlemen, first I would like to thank you all for coming to witness the marriage between myself and my lovely bride, Bridget. I've known Bridget for four years now and I know she's going to make me the happiest man alive. I say this with conviction, not only because we love each other, but because of her wonderful family background. First, there's her mother,' Michael pointed to Mary. 'What an example she is to all of us: for many years raising a large family on her own, while running a successful business. Never, in those four years have I heard Mary O'Dwyer once complain about anything or anyone. Second, is the loyalty and trust that exists between the siblings of that family. To me, they're a perfect example of what an Irish family should be.'

While Mary blushed, Jane could hardly keep a straight face. She thought, if they only knew the real truth.

Bridget tipped Michael's hand. He bent down and she whispered something in his ear.

Straightening up, Michael said, 'Oh, my wife!' (He smiled boyishly as he said the word.) 'My wife! Sounds great, doesn't it. Anyway, she's telling me not to forget to propose the toast to the beautiful bridesmaids. Apparently that is now my function.' Michael pointed out our Nancy and Jane seated at different ends of the top table, then indicated young Eileen, 'And our lovely flower girl.' He raised his glass and said, 'Could I ask you all to stand and raise your glasses in a toast to the lovely bridesmaids, Nancy and Jane and our lovely flower girl, Eileen.'

Except for the bridesmaids and the flower girl, everyone in the room stood up and raised their glasses murmuring, 'To the bridesmaids and the flower girl.'

Michael then noticed people getting fidgety and said jocosely, 'No doubt, you'll be relieved to hear that's the end of the speeches. Just enjoy the rest of the afternoon.' He sat down looking relieved that his speech was over. But his relief was short-lived. The best man whispered something in his ear. As people started stirring, Michael shot up again. 'Sorry everyone!' he said. 'I forgot something very important—the Management and Staff of this beautiful hotel. I'd just like to thank them very sincerely for their graciousness in serving such a wonderful meal. That's it.' He sat down.

As the people at the top table started moving on to the floor to visit with the other guests, Willie tipped Peter behind Nancy Pete's back, 'What's next?' he whispered curiously.

'I'll try and organize something,' Peter whispered back.

Just then Nancy Pete hoisted her huge weight out of the chair and whined, 'Peter I want to go home.' Moving away, she articulated emphatically, 'I'm going to the toilet. Be ready to leave when I get back.'

Peter looked thoroughly aggravated. He wondered what to do about the Willie and Jane situation? Suddenly his eyes lit on Lily in the distance, chatting with Sean, their cousin from the country. That had to be the solution, he decided. With the 'ball and chain' demanding that they leave immediately, he had no option. Lily would have to handle the situation for him.

Apologizing to Lily and Sean for interrupting their conversation, Peter pointed to Willie saying, 'Lily, we have a situation that needs your attention.'

'But of course,' Lily smiled collusively. Excusing herself, she said to Sean, 'Sorry Sean, but I have some pressing business to attend to.'

Sean smiled a foxy smile and nodded in Willie's direction. 'Your latest beau, I presume?' he said jocosely. 'What will the mother say?'

'Oh, to hell with that!' Lily said as she moved away with Peter. 'What's up?' she asked.

'Nancy is demanding I take her home,' Peter said. 'Could I ask you to look after Willie until Jane can extricate herself and join him.'

'Ach, I wish to God you'd stay,' Lily said, looking very perturbed. 'Jane wanted you to be at Willie's side — emphasizing the fact that he's your friend — when Mother got around to talking to him.' She looked around her, 'Where is Nancy Pete anyway?'

'Gone to the toilet.'

They could see that Mary was now working her way down the room visiting with groups of guests. Jane doing likewise with other groups. But her anxious eyes were mostly on her mother's progress. Timing was really important because the plan was that she would be sitting with company — which included Willie and hopefully Peter and Lily — when the mother arrived to visit with Willie. Peter could then make the necessary introductions.

Suddenly Lily had an inspiration. 'I'm off to the Ladies Powder room to intercept Nancy Pete,' she said to Peter. 'You never know, I might be able to talk her out of going home.'

'Fat chance!'

As she was about to leave the worst happened. Our Nancy appeared out of nowhere. Slouching down beside Willie, she hailed him flirtatiously, 'Don't you look smart in your uniform!' she said. Then she was all over him, fiddling with the buttons on his tunic.

'I came with Peter,' Willie said, looking most uncomfortable at the hand that was roving between his buttons.

Lily grabbed Peter's arm and drew him away from the table out of earshot. 'Jesus Christ!' she raged. 'That wan! She can't keep her bloody paws off him!'

'Language, Lily!' Peter chided. Lily was deaf to Peter's rebuke.

Flaming mad and spluttering, she said, 'Hasn't she gone and upset the whole bloody apple cart.'

'What do we do now?' Peter asked.

'Pray for a bloody miracle,' Lily said. Then inspiration. 'Stay here! Don't move!' she said. Then made a beeline for cousin Sean's table. 'Sean,' she gasped, leaning over him, 'Could you do me a favor?'

'Course, anthin for my favorite cousin.'

'It's our Nancy,' Lily said. 'She fancies my boyfriend.' She nodded towards Willie. 'Could you manage to get her away from him on some pretext or other? Preferably to talk about hairdressing.'

An understanding smile from Sean. 'Well, now, me dear,' he said, fondly touching his hair, 'as my hair is naturally curly, I don't really need a perm. But my Siobain might be interested in getting some advice about her hair.' With that Sean turned to Siobain sitting next to him and explained the situation to her.

'Sure,' Siobain agreed, 'anything I can do. Only don't ask me to walk across the room in my condition.' Siobain was heavy with child.

'Siobain's hair is a mess,' Sean said, giving Lily the wink. She definitely needs to do something with it. Leave it to me; I'll entice your Nancy over to our table .

'Sean and Siobain, you're absolute angels!' Lily gushed, then gave Sean his instructions. 'Wait a few seconds until I rejoin them. Then just saunter over casually.'

Lily joined the other three — Peter, Willie and our Nancy. Noticing Mary getting close, Lily gave Sean the beck to make his move. As soon as he arrived, Lily took off in search of Nancy Pete. At the exit she looked back in time to see Sean and our Nancy crossing the room. Thankfully, Sean had succeeded in luring Nancy away from Willie. Lily found Nancy Pete standing in a long queue outside the Ladies' Powder Room. She thought, that'll take care of her for a while. Best say nothing. Leave well alone.

Meanwhile, Jane felt the time had come for her to join Willie. With a face that glowed with happiness, she stood in front of him. 'Gosh, it's wonderful to see you,' she said grasping his hand.

'And aren't you looking gorgeous,' Willie said squeezing her hand.

'Ahem!' Peter exclaimed loudly. Then threw his eyes in the direction of Mary bearing down on them. 'Look out!' he said. Jane pulled her hand away from Willie's.

Mary arrived. Peter made the introductions. Shaking Willie's hand, Mary said, 'So you're Peter's good friend?'

'Yes,' Willie replied. 'We go back a long way.'

'If I'm not mistaken,' Mary said, 'you two met originally in the Frongoch Prisoner of War camp?'

'No,' Peter put in, 'we actually first met in the Stafford Prison.'

'Well, Willie,' Mary said candidly, 'you certainly stood out in the crowd in that uniform. Was there a special reason for wearing it?'

Peter interjected. 'Yes, Willie was a pallbearer for Thomas Ashe at his funeral this morning. You remember that patriot who was on hunger strike in Mountjoy prison and whose death was brought about by forcible feeding?'

'He was a good friend of mine,' Willie added, looking desolate.

'I'm so sorry,' Mary sounded genuinely sympathetic. 'I read

about it in the newspaper. It was a horrible business. The way they treated him was outrageous.'

'An animal wouldn't be treated the way he was,' Peter vociferated.

'That's why I'm in uniform,' Willie said. 'Personally, I didn't think it was suitable garb for a wedding, but Peter convinced me otherwise at the cemetery.'

Peter threw in. 'Well, if he'd gone home to change, he wouldn't've been here in time for the reception.'

Mary seemed comfortable with the explanation. 'Well, Willie,' she said cordially, 'whatever about the garb, you're more than welcome.'

She turned to Jane. 'Bring Willie back to the house afterwards, Jane,' she said. 'I'm sure he could do with some cheering up.' This was music to Willie and Jane's ears. They tried not to look too pleased. Both had the same thought; if she only knew how marvelously she played into our hands. 'Will you excuse me now, Willie,' Mary said politely. 'I must have a word with Sean and Siobain, over there. As Siobain is expecting a baby, I imagine they won't be coming back to the house. Still I'd like to invite them.'

When Mary left, Peter roared laughing. Looking pleased as be damned, he said to Jane and Willie, 'Okay, you love birds, the Mother has now been fittingly introduced, may your future be a happy one.' He winked artfully at Jane. 'Bring Willie back to the house and let's hope it'll be the first of many visits.' Then throwing his eyes up to heaven, he added, 'As for me, I will arise and go now, and fetch to my 'ball and chain.''

Arriving back to the banqueting room, Lily met Peter at the exit. 'Hold your horses,' she told him. 'Your Nancy is in a long queue outside the Ladies' Powder Room and it looks like she's going to be there for sometime.'

'She'll be like ten divils when she gets back!'

'Are you coming back to the house?' Lily asked.

'You must be joking!' Peter said. 'The ball and chain wishes to go home. And the ball and chain must be obeyed.'

'Why don't you come later?' Lily suggested.

'Do you think she'd let me?'

Lily got very agitated. 'Don't ask her, just come,' she said. Wouldn't it be nice for Willie if you were there?'

'Ach, I'll do my best,' Peter said. 'But don't bank on it.'

Jane's joy at being with Willie knew no bounds. As they sat on their own chatting about commonplace things, like the Kilkenny result and how Jane's job almost stopped her getting to the wedding, in the back of Willie's mind he was thinking, why the hell am I talking shop to her when I want to tell her how much I love her?

Suddenly he blurted out, 'Seeing you like this, Jane, looking so gorgeous, my body aches to hold you.'

Jane could see profound longing in Willie's eyes. She too craved a big, bear hug and maybe a kiss. But like always, this was neither the time nor the place. 'Much as I want to feel your arms around me,' Jane said, her eyes twinkling, 'unfortunately it's much too public.'

'It's just I can't believe you're here beside me in the flesh,' Willie said. 'You've no idea how distracted I was looking at you in the distance for so long.'

'Me too,' Jane said. 'But, oh! Willie! It was such a lovely surprise when Lily, bless her heart, came to the top table and told me it was you in the uniform! I swear to you, every nerve in my body started to tingle.' Jane's eyes gleamed with amusement. 'To be honest with you,' she said, 'I didn't hear a word of the speeches. All I could think of was, please God, let them be over soon, so that I can be with Willie!'

Willie laughed. He found Jane's frankness so refreshing. 'It must be mental telepathy,' he said. 'I felt exactly the same during those speeches.'

Lily and Peter joined them. 'I've been granted a temporary reprieve,' Peter said laughing. 'The ball and chain is stranded in a long queue outside the Ladies' Powder Room.'

Jane and Willie roared laughing. Peter's comment jolted them out of the magic they'd woven around themselves for the past ten minutes.

Lily spied our Nancy coming towards them after her visit with Siobain. 'Christ!' she raged. 'Here she comes—our raptorial sister—watch her go into action.'

Right enough, just as predicted, our Nancy planted herself beside Willie.

'Mother tells me you're coming back to the house,' she said to him. 'Can I be your escort?'

Willie put his arm across Jane's shoulder. 'I already have one,' he said giving a lopsided smile. 'Thank you all the same.'

Our Nancy suddenly jumped up. 'Oh!' she said, self-importantly, pointing to a middle-aged man on his way to the exit. 'There's Jim Maloney. I need to talk to him.' With that she was gone.

Lily puffed out her relief. 'Thank God for Jim Maloney,' she said making no effort to hide her sarcasm.

Peter said in a low tone to Lily, 'I take it our Nancy has a crush on Willie?'

'Our Nancy has a crush on anything in pants,' Lily scoffed.

'Mew! Mew. !' Peter made cat noises. 'Now who's the pussycat?'

Lily didn't get a chance to answer. Because just then Bridget and Michael appeared on the dais dressed in their going-away suits. Looking blissfully happy and stunning in her red suit, Bridget was now ready to throw the bridal bouquet to the many hopeful young women present.

Peter said to his sisters, 'Off you go, girls. Find out who's going to be the next bride?'

Jane was reluctant. But Lily insisted. 'Of course you must join in, Jane,' she said, pulling her to her feet and pushing her ahead of her up the room to join the throng of single females eager to catch the bouquet. Bridget turned her back and threw the bouquet high in the air. It was caught by a young cousin.

For Jane the rest of the day was like a dream come true. She kept asking herself, could this really be happening? Was Willie here beside her openly with her mother's knowledge?

Back at the house there was more food and drink and socializing. Thankfully, this time the music was supplied by a phonograph — a wedding present Bridget insisted should be put to good use — sparing Jane the chore of playing the piano. Jane did, however, accompany a number of the singers. But each time Willie sat up at the piano close to her.

Eventually our Nancy concluded that Willie was out of her reach. No sense in trying to hang my hat there, she thought. Where Jane is concerned, he's like a bloody leech.

Noticing Jane and Willie's attachment, Mary had mixed feelings. The one thing she didn't want was her daughter marrying a renegade republican. However, she decided to say nothing. Jane was young. No doubt she'd have many romantic attachments before she finally settled down with the right man.

By midnight Willie was really exhausted and more than ready to retire. Taking his leave of Jane he said, 'How about a walk by the river tomorrow after Mass?'

'Lovely,' Jane said. 'Call for me here at the house.' Her happiness showed in her smile. 'T'would be the best way to make Mother realize how things will be between us in the future.'

'Good idea.'

Chapter XX

At the Annual Convention held in the Mansion House on October 25th, 1917, DeValera was elected to the Presidency of Sinn Fein. This election was significant for one thing: a short time before the event Arthur Griffith, a Sinn Feiner and a good friend of Collins, decided not to challenge it and stood down. Though he probably could have carried the vote. Instead he was elected Vice President. Austin Stack and David Figgis became joint Honorary Secretaries with Liam Cosgrave and Laurence Ginnel, Honorary Treasurers. The Executive Council consisted of twenty-four persons of whom Collins was one. Harry Boland — a good friend of Collins — was also elected to the Executive. Before this election Collins suggested to Willie that he might consider being a contender, but, feeling he'd be considerably out of his depth, Willie declined.

The Sinn Fein Convention involved a great deal of preliminary discussions between the different factions: Griffith's followers — the Irish Nation League (conservatives chiefly-) and the IRB which consisted of the 1916 revolutionary wing, Brugha, Collins, DeValera and Count Plunkett. It meant hammering out a common platform between the moderates and the revolutionaries. However, as it turned out, it was highly successful. It united these hitherto diverse national forces (both of which were opposed to the Irish Parliamentary Party) in agreeing on the leadership question and in presenting a constructive and positive policy. DeValera's skill in negotiation was seen to have considerable effect in these preliminary negotiations. He dominated the 1917 Convention. He achieved his desire by having his economic and abstention programs accepted by a nation wide organization instead of the extremely limited one with which he had worked in the years before 1916. Two days later, at a Convention of the Volunteers, DeValera was again elected President.

The most significant point to emerge from this Convention was the instigation of a policy empowering the Executive to declare war against Britain should the British Government press its threatened plans to extend conscription to Ireland. Because the Great War was going so badly for them. Here again the IRB was the domineering influence: Collins became Director of Organization and was elected a member of the Executive of the Volunteers. Brugha was appointed to the position of Chief of Staff. In the drafting of the new Constitution for the volunteers, Collins did a first rate job: a great many points were straightened out, a certain amount of success achieved and the name of Collins was beginning to be known as a person of consequence.

At this time, Willie found that Collins brought a new excitement to his life. With Jane working days (Monday to Saturday) from nine to six and himself idle during these hours, Collins' invitation to work as a volunteer in his office was a godsend. To Willie's mind, Collins office typified unimaginative chaos. But Collins himself apparently found the overcrowded presses stuffed with documents, tables laden with files, scattered copies of *The Times* and *Manchester Guardian,* his desk heaped with reports and bundles of papers ranging round his typewriter, quite normal and workable.

When Willie suggested a tidying job to bring some order to the office, Collins explained, with a transient flash of mirth, 'Believe it or not, Willie, out of the chaos that exists in my office, and with a glance at the maps on the walls, I can actually tell every man who is hostile, friendly or useful to me.'

A table was allocated to Willie to work on. But he found it increasingly difficult to get anything done: so much time was wasted looking for documents and files. What was badly needed was a filing cabinet that would get things organized and into shape. 'You've got to be joking!' Collins laughed derisively at Willie when he mentioned the word filing cabinet. 'That's one luxury we definitely cannot afford.'

But Willie had other ideas. At a recent meeting he overheard Harry Boland (who owned a tailor shop in Abbey Street) mention that he was in the process of replacing his current filing cabinet and it was costing him a fortune. Willie thought, Harry's the man to approach. Won't he have to dispose of his old filing cabinet?

Within ten days of joining Collins' volunteer office staff, Willie had a filing cabinet, complete with a competent filing system up and running. It was done in Collins' absence.

'You mean to say, Willie,' Collins said on discovering the orgy of organization that had taken place in his office, 'I'll be able to put my finger on everything I need without having to rake through piles of papers?'

'Just so,' Willie grinned.

More to the point, Collins now trusted Willie so implicitly he let him into secrets (as he put it), 'I wouldn't tell my best friend.' Along with that he allowed Willie to hand deliver important, secret letters and documents to members of both Executives — Sinn Fein and The Volunteers — in their different, secret business houses. And though Collins hated to let his bicycle out of his sight (his emergency transport, as he put it), once in a while he allowed Willie to use it, saying, 'For God's sake, don't leave it unattended. If necessary, bring the bloody thing into the building with you.'

For a while Willie got the impression that Collins was treating him as Ashe's successor. Plainly, Ashe's death was a blow from which Collins was only slowly recovering. On one occasion he said to Willie, 'I grieve for Ashe as perhaps no one else grieves. And yet our comradeship was not of a long duration. He was a man of no complexes, doing what he did for Ireland always in a quiet way.'

§

Never was Willie's happiness more firmly in his grasp than after Bridget's wedding. On most Sundays — his day off — he was able to call openly to the O'Dwyer home to collect Jane to bring her out for the day on the tram sometimes to Kingstown sometimes to

Howth. However, once when the weather was bad, they were forced to stay indoors and have tea with the family, which now comprised Mary, Jane, our Nancy and young Eileen. Early on the atmosphere was pretty strained. Sorely missed were Bridget and Lily (back at school) who could always be depended on to be helpful. Jane could tell that Willie was most uncomfortable.

Our Nancy flirted with him continually even as he tried to have an intelligent conversation with her mother, whom she sensed didn't particularly approve of him because she immediately quizzed him about his politics, ending up saying prejudicially, 'I understand, Willie, you're quite involved with that scoundrel, Collins?'

Willie felt this was a moment when he had to be guarded in his reply. 'I'm not really that involved,' he said. 'But I do see him once in a while.' No more than he would tell Jane about the bond that now existed between himself and Collins, would he acquaint the mother with the fact that presently he was probably one of Collins' right-hand men.

At this point, our Nancy changed the subject. 'Tell us, Jane,' she said, 'What happened with 'the bull' on the Monday following Bridget's wedding? You were expecting to be fired?'

'Oh that!' Jane grinned, grateful for her sister's timely intervention. 'I thought you all knew what happened.'

'Not me,' our Nancy said. 'I didn't hear a word.'

'Well, Jane chortled looking at the ceiling, 'someone up there, must've put in a good word for me. Because on that Monday morning Miss Bullingsworth was missing. It transpired later that she was in the hospital having her appendix out. She's still out sick.' Jane joined her hands together prayer-wise. 'I only hope and pray that her illness will blot out the memory of my grievous misconduct.'

'So you still have to face her?' Eileen put in.

'Fraid so.'

Once again Mary stubbornly returned to the subject of Willie's involvement in the fight for Irish freedom, asking him the question, 'do you intend to continue fighting for the Cause?'

Willie looked at Jane. Fearful of giving the wrong impression, he pondered the question. A lot was riding on his answer — his and Jane's future for instance. Jane noticed how flushed he was as he sought to answer the question diplomatically. She wished to God her mother would desist. But right now she seemed hell bent on finding out all she could about Willie and his politics.

'Well,' Jane intervened, trying to keep the irritation out of her voice, 'If you could call volunteering in the bye-elections, working for the Cause,' she smiled at Willie, 'then I suppose you could say he's still working for the Cause.'

Working as opposed to fighting,' Mary said sardonically.

'Oh please, God!' Willie sounded quite emotional, 'The fighting is over.' He smiled whimsically. 'We've great hopes that the successes of the bye-elections and the fact that those elected will not be taking their seats in the Westminster Parliament, will convince the British that the time has come for the Irish and the British to sit down together and negotiate.'

Willie's reply seemed to satisfy Mary. She stood up. 'I'm sorry. I'm afraid I have to leave,' she said. 'My shop awaits me. Unlike the rest of you who have the day off, my job never finishes.' With that she left the room.

Once again Jane threw her eyes up to heaven while our Nancy remarked cattily, 'That's the Mother doing her usual martyr act.'

With Mary gone, our Nancy invented an excuse to get away. She certainly didn't feel like staying to watch the love birds holding hands and looking into each other's eyes for the rest of the evening. This left young Eileen, who rushed from the room and came back excitedly waving a pack of playing cards.

'Do you play cards by any chance?' she asked Willie, her eyes alight with anticipation.

'I've been known to,' Willie answered. 'What game do you have in mind?'

'The only two she knows,' Jane said jauntily. 'Old Maid and Beg o' my neighbor.'

'I'm quite prepared to learn a new one,' Eileen said bursting with enthusiasm.

'Right,' Willie said joining in her enthusiasm. 'We'll play your games first. Then how'd ye feel about learning twenty-five?'

'Oh! That'd be great altogether,' The prospect of learning a new card game appealed very much to Eileen.

By the end of the evening, despite his early discomfort at Mary's probing, Willie began to feel at home. He attributed this, not only to Jane's presence, but to the pleasant atmosphere created by Eileen with her funny card games and her silly jokes. She really was a sweet child.

§

Christmas Day, 1917, was a happy occasion for Jane and Willie. The fact that our Nancy let it be known that she was really and truly in love with Gerald Quinn, a handsome, twenty-four-year-old Second Lieutenant in the British Army, and was able to persuade Mary to invite him to Christmas dinner, made it easy for Jane to invite Willie. Other factors which contributed to the enjoyment on Christmas Day were having Lily home from school, and Bridget and Michael joining them for the dinner at the last minute. As she listened to the happy banter in the room, Jane was remembering old times when family and guests were seated around the table wearing funny paper hats.

Today even Mary joined in the gaiety. It would seem she thoroughly approved of our Nancy's choice of new boyfriend. The son of Irish immigrants — who lived in England — Gerald was a real charmer. He had very nice manners and a nice accent. But more to the point, he was catholic. Our Nancy and himself entertained everyone telling how they met originally.

'When the Mass ended,' our Nancy said, 'I stepped out of the pew and low and behold if my high heel didn't land bang in the middle of Gerald's foot.'

'Ouch!' Gerald chuckled, chipping in. 'It hurt! But then when I looked up and saw the pretty face of the person who'd done this dastardly deed, naturally I forgot the pain.'

'Well, if you did, you certainly didn't show it,' our Nancy said, trying to keep the laughter out of her voice. 'You should have seen the agony on his face,' she said. 'You'd swear it was an elephant that trod on his foot.'

There was much laughter in the room.

'But of course,' Gerald giggled, 'I was determined to get your attention.'

Our Nancy continued. 'You certainly got that. Would you believe,' she said to the others, again trying to hold in the laughter, 'he limped so badly I practically carried him out of the church. Was I mortified?'

Eileen chipped in sympathetically, 'But surely you felt guilty about hurting his foot?'

'Of course, I felt guilty,' our Nancy said. 'He made sure of that. Didn't he lean on me the whole way down Dominick Street.'

Again there was much laughter.

'It was the best strategy to get to know you,' Gerald said gleefully.

'Well, you certainly rubbed it in,' our Nancy said, 'with your moaning and groaning.'

'If I hadn't acted the way I did,' Gerald said bubbling with mirth, 'I wouldn't be sitting here in the midst of this wonderful Irish family enjoying the delights of a fabulous Christmas dinner.'

'And the rest is history,' Michael put in jocularly.

'Hopefully!' Gerald added taking another sip of wine.

The hilarity of their story had everyone in stitches laughing. Moreover, the attraction between our Nancy and Gerald was pretty obvious.

As Bridget said to Jane when they were washing the dishes later. 'Well, anyway, he's a hell of an improvement on Claude...the hairdresser.'

'I've a hunch, he's going to be *the* one,' Jane said.

As soon as the dinner was over, much to the surprise of the family, Mary stood at the tree handing out small gifts to everyone present.

'Holy Moses!' Jane said to Lily, 'She must be losing it! Closing the shop for the day. Distributing presents from the tree to all and sundry. What on earth's got into her?'

Lily answered, 'It's about time she got the message that Christmas is a day to be enjoyed and not for slaving in that bloody shop.'

Shortly afterwards, Peter, Nancy Pete (heavy with her second child) and their bawling toddler, Colbert, arrived, laden with gifts, to make their Christmas visit and in the process make a lot of people uncomfortable because accompanying the child's tantrum was the parents' bickering.

Barely in the door, Nancy Pete started biting the head of her husband. 'I told you we shouldn't have come,' she shrilled at him.

'It's Christmas!' Peter threw at her accusingly. 'What's so terrible about a son wanting to visit his mother and his family?'

'Oh nothing, I suppose,' Nancy Pete said, then added petulantly, 'as long as you look after your cranky son and don't expect me to do it.'

Intervening, Bridget thrust a glass of wine into Nancy Pete's hand. 'Happy Christmas,' she shouted over the din being caused by the child. 'Come and sit down. You're very welcome.'

Meanwhile Mary took Colbert's hand and lead him to the Christmas tree, saying, 'Let's see what Santa put on the tree for you?'

Seeing the tree all lit up with candles, Colbert's eyes widened with surprise and excitement. He stopped crying. His eyes then fell on a large toy horse placed under the tree. 'Want,' he said, pointing to the horse. Mary picked it up and put it in his arms. A huge smile spread over Colbert's face. He ran to his Daddy to show it to him, saying, 'Hoss! Hoss!'

'Did you say thank you to Gran?' Peter asked him. Colbert looked coyly at Mary, then hid his head in his father's legs.

Mary said, 'There's no necessity to thank me; t'was Santa Clause who brought it.' Colbert now started rubbing his eyes. It was obvious he was very tired. Feeling like she was walking on egg shells, Mary approached Nancy Pete. 'He seems very tired?' she said to her.

'That makes two of us,' Nancy Pete complained.

'Do you think he might sleep in my bed?' Mary asked timorously.

'Good idea!' To Mary's amazement, Nancy Pete was actually agreeing with her. 'The only thing is,' Nancy Pete whimpered, 'I'll have to stay with him.'

'Well then,' Mary said, sounding practical, 'why don't the two of you rest on my bed. Nancy, you look worn out.'

For the first time in her life Nancy Pete gave Mary a grateful hug. 'Thanks, Mother,' she said her eyes brimming with tears. 'I'm so glad someone understands.'

There was a great release of tension when Mary, Nancy Pete and Colbert left the room.

Lily grabbed Peter and pushed him towards the piano, 'Come on, Peter,' she said, 'tickle the ivories and let's have a dance.'

As our Nancy and Gerald danced together looking adoringly into each other's eyes, it was patently obvious that there was a great attraction between them. They laughed and joked incessantly and Nancy never looked more beautiful.

It has to be love, Jane thought. It more or less explained why our Nancy was so affable of late; like offering to help with the Christmas decorations two nights ago. That was a definite first. Nonetheless, she didn't pass up the opportunity to use Jane to get discount off her Christmas shopping. Particularly the new, violet-colored velvet dress she was wearing this evening; it went between Jane and her rest. Because had she seen it in time in the store, that dream of a dress would be on her back and not our Nancy's. Her own green two-piece (with embroidered bodice) looked positively dowdy beside it. Jane lived in hopes that this love affair between our Nancy and Gerald would last. Maybe then herself and Willie could look forward to a bit of peace.

Willie, on the other hand, wasn't too comfortable having to fraternize, as it were, with a member of the opposite camp. Collins would call it 'hobnobbing with the enemy.'

DeVALERA

Chapter XXI

The year 1918, contrary to many expectations, opened on a somber note for Sinn Fein. Three successive defeats were recorded against their candidates. On February lst at the South Armagh bye-election, Dr. MacCartan was defeated. On the 22nd of March at the Waterford bye-election, Dr. Vincent White was defeated (though there was little hope of success here, the seat being retained by John Redmond's son.) And on the 2nd April, at the East Tyrone bye-election, Sean Milroy was defeated. This chain of events kept Willie out of Dublin. His resourcefulness during these bye-elections made him one of the brightest stars in the campaign's galaxy.

However, despite all the defeats, the balance was more or less maintained by the success of the anti-conscription campaign. At the Mansion House, an event of historic importance occurred. Leaders of Sinn Fein, the Irish Parliamentary Party and the Irish Labor Party met and passed a resolution against conscription. In this they had the assistance of the Catholic Hierarchy. Enormous crowds signed a pledge in furtherance of the resolution. A National Defense Fund raised a huge sum of money to fight the British authorities' efforts to suppress any support of the resolution and the Newspapers' Fund. Finally, the Irish Labor Party called a one-day Strike in further support.

In one of his confidential chats with Willie, Collins told him, 'Aside from the primary object of the meeting of the three parties, the chief topic of interest is the fact that the Irish Parliamentary Party have at long last recognized that others are also entitled to speak for the country as against the days when they did all the speaking.'

Willie remarked, 'So it seems as far as the Irish Parliamentary

Party is concerned, their power is nearing its end.'

'Exactly.'

§

During these months, it went without saying that Jane saw precious little of Willie. He'd barely finished campaigning for one election when he was off again campaigning for the next one. Jane felt his absence keenly. Particularly as our Nancy's romance was thriving. Not only did Gerald see her weeknights, but the fact that he was 'duty officer' only one Sunday in every four, meant he was a regular visitor for dinner on Sundays; a situation that seemed to have Mary's whole-hearted approval. Though she was pleased for our Nancy, Jane couldn't help feeling envious. She was acutely aware that, whereas Gerald was continuously around and very attentive to our Nancy, Willie was never there to be attentive to her. Of course, he had valid reasons for his absence, but it didn't make things any easier.

Having lunch with Philomena one day in the Store Café, Jane voiced something of the frustration she was feeling about Willie. (As it happened, a few weeks earlier Philomena confided in Jane that herself and her boyfriend had just broken up. At the time she didn't want to talk about it.) Notwithstanding this, their brief chat gave Jane the opening she needed to talk to Philomena about the problems in her romance.

Philomena consoled her saying, 'At least Willie's still your boyfriend. In my case Jimmy told me straight out: 'we're finished; I'm in love with someone else.' '

'How long were the two of you walking out?' Jane asked.

'Three years.'

'That's a very long time.'

'You can say that again,' Philomena said disconsolately. 'It's three fecking years down the drain.'

'Are you very cut up about it?'

'Naturally, I'm cut up about it,' Philomena said. 'I was expecting to marry him. But then,' she said philosophically, 'wasn't it better to find out sooner than later the kind of person he was?' Sounding really bitter, she added, 'It's probably good riddance to bad rubbish.'

Jane and Philomena (now 'playing the field' as she called it) became firm friends. Whenever they could during lunch breaks, they candidly discussed their love lives. On one such occasion Philomena remarked, 'Jane, we have to see life as it is, not as we want it to be.' Jane marveled at Philomena's common sense approach to life. She always felt good after talking to her.

On a Monday in May when Willie was away working for the East Tyrone bye-election, Jane was in the staff cloakroom getting ready to go home when Philomena bounced in giggling and laughing and full of beans. 'Ever been to the National Gallery?' she asked Jane.

'No,' Jane answered, looking quizzically at her. 'Have you?'

'Not yet,' Philomena said. 'But I was thinking that maybe if you're free tonight...?'

'I'm continually free these days,' Jane interjected.

'Well, then, how about the two of us meandering over to the National Gallery tonight? I understand it's hosting a Yates Exhibition. And the Gallery will be open till ten.'

'Though I'm not into art,' Jane said, 'going to the Gallery would certainly be an improvement on reading my book for the rest of the evening.'

'Let's do it,' Philomena enthused. 'You never know who you'll run into there.' She couldn't keep the eagerness out of her voice. 'What with all those pretentious, arty types, it could well turn out to be a interesting experience.'

'Are you trying to lead me astray?' Jane said joining in the spirit of the moment.

'Do you think it's possible?' Philomena laughed a good natured laugh.

'Huh!' Jane reflected. 'I doubt it.'

'See you in the Lobby of the Gallery at eight then,' Philomena shouted over her shoulder as she disappeared through the door.

It seemed the Lobby of the Gallery was a rendezvous for many of the patrons. There was no sign of Philomena when Jane arrived. Until suddenly this weird looking stranger sidled up to her and whispered, 'Do you think I'd pass for an art critic?'

'Sweet Mother of God!' Jane ejaculated. She couldn't believe her eyes. Philomena had undergone a total metamorphous trying to look arty. First there was her hair in a chignon. Then there were those heavy, horn-rimmed glasses making her look intellectual. Next the clothes — a old muskrat jacket with a beaver collar and matching beaver hat. Add to this the jewelry, the long earrings, and fingers covered in rings, and you had the perfect bohemian. She carried a walking stick, 'for effect' (as she put it). In total bewilderment, Jane whispered, 'Where on earth did you get the clothes?' She was terrified she'd be overheard.

'In a trunk in our attic,' Philomena whispered back. 'They belonged to my grandmother. As a child I used to dress up in them all the time'

Jane looked around to see if Philomena's appearance was impacting on the people in any way. But nobody seemed to notice. Come to think of it, a lot of the women were dressed just as flamboyantly. Philomena fitted in perfectly. Her acting too couldn't be more appropriate. Leaning on Jane's arm for support (mi-ah) they slowly made their way towards the Long Room where the Yates Exhibition was being held.

The room was a buzz with the babble of hundreds of patrons 'dressed to the nines' (as Philomena put it.) They stood in groups around each painting extolling the virtues of Yates magnificent form and imagery.

Holding tight to Jane's arm (giving the impression she was afraid she'd fall), Philomena pointed to an empty space in front of the last few paintings. 'Come and have a look,' she said loudly to Jane in her best Anglo-Trinity accent. 'This is the painting I was telling you about.' She pointed to a delightful landscape painting in oils.

As they lumbered towards the painting it was all Jane could do to contain her laughter. Standing before the painting, studying it closely, then standing back from it, anyone would think they were experts. During this time Philomena leaned on Jane's arm as if her life depended on it. Suddenly a group of patrons gravitated in their direction.

The next thing Jane felt a heavy hand on her shoulder and heard the loud tones off Percy's voice declaring in his best Oxford accent, 'As I live and breathe, if it isn't the smart, young hatter from the Store.' As he came face to face with Jane, his lascivious eyes devoured her.

'Jesus!' Philomena whispered turning her head away. God! she was thinking, if he recognizes me I'm in deep shite.

'And this must be your mother,' Percy indicated Philomena's back.

'Ah! Well, No! Not really!' Jane muttered, inwardly cringing. Just then she heard another familiar voice coming from a group nearby. Nancy Pete, looking nice and slender after giving birth to her second son, Heuston, was bumbling away, laying down the law arguing with someone about one of the paintings.

'Excuse me,' Jane said to Percy, 'but I've just seen someone my friend and I wish to talk to.'

With that she grabbed Philomena by the shoulder and shepherded her hastily through the crowds across to Nancy Pete's group where she hoped to be out of danger. She couldn't help thinking: Imagine it — *me* relying on Nancy Pete to get me out of this jam!

Nancy Pete's gushing was overwhelming. 'Why Jane!' she greeted her with astonishment, 'I didn't know you were interested in art?' Then after staring at Philomena long enough, she added, 'but your friend looks the part; no doubt she's had a good influence on you.' Jane made no attempt to enlighten her. 'What's your artist friend's name?' Nancy Pete asked Jane quietly. 'I'd like to introduce the pair of you to my friends.'

Before Jane could answer, Philomena, smiling sweetly, blurted out 'Philomena DeFelice.'

Gasping with astonishment, Nancy Pete uttered, 'You're one of the Connemara DeFelices?'

'Yes, actually,' Philomena answered brazenly.

'People!' Nancy Pete's voice went up a few decibels as she got the attention of the patrons in her group. 'First let me introduce my sister-in-law, Jane O'Dwyer,' she indicated Jane. Second, I have the great honor to introduce Jane's friend, Philomena DeFelice.'

Shock waves ran through the company at the mention of the name.

'Not one of the Connemara DeFelices!' a woman exclaimed incredulously, holding her hand to her throat.

'But of course,' Philomena said boldly, once again using her best Anglo-Trinity accent.

In her haze of discomfort Jane didn't catch the name of any of the people she was being introduced to.

'Are you living in Dublin now?' a professorial gentleman asked Philomena.

'No, just here for a few days,' Philomena said pertly. 'I'm so glad my visit coincided with this incredible exhibition.' Jane was totally stunned by Philomena's performance; it would beat Nancy Pete's any day. Philomena then looked critically at the clock on the wall. 'But now,' she said, totally in control, 'I'm afraid we must tear ourselves away.'

'Oh! Do you have to leave so soon?' another female patron appealed to her.

'Fraid so. I've so little time and so much to cram into it,' Philomena said apologetically. 'I still have another pressing engagement to fulfill this evening.' She turned to Jane and said, 'Best go now before it gets too late.' With that she laid her hand on Jane's arm supposedly for the physical support. Then leaning heavily on her stick, she nudged Jane, 'Let's go.'

§

On the 12th May, 1918, General French was appointed Military Viceroy to Ireland by the British Government. The day following this announcement, when Collins arrived into the office on Bachelor's Walk, Willie could see he had a bee in his bonnet. For a while Collins was silent. Bad sign. His mannerisms were now so well known to Willie, he knew if he waited long enough Collins would divest himself of whatever was bothering him. It came at last fifteen minutes later.

'This new appointment of General French as Viceroy,' Collins blurted out, 'has me worried. It has all the hallmarks of trouble and strife.'

'What makes you say that?' Willie asked.

'He has the reputation of being a shit-disturber of the highest order: a real mischief-maker.'

'So what great plans have you in mind for him?' Willie asked.

'At this stage, we sit tight,' Collins face showed real concern. 'We'll just have to wait and see, exercise extreme caution and do our best not to provoke him.'

On the morning of the 17th May, Harry Boland charged into Collins' office in a whirl of panic.

'Jesus! Mick,' he exclaimed, producing a sheet containing a list. 'This is a 'wanted' list issued by Dublin Castle. It has the names of all the prominent members of Sinn Fein and the IRB on it. Including elected members of parliament.'

'You're pulling my leg.' Collins took it as a joke.

'Swear to God, I'm not!' Boland said looking very troubled.

'Where did the list come from?'

'Well, it originated with Joe Kavanagh.'

'Do you mind me asking,' Willie interjected, 'but who is Joe Kavanagh?' He hadn't heard the name mentioned before; that made him curious.

'He's a detective in the G. Men Division,' Collins told him. 'One of our main sources of information in the Castle.'

'Well, anyway,' Boland continued, 'Kavanagh gave the list to Gay, the Librarian in Capel Street, who dispatched it promptly to me.'

Collins studied the list. 'Even I'm on it,' he remarked.

'We're all on it,' Boland said. 'But according to Kavanagh, the most important thing about this list is the fact that they intend arresting all those people tonight in a gigantic round-up.'

Perplexed, Collins asked, 'Did Kavanagh happen to mention what Britain's explanation for this round-up was?'

'Their explanation! That's the big joke!' Boland scoffed. 'According to the Brits, they've uncovered a pro-German plot in which Sinn Fein and the IRB are involved,' he said. 'It's their way of blinding the Americans to the true fact.'

'Which is?' Collins asked.

'The Resolution we passed against Conscription.'

'A pro-German plot!' Collins exclaimed. 'I've never heard such a load of horse shit in all my life! What next?'

Boland said, 'We both know it isn't true, but what can we do about it?'

'We'll just have to get word to everyone on that list not to be in their homes tonight when the bloody G. Men swoop in,' Collins said. He stopped to think. Consulted the list again. 'There's a meeting of the Volunteer Executive this evening,' he said. 'I'll certainly see to it that all the members on that list who are present are notified.'

'Joe O'Keeffe has undertaken to warn the Sinn Fein Executive at their meeting tonight,' Boland said.

After studying the list for the umpteenth time, Collins contemplated for a moment, then said, 'I get the feeling I'll be working overtime peddling that bicycle of mine for the rest of the day. No,' he said positively. 'Better not take a chance on them being at the meetings. All these people should be informed in person in case any of them fall through the cracks.'

'Let's break the list into three parts,' Boland suggested realistically. 'That way the three of us can share the burden of visiting each and everyone of these people today and give them timely warning.'

The next hour was spent making three lists, one for Collins, one for Boland and one for Willie. The Collins office then closed for the day.

Willie spent the rest of the day walking and tramming to the addresses on his list. If the person in question wasn't available, he was instructed to leave a note saying that Collins wanted him to attend an extremely important meeting of the Volunteer Executive that evening, the 17th May. It transpired that each member he visited was available to talk to, so he didn't have to leave any notes. Each of them took the warning seriously and thanked him profusely for his trouble.

On his way to the Tivoli that evening, Willie hoped to God Finbar would be there so that he could ask for time off to attend some of the meetings. His mind was in turmoil. He desperately needed to know what was going to happen. But Finbar didn't turn up. Willie found it exceedingly problematic to focus on work. His mind was continually occupied with that 'wanted' list. For the first time in a long time, he was butter-fingered; had great difficulty getting the reels into the projector. To add to his misery a reel dropped on the floor and rolled all over it.

Collins meantime was having a hard time trying to convince Griffith and DeValera and other members of the Sinn Fein Executive to go into hiding tonight. Earlier, having divulged the names on the 'wanted' list to his own Volunteer Executive meeting, he adjourned the meeting early and left the members to mull over the situation. Then, he cycled over to Harcourt Street to attend the Sinn Fein Executive meeting where he ran into real trouble. Both DeValera and Arthur Griffith demurred about going into hiding.

DeValera, as usual stood up and made a speech. 'There are three courses open to us,' he said. 'We go into hiding, we meet the arrests with resistance or we let the Government take us into custody. Personally, I favor going into custody.' This was said very doggedly. DeValera then continued. 'Such a course of action could be most advantageous to Sinn Fein in the forthcoming Cavan bye-election.'

Collins argued, 'We're dealing with an unknown quantity in this General French fellow. It's possible we could all end up in jail. Then where are we?'

'Well,' DeValera said, 'each man is entitled to his belief. For myself, I intend to sleep in my own bed tonight.' He looked at Griffith, who nodded assent.

That night Willie hardly slept worrying about the fate of his comrades. Collins in particular.

As for Collins, he spent the night cycling round the city once again delivering warnings. However, somehow by accident he managed to come into the center of the operation when he arrived at Sean McGarry's house to warn him. He was just in time to witness Sean's arrest from a distance. As a result, Collins spent the rest of the night sleeping safely in Sean's house.

Chapter XXII

As Willie was dressing the following morning, there was a light tap on his bedroom door. Opening it, he was surprised to find Sadie standing outside looking extremely agitated.

'I've an urgent message for you,' she said dolefully.

Willie's heart hammered so fiercely he could hear it in his ears. He sensed bad news. 'It's Collins?' he groaned. 'They've arrested him?'

'No,' Sadie said. 'It's not as bad as that; at least I don't think it is.'

'For God's sake tell me,' Willie exclaimed passionately, 'What's happened?'

'First the message,' Sadie said. 'A young lad delivered it a while ago. You're not to go next or near the Bachelor Walk building today. For that matter, any other days until further notice. It's for your own safety.'

'Did the young lad say anything about what happened last night?' Willie asked. 'You know, about the threatened arrests?'

'No,' Sadie said. 'He couldn't throw any light on it. I did ask him because there's a paragraph in this morning's *newspapers* saying a number of prominent Sinn Fein members were arrested last night on conspiracy charges.'

'Did it give any names?'

'No,' Sadie said in a quiet voice. 'It was a brief paragraph. Just enough to worry us.'

Later that morning Willie dropped into Harry Boland's shop in Abbey Street. He was frantic to know what happened the night before.

Damien, Harry's assistant told him, 'No, Harry's not in yet. I'm just as much in the dark as yourself about what happened last night. And with Harry not checking in, I fear the worst.'

As Willie was talking to Damien, two G. Men arrived. After showing their badges to Damien, they said, 'We have a warrant to search these premises.' One of them produced a parchment.

As Willie moved towards the door, he said to Damien, businesslike, 'Right, I'll call on Friday to collect the suit.'

Damien caught on. 'I promise it'll be ready by then.' He grinned mischievously. 'Got to look your best at that wedding on Saturday.'

After leaving Boland's Outfitters, Willie made a beeline for The Independent House down the street. Please God, he thought, let Peter be around. But when he asked for O'Dwyer at Reception he was told that he was out on assignment.

'The best time to catch him in here is generally before nine or after five,' the receptionist told him.

With time on his hands Willie thought about what he should do next? Should he visit some of the addresses he was at yesterday? No, he decided. Too risky. All those places were bound to be under surveillance. Would it be an idea to take Jane to lunch? At first he was inclined to dismiss the idea on the grounds that if he told her about last night's happenings she might be worried about his safety. But then when he thought about her lovely smiling face, he changed his mind. I could do with a nice distraction, he thought. And what could be nicer than seeing Jane. It would be a way of making up to her too for all his absences of late. A nice surprise. There would be no need to say anything about what was troubling him at the moment. Anyway, at this moment she'd no idea how much he was caught up in Collins' work. And that was the way he wanted it to remain.

Jane, loaded down with hat boxes—replacement hats—was passing by the entrance, en route to the millinery department, when she spied Willie's tall frame coming through the main door. At the sight, of him, her face lit up with delight.

Not noticing her behind the boxes, Willie headed for the Millinery Department. Until he heard Jane's voice shout, 'Willie!' and she eventually caught up with him. He turned around. He thought, what a vision of loveliness she was, even behind those awkward looking boxes.

Catching his breath, drinking in her beauty, he smiled a warm smile and gasped, 'Jane!'

'This is a surprise!' Jane gaped at him in wonder.

'Here,' Willie tried taking the boxes from her, 'let me help you with those.'

'No, unfortunately this time I must refuse your chivalry,' Jane said with a twinkle in her eye. 'It's my job. Wouldn't it look funny now if I were to arrive at the counter with a handsome attendant doing the donkey work.' She laughed her wonderful laugh. 'Not to mention the rumors that would fly around the store like pig squat afterwards.'

Willie laughed heartily. Jane's talent for describing things never failed to amuse him. 'Naturally I don't want to embarrass you,' he said. Then hurriedly, asked, 'Could you manage lunch with me at our 'retreat' today?'

'Oh! That'd be lovely!' Jane said her heart pounding with pleasure. 'I wasn't expecting to see you until Sunday.'

'Right, I'll see you there at one o'clock,' Willie said moving away abruptly. 'Best not to delay you now; you're busy.' With that he was gone.

Jane wondered about the suddenness of his departure. Other times when he dropped in he was quite disposed to wait until she was free to talk to him. Why act so strangely today? Come to think of it, he didn't look at all well. He was very gray in the face. She could tell he was worried about something? What? she wondered. She wished to God he'd take her into his confidence; take her word for it that she didn't mind when he was out of the city. (Though she minded very much, she certainly wasn't going to tell him.) Anyway, didn't it make their reunions that much more enjoyable.

Lightening struck. That's it! she decided. Today he's going to tell me about another bye-election in the country. And he'll be full of guilt and recriminations. How she hated seeing him that way. All she wanted was for him to be happy.

Lunch was not a great success. As Jane prattled away telling Willie about her adventure with Philomena in the National Gallery the previous Monday, though he laughed a lot at her wonderful, vivid descriptions, his laugh had a hollow ring to it. Jane could see plainly that she hadn't his full attention: he was so preoccupied with whatever was worrying him. Every few minutes he'd fall silent. Along with that his eyes were smudged with fatigue.

Eventually, after studying him solemnly, Jane asked, 'Are you feeling unwell, Willie?'

Willie didn't answer immediately. He looked at her with no expression in his eyes. 'Sorry,' he said eventually, 'I'm not feeling the best. I think I'm coming down with something.'

'I think you are too,' Jane said. 'You haven't touched your lunch and you look very tired.'

Willie shook himself as if he was shaking off a bad dream. 'Jane,' he said, 'I'm afraid this lunch wasn't a good idea. I'm not the best company for you today.'

Jane said, 'I think you should go home immediately, have a hot lemon drink, take a couple of aspirin and stay in bed for the rest of the day.'

Willie reached over and took her hand in his. 'My lovely Jane,' he said sounding very contrite, 'I wanted to make it up to you today for being absent so much, but look at me, what am I but a junkyard of disappointments, let-downs and broken promises.'

'Please, Willie!' Jane admonished him. 'Don't talk like that. I told you before I understand that you have to be absent from time to time.' She couldn't shake off the lurking feeling that something sinister had happened which he was hiding from her.

'But these absences of mine happen too frequently, 'Willie said. 'I'm neglecting you.'

'You're not neglecting me,' Jane insisted. She thought, here it comes; he's about to tell me there's another bye-election coming up.

But he surprised her saying, 'You're so patient with me, Jane. I don't know how you put up with me?'

'Because I love you.'

Willie squeezed her hand tightly, 'And I love you too,' he said. 'But sometimes I wonder if I'm not standing in the way of your finding someone else who has a real future. I'm a glorious flop. What have I got to offer you?'

'Don't say things like that,' Jane could feel her blood chilling. 'You're not feeling well today,' she said striving to make herself sound chirpy. 'Go home, dose yourself, have a good sleep and tomorrow you'll feel on top of the world.'

'Always the super optimist,' Willie said with a wry smile.

Jane glanced at the clock on the wall. 'Gosh!' she exclaimed in horror, 'Will you look at the time. I have to get back to work.' Planting a hurried kiss on his lips, she asked, 'Are we seeing each other on Sunday?' As she waited for his answer, she fully expected to hear about another bye-election.

Again he surprised her. 'Of course,' he said.

'No bye-elections in the offering?'

'Not for the moment anyway.'

When she was gone, Willie thought, why is it when you want to say what's on your mind, you feel like a damn fool. But then, he thought, even if I wanted to, how could I tell her about what's going on, when I don't know myself?

Better to be sure than sorry and keep silent. That experience in Boland's Outfitters this morning shook him badly. It made him realize how close he came to being detected as one of Collins' associates by those G. Men. Collins was right, 'You never knew where the hell they're going to pop up next.'

As he had a few hours to kill before he reported for work, Willie decided to take Jane's advice and go home for a short nap. Along with everything else he was suffering from a terrible lack of sleep. The aroma of Sadie's baking met Willie at the door when he arrived home.

Sadie called from the kitchen, 'That you, Willie?'

'Yes, Sadie.'

'Could you come in for a minute?' Willie hurried towards the kitchen. 'I found out the names of the people who were arrested last night,' Sadie said. Her eyes glittered with venom.

Anxiety surged through Willie. 'You did?' he said. Then trying to keep the terror out of his voice, he asked, 'Was Collins among them?'

Sadie blessed herself. 'No, thank God!' she said. 'But the list of those arrested reads like an A. to Z. of the most important people in Sinn Fein.' Sadie picked a folded sheet of paper off the dresser and proceeded to read out the names.

'Those arrested,' she said, 'included Arthur Griffith, W.T. Cosgrave, Eamon Devalera, Count Plunkett, Doctor Richard Hayes, Doctor Brian Cusack, Sean Milroy, Joseph MacGuinness and Countess Markievicz.'

As he listened Willie clenched his teeth to stop his jaw from trembling. 'My God!' he cried in horror, 'that's most of the leaders gone.'

'You can say that again,' Sadie answered dolefully. 'And for good measure, the captives were herded off to a waiting gunboat at Kingstown.'

'How did you find out about it?' Willie asked curiously.

Sadie touched the side of her nose with her forefinger. 'Oh!' she said, 'Not meaning to give you a smart answer, but I have my sources. Sources which have to remain anonymous.' Suddenly it struck Sadie that Willie looked most unwell. 'God!' she exclaimed, 'you look like death. Are you ailing?'

'Oh, it's nothing,' Willie assured her. 'Just lack of sleep. I thought I'd grab a quick nap before going to work this evening.'

Sadie poured milk into a saucepan. Bless her heart! she said, 'I'll make some hot milk for you and lace it with a drop of the 'crater'; that should help you to sleep.'

That evening Willie went about his work in a stupor of anxiety and uncertainty. Once again Finbar didn't put in an appearance. As he worked, Willie couldn't get Collins out of his mind. Where could he be hiding? he wondered. Where could he start looking for him? Who was there left to contact now that most of Collins' comrades were arrested? He had great hopes of Finbar turning up tonight and shedding some light on what was happening? In his turmoil Willie managed to get the reels mixed up. After the first reel finished, instead of putting on the second one, he put on the third by mistake. This did not go down well with the patrons who were determined to let him know.

The revolt started with an aggressive 'shawlie' standing up and shouting, 'They must take us for right eejits. Look at that. Why don't they show us the right picture?'

She was gradually joined by other malcontents who screamed and yelled, 'Show the picture! Show the picture! We paid our money!'

Willie was in a fog of confusion. He realized his mistake, but for the life of him, he couldn't put his hand on the second reel. He stopped the projector and, in desperation, turned on the house lights. He remembered clearly that earlier he had the second reel in his hand in readiness to go on when the first reel ran out. But the question was, where had he put it? As the commotion continued in the auditorium, he searched desperately for the second reel. But the damn thing was nowhere to be found. Next, there were patrons hammering on the door of the locked projection room, shouting obscenities. They sounded so furious, Willie thought, if they could get their hands on me, they'd string me up.

Into the middle of this fracas came Finbar. Willie could hear his calming voice outside the door saying to the mob, 'All right, everybody, calm down. It's probably a glitch. Go back to your seats. We'll have everything up and running in a few minutes. If not, you'll get your money back.' Willie then heard the clatter of people's feet going down the bare staircase. He guessed the outraged patrons were returning to their seats. Finbar then let himself in with his key. 'What the hell is going on?' he asked Willie grinning amicably.

Willie now puce in the face with the humiliation of it all, answered, 'apparently I put the third reel on by mistake. But the trouble is now I can't find the second one.'

'Are you sure the agents sent the second one?' Finbar asked. 'They have been known to make mistakes in the past.'

'No this isn't their mistake,' Willie said mortified. 'It's mine. The second reel was definitely included in the package. I know because before I started I had it in my hand ready to put it on when the first reel ran out. Stupidly, I must have put it somewhere other than the usual place. And now I can't find it.' Finbar started to search. The first thing he did was lift a sheet of paper off a box and there it was — the second reel sitting on the box. 'Oh! Thank God!' Willie exploded, as relief surged through him.

'Get it on as quick as you can,' Finbar said handing him the reel. 'I'll see to the house lights.'

'You heard the news, I suppose?' Finbar said to Willie as soon as the second reel was operating smoothly and peace and quiet was restored to the auditorium.

'You mean about the arrests?'

'What else is news?'

'Would you have any idea where Collins might be?' Willie asked gravely.

Finbar detected great distress in Willie's voice. 'My guess is he's probably on his bicycle commuting between a number of addresses,' he said. 'Strange as it seems, the British authorities haven't one single clear picture of him, which means they haven't a clue what he looks like. With the result that the bauld Mick can cycle boldly and freely around Dublin unrecognized by everyone except his closest friends and comrades.'

Willie remembered a former conversation he had with Collins in Frongoch, when he declared unequivocally that under no circumstances, would he allow his photograph to be taken by the British. 'I'm camera shy,' was the way he put it. The man was amazing. Along with everything else he appeared to be telepathic. His anominity was certainly paying off now.

'You've seen him since the arrests, then?' Willie asked anxiously

'Yeah. I had a quick pint with him on O'Donovans this morning,' Finbar answered. 'He's quite shaken.'

'By any chance did he mention my name?' Willie asked.

'As a matter of fact he did,' Finbar said. 'I've message for you from him. He said to tell you that he'll be in touch with you as soon as the dust settles.'

§

At lunchtime the following day Jane confided in Philomena her fears that Willie might be cooling off.

'What on earth makes you think that?' Philomena asked. 'Didn't you have lunch with him yesterday?'

'Yes, but I got the distinct impression he would've preferred to be sitting somewhere else other than in that café with me.'

'You don't think there's somebody else?'

'I don't know,' Jane said despondently. 'Well, after hearing about your experience with Jimmy, do any of us know? He made a statement that has me terribly worried. I couldn't sleep last night thinking about it.'

'What was it?'

'When he was apologizing for being absent so much, he said,' Jane paused to think for a second, then resumed. 'I want to get the words right,' she said. 'Yes, his exact words were, 'I wonder if I'm not standing in the way of your finding someone else who has a future. I'm a glorious flop. What have I to offer you?' The words were like a knife twisting in my gut. They kept buzzing in my brain all night.' Tears glistened in Jane's eyes.

'He's your first boyfriend?' Philomena said.

'Yes, he's my one and only boyfriend,' Jane answered. 'I couldn't imagine life without him.'

'Ach, maybe he was having a bad day?'

'Or he was gently trying to give me the brush-off,' Jane said dejectedly.

'Have you arranged to see him again?'

'Yes, on Sunday,' Jane said, 'but it wouldn't surprise me one bit if he canceled that too. I never know from one week to the next if he's going to disappear.'

It was obvious to Philomena that Jane was feeling extremely insecure about Willie. How well she knew the feeling; those awful months prior to the day Jimmy came straight with it. All along she'd made a point of ignoring his hints and innuendos, telling herself, he's my fella, he loves me, he's going to marry me. She was so naive. But now she knew better. The affair finally ended that last night when, without putting a tooth in it, he mercilessly spelt it out: 'It's over, Philomena,' he said bluntly. 'I won't be seeing you again.' Men are such shites, she thought vehemently. However, she decided, Jane was upset enough without her adding to it by suggesting that Willie's words might be symptomatic of a break up.

Jane said, 'Did I mention that he looked very ill and when I referred to it he admitted he didn't feel the best.'

'There's your answer then,' Philomena proclaimed. She decided it was not the time to dwell on the significant indicators that lead up to her own break up with Jimmy. T'would only be heaping coals on the fire. At this stage Willie should at least be given the benefit of the doubt. Time, of course, would tell. But right now Jane needed a distraction. And what could be a better distraction than discussing one of Philomena's pet peeves. 'When it comes to sickness,' she said, 'men are the world's worst! They'll suffer in silence until some woman, either calls the doctor or takes them by the hand to the doctor. I know this because my mother goes through it all the time with my father. The way he carries on would drive any woman insane. There he is suffering like hell and my mother literally has to drag him to the doctor. Then later on she has to stand over him with the medicine bottle making sure he takes it. He's like a bloody baby.'

Jane laughed. 'I wouldn't know; my father died when I was eight years old.'

'Look, Jane,' Philomena took her hand. 'Don't come to any silly conclusions about Willie until you see him on Sunday. If he's feeling better, maybe you could broach the subject of your future together. But,' Philomena screwed up her face, 'if he's feeling sick,' she shook her head resolutely, 'don't even mention the subject. Take my word for it, the worst possible time to discuss things of that nature with a man is when he's sick.'

'You're such a good friend,' Jane said warmly. 'Where would I be without your help?'

'Well, if talking about it helps,' Philomena said, 'I'm a good listener.'

§

When Jane arrived from nine o'clock Mass on Sunday, Essie, the new girl in the shop, informed her that a young man was waiting in the parlor to see her.

'My name is Ronnie White,' the young man said proffering his hand. Jane would put his age at about fifteen. 'I've come to deliver a message from Willie,' he told her as they shook hands.

'He can't see me today?' Jane interjected, a lead weight bearing down on her heart.'

'No, he can,' Ronnie contradicted her. 'It's just that he's being delayed and he's going to be late.'

'How late?'

'Seven o'clock,' Ronnie said. 'He wants you to meet him at the Pillar.'

'I'll do that,' Jane said pertly, giving the impression that this was quite a normal arrangement.

'Thanks, Ronnie, for bringing me the message.' As Ronnie moved to go, Jane was suddenly conscious of the frailty of his appearance, not to mention his somber expression. She hastened to ask, 'Could I offer you breakfast or a cup of tea or something?'

Ronnie beamed genially. 'Breakfast would be very nice.'

Jane thought, he's so thin; he certainly looks like he could do with a decent meal. 'I'll have to ask you to come into the kitchen,' she said.

'With pleasure.' Ronnie followed Jane into the kitchen. Thankfully it was empty. Obviously our Nancy and Eileen had gone to a later Mass, because the used pan was still on the ring of the cooker and the dirty dishes were in the sink. Sunday being Charmaine's day off, the girls made their own breakfasts. Not being a work day or school day, it was common practice for the family to eat big breakfasts. So Jane proceeded to cook rashers, sausages and eggs and make toast for herself and Ronnie.

Ronnie's eyes nearly popped out of his head when Jane put the plate in front of him. He rubbed his hands together in anticipation. 'Gosh! This is my lucky day,' he said tucking ravenously into the food.

When Jane joined him at the table, she asked, 'Did Willie give any reason for being late?'

'No,' Ronnie said. 'Actually, I didn't get the message direct from Willie.'

'Why not?'

'Because apparently he had to go out of the city early this morning,' Ronnie said. 'T'was Finn asked me to deliver the message.'

'Well, that is strange.'

'We're living in strange times, Miss,' Ronnie said.

'How do you mean strange times?'

'Well, with all those arrests the other night.'

'What arrests?'

'The arrests of all the Sinn Fein leaders.'

'Oh! I didn't know.'

'Did you not see it in the newspapers, Miss?' Ronnie asked.

'No,' Jane expressed surprise. 'Was it in the papers?'

'Course, Miss,' Ronnie said shoving a sausage into his face.

'Obviously I haven't been reading the right papers.' Jane remarked.

'Oh, you could easily have missed it,' Ronnie said. 'It was just a brief paragraph.'

'Was Michael Collins arrested?' Jane thought, maybe that was what was bothering Willie the other day.

'No. Thank God! Mick was one of the few who escaped.' Ronnie lowered his voice to a whisper, 'I'd say that's where Willie is this morning. With Collins.' He looked over his shoulder furtively. 'Don't tell Willie I told you this, but Mick had to go into hiding. He's wanted by the British authorities. They're scouring the city looking for him.'

Jane's hand flew to her mouth. What Ronnie was telling her could have serious implications for Willie: with Collins in hiding, where did that leave him? Leading Ronnie to the hall door she appeared calm and composed, but inside she was trembling.

§

The rickety bus bringing Willie back to the city from Balbriggan on that Sunday provided him with the first opportunity to ponder the past twelve hours. The night before, just as the picture was ending, Finbar burst into the projection room.

'Willie,' he said breathlessly, 'Collins wants to see you tomorrow.'

'Oh!' Willie expressed surprise as he eyed him quizzically. 'In the name of God where's he at?' he queried.

'That's just it!' Finbar said, ill at ease. 'He's not in the city.'

'Well, where is he?'

'You'll know that when you get there,' Finbar said, maintaining silence about Collins' whereabouts. 'I'll be driving you there, but unfortunately you'll have to find your own way back; because of other commitments, I can't dally when I drop you off. It means an early start.'

'How early?'

'Half-seven in the morning,' Finbar answered. 'I'll call for you. We'll be going North.'

'You can't mean the North of Ireland?'

'No! Not that far.'

Willie was momentarily speechless. Then he asked, flustered, 'Any chance I'll get back in time to see my girlfriend? I have a date with her tomorrow.'

'What time is the date?'

'Midday.'

'She lives in the city?'

'Yeah.'

'Better be on the safe side,' Finbar said craftily. 'I'll get young Ronnie to deliver a message saying you can't make it.'

'No,' Willie said defiantly. 'That's not good enough.'

'All right then, I'll ask Ronnie to say you'll be delayed?'

Willie thought for a moment, then said positively, 'Tell Ronnie to say that I'll see her at the Pillar at seven. Otherwise I'm going to be in scalding water.'

'Okay, Okay!' Finbar said. 'Simmer down. I'm sure there'll be a bus of some sort that'll transport you back to the City later in the day.' He took a notebook from his inside pocket, opened it on a blank page and handed it to Willie. 'There,' he said, 'jot down her name and address.'

The meeting with Collins took place in an imposing, palatial room of a secluded mansion belonging to some absent Anglo/Irish aristocrat, not expected to return till June. It was very much off the beaten track; located somewhere near Balbriggan. Among the group at the meeting were, Collins, Boland and six brigade commandants, whom Willie was introduced to but immediately forgot their names and their regions.

Collins opened the meeting saying, 'With most of the leaders gone we're in a situation of near crisis.'

One of the commandants spoke up. 'I think we should call an end to the fight for the moment,' he said. There were murmurs of assent from some of the other commandants.

Collins and Boland spoke up simultaneously, 'Not on your life, Hugh!' Collins said.

'No way!' Boland said. 'We carry on as best we can.'

'How can we?' Willie asked.

'We'll just have to work harder and make do,' Boland said.

Collins put in, 'Myself and Harry have no intention of hiding out in this house indefinitely. As soon as the dust settles we'll be back running things in Dublin.'

A discussion followed in which the names of volunteers — still free and still involved in the fighting — were bandied about as people who could tentatively occupy meaningful positions. 'All of which,' Collins finished by saying, 'will have to be sorted out at a later date and at another venue.' He then turned to Willie. 'This is where you come in, Willie,' he said with a guileful grin. 'I'll have great need of your administrative prowess setting up, not one but two or three offices, which hopefully will thwart the British.' He scratched his head. 'I'm sure you're all aware that I head the 'wanted' list. So the only way I can survive is to keep the authorities guessing about my whereabouts.'

'Any idea where these offices will be located?' Willie asked.

Collins referred to Boland. 'Harry there has made a list of possibles.'

Boland dug into his inside pocket and produced a list which he handed to Willie. 'They're all more or less back rooms in buildings throughout the city,' he said. 'Maybe you could vet them and report back to us.'

Collins butted in. 'When you've found the right offices, Willie,' he said, 'we'll see to it that you have lots of assistance setting them up.'

Complimented, Willie said, 'Thanks for your confidence.' He looked at the list. 'I'll start looking first thing in the morning.' Then with a shaky laugh, he added, 'This evening I have a heavy date in the City at seven. Any chance I could get either a lift or a bus from here?'

One of the commandants answered, 'Yes, there's a bus that runs from Drogheda through Balbriggan around twenty past five. That should get you into the city in time.' He looked at the clock on the wall which showed twenty past four. 'You'd want to hurry though, it's quite a hike to Balbriggan.'

Collins looked at Willie and grinned. 'Go on, By!' he said. Then looked quizzically at the rest. 'As we're going to be discussing strategy we can spare Willie?' he said.

The hike to Balbriggan took Willie practically an hour. And had bus driver not been so accommodating, stopping between recognized stops, he'd never have made it.

§

Jane was at the Pillar promptly at seven. Until this evening she never realized what a popular rendezvous the Pillar was. Pushing her way through the milling crowds of people meeting there, she searched for Willie. Because of his height, he always stood out in a crowd and she expected to be able to see him immediately. But he wasn't there. For the next twenty minutes, different people came and went. But still there was no sign of Willie. Jane didn't know whether to be worried or annoyed. She walked around the Pillar at least twenty times. She found this whole arrangement of meeting Willie there very mysterious. Why couldn't he have called to the house? Why the change in meeting place? How much was he involved with the people who'd been arrested? Her mind was a whirlpool of distressing thoughts. Maybe at this very moment he was languishing in some jail having been arrested himself. God! The uncertainty and the tension was driving her crazy.

'I'm terribly sorry for being so late,' Willie's voice in her ear jerked her back to reality. Surreptitiously he'd sneaked up on her.

Without thinking, Jane impulsively threw herself into his arms. 'Oh! Thank God you're safe!' she said fervently, her happiness at seeing him showed clearly in her face.

'Of course I'm safe, sweetheart,' he said when he released her. 'Did you think I was in danger?'

'No,' Jane tried to make light of it. 'It's just I was a bit mystified about meeting you here at the Pillar rather than at home.'

'Oh that!' Willie laughed it off. 'As I was out of town, I thought I'd save time meeting you here.' He took her elbow and propelled her away from the crowds. 'Let's walk up towards the Green,' he said. 'It'll be quieter there.'

Pushing their way through the crowds packing the city this fine Sunday evening, made conversation impossible. Until they reached

Saint Stephen's Green. During the day Jane had made a decision. She would ask Willie straight out how close he was to Collins and exactly what their relationship was. The chat with Ronnie this morning opened her eyes to a lot of things. Now, more than ever, she was convinced that Willie was withholding many secrets from her. As they held hands walking through the gardens of the Green — so beautifully manicured and pristine — Jane's troubled mind seemed to find peace at last.

'So what was the mad rush out of the city this morning all about?' she asked Willie, doing her best to sound casual.

Willie indicated some vacant seats in a deserted area near the pond. 'Let's sit down, Jane,' he said.

'Oh, I should have brought bread to feed the ducks,' Jane exclaimed. 'It used to be one of my favorite pastimes when I was a child.'

When they sat down Willie said, 'Jane, I'm afraid I have a confession to make which may upset you.'

'Sounds serious!' Though Jane's heart was thumping, she put a lot of effort into sounding relaxed.

Willie took her hand and said solemnly, 'It is serious.' He took a deep breath. 'I wanted to spare you this, but in view of recent developments, I have to tell you.'

Jane's blood ran cold. 'You mean the arrests?' she murmured.

'Yes,' Willie said. 'You know about them?'

'Yes.' Not wanting to betray Ronnie's trust, Jane didn't elaborate. 'Who exactly was arrested?' she asked.

Willie told her the names.

'My God!' Jane declared. 'That means all those people who were elected are in prison?'

'Exactly.'

'But why?'

'Isn't it obvious?'

'Not to me, it isn't.' Jane looked bewildered. 'Weren't they elected by the people in a just and fair election?'

'Try telling that to the British,' Willie said. 'No,' he went on, 'the

British are most unhappy about the results of the Irish elections: first because the Sinn Fein members refuse to take their seats in the Westminster Parliament and second because of the Anti-Conscription Resolution passed by the Sinn Fein Executive recently. It really hurts them.'

'So where does Sinn Fein go from here?'

'That's what I was involved in today with Collins.' Willie said. 'Collins is number one on a 'wanted' list. He has to go into hiding for the time being.'

'Does that mean he'll have to give up the fight?' Jane asked.

'No,' Willie said unequivocally. 'To be absolutely frank with you, Jane, I think he's now more determined than ever to see Ireland freed from the clutches of the British.'

'But if he's in hiding how can he achieve that?'

'Through his many loyal followers.'

'Including you?' Jane chipped in.

'Yes, including me,' Willie said. He put his arm across her shoulder pulling her close to him. 'Jane, I don't want to worry you,' he said, 'but between the arrests, the 'wanted' list and my association with Collins, my safety and the safety of the friends with whom I associate, could well be in danger.'

'That's why you asked to meet me at the Pillar?' Jane said, beginning to understand a little of the circumstances.

'Yes, my calling to your house could implicate you and/or your family,' Willie said. There was a severity in his face that pierced Jane. It went right down through her ribs into her stomach and seemed to twist her gut. Willie had tears in his voice as he said bluntly, 'Jane, I'm afraid we're going to have to stop seeing each other.'

Jane's hand went to her throat. She swallowed deeply a number of times before she said, 'Oh, my God!' It came as a soft groan. She threw herself into Willie's arms. 'I love you Willie; I can't bear the thought of not seeing you.' Terrible! Terrible! Terrible! The words were yelling in Willie's ears as he held her tightly in his arms and kissed her passionately, her face, her neck, her lips.

'Darling Jane, it breaks my heart to have to say those words,' he said. 'You know I love you dearly, but I can't risk your safety. Even at this very minute I could be under surveillance.'

'Please! Willie?' Jane implored, 'All I want is to be with you.'

'Jane, we must be sensible,' Willie said holding her two hands in his. 'T'would only be a temporary separation until such time as the British authorities stop conducting their crusade against Sinn Fein and its associates.'

'That could be another seven hundred years.'

'Darling Jane!' Willie touched her face tenderly with his fingers. 'How much I'm going to miss your lovely face and your marvelous wit.' He pulled her back into his arms. 'Be patient with me, Jane,' he said. 'Things have got to get better.' He stood up and bowed his head in obeisance to give authority to his words. 'And now,' he said, 'I'm going to have to put you on a tram and send you home alone.'

'Can I write to you?' Jane asked as they waited at the tram stop.

'Yes, of course. And I promise faithfully to reply. But,' he cautioned, 'you must destroy my letters after you've read them and I'll destroy yours.' When the tram came, Willie kissed Jane good-bye. 'Chin up, darling,' he said. 'We've weathered worse storms than this.'

With that he disappeared into a lane way beside the tram stop.

Chapter XXIII

Collins decided on four offices in different places, which were at best, temporary; because he reckoned they were liable to a visit from a raiding party at any time, day or night. Often he received warnings of an impending raid. On one such occasion, early on, the raid actually took place when Collins was on the premises. As the raiding party was coming up the stairs, Collins, with a bundle of important documents in his hand, met them and brushed past them. He was out and walking the street before the raiders had time to think.

A few yards from the building Collins, his cap pulled down over his eyes, ran into Willie on his way to see him. Grabbing his arm and indicating the building, he turned him around, saying, 'Turn back, Willie. The enemy is within.' Then under his breath importuned, 'For God's sake cross the street; don't be seen in my company.'

Willie did as he was told. But, once again, the situation brought home to him how close he'd come to being identified as an associate of Collins. (Still Number One on the 'wanted' list.) He thought, wasn't I lucky to run into him! He was so quick off the mark tipping me off. Unlike Collins—who reminded Willie of a persistent garden weed that was trampled on over and over but always grew back straighter and stronger then ever—Willie was finding these close brushes with the British authorities very unnerving. The more they occurred the more convinced he was that he'd made the right decision regarding Jane. But God how he missed her!

In his capacity as a general factotum to Collins during his free time, Willie was mesmerized by the man's ability to tackle the crisis head-on following the arrests; his organizational skills were inestimable. In Boland's case too. Willie could see he was a man of selfless energy and determination. Though everybody looked on Boland as little more than a foil for Collins, it was obvious to Willie that he was much more than that. Collins in boyish good humor, Collins in a rage and so on, Boland was always there. He and Collins worked desperately to heal the threatened breach between those who wanted to call an end to the fight and those who didn't. It was a case of make-do, with both men shouldering more responsibility than would normally be the lot of ten men. Despite being Number One on that wanted list and taking on the roles of Adjutant General of the Volunteers, Director of Organization and Director of Intelligence, which were thrust upon him after the arrests, Collins still managed to cope—working sometimes eighteen hours a day. With the result that he became famous almost overnight. With Alderman Tom Kelly and Boland (who were joint Secretaries of Sinn Fein), Collins now strove his mightiest to piece together the crumbling framework of the movement.

In the reorganization of the volunteers, Cathal Brugha continued to hold the position of Chief of Staff. The rift between himself and Collins seemed healed for the moment anyway. Though he complained endlessly about the burden he was carrying, Brugha, nonetheless concentrated on tackling the threat of conscription in a more forthright fashion than Collins was prepared to accept. In the event of conscription becoming law in Ireland, some of the measures formulated by Brugha were so extreme, they included the shooting of British Cabinet Ministers. His standpoint was quite ruthless.

One morning when Willie arrived into Collins' office, he found Collins and Boland laughing hysterically. Collins let Willie into the joke. 'Would you believe the Chief of the British Imperial General Staff the bauld Field Marshall Sir Henry Wilson himself—has made a statement calling our Volunteer Army a ragtime outfit formed hastily from lawless members of the population.'

'Little does he know,' Willie said. Through conversations he had with Collins and Boland, he knew that the code of efficiency and discipline of Volunteers was as high if not higher than that of the British Army and its subsidiary—The Royal Irish Constabulary. Collins then went on to explain to Willie that disciplinary matters were dealt with first by the local Brigade Commanders, and if beyond their measure, by General Headquarters in Dublin.

At a later date, Willie was witness to Collins reprimanding a Volunteer from Kerry for not pulling his weight during a skirmish. Collins explained to Willie afterwards: 'The continued success of the Volunteers is entirely dependent on strict discipline, nothing should be allowed to contaminate efficiency and morale. In this way we'll have a highly efficient, reliable and soldier-like atmosphere pervading even the smallest task the local brigade commanders are called upon to perform.'

The method of warfare employed in the odd skirmish by the volunteers was unique at this time; it was preceded only by tactics used by the Boer Army in 1899-1901, though not as efficiently. The pattern as practiced by the Volunteers, proved its value; insofar as a limited number of soldiers, though lacking in arms, and having taken into account certain inferiorities of the enemy, could eventually prove themselves superior. As far back as Frongoch, Collins preached this form of warfare. Guerrilla warfare he called it. 'Strike the objective and run like bloody hell.' (His words.) Willie thought if he had a halfpenny for every time Collins repeated this line, he might be a millionaire. 'In any engagements,' Collins contended, 'the element of surprise is the factor which makes for victory. It's the only form of warfare the Volunteers can employ, because they're invariably out-manned and out-gunned. Along with that, this type of surprise action is something not governed by the British Army handbooks.'

Time would tell that it was the failure of the British commanders to appreciate the efficiency of the Volunteers which went a long way towards the ultimate failure of the British forces. From Field Marshall, Sir Henry Wilson in London, to the various army commandants in Ireland, all were guilty of not assessing at face value the efficiency of the Volunteers, who at this time were only engaged in the odd local skirmish. Nor did the Royal Irish Constabulary fare any better than the military. Their garrisons, dotted throughout the land, were subjected occasionally to sudden lightening strikes by the Volunteers who relieved them of their armory. In open country the story was the same, though more often than not, less than a third of the Volunteer force was armed with anything from the most ancient of rifles to a modern revolver.

Gradually, Willie was learning that what remained of the Executive, the General Headquarters or the Army were structured in such a way as to permit flexibility in the exchange of duties. Since, according to the British, it was an outlaw organization, its members were liable to arrest at any time. It was therefore essential that the whole organization should be very adaptable. In practice, none of the Departments of the General Headquarters kept religiously to its own sphere of work: every man was possessed of a reasonable knowledge of the workings of departments other than his own. Therefore, in the case of an arrest being made involving the loss of a particular member of staff, the vacancy was filled with the minimum of trouble.

'Of course,' Collins explained to Willie on one occasion, 'our unorthodox ways of doing things is a cause of great wonder to those British bastards who are only familiar with their own rigid orthodox methods.'

'In the event of you being arrested,' Willie asked, 'who's going to replace you?'

'How would you like the job?' Collins asked jocosely.

'I wouldn't be even half capable of doing it,' Willie answered looking quite serious. 'Considering most of the executives have been arrested, I don't know how you manage to keep things rolling. You must have at least three brains.'

'It's team work,' Collins said grinning.

'But without your leadership,' Willie said passionately, 'there would be no team.'

§

Lily being home from school for good provided Jane with a certain amount of consolation and diversion. To say the least, it was a relief to be able to talk to someone frankly about her anxiety concerning Willie and the secretive work he was doing for Collins.

One night when they were going to bed, big-hearted Lily suggested, 'Let's do a joint Novena to Saint Jude; he's the patron saint of the impossible. And remember, two prayers are better than one.'

'What do we ask for?'

Lily thought for a moment, then said, 'I think we should ask for this bloody small war, as it's called in the newspapers, to be over soon.' Lily opened her handbag and produced a picture of Saint Jude. Handing it to Jane, she said, 'The prayer to Saint Jude is on the back.'

'No,' Jane protested. 'It's your prayer; I can't take it.'

'For heaven's sake,' Lily insisted, 'take it. I know it off by heart.'

As Jane took the picture she asked, 'Has he ever answered your prayers?'

'Yeah, once — the time I was nearly expelled.'

'What!' Jane exclaimed, her face filled with supreme surprise. 'In the name of God! When was that?'

'You didn't hear about it?' Lily looked just as surprised.

'Not a word.'

'Of course, that was Mother hushing it up,' Lily said. 'The beginning of the term it happened.' She then went on to relate the details. 'When I was being carted off the hockey pitch after Fionula McCarthy deliberately hit me instead of the ball, that auld witch Sister Agnes, overheard me saying, *Jesus Christ almighty! The bloody bitch did it on purpose!*'

'So what happened?' Though it was serious, Jane was splitting her sides laughing.

'Wasn't I hauled up before the Reverend Mother. You know the Principal.'

'And?'

Lily adopted Reverend Mother's harsh voice:

'Miss O'Dwyer,' she says, 'we cannot put up with your obscene language any longer; it's such an atrocious example for the other students, particularly the younger ones.' At this stage,' Lily added, 'she was staring at me through her pince-nez, the nostrils quivering. I says to myself, here it comes, they're going to expel me. I didn't mind so much for myself, but then I started thinking about Mother. And the scandal in the family. Imagine it! One of the O'Dwyer girls being expelled from Sienna Convent! Silently I said the prayer to Saint Jude while Reverend Mother droned on, 'If you were anybody else but Father Vincent's grandniece, you'd be expelled on the spot. But because of your uncle's intervention, we're prepared to excuse you this time. However, should this appalling language ever come out of your mouth again under this hallowed roof, we'll have no option but to expel you.' ' Lily laughed. 'So you see, Jane,' she said, 'Saint Jude worked the oracle.'

Jane said, 'I can't believe this happened and none of us heard a word about it. Mother amazes me!'

'Oh, there was such a stream of fecken letters toing and froing between Mother, Father Vincent, Reverend Mother and myself, I lost count,' Lily said. 'Naturally, Mother wrote about the disgrace I was bringing on the family, preaching that three of her daughters had already been educated by the Sisters of Sienna Convent ahead of me and there was never a complaint. But there was I, the evil one, ruining the reputation of the family. And Eileen still to be educated. On the other hand,' Lily continued, 'Father Vincent's letter was more conciliatory. He says: 'Sometimes the Lord sends us crosses which upset and frustrate us. And although we feel like swearing at Him, we must exercise control. My dear niece, pray to Our Blessed Lady. Ask her to give you the strength and the will power to refrain from using obscenities when things go wrong and you feel frustrated.' '

Jane burst out laughing. 'Well, Lily,' she said, 'this is the best laugh I've had in a long time. But I still can't get over Mother's secrecy.'

'I'm so glad somebody is enjoying it,' Lily said. 'But, ever since that episode, it's been a real strain having to watch my every word.

Thank the Lord I'm out of that school for good.'

'Do you think you're cured of the cursing and swearing?' Jane asked.

'Somewhat,' Lily answered with a glint in her eye. 'Of course, if I go down to the cousins' farm to help out with the hay making, it'll all start again: that's where it came from in the first place,' she said. 'Those farm lads are never done f...ing and blowing when the rain is belting down and they're trying to get the harvest in.'

Jane hoped to God Lily wouldn't go to the country this summer. It was so lovely having her around again. She thought, who would she have to talk to about Willie and his secret activities? Who would console her when she was missing him so much and felt so insecure? There was only one person who fitted the description and that was Lily. She was such a pal. So understanding, so helpful and so funny.

But Lily had other ideas. Terrified she'd be roped into working in the shop, she pleaded with the mother, telling her that the cousins depended on her to help out with the harvest every summer. And Mary, feeling she owed a debt of gratitude to Aunt Maggie and Uncle Tom for supplying the milk that helped to put the O'Dwyer Family Dairy on the map, acquiesced and put up no objection.

So in the middle of August Lily packed her bags and left to do her usual two weeks stint helping with the harvest on Uncle Tom's farm. 'And,' as she put to Jane, 'brush up on some new swear words.'

§

The Sunday morning after Lily's departure to the country, Mary remarked to Jane and our Nancy over breakfast, 'I notice your two boyfriends haven't been around much lately. Have you stopped walking out with them?'

Jane was totally stunned by the question. How could she answer it? How could she tell the truth that because of Willie's association with Collins (who now had a price of ten thousand pounds on his head) he feared for the family's safety should he be seen either entering the house or in the presence of a member.

So it was a great relief when she heard our Nancy answering positively, 'Well, as far as Gerald and I are concerned,' she asserted, 'We haven't stopped walking out. It's just that he's been posted to the back of beyond down there in County Tipperary. Apparently, the British Army needs bolstering up to deal with those stupid Irish Volunteers who are wreaking havoc there.'

'How do you mean, wreaking havoc?' Mary asked, intrigued.

'Aren't they attacking barracks and military establishments all over the area,' our Nancy said. 'Taking as much armory as they can lay their hands on.'

'Don't tell me they're about to start another rebellion?' Mary was aghast.

'Ach, I think the authorities have it more or less under control,' our Nancy said. Then without attempting to disguise her disdain, she added, 'Gerald tells me that Field Marshall, Sir Henry Wilson, the Chief of the Imperial General Staff, calls the Volunteers *rats, gunmen and murder gangs.*'

For seconds Mary looked shocked. 'My God!' she exclaimed. 'What is the country coming to at all?' She then turned her attention to Jane. 'So what's happened to Willie?' she asked. 'He hasn't been around for ages.'

Jane's stomach gave a great lurch. St. Jude! she thought, please help me!

Suddenly at that moment there was very pronounced crash in the parlor. All three jumped up from the table and charged in that direction. They were just in time to see a stray cat flash through the open window. Shattered china littered the floor around the piano. Somehow the cat had managed to toss a large, valuable vase, originally sitting on top of the piano, on to the floor, breaking it into many fragments.

The next ten minutes were taken up with the two girls cleaning up the mess with brushes and pans. Mary, visibly shaken, stared at a large chunk of china in her hand. 'It's been in the family for generations,' she said solemnly. 'It was a very valuable antique.'

'Anyway, it could be repaired?' Jane asked.

'Not a hope,' Mary said. 'Look at it, it's practically in smithereens. It's a great loss. But maybe it broke a bigger cross.'

Jane, meantime, couldn't help thinking that her mother's loss was her gain. The way Saint Jude had responded so quickly to her prayer. At that precise moment when she was racking her brain trying to find an answer to her mother's complex question, he created the diversion and saved her the distress of trying to explain Willie's absence. She was sorry that it had to be at her mother's expense, but for her it was nothing short of a blooming miracle. There and then she decided to start a Novena to Saint Jude for herself and Willie.

She thought, won't Lily be chuffed when I tell her about this miracle: a stray cat saving my bacon immediately after I'd prayed to Saint Jude! She was now more than ever convinced that Saint Jude was the 'saint of the impossible.' Nevertheless, she still had to think up a convincing explanation about why Willie wasn't around. Sooner or later someone – mother our Nancy, or even Eileen — was bound to bring the subject up again. And what could she possibly say? She had written to Willie shortly after their last meeting two months ago. But heard nothing from him until a letter arrived last week. They were two awful months. Watching the post every day for a letter. Heartbroken when there wasn't one. Worst of all was the effort trying to appear cheerful and happy in front of the family; at all costs she had to give the impression that everything in her life was absolutely normal, when everything was anything but. Mother could be so perceptive too.

Then, after she'd given up all hope of ever hearing from Willie again, his letter arrived and her heart took wings. However, though she appreciated that he had to be extra careful about the words he used — in case the letter should fall into the wrong hands — it was anything but coherent. Mainly he talked about how much he missed her. Then went on to reminisce about the happy times they'd had together. And, except for telling her about the night the projector broke down and they had to give the money back to all the patrons, there wasn't a mention about his secret life working for Collins. Nothing about his activities. Nothing about where he was or what he was doing? The envelope was postmarked Dublin. That at least told her he was in Dublin when he wrote the letter. So many times during the past two months she wanted to just drop into the Projection Room at the Tivoli and see him. But, he was so worried about her safety that last time they were together, and made such a strong case against her being seen in his company, how could she possibly go against his wishes? More to the point, he'd probably hate her for taking such a liberty after all his warnings.

This Sunday she would sit down in her bedroom and write two letters: one to Lily telling her, first, about the Saint Jude miracle with the stray cat breaking the vase. And second, asking for her help in formulating a convincing lie explaining Willie's absence to the family. She didn't want to over strain Saint Jude with this particular petition because the big one — please let this little war be over soon, so Willie and I can be together again — was coming up in the Novena.

In a postscript Jane added, 'I'm about to tackle writing a reply to Willie's letter. But for the life of me I don't know what to say in case I put my foot in it.'

Because of the extraordinary tact she had to exercise, Jane found the writing of Willie's letter an impossible task. Despite her efforts to conceal her real feelings, hard as she tried, her anxiety and heavy heart seemed to trickle through the lines. It definitely wouldn't do. Willie knew her as a happy, jolly person. So he'd expect a happy, jolly letter. Not a morbid one full of woe. She had resigned herself to spending the whole of Sunday afternoon writing this letter to Willie, but with her thinking so indeterminate, at least a dozen crumpled pages ended up in the waste paper basket. She thought, the whole situation is so abnormal and artificial, not only can I not give vent to how I feel, but I daren't sound curious or critical or ask awkward questions. So what does one write about when one's mind is preoccupied with questions one dare not ask? Jane wracked her brain for ideas to write about. None came.

After two wasted hours trying to get started on the letter, she yielded unhappily to defeat. Willie's letter, she decided, will just have to wait till another day. 'Silence is golden', the quote came to mind. Maybe that was the answer. She went back to Lily's letter and added another postscript:

'I've now spent two hours trying to compose a letter to Willie. But it's impossible. Except to say, I love him and miss him, there's precious little I can say. Come to think of it, even the word 'miss' could be misinterpreted if it were to fall into the wrong hands. Ah, heck! I give up! I wish to God you were here to help me put the right words on paper. Write soon. Jane.

Dear Jane,

This has to be a quick note as Sean is going into the village any minute now and I'm depending on him to post it.

Regarding the letter to Willie. If I were you I'd forget about it. After all it took him two bloody months to write to you. I say, give him a taste of his own medicine. Let him wait.

Regarding the explanation to the family about Willie's absence, the only suggestion I can think of is, say he's working down the country for the moment. Well, wasn't he away a lot last year working for those bye-elections?

Oh! I've just had a thought! What would you think about having a chat with Peter about things? Maybe he'd know what's going on with Willie?

Got to go. Sean's knocking on my door.

Come the weekend I'll write you a long letter.

Keep your chin up. I'm worried about you.

God bless,

Lily.

It was typical Lily letter. No date, no address, just supportive and consoling words. God bless her.

§

'Right!' Peter said to Jane when he arrived back to the kitchen. 'Now that the little rascals are settled down, we'll be able to hear our ears.' While he was away Jane had started into washing up the dishes in the sink. 'Leave those,' Peter said taking the drying up cloth out of Jane's hand, 'you came for a visit not to do my chores.' He pointed to a chair at the table. 'Sit down and take the weight off your feet while I make us a nice cup of tea.'

It was Wednesday night. Nancy Pete's night out, when Peter did his husbandly duties. 'So what's the problem?' he asked Jane as he filled the kettle.

Jane swallowed hard before she answered. 'It's Willie,' she said.

'What about Willie?' Peter could see that Jane was very troubled. 'Don't tell me you've broken up with him?'

'No, it's nothing like that,' Jane said. 'It's just I never see him these days.'

'You think he's cooling off?'

'No, not that either.' Jane was silent. Sadness seemed to overwhelm her.

'For God's sake, Jane,' Peter said fondly. 'I'm your brother. You can tell me. I promise it won't go beyond these four walls.'

'It's a long story.'

'Try starting at the beginning,' Peter said. 'I'm all ears.'

Jane then proceeded to tell Peter what transpired the last time herself and Willie were together. She finished up telling him about Willie's recent letter which told her exactly nothing.

'Well,' Peter said soothingly, 'Maybe what I'm about to tell you might explain Willie's silence.' He gave a wry smile. 'If I wasn't married now with two children, my Nancy, could possibly be in the same boat as yourself at this time.'

'How do you mean?' Jane asked.

'I'd probably be gobbled up in Collins' machine too.' Peter pursed his lips for a moment. 'Jane,' he said gravely,' I don't know if I should be telling you this; it's top secret.'

'Oh! Please do,' Jane pleaded. 'I promise I won't mention a word to a soul.'

'Since the arrests of the leaders,' Peter told her, 'even though there's a price on Collins' head, he still holds the positions of Adjutant General and Director of Organization, which means he has to deal with thousands of directives and queries from all over the country, all of which he insists on answering himself. Along with that, he has to fill in for the people who were arrested. This includes dealing with the newly appointed directors: M.C. O'Reilly, Director of Training, formerly Collins' commandant in Frongoch. Then there's Michael Staines, Director of Equipment, Dermuid Hergarty, Director of Communications, Dick McKee, Commander of the Dublin Brigade. The man is worked to death. I know this because of my involvement with the two journals—*An tOrlach*—the official journal for the Volunteers and the Manual entitled *Organization Scheme,* which instructs the Brigade Commanders. Working on those publications requires me to keep in touch with Collins and Piaras Breaslai, the Editor of *An tOrlagh*. With the result that I'm getting an insight into the monumental load Collins is carrying since the arrests.'

'So that's where Willie comes into the picture?' Jane quietly queried. 'He helps Collins cope with the load?'

'Exactly,' Peter concurred. 'Willie, being free in the daytime, is very useful to Collins. Also because he's not married, Collins looks upon him as a free agent and leans heavily on him.'

'But isn't Willie running a terrible risk being associated with Collins when he (Collins) is number one on the wanted list?'

'No more than the other directors are,' Peter said. 'In fact,' he stopped to think, then continued. 'Every time I had to visit Collins to talk about *An tOrlagh*, I could've been in great danger too. Mind you, Collins has a great set up. His devoted friend, Batt O'Connor, a master builder, has cunningly built secret cupboards and a secret room for sleeping quarters in a couple of his offices. As a matter of fact, on one occasion I was actually in the secret room with Collins listening to the raiders tramping all over the house as they searched for him.'

'My God!' Jane said, her heart fluttering. 'You must've been shaking in your boots?'

'Shitting in my trousers would be more like it,' Peter laughed. 'God! It was incredibly eerie,' he added grimly. 'After that experience I decided to skip Collins and deal directly with Breaslai. After all, I can't afford to be taking such risks when I have a wife and two children to look out for.' Peter continued, 'People say that Collins is a psychic; either that or his comrades love him so much, they'll literally put their lives on the line to make sure he's safe.'

'Maybe, like the proverbial cat, he has nine lives,' Jane said.

'That too,' Peter said laughing. 'But going on my knowledge of him in Frongoch, I think it's all within himself. Ironically, the training he got in the Civil Service and the Post Office in England contributed greatly to his organizational skills. As for his memory! It's amazing! It seems to soak up information and retain it just like blotting paper. So, you see,' Peter said as he poured another cup of tea for Jane, 'Willie is probably under a lot of pressure working for Collins. I know Collins is very fond of him and depends on him a lot. At the same time, Mick doesn't force anyone to do anything against their better judgment, their conscience or their beliefs.'

The front door slamming indicated that Nancy Pete was back.

Putting two fingers to his lips, Peter said, 'Not a word to the ball and chain.'

Nancy Pete entered. She nearly had a fit when she saw Jane. 'Christ Almighty! Peter, you're entertaining in the kitchen!' she thundered. 'Why the hell couldn't you light a fire in the drawing room?'

'It's much cozier in here,' Peter said calmly.

'It may be cozier,' Nancy Pete said disdainfully, 'but do we have to inflict all those wet nappies drying out on the line above, on our guests?'

Peter looked up at the wooden laths that served as a clothesline high above their heads at the ceiling. Right enough, it was overloaded with wet baby clothes and nappies.

'Didn't even notice them,' Peter said languidly.

'You'd notice them if you'd laundered them and hung them there,' Nancy Pete said waspishly. 'Trouble is you're too damn lazy to light a fire.'

Peter ignored the insult. 'I take it the play was disappointing then?' he said, by way of a diversion.

'Oh, the play was all right,' Nancy Pete snorted. 'It's coming back to this mess that irritates me.' She waved her hand to take in the sink full of dirty dishes. 'And just to add to my miseries,' she said angrily, 'the dishes are still there.'

Jane's anger at Nancy Pete's attack on her brother made her chest heave and puff like the bellows hanging by the stove. If I had my way, she thought, I'd kick that wan's arse so hard she'd never sit down again. Instead she stood up, looked at the clock and said, 'Gosh! Look at the time! I have to go.'

Peter walked her to the hall door. Opening it, he said, 'Go easy on Willie. He really does love you, you know.' Then after hugging her, he added, 'No matter how difficult it is, write that letter to him. You've no idea what a difference it'll make in his life.'

'All right,' Jane said. 'Now that I've had these few words with you, maybe it'll come easier to write that letter.'

'Please don't mention to anyone, including Willie, what we talked about tonight,' Peter said anxiously. 'You're privy to that information in the strictest confidence.'

'Course not,' Jane assured him. Impulsively, she gave her brother another hug. 'Thanks a million for all your help,' she said.

'Anyway,' Peter told her, 'if you ever want to have a chat about things, I'm on my own here most Wednesday nights.'

'I may take you up on that,' Jane said brightly. Then left.

Chapter XXIV

In his work as Adjutant General and Director of Organization, the real Collins emerged. He was a man who was both fastidious and methodical. Despite the conditions under which he worked — alternating between his various offices — he had the trained Civil Servant's hatred of loose ends and anything which resembled untidiness. Willie discovered this from his experience working for him and from reading directives issued by him in which he upbraided brigade commanders and intelligence officers for seemingly small details they'd overlooked.

A good example of this was a directive from him dated 15 September, l918 to Michael Lacy of the Mid-Limerick brigade; in it he demanded 16/8d for copies of *An tOlagh* allocated to his brigade and still not paid for. He finished the directive by saying, 'As far back as the 31st August, 1918, I requested this bill to be paid. Now, I do not request, I insist.'

From time to time Collins spoke to Willie about all manner of men he had to deal with. Of some he spoke very highly of others he said nothing at all. The former he was always at great pains to disguise from them anything which might have the look of too much praise, but he didn't spare his feelings for those whom he considered to be valueless to the fight. 'Many's the time,' he said laughing, 'more than one commander has found himself being chased down the steps of this irate Adjutant General's office.'

Willie was beginning to realize it was useless attempting to pull the wool over Collins' eyes: he carried around in his head a mass of information regarding the doings of every brigade.

A typical example happened on an occasion when Willie was on duty. A brigade officer from the country was in Collins' office awaiting his arrival. He told Willie:

The last time I arrived in Dublin to see Collins, it was late at night. I'd little hope of seeing him until the following morning. But to my surprise, I was directed to his office and found him still hard at work reading and commenting on a mass of papers in front of him. As I entered the room he asked me 'Do you know Breffini Moran?' I said I didn't. 'Well,' says Collins, 'he's an idiot and the sooner someone tells him so the better for us and for him.'

That was my introduction to the man who was universally admired by the men of the brigades.

Then it seemed Collins' manner changed in a moment. He told me to sit down, gave me a cigarette, asked me the purpose of my visit. I told him, arms and ammunition were in great shortage. To my amazement, he began to reel off a list of skirmishes which my brigade had had with the enemy. 'Not bad,' he commented. Then began to pace the room. He says, 'If I had a few more brigades of the quality of yours, I'd be happy. Luckily, the good ones outnumber the bad by a fair majority.' He went on, 'Would it surprise you to know that in some brigades there's never a shot fired except at a bird?' That would surprise me, I said. He thought about it for a moment then asked, 'How about that last job you were allocated?' Went smooth enough, I said. 'Haven't got the report to hand yet,' Collins said, by way of explanation as to why he didn't know the facts. 'How did the lads fare? No casualties, I hope?' he asked. No, thank God! We'd no losses, or casualties, I informed him. He was full of enthusiasm. 'Grand,' he says. 'It deserves a drink.'

And off we went to Vaughan's Hotel.

§

'Bugger it!' Collins made little effort to hide his exasperation.

'What's up?' Willie asked.

'The fecken usual!' Collins lifted his head out of the ocean of paper that surrounded him. 'They're all looking for arms and ammunition.'

'The Brigades?'

'What else,' Collins hissed. 'I've never read anything like the grumbles and grouses issuing from them.' He held up a huge sheaf of papers. 'There's not one in there that isn't looking for more arms and ammunition. What do they take me for? I can't work bloody miracles.'

'What about Staines?' Willie asked. 'Isn't he supposed to be in charge of equipment?'

'Staines' begging memorandum tops the heap.' Collins read it out for Willie: ' 'Mick,' he read, 'how can a unit of fifty men, only half of whom are armed, work on the basis of seventeen rounds of ammunition?' '

'He's more or less tossing the problem into your lap?' Willie said. 'So what are you going to do?'

'There's only one thing I can do,' Collins said. 'Issue a strong directive to each brigade commander to step up the raids. What they're capturing is a mere one thousandth of what we really need. They know well the purchase of arms is very difficult and always dangerous for those engaged in that very vital task.' Collins stopped to think, then nodded his head decisively. 'Yes, that's the solution,' he said. 'I know t'will worry them all when I tell them that for the moment their allocation of arms and ammunition must remain as it is. That's got to be it,' he said doggedly. 'And no if, ands or buts about it.'

Although Collins sounded tough at this moment, Willie knew from experience, he would stand on his head for any of those brigade commanders. Despite all his pressures, to Mick's mind, no one was insignificant. He worried about his 'lads' as he called them. Anyone who came to Dublin to see Mick Collins was sure of a hearing. He was never too busy and nothing was more important than the man waiting to see him. What could be done was done. Sometimes the almost impossible was achieved. If by attending to a particular want that made a man or a group of men happier, Collins saw to it that it was done.

Willie could see how these personal attentions of Collins endeared him to the men of the brigades. He was especially considerate to those in trouble or, in particular, to relatives of men killed or captured.

§

This Halloween night heading in the direction of Francis Street and the Tivoli to see Willie, Jane pondered the extraordinary factors that brought about this situation.

It started this morning. Out of the blue Willie appeared in the Department Store looking for her when she was in the Stock Room trying to solve the mystery of a missing hat. This particular hat was probably one of the most expensive carried by the Store. It was being held for a wealthy customer who couldn't make up her mind whether to buy it or not yesterday. She paid a deposit on it and said she'd bring her mother in this morning to help her make the decision. Jane remembered distinctly putting the hat in the usual 'on hold' shelf. But for the life of her she couldn't find it now. And the customer and her Mother were at the Millinery Department counter waiting for it.

Suddenly in the midst of her search, Philomena arrives in the Stock Room all excited and announces, 'Your Viking boyfriend is upstairs. He'd like to have a word with you.'

'Sweet Mother of God!' Jane ejaculated. 'I can't leave here until I find that bloody hat.'

'Right!' Philomena said. 'I'll take over here. You go.'

As Jane mounted the stairs from the Stock Room, she thought, why do things like this have to happen to me? After all those months not seeing him, he picks the worse possible moment to reappear. She wanted so much to see him, but now, with the customer waiting at the counter for her hat, she wouldn't have time to dawdle.

The sight of him, standing so tall and upright beside the entrance, facing out, awakened those tender, racing feelings in her blood and on her skin. As she rushed towards him, she had a crazy impulse to throw herself into his arms, but just in time realized where she was. When she arrived at his side, he turned and gave her that lightening up smile that always slayed her emotionally.

'Willie!' she gasped. 'This is a surprise!'

'I hope I haven't picked a bad moment?' he said.

'No, not at all,' Jane assured him, feeling a right hypocrite. If she were to tell the truth, she'd have said, this particular moment couldn't be more diabolical.

Willie said, 'It's about a job I thought you might be interested in?'

'What is it?'

'You read music, don't you?' Willie asked.

'Yes,' Jane said, looking totally mystified. 'Is the job to do with music?' she asked.

Willie hesitated, thinking. 'It's a bit complicated,' he said. 'Do you have a few minutes to spare? Maybe we could have a quick cup of tea in the café upstairs?'

Jesus! Jane thought, what can I say? If I say no, I'll probably never see him again. If I say yes, I'll probably lose my job. I just can't win.

Willie noticed her indecision. 'Bad idea?' he said.

Just then Jane saw Philomena arrive at the top of the stairs on her way from the stock room. She had the missing hat in her hand. She waved the hat triumphantly in the distance for Jane to see, mouthing the words, 'Take your time.'

Breathing a sigh of relief, Jane gushed. 'No, no! It's a great idea.'

After the tea arrived on the table, Willie said, 'About this job.'

'Sounds very mysterious,' Jane remarked.

'Well, I think it's different from anything you've ever done before,' Willie said.

'I'm on tenterhooks,' Jane said. 'What on earth is it?'

'It's playing the Pianola in the Tivoli Cinema for the pictures on Saturday nights.'

'A pianola,' Jane said. 'That's a player piano?'

'Right,' Willie answered. 'But part of the job would entail turning off the mechanical part of the instrument for short periods and playing it like an ordinary piano. You'd need special sheet music, which we'd supply; that is, if you take the job?'

'Is this a new innovation in the picture world?' Jane asked.

'Not really,' Willie said. 'It's just that Fergus, the lad who normally plays the pianola for the pictures, announced last night that he had another job on Saturday nights which means he won't be able to do the needful for us any more on Saturday nights. So I thought of you.'

Jane silently whispered a prayer of thanks to Saint Jude. She thought, if I take this job, I'll be able to see Willie regularly every Saturday night. 'All right,' she said brightly. 'How soon can you get the music to me?'

'Could you come to the Tivoli tonight?' Willie asked diffidently.

'Of course,' Jane said. 'What time?'

'Could you make it as soon as you finish work?' Willie answered.

'That would give Fergus time to show you the ropes. And maybe you could try out the instrument at the same time.'

Though Jane was ecstatic at the prospect of seeing Willie again this evening, her joy was marred somewhat by the worrying situation that developed later in the store.

At lunch time Philomena told her, 'I'm afraid, Jane, we have a problem regarding that hat; you know, the one that was missing this morning.'

'But I thought you found it?' Jane said, alarmed.

'No, the hat I waved at you wasn't the one we 'put by' for the customer,' Philomena disclosed unhappily. 'I was forced to find another one like it.'

'Sweet Mother of God!' Jane exclaimed. 'What could have happened to the original?'

'That's the big mystery,' Philomena said.

'Holy Moses!' Jane uttered. 'I'm going to be in terrible trouble over this.'

'I didn't mention a word to Kathleen,' Philomena said comfortingly. 'Well, I was sure it would turn up.'

Jane said, confused, 'Maybe I didn't bring it to the Stock Room after all.' She thought for a moment, then said, 'is there the slightest possibility that it could've been put into a drawer in the department?'

'No. I searched high and wide,' Philomena said gloomily, 'systematically going through every single drawer behind the counter. But there's not a trace of it, or the box.'

'How did you manage the sales docket?' Jane asked. 'The copy of the deposit slip would've been in the box with the hat?'

'I just issued the receipt for the whole amount, less the deposit.'

'That means the copy of the deposit slip is missing too.' Jane sounded desperate. 'It's the end of the month; time to hand over the up-to-date inventory to the Bull. How on earth am I going to explain the missing hat?' There was misery in her voice. 'I can see myself being fired over this.'

'It's bound to turn up sooner or later,' Philomena said, optimistically.

Fergus — in his thirties — turned out to be an excellent demonstrator of the pianola, which was placed to the right of the screen in the auditorium of the Tivoli. Jane was amazed at the authentic sounds it produced. Nor could she believe how easy it was to play. Using it as a player piano was simply a matter of opening the door on the front, lacing a parchment covered in square holes on to two reels inside, closing the door and using the large pedal underneath to operate it. One didn't need to be a musician to play a pianola mechanically. The pedal did all the work, moving the scroll over the reels to produce the music. Playing it as an ordinary piano, however, was a different proposition. One definitely had to be a pianist. After switching the lever, on the front of the instrument, to the 'off' position, it was now up to the pianist to produce the music. In other words, he or she had to be a musician capable of reading sheet music. This was where Jane scored. She found the music easy to read.

As she was playing one of the piano pieces, Willie arrived in the auditorium; up to this he'd been busy setting up the projectors for the evening's entertainment. Fergus moved away from the pianola to talk to him.

'She's a natural,' he said. 'She catches on fast.'

'What did I tell you,' Willie said proudly.

When Jane finished the piece, Willie joined her. 'Sounds great,' he complimented her. Then asked, 'How would you feel about taking the job?' Before she had time to answer, he asked Fergus. 'What's the pay like?'

Fergus stroked his chin thinking. 'Uh! For a Saturday night,' he said, 'probably about a half-crown an hour.'

'So?' Willie looked inquiringly at Jane, 'What's the verdict?'

Jane didn't have to think twice. As far as she was concerned, she didn't give a damn if she didn't get a penny. The thought of seeing Willie every Saturday night was compensation enough. 'Oh, I'd love to do it,' she said stroking the cabinet of the pianola. 'It's an absolute dream to play.'

Willie said, 'We'll see you then on Saturday night around…?' he looked curiously at Fergus, 'What time?' he asked him.

'A quarter to seven,' Fergus answered, handing Jane copies of sheet music. 'Here, try these numbers out on your own piano,' he said.

'Thanks a million for doing the needful,' Willie said, looking lovingly into Jane's eyes. He then turned to Fergus and said, 'Would you mind walking Jane to the door, I've got to get back to the projection room.'

As she walked towards the door, Jane couldn't help wondering would this be the routine every Saturday night? She'd play the pianola, he'd be locked in the projection room and at the end of it all, she mightn't even get to see him? The least she expected this evening was a hug at the door. Though he talked about how much he loved her in his last few letters, he was still keeping a distance between them.

Jane spent the next two days frantically searching the Stock Room for the missing hat, without success. Thankfully the Bull was away on one of her buying sprees. And the two girls agreed that for the moment Kathleen wouldn't be put in the picture.

However, at lunch time the second day, Philomena, looking nervous and upset, asked Jane, 'How many more shelves are left to be checked in the stock room?'

Troubled, Jane said, 'Only three.'

Philomena shuddered. 'What on earth could've happened to that hat? You're sure you've checked and double checked every shelf?'

'Every nook and cranny,' Jane answered, the increasing nervousness showing in her voice. 'It's just disappeared into thin air.' Suddenly she sounded more positive. 'I'm fast coming to the conclusion that that hat was stolen.'

Philomena asked, 'By any chance did you leave the door open at any time?'

'No,' Jane was very definite. 'I'm absolutely scrupulous about locking that door every time I leave the Stock Room,' she sighed wearily. 'Don't you remember I handed you the key out of my pocket yesterday?'

'Yes, of course,' Philomena said. 'And I made sure to lock the door as I was leaving.'

'And you returned the key to me later on,' Jane said.

'So there were no slip ups made by either of us,' Philomena said. 'But gosh, Jane! We can't leave it any longer to tell Kathleen.'

'Holy Mother of God!' Jane sounded like she was choking. 'She's going to think I stole it.'

'Don't be silly.'

'Well, from her standpoint,' Jane said, 'it'll be the only logical explanation. I'm the thief.' She groaned at the thought. 'Please,' she pleaded with Philomena, 'could you leave off telling Kathleen for just one more day?'

Philomena considered her plea. 'Ach,' she said eventually, 'I suppose I could.' Then more cheerfully, she added, 'My gut feeling tells me that that hat will turn up when we least expect it.'

Coming up to half-five, Jane, the sweat lashing off her, was standing on the ladder for the umpteenth time re-checking the top shelves, when she heard Percy's posh voice addressing her suavely,

'Lost something?'

Turning round she saw him standing in the doorway grinning like a Cheshire Cat. Jane felt a jolt as if someone had punched her in the chest. It was now sticking out a mile that this stupid eejit had something to do with the disappearance of that hat: somehow or other he managed to get into the Stock Room and pinch it.

'Just a hat,' she said. On the surface she appeared calm and composed, but inside she was trembling and actually felt sick.

'By any chance would it be a hat with a deposit on it?'

That did it.

'Jesus! Jane burst out, losing control. 'You dismal fool!' she screamed at him angrily. 'You're the thief! You damn well took it!'

'However did you guess?' Percy said with a derisive grin.

'However do you think?' Jane said waspishly.

'Well, as it happens I do have the hat,' Percy said. 'But it's going to cost you to get it back.' His face smirked with satisfaction.

'Cost me what?' Jane asked cuttingly.

'An evening spent with me at the ballet,' Percy answered, again with that stupid grin on his stupid face.

'I told you before I have a boyfriend.'

'Who cares?' Percy said. 'If you want your hat back, that's the price. Take it or leave it.'

'I'll report you.'

'Go ahead,' Percy said defiantly. 'It'll be your word against mine. And,' he sneered, 'who's going to believe an apprentice over the Managing Director's son?' He looked at his watch. 'You have exactly three minutes to make up your mind.'

Jane calmed down. She realized this was not a moment to prevaricate; this unscrupulous bastard had out maneuvered her totally. One thing was certain, she wanted that hat back, no matter what the cost.

'All right,' she said yielding unwillingly. 'When and where is the ballet?'

'It's tonight in the Gaiety,' Percy had that sickly grin on his face again. 'I'll bring the hat and you can wear it.'

'You'll bring the hat, but I definitely won't wear it,' Jane said resolutely.

'Whatever! Suit yourself,' Percy said. 'See you at the Gaiety then at half-seven this evening.'

As he was leaving, cheeky as you like, he said, 'I'll be the one carrying the hat box.'

Jane decided not to tell Philomena in case she might try to dissuade her. As she saw it, she really had no choice. And even though there was no guarantee that she'd get the hat back, she had to take a chance and go through the tedium of sitting beside that stupid jackass for the duration of the ballet. When Jane met Percy he was dressed to the nines in a full dress suit complete with tails. He handed her a bunch of flowers and a box of chocolates which left her momentarily dumbfounded. However, determined not to show weakness, she quickly regained her equilibrium and without as much as a 'thank you' immediately asked, 'Where's the hat?'

'Oh, I checked it in with my coat at the cloakroom,' he told her. Then asked, 'Would you like me to check your coat in?'

'No, thank you,' Jane said. 'The only reason I'm here is to get the hat back.'

'In time,' Percy said laconically. He then escorted her up the stairs to a Box. Jane thought, would anyone believe it! Me on my own with Percy — who already presented me with a bouquet of flowers and a box of chocolates — here in a Box at the Gaiety Theater. Nonetheless, Jane came armed with a long hat pin in her hat in case he tried anything on. Strangely enough Percy turned out to be the perfect companion. The ballet was *Swan Lake*. As the story unfolded, he explained what was happening. Then during the intermission he surprised her further by going outside and arriving back with a tray containing a cup of tea and a plateful of biscuits for her and a whiskey-soda for himself. During the second half, Jane, on alert, waited for the unwanted advances. But they never came.

When the show ended, Percy retrieved the hat box from the cloakroom and presented it to Jane. 'Open it,' he ordered. Jane opened it. Right enough the hat was there as was the Deposit slip. She let out a sigh of relief. Outside the theater Percy hailed a cabby.

Jane said very decidedly, 'I can easily take the tram from here.'

'Not on a date with me, you won't.'

Jane yielded. But now under the cover of darkness in the cabby, she definitely anticipated the worst. But, surprise, surprise, Percy still kept his hands to himself.

'How did you get into the Stock Room?' Jane asked him.

'With the key, of course.' Percy's tone of languid assurance was most irritating. 'I have access to the keys of all the rooms and offices in the building,' he said. Then he added, 'Don't worry, I won't be trespassing on your territory again, I won the bet.'

'What bet?'

'The one I have with a chap I gamble with,' he said complacently. 'Recently I bet him a hundred pounds that I'd get you to accompany me to the ballet. He was in the audience tonight and saw for himself.'

Jane turned the full force of her anger on him. 'You really are contemptible,' she said. 'All the misery you've caused me during the past two days searching for that hat.'

'Contemptible I may be,' Percy smirked, 'but winning is all important to me. After tonight I'll be one hundred pounds to the good. Not to be sneezed at, eh?'

When they finally reached home, Jane jumped out of the cab, ran like a rabbit clutching the hat box and disappeared inside. Later, getting ready for bed, after telling Lily the end of the saga of the missing hat, Jane remarked, 'I know it sounds crazy, but I actually enjoyed that stupid twit's company at the ballet. I couldn't find fault with it.'

'Don't tell me you're falling for the bugger?' Lily, in bed stared incredulously at her sister.

'Not on your life!' Jane said. 'However, it was interesting to see how the other half lives.' She smiled wryly. 'Because I can't see Willie ever being able to afford to shower me with such luxuries.' Jane thought for a moment. 'I don't think I'll mention it to him; it might undermine his self-confidence even more.' As there was no response from Lily, Jane was suddenly aware that she seemed to be only half listening. Worried, she asked, 'Is something the matter?'

Looking solemn, Lily said, 'I've something to tell you.'

'Good, I hope?' Jane sounded concerned.

'Perhaps, in the long run, it might turn out to be good.' Lily said, not sounding terribly positive.

'What is it?' Jane asked anxiously. Lily's demeanor worried her. Something was obviously bothering her.

'Well, it's not definite yet,' Lily said, 'but I'm hoping to get a certain job.'

'But sure that's marvelous!' Jane said, relieved and excited.

'Where is it and when will you know?'

'It's in O'Grady's of Capel Street,' Lily said, 'and I should know by early next week.'

'That's the shop that sells farm machinery?'

'Yeah,' Lily said. 'It has a Gardening Section too. That's where the job is.'

'Well, aren't you the secretive one!' Jane said frivolously. 'You never said a word.'

'Ach,' Lily said, shrugging. 'I didn't want to say anything until I was sure I had the job. Wouldn't I feel a right eejit now if I talked to all and sundry about a job I mightn't even get…'

'You're right! I suppose,' Jane said. 'Still you could've told me quietly.'

'I wanted to,' Lily said, 'but you've been so busy of late with so many things going on in your life: playing the pianola at the Tivoli, losing the hat and having a date with the boss' son.' Lily laughed. 'What an exciting life you lead.'

'Exciting! You've got to be joking!' Jane exclaimed. 'Except for the pianola, the rest was extremely stressful. However, I am sorry I've been so preoccupied with my own affairs of late but,' she said encouragingly, 'that job sounds like it was made for you. What with your experience working on the farm, learning all about the machinery, the soil, the seeds and how to grow things.'

'I sincerely hope that O'Grady's think the same,' Lily said with an oblique smile. 'Needless to say I'll be on tender hooks till I know I've got the job. Because,' she said dolefully, 'you and I know what the alternative will be if I don't.'

'Slaving in the family dairy,' Jane said.

Thankfully, when Lily called to O'Grady's Shop on Monday, much to her relief, she was told that the job was hers and she could start immediately.

Mary wasn't too put out when she heard about Lily's new job. She thought, God knows best. Had Lily opted to work in her Dairy, her volatility and foul language could well prove a big embarrassment.

Chapter XXV

On the 11th of November 1918, with the signing of the Armistice, the Great War in Europe ended. Shortly afterwards, Collins told Willie, 'The British Government's attention is now fully focused on Ireland. Finished with the German war, I'm told they're now ready to sweep the Irish board clean of what they call the 'unruly elements'—that's us,' he laughed. 'But first they have to dissolve parliament and call a general election.'

The general election was ultimately fixed for the 14th December. Sinn Fein then issued its MANIFESTO to the Irish people as follows:

The coming General Election is fraught with vital possibilities for the future of our Nation. Ireland is faced with the question whether this generation wills it that she is to march out into the full sunlight of freedom, or is to remain in the shadow of a base imperialism that has brought and ever will bring in its train naught but evil for our race. Sinn Fein gives Ireland the opportunity of vindicating her honor and pursuing with renewed confidence the path of national salvation by rallying to the flag of the Irish Republic. Sinn Fein aims at securing the establishment of that Republic.

1. By withdrawing the Irish Representation from the British Parliament and by denying the right and opposing the will of the British Government, or any other foreign Government, to legislate for Ireland.

2. By making use of any and every means available to render impotent the power of England to hold Ireland in subjection by military force or otherwise.

3. By the establishment of a constituent assembly comprising

persons chosen by Irish constituencies as the supreme national authority to speak and act in the name of the Irish people. And to develop Ireland's social, political and industrial life, for the welfare of the whole people of Ireland.

4. By appealing to the Peace Conference for the establishment of Ireland as an Independent Nation. At that Conference the future of the nations of the world will be settled on the principle of government by consent of the governed.

The Manifesto went on to point out that Ireland's claim to her freedom was based on its possession of a distinctive culture and social order older than many, if not all, of the present belligerents. And not on any accidental situation arising from the war. Nearly every generation and five times within the past 120 years, our people challenged in arms the right of England to rule this country. On these incontrovertible facts is based the claim that our people have beyond question established the right to be accorded all the power of a free nation.

Sinn Fein represents the old tradition of nationhood handed on from dead generations; it stands by the Proclamation of the Provisional Government of Easter 1916, reasserting the inalienable right of the Irish Nation to sovereign independence, reaffirming the determination of the Irish people to achieve it, and guaranteeing within the independent Nation equal rights and equal opportunities to all its citizens.

Believing that the time has arrived when Ireland's voice for the principle of National self-determination should be heard above every interest of party or class, Sinn Fein will oppose at the Polls every individual candidate who does not accept this principle. The present Irish members of the English Parliament constitute an obstacle to be removed from the path that leads to the Peace Conference. By declaring their will to accept the status of a province instead of boldly taking their stand upon the right of the nation, they supply England with the only subterfuge at her disposal for obscuring the issue in the eyes of the world. By their persistent endeavors to induce the young manhood of Ireland to don the uniform of our seven-century-old oppressor, and place their lives at the disposal of the military machine that holds our Nation in bondage, they endeavor to barter away and even to use against itself the one great asset still left to our Nation after the havoc of centuries.

Sinn Fein goes to the polls handicapped by all the arts and contrivances that a powerful and unscrupulous enemy can use against us. Conscious of the power of Sinn Fein to secure the freedom of Ireland, the British Government would destroy it.

Sinn Fein, however, goes to the polls confident that the people of this ancient nation will be true to the old cause and will vote for the men who stand by the principles of Tone, Emmet, Mitchell, Pearse and Connolly; the men who disdain to whine to the enemy for favors, the men who hold that Ireland must be as free as England, or Holland or Switzerland or France, and whose demand is that the only status befitting this ancient realm is the status of a free nation.

Issued by the Standing Committee of Sinn Fein.

The election in Ireland resulted in an overwhelming victory for Sinn Fein. Out of a total of 105 seats for Ireland, 73 went to Sinn Fein. Of course, the electoral register now had changed out of all recognition. It was three times larger than for the last election in 1910 and included, for the first time, women over thirty and all men over twenty-one.

A number of factors favored Sinn Fein. The Irish Parliamentary Party was seen to be on the defensive from the very beginning: not only because it had lost a number of sensational bye elections, but also because they suffered a number of public defections to Sinn Fein while the campaign was in progress. The Party was unable to raise candidates for even a quarter of the Irish seats. So, in effect, Sinn Fein had almost swept Ireland clean of British political influence. Among the Irish leaders, Collins gained the seats for West Cork and Armagh, DeValera (still in jail) for East Clare and County Down and Arthur Graffith (also in jail) won Cavan and Tyrone/Fermanagh.

§

It goes without saying that from the day the war ended—a short time after Jane started playing the pianola in the Tivoli—until after the general elections in mid-December, Jane saw precious little of Willie. Once again he was caught up in the election campaign. This time, with others, he campaigned full time for Collins, commuting between West Cork and Armagh. He was so busy he ceased writing. So all Jane's wonderful fantasies about seeing him every Saturday night after the pictures ended, faded like the sunset. When Finbar wasn't available, a young lad named Milo, filled in for Willie. Milo had little or no experience of how to project pictures. On one occasion it took him so long to change the reels the audience ended up in total revolt. On this occasion Jane came to the rescue: though deafened by the din of the yelling and screaming, she played some light, popular songs of the day which gradually appealed to this disgruntled audience. Eventually they simmered down and joined in a sing-song.

When the election was over, Jane's heart soared with happiness at the thoughts of Willie being back in Dublin free to be with her again. (She hoped?) Also bringing joy to her heart were thoughts of Christmas. It was her favorite time of year. A time when the city was alive and vibrant with the hustle and bustle of Christmas shoppers. Add to this the brightly decorated shops so temptingly inviting. But for Jane—now a fully fledged salesperson—this was a particularly wonderful Christmas. Having completed her apprenticeship, she was transferred to the Jewelry Department where there was a vacancy. Needless to say, selling jewelry appealed more to Jane than selling hats.

On the Wednesday night after the results of the election were announced, Jane paid Peter a visit. To say he was ecstatic would be putting it mildly. Rubbing his hands together excitedly, he exclaimed, 'This victory should definitely change the course of Irish history. The people have spoken. The British Government will have no alternative now but to sit down with an Irish parliament, based here in Ireland and negotiate with it.'

However, uppermost in Jane's mind now was the question of how this situation would affect her and Willie's relationship. 'Does this victory mean that Willie can stop worrying about being arrested on account of his association with Collins?' Jane asked Peter tentatively.

'Not only can Willie stop worrying about being arrested,' Peter said confidently, 'but the British authorities will now have to release all the leaders they arrested in May.' He grinned roguishly. 'Aren't the majority of them now elected members of the new Irish Parliament, anyway.' Peter's laughter was full of merriment. 'Our parliament will be full of ex-jailbirds.'

Peter's joviality brushed off on Jane. 'Gosh!' she said excitedly, 'things are at last looking up for the Irish, aren't they?'

'They certainly are.' Peter produced a bottle of port wine and two glasses. 'I don't do this very often,' he said, 'but tonight, Sis, we have something really worthwhile to celebrate.' He poured the wine into the two glasses and handed one to Jane, saying, 'I know you're under age, but this is a truly special occasion.'

'And I suppose it's any port in the storm,' Jane said, facetiously.

Raising his glass, Peter pronounced, 'Here's to the new Irish Republic.'

'Under age or not,' Jane said, 'I'll drink to that.'

Yes, Jane thought sitting on the tram trundling towards Sackville Street, this is going to be a wonderful Christmas. Apart from Peter's joy and exhilaration about the general election, since the results were announced, Jane couldn't help noticing the happy mien of the people generally. With so many happy, smiling faces, an abounding air of optimism prevailed throughout the city. It was particularly noticeable in the shop; if customers weren't expressing relief about the Great War being over, they were marveling at the result of the general election.

§

When the show in the Tivoli was finished the Saturday night before Christmas, to Jane's intense joy, Willie walked her as far as the corner of Parnell Street. After he'd kissed her goodnight and was about to take his leave, she asked him if he'd do her family the honor of having Christmas dinner with them?

Before answering, Willie regarded her thoughtfully, then asked, 'Will Gerald be there?'

'I suppose he will,' Jane said, thinking, what kind of a question is that? However, she asked, 'Would that worry you?'

'It wouldn't worry me unduly,' Willie said with a wry smile, 'but insofar as we're opponents in this small war, it might cause some embarrassment to your family.'

'It didn't embarrass my family last year,' Jane said, keeping her voice light and cheerful.

'We didn't get around to discussing politics last year,' Willie answered. 'But in view of recent developments, someone is bound to bring up the subject sometime during the evening; it's inevitable.'

A feeling of concern crept over Jane. She gave a shaky laugh. 'Supposing I were to tell you that politics will be taboo in our house on Christmas Day,' she said. 'Would that make a difference?'

Willie had to smile at Jane's innocence. 'My sweet innocent Jane,' he said. 'T'would be like trying to push back the tide asking Irish people to refrain from discussing politics, at this time.' He went on, 'Whether they're for or against an Irish Republic, it's the one topic that's on everybody's mind and lips these days.'

There was a moment's silence. Jane wasn't sure how to answer him. Then suddenly she drew herself up and assumed a confidence she was far from feeling. 'If you ask me,' she said, displaying unusual dignity, 'I can't see anything wrong with people having a healthy debate about any subject, be it politics or otherwise.'

Willie roared laughing as he pulled her into his arms. 'Jane,' he said, 'how much I love you; your mind, your spirit your optimism.'

'You'll come then?' Jane asked timorously.

Willie still hesitated. 'I'm not sure,' he said. 'The last thing I want is to embarrass you or your family.'

'For God's sake!' Jane tried not to sound irritated. 'Isn't our Peter of the same mind as yourself about Irish politics. If he wasn't married with children, he'd be as much involved as you are.'

'Darling Jane!' Willie released her and looked ardently into her big brown eyes. 'As only you can, you've convinced me. I capitulate.' He smiled warmly. 'T'would give me the greatest pleasure to be present at your family's Christmas dinner. And thank you for inviting me.'

Jane felt it was the mention of Peter's name that persuaded Willie to come. 'Oh, Willie!' she said throwing herself back into his arms, 'I'm so relieved!' Then with a slight sob in her voice, she added, 'Christmas Day wouldn't be the same without you.'

As Jane wended her way down Parnell Street, she looked skywards and murmured: Thank you, God for telling him to come. Apart from wanting him there, I want Mother to see he's still part and parcel of my life; something she'll just have to get used to.

Christmas Day in the O'Dwyer home produced two big surprises. The first surprise happened after the Christmas pudding was served. Sate with food and drink, the company was now filled with festive light heartedness. Apart from the whole O'Dwyer clan (less Peter and his family) the company included Michael, Willie and Gerald. As they indulged in pulling Christmas crackers and exchanging jokes and anecdotes, out of the blue, our Nancy suddenly shot up, and to everyone's surprise, pragmatically tinkled a glass tumbler with a spoon.

'Could we have a bit of hush here,' she shouted. As soon as the noise died down, our Nancy, her eyes sparkling with excitement, said, 'I have a special announcement to make.' She stopped, smiled at Gerald, then apologized. 'Correction; Gerald and I have a special announcement to make.'

'You're engaged?' Eileen interjected excitedly, stealing our Nancy's thunder.

'Yes, Eileen,' Our Nancy looked surprised. 'How did you know?'

'Special announcements are always about engagements,' Eileen said matter-of-factly.

'Well as it happens,' our Nancy said, 'you're absolutely right,

Eileen. Gerald and I are engaged to be married.'

Eileen scrutinized our Nancy's left hand. 'I don't see an engagement ring?' she said, bold as you like. Our Nancy screwed up her face. At that moment she could willingly have wrung Eileen's neck.

'It's coming,' Gerald butted in. 'In early January.'

'Good!' Eileen smiled her approval. 'What good is an engagement without the ring?' she said.

Though Eileen's forthrightness over shadowed our Nancy's startling news somewhat, it brought forth bursts of laughter from the Company. Nonetheless, Mary didn't hesitate to show her approval of the engagement. Quickly she was up on her feet rushing over to embrace Gerald, saying with enthusiasm, 'Welcome to the fold of the O'Dwyer family.' The delight in her face bespoke the fact that she wholly endorsed this union. After congratulations and good wishes were exchanged and the celebratory drink was being imbibed, it was only natural that the subject of the engagement would take possession of the room.

Eileen, uninhibited, started the ball rolling asking questions like, 'When is the wedding going to be? Can I be a bridesmaid or flower girl? Where will it be held? Here or in England?' Unwittingly she was doing the family a favor asking questions they wanted to ask but were too polite to do so.

'Woe! Slow down!' Gerald said to Eileen. 'We've only just become engaged.'

Our Nancy explained, 'Gerald doesn't know where his job will take him next; whether he'll be allowed to stay in Ireland or be sent back to England.'

'Yes,' Gerald took over from our Nancy. 'It really depends on how things pan out here in Ireland in the immediate future.'

'You mean on account of the result of the recent general elections?' Mary asked.

'Exactly, Mrs O'Dwyer,' Gerald said with elaborate politeness. 'I'm hoping that once and for all those elections will settle the question about the British getting out of Ireland. Now that enough Sinn Fein members have been elected, the Irish should be allowed to get on with it and form their own government.'

Sitting beside Willie, Jane squeezed his hand under the table.

'If it was a case of the Irish being allowed to form their own Government,' Willie said, diffidently, 'I suppose you'd be returning to England?'

'Not necessarily,' Gerald said. 'If Ireland had its own Irish Army, I'd certainly apply to be a member of it.' He smiled engagingly at Willie, 'I am Irish after all.'

Willie gasped. This was the second surprise of the evening. 'You mean to say,' he tried not to sound too startled, 'you'd actually leave the British army to join the Irish one?'

'Exactly that,' Gerald answered. 'Of course, I may be jumping the gun here; we none of us know what the future holds for Ireland. So it's difficult to make solid plans till we see what way the wind blows.'

As Mary was distributing gifts from the Christmas tree to family members from each other, to guests from family members and visa versa, Peter arrived with Colbert (now two-and-a-half) and without Nancy Pete. (A popular arrangement with most of the company — if they'd admit to it.) For a change, Peter was his own boss; away from the jarring voice of the ball and chain.

Peter was barely in the door when Eileen caught hold of his arm. 'Our Nancy and Gerald are engaged to be married,' she jabbered enthusiastically.

Peter's face showed great pleasure at the news. After congratulating the couple, he said roguishly to Gerald, 'Do you realize what you're letting yourself in for? A family of nattering females?'

'Aye,' Gerald replied with a winsome smile, 'but what charming, nattering females they are!' To be sure Gerald was well endowed with the gift of the gab.

Colbert, this year, was even more over-awed by the Christmas tree. Like last year, Mary had made sure there were toys on the tree for the two grandsons.

On receiving his box of toy soldiers, Colbert said, 'Dih for Oosta. I give.'

Mary looked quizzically at Peter. 'Interpret?' she said.

Peter enlightened her. 'He wants to give the soldiers to his brother, Heuston,' he said.

'No,' Mary said gently to Colbert, 'This is *your* present; the soldiers are for you.' She then picked a medium-sized teddy bear from behind the tree and handed it to Colbert saying coaxingly, 'Teddy is for your baby brother, Heuston. That'll be *his* present.'

Colbert's eyes lit up with delight as he took the teddy bear and hugged it to his chest. 'No. Teddy my,' he declared obstinately.

Seeing the dismay on his mother's face, Peter intervened. 'Never mind, Mother,' he said. 'We'll sort it out later on.'

Colbert then proceeded to hold the ladies attention telling them that Santa had brought him 'a mo-ca,' and how he'd seen the baby 'eesus' in the kib at Ma dis moning.'

Meanwhile, Peter and Willie talking politics were joined by Gerald.

Willie said to Peter, 'Gerald has just been saying that he would join the Irish army when it's mobilized.' He gave Gerald a complicit smile. 'You don't mind me telling Peter this, I hope?' he said.

'No, not at all,' Gerald assured him. 'As long as it stays in this room and doesn't reach the ears of the British authorities.'

'Not a chance,' Peter said. 'As the saying goes, 'Careless talk costs lives.'' His eyes carried a wealth of good will. 'T'would be absolutely fantastic if the Irish Army could recruit professional officers of your caliber; all that training and capability.'

'Oh, I'm not the only one,' Gerald said enthusiastically. 'There are lots of Irish commissioned officers in the British army presently who'd be only too glad to join an Irish Army if and when it's in place.'

Chapter XXVI

The next step for the men whose hearts were set on independence for Ireland was the planning of the formation of a native government. They wasted no time. On the 21st of January, 1919 an Irish parliament (Dail Eireann) came into being in the Mansion House, Dublin. Outside the Mansion House that day American flags were waved, together with the Republican Tricolor, by cheering crowds, symbolizing the hope they felt that at the Peace Conference, due to be held in Paris, the American President, Woodrow Wilson, would insist on recognizing the rights of small nations, including Ireland.

This first meeting of Dail Eireann was supposed to consist of those members who were elected in the recent general election. But as it turned out that day, it was a sadly depleted assembly. Because out of the 73 seats gained, 36 of the victors were in prison, 4 were out of the country and 5 were unable to attend, among them Collins and Boland. Along with that, despite the fact that the Irish Parliamentary Party members and the Unionist party members were invited to attend, none of them did so. Yet for all its lack of representation the Dail provided a heartwarming sight for those nationally minded enough to care about a native government. Cathal Brugha, who was appointed acting President until DeValera's return, delivered the opening address in Irish.

However, on the very day the Dail was meeting for the first time, a clandestine incident was taking place in County Tipperary. Two Irish constables of the Royal Irish Constabulary, who were escorting a cart carrying gelignite to a quarry at Solohedbeg, were set upon by masked Volunteers and shot dead with revolvers at point-blank range. The killings were carried out by two young Volunteers,

Dan Breen (Commandant of the third Tipperary Brigade) and Sean Tracey who had received no orders from Collins or anyone else.

'If we were to wait for orders from Headquarters or Dail Eireann,' Breen said later, 'nothing would have happened.' After that, all around Ireland a picture of Breen was posted saying a REWARD of one thousand pounds would be paid by the Irish Authorities to anyone who would supply information about the whereabouts of this man.

At the time of this incident Collins wasn't even in the country. A week before the opening of Dail Eireann, Collins spoke to Willie about a plan being mooted between himself and Harry Boland, to try and gain DeValera's escape from Lincoln jail. 'If I can fix it with Finbar,' Collins said to Willie, 'how would you feel about helping us out?'

'Of course, I'd like to help,' Willie told him, 'but what exactly would my role be?'

'Your role would be to act as the look-out with Frank Kelly, when Boland and myself are opening the lock of the prison,' Collins told him.

Willie was aghast, 'You've actually got the key to the lock of the prison?' he said.

'Hopefully,' Collins smiled whimsically producing a key.

'How on earth did you manage that?'

'It took a bit of doing,' Collins said, 'but t'was the bauld Dev himself who worked the oracle: demonstrating amazing ingenuity, he smuggled out an impression of the key on a piece of soap. However,' he went on, 'first of all we need to talk to Finbar about letting you off.'

Willie said, 'I doubt we'll have any trouble getting Finbar's permission.'

'Still, the least we can do is pay the man the compliment of asking him anyways,' Collins said.

That night as Willie was tidying up after the pictures ended, Finbar arrived. 'So, tomorrow night you're off to England on an errand of mercy?' he said to Willie.

'Collins has been talking to you?'

'Yeah,' Finbar said. 'Don't worry about the job; it'll still be here when you get back.'

'Thanks,' Willie said. 'I really do appreciate your patience putting up with the inconvenience.'

'And I appreciate your courage participating in such a dangerous mission,' Finbar said, sounding very earnest. He touched Willie's arm affectionately. 'Be on your guard, lad,' he said. 'Be extra vigilant. Take good care.'

It wasn't until that moment that Willie realized just how risky the mission he'd agreed to be part of was going to be. He was cognitive of the fact that there would be a certain amount of risk, but Finbar's ominous words put the wind up him crosswise. However, he'd little time to indulge the worry. Because the following evening Collins, Boland, Kelly and himself set forth on the Mail Boat from Kingstown across to England.

At the end of their journey they stayed in a run down, seedy looking house in Lincoln, rented by a sympathizer. With a lot of help from inside the prison, a plan was devised whereby a key concealed in a cake would be smuggled into DeValera in Lincoln Prison. However, things did not go according to plan. First, this key turned out to be too small. Then a second key was made. But once again it proved a failure. The third attempt was successful, chiefly because the smuggled in key was a rough-cast one fixed by a prisoner afterwards with tools that were also smuggled in. Even so, early on, this attempt seemed doomed to failure too.

On the night fixed for the possible escape, February 3, 1919, Collins, Boland, Kelly and Willie approached the prison building. Leaving Kelly and Willie at points near the prison to keep the lookout for anyone approaching, Collins and Boland went ahead to do the job on the outer gate to which Collins had the key. As Dev and two other prisoners, Sean Milroy and Sean McGarry, walked impatiently up and down on the other side of the gate, Collins fitted the key into the lock. Then disaster struck. The key turned partly in the lock then broke, leaving the lock half-jammed. DeValera in a fit of rage thrust his key into the lock and to everyone's relief the broken half of the other key fell out and his own key opened the gate. The prisoners were free.

Willie and Kelly, meantime, became alarmed at the sight of two British soldiers and their girl friends occupying the stile through which the escaping prisoners, together with Collins and Boland would have to come. Before they had time to warn the escaping party, Boland was the first to arrive.

He surprised Willie, who was hiding behind a wall close by, by being equal to the occasion. As he brushed past the soldiers, he raised his hat and in a good imitation of an English accent, said, 'Good night, chaps!'

The soldiers muttered something nebulous and continued to give their attention to their girlfriends. Consequently, the escaping party sailed by unnoticed.

On Collins' instructions, the party broke up. One lot went to stay with friends in Manchester, the other lot to stay with other friends in Sheffield. As per instructions from Collins, Willie found his way to Liverpool on different buses. He crossed the Irish Sea inconspicuously mixed up with a lot of bodies on the floor of the Mail Boat, plus he caught up on his sleep.

As for Kelly. The story went that he got lost in the fields around Lincoln trying to find a safer way to escape. He eventually surfaced in Ireland a few days later.

On March 8, 1919, the British Government released all political prisoners, chiefly because of a devastating outbreak of influenza which resulted in the death of one prisoner, Pierce McCann in Gloucester Jail on the 6th of March.

§

On April 1, 1919, the Dail, in private session in the Mansion House, Dublin, appointed DeValera as Priomh Aire (First Minister) a term translated in the official report as President. At three further private meetings held on April 1, 3, and 4, the President appointed a cabinet, which included Collins as Minister of Finance and Griffith as Minister of Home Affairs. To all intents and purposes, in defiance of both the British authority in Ireland and the Government in London, the native government of Dail Eireann literally took over governing the country. It set up its own Courts of Law and established its own Departments of Home Affairs and Finance. The Dail, in fact, put into operation Griffith's plan of Sinn Fein (literally 'Ourselves'—Self Reliance,) which had evolved between 1900 and 1905. It was a composition of passive resistance and self-reliance. Collins realized that Arthur Griffith was far and away the man of experience in political theory. For a long time he had been the man in the background, quietly formulating his ideas, working out a policy and now he was putting it to the practical test, all without the blaze of glory which surrounded DeValera.

Talking to Willie afterwards, Collins went to great pains to point out Griffith's impressive part working for the Cause. 'Griffith,' he said, 'is the *father* of the independent movement. Didn't himself and Willie Rooney launch the paper *The United Irishman* as far back as 1899 with himself as Editor? That paper had the backing of the Irish Republican Brotherhood. Not to mention his role in the Irish Neutrality League — the league that actively opposed the enlistment of Irishmen into the British Army: in October 1914, he joined forces with James Connolly (the President of the league,) Countess Markievicz, Sean Milroy, Francis Sheehy-Skeffington, William O'Brien and Major John McBride. At the time he was Editor of such publications as *The Irish Worker, Sinn Fein* and *Eire*. And the I.R.B. paper *Irish Freedom*. Unfortunately, shortly afterwards these papers were put out of action by the British military and the police raiding and dismantling their printing works.' Collins face glowed as he continued to extol Griffith's virtues. 'And though, through no fault of his own, he took no part in the 1916 rebellion (his offer to be part of it was declined on the grounds that his services might be required in the future as publicist and national philosopher), early in May he was imprisoned in Wandsworth and then in Reading, from which he was released on Christmas Eve, 1916.'

This history lesson about Griffith was an eye opener for Willie. Up to this, he'd looked on Griffith as a dour, silent man. 'What you're telling me,' he said to Collins, 'surprises me. All along Griffith gave me the impression that he was a man who had little to say.'

'Ah! That's because he's a thinker, not a talker like myself,' Collins laughed. 'Would you believe he refused an offer of a thousand pounds to work on a New York paper early on in his career?'

'He sounds like a man with great strength of character,' Willie said.

'Yeah,' Collins affirmed. 'Imagine refusing such riches: instead of living like a lord, he opts for a life of near poverty and concentrates on founding the national ideal. One cannot but admire the man.'

'In relation to DeValera, where would you place Griffith politically?' Willie was suddenly very curious about these two men.

'Griffith is definitely a politician,' Collins said. 'But the 'long fella' — Dev,' he shrugged, 'I'd say he has no political experience whatsoever.' He smiled wryly. 'What's more he only consented to the I.R.B. on his terms. But even though he lacks political experience he has ably demonstrated his willingness and devotion to the Cause' Collins nodded his head approvingly. 'No doubt you've noticed his uncompromising attitude towards the British.'

'Yeah. I did, sort of,' Willie said. 'Considering he's not a hundred per cent Irish, it's quite surprising.'

'Yeah,' Collins agreed. 'Born as he was in Manhattan in America, of Irish and Spanish parents, it *is* remarkable.'

'All of which saved him from execution,' Willie interjected.

'True for ye!' Collins said. 'Ach,' he went on, 'we should consider ourselves lucky that because of his birthright, he was the one and only leader spared execution.'

'Listening to his pre-election speeches,' Willie said, 'I got the impression he was capable of rousing feelings of great emotion — both of love and hate.'

'That's our Dev all right!' Collins acclaimed. 'As an orator he's the least emotional of men, yet he speaks with an apparent sincerity that gets to the people.'

Willie could see that between Eamonn DeValera and Collins there existed a great difference of character — humanity. With Dev there was an apparent lack of warmth towards his fellow beings, whereas with Collins it was the direct opposite – an excess of humanity.

That day Willie took away with him a very different impression of Griffith. He decided he had inordinately misjudged the man. According to Collins, Griffith had a great brain. 'He's a humble man,' he said, 'who doesn't seek celebrity and who certainly doesn't get the respect and admiration which is his due.'

Where DeValera was concerned, Willie himself had already perceived that he was a proud man who, since he became President of Dail Eireann, had adopted a condescending and kingly attitude towards his colleagues. He became sacrosanct in his own mind and couldn't bear to think that anyone could honestly differ from him.

§

January, 1919 was a big anti-climax for Jane. Mostly because she'd seen so much of Willie over the Christmas period. Come January, he disappeared again.

During the festive season, apart from his frequent visits to the house, which included the Christmas Dinner and the ringing in of the New Year, they'd attended a number of Christmas celebrations together: a Choral Concert in Christ Church Cathedral, a Christmas Concert in The Mansion House, where she met and was able to put a face on some of the patriots Willie talked about and of whom the papers wrote about. Life around Christmas was a whirl of activity and excitement. And smiles came easily to Willie. Jane sensed it was his optimism about the future. He confided in her that as a result of the general elections, Ireland would now have its own Irish parliament. And with Collins' help he'd great hopes of getting a decent job in the Government — the Civil Service possibly. Truly the future looked much more positive.

At Sadie's party in Carlingford Avenue on Saint Stephen's Night, Willie even went so far as to whisper the words, 'How much I want to marry you, Jane,' into her ear as they danced. He said it in a teasing sort of way. But later when he was saying goodnight to her, he brought the subject up again. 'Darling Jane' he said, 'I'd marry you in the morning if I had a decent paying job.'

Jane felt such a warm glow inside. 'Are you proposing to me, Willie?' she murmured softly.

'God, Jane!' he said, 'how I wish I could come straight out and say, will you marry me, Jane?'

Jane interjected eagerly, 'And I would say *yes*, Willie! I will marry you.'

'But Jane, we have to be realistic,' Willie said with an uneasy smile. 'Until the day I'm secure in a good, steady job and not penniless, I'm in no position to propose marriage to anyone.'

'Things can change,' Jane said optimistically.

'Please God they will,' Willie said. 'But it's got to be for the better.'

Jane threw her arms around Willie's neck. 'Let's get secretly engaged,' she said her eyes brimming with excitement.

'Of course, if it makes you happy, Jane,' Willie said with a sigh, 'we can be secretly engaged.' He smiled a fervent and supportive smile. 'Trouble is I want to shout 'I'm engaged to the most wonderful girl in the world," from the roof tops.

One day during the second week of the New Year, Willie dropped in to see Jane in the store. It was the first time he'd seen her serving behind the jewelry counter. Looking very attractive in her smart uniform (black dress with white collar and cuffs) she was showing a middle-aged male customer — having difficulty making up his mind — a selection of pendants. Willie waited patiently as the customer handled the different pendants individually and hemmed and hawed over each one for seconds. Then, Jane, politely endeavoring to expedite the sale, placed the pendants around her own neck one after another. Still he couldn't decide. Eventually he indicated graciously that none of them were suitable, and left.

'And you think your job is bad,' Jane laughed as she turned to Willie. 'Would you believe he's been here for,' she looked at the big clock in the center of the store, 'half an hour. At least you don't have to contend with that sort of thing in your job.'

'No, Thank God! I don't,' Willie said. 'I doubt I'd have your patience.' He smiled whimsically. 'Of course,' he said 'he was a man; it could well be he was more interested in the salesgirl than he was in the merchandise.' He laughed waggishly. 'That's it,' he said, 'he couldn't drag himself away from those adorable, big, brown eyes.'

'Oh! Big joke!,' Jane laughed with him. Then she suddenly became concerned. 'What are you doing here anyway?'

Looking extremely contrite, Willie told her, 'I just dropped in to tell you that I'm going to be missing for the next week or so.'

Jane did her best to look unperturbed. 'Where are you off to this time?' she asked nonchalantly.

'England.'

Jane knew better than to ask questions like, 'Why?' or, 'What part of England?' It was an unspoken agreement that unless he volunteered the information, she didn't ask annoying questions. This was one of those times when he wasn't being frank and open about the details of his trip. So she just had to curb her curiosity.

Willie broke into her thoughts. 'I'll see you when I get back,' he said and moved away. Now it was the middle of February and she hadn't heard a word from him since that day in January. Not even a card. As each day passed her imagination ran riot. Could he possibly have been arrested in England? she wondered. The way he told her was so cryptic, she got the impression that the job in England was cloaked in secrecy.

To add to her misery, the previous Saturday night after playing for the pictures, she ran into Finbar. Mustering up the courage, she asked him casually, 'Any word from Willie in England?'

'Not a syllable,' Finbar said. Then trying to be funny, he called after her, 'Maybe he got a job over there projecting better pictures.'

To Jane's mind it was anything but funny. On the home front too she was continually making excuses for Willie's absence to her mother, our Nancy, Gerald and Eileen. For instance, at lunch time this past Sunday she felt awful when Gerald made a point of asking her, 'What's happened to Willie? I haven't seen him since Christmas day?'

'No more than the rest of us,' Mary interjected, looking curiously at Jane.

At this point, Lily (God bless her) conveniently interposed by knocking over a full glass of water on the table, a lot of which landed on Gerald's lap.

Lily jumped up from the table exclaiming, 'God! I'm terribly sorry, Gerald.' Then, to our Nancy's horror, she started dabbing the moisture on Gerald's fly with her serviette. Shocked, Gerald shot out of his chair and started brushing off the moisture with his own serviette. Meantime Jane rushed towards the scullery to get a towel to mop up the mess on the table. While she was out of the room, Lily went even further with her meddling. 'You can't possibly stay in those wet trousers,' she said to Gerald.

'Oh, don't worry about it,' Gerald said, his face puce with embarrassment. 'They'll dry out in no time.'

Jane arrived back with the towel and proceeded to mop the mess on the table. Excelling herself, Lily grabbed a newspaper from a side table, handed it to Gerald, and said, 'Push a few sheets of this inside the front of your trousers until they dry out; that's the solution.' Then turning to Mary, looking innocent as you like, she added, 'Isn't that so, Mother?'

'Yes, Lily's right,' Mary said. 'It's not good to let wet clothes dry into you; it could give you rheumatic fever.'

'Yes,' Eileen joined in the controversy. 'Mother is very strict about us not letting wet clothes dry on us,' she said to Gerald. 'As a matter of fact, on the days its raining, Mother makes sure that there are sheets of newspaper tucked in a bag with my lunch, in case my stockings get wet on the way to school. She's very fussy about things like that.' Eileen laughed. 'Those times,' she continued, 'the kids at school laugh and jeer at me and call me paper stockings.'

Everyone laughed but our Nancy. Mary interjected, 'Let them sneer and jeer,' she said to Eileen. 'You don't get laid up very often as a result of those precautions.' She then turned to Gerald. 'Off you go upstairs to the bathroom,' she directed him, 'and put the paper down inside your trousers.' Gerald left her room armed with the newspaper and looking very sheepish.

The door had hardly closed behind Gerald, when our Nancy went into the attack against Lily. 'You awkward, bloody fool!' she screamed at her. 'You did a massive job of embarrassing him.'

Mary intervened. 'For goodness sake, Our Nancy!' she said, shaking her head disapprovingly at her language, 'It was an accident.'

'It wasn't an accident,' our Nancy's voice was full of venom. 'She did it on purpose.'

Jane was afraid to open her mouth for fear someone would remember the question that started the incident off – Willie's absence.

Mary said, 'Why would she do such a thing?'

'Because she's as jealous as sin of the fact that I have a fiancee.'

'Me jealous of you!' Lily spat the words at our Nancy. 'You've got to be joking. However,' she said, superciliously, 'I do hope that drenching won't affect his performance.'

'Goodness Lily!' Mary burst out, exasperated, 'do you have to be so crude and vulgar.'

Throughout all this commotion Jane wanted to shout at the top of her voice at our Nancy, you're not the only one who has a fiancée; Willie and I are secretly engaged. She wondered would the time ever come when she would be in a position to let this fact be known?

Later when Jane and Lily were out walking, they laughed heartily reminiscing about the lunch time incident. Lily topped it off saying, 'For our Nancy's sake, I hope Gerald's wick isn't permanently dampened.'

Jane couldn't stop laughing. 'God, Lily! You're a howl!'

'Well, it gave you a bit of a laugh anyhow,' Lily said, looking quite self-satisfied. 'It also got your mind off Willie for a while.'

'It certainly did,' Jane said. 'Though when you threw that water over Gerald and started patting him, t'was all I could do not to burst my sides laughing.' She stretched across and squeezed Lily's shoulder. 'Gosh, Lily!' she said, 'I don't know what I'd do without you; the way you continually come to my rescue.'

'Two things were in mind when I threw over that glass of water,' Lily said with a mischievous glint in her eye. 'One was to rescue you, the other to practice a bit of one-up-man-ship on that smug Nancy bitch.'

'Nonetheless, you got me off the hook,' Jane said.

'When Gerald asked about Willie I was completely stuck for an answer.'

'Still no word from him?' Lily asked, concerned.

'No nothing.'

'Keep your chin up,' Lily said. Then more assuredly, 'Like the proverbial bad penny, he's bound to turn up eventually.'

Having Lily at home full time was very comforting for Jane; between them they shared so many confidences and so many laughs. They had no secrets from each other, except the big one — Jane's secret engagement to Willie. At times Jane felt quite guilty about it. But she had given her word to Willie. And much as she loved her sister, there were times when Lily, in a fit of pique, inadvertently blurted out things she shouldn't. For instance, had she known Jane's secret at lunch time today, it was quite conceivable she'd have blown the gaff. And where would that have left Jane?

§

The following Saturday night when Jane arrived at the Tivoli to play for the pictures, much to her delight she was met at the door by Willie. 'Mother of God!' she exclaimed, 'You're back in one piece.' At the sight of him, her heart felt it would burst with happiness.

Willie gathered her into his arms. 'Yes, sweetheart,' he said, squeezing her tight. 'I'm back and very glad to be back.'

After he released her, Jane asked, 'Can you talk about it?'

Willie tipped his nose with his forefinger. 'Afraid not,' he said, giving her that most, endearing grin.

Jane winced with disappointment. She veered from exuberant hopefulness to depressing hopelessness. Suddenly she was riddled with doubt. Was this secrecy of Willie's to be the pattern of their future together? If so, the future looked pretty bleak. A feeling of agitation overtook her.

Her changed demeanor was immediately obvious to Willie. Contritely he said, 'Darling, Jane, you know very well, I'd...'

He was interrupted by Finbar slapping him on the back. Squealing with pleasure, he said, 'The wandering boy has returned!' He aimed a wink at Jane.

Jane's face struggled with the contraries of inward anxiety and outward sociability. The best she could do was nail a smile on her face as she nodded affirmation. Then abruptly she excused herself saying, 'Sorry, I can't dally, I've a job to do.' On her way to the pianola she had trouble fighting back the tears.

That night she played anything but well. Her thoughts were not on the job; Willie occupied them full time. She wondered how much longer she could go on bottling up her resentment about his secrecy. He knew very well, she was in sympathy with the Cause. But the way he carried on you'd think she didn't give a damn. What could she do to convince him that she could be trusted?

§

'Why can't you tell me, Willie?' Jane sounded more determined than ever to get an answer to her question. 'Don't you trust me?'

They were in their retreat in Liffey Street drinking cups of cocoa after the show.

'Good Lord!' Willie said, startled. 'Of course I trust you! It's nothing like that.' He scraped around his mind looking for an answer to the question about what he'd been doing during the past three weeks? He daren't tell her the truth. 'What can I say?' he said, hot embarrassment bleeding into his face and neck.

'You can stop keeping secrets from me,' Jane said and held her breath for his reply.

'Even if the telling of those secrets compromises you and your family?'

'Oh we're back to that again?' Jane tried hard to fight down her impatience.

Willie's answer was to stare out the window because he wasn't sure what else to do or to say. A look that was akin to torment held his face.

Noticing it, Jane thought, he's wrestling with some inner conflict. He looked so discomforted she began to feel pity for him. Stretching her hand across the table she covered his saying, 'I'm sorry, Willie. I don't want to upset you. It's just when people ask me where you are and why you're missing so much, I don't know what to say.'

'Who's been asking about me?' Willie's voice was filled with suspicion.

'Oh, just the family, Mother, Gerald, people like that.' Jane was now as flushed as he was. 'At times it can be very awkward,' she said. She was finding this conversation hard going. She didn't like the look on Willie's face. As they fell silent, her mind churned trying to think of something light and airy to say to relieve the tension.

After a minute, Willie perked up. He suddenly realized it was up to him to reassure her. Placing his other hand over hers, he said, 'Darling Jane, I swear to you as soon as I'm secure in the knowledge that this country is going to be a republic, there'll be no more secrets between us.' Then flashing one of his most irresistible smiles, he added confidently, 'and believe me, this could happen sooner than later.'

'Something important is about to happen?' Jane's face lit up with expectation. 'Can you even tell me about that?'

'Yes, I can,' Willie answered. 'Because it's going to be public news any day now.'

'What is it?' Jane could hardly wait for his answer.

'It's how the Peace Conference coming up in Paris, could greatly benefit Ireland.'

'How?'

'Woodrow Wilson, the American President, will be in attendance. We've great hopes he'll recognize Ireland's right to independence.'

'My God! Wouldn't that be wonderful!'

'Should it happen, the country would be halfway towards independence,' Willie said profoundly. 'Britain would be called to heel and they'd have no option but to recognize Ireland as an independent state.'

Although Jane seemed reasonably appeased by this news, she was watching him closely. Her gaze was steady and patient. He found it quite disarming. God! he thought, will this small war ever be over? Will the time ever come when I can be frank and open with Jane about what's happening in my life?'

§

'With the reappearance of DeValera on the scene,' Collins informed Willie, 'there are now three men of outstanding ability in the Dail Cabinet: DeValera, Arthur Griffith and, even if I say so — myself.'

'Your modesty is overwhelming,' Willie said laughing.

'Why not?' Collins laughed with him. Then got serious. 'Of course, there is a fourth to be reckoned with, namely the indomitable Cathal Brugha. His opinions, although at times misguided, are of immeasurable influence.'

Working with Collins, Willie could see that despite the fact that there was bitterness between Brugha and Collins, there was a link of sorts there. They both had the adventurer spirit, though of the two, Brugha was the most headstrong.

Some weeks later when Collins was having a drink with Willie and Peter, he confided in them that at the next meeting of the Sinn Fein Executive, he intended to announce, what in his view, was the only policy now open to them. 'The sooner fighting is forced and a general state of disorder created throughout the country,' he said his face set in lines of determination, 'the better it will be for the country.' He went on, 'Obviously some of the members will feel uneasy about this, but Ireland is likely to get more out of a general state of disorder than from a continuance of the situation as it now stands.'

'So, it's back to violence is it?' Peter asked.

'Whatever it takes,' Collins answered wearily.

'Personally, I have to agree with Mick,' Willie said to Peter. 'The country seems to be stuck in a stalemate presently; and there's no sign of it letting up.'

'Do you think you'll get enough support?' Peter asked Collins.

'I don't think,' Collins said, 'I know.' He turned to Willie.

'Willie,' he said, 'from time to time, you've read some of the memoranda that cross my desk daily from brigade commandants, flying columns and the ordinary man in the street. What do they tell you?'

'Oh, they're very much in like mind as yourself; impatient to let the British know that the fight isn't over.'

'So you see, Peter,' Collins said, 'we've no option but to create mayhem to get the British Authorities' attention. Because despite the fact that the IPP has been virtually wiped out by the 73 Sinn Fein members who won most of the Irish seats and who insist on not attending the Westminster Parliament, Britain has no intention of recognizing our Irish Parliament.'

'I noticed the list of new revolutionaries keeps getting longer,' Willie said. 'And most of them are in favor of action.'

'Between notes, interviews and word of mouth, that list grows by the hour,' Collins claimed cheerfully. He then turned to Willie. 'Willie,' he said earnestly, 'would you be interested in becoming a Brigade Commandant? Going back into the field? I ask you this because you were once a crack shot?'

Willie was staggered by the question. 'Be gorra!' he gasped, 'I doubt very much I'd be a crack shot now; it's such a long time since I trained in the Kimmage Garrison.'

'Would you think of giving Sinn Fein a hand with the training of the new recruits in that warehouse you found for them recently. He sighed heavily. 'As long as it lasts.'

'Unfortunately they train at night,' Willie said. 'And much as I'd like to, either train or help with the training, I've still got to earn the pennies.'

'Of course,' Collins said, 'you're busy showing the pictures at night time.'

'However,' Willie said, 'I'll think about it.'

'No harm done if you decide against it, By,' Collins said amicably.

A young man with his hat pulled well down over his face joined them in the snug.

'The hard Daniel!' Collins greeted him. 'How goes it?'

Daniel removed his hat. Willie and Peter immediately recognized him from the REWARD photograph, posted all around the city, as Daniel Breen.

'Not so good,' Breen said disconsolately.

'Before you go any further,' Collins said, 'what are you drinking?'

'I'll have a pint of Guinness.'

'Give us another pint of Guinness there,' Collins called to the barman. He then turned to Willie and Peter. 'In case you haven't recognized him,' he said with affection, 'this is the infamous Daniel Breen who has a price of a thousand pounds on his head.' He indicated Peter and Willie to Breen. 'Meet two of my stalwarts from Frongoch,' he said, giving their names. He grinned at Breen. 'Aren't you the brave man,' he said, 'showing your face in the city of Dublin.'

'Jaysus, Mick!' Breen said irritably. 'What else can I do? I send you memorandum after memorandum requesting ammunition, and what do I get — silence.' He continued: 'How the hell can I carry on a guerrilla war if I can't supply the troops with ammunition? We're practically reduced to fighting with hay forks.'

'I'm really sorry, Daniel,' Collins sounded genuinely sympathetic. 'If I could lay my hands on a supply, you'd be the first to get it. I know the marvelous job you're doing down there in Tipperary.'

'Too much time is being wasted,' Breen said, troubled. 'We could have blown up a dozen barracks in the past month if we had the ammunition.'

Collins said, 'Bear with me, Dan. I'm working hard on it. Soon I should have results.' He lowered his voice. 'As Minister of Finance,' he said, 'I'm now in a position to start raising money. Next week the Office of the Finance Minister will issue bonds to the value of one pound and multiples.'

'How on earth are you managing that?' Peter asked.

'Just between us,' Collins whispered, 'as a precaution against the Authorities investigating, the money will be banked in the name of various citizens.' He grinned boyishly. 'It's looking good.' Turning to Breen, he said, 'Please God, in a few weeks you'll have your ammunition.' Collins then went on to tell Breen about the policy he intended putting to the next Sinn Fein Executive Meeting — the one about fighting and creating a general state of disorder throughout the country to get Britain's attention.

'It's music to my ears,' Breen said, looking totally gratified.

Chapter XXVII

At the O'Dwyer family lunch the following Sunday (at which Willie couldn't be present) our Nancy announced that herself and Gerald would be 'tying the knot' the following June.

'As the Great War is over,' she explained, 'there's nothing to hinder us now from getting married.'

'Yes,' Gerald supported her, 'I was so lucky to be posted to Ireland during that period.' He lifted Nancy's hand lovingly to his lips, adding, 'Apart from meeting my lovely Nancy, I didn't know from one day to the next if or when I'd get the call to serve at the Front.'

The news was received with great jubilation by Mary and Eileen. While Jane and Lily coated their faces with agreeable expressions, as congratulations and best wishes were exchanged all round.

Then Eileen, with childish exhilaration, rushed in saying, 'Oh! Can I be a flower girl again?' Her face glowed expectantly.

'Don't be silly, Eileen,' our Nancy said, irked 'It'll be a long time before we get round to discussing things like that.'

Eileen's face dropped a foot. She then looked appealingly at Gerald, who responded by taking her hand in his. 'Eileen, my old segoocheria,' he said, 'the wedding wouldn't be the same if you weren't there as our flower girl.'

Eileen threw her arms around Gerald's neck. 'Gerald you're an angel!' Her voice exuded delight.

'Now,' our Nancy said, looking askance at Gerald, 'when you two have finished being so lovey dovey, could we discuss an issue of importance concerning the immediate future?'

'Which is?' Mary asked. She could tell our Nancy had a bee in in her bonnet.

'Gerald's parents are coming from England to meet my family the Easter weekend.'

'Sounds perfectly reasonable,' Mary said. 'I suppose you'll be booking them into the Gresham Hotel?'

'That's the point.' Our Nancy looked uneasily at Gerald. Gerald spluttered as he got his tongue round, 'We were wondering if...they could stay here?'

'In this house, you mean?' Mary looked startled.

'Yeah,' our Nancy said bluntly.

Gerald intervened. 'You see, Mother doesn't like sleeping in hotels; she says the sheets are never properly aired.'

Mary, perplexed, looked at Jane and Lily. 'I suppose we could manage it all right?' The question was directed at them.

Jane answered, 'Well, if our Nancy moved into Eileen's room that would leave her room free for the visitors.'

'Charlie and Maureen,' Gerald said pointedly.

'I take it they'll be the only members of your family coming?' Mary asked with drawn brows.

'That's right,' Gerald reassured her. My sister and brother usually go on field trips with the school at Easter.'

§

For the first time in her life, our Nancy inherited a relatively big responsibility - the chore of getting her bedroom ready for her prospective in-laws. Lots of things needed to be done. Because without Bridget — the one with an instinct for order and tidiness — the bedroom had become a veritable dump. Now our Nancy had her work cut out for her transforming this dump into a presentable bedroom. Going on Mary's instructions, the first thing she had to do was empty the room of all her belongings. That done the floor would need to be swept and washed with a mop. Next came the furniture; it would have to be dusted and polished. Then came the beds; they'd need clean blankets, linen and bed spreads.

When our Nancy tried to palm the cleaning work off on Chairmaine, Mary wouldn't hear of it. 'This is your responsibility,' she told her. 'Charmaine has enough to do looking after the rest of the house.' So Mary left her to it, thinking, it'll be good training for her.

Around half-eleven, two nights before the visitors were due to arrive, our Nancy started transferring her belongings into Eileen's bedroom. Eileen, a great sleeper, slept through it all, but on awaking next morning was staggered to discover that, thanks to her sister, her room had now become the dump. The rest of Eileen's day was spent restoring order in her bedroom. She couldn't live with this mess. With our Nancy's clothes and accouterments taking up most of the storage space in Eileen's bedroom, her own clothes ended up in a suitcase under her bed.

The visitors were due to arrive around tea time on Good Friday. It suited Mary admirably. When the shop was closed for the three hours of the crucifixion, she would prepare the evening meal, which was fish. After which she'd attend the Good Friday Stations of the Cross. Gerald was meeting his parents at Kingstown and bringing them by tram to the O'Dwyer house.

Gerald's mother, Maureen, was a small woman with a white, vacant face and little to say. Her husband, Charlie, on the other hand, more than made up for Maureen's shortcomings in the babble department. Well-dressed, stout and loud-mouthed, he brought more than a breath of gregariousness to the O'Dwyer home. One thing that got on Mary's nerves was his loud, hearty laugh. He laughed at everything, whether it was funny or not. And from the pained expression on his wife's face, it was obvious he got on her nerves too.

Eating the evening meal in the company of Mary, our Nancy, Jane, Lily, Eileen and Gerald, Charlie was particularly loud and more or less monopolized the conversation. It seemed there wasn't a subject on which he wasn't an expert. He told off-color jokes, ending each one with a loud guffaw, and a wink and a poke of the elbow at either Mary or Lily sitting each side of him.

'I say, if we don't take risks,' Charlie said to Mary, 'we might as well be dead. Am I right missus?'

'Of course you're right,' Mary's ability to reason things came in handy. 'Tell me a success story that doesn't start out as a gamble?'

Charlie roared laughing. 'At last, I've met a kindred spirit,' he said. 'Talking about spirits, would you have a drop in the house?'

'A drop of what?' Mary asked, bewildered.

'A drop of the crater.' Another wink and an elbow at Lily this time.

Ah! Lily thought, he's a drinker! His secret is out. She'd seen enough of this kind of behavior when she was helping out on the cousin's farm. Regularly on Saturday nights the farm hands came back from the pubs overflowing with this kind of palaver.

Mary jumped up. 'I think we might have some port wine left over from Christmas,' she said, then left the room.

'I can't believe there's not a pub open in Ireland today,' Charlie sighed.

'It's Good Friday,' Gerald told him bitingly. 'Everywhere and everything is shut down.'

'Even shebeens?' Charlie queried.

If looks could kill, Maureen's flinty stare at Charlie would have him dead. But Charlie knew better than to look in her direction.

Before anyone could say anything, Mary reappeared carrying a bottle. 'I'm afraid port wine is the best we can offer,' she said handing the bottle to Charlie. 'Unfortunately, the public houses are all closed today, otherwise I'd send out for a bottle of whiskey or brandy or something.'

'Oh, this will do fine,' Charlie's eyes lit up. He half filled one of the empty tumblers. Holding up the bottle he addressed the company, 'Anyone like to join me in a tincture to celebrate this auspicious occasion?' he asked, motioning to Mary.

'No,' Mary graciously declined. 'Not on Good Friday.'

'Gerald?' Charlie, unabashed, waved the bottle at Gerald.

'No thanks, Dad.'

Mary then brought up a subject that was close to her heart. She addressed Maureen. 'Any priests in your family?' she asked.

'No, I'm sorry to say there aren't any in our immediate family,' Maureen said. 'However, I do have a distant cousin who's a priest.'

'Well then, that's settled,' Mary averred. And without as much as a by your leave to the engaged couple, announced, 'This time we'll have Father Vincent celebrating the marriage.' Then as an afterthought, she turned to our Nancy and asked, 'Is that all right with you?'

'Nice of you to ask, Mother,' our Nancy said with an abundance of sarcasm. She hunched her shoulders, 'Whether we like it or not,' she said, 'I suppose we'll have to put up with it.'

'How can you be so disrespectful?' Mary asked, shocked. 'Father Vincent is a living saint; if he's free to be the celebrant, you should be down on your knees thanking God that such a reverend and holy man is solemnizing your union.'

Our Nancy rolled her eyes showing her boredom.

Charlie tried to be funny. 'So what has that got to do with the price of spuds?' he asked. Most of the company burst out laughing. The tension eased. Charlie went on, 'Once you've sorted out the celebrant of the marriage, everything else is cheap whiskey,' he said. 'Am I right, Missus?' Charlie guffawed loudly and gave Mary another elbow.

Later when Lily and Jane were washing the dishes in the scullery, Jane asked Lily, 'So what do you think?'

'Well, Lily said,' as far as the mother is concerned, she has a face on her that that would sour milk. As for him, if he guffaws any more he'll swallow his ears.'

They both went into kinks of laughter.

'I take it you wouldn't like having them as your in-laws?' Jane said when she stopped laughing.

'There isn't much one can do about in-laws,' Lily said wisely. 'Like family, you can't choose them.'

Next day, Saturday — a working day for the O'Dwyer adults — Gerald took the parents out for the day on the tram to Dalkey. Before leaving he told Mary not to bother about food for them. They would dine out. Mary was grateful for his thoughtfulness. Up to that she'd been racking her brain trying to work out how she'd manage to run the shop (on one of its busiest days of the year) and still be a good hostess.

As they were leaving, she asked, 'Are any of you interested in attending the Easter Ceremonies tonight?'

'But, of course,' Charlie replied with great exuberance. 'What time do they start?'

'At ten,' Mary said. 'But if we want to get a decent seat, we'd need to be in the church by nine.'

'No problem,' Charlie enthused.

'I take it Nancy will be in attendance?' Gerald asked.

'Yes,' Mary answered. 'The whole family will be in attendance.'

'It's Dominick Street Church?' Gerald queried.

'Yes,' Mary laughed. 'Where you first laid eyes on our Nancy.'

'Never to be forgotten,' Gerald said laughing with her. 'We'll be back in good time.'

Nonetheless, up to the time the family left for the ceremonies, the travelers hadn't returned.

'They've probably gone straight to the church,' our Nancy said, with conviction.

The church was filling up fast when the family arrived. As there was no sign of the travelers, Mary suggested they take a pew near the entrance and hold three seats in reserve. That way they could nab the travelers as soon as they arrived. At three minutes to ten, just before the priests came on the alter, our Nancy spotted the travelers coming through the entrance. She waved to them indicating the seats in reserve. Pushing their way through the crowds, they finally joined the family in their pew.

Only then did our Nancy notice their strange demeanors: Charlie was noticeably staggering and smelt like a brewery, Maureen looked grimmer than ever and Gerald looked flustered and embarrassed. The reserved seats ran from the opening of the pew to where our Nancy was sitting. Gerald came in first and took the seat next to her. He was followed by a stumbling Charlie who leant across Gerald and said to our Nancy, 'Jaysus! I'm sozzled!' Whereupon he slouched down in the seat, reclined heavily against Gerald and went to sleep.

'How did he get like that?' our Nancy asked Gerald in a whisper.

An exceedingly troubled Gerald whispered back, 'It's a long story. I'm terribly sorry! I tried to dissuade him from coming, but he insisted.'

Looking beyond Charlie to Maureen, our Nancy wasn't surprised to see her woebegone expression. She turned her attention to Gerald. 'It's all right,' she whispered reassuringly, 'I'm sure it's not your fault.'

Mary, sitting at the other end of the pew, was impervious to the situation for the moment.

The priests arrived on the alter. Everybody stood up except Gerald and Charlie. As Charlie's prop, Gerald daren't move. Halfway through the ceremonies, Charlie started snoring loud enough to waken the dead. Gerald went into action immediately; first he shook his father gently. Then when he got no reaction, he put his arm across Charlie's shoulder and strenuously jolted and jerked him. But all to no avail. Charlie let out a loud snort and if anything, his snores got louder. Meantime, people's heads started turning round to see where the rasping noise was coming from; they obviously found it very distracting.

Only now did Mary realize what was happening.

Our Nancy whispered aggressively to Gerald, 'Get him out of here.' She was thinking about all those people who were staring: for sure Charlie was making a holy show of the O'Dwyer family.

As luck would have it, another drunk on the other side of the church caused a diversion: he joined Charlie in what was the nearest thing to a snoring contest. With heads about turning in the direction of the other drunk, focus was mercifully taken off Charlie for the moment.

At this stage, Maureen took control. Small and all as she was, she succeeded in bringing Charlie alive by giving him an unmerciful elbow in the ribs. After a series of loud snorts, Charlie opened dazed eyes and looked around him. Anticipating an excessive verbal reaction, Maureen quickly clapped her hand over his mouth and half whispered viciously, 'Utter one, single word and so help me God! I'll brain you!'

For the rest of the ceremonies, peace and quiet was restored to the O'Dwyer pew. But the other drunk snored on sporadically. Just before the final blessing, Maureen gestured to Gerald that they should leave now before the crowd started moving. Gerald agreed. All he could think about was getting Charlie to bed as quickly as possible. Because the last thing he wanted was Mary to have the experience of his father in this condition.

He whispered to our Nancy, 'Mam thinks we should go before the end.' Nancy stirred. Gerald restrained her saying, 'You stay. Let Mam and I get him to bed before the rest of you get home. Otherwise, it'll be bedlam with him in this condition.'

Our Nancy handed him the key to the house. 'Good idea,' she said.

When the family eventually arrived back at the house, all was quiet. Charlie and Maureen had retired for the night. After Gerald kissed our Nancy goodnight, he said, 'About tomorrow, Sunday, I'll call first thing in the morning to collect them.' Sheepishly, he asked, 'Do you think you could tolerate being in their company with me for most of the day?'

The urgency in his voice forced our Nancy to say, 'Why not?'

'That's my girl!' Gerald's sigh was very audible. Then he asked, 'Can you think of anywhere we could take them that'd be miles from the nearest pub or licensed premises?'

'Phoenix Park.'

'Perfect.' Gerald hugged her. When he released her he said, 'Let's make it a picnic.' Forestalling any objection she might make, he added, 'I'll bring a basket of food from the Mess. You needn't do anything.'

'That'd be grand,' our Nancy smiled indulgently. 'As a matter of fact,' she said, 'as it's Easter Sunday there's bound to be lots of matches — football, hurling and the likes — being played up there. That should keep Charlie entertained for a while.'

Sunday evening, Mary arranged to give a dinner party to introduce their guests to other members of the family and friends. Apart from the immediate family, they included, Peter, Nancy Pete, Michael, Bridget and Willie. With Jane and Lily's help, Mary spent the afternoon preparing a lavish meal of roast lamb with all the trimmings — roast potatoes, peas, carrots, gravy and mint sauce. After which Mary's famous desert — trifle smothered in whipped cream — would be served. Before the travelers returned, except for Peter and Nancy Pete, everyone who was invited was present.

When the travelers did appear, for a change Charlie seemed to be going through a bout of taciturnity. After the introductions, he was struck dumb. Gerald put this down to three things: a surfeit of fresh air, an inordinate amount of walking, but more important, a lack of alcohol. (Except for one bottle of ale, supplied by the hamper, it had been an excessively dry day for Charlie.)

However, in Charlie's mind there was a bigger reason for his silence. Apart from the lack of alcohol, he realized he was in the company of a group of very intelligent young people. Sure, one had only to listen to their manner of discussion to realize this. Especially, Michael and Willie. He thought they were two of the brightest lads he'd met in a long time. Drinks were served as the company waited for Peter and Nancy Pete to arrive. (As usual they were hours late.) In the beginning, Gerald saw to it that his father's whiskey was well watered. But unfortunately he didn't take the precaution of putting the bottle out of sight. And Charlie, with the thirst that was on him, naturally took advantage of the oversight: surreptitiously he doubled up on every drink.

Three drinks later Charlie was in that state that presages outright drunkenness. He then took over the conversation, regaling the company with anecdotes and jokes, some of which were in glaring bad taste. To everyone's relief, Peter and Nancy Pete's arrival interrupted the flow. Needless to say, Nancy Pete, a terror for the lime-light, commanded everyone's attention, reducing Charlie to a mute.

Entering the room she made straight for Gerald. 'Ah! The happy bridegroom-to-be!' she exclaimed, giving him a juicy kiss on the lips. Gerald looked mortified. But now Nancy Pete had passed on to Charlie and it looked as if he was about to get the same treatment.

Until Mary intervened, taking her elbow and saying stiffly, 'This is Mr. Charles Quinn — Gerald's father.' Thankfully, Mary's intervention had the right effect on Nancy Pete; for once she used discretion and offered Charlie her hand.

When all the introductions were over, Mary suggested that Peter and Nancy Pete might like a drink. But Peter, embarrassed about being so late, declined, saying, 'We've held you up long enough, let's eat.'

Nancy Pete gave her husband a withering look. 'You speak for yourself,' she expostulated. 'I'd like a drink and I intend having one.' Whereupon Mary trust a glass of wine into her hand. The last thing Mary needed now was a bickering match between her son and his wife.

During the meal Nancy Pete sat beside Charlie. As usual, she tediously monopolized the conversation, boring him to distraction with the litany of her domestic problems — two babies in the space of three years, an acting career she had to abandon, a journalist husband who was constantly missing. Charlie was more interested in hearing what the young men were talking about. It would seem they were discussing Irish politics — a subject close to his heart.

Nancy Pete was in the middle of a sentence when he cut her short by joining in the young men's conversation. 'That was helluva, daring feat Sinn Fein brought about in Lincoln,' he said, butting in.

'Which one was that?' Michael asked.

'Arranging DeValera's escape from the Lincoln Jail,' Charlie answered. 'I suppose that man Collins had a big hand in it?'

'Yeah,' Peter answered him. 'T'was an incredible accomplishment.'

Michael interjected, 'Strange, this is the first I'm hearing about it. Was it reported in the newspapers?'

'Just a few lines,' Peter said.

'Well,' Charlie said, 'you'll be glad to hear the English newspapers had a field day with that story.'

Jane was curious. 'When did this happen?' she asked.

'Back in February, I think?' Charlie looked at Peter for confirmation.

'That's right,' Peter nodded compliance.

Jane felt a big stone develop below her throat. Willie's secret was out. She stared at Willie for a long moment, her face a mixture of annoyance and worry. He stared back. His guilt was very evident.

Jane's wounded expression aroused Peter's suspicion: he concluded that somehow or other Willie had been involved in the DeValera escapade. And Jane had, as usual, been kept in the dark. Shrewdly changing the subject, he pronounced, 'Tomorrow's newspapers will have news of the Peace Conference in Paris.'

Jane could see Willie's eyes spark with interest.

'You're serious?' he said to Peter.

'Yes, I'm very serious,' Peter said solemnly. Suddenly the room was taut with tension. Peter cogitated for seconds. The group, all ears, patiently waited for him to continue.

'Well, tell us what you know,' Willie eventually pleaded, 'the suspense is murder.'

'I'm afraid the news is not going to be good,' Peter said dejectedly. 'From what I heard, it seems that the American President, Woodrow Wilson, has decided not to disturb this moment of allied triumph by quarrelling with the British Prime Minister, Lloyd George, about Ireland's independence.'

'What?' Charlie screeched indignantly. 'The bloody auld gobshite—licking British arse!'

For seconds there was a stunned silence. Hard to say whether it was the result of Peter's announcement or Charlie's coarse outburst. One thing was certain, Maureen wished the ground would open and swallow her.

Until Lily exploded with laughter and broke the spell, saying, 'Trust you, Charlie, to put your stamp on it.'

Willie, shocked for seconds into silence by the bad news, suddenly burst out ruefully, 'So, it's a non-starter?'

'Fraid so,' Peter said. 'It's a terrible disappointment! The Irish people had such high hopes of that Conference helping to bring about an Irish solution. But now, with the American President throwing his support behind Britain, it definitely puts the kibosh on any hopes the Irish nation had of America helping in its struggle for independence.'

'So what will Sinn Fein do now?' Charlie asked. It was a rhetorical question which no one tried to answer.

The silence gave Nancy Pete a chance to have another innings. 'Enough about gloomy politics,' she spluttered. Then turning to Mary, she asked, 'Can I have another glass of wine, please Mother?'

'I'll get another bottle,' Eileen volunteered.

Lily's heart went out to Jane, who's face had gone a grainy white. She knew exactly how she felt. The bloody Conference in which herself and Willie had placed so much hope, had now hopelessly let them down. God only knows what's going to happen now, she thought. At this moment their future looks awfully grim.

As all the guests were leaving at the same time, Jane had no chance to talk to Willie. After giving her a peck on the cheek going out the door, he said, 'I'll see you for lunch during the week.' It was obvious to Jane that Willie didn't want to talk to her about Peter's unhappy revelation.

The following morning, to the family's relief, Charlie and Maureen made their departure, saying they'd had a wonderful time and were eagerly looking forward to coming over for the wedding in June.

'You know something,' Lily said to Jane later, 'the reason Maureen wanted to stay in a private house in Dublin is as plain as the nose on your face.'

'How do you mean?' Jane asked. 'I thought she was afraid of damp sheets.'

'Damp sheets my arse!' Lily exploded. 'The reason she wanted to stay in our house was because Charlie has a drinking problem. If they stayed in a hotel, he'd probably spend most of his time in the bar.'

'Good Lord!' Jane exclaimed, 'I sincerely hope that doesn't mean a repeat performance in June?'

'I'd say it does,' Lily said. 'Not only that, but more than likely they'll have the sister and the brother along too.'

'Sweet Mother of God!' Jane exclaimed. 'Mother will have a fit if she has to go through that nightmare again.'

Chapter XXVIII

On Easter Tuesday — the third anniversary of the Easter Rising — Collins addressed a meeting of the Volunteers in the Warehouse where they trained.

'As a result of the outcome of the Peace Conference,' he said, 'the only option left to us Irish now, is to start a reign of terror against the Royal Irish Constabulary. That should get the attention of the British.' He smiled wryly. 'Further, going on the advice of my intelligence network, the policemen in the RIC who are to be targeted will be picked by me personally. They will be policemen who are considered dangerous or obnoxious to the Volunteers.'

There was a lull, then Collins continued.

'The South is itching to get this war started,' he said. 'When it comes to terror and counter terror, ye can't beat the South. Already the place bristles with guns and steel and the tension and devilry of war is abroad throughout the countryside. God bless them! They can't wait to wage an almighty guerrilla war against the British.'

For seconds after Collins stopped talking there was a marked, unusual stillness, without a cough, a rustling of paper or the shuffling of shoes. A cloud of unease seemed to pervade the place.

'So what do you say, lads? 'Collins asked anxiously, breaking the silence.

A dissident voice from the back called out, 'Surely there must be some alternative to that kind of violence?'

Collins stretched his neck in the direction of the voice. 'Can you give me one?' he asked.

Mumbling the voice said, 'Not really.' Then raising his intonation, the voice asked, 'Are you sure we've exhausted every means, every channel, every avenue, other than war, to solve the Irish problem?'

'My God! If the result of the General Election isn't enough proof for the British and the world, that the whole Irish nation wants independence, what's left?' Collins spoke with remorseless determination.

'So I reckon it has to be out and out war,' Willie supported Collins from the floor.

Looking sorry but resolute, Collins said, 'Unless the British have a big change of heart, it looks very like it.'

'There's little hope of that,' another voice in the crowd said. 'You're right, Mick. The result of the elections didn't make a blind bit of difference to the British. It has to be war.'

'So if any of you want to opt out,' Collins said, 'now is the time to do it.' His voice softened. 'And you can take it from me there'll be no hard feelings.'

Someone at the back started a slow clap. Gradually the rest joined in until it developed into a thunderous acclamation.

Collins took this as a vote of confidence. When the din died down, looking very gratified, he said, 'Thanks, lads!' Then in a more serious tone. 'Now this is where I have to tell you some really unpleasant facts.' He stroked his chin in reflection, then resumed speaking. 'Sometime in the future you may be asked to do things that appall you and that seem unconscionable. All I can say is, try to bear in mind that you are doing these acts to gain freedom for your country. No matter how evil, balm your conscience with the thoughts of the atrocities perpetrated by the British against the Irish for the past seven hundred years. Remember the Leaders of the 1916 rising who were taken out and shot like dogs without the benefit of any kind of trial.'

Somebody said, 'In for a penny, in for a pound.'

'That's the spirit,' Collins answered.

After the meeting Collins spoke to Willie. 'Did you give any more thought to joining the volunteers training sessions?' he asked him.

'Yes, as a matter of fact, I did,' Willie told him. 'After I heard the result of the Peace Conference, I made up my mind. I've arranged with Finbar to have Monday nights off.'

§

Four weeks later, Willie was holding a council in a little mill among the hills. Thirty men were lined up in the top room, gripping ash plants and rifles. The stream rippling below could be seen through the open window. Willie finished giving instructions and the men broke into waiting groups.

'Fall in! Quick march!' Willie shouted.

The thirty men filed down the stairs out into the falling darkness and up the hill slopes, Willie leading. A mile further onwards the main road reappeared. A sharp command from Willie split the company into two sections. One of which (ten volunteers) marched away while Willie remained with the larger body which climbed the slopes and pressed on higher and higher above Dublin. Underneath, a quarter of a mile away, lay the square barracks that would be the target that night. Higher and higher above the slopes into the forest behind went the young volunteers. For the next couple of hours twenty men marched and counter-marched as the drill terms were shouted by Willie, and Dublin grew dimmer below.

Then in twos and threes the absent section of the company returned. Willie looked attentively at the shotguns they carried. They had been arms-raiding the great houses in the neighborhood. Farmers, doctors and retired colonels had paid their toll to the invisible army. Again sharp orders from Willie and the company faded down the slopes in sixes and sevens, gripping weapons and clanking petrol cans, down to the square barracks which dominated the cross-roads.

Rifle shots rattled on steel shutters. Prolonged firing shook the lonely hillside. Volunteers closed in and the circle was contracted in a series of short rushes. Something crashed on to the roof of the barracks and a tongue of flame shot up, lighting up the circle of attackers outside. A white flag was thrust through an upper window.

The Sergeant and his six constables threw their arms into the road and came out slowly with hands above their heads. The attackers bound them and left them on the roadside. Bodies of volunteers rushed inside the barracks. After relieving it of all its ammunition, they dashed petrol on the walls. The stinking flames then screamed to life skywards in a red glare.

Far below shone the searchlights of a military lorry where khaki forms peered across felled threes which blocked the main road. One volunteer rolled in agony on the ground as flames played round his petrol soaked hands. He was borne into the darkness moaning, while his companions muttered imprecations on his failure to obey the warnings whispered as the waiting circle prepared the final onslaught. For the young volunteers, that night was a lesson in the right and the wrong way to use petrol when demolishing enemy buildings. A lesson they wouldn't forget in a hurry.

The last dark form darted up the hill slopes and the wailing voice of the unfortunate burnt victim died away. The dawn would reveal the bound sergeant and constables on the road at the crossroads, the burnt-out barracks and the woods and the hills behind. Tonight's work was typical of the guerrilla struggle; its echoes were heard that night in many counties in Ireland – the arms raid, the sudden attack, the ruined barracks and the escape of the Invisible Army.

Afterwards, thinking about his first successful sortie as a brigade commandant, Willie felt a rush of pride and elation. Trouble was he could never utter a word of it to anyone who wasn't in the movement.

§

Collins bent over his heaps of documents, sometimes with furrowed brow, sometimes with transient flashes of mirth in his lively eyes. Sometimes he swore loudly, sometimes he sighed. As he brooded over his desk in silence, Willie, at his own desk a distance away, brooded over his traumatic experience as a brigade commandant, directing operations in the mountains the night before. He brooded too on the surprise reception he received from Collins early this morning when he arrived in.

Before he could open his mouth, to his amazement, Collins hailed him as 'the conquering hero,' adding, 'That was a superb job you did on those bobbies in the mountains last night.'

Willie, all set to give him a blow by blow about what happened, wondered about the speed with which the news of the operation reached Collins' ears. 'How on earth did you come by this news so quickly?' Willie asked him.

'My intelligence network.'

'Already?' Willie gasped. 'But it only happened a few hours ago.'

'Yes, already,' Collins said complacently. 'My network never lets me down; it's forever on the ball.'

'My God!' Willie exploded, 'it's like they're omnipresent.' He tried to make light of it by a mirthless laugh. 'A body can't scratch themselves without them knowing about it.'

'They're efficient all right,' Collins said. Then looking well pleased with himself, he added, 'But more important, they're loyal.'

'Do I know all of them?' Willie asked.

'You probably do,' Collins said. 'But you may not be fully cognizant of the roles they play. Particularly the ones at the top.'

The following night when Willie finished work he was surprised to find Collins waiting for him at the exit.

'Ah! Willie!' Collins greeted him jovially. 'It's a fine night; I thought you and I might take a walk.'

Willie's heart practically leaped into his throat. He thought, a quarter to twelve at night! A strange time to be going for a walk. The request filled him with suspicion. He wondered what Mick could be up to now?

'Is it not a funny time to be taking a walk?' he challenged Collins. 'What's up?'

'Wait for it, By,' Collins brushed aside his question. He was all business.

'If you say so,' Willie concurred reluctantly. He could see that Collins was in one of his mysterious moods. So it was not a time for questions. They set off walking through the streets of Dublin and ended up at a Police Station. Willie was appalled. 'Surely we're not going to burn this one down without back up?' he said.

'Wait for it, By,' Collins repeated. They entered the Police Station and were met by the Sergeant in charge. 'Meet Sergeant Broy,' Collins said to Willie introducing him. 'He's one of my Irish Republican Brotherhood friends.'

Willie shook hands with Broy, nodding perceptively. 'I take it you're a member of Mick's intelligence network?' he said.

Broy looked askance at Collins seeking the right answer.

'It's all right, Broy,' Collins said, reassuringly. 'Willie and I go back as far as Frongoch.' Sounding extremely gratified, he added, 'He was the Commandant in charge of that operation in the Dublin mountains night before last.'

'Oh Good! Good! You did a great job" Broy said to Willie. He then turned to Collins and said, 'Things are all set up for you, Mick. Follow me.' Collins and Willie followed Broy upstairs to the Inspector's Office. Pointing to the filing cabinets, Broy said to Collins, 'You should find all you need among that lot.' Then moving towards the door, he said. 'I'll leave you to your work. It's best I stay downstairs in case of an emergency.' At the door he turned back. 'I'll give the three raps on the wall should anything untoward crop up.'

Feeling the continuous drum beat of his heart, Willie spent the rest of the night in the room with Collins, going through the files, noting names and addresses of detectives engaged in political work. When they left the building, Willie's curiosity got the better of him.

'If you don't mind me asking, Mick,' he said, 'what do you intend doing with that list?'

'Everyone on that list will be sent a warning telling them to change their job,' Collins said. 'Should they ignore that warning, someone in our 'special squad,' will 'rub 'em out' — as Breen would put it.'

§

Willie continued seeing Jane on Saturday nights after the pictures and on Sundays; sometimes partaking of lunch in the family home. But most times, weather permitting, having picnics on beaches either on the North side or the South side of the city. Once when Jane suggested a hike in the mountains, Willie's worried expression was a cause of concern.

Before she had time to explore his concern, Willie chipped in with a shaky laugh and said, 'Let's make it the sea; I love watching the white capped waves, the sea gulls and the fishing boats. And the air is so exhilarating'

Jane detected the false cheer in his words. More to the point, since the night of the dinner party, when Peter announced the result of the Peace Conference, she sensed a major change in Willie; a change for the worst. Nowadays, she was never fully relaxed with him. His demeanor suggested something very disturbing was troubling him. Whatever it was, he made sure not to tell her about it. At times she felt so on edge with him, she had to stop to choose her words before she opened her mouth. Clearly any discussion about politics was taboo; the once or twice she mentioned politics, he went silent. Moreover, the silences were becoming much too frequent; they clamored loudly in Jane's ears. In order to keep the conversation light and breezy she had to resort to talking about our Nancy's upcoming nuptials ad infinitum. Which if truth were told, was not one of her favorite subjects. And judging by Willie's expression was not one of his either.

However, the Sunday after the wedding invitations went out, Jane had to find out where he stood.

'You're coming to our Nancy's wedding, I hope?' she said to him as they were packing up after finishing their picnic on the beach in Portmarnock.

Willie hesitated, then said tersely, 'I'd very much like to.'

'Was that a yes or a no?' Jane said in a falsely bright voice.

'Hopefully, it's a yes.'

The words were said with such a lack of enthusiasm, Jane decided, he's trying to let me down lightly, he's not coming.

When Willie saw Jane's woebegone expression, he suddenly felt conscience stricken. I'm not being fair to her, he thought. As usual, much as I'd like to confide in her what's happening in my life, I daren't. If she had the slightest inkling that I was a part-time brigade commandant, she'd be worried sick. Reaching out to her, he pulled her into his arms. 'Darling, Jane,' he said. 'You'll have to forgive me if I don't sound overly excited about going to the wedding. I've so much on my mind these days.'

'And you can't talk about it?' Jane said, her beautiful brown eyes filled with supplication.

'Unfortunately, I can't,' Willie said ruefully. 'Not to you, anyway. T'would be too dangerous.'

'Oh my God!' Jane words were like a scream. 'You're involved in something really dangerous.'

'No, no, it's nothing like that,' Willie hastened to assure her. 'It's just that there's so much happening on the political front that's anything but agreeable.

'And you definitely can't tell me about it?' Jane said glumly.

'Maybe I could tell you a certain amount,' Willie said. But then thinking better of it, his lips tightened. It was obvious he was wrestling with whether or not to confide in her.

'Well, go on,' Jane urged. 'Tell me the certain amount?'

Willie started to talk again. 'I'm telling you this in the strictest confidence,' he said. 'You must give me your promise not to breathe a word of it to anyone. Not even to Lily.'

'Of course, you have my promise,' Jane said. 'As for Lily, though I love her dearly, there's no way I'd confide secrets of that nature to her.'

Willie paused then took the plunge. 'I heard today that DeValera is making a trip to America,' he said. Telling her this, he thought, is the lesser of two evils; hopefully, it will be enough to distract and appease her.

'When?' Jane asked.

'Sometime in July.'

'What does he hope to achieve?'

'Jane,' Willie said in a strained voice, 'the reason for the secrecy is because Dev'll have to be smuggled out of Ireland. Should word of his trip be leaked to British intelligence, they'd definitely put a stop to it.'

'So, go on!' Jane urged further, crossing her heart. 'I've given my word. Tell me what Dev's mission will be?'

'Dev's reason for going to America is to try to raise a loan to provide financial backing for Dail Eireann.' Once again Willie hesitated, nodding his head negatively. 'I really shouldn't be telling you this,' he repeated again.

'Ach, Willie, how many times do I have to say you can trust me?'

'Believe me, Jane, I do trust you,' Willie said earnestly.

'Well, if you trust me, Willie, you'll tell me the whole story?' Jane said. 'Now that you've aroused my curiosity, what else is there to tell about DeValera's trip to America?'

Jane was so impassioned, Willie decided it wasn't fair to be giving her bits of the story; having gone so far he should tell her the rest. 'I'll say one thing for you, Jane,' he said, 'you're very persistent: you don't give up easily.'

'A bit like yourself,' Jane smiled.

'Well, all right,' Willie said. 'As you're so insistent, I'll tell you what I know.' He continued. 'When Dev is in America he hopes to persuade either or both the major American political parties—Democrats and Republicans—to include in their election platform a plank recognizing the Irish Republic. In effect, it could mean the next American Government could possibly recognize the Irish Republic. As you know the outcome of the Peace Conference, was construed by the world as America being opposed to the Irish National demands.'

'But sure isn't Dev's trip to America a great step forward?' Jane said, with enthusiasm.

'Maybe so, maybe not.' Willie let out a great sigh.

'Oh, Willie!' Jane said encouragingly, 'you've got to look on the bright side. If I were in politics, I'd say Dev's trip is an excellent idea.' She smiled a slow smile. 'I'm told there are lots of wealthy Irish Americans only dying to help the Cause financially.' She hoped to God that speaking so positively would cover up her own insecurity.

'Like always,' Willie said, looking at her ardently, 'you're right, Jane. I've got to think positive.'

Jane took Willie's hand in hers. 'Willie, my love,' she said, 'you know very well I don't mind waiting until Ireland is free and life is back to normal. Someday, somehow, we'll manage to walk down that aisle together.'

'I'd like nothing better than to be able to believe that,' Willie gave a strangled laugh, 'but every time there seems to be a light at the end of the tunnel, it's swiftly snuffed out and Ireland reverts to drowning in the quagmire of British oppression.'

Chapter XXIV

The night before the wedding, Baby Heuston was running a temperature and kept his parents up most of the night.

'He's probably only teething; his cheeks are on fire,' Peter told Nancy Peter after his third trip to the baby's bedroom.

'Don't be stupid!' Nancy Pete hurled the insult at her husband. 'He's running a temperature; it's obvious that whatever is wrong, it's more than teething.'

Peter ignored the insult. 'There must be something you can give him to ease the pain?' he said.

'I've already given him baby aspirin.'

'What did you give Colbert when he was like that?' Peter asked.

'Like what?'

'Teething.'

'Once and for all, he's not teething!' Nancy Pete fired at him. 'Is that too much for that thick, stupid skull of yours to grasp?'

Suddenly the child stopped crying.

Nancy Pete rushed from the room, her face drowning in anguish. 'Jesus Christ!' she screamed, 'the child is dead.'

Peter followed her, his legs like jellies. He was prepared for the worst. When he reached the baby's room, Nancy Pete stood motionless staring into the crib. Strangely, there were no hysterical yelps issuing from her. Instead, she turned to Peter and threw herself into his arms. 'Oh, thank God!' she said breathlessly. 'He's all right; he's sleeping soundly.'

Releasing her from his embrace, Peter took a look for himself. Gone was the redness from the child's cheeks. He seemed to be sound asleep and breathing normally. It was now five o'clock in the morning.

When Colbert woke them at half-seven, Peter was utterly fatigued and groggy from lack of sleep. To add to his miseries, Nancy greeted him with, 'We can't possibly go to the wedding today; you'll have to get some else to stand in for you.'

Peter gritted his teeth. At this hour of the morning, feeling so wretched and fatigued, he was in no shape to argue the point. 'Do you want me to fetch the doctor for Heuston?' he asked tentatively.

'No, he seems all right for the moment.'

'Well then, there's nothing to prevent us from going to the wedding,' Peter said. 'Didn't we go through the same amount of teething bouts with Colbert?'

But Nancy Pete wasn't there. She'd left the room. She wasn't going to listen to any further arguments.

When Baby Heuston woke at nine o'clock, Peter searched his mouth with his finger. There it was, the new tooth. It had pushed it way through during the night. This reinforced Peter's decision to discharge his wedding duties today. Regardless of how his wife felt, this time he definitely wouldn't let the family down. He'd be there in his 'monkey suit' as arranged, to escort his sister down the aisle.

Peter was in the middle of dressing in his morning suit when Nancy Pete, still in her dressing gown, joined him in the bedroom. 'I won't be coming,' she said.

'Oh!' Peter endeavored to appear disappointed. 'Why not?' he asked. 'The kids are fine. And your mother is quite capable of looking after them.'

'Not as capable as their own mother.'

'Oh, come on now, Nancy, for God's sake!' Peter said. 'We've been through all this before with Colbert.'

'Nevertheless, you never know with babies,' Nancy Pete said. 'Teething symptoms can sometimes mask a more serious illness.' Nancy Pete was at her most dramatic. 'Anyway,' she continued,

'I've made up my mind, I'm definitely not coming.'

'You'll be missed,' Peter said as he left the room. He was thinking: Boy! Will she be missed! If it's only for the insults and the faux pas she makes!

§

In the O'Dwyer household the wedding arrangement were progressing according to plan. There appeared to be no hitches: the situation with regard to Father Vincent being the celebrant of the wedding and the accommodation problem for Gerald's family had been amicably settled. The latter sorted out by Gerald booking his family into a temperance hotel in Harcourt Street. As the Reception was being held in the Shelbourne Hotel on Saint Stephen's Green, once it was over, his family — Father, mother, sister and brother — could easily walk to their own hotel without bothering anyone and without incurring the expense of a cabby.

Having the Reception in the Shelbourne Hotel was not particularly popular with Mary. She'd set her heart on the Gresham Hotel in Sackville Street where she'd be close to the shop in the event of an emergency. The Shelbourne was miles away on the other side of the city. Something else that didn't please her, was the ceremony taking place in the Pro Cathedral church, rather than the Dominick Street parish church. Our Nancy insisted on this and no amount of pleading and arguing would change her mind. If you please, she didn't want the church swarming with the local, gawking and gossiping 'shawlies.'

Once again Jane was a bridesmaid. But instead of Lily being the second bridesmaid, our Nancy contrarily opted to have Bridget as her matron-on-honor.

'If that isn't a bare-faced insult,' Lily burst out to Jane when she first heard about the arrangements, 'I don't know what is.'

Along with that Eileen was told there would be no flower girl: the bride had too many more important things to attend to. Needless to say, Eileen was extremely disappointed.

'Jesus! Lily spluttered to Jane when she heard Eileen's news, 'like always, that wan has everything cut and dried.' Though she felt bitter about the snub to herself, she could have strangled our Nancy for disappointing Eileen. 'She's a heartless bitch!' she said vehemently. 'The child was so looking forward to being a flower girl.'

Jane felt sorry for both Lily and Eileen. However, in Lily's case, it wasn't terribly surprising. Considering the animosity that existed between the two sisters, wouldn't our Nancy get great enjoyment denying Lily the pleasure of being one of her bridesmaids. But Eileen's case was different; denying the child the thrill of being a flower girl was really mean spirited.

'Personally,' Jane told Lily, 'I'd just as soon not be her bloody bridesmaid.'

'Well,' Lily said bitterly, 'I hope it keeps fine for her.'

Lily's remark was strangely prophetic. The weather definitely didn't oblige: just as our Nancy was leaving the house, the rain bucketed down and continued bucketing for the rest of the day.

Willie was pleased to see Peter on his own at the wedding. And to find out that they would be seated beside each other at the Reception. It meant they could have a frank and open discussion about political affairs, without Peter having his head constantly bitten off by that wife of his. Peter was a different person when she wasn't around. Throughout the breakfast Willie couldn't help noticing how easy going and relaxed he was out of her company. He was remembering the Peter he knew in Frongoch: no matter how bad things got, Peter O'Dwyer was a free spirit who didn't let anything get him down. In many ways, he reminded Willie of Collins. (Except that Collins didn't have a ball and chain perpetually putting him down.)

'Do you know what the situation is regarding DeValera's trip to America?' Peter asked Willie quietly as they were eating. 'Has a date been fixed?'

'Oh yes,' Willie said. 'It's been fixed at last. It's the nineteenth of July, please God.'

'That's definite?'

'Yes,' Willie said. 'What held things up was the argument between

Dev and Collins about Boland accompanying Dev to America. Needless to say, Collins was dead against it.'

'What!' Peter's eyebrows shot up with the shock. 'You mean to say Dev wants Boland to accompany him?'

'Just that,' Willie said grimly. 'He insists if Boland doesn't go he won't go either.'

'That's blackmail,' Peter said solemnly.

'Exactly,' Willie said. 'Unfortunately, Dev finally got his way with a very reluctant Collins. So on the nineteenth of July both Dev and Boland will travel to America.'

'That's unbelievable!' Peter said. 'Sure Boland is Collins' best friend and teammate. It looks as though Dev is cashing in on that friendship.'

'Collins feels betrayed by both of them,' Willie said.

'You're not telling me that Boland wants to go?' Peter said very surprised.

'Hard to say,' Willie said. 'He hasn't said yes, aye or no throughout all the arguments.'

'Maybe Boland is infatuated with the idea of seeing America,' Peter reasoned. 'Well, wouldn't it be a fabulous opportunity for him.'

'Collins will be absolutely lost without him,' Willie put in. He lowered his voice. 'The thing that worries me most about this business is that I may be asked to fill Boland's shoes in his absence.'

'Which I take wouldn't sit well with you?' Peter said.

'Well, as it is,' Willie said, 'I feel I've more than enough on my plate, what with the job along with working for the Cause, without becoming Collins full-time teammate.'

'And you're worried about neglecting Jane?' Peter put in sagaciously.

'You put your finger on it; I love Jane to distraction,' Willie said, flushed. 'I want to marry her. But I have so many secrets from her and let her down so often, I wonder how much longer she'll put up with me?'

'Jane loves you too,' Peter said. 'That I can vouch for.' He looked at Willie with great sympathy. 'Maybe if you let her into some of the secrets...'

'I do tell her the odd one,' Willie interjected. 'Mostly about things that are going on generally in politics. But I daren't mention some of the risks I'm taking myself. For instance, were I to tell her that I'm now a part-time brigade commandant, she'd probably have a fit.'

This was news to Peter. It seemed to stagger him. 'My Goodness!' he said, 'You're actually a brigade commandant?'

'See now,' Willie said. 'Even you're shocked.'

'No, not so much shocked,' Peter said, 'as filled with admiration.' For a split second he was silent, then said, 'You took Collins up on his proposition; the one he made that day we had the jar together?'

'Exactly,' Willie said absently. 'With so many things going awry in his life, I hadn't the heart to refuse him.'

'How long have you been a operative then?' Peter asked, inquisitively.

'About a month.'

'Have you participated in any missions yet?' Peter's eyes were alight with curiosity.

'Yes, I was the leader in a mission carried out by thirty of us up the Dublin Mountains recently; we burnt down the police barracks.' Willie then became very anxious. 'For God's sake don't mention a word of this to Jane,' he said.

'Course not,' Peter reassured him. His face split into a gleaming smile. 'Well, Willie, he said, 'you never cease to amaze me.' His eyes were full of admiration. 'You have my heartiest congratulations.'

An excited voice came from behind. Lily's.

'Sounds intriguing!' she said to Peter, 'Why are you congratulating Willie?'

Peter turned to face her. 'It's very bad manners to eavesdrop, young woman,' he said. 'I suggest you watch it, because if you do it often enough you're bound to hear something unflattering about yourself.'

'Ach come off it!' Lily said coaxingly. 'Tell your curious sister Willie's good news.' She wondered could it possibly be that Willie had decided to pop the question to Jane?

Lost for words, Peter looked quizzically at Willie. 'Oh, it's just that I came first in a shooting contest and won a medal for it,' Willie said grinning genially.

'Well, isn't that great!' Lily said in a dull voice.

Meanwhile, seated at the end of the top table, Jane was still reeling from the shock of discovering that Percy was the groomsman who was her partner in the bridal group. When herself and Bridget arrived at the alter ahead of the bride, she couldn't believe her eyes when she saw him standing there in his morning suit next to the best man — an army officer. Throughout the ceremony, she thought, Sweet Jesus! Am I going to be stuck with this stupid jerk for the rest of the day? (She'd been informed by our Nancy beforehand that the bridesmaid and the matron-of-honor would be seated beside their respective male partners during the meal.) The day was going to be endless. What with all those long-winded speeches. She could see Willie in the distance sitting and chatting with Peter. She thought, how I envy Peter; if only we could swap places. I couldn't have had a worse companion for the day. And I can't even talk to anyone about it!

Lily was, as usual, sitting with the country cousins. And from the way her head was thrown back laughing heartily, she was obviously having a wonderful time. Jane thought, about the irony of life: had Lily been the second bridesmaid, she'd have had Percy as her partner. And without a doubt, she'd be the one to put him in his place. Whereas in Jane's case, as an employee, she would be expected to threat the Managing Director's son with great respect. Notwithstanding Jane's fears, to give Percy his due, early on he did try to be pleasant; the shop or the episode of the hat were never mentioned.

On the other hand, from the start, he flirted wildly with her. She noticed too that he called the Wine Waiter a number of times for refills, which meant he was getting stocious by the minute. Gradually, the flirting became more brazen: he did things like putting his hand on her knee and squeezing it, stretching his arm across her shoulder, pulling her towards him trying to kiss her. Then his behavior became totally obnoxious when he leaned under the table and put his hand up her skirt. This was too much for Jane. She stood up and excused herself to go the Ladies Powder Room.

Lily found Jane leaning over a basin in the Ladies Room taking deep breaths. At the sight of her sister Jane's relief was profound. At last someone to talk to; the very best person at that. When Lily saw Jane rushing from the dining room, her face panic-stricken, her eyes big and anxious, she sensed something was radically wrong. Earlier, she'd noticed Jane looking extremely tense at the top table and put it down to nerves or boredom. However, not long afterwards, when she looked once again in Jane's direction, it was very evident what the problem was; the groomsman beside her seemed to be making very improper advances towards her. If she was seeing right, Jane was pulling away from him as he tried to kiss her. This was what induced her to follow Jane to the Ladies Powder Room.

'What the hell does that fellow think he's doing?' Lily burst out from the door. Thankfully, the Powder Room was empty.

'My God!' Jane said patting her face with a paper towel. By now she was soaking in perspiration and looked close to tears. 'Have you any idea who he is?' she asked Lily.

'Not a notion,' Lily said, then added sardonically, 'and from what I've seen of his behavior, he's no gentleman.'

'He's Percy. You know, from the shop,' Jane said. 'The Managing Director's son.'

'Percy!' Lily stared in disbelief. 'In the name of God, how did he become a groomsman? He's not even in the army!'

'He's filling in for another friend of Gerald's who had to return to England in a hurry; something to do with a family emergency.' Jane looked miserable. 'God! I hate going back to that table again.'

'I've an idea,' Lily said. 'As you're sitting on the very end of the table, with no one beyond you, what would you think about me bringing up an extra chair and sitting either alongside you or on the end?'

'Would you do that?' Jane said looking greatly relieved.

'Course, I'd do it.'

'That'd be marvelous.' Jane said. Then after she had a little think about it, she pleaded, 'But Lily, you wouldn't make a scene, would you?'

Lily started to laugh. 'Now wouldn't this be a marvelous opportunity for me to create a furor at my dear sister's wedding; timing would be perfect.' Laughing heartily, she continued, 'The bitch'd be convinced I did it on purpose to embarrass her and ruin her wedding.'

Jane caught Lily's arm anxiously. 'But you wouldn't start a row or use bad language at the top table, would you?' she said fearfully.

'Course not,' Lily said, her eyes glowing with mischief, 'there's more than one way to skin a cat.'

Jane checked her watch. 'Gosh,' she said anxiously, 'they haven't even started the speeches yet. And they could go on for hours.'

'Well, at least we've only the one priest to put us to sleep at this wedding,' Lily said. Then she was all business. 'Right,' she said with aplomb, 'once and for all let's put this fella in his place. You go back to the table. I'll find a waiter to bring my chair up to the top table and sit beside you.'

'Lily, you're an angel!' Jane said, heady with relief. At the door she turned back. 'Please, Lily!' she pleaded, 'remember—no shouting or bad language.'

'Don't worry, Jane, I'll be the soul of discretion.'

Jane was barely settled back in her chair when a waiter arrived with another chair, followed by Lily carrying her plate and cutlery. On Lily's instructions the waiter put the chair at the end of the table beside Jane. Nobody at the table seemed to take any notice, except Percy. When he saw Lily sitting on the end of the table, he raised surprised eyebrows.

'What's going on?' he said in a very slurred voice.

'This is my sister, Lily,' Jane introduced Lily to him. Adding, 'Lily meet Percy.'

'Delighted to meet you, Percy,' Lily said in her best accent, stretching across the table to shake his hand.

'Why is your sister joining our table?' Percy asked perplexed. The slurring was now more pronounced and the face was full of suspicion.

Lily leaned across the table, stared ardently into his eyes and in a low tone said, 'I noticed you in the distance; you remind very much of a young man I was very fond of.'

'What happened to him?' Percy asked.

'It's a long story,' Lily said. Then giving Jane a conniving smile, she asked her politely, 'Would you mind changing places with me for a few minutes, Jane, so that I can tell Percy the full story.'

Jane was up like a shot. 'Course.'

Lily settled into Jane's chair and proceeded to make up a yarn about this wonderfully, handsome young man she was mad about.

'So what happened to him?' Percy repeated the question, this time putting his hand on her knee and squeezing it. Lily was ready for him. Concealed in her hand was a small hat pin. This was plunged into the hand on her knee. 'Jesus Christ!' Percy let out a loud shriek. 'What have you done to my hand?'

Looking innocent as a newborn babe, Lily said, 'Sorry! Is something the matter?'

Holding his hand, Percy looked at her like he could strangle her. 'You're a witch!' he said. Then stood up, staggered from the table and continued staggering down the room, till he finally disappeared through the exit.

Smiling wickedly, Lily indicated the hatpin in her hand to Jane, 'God bless whoever invented these,' she said.

Strangely, nobody seemed to notice what was going on at the end of the table. Except for Maureen who was seated next to Percy. Leaning across, she whispered to Lily, 'I'm glad someone had the gumption to put that awful creature in his place.'

The three laughed conspiratorially.

Percy was missing for the rest of the day.

'Probably went to the hospital to have his hand seen to,' Lily said offhandedly to Jane, later on.

'Jesus, Lily!' Jane said, her eyeballs on stalks with worry. 'I hope you didn't injure his hand seriously with that hat pin.'

'Pity about him!'

'But suppose he gets blood poisoning, or an infection or something in the hand?'

'Suppose he has to have his hand amputated!' Lily roared laughing. 'That's one hand that deserves to be put out of action.'

Thankfully, Father Vincent was suffering from laryngitis so the guests were spared a long, tedious sermon. He just had enough voice to wish the couple every blessing in their marriage and in their future. Then, with our Nancy directing operations — giving the other speech makers their instructions to 'keep it short' — things moved rapidly and smoothly, until the bride and groom made their departure for their honeymoon in Greystones.

Then the fun commenced with Charlie who had knocked back a fair few whiskeys. Approaching Mary, he slapped her on the back and said raucously, 'So where do we go from here, Mam?'

Mary gave him a look of incomprehension which to an ordinary person would have been answer enough. But in this instance she was dealing with a drunk. The worry of Charlie arriving on her doorstep in this condition clamped down on her throat, rendering her speechless for seconds. However, being Mary, her mind quickly picked up the thread of what the consequences would be if she didn't put him off. 'Well,' she faltered, 'I don't know what arrangement the young people have made for afterwards, but as far as I'm concerned, I'm going home to rest. It's been a long day.'

'Surely there's a 'knees-up' somewhere?' Charlie protested.

'What do you mean a 'knees up'? Mary feigned puzzlement.

'A good old fashioned hooley.' Charlie clasped his hands in anticipation.

'Nothing that I know of,' Mary tried to sound as negative as possible.

Just then Eileen arrived. 'Everyone's going back to our house,' she announced excitedly. She touched Charlie's arm, 'You're coming too I hope?' she added.

Mary's look at Eileen couldn't be more contemptuous. Here she was doing her best to put Charlie off. Now, if she was to save face, there was no alternative but to invite him and his family back. 'Oh!' she said to Eileen, blushing scarlet, 'that's news to me.' Then turning to Charlie she said, 'but of course you and your family must come if everyone else is coming.'

As it turned out Charlie arrived alone by cab. Evidently his family was disinclined to go through the embarrassment of seeing him make a fool of himself again.

Mary told Bridget, who was helping to serve the drinks, 'Water Charlie's whiskey as much as possible.'

However, the warning was unnecessary. When Bridget arrived with his drink, Charlie had passed out on the sofa. Here he snored his way through the evening's festivities; the eating, the drinking, the music, the entertainment and the dancing. He missed it all.

'What a pity our Nancy isn't here to witness this reprehensible sight,' Lily said to Jane, indicating Charlie on the sofa with his mouth wide open. 'She was so bloody righteous about everything being absolutely perfect on *her* wedding day.'

'With a father-in-law like that,' Jane said, 'who'd envy her? Sure you couldn't bring him anywhere. He makes such a show of himself.'

Thankfully, Charlie came alive at twelve o'clock when everyone was was leaving. He seemed fresh as a daisy after his long sleep. He thanked Mary profusely for a wonderful evening. Then sticking out his robust chest, announced, 'Now that the rain has stopped, the walk to Harcourt Street will be great exercise for me; do me a whale of good.' He departed under his own steam.

The O'Dwyer family let out a collective sigh of relief when they saw him disappear into the darkness.

Chapter XXV

As anticipated, Willie became one of Collins chief confidants. Collins kept no secrets from him. Sometimes Willie felt quite overburdened by knowing so much. What if he was arrested and tortured? Collins even went so far as to tell Willie about Joe, his IRB spy in Dublin Castle who fed him really important information. According to Collins he was number one in his intelligence network. Meantime, Collins alternated between his roles as Finance Minister, organizing vast loans for the Irish Republic, while directing in Dublin and coordinating throughout the country the activities of the volunteers. By now Collins, with relentless single mindedness and efficiency had set about creating the general state of disorder he'd formerly talked about. Going on information supplied by his intelligence network, a reign of terror began against Irish policemen in Dublin and around the country. Notwithstanding the fact that DeValera and Boland had gone to America intent on procuring recognition for the Irish Republic, Collins, who stayed home, maintained that 'the fight must go on.'

During one of the many conversations Collins had with Willie, he complained, 'Dev is probably not the best person to represent Ireland in America; he's so bloody fastidious. Even mulling over a minor press statement, takes him days. He refuses to be rushed making the simplest statements.' Collins went on, 'With him in the saddle, I don't anticipate decisions being made in a hurry in America. So I'm not holding my breath.'

'Isn't he nice and safe over there too?' Willie remarked cuttingly. 'Whereas you've been left holding the combat zone.'

Collins grinned. 'You might say that,' he said. 'However, I'm convinced, despite his slowness, Dev has a singleness of purpose. He may be slow but he's sure.'

'Like the tortoise,' Willie put in laughing. 'So you think he'll eventually deliver?'

'Yeah. Eventually is the operative word,' Collins looked towards heaven,' but we'll need divine patience waiting for it.'

Mechanically going through memoranda and notes at this time, Willie came across some notes from Volunteers who expressed dissatisfaction and shock at the amount of bloodshed. One such note, signed by four volunteers, said bluntly, 'Is this bloodshed necessary? It seems like we're forcing an open door.' Another one, said, 'Why fire a shot when we have the country behind us?'

On reading these notes out to Collins, fired up, Collins would ask, 'What are they talking about? Are they happy to see the country stagnate and never move forward? With an attitude like that, they're not worth a roasted fart to their country.' Nevertheless, ninety per cent of the correspondence praised Collins for continuing the fight. And Collins was greatly heartened.

Through his intelligence network, Collins learned that an arrest warrant had been issued for him, putting a price on his head—dead or alive. Despite this, Collins, undeterred, seldom bothered to disguise himself, but rode freely around Dublin on his bicycle, relying on the efficiency of his intelligence system and his hand-picked 'squad' to protect him, which they did magnificently. Not once did they let him down. On one occasion Collins broached the subject to Willie about joining his hand-picked squad. But Willie declined on the grounds that he could never kill someone deliberately. It was one thing to be a soldier in a war, quite another to be a cold blooded assassin.

Afterwards, Willie felt relieved that once and for all he had made clear to Collins his point of view regarding killings.

'It's no reflection on you, By,' Collins told him calmly. 'You need to have the stomach for it. Most of those assassins are young, bloodthirsty nationalists, who, unlike yourself and myself, haven't been through the mill as yet.'

'Is Mick around?' a girl's voice asked Willie as he mulled over a mountain of documentation. Looking up he saw a young girl — not more that sixteen — asking the question.

'Who wants to know?' Willie asked.

'The girl produced a bulky package. 'This package from my father is to be delivered into his hands.'

'And who might your father be?' Willie asked.

'I'm not supposed to say.' The girl looked quite resolute. 'My instructions are very clear,' she said. 'This package is to be given to Mick Collins and Mick Collins only.'

'What's in it?' Willie asked.

'How would I know!' The girl's mouth puckered doggedly.

'Well, Mick isn't here,' Willie said. 'You've either got to trust me and leave the package with me, or come back.'

'I can't come back,' the girl said. 'It's too risky.'

Willie plucked up his ears. 'I'm one of Mick's assistants,' he said. 'You can trust me.'

'Did you fight in the sixteen rising?' the girl asked.

'I did,' Willie said, 'and I spent time with Mick in the Frongoch prison.'

The girl seemed to relax. 'So did my father,' she vouched.

'That's where he met Mick.'

'That's where I met Mick too.' Willie smiled a slow smile. 'So now that we've established that your father and I were jailbirds together with Mick,' he said, 'perhaps you'd tell me your father's name? More than likely I know him.'

The girl seemed to gain confidence from this statement. 'His name is Peadar O'Dea,' she said.

'Oh I remember him!' Willie's face was full of animation. 'He was the best kicker on our Frongoch football team; scored most of the goals.'

'Oh! Isn't that interesting now?' the girl said, a hint of excitement in her voice.

'Yes, I was the goalie.'

'Well,' the girl said, now sounding more confident, 'in that case, I suppose I could leave the package with you.'

'Can you tell me what's in it?' Willie asked. 'If there was a raid by the constabulary, I'd need to know.'

'Ammunition,' the girl said bluntly. 'According to my father, from time to time I may be dropping other packages off for Collins.'

Willie smiled. 'I take it your father is the 'keeper' of the ammunition?'

'I don't know about him being the keeper,' the girl said. 'What I do know is bulky packages disappear regularly under the flooring of our front room. Later those packages are collected by young men in trench coats and slouch hats.'

'For someone so young,' Willie said, 'you're very intelligent and sophisticated.'

'Living with my father, I'd have to be,' the girl retorted. 'Not only do we have young men dropping in to collect ammunition, but sometimes, without warning, they drop in and sleep on the floor of the front room. They're 'on the run'; that means they're wanted by the Castle.'

'How does your mother feel about all this activity?' Willie asked, puzzled.

'She's dead,' the girl said sadly. 'A casualty of the rising; she was in the Cumann ne mBan.'

'How long do the young men stay in hiding at your place?' Willie asked.

'Until a seafaring man calls and takes them aboard his vessel,' the girl told him. 'That way they're beyond Mister Healy's grasp; he's head of the detectives in the Castle.'

'You amaze me; you're so knowledgeable,' Willie said.

'My father saw to it,' the girl answered him. 'He made sure I learned about bandages, wounds and the makes of arms in the drill halls.' She prattled on. 'And I regularly attend Countess Markievitz's meetings. She's a bit mad, but mad in the right sense; good to the poor. Did you know her hair turned white when she was in jail?'

Willie was astounded that someone so young could be privy to so much information. Considering her age and the fact that she' lost her mother in the rising, he couldn' help but admire her pluckiness. He wondered did she have any idea the danger she was in carrying such hazardous packages? He came to the conclusion that she was being shamelessly exploited; no other word for it. Such were his thoughts when Collins arrived.

'Well, if it is isn't the beautiful Sive,' he exclaimed, giving Sive's shoulder a squeeze. Indicating the package still in her hands, he added, laughing, 'our angel deliverith!' Sive smiled a brilliant smile. Like everyone else, she seemed totally devoted to Collins. 'I hope this is the start of many such deliveries?' Collins pronounced giving her a collusive wink.

'You're a hard man to find,' Sive told him. 'This is the fourth place I called to this morning; nobody knew where you were.'

'My sweet child!' Collins pronounced solemnly, 'it's the only way I can survive.' Then he added, 'Were it not for my network and all the help I get from people like Willie there (who doesn't know, from one day to the next, where he's going to be based), I couldn't keep going.'

Willie thought, what Mick was saying was so true. Late every evening, someone left a message with Sadie telling Willie which address he was to work at the following day.

When the young girl left, Collins said to Willie, 'Could you leave what you're doing and bring this package Sive delivered over to Aungier Street; you know the address. The squad are having their meeting there midday today. I'll be joining them later.'

§

Claremorris,
Co. Mayo,
15th September, 1919

Dear Willie,
This letter will probably come as a surprise. I trust you're keeping well and that the film industry is thriving. It's been such a long time

since we heard from you.

My reason for writing is to tell you that our sister, Monica, and her brand new husband, Tom, have just arrived from Chicago for a short visit. They would very much like to see you. But as their stay in Ireland is short, it isn't possible for them to travel to Dublin.

So we were wondering if you could manage to make the trip to the West sometime during next week? I realize this is very short notice. But you know the way it is with Americans. They don't believe in giving prior notice to their Irish relatives; they just arrive. Anyway, if you can make it, we'd all love to see you.

All here are in fine fettle.

> *God Bless,*
> *Your fond brother,*
> *Martin.*

As the train streaked through the Irish countryside heading West, Willie had lots of time to reflect on this journey. He wondered how his parents would receive him this time? Would their attitude have mellowed in the interim? Naturally he was thrilled at the prospect of seeing Monica again after such a long time. She was next to him in age. As children, they got on like a house on fire; played together most of the time. With the result she became something of a tomboy. But the real worry now was how to deal with questions about his life posed by Monica and/or her husband. In view of his parents' attitude last time, prohibiting talk or discussions about the 1916 rising or Willie's incarceration in Frangoch, he decided the best strategy this time would be to sing dumb should the subject of the Cause, or anything pertaining to it, arise. As the train got closer to his destination, sadly, Willie had to come to terms with the fact that in this part of the country, 'silence was golden' when it came to Irish politics.

His other worry concerned Jane. This week she would be spending her annual holiday (her first since she started working) at the sea with her friend Philomena in Courtown Harbor, County Wexford. When the holiday was in the planning, Willie promised he'd spend the Sunday with her.

A fact warmly welcomed by Finbar, who said to him, 'Why don't you take the week. You work too hard. Everyone's entitled to a break.' Though Finbar was a pushover allowing him to take this trip, he felt really bad having to tell Jane about his change of plans. But like always, she was her usual stoic self about it.

'She is your sister after all,' she said, her blazing smile covering her disappointment. 'God only knows when you'll see her again.'

When the train shrieked into the Claremorris Station, Willie was glad to see Martin standing on the platform.

'Great you were able to make it, Willie,' Martin greeted him warmly. Then took the bag out of his hand. 'I have the trap waiting outside,' he said.

'So how is our American sister?' Willie asked Martin as the trap plodded along the country road.

'In fine fettle.'

'What's the husband like?'

'Seems like a nice fella.' Martin was curt as ever. Willie thought, well, Martin hasn't changed anyhow. He's still a man of very few words.

When they arrived at the farm, Monica came tearing out of the house to greet them. Bristling with excitement, she threw her arms around Willie. Then releasing him, she stood back and studied him.

'My, but haven't you turned into quite the Adonis!' she said beaming at him. 'The last time I saw you, you were a long, thin, scrawny looking youth with no flesh on your bones.' From the admiring way she sized Willie up, it was clear she was impressed with his appearance.

'And you don't look so bad yourself,' Willie said giving her another hug. What he saw was a handsome young girl in her early twenties, red-headed, blue-eyed and filled with the joie de vivre. And why wouldn't she be? he silently asked himself. Just married. On a honeymoon with a man she probably adored.

Tom turned out to be quite a bit older than Monica. Dark and handsome, Willie guessed, of Italian origin. He greeted Willie warmly, hugging him first then kissing him on both cheeks. His greeting was in stark contrast to the limp hand shakes Willie got from his parents, Ellen and Patrick.

'Dying to hear your news,' Monica enthused as soon as Willie sat down and she'd handed him a glass of whiskey.

'Well, for starters,' Willie said, handing her back the glass, 'you can take three-quarters of this drink back; I wouldn't drink that much in a week.'

'But you're a city person!' Monica poured some of the whiskey back into the bottle. 'A man of the world, a man in the film business, no less!'

Willie felt like laughing heartily at the irony of it. If she only knew, he thought. At the same time he was grateful she'd chosen to talk about the pictures rather than politics.

Monica prattled on. 'You know, Willie,' she said, 'you're in the right business. Film business is big business in the States.'

Willie smiled indulgently. 'You don't say?'

Tom interjected, 'what exactly is your role?' he asked Willie curiously.

'Oh! I'm just a simple, unimportant projectionist,' Willie said unpretentiously.

'There's no such thing as a simple, unimportant projectionist,' Monica asserted. 'According to what I've heard, the projectionist has a very powerful role to play in the showing of the pictures; if he wasn't there, there'd be no pictures. Have you ever thought of that?'

'Well put, Sis,' Willie said. 'I wish everyone appreciated me as much as you do.'

'You know something, Willie,' Tom said with enthusiasm. 'You'd do very well in the States.'

'Would you think of emigrating?' Monica asked excitedly, her face lighting up.

'Pity he wouldn't!' the words were like a growl coming from his mother's mouth. Clearly, because of his republican ideals, Willie was still an object of vituperation in his mother's eyes.

There was a little pause, which he filled, saying, 'Enough about me, what about yourselves?'

'Oh, we're doing fine,' Monica said throwing her arm affectionately around Tom's neck. 'We're in the family grocery business.'

'It goes without saying that people have to eat,' Tom said lightheartedly. 'Hence, so far we've been fairly successful.'

Willie said, 'You're in one of the best businesses.'

'What about romance?' Monica asked Willie, changing the subject. 'Have you a girlfriend?'

'I have, as a matter of fact. 'Willie smiled thinking of Jane. 'By the same token, her family are in the dairy and grocery business too.'

'In Dublin?' Monica asked inquisitively.

'Yeah,' Willie said. 'Right in the heart of the city.'

'It's hard work,' Tom said.

Later while they were eating supper, much to Willie's unease, Tom brought up the very subject he hoped to avoid—Irish politics. Addressing Willie, Tom said, 'You know anything about that guy DeValera who came to America to raise funds?'

'I read something about it in the newspapers,' Willie said nonchalantly. 'Why do you ask?'

'Well, from what I read in the American newspapers,' Tom said, 'he's not doing a very good job.'

'Why is that?' Willie asked, making a supreme effort to sound indifferent.

'According to a New York paper,' Tom said, 'DeValera's attitude has earned the animosity of two prominent Irish American leaders—Judge Coholan and John Devoy.'

'How on earth did he manage to do that?' Willie asked, still trying hard not to sound too interested.

'Well, going on what I read later in a local newspaper,' Tom said, 'it stated that Mister DeValera—representing the Republic of Ireland—was a very arrogant man who made many gaffes; one in particular was very offensive to the American Congress.'

'As bad as that?' Willie gasped.

'Reading between the lines,' Tom said, 'I got the distinct impression that that man DeValera has done a good job alienating Irish-American sympathy.'

Ellen butted in. 'He's probably one of those stupid, Irish revolutionaries,' she said viciously. 'What can you expect?'

With a couple of sentences Ellen succeeded in putting an end to the conversation. The company then went on to discuss desultory matters. Later in bed Willie couldn't sleep thinking about Tom's revelations regarding DeValera. His mind was a firestorm. He thought about Collins working himself to death, taking terrible risks, dealing with the invisible army, gun-running, flying columns, new revolutionaries, raising funds and for good measure, topping the British Authorities 'wanted' list. While Dev was having the life of Reilly in the States; true to form, playing God and making an unholy mess of things. Instead of fund raising, he was getting the Irish-American people's backs up. How could the Republic ever hope to get American recognition when an arrogant bastard the likes of Dev was doing the negotiating?

Since DeValera and Boland's departure, the few and far between letters sent anonymously to Collins, and usually passed on to Willie, were penned by Boland. These letters were totally uninformative; they said little or nothing. Just made references, without specifics, to how hard the two of them were working, the numbers of wealthy Irish Americans they hoped to meet and the amount of traveling they had to do. Except for saying they had raised a certain amount of money—which to Willie's mind was trivial—it would appear they were not meeting with any great success. Willie wondered if he could possibly learn more about the situation from Tom without arousing suspicion? One thing was certain, he'd have to nab Tom on his own. The matter definitely couldn't be discussed in the presence of his family.

Next morning at breakfast the chance to talk to Tom presented itself when Willie found him breakfasting by himself in the kitchen. The parents and Martin were away doing their farming chores and Monica had elected to have her breakfast in bed. Willie broached the subject diffidently, saying, 'Tom, I was most interested in what you had to say about DeValera last evening. Could you elaborate a little more on it?'

Tom looked up from his plate of rashers, eggs and home-made brown bread. Grinning, he said, 'You're mixed up with that business of fighting for the Cause aren't you?'

'I'm mixed up with a certain amount of it.' Willie decided to play safe. Nodding towards the outside door, he added, 'Of course, the parents have no time for it; it's a non-subject in this house.'

'I gathered as much,' Tom said, 'by the abrupt way Ellen put an end to the conversation last evening.'

'Can you tell me anything more about what DeValera is up to in America?' Willie asked. 'The reason I ask is, it's costing a lot to keep him there and if he's not doing the job properly it's a terrible waste of precious money.'

'I see your point,' Tom said. 'Well, I don't know that I can add much more to what I said last night. As far as I can make out, there are some very wealthy Irish Americans sympathetic to the Irish situation. These people have contributed generously towards financing your Irish Parliament…'

'Dail Eireann,' Willie interjected proudly. 'Irish for the Irish parliament.'

'Dail Eireann,' Tom repeated. 'I like the sound of that. Anyway,' Tom went on, 'to make a long story short, this guy DeValera wasn't content with just collecting money. No, he had the audacity to demand that the American Government recognize the Irish Republic which would mean America having to oppose Article 10 of the League of Nations Covenant.'

'Article 10 of the League of Nations Covenant,' Willie repeated, puzzled. 'What's that all about?'

'As you probably know,' Tom said, 'the League of Nations Covenant is an International Covenant.'

'Yeah, I know that,' Willie said. 'Go on.'

'Well, as far as I can gather,' Tom said, 'in a nutshell, Article 10 is construed as being opposed to Irish National demands. So short of changing our American Constitution, there's no way America can recognize an Irish Republic at the moment. However, things can change.'

'You mean there could be a change of Government in America and Woodrow Wilson would no longer be President?'

'Exactly,' Tom said, then looked quite irritated. 'But try telling that to your Irish friend, Mister DeValera.'

'He's no friend of mine,' Willie said, trying not to sound too bitter.

'Frankly, Willie,' Tom said solemnly, 'I'd be inclined to think that your country has put its money on the wrong horse sending such an arrogant, overbearing man to represent it.'

Willie stayed on in Mayo for the rest of the week. Having Monica and Tom around made a tremendous difference. For the first time in years he was enjoying a visit home. For the American newlyweds it seemed the Welcome Mat was rolled out with a vengeance by relatives and friends. Practically every evening there was an invitation to some relative or friend's home. On each occasion, Monica insisted on Willie accompanying them. It was clear to her that he was as much a stranger to Mayo as she was.

On these occasions Monica made a point of telling everyone that Willie now worked in the 'film' business in Dublin. People were fascinated by this extraordinary phenomenon. Imagine moving pictures on a screen! Never in their lives had they heard the likes. With the result that most of Willie's time was spent explaining how the film system worked. Plus answering non-stop questions. At most of these functions, Monica, having captured everyone's attention, would state categorically, for Willie's benefit and the benefit of the people present, 'Willie's expertise is wasted in this country! Tom and I are trying to get him to come to America where he could make a fortune.'

Willie thought, if only it was as easy as that.

Throughout the week the people's fascination with the film business monopolized Willie's conversations. With the result that politics were never mentioned. However, he did confide in Tom eventually; telling him the full story about his participation in the 1916 rising and his imprisonment in Frongoch.

Showing great admiration and respect, Tom said, 'Don't worry, Willie, not a word of this will I mention to Monica until we're back on American soil.' He then added, 'Thank you for taking me into your confidence.'

Strangely, as Willie was telling Tom his story, a sense of reconciliation surged through him. A lot had to do with the fact that, unlike the last time he visited and was muzzled, this time he was able to open up to someone, albeit an American, an Italian one at that.

The night before the couple left, Ellen and Patrick gave a party for them. As far as Monica was concerned she hardly participated; she was too busy trying to persuade Willie to make the decision to emigrate to America. She went to great lengths explaining about how easy it would be to get American citizenship and how honored Tom and herself would be to sponsor him.

'It would be no problem,' she told him with exuberance, 'and as far as jobs in the film industry are concerned, there would be a massive demand for your services. Besides,' she went on, 'wouldn't it be marvelous for our brothers, Jack and Michael and their families to have you around? We all live close to each other over there and see each other on a regular basis.'

'T'would be one big happy family,' Willie said with a smile to cover the negativism he was feeling.

'Now you've got to promise me you'll think about it,' Monica insisted.

'All right, I'll think about it,' Willie said, knowing full well that there wasn't a snowball's chance in hell he'd ever forsake his native land.

Chapter XXVI

'I've established a regular IRA Intelligence staff,' Collins told Willie the first time he saw him after his sojourn in The West. 'Along with Joe O'Reilly, I've managed to acquire two more dependable people — Liam Tobin and Frank Thornton. I'm sure you already know them?'

'Yeah, I'm well acquainted with them all right,' Willie said, sounding pleased. 'It's a good move, Mick. Hopefully t'will ease your burden a bit.'

'The reason I'm telling you this,' Collins said, 'is because in the future you'll probably see these three men frequently trotting in and out of our offices. O'Reilly in particular.'

Afterwards, Willie noticed Collins' increasing dependence on O'Reilly: he was courier, clerk, messenger boy, right-hand man to Collins. He was, in fact, the nearest thing to Boland's replacement. And Willie was thankful for it. It tended to make life easier for him. In the main because O'Reilly gave generously of his time to Collins which, in turn, helped to lessen Collins enormous burden. Plus, Willie was free to concentrate on bringing some order to the inherent chaos that existed in the offices. In particular, he wanted to set up a system whereby, in the event of a raid, classified documents could be hidden away in an orderly fashion. Up to now, when a raid occurred, some of these documents were jumbled together any old how with other documents which, not only made the sorting out difficult afterwards, but there was always the chance that some unauthorized person would get a look at them. The present system was much too haphazard.

After his return, Willie agonized for days over whether or not to tell Collins what he'd heard about DeValera's activities in America. He was sorely tempted to divulge what he knew. But eventually, decided not to mention anything. God! he thought, the man is carrying a heavy enough burden without me adding to it.

Two weeks later another letter arrived from America. It mentioned about sums of money raised, otherwise it was filled with the usual ambiguities. Reading the letter, Collins face flushed red with fury.

'God damn them!' he cursed. 'Why the hell can't they tell me the full facts about what's happening over there and stop beating about the bush.' Around this time Collins, in a confiding mood, told Willie of the existence of Vinny Byrne now the leader of the squad. 'Eighteen-year-old Vinny,' Collins declared, 'is a cold-blooded killer if there ever was one; many's the executions he's carried out on Irish policemen over the past year. He takes killing in his stride; doesn't bat an eyelid.' Collins continued expansively. 'One such execution was that of a high profile Detective Sergeant who was on that list we took from the police station. Remember that night?'

'Will I ever forget it?' Willie said. 'I was shaking in my britches.'

'Afterwards,' Collins said coolly, 'that fellow got a warning to get a new job or else.'

'I take it he didn't get the new job?' Willie said.

'No,' Collins answered, 'and I'm afraid we had to make an example of him.'

Throughout 1919 the squad continued to carry out a series of ruthless killings. It was the reign of terror against policemen Collins promised earlier. By the end of 1919 fourteen Irish policemen had been shot and killed and more than twenty others seriously wounded. These killings struck terror into the heart of the British establishment in Ireland. Though Collins was 'on the run' from September 1919, he was totally fearless. Sometimes cycling through the city, he'd go so far as to actually stop to chat and joke with a policeman on point duty.

§

One day the week before Christmas, Peter was surprised to find his mother waiting for him in his office when he arrived back from an assignment. It spelt trouble.

'Something's wrong, Mother?' he said anxiously.

'Something's very wrong,' Mary's mouth was in a hard line.

'Well, what is it?' Alarm bells went off in Peter's head.

'It's about that young man, Willie, who's walking out with Jane.' The prejudice in her voice was unmistakable.

'I see nothing wrong with that,' Peter said. 'He may be only a film projectionist, but there's no reason to hold that against him.'

'It's nothing to do with that,' Mary asserted.

'Well, what is it to do with?' Peter sounded impatient.

'It's how he connected to that Collins man.'

'Piffle!' Peter proclaimed. 'All he does for Collins is a bit of office work now and then.'

'No one with an ounce of self respect,' Mary said prejudicially, 'would be seen in the company of Michael Collins or his associates.'

'What do you know about Collins, anyway?' Peter asked. He was surprised at the trend this conversation was taking.

'I know what I read in the newspapers,' Mary said.

'Such as?'

'The murders Collins and his henchmen are carrying out on our police force,' Mary said with disgust. 'And it's common knowledge that there's a price on his head.'

'So you're blaming Willie for Collins' sins?' Peter said, trying to maintain a facade of calm control. 'There isn't a scintilla of evidence to prove that Willie is involved in any of those killings.'

Mary, now very agitated, said, 'The mere fact that Willie is associated with that criminal, is enough for me.'

'What do you want to do about it?' Peter decided his mother had to be given a hearing.

'I want you to speak to Jane,' Mary said. 'Tell her she's got to give up seeing Willie.'

'Mother, you're being most unfair and must unjust!' Peter

exploded. 'Have you any idea how much Jane loves Willie?'

'If she doesn't give him up now, she'll rue the day,' Mary said bluntly.

'Have you spoken to Jane about this?' Peter asked, alarmed.

'No,' Mary said. 'I thought it would be better coming from you.'

Peter sighed. 'So, let's be clear here,' he said, very agitated. 'You actually want me to ask Jane to give up Willie?'

'Exactly,' Mary said. 'I don't want that man under my roof ever again; it's an affront to our family forcing his company on us.' Mary felt so strongly her face looked like it was ready to burst through her skin. 'Alternatively,' she add, 'you could tell Willie he's not to see Jane again.' She hunched her shoulders. 'You decide.'

For seconds Peter stared at her open-mouthed. 'Mother!' he said in a chilly voice, 'this has come as a dreadful shock! I've known Willie for three and a half years. We're very good friends. He's one of the most decent, sincere people I've ever met, and he's very much in love with Jane.' Peter scratched his head. 'If I stab him in the back like this, what kind of friend does that make me?' Peter studied his mother's hard expression. 'I can see, however, that you've judged him and condemned him without knowing the true facts.'

'The true facts are I don't like people who support criminals,' Mary said caustically. 'Those poor policemen, only doing their duty, were shot down like dogs. Most of them are family men. This Christmas a lot of wives will be widowed and children orphaned because of that man Collins' criminal activities.

At that moment a young man stuck his head round the door. 'Sorry, Peter,' he said, 'but Hugh would like to have a word apropos your assignment this morning.'

Peter shot up from his desk. 'Course,' he said, 'I'll be there directly.' When the young man disappeared, he turned to Mary. 'Mother,' he said, 'have you any idea the invidious position you're placing me in demanding that I tell Jane and Willie they're not to see each other again? It's unconscionable.' The more he thought about it the more irritated he became. 'In the name of God, where ever did you get the idea that Willie is a criminal? His relationship with Collins is merely...'

'I didn't say he was a criminal,' Mary interrupted aggressively, 'I said he's associating with a criminal who murders policemen.'

'Maybe you didn't actually call Willie a criminal,' Peter said mutinously, 'but you certainly inferred it by your outlandish allegations against him. Allegations which are totally unfounded. For God sake, Mother!' Peter asserted strongly, 'Willie's no criminal. He had no hand, act or part in those killings. Get that out of your head.' He made for the door, then stopped and said, 'I need time to think about this.'

'You don't have much time,' Mary said threateningly.

Peter turned back. 'How do you mean I don't have much time?' he asked, baffled.

'Well, either you tell Jane immediately or I do,' Mary said. 'I don't want Willie at my dinner table this Christmas.'

Peter's face now showed the anger he was feeling. 'So,' he said, 'you're issuing me with an ultimatum?'

'You might call it that,' Mary's eyes were steel.

Peter's brow furrowed deeply. 'Right,' he said decisively. 'I don't want you to open your mouth to Jane about this until I've had a chance to talk to her.' He rammed his head aggressively in his mother's direction. 'Got that?' he shouted at her.

'Loud and clear,' Mary answered tersely.

Peter left the room abruptly. God! he thought as he climbed stairs, how am I going to deal with this? What on earth am I going to say to them? He knew Willie was inextricably involved with Collins. But, he thought, what right have I to ask him, or anyone else, to make a choice? He wondered if there was any possible way they could reach a compromise whereby the couple could meet in secret? If they agreed, he'd certainly be prepared to help any way he could. He couldn't remember when he last saw his mother so angry. My God! he thought, she's determined to split them up.

§

The Christmas rush was well and truly in full swing in the Henry Street Department Store when Peter called to see Jane. The Jewelry Department buzzed with customers. And Jane and the other assistant looked frazzled trying to cope with the numbers.

Nonetheless, Jane registered Peter's appearance immediately. She thought, he's probably here to buy Nancy Pete's Christmas box. 'I'll be with you in a minute,' she called out cheerfully to him.

'No hurry,' Peter responded.

Gradually the customers thinned out and Jane was eventually free to attend to him. 'Well, this is a surprise!' she said lightheartedly. 'It's not very often my brother pays me a visit. I suppose you're here to buy a Christmas box for your wife?'

Peter thought gloomily, *if she could read my mind, she'd know I'd much prefer to be anywhere else at this moment.* 'No,' he said out loud, then stopped abruptly to think. 'Though it's not a bad idea. I still have to get her something. What would you recommend?'

Jane indicated long and short strands of beads, necklaces, in multiple colors and designs displayed in the show case under the counter. 'Those beads are all the rage at the moment,' she said. 'I'd say they'd suit your Nancy down to the ground.'

'Yes, I suppose you're right,' Peter said, with a blank expression. 'She does seem to go in for that type of thing.'

Peter's unusual solemnity worried Jane; normally he was such a cheerful, bubbly person. *That row between himself and Nancy Pete must've been quite something, she thought. So what's new?* Opening up the back of the showcase, she took out strands of beaded necklaces in assorted colors and designs and placed them on the counter. 'Anything there you think she'd fancy?'

Peter grabbed a strand that had all the shades of green. 'I think this one,' he said, still looking very grim-faced.

'Is something the matter?' Jane had to ask the question. She found her brother's apathy quite disturbing.

Peter smiled an oblique smile. 'Isn't there always something the matter when you're married to a ball and chain and have two bawling kids, to boot,' he said handing Jane the green necklace. 'I'll take this one.' Then he inquired, 'Any chance of a box?'

'Certainly,' Jane pulled a box out of a drawer behind the counter.

As she was arranging the necklace in the box, Peter got his courage up. 'As a matter of fact,' he said, 'I was wondering could we have lunch together today?'

Jane looked surprised. 'Sure,' she said. 'I usually have lunch in the store cafeteria with the girls. But I can easily change that.'

'Good,' Peter said as he paid for the jewelry and took the bag displaying the store's logo. 'See you in Clery's restaurant at one.'

Jane's bewildered stare followed him as he made his way towards the exit. Something's definitely wrong, she decided. It's more than an ordinary 'bull and cow' with Nancy. There wasn't time to dwell on it, however, as once again a queue had formed at the counter.

§

Jane had the fish. Peter the steak. Jane could tell that Peter was still very troubled. 'All right,' she said, 'out with it. What's bothering you?'

Peter gritted his teeth and tried to make his voice sound casual. 'I'm afraid,' he said, 'it concerns you.'

'Me!' Jane exclaimed. 'What on earth have I done?'

'It's not what you've done,' Peter said toying with stirring the sugar in his tea, afraid to meet her eyes. 'It's what's being done to you.'

A feeling of panic crept over Jane. 'For God's sake, Peter,' she said, 'what is the matter? Has something happened to Willie?'

Peter lifted his head and saw her face was filled with inordinate distress. 'No, nothing's happened to Willie,' he hastened to assure her, 'but it does concern him.' He tried hard to suppress his feelings of anger as he took the plunge. 'Mother has decided you'll have to give up seeing him.'

'What!' Jane's face went a greenish white with shock.

'Blast her!' Peter said. 'She came into my office yesterday and told me that if I didn't tell you to break up with Willie, she would.' His heart now filled with rage against his mother placing him in this position. 'She doesn't want him under her roof ever again.'

'But why? What reason did she give?' Jane had trouble fighting back her tears.

'Oh, she's been reading in the newspapers about Collins and his reign of terror against Irish policemen. She contends that Willie is associating with a dangerous criminal.' Peter took a sip of tea before continuing. 'She's determined you should have nothing more to do with him.'

Jane's body went numb. She let out a wail. 'Oh my God! You can't be serious?' Then suddenly she was shaking with anger and an overwhelming sense of futility. 'I can't live without him,' she whispered.

'Look, Jane,' Peter said, making feeble gestures, 'I argued with her and disagreed vehemently with her, but it was like talking to a stone wall. Her mind is made up. She's adamant. She wants you to have nothing more to do with Willie.'

'What should I do?' Jane whispered, the tears rolling down her face. 'I love Willie. I can't give him up.'

'I know that,' Peter said. 'You've more than proved your love. Throughout all his unexplained absences, you've waited patiently for him to turn up, not only have you shown love, but you've shown staunch loyalty.'

'How can I tell him?' Jane whispered, flicking the tears away. 'At the best of times Willie is not the most confident person in the world. He'll probably take this as an assault on his character.'

Drumming his fingers on the table, Peter said with a quelling look., 'Maybe I could help a bit. After all he's my friend too.' Then he added scornfully, 'And there, but for the grace of the ball and chain and two bawling kids, go I.'

'How could you possibly help?' said Jane miserably.

'There's such a thing as secret meetings,' Peter smiled a watery smile. 'I could help the two of you to arrange them.'

'Willie would never agree to that,' Jane said despondently. 'He's so damn proud. And he's so terrified all the time of putting me in danger.'

'Jane,' Peter said sounding very serious, 'you must realize that Willie is truly concerned about your safety, because, he is involved in what one might call very unsavory work for Collins.'

'Oh Peter!' Jane burst out unhappily, 'this is the end of us.'

'It doesn't necessarily follow,' Peter said. 'Just think of it as a postponement of your relationship until this small war is over and things are back to normal.'

'Jesus!' Jane burst out as the thought struck her. 'This means Willie can't come for Christmas dinner! In the name of God, how am I going to explain that to him?'

'Would you like me to talk to him?'

'Yes,' Jane answered impulsively, then suddenly changed her mind. 'No, no!' she said very agitated. 'It has to come from me. Otherwise he'll think I'm too much of a coward to do my own dirty work.'

'Look, Jane,' Peter said wearily, 'if there's anything I can do to help, for God's sake tell me.'

'Sweet Mother of God!' Jane exclaimed, 'how can I tell him the real truth? That Mother has banned him permanently from our house and he's not welcome to come for Christmas dinner!' Jane looked agonized. 'I ask you, what kind of Christmas spirit is that?'

'That's a tough one!' Peter mulled over it, then his face brightened. 'What about telling him a white lie about Christmas?' he suggested. 'Like…this year the family is going to Bridget's house for Christmas dinner. The house is too small to fit everyone. So it has to be just the family?' Peter was grasping at straws.

Relief drained some of the tension from Jane's face.

'Jane,' Peter continued, 'for the moment say nothing to Willie about breaking up; just tell him about the new Christmas arrangements. After Christmas we'll work something out.'

'What an angel you are, Peter.' Jane's relief was profound. 'If I were to tell Willie the real truth, t'would definitely be the end of us.'

'Take heart, honey,' Peter said. 'Every cloud has a silver lining.'

§

The Saturday night before Christmas, Willie met Jane as usual after the show. The first thing he noticed was her pallor and the big black circles under her eyes. She looked anything but healthy.

'Goodness, Jane!' he exclaimed, 'you look terribly ill.'

'Oh, it's just Christmas fatigue; the store is so busy.' Jane brushed the remark aside and smiled her lovely smile, giving the impression her life was perfect. Truth was she hadn't slept a wink since her meeting with Peter a few days ago.

'Are you sure you're not coming down with something?' Willie asked. He sounded really concerned. 'Maybe you should be at home in bed.' They were walking towards their Cafe retreat in Liffey Street.

'Stop worrying,' Jane said, a little too brightly for Willie's liking.

'No, I mean it,' Willie said putting his arm across her shoulder and squeezing it. 'I couldn't bear it if anything happened to you,' he said earnestly. 'You're the light of my life, Jane, don't you know that?'

Jane was thankful for the darkness. He couldn't see the tears trickling down her face. When they arrived at the cafe, she hurriedly excused herself to go to the communal toilet. Somehow or other she had to fix her tear-stained face. A dab of powder from her compact and a dab of rouge (acquired recently in the store) were a bit of a help. When she got back Willie had ordered their cocoa and biscuits.

'I hope you don't mind; I ordered,' he said. 'I want to get you home to your bed as quickly as possible.'

'Oh, stop mothering me,' Jane laughed. 'I'm fine. It's just that it's been a very hectic week in the store.'

'You're sure you're all right?' Willie badly wanted to hug her.

'I'm certain,' Jane smiled her dazzling smile. Willie dug into his pocket and produced a small box wrapped in Christmas paper which he pushed across the table towards her.

'By rights,' he said, 'this should go on to your family's Christmas tree.' He grinned as he continued. 'Because strictly speaking, according to custom, it shouldn't be opened until Christmas Day. But, as I won't be there to see your reaction when you open it, I'd like you to open it now.'

The mention of him not being there on Christmas Day made Jane's face go brick red. For the moment the gift was forgotten.

'You won't be there?' Jane spluttered nervously, her eyes like saucers. 'Has Peter been talking to you?'

'No, what would Peter have to talk to me about?'

'Oh, just the Christmas arrangements,' Jane said giving him an uneasy smile. 'You see, this year...'

'Yes, I've been meaning to talk to you about that,' Willie interjected. 'This year I'm afraid I won't be spending Christmas in Dublin.'

'Oh! you won't!' Jane couldn't hide her surprise.

'No, believe it or not, there's great pressure on me to spend the festive season with my family in Mayo.' Putting his hand over Jane's and sounding very contrite, he added, 'You don't mind, darling, do you?'

Jane could feel the lump of tears melting away out of her throat, her relief was so profound. It was like a reprieve.

'Of course, I don't mind,' she said happily. 'I think it's great that you're going to spend Christmas with your family. It seems like ages since you did so.'

'Not since 1916 when I came home from Frongoch,' Willie said, bitterly. 'It was not a good reunion: my parents made no secret of the fact that they were entirely ashamed of my political activities — the sixteen rising and my incarceration in prison. Plus, any mention of Irish politics was strictly taboo.' Willie roared laughing. 'But since Monica's visit my family's attitude has changed completely towards me. Bless Monica! She went to such lengths to let them and the local people know how important my job in Dublin as a film projectionist was. Now they talk about it like I'm a blooming genius —'Imagine, one of our lads being able to project moving pictures on to a screen?' they say. 'T''is a great wonder altogether.' '

For the first time in days, Jane was able to laugh naturally.

'Yes, I spent hours trying to explain to all and sundry the technicalities associated with showing moving pictures,' Willie said, getting carried away with enthusiasm. 'And now, of course, relatives and friends over there look on me as a bit of a celebrity.' Suddenly Willie remembered the box Jane was clutching. 'Well,' he said, 'aren't you going to open your gift?'

'Yes, of course,' Jane said with eagerness. 'It's just I was so fascinated hearing about the hero worship you've whipped up for yourself in the West.'

As Jane tore the wrapping off the box, Willie looked on with the anticipation of a small boy watching a parent open his gift. The padded jewelry box held a beautiful, silver locket on a chain. Jane opened the locket. Inside was an inscription which read, *To my lovely Jane from her ever loving Willie - December 1919.*

The lump of tears was back in Jane's throat.

Smiling through her tears she said, 'Oh Willie! It's beautiful! If we weren't in a public place I'd show you just how much I love it and how much I love you.'

When they reached O'Dwyer's hall door, Willie said with arching eyebrows, 'Now's your chance to demonstrate how much you love my present and how much you love me.'

'Need you ask?' Jane whispered, throwing her arms around his neck, kissing him passionately. The pain in her heart was unbearable.

'I'm going to miss you terribly,' Willie said, when he released her. 'You're the one thing in my life that makes it worth living.'

As the tears were coming fast, Jane felt she had to get away in a hurry. It wouldn't do if he kissed her again and found her face drenched in tears.

'Willie,' she whispered, 'I'm feeling very chilly, I think I'd better get to bed.'

'Sorry!' Willie said. 'Of course you must get to bed as soon as possible. You've got to take care of yourself, even if it's only for my sake.' Touching her delicate skin with anxious fingers, he said,

'Happy Christmas, darling. Now,' he added, 'I'll be away till the first of January. But remember, Sweet Jane, you'll be constantly in my thoughts and I'll be counting, not the days, but the hours till I see you again.'

'Happy Christmas, Willie,' Jane muttered as she hastily put the key in the door. 'I'll miss you too,' she said and was gone.

§

Throughout Christmas Day Jane felt nothing but unrelenting misery. She moved through the day like an automaton. Aside from the transformation in her demeanor, she looked like a ghost. When it came to helping out or participating in the activities, she took the line of least resistance and did the minimum. A lot had to do with the ill feeling she harbored towards her mother; she could hardly bring herself to speak to her. For Mary's part, never once did she mention Willie's name. It was eerie.

Until Gerald brought up the subject of Willie's absence at the dinner table. 'Willie's not here this year?' he remarked inquiringly.

Mary was quick to answer, 'No, he couldn't make it this year.'

'I'm really sorry about that,' Gerald sounded genuinely disappointed. 'I was quite looking forward to seeing him again.'

'Can't be helped,' Mary said dismissively, then skillfully changed the subject to Bridget's pregnancy. 'Isn't it marvelous!' she said. 'Our Bridget expecting a baby in February.'

'Mother!' Bridget exclaimed blushing, 'I'd prefer if we didn't discuss it.'

Bridget's pregnancy had been very precarious; she'd come close to miscarrying in the last month. Hence, at this moment, she should have been at home in bed, resting. But she had made the effort to come to her mother's Christmas dinner. However, she and Michael left immediately afterwards. It was another disappointment for Jane. She wanted so much to talk to Bridget—the family's rock of sense—and tell her a little about what she was suffering. But then reasoned that Bridget had enough worries of her own without her adding to them.

On the other hand, when Lily first heard about the situation, there and then she wanted to rush in like a bull and confront her mother. 'How dare she!' she barked, bristling with fury. Then instinctively added, 'Do you want me to sort her out, Jane?'

'No, no. For God's sake, Lily! No!' Jane pleaded, 'I don't want a row.'

'But she's forbidden you to see Willie,' Lily thundered. 'What in God's name are you going to do after Christmas when he's back?'

Jane dissolved into tears. 'I don't know,' she whispered frantically. Then quickly pulled herself together. 'But I don't want you to intervene with Mother on my behalf. T'will only make matters worse.'

However, despite Jane's appeal to Lily not to kick up a storm with her mother, Lily couldn't abide it. On Christmas night, after the guests had departed, Jane, having made her contribution to the clearing up, disappeared into her bedroom. This left Lily on her own doing the dishes with her mother.

Suddenly, Mary brought up the subject of Jane. 'Is Jane not feeling well?' she asked. 'She looks a very bad color?'

'You're a fine one to be asking that question!' Lily retorted viciously.

'What do you mean?'

Mary's feigned ignorance infuriated Lily even more. 'What do you think I mean?' she fumed.

'I haven't the foggiest notion what you're talking about?'

'Oh, it suits you to forget,' Lily barked at her. 'You've only taken a sledge hammer to Jane's heart.'

'By that should I deduce that you're referring to Willie?'

Lily turned on her like a raging bull, 'Who the hell are you to tell Jane who she can or cannot see?'

Mary flinched. 'I'm her mother,' she said. 'And I've nothing but her best interests at heart.'

'For someone who's a daily communicant,' Lily said bitingly, 'you haven't an ounce of Christianity in you.'

Mary froze. Her throat constricted and her lower lip began to tremble. Lily's words had struck home. Lily then decided she'd said enough. She left Mary in the kitchen to mull on it. 'As if any words of mine would make a difference,' Lily said to Jane later when she was getting ready for bed. 'The auld bitch! She's no interest in anything but her bloody shop!'

During the night Jane's sleep was disturbed many times by Lily's constant trek to the bathroom. Then around three o'clock in the morning, Jane became aware of loud groans coming from Lily's bed.

'Lily,' Jane called out in the darkness, 'What's the matter?'

Lily didn't answer, but continued to groan. Jane groped in the darkness for the string to the gas light. Finding it eventually, she pulled on it and flooded the room with light. To her horror she found Lily writhing in her bed outside the bed clothes, her face was pure white. She looked like she was unconscious.

'Oh my God Lily!' Jane called out, 'What is the matter?'

When there was no response from Lily, Jane put her hand on her brow. Her sister was burning with a fever. 'Sweet Mother of God!' Jane was worried threadless. 'I'd better get Mother …Mother! Mother! Come quickly!' Jane shrieked as she rapped on Mary's bedroom door.

Quick as a blink Mary was at the door. 'For God's sake! What's the matter?' she asked as she dragged on her robe.

'It's Lily,' Jane screamed. 'She's very ill; she looks like she's unconscious.'

Mary dashed into the girls' room. One look at Lily was enough to tell Mary that her daughter was seriously ill.

'Get dressed quickly,' she said to Jane, 'and fetch Doctor Cleary.'

Jane didn't wait to get dressed. She threw on her winter coat over her night gown, thrust her feet into her shoes and flew out the hall door.

'I'm afraid it's typhoid!' the doctor pronounced after examining Lily. 'We'll have to get her to the hospital immediately.'

'Is she going to be all right?' Jane asked, her eyes filled with terrible pain.

'Hard to say,' the doctor answered. 'Depends on how far advanced it is. How long has she been complaining?'

Mary looked at Jane for the answer. 'As far as I know,' Jane said, 'it only started last night.'

'How long has she had the diarrhea?' the doctor asked.

'She had a touch of it a few days ago,' Jane said, 'but I thought it had cleared up.'

'That's when I should have been called in,' the doctor said, concerned. 'A few cases of typhoid have been reported in Dublin in the past month. Anyway,' he went on, 'I'd better get the ambulance here as quickly as possible. Until we get her to the hospital we won't know how serious it is.' The doctor looked perturbed. 'Meantime, to be on the safe side, anyone who's had a lot of contact with her over the past few days will have to be tested.'

Alarmed, Mary looked at Jane. If any one looked the part for the past few days, it was Jane.

'I take it you're not on the telephone?' Doctor Cleary interrupted Mary's thoughts.

'Not so far.'

'Right. I'll call an ambulance from the Rotunda Hospital and be right back,' Doctor Cleary said and left in a hurry.

He was back very quickly. Practically on his heels the ambulance arrived. As the attendants fixed Lily on the stretcher, the doctor asked, 'Any one else in the house whose been in close contact with the patient?'

'Just ourselves,' Mary indicated Jane and herself, 'and my youngest daughter, Eileen.'

'Get her up,' the doctor said. 'She'll have to be tested. Now,' he went on, 'I want the three of you to accompany Lily and myself in the ambulance to Jervis Street Hospital where the tests can be carried out. Hopefully, you'll all be cleared and there'll be no necessity for any of you to be placed in quarantine.'

As soon as they reached the hospital, Lily was whisked away on a gurney by two female members of the nursing staff. After a quick word with the middle-aged nurse on duty, Doctor Cleary introduced her to the members of the O'Dwyer family as Nurse O'Brien.

'This nurse will look after you from here on,' Doctor Cleary told them. He then touched Mary's shoulder sympathetically, saying, 'Mrs. O'Dwyer, I have to go, but I'm leaving you in good hands.'

'Now,' Nurse O'Brien said, matter-of-factly, to the group, 'if you'll follow me to the laboratory, we'll get you all tested.'

They followed her through a labyrinth of corridors to the laboratory. Here the nurse took all their temperatures. Thankfully when she finished, she said, 'Well, you're all normal; that's a good sign.' After that, each of them had a needle inserted into their buttocks extracting blood. When she had finished taking blood, the nurse looked at her watch and said, 'The laboratory technician should be in any minute now, so we shouldn't have to wait too long for the results.' She smiled encouragingly. 'Hopefully, they'll prove negative and we'll be able to let you go home. But should any of the tests be positive, I'm afraid it'll mean quarantine for at least a week for the person concerned.'

'When will we know the prognosis on Lily?' Mary asked, her body shaking with apprehension.

'Doctor Cronin's assistant is now attending to Lily,' Nurse O'Brien said. 'No doubt he'll talk to you soon.'

'How soon?' Mary asked.

'Could be an hour or so,' Nurse O'Brien answered. 'We never know.'

'If she has typhoid what is the situation?' Mary asked.

'To be honest with you,' the nurse said, 'it all depends on what stage it's at. Unfortunately, when it's advanced we can never tell if the patient is going to make it through the crisis.'

'The crisis?' Mary repeated.

'In layman's terms,' Nurse O'Brien said, 'when the fever peaks.'

'Oh my God!' Mary gasped in horror. 'How long does it take to reach the crisis?'

'It varies.'

'Is it hours or days?' Mary asked holding her breath. She knew she was being a nuisance asking so many questions, but she had to know.

'Unfortunately it could be days,' Nurse O'Brien said. Then seeing the three stricken faces, added optimistically, 'but you know, it still has to be confirmed that she has typhoid.' She looked around the laboratory. 'We're finished here,' she said. 'Now if you'll follow me I'll bring you to the Waiting Room where, I hope, we won't have to delay you too long.'

In the Waiting Room — situated beside the hospital entrance — Nurse O'Brien said, 'I'll be back as soon as I have the results of your tests.' Then seeing Mary's distress and hearing Jane and Eileen's quiet sobbing, she added, 'Keep your chins up. Please God, the news about Lily will be good.' At the door she turned back and with a bright smile said, 'Good luck.'

It seemed like an eternity before the doctor appeared; thought it was only about thirty minutes. He was a tall, spare man with penetrating eyes, probably in his fifties. Up to the moment he arrived, except for the sounds of quiet weeping and sobbing, silence reigned in the Waiting Room. Clearly, the family was totally shattered.

Jane found the reality of the situation overwhelming: that Lily — her wonderful sister, her best friend — could actually be going to die. As for Mary, for the life of her, she couldn't stop thinking about Lily's last angry words flung at her in such a rage: *For someone who's a daily communicant, you haven't an ounce of Christianity in you! For someone who's a daily communicant, you haven't an ounce of Christianity in you.* The words pounded in her head like a grating drum.

'I'm Doctor Cronin,' the doctor announced coming towards Mary with outstretched hand.

Mary practically jumped out of her skin at the sound of his voice. 'My God!' she gulped, first holding her hand to her mouth, then taking his hand. 'How is she, Doctor?' she asked, looking piteously at him.

'I'm afraid it's typhoid all right,' Doctor Cronin said. His voice was kind; he spoke softly. 'Now, I have to be honest with you, Mrs. O'Dwyer, it's a bad case.' He looked very grim. 'For the time being she's been placed in the isolation ward which means definitely no visitors.'

Mary shuddered.

Eileen, the tears streaming down her face, impulsively asked the crucial question, 'She's not going to die, is she?'

'Well, let me put it this way,' the doctor answered, 'she's going to need all the prayers she can get.' He then beckoned to Mary. 'Mrs. O'Dwyer,' he said, 'could I have a word with you in private?'

Mary jumped out of her seat. Sweet Mother of God! she thought as she followed him through the door, he's going to give me bad news.

They stood talking just outside the room. Though Jane couldn't hear their conversation, from her vantage point, she had a clear view of her mother's facial expression and body language; they clearly indicated bad news.

'Saint Jude, worker of miracles! Jane silently prayed to her favorite saint, 'please let my loving sister live.' Then, as tears cascaded down her cheeks, she added, 'If you'll spare Lily's life I'll make the supreme sacrifice — I'll do what Mother wants and give up Willie.'

Mary, her face a mask of misery, came back into the room. 'The only thing that will save Lily now,' she said despairingly, 'is prayer.'

All Jane could do was cry. She was brokenhearted.

Eileen burst out through her tears, 'She can't leave us, Mother, she can't die. I can't bear to lose another sister.'

Eileen's outburst had a bad effect on Mary. For the first time during those desolate hours she allowed the tears to flow. She then grabbed Eileen in a close embrace and they cried bitterly leaning on each other.

'Well, I've good news for you regarding your tests,' Nurse O'Brien breezed into the room. 'You're all clear.' Then sensing the tension, she added, 'I take it the news about Lily isn't good?'

Mary stood back from Eileen and wiped her tears with her handkerchief. 'No,' she answered. 'The doctor has just spoken to me.' Her voice broke. 'All we can do now is pray.'

After studying the family closely, Nurse O'Brien said, 'You all look absolutely whacked. I think you should go home and have a sleep.'

Mary said, 'The other two can go. I'll stay.'

'Well, if you feel more comfortable doing that,' Nurse O'Brien said, 'by all means do. But you look so worn out. And you know there isn't much you can do here but wait.'

'Whatever it takes,' Mary said.

'From my own personal experience,' Nurse O'Brien went on, 'there won't be any change in Lily for at least twelve hours.' She produced a bottle of pills, saying, 'these are mild sedatives guaranteeing at least three hours sleep. I think you should all go home, take one of these and get some rest.'

Jane placed her hand on her mother's arm soothingly. 'Mother,' she said, wisely, 'I think Nurse O'Brien is right: we've had a very trying night. We'll need all our strength for what's to come.'

'Maybe you're right,' Mary said.

'Your daughter's absolutely right,' Nurse O'Brien, agreed as she handed each of them a pill.

As Jane and Eileen, looking and feeling frail and groggy, mounted the stairs to go to bed, Mary said to Jane, 'I'll send one of the girls from the shop round to the Henry Street Store to say you'll be late coming in this morning.'

Jane stopped in her tracks. She'd completely forgotten the store, the Stephen's Day Sale (the biggest sale of the year) — everything. At this moment her only thoughts were of her beloved sister lying close to death in Jervis Street Hospital.

'Thanks Mother,' she said with reserve, then carried on up the stairs.

As for Mary, not unexpectedly, she headed straight to her office, took off her overcoat, donned her shop coat. Sleep or no sleep it was business as usual.

Chapter XXVII

Willie awoke on Christmas morning to the sound of a blackbird somewhere testing his throat and far across the bog he heard a curlew. Opening the curtains of his bedroom, he observed the waking landscape. He'd forgotten how gray and bare it could be in winter. Just flat bog punctuated by scraggy evergreens clutching at the rocky soil. A few bare trees with ice coating their branches. Clumps of withered, yellow grass providing the only patch of color.

Claremorris in the Winter was no wonderland. Still, he was glad he'd come. It was remarkable how much his parents' attitude towards him had changed. The night before they inundated him with questions about his film work. What exactly was involved? What exactly was his role?

'You know,' Ellen said, 'when Monica was here we couldn't get a word in edgewise. Everyone, but your father and I, got their spoke in asking questions. But being in the background, we heard little or nothing.' She gave an engaging grin. 'All we heard was people singing your praises. Telling us what a clever lad Willie turned out to be.'

'Maybe now that we have you to ourselves,' Patrick said, 'you might enlighten us?'

They listened attentively as Willie explained in detail the mechanics of showing films. How it worked. He then went on to tell them what exactly was entailed in being a film projectionist.

'By the sound of it,' Ellen said fascinated, 'sure t'is a marvel altogether. I'd love to see one.'

'Why don't you come to Dublin and be my guest?' Willie said positively.

Ellen looked at Patrick. 'What do you think, Patrick?' she asked her husband.

Patrick removed the pipe from his mouth. 'I can't see why not,' he said.

'We have a matinee at lunchtime on Saturdays,' Willie said. 'You could come on an early train in the morning and catch the late train home the same day. That'd save you the expense of a hotel.'

Ellen's hand hit Patrick's knee enthusiastically. 'Let's do it,' she said, her face suffused with pleasure at the thought.

On Christmas Day it seemed Willie couldn't get away from the subject of the 'pictures.' It started after Mass when people gathered around him full of questions. Then throughout the day as people, relatives and friends, dropped in to pay a visit, the inquiries and questions continued ad infinitum. The big news was, of course, that Ellen and Patrick were going to Dublin in the near future to see the 'pictures.' Neither of them had ever been further than Galway.

'Has to be a first time for everything,' Martin said, giving Willie an exaggerated wink.

On Christmas night when the visitors were gone and the parents retired totally exhausted after a hectic day of entertaining (all in Willie's honor), Martin said to Willie as they supped a couple of beers, 'There's a ceilidhe in the Ballyhaunis Hotel tomorrow night, would you be interested in going?'

'Would I ever!' Willie jumped at the chance. 'T'would be a real treat to get away from explaining the ins and outs of the picture business.'

'I thought you could do with a break all right,' Martin said.

Driving in the trap to the ceilidhe, Willie was surprised to learn that his brother, Martin, was walking out with a girl named Caith. Around Peter's own age, Caith was handsome, with an oval face. On acquaintance she appeared to be warm and intelligent. Plus she was a very good dancer. The ceilidhe turned out to be a great occasion altogether. With the girls in the majority, a lot of the dances were 'ladies choices.' So, when this handsome stranger, Willie—who turned out to be a good dancer—arrived, there was a ferocious rush on him.

Halfway through the evening, a girl with short, blond hair and big blue eyes, asked Willie to dance. She appeared outgoing and charming. As they danced, she smiled at him coyly and said, 'You don't remember me, do you?'

Willie looked hard at her. No question about it, she did look familiar. He had an uncanny feeling that sometime in the past their paths had crossed. But when and where? That was the big question. He looked puzzled.

'You used to pull my hair in the second class,' she said, her face bathed in a lovely smile. 'T'was long then in braids — my hair that is.'

Her smile stirred a tendril of memory in Willie. 'Of course,' he said, recognition darting across his face. 'Well, honest to God!' he exclaimed, 'if it isn't Aine Ni Muracha!'

At that precise moment, Aine left Willie to do the chain in the dance. When it finished and she joined him again, she said, 'The very one.'

'My Goodness!' Willie said, standing still staring at her.

'Willie,' Aine nudged him, 'we'd better keep dancing.' She pointed to the other dancers in the set waiting patiently for them to cross over.

Abashed, Willie said, 'Sorry,' to the other dancers, 'I've just met an old friend.' After that, he displayed great dexterity handling the complicated movements in the set.

When that dance was over they withdrew altogether from the dance floor. And over glasses of lemonade spent the rest of the evening giving accounts of their lives. Aine told Willie about her nursing career; how she was doing her internship in Jervis Street Hospital in Dublin and how she was only home for a visit with her family in Ballyhaunis for the Christmas. Tomorrow she would return to Dublin.

Willie took to her instantly and proceeded to tell her about his career as a film projectionist. Like everyone else in Mayo she was intrigued.

'I did manage to get to see one film in the Tivoli Cinema,' she said, looking quite excited. 'Imagine you having the job of projectionist!'

'Oh, there's nothing to it really,' Willie said modestly. 'Once you get the hang of it.'

Somehow or other Aine maneuvered the conversation round to politics. 'You know something,' she said, 'the people over here haven't a clue about what's going on politically in Dublin, or, for that matter, all around the country.' She sighed. 'I'm doing a line with one of Collins' volunteers, so I know a thing or two about what's happening. However, I daren't mention the subject here in Mayo. And I certainly daren't mention the fact that I have a boyfriend who's sympathetic to the Cause.'

Willie put his hand on Aine's arm companionably. 'We're kindred spirits,' he said, sounding very relieved. 'I too am a member of Collins secret army, but like you say, the Mayo people turn a deaf ear whenever the subject of the Cause comes up.' Willie smiled broadly. 'It's so refreshing to hear someone from Mayo say what you've just said.'

Aine shook her head negatively. 'Things are not looking good for the Irish presently, are they?' she said passionately. 'I don't think we're ever gong to get Home Rule.'

'As far as I know,' Willie said confidently, 'Collins is way past wanting home rule. He now wants an Irish Independent Republic. He's made up his mind, he won't settle for less.'

Later driving home in the trap, Martin unexpectedly opened up to Willie. 'Cait and I hope to be married the summer after next,' he told him.

'That's fantastic news,' Willie said. 'Do the parents know?'

'Not yet,' Martin said, 'They'll probably have a fit.'

'So, when do you intend telling them?'

'Well, I'm about to start working full time for a local builder, whereby I'll be doing all the carpentry work for the six houses he hopes to build. It entails making and fitting the rafters for the roofs, staircases, windows, doors and anything else that needs doing in the carpentry line.'

'I hope you've signed a contract with this builder?' Willie said, concerned.

'Oh yes, I have John O'Riordan, the local solicitor, handling things like that for me; all the documents are now signed and sealed.'

Though Willie was very pleased for his brother, he couldn't help feeling envious. 'When does the work commence?' he asked.

'We hope to be working on the site by the first of March, weather permitting,' Martin said. 'Two of the foundations are already in.'

'That's great news altogether,' Willie said. 'Any chance you'd get one of the houses for yourself?'

'Exactly what I have in mind,' Martin laughed, then pondered a while. 'What about yourself?' he asked. 'You do have a girlfriend?'

Willie sighed heavily. 'Yes, I have. I love her dearly. And we're unofficially engaged. But my prospects are so dismal, I can't even think about getting married.'

'Doesn't your job pay well?' Martin asked.

'A pittance,' Willie said disconsolately. 'There's no way I could afford to get married on it. Besides there's all this business I'm involved in with Collins.'

'Oh! You're still working for him?' Martin interjected, surprised. 'I thought all that was behind you since you got the job?'

'Believe me! It's far from being behind me,' Willie said dismally. 'The job is just a front. If anything, I'm now more involved than ever in fighting for the Cause. So how could I ask any woman to marry me under the circumstances?'

Martin went silent for a moment. Obviously he was trying to absorb what Willie had said. After a while he said quietly, 'You're right, Willie; you couldn't possibly ask any woman to share that kind of a life with you.' After a while, Martin asked, 'Is there any hope at all of an independent Ireland ever materializing?'

'Well, Collins has great hopes,' Willie said. 'And at least we have the Dail.'

'The Dail?'

'Yes, our own Irish Parliament.'

'Oh yes, I read about that.' Martin said rubbing his hand across his chin pondering. 'But it doesn't seem to be achieving anything, does it?'

Willie thought: Why am I not surprised hearing that kind of negative remark from someone living in this part of the world? Just like Aine had said, 'The people around here haven't a clue.' All he could say in reply was, 'It takes time.'

Willie didn't blame Martin for his ignorance. The situation with Collins was so damn complicated it would take a month of Sundays to explain it all to Martin or anybody else in Mayo, for that matter. However, he felt the trip was well worthwhile. Apart from patching up his relationship with his parents, it gave him time to clear his head; to ponder on the political scene at the moment.

Willie rang in the New Year — 1920 — in his Uncle Joe's big house in Ballyhaunis, surrounded by family, uncles, aunts, cousins and friends. Singing Auld Lang Syne, he suddenly missed Jane desperately. He was remembering this time last year when she was in his arms. As he raised his glass welcoming in the New Year, silently, he said, 'Happy New Year, Jane! Please God during this coming year we'll find some way to tie the knot.'

§

27th December, 1919

Dear Willie,

This is probably the most difficult letter I'll ever have to write. It breaks my heart to have to tell you that I cannot see you again. Unhappy circumstances, over which I have no control, force me to put an end to our relationship. It would take too long here to go into the reasons for my decision. Suffice to say, the decision wasn't taken lightly.

In our lives our paths go in very diverse directions. This is not to say it's a reflection on you in any way. No. I cannot but admire the tenacity you've shown pursuing that dream of yours. Such dedication deserves reward. I sincerely hope that some day you'll realize that reward and that dream.

In case you're thinking there's another man, there isn't. You'll always be my one true love. But at this unhappy time, I think it's best to make a clean break.

Please, please, don't try to contact me. I'll need all the strength and will power I can muster to keep away from you.

Take care of yourself, dearest Willie.

God bless.
Jane.

P.S. I told Finbar to get someone else to play the pianola on Saturday nights as I won't be available.

This letter was waiting for Willie at his digs in Carlingford Avenue when he got back from The West. Reading it, his body shook and he felt nauseated. He was in shock. Obviously something fearful had happened to Jane during his absence. What could it possibly be? he wondered. The shakiness in her hand writing communicated that she was extremely disturbed. But the ambiguity of the words 'unhappy circumstances' were baffling. What unhappy circumstances could she be referring to? Her letter seemed totally irrational: except that she was feeling a bit off color, they parted on the best of terms before Christmas. Perhaps it was a health problem? If so, why not say so in the letter? I want an explanation, Willie thought. I just can't let it go at that. We love each other. At least she admits to that. So why this awful letter breaking us up? When two people love each other as we do, they stick together through thick and thin. They support each other.

Sleep did not come easy to Willie that night. He lay awake for hours. It wasn't until the night came to an end and the rectangle of gray dawn light appeared around the blind on his window like a picture frame, that he drifted off to sleep. Then he had the awful nightmare: Jane clinging to the face of a cliff and he trying desperately to reach her. He eventually woke in a leather of perspiration around ten o'clock. During those wakeful hours, Willie made a decision. He would drop in to see Peter O'Dwyer in his office first thing the following morning. Somehow or other he had to solve the mystery.

At the Reception Desk in the Independent House, Willie was told that Peter O'Dwyer was on leave of absence. The clerk couldn't say for how long. Walking down the steps from the Independent House filled with disappointment, inspiration suddenly struck Willie. I'll go round and see my friend and ally, Lily, in her shop in Capel Street, he thought.

In O'Grady's of Capel Street, Willie fared no better. The young lad holding the fort while the boss was at lunch, informed him that as far as he knew Miss O'Dwyer was on sick leave. My God! Willie thought in frustration, it's like there's a conspiracy abroad to stop me finding out what's happened to Jane. He wondered who else he could approach? Certainly not the mother: he had a sneaking suspicion that somehow or other she had a hand in this whole business. That left just Jane herself. No, he concluded, Jane's wishes had to be respected; under no circumstances should he encroach on her in the Department Store.

Ambling along the Quays, Willie decided he had to find something to take his mind off Jane. The best place for that was with Collins. But once again he was thwarted: he found Collins' office on the Quays barred and bolted. He thought, best take a tram up to Harcourt Street. Even if Collins is missing, someone else is bound to be there. As the tram trundled along by the side of Saint Stephen's Green, Willie suddenly had inspiration. Peter O'Dwyer, he thought, he's on leave. His flat is only a short distance away.

Impulsively, he jumped up in the tram and got off at the next stop. It took three rings on the bell before the door was opened by Nancy Pete, who, to say the least, looked terrible.

'Willie!' she gasped.

Before she could say anything else, Willie asked, 'Is Peter in?'

'No,' Nancy Pete said, 'he's at the hospital.'

'Is he ill?' Willie asked anxiously.

'No,' Nancy Pete said, looking puzzled. 'You'd better come in,' she said with a quiver in her voice.

Willie followed her into the drawing room. 'If Peter's not ill, what's—'

Before he finished the sentence, Nancy Pete interjected, 'It's Lily,' she said with a sob in her voice. 'You haven't heard?'

'No,' Willie said. 'I was in the West of Ireland for the Christmas. Just got back last night.' He shuddered as he asked the question. 'Has something happened to Lily?'

'She's dying.'

'Jesus!' Willie hand went to his mouth in horror. 'What happened to her?' he whispered because his voice had left him.

'She took bad on Christmas night,' Nancy Pete said in a low tone. 'They say it's typhoid. She's been in a coma ever since.'

'Oh my God!' Willie's sense of foreboding increased as the tears began to roll down Nancy Pete's face.

'We got word last night that the end was imminent,' Nancy Pete said with a sob, 'so between them, the family are keeping a twenty-four hour vigil at the hospital.'

'Which hospital?' Willie asked, his heart thumping.

'Jervis Street,' Nancy Pete answered. She then went on to tell him, 'She received the last sacraments last night.' Nancy Pete now sobbed uncontrollably. Eventually she pulled herself together. 'When I saw you at the door,' she said, 'I thought you were bringing me the bad news that Lily had passed away.'

Totally stunned, Willie slumped into a chair.

Just then little Colbert ran into the room. 'Mammie, Mammie, I want bickie,' he said pulling aggressively at his mother's skirt.

Nancy Pete dashed her tears away with the back of her hand. 'Yes, yes, darling,' she said, 'I'll get you a bickie in a minute. Just be a good boy while I talk to your Uncle Willie.' Making for the cocktail cabinet, she said to Willie, 'You look like you could do with a stiff drink.' With that she produced a bottle of whiskey and two tumblers from the cabinet and proceeded to pour two full glasses of whiskey — one for herself and one for Willie.

'Mammie, Mammie,' Colbert nagged at his mother, still pulling her skirt. 'Want bickie.'

After handing Willie a full glass of whiskey, Nancy Pete excused herself to go to the kitchen to get the child a biscuit. Willie was grateful to see her leave. Somehow or other he had to get rid of most of this drink. He knew of old how heavy Nancy Pete's hand was pouring drinks not to mention her determination to get the drink quaffed. Desperate to find a dumping place, his eyes eventually lit on a beautiful, tall, potted plant sitting in the corner of the drawing room. Well, if it kills the plant, Willie thought, as he poured most of the whiskey on top of it, it can't be helped. Things are bad enough without me getting sozzled and staggering out of here.

Nancy Pete arrived back in the room. She noticed Willie's practically empty glass immediately and tried to replenish it.

'No,' Willie insisted putting his hand over the top of the glass. 'For God's sake! I've had enough.' He looked at his watch, then stood up to leave. 'I'd best go,' he said. 'By the time I get home and have some dinner, it'll be time to go to work.' He didn't know what else to say. This woman was so well meaning, he didn't want to sound ungrateful.

'Why don't you let me make you a sandwich?' Nancy Pete offered.

'Oh, no, no!' Willie demurred. 'Sadie will have a great, big dinner ready for me when I get back to the digs.'

Once again Colbert was in the room pulling his mother's skirt. 'Mammie, Mammie, mo bickie?' he was saying.

It was time for Willie to leave. Nancy Pete saw him to the door. 'If you call into the dairy,' she said, 'they'll be able to tell you there what's happening with Lily.' Her eyes filled with tears. 'But the last word I heard was that she was fading fast.' Once again she burst into tears. Willie put comforting arms around her and she sobbed on his shoulder.

What do I do now? Willie thought as he shambled along Leeson Street filled with uncertainty and indecision. Considering what he'd just heard about Lily, where Jane was concerned, he was now more confused than ever. Surely she must be suffering agonies over her dying sister; they're so close. So why wouldn't she turn to him for comfort and consolation, instead of shutting him out? It didn't make sense. The worst of it was, there seemed no way to elucidate the mystery surrounding Jane's letter. Presently, the O'Dwyer family would be going through hell. Were he to approach any of them, they'd possibly consider it an encroachment on their grief. And who could blame them?

In the throes of wondering what to do next he suddenly remembered Aine, the girl he met at the ceilidhe in Ballyhaunis. It was a fortuitous meeting, surely. Didn't she say she was an intern nurse in Jervis Street Hospital? Would he ever be lucky enough to get hold of her if he went to the hospital now? Though he feared the worst, he had to know. It was worth a try anyway. One thing was certain, this terrible news about Lily put to rest any ideas he had about joining Collins.

Willie couldn't believe his luck when he found that Aine was on duty that day in Jervis Street Hospital. He didn't mind one bit having to wait thirty minutes in the Waiting Room for her.

'Well, if this isn't a huge surprise,' Aine exclaimed pleasantly when she saw Willie, 'I don't know what is.' Then she noticed Willie's deathly pallor and inquired anxiously, 'Are you ailing, Willie?'

'No, it's not me,' Willie answered. 'It's a very good friend of mine — Lily O'Dwyer — she's a patient here. I understand she's very poorly. As you know,' he went on, 'I was away in the West for the Christmas holidays and I've only just now heard about her illness. Apparently she was diagnosed with typhoid. I'm really worried about her.'

'I can see that.'

'Any chance you could find out how she's doing?'

'Oh, that patient!' Aine intoned solemnly. Her lips tightened as she considered Willie's request. 'Could you wait just a minute,' she said, 'and I'll see what I can find out.' With that she left the room.

It was at least fifteen minutes before Aine returned looking grim-faced. 'Well, from what I can ascertain,' she said earnestly, 'Lily is hanging on to life by a thread.' Then trying to put a brave face on it, she remarked, 'Of course, Willie, where there's life, there's always hope.'

Willie said, his voice low and calm, 'I take it her family are with her?'

'No, they're not actually in the room with her,' Aine told him. 'As she's highly infectious, she's in the Isolation Ward. However,' she continued, 'a private room with two beds has been placed at the family's disposal in case of an emergency. Since Lily's admission apparently the family have a rota in place whereby at least two members occupy this room around the clock.' Aine looked thoughtful, then said, 'Would you like to speak to one of the family members who's on duty?'

'No,' Willie said without hesitation. 'I don't want to bother them.' For an instant he seemed nonplused, then became decisive. 'What time do you finish your work?' he asked.

'Round six.'

'Would you mind if I called in to see you before six for an up-to-date report on Lily's condition?' Willie asked. 'I'll be on my way to work.'

'That'd be fine,' Aine said. Then seeing him looking so downcast, she touched his arm sympathetically. 'Willie,' she said, 'the fact that Lily has battled death this length of time is a good sign; she must be physically very strong. Keep the faith.'

Sitting on the tram going back to his digs, Willie thanked the Lord for having met Aine at the Ceilidhe. Little did he think that night he'd be enlisting her help so soon relative to this situation; a situation made worse by Jane's letter, which forced him to keep his distance. He thought, Aine obviously has the impression that Lily is my girlfriend; otherwise why would she go to such lengths to get the information for me? He felt he should enlighten her, but on reflection decided the situation was much too complex to explain. In the name of God where would he start? Besides, if Aine knew the patient wasn't in fact his girlfriend, she mightn't be quite so forthcoming.

Later that evening when Willie called to the hospital to see Aine, she told him, 'The good news is, Lily's fever has broken. The bad news, her temperature is still high; it doesn't bode well for a quick recovery. And she's in a coma.' She then went on to say, 'The doctors are now faced with a situation whereby ulcers may have been produced in the intestine. If that's the case,' she shook her head ruefully, 'those ulcers could make holes in the intestinal wall and could lead to the contents of the intestine spilling into the abdomen.'

Willie got the feeling that Aine was seizing the moment to impress him with her medical acumen.

Seeing his look of total puzzlement, Aine said, 'Obviously you can't make sense of all this medical jargon?'

'You're absolutely right,' Willie scratched his head, then said, 'Aine, do me a favor; cut to the chase and tell me if Lily is going to recover?'

A despondent look crossed Aine's face. 'I wish I could say she is,' she said. 'She's been in hospital long enough for the treatment to be having an effect: by now she should be showing some signs of improvement. But…'

'She isn't.'

'No,' Aine sighed. 'It's not a good sign.'

Willie went to work with a heavy heart.

On his way to work each evening, Willie continued to call in to see Aine at the Hospital to get an up-to-date report on Lily's condition. Though she was always in a rush, Aine took time to talk to him. Invariably, it was the same story; Lily was still on the critical list and still in a coma.

However, on the Friday of the second week, when Willie made his usual call, Aine greeted him with a happy face. 'I'm so glad to tell you, Willie,' she said, 'The typhoid is under control at last. Lily's condition has been upgraded to stable. She's no longer infectious. So she's allowed to have visitors — family only.'

'That's great news,' Willie enthused. Then asked, 'Is she conscious?'

'No,' Aine said. 'She's still in a coma.'

'What are her chances of coming out of the coma?' Willie said, concerned.

'Unfortunately, we never know,' Aine said. 'But Doctor Cronin has a theory; he believes that if someone very familiar to the patient talks to them continuously, there's a chance of penetrating the coma and making a breakthrough.'

'So, is anyone doing that?'

'Well, rumor has it,' Aine said, 'that Lily's sister, Jane, spent the whole of last night talking to her.'

'My God!' Willie exclaimed, 'how could she possibly keep talking that length of time? It must've been a terrible strain.'

'From what I heard, she didn't just talk,' Aine said, 'she read out loud part of the time.'

'I take it with no success?' Willie said.

Aine said, 'No, not so far. But according to Doctor Cronin, it could take weeks before it has an effect, if it works at all. There's no guarantee.'

The more Willie thought about Jane's dedication to her sister, the more he was convinced that Jane was deranged with grief over Lily when she wrote that letter.

During those two weeks Willie took time off from working for Collins. Being so stressed he was convinced he couldn't concentrate long enough or hard enough to meet Collins' expectations, and the last thing he needed just now was to be diminished in the eyes of 'the great one.' He spent lots of time walking and thinking about Jane, and praying hard that Lily would soon make a sound recovery. Until such time his hands were tied. Jane would continue to be unapproachable as long as she was preoccupied with nursing Lily back to health. He couldn't or wouldn't impinge on that.

So it was a nice surprise for Willie to find Peter having a quick pint with Collins at lunch time the following Sunday in Flanagan's Pub.

'Hello stranger,' a haggard looking Peter greeted Willie when he entered the snug. 'Where have you been hiding?'

Offhand, Willie couldn't think of a light rejoinder. 'Well,' he said, 'I went home to the West to see my folks for Christmas.' He endeavored to sound calm and factual.

As ever bristling with energy, Collins roared through the hatch, 'Bring us another pint a Guinness there, Benjie.' He then turned to Willie. 'So the wanderer has returned,' he said. 'That was a long break, Willie?'

By way of explanation Willie said, 'As a matter of fact, when I called into the office on the Quays early last week, I found it barred and bolted.'

'Yeah,' Collins gave a watery smile. 'Got word we were about to be raided.' He nodded collusively, 'Came from the usual source.' He lowered his voice, 'By the way, we've acquired a new office, a shed at the back of Little Strand Street.'

'So we won't be using The Quays office any longer?' Willie said.

'Fraid not. Too risky.' Collins went on to talk about how useful Willie's administrative prowess would be setting up the new office. Suddenly he stood up. 'Have to go,' he said. His eyes were full of mischief, 'Got to see a man about a horse.'

'Oh, it's upgraded to a horse, is it?' Willie said flippantly.

'You get the picture?' Collins laughed. He wrote on a slip of paper then handed it to Willie. 'That's our new address,' he said. 'Maybe you'd join us tomorrow?'

'Sure,' Willie said. As soon as Collins was gone, Willie pulled his chair close to Peter, who seemed unusually silent. 'How is Lily?' he asked.

'Not good.' Peter sounded very bleak. 'Nancy told me you called to the house. I was half expecting you to turn up at the hospital to give the family, and a certain party, a bit of moral support?'

'And I would have only...' Willie dug into his inside pocket and produced Jane's letter (carried close to his heart) 'for this,' he said, handing the letter to Peter.

Bewilderment crossed Peter's face as he read the letter. When he finished, he appeared to be shocked into silence.

Willie broke the silence. 'Can you shed any light on why Jane would write such a letter?' he asked. Now they were alone, he felt they could talk openly. Peter's look was hard to read: it was as if he was struggling to find the right words.

Finally he said, 'Willie, one thing you must understand is that presently the O'Dwyer family is very cast down.' He cogitated for seconds. 'The only explanation I can come up with about that letter,' he said, 'is that Jane was so demented about Lily, she was driven to writing it.' He then went on to explain about his mother's ultimatum to him before Christmas, telling him in no uncertain terms, that if he didn't tell Jane to stop seeing Willie, she would. Rushing on, he said with great sincerity, 'Believe me, Willie, I was totally opposed to the idea of you two breaking up because of my mother's stupid prejudice. And I said so to Jane when I explained it all to her.'

'How did she take it?' Willie asked earnestly.

'Badly; she was brokenhearted,' Peter said. 'Sobbed like a baby.'

'Oh my God! If only I'd known,' Willie said tersely.

Peter continued, 'I even went so far as to suggest to her that I'd be quite prepared to help the two of you to meet in secret; arrange places and times, that sort of thing.'

Willie could see that Peter was greatly distressed. 'I'm terribly sorry to be bothering you with this problem at a time like this,' he said. 'Considering the load you're carrying with Lily's illness, you can do without me adding to it.'

Peter looked solemn and tearful. Suddenly he covered his face with his hands and his body shook with sobs. Willie felt such a wave of pity for him, he could hardly speak. The best he could do was put his hand on Peter's shoulder and squeeze it sympathetically. Gradually Peter brought his emotional outbreak under control. Willie handed him a handkerchief.

'Sorry,' Peter said, as he mopped his tears. 'It's just I can't come to terms with Lily dying.'

'But I understood she was upgraded to stable,' Willie said.

'Who told you that?'

'Aine, a nurse friend of mine,' Willie said. 'She's training in Jervis Street Hospital. I met her over the Christmas in Mayo. T'was a meeting that turned out to be very useful. Because since the day I heard about Lily from your Nancy, Aine kept me informed about her progress.'

Peter asked, 'Did she tell you about Lily's heart?'

'No,' Willie said, troubled. 'Is there a problem?'

'There could be,' Peter said sadly. 'It seems Lily has a dickey heart since she had rheumatic fever as a kid.'

'That's a big worry,' Willie said.

'It is Willie,' Peter nodded his head dejectedly. 'The truth of the matter is Lily's far from out of the woods. According to the doctor, the coma could pose a big threat to her heart.'

'You mean...?'

'Yes, at any moment it could give out.'

'You're very fond of her?' Willie said.

'Yes,' Peter allowed a small smile to flash across his face. 'Despite all her cursing and swearing, I love her dearly. She has a heart of gold.'

'If you feel so upset about her,' Willie said, 'how on earth is Jane holding up? Those two are joined at the hip.'

'You can say that again,' Peter said. 'My heart goes out to Jane. She's killing herself. Since the visiting ban was lifted three days ago, she literally hasn't left Lily's side. Day and night she sits by the bedside talking and reading to her.'

Willie said, 'At that rate she's getting very little sleep...'

'At best, three hours out of twenty-four,' Peter said.

'She is killing herself,' Willie agreed. 'But surely someone can relieve her?'

'Oh, she's being relieved all right,' Peter said. 'But she won't budge. She insists she's the one who has to do the talking to Lily. If you ask me, Willie, I think she's made a 'cause' of Lily's illness.'

'She's been off work then for quite a while?' Willie asked.

'When Lily was in quarantine and couldn't have visitors, I managed to convince her to go back to work,' Peter said. 'She definitely needed a distraction. But since Lily is now out of quarantine and no longer infectious, Jane never leaves the place. She snatches a few hours of sleep every night in the room the hospital allocated to the family. As far as I know she's on indefinite compassionate leave from work. Oh, Willie!' Peter said passionately, 'she looks terrible. How I wish to God you two were together and you were in a position to help her.'

'But her letter said...'

'I know, I know,' Peter shook his head dejectedly. 'I don't know what to tell you, Willie,' he said, 'except to say, that like the rest of us, we must wait and see and pray to God that Lily soon recovers. At the moment everything is topsy turvey.'

§

In the bright, airy room Lily had been moved to, Mary sat by her bedside reading out loud. The chosen book was *Jane Eyre* — one of Lily's favorites. Presently, Jane - a victim of exhaustion — dozed in an easy chair in a corner of the room. Though Lily looked a better color, there still wasn't a stir out of her. Suddenly the door opened and a strange nurse entered. She approached Mary.

'Mrs. O'Dwyer,' she said in a low tone, 'there's a phone call for you at Reception. They said it was urgent.' A frightened look washed over Mary's face. What, she wondered, could be so urgent that it needed a phone call to the hospital? Her sense of foreboding increased as she left the room.

Mary's movements going out of the room disturbed Jane. Startled, she shot out of the chair. Her face was drained of color except for the big, black rings circling her eyes. Swiftly she moved into the chair vacated by Mary at Lily's bedside. Leaning over Lily, she croaked, 'Lily, please, please open your eyes. I can't bear to see you like this.' She picked up the book from the bed where Mary had left it. She intended to continue the reading. But this time when she opened her mouth, the only sound that came out was a whisper; her voice was completely gone. What have I done to deserve this? she thought. Looking up at the ceiling she pleaded in a whisper, 'Oh God! Please give me back my voice so that I can at least talk to Lily.'

Reduced to silence, Jane sat in the chair, never taking her eyes off her sister's face. Strangely she began to think about Willie. She wondered if he was feeling as miserable about receiving her letter as she was about writing it? It was now three weeks since she posted it. As she hadn't heard a word from him, she assumed he was accepting the situation. She pondered awhile about seeing him again.

No, it wasn't possible. She'd made a pact with the Almighty; if He spared Lily's life, she'd never see Willie again. She looked dismally at Lily's still form in the bed. But it seemed that God and Saint Jude had abandoned her. How much longer could Lily hold out? With her heart so weak, the longer the coma lasted the worse her heart would get. She had the dreadful feeling that the sacrifice she was making would be for nothing. As the tears spilled down her cheeks, she prayed silently and earnestly. Dear God and Saint Jude, don't take Lily from us. Please, please let her live!

Mary arrived back in the room. 'Trouble never comes alone,' she said dully and mechanically.

'What's up?' Jane whispered.

'It's Bridget!' Mary said putting her coat on. 'She's been in labor all night. She's having a very difficult time. That was Michael on the phone asking if I could go over to the Rotunda Hospital for a few hours. He has to be in Court in an hour.' She nodded towards Lily. 'However, you won't be on your own for too long. I prevailed on your selfish sister, Nancy, to come to the hospital and relieve you.'

'How ever did you manage to contact her?' Jane whispered.

'You've lost your voice!' Mary said, amazed.

Jane nodded her head silently, looking miserable. Then whispered, 'What about our Nancy? Did you actually speak to her?'

'Yes I did,' Mary answered positively. 'I phoned the Main Office in the barracks from the Reception here and insisted on speaking to her. I told who ever answered the phone that it was a matter of great urgency. So they eventually got her to the phone.'

'I'm sure she welcomed your request with open arms,' Jane whispered, being sarcastic.

'Pity about her!' Mary conjured up a small smile. 'At least she has her voice. She can do some reading to the patient.'

It was a good hour and a half before our Nancy arrived. Typical of her insensitivity, her opening remarks to Jane were, 'This is most inconvenient; I'm supposed to be chairing a meeting of the Ladies' Committee for the army's Annual Ball next month.'

Jane could only whisper, 'I'm sorry if you're being discommoded. But as you can see my voice is gone and I'm not much use to Lily.' Jane moved out of the chair beside Lily leaving it free for Nancy to occupy it.

'What do you want me to do?' our Nancy asked irritably as she sat down.

Jane handed her the *Jane Eyre* book. 'Just read this to her as loud as you can,' she whispered. 'Start from where the marker is.'

As only our Nancy could, she looked skeptically at Jane. 'You know very well, Jane,' she growled, 'I was never a good reader. At school you were the one who got the honors in English for reading and writing.'

'Well, if you don't want to read, just talk to her,' Jane whispered, now irritated to the point of fury. But being voiceless was unable to give vent to it. All she could do was whisper, 'She hasn't heard a human voice for two hours now.'

Our Nancy leaned over Lily. 'Lily,' she roared, 'it's your bitchy sister, Nancy. Will you for God's sake snap out of it and come alive.'

The next instant brought forth a scream from our Nancy.

'Jesus Christ!' she exploded. 'She's opened her eyes!'

Quickly Jane rushed to the other side of the bed. Right enough Lily's eyes were open, but not focused. All Jane could do was cry and whisper, 'Oh, thank God! Thank God!' She turned our Nancy. 'Say something to her,' she entreated in a whisper.

'Like what?' Our Nancy sounded totally irritated.

'Talk about the weather. Talk about anything that comes into your mind. Just talk to her,' Jane's voice was fraught with anxiety.

'Okay,' our Nancy grudgingly turned her attention to Lily. 'Lily,' she said, 'do you know that it's a glorious day outside; the sun is shining, the birds are singing, the buds are on the trees. Spring has arrived at last.'

Slowly Lily turned her head in our Nancy's direction. 'Our Nancy,' she said, 'what the hell are you doing here telling me that spring has arrived?'

Our Nancy was struck dumb.

All Jane could do was ball crying. 'Oh thank God, thank God!' she whispered over and over again. 'You've come back to us at last, Lily.'

Lily looked in Jane's direction. She put her hand over Jane's. 'Jane,' she said, 'why are you whispering?'

'I've lost my voice,' Jane whispered close to her ear.

Lily said to Jane, 'I was dreaming you were talking to me?'

'And she was talking to you,' our Nancy burst out. 'Hasn't she lost her bloody voice on account of talking to you for the past week.'

Lily squeezed Jane's hand. 'Dear Jane,' she said,' it wasn't a dream. I did hear you. And it wasn't wasted.'

Suddenly Jane realized the seriousness of the situation. She pressed the emergency button hanging over Lily's bed.

Quick as a flash Nurse O'Brien was in the room. She was struck immediately by the animation on the faces of the two sisters. 'Oh!' she said excitedly, 'by the looks of you, the patient must have regained consciousness?'

'Yes,' our Nancy said. 'She has and she's as cheeky as ever.'

The girls moved away from the bed allowing Nurse O'Brien to do what she had to do to take Lily's pulse. After looking at her watch for seconds as she held Lily's wrist, she looked up and said positively, 'It's steady, thank God.' Then added, 'Still I'd better get Doctor Cronin to have a look at her.'

'Do you want us to leave?' Jane whispered.

'That might be a good idea,' Nurse O'Brien said.

Jane took Lily's hand in hers. 'Lily,' she whispered, 'while the doctor is examining you, our Nancy and I will wait outside.'

'Please come back,' Lily pleaded.

'You bet I will,' Jane reassured her. Lily then closed her eyes. Jane looked at Nurse O'Brien panic-stricken. 'My God! Nurse,' she croaked, 'has she gone back into the coma?'

Nurse O'Brien leaned down over Lily. 'No,' she said. 'She's sleeping.'

'Come on, Jane,' our Nancy hustled her. 'We'd better do as the nurse said and wait outside.'

Though our Nancy wanted to wait in the comfort of the Waiting Room, Jane opted to linger in the corridor outside Lily's room. Shortly afterwards, Nurse O'Brien, accompanied by a strange young doctor, came along the corridor and entered Lily's room. As Jane paced up and down, trembling and quaking with fear, hoping to God the doctor's report would be favorable, our Nancy rambled off. After what felt like a very long time, but probably was no more than minutes, the door opened and the doctor and Nurse O'Brien emerged.

The doctor could see that Jane was very distraught as he approached her. 'I'm Doctor Grogan,' he introduced himself to Jane. 'I take it you're Lily's sister?'

'Yes,' Jane croaked, her voice barely above a whisper.

'Well now,' Dr Grogan said, 'though Lily is out of danger, she has a long way to go before she makes a full recovery.' He looked at Jane with great sympathy. 'I'm afraid I'm going to have to ban all visitors for the time being.'

'But I promised her, I'd come back,' Jane whispered sounding desperate.

'Well, she's sleeping now,' the doctor said. 'There's no necessity to go back.'

'So when will she be able to have visitors?' Jane whispered.

Doctor Grogan whispered back, 'Not for at least a week, maybe longer.' The doctor then looked at Nurse O'Brien. Screwing up his face he said, 'Tell me, Nurse, why are we whispering?'

'Seems to be catching, doctor,' Nurse O'Brien replied laughing heartily. 'Jane has been reading to Lily continually for the past week. As a result she's lost her voice.'

'Very commendable,' Dr Grogan said, out loud this time. 'But don't you think we'd better give her some medication for that throat of hers?'

'I'll attend to it, Doctor,' Nurse O'Brien said.

'Now,' Dr Grogan turned to Jane, 'as things stand,' he said, 'Lily has an awful lot of ground to make up. To be utterly candid, I feel that visitors traipsing in and out to see her would be much too much excitement for her. What she needs now is complete rest. No fuss. No agitation. Especially, no stress.' He paused for a second, then continued. 'Keen as you are to visit with your sister, I'm sorry to say visitors of any kind could be very detrimental to her recovery.'

When the doctor left, Nurse O'Brien said to Jane, 'Wait at the Reception for me and I'll bring you something for that throat of yours.'

Jane went in search of our Nancy. She found her, eventually, in the Reception area talking to a very attractive blonde nurse, whom she introduced to Jane as Aine.

As soon as the introductions were complete, Aine said to Jane, 'Your sister tells me that Lily has come out of the coma?'

'Yes,' Jane croaked.

'That's wonderful!' Aine said. 'I'll be able to tell Willie the good news when he calls in this evening.'

'Willie!' Jane gasped in a whisper. Her breath caught in her throat at the sound of his name.

Aine rushed on to explain. 'Yes, Willie — Lily's boy friend — he's been calling in most evenings on his way to work to inquire about her.'

Our Nancy pealed with laughter. 'Willie's not Lily's boyfriend,' she asserted, 'he's Jane's.'

Aine looked nonplussed. 'I'm so sorry, Jane,' she said, 'I thought he was Lily's boyfriend.'

'What on earth gave you that idea?' our Nancy inquired curiously. 'Did he say Lily was his girlfriend?'

Aine looked bewildered. 'No, not in so many words,' she said, 'but he seemed so concerned about her, I took it for granted she was his girlfriend.' Aine noticed that Jane's face had gone a deep shade of red. 'Sorry,' she said to Jane. 'Obviously I got the wrong end of the stick. You see,' she went on to explain, 'I met Willie at a ceilidhe in Ballyhaunis over the Christmas. In the course of the evening I told him I was doing my internship in Jervis Street Hospital in Dublin. Picture my surprise when he arrived in during the first week of January to inquire about Lily. Since then he's been coming in most evenings to find out how she is.'

'Who could blame you for coming to that conclusion,' our Nancy laughed heartily. 'I can't wait to tell Lily; won't she have a good belly laugh about it!'

Jane was speechless in every sense of the word. All she could think about was this very attractive girl, Aine, being held in Willie's arms as they danced. She could just imagine them looking into each other's eyes, laughing and joking. And because that wasn't bad enough, later on, Willie uses Lily as an excuse to see Aine on a regular basis at the hospital, adding insult to injury. A knife twisted in her heart.

§

Michael's call to Mary in the hospital soliciting assistance for Bridget in labor (as he thought) turned out to be a false alarm. Because later that afternoon Bridget's pains stopped abruptly and the doctor discharged her.

'The pains you're experiencing, Mrs. Barry,' he told Bridget, 'are not the real thing.' He then went on to say, 'In any event, I'd prefer if you went full term; needless to say full term babies are much stronger and healthier.' Handing Bridget a prescription, he said, 'I'm giving you something to help you relax. I want you to go home now and rest as much as possible for the rest of your pregnancy. Do that and you'll surely go the full term.'

Painfully aware of the complications that could occur with a premature baby, Bridget was inordinately relieved to hear these words from the doctor. She prayed to God to let her go the full term and thankfully her prayer was answered. Another three weeks would pass before real labor began. It was unfortunate, however, that Michael, once again, had to be in Court on the actual day.

So Mary found him on her doorstep early in the morning pleading with her to stand in for him at the Rotunda hospital where he'd just left Bridget. 'I really wanted to be there for Bridget,' he told

Mary, 'to give her support and encouragement in the run-up to the delivery time.'

Mary was very touched by Michael's concern. Though he was a bit of a fusspot, she couldn't help thinking he was a wonderful husband. Unlike when she was having her babies — as was the case with most Irishmen — at the first signs of labor, John deposited her in the hospital straight away. Then he was gone; he couldn't wait to get away. Only when the babies were born would he deign to put in an appearance. And then he drooled all over them. But never in his life did he allow himself to be laid open to the pain and suffering that went into the birthing of a baby. Michael was one in a million. If he could, he would've been by Bridget's side staunchly helping her through every pain before the birth (if that was possible.)

Bridget's labor lasted roughly six hours. Although she would have preferred to be on her own with just the nurses, she felt she should be grateful to her mother for making the effort. But if truth were told, as each excruciating pain assaulted her wracked body, she was hard pressed to exercise self-restraint in front of the mother. Mary hated fuss and hysteria. That meant Bridget had to deny herself the luxury of giving vent to the yells and screams considered normal during labor.

Between each pain Mary talked at length. Obviously thinking she could divert Bridget's attention from the pains. (As if anyone could do such a thing at a time like this.) Bridget thought, having borne seven children herself, wouldn't you think she'd know better. One of the things Mary talked about was Lily's progress. She told Bridget that for the time being, Lily could only have one visitor at a time, and that visitor had to be family. 'Apparently,' she said, 'the rheumatic fever she had as a child left its mark on her heart.'

'Oh! That could be very serious,' Bridget gasped out between deep breaths, preparing for the next surge of pain.

'According to the doctors the typhoid aggravated the heart condition,' Mary continued. 'So they're continually monitoring her heart. That's why they insist on keeping her quiet.'

'Thank God she's on the mend,' Bridget spattered, writhing and squirming in the bed as another gigantic pain took possession of her. Then she let out an unmerciful scream, 'Oh my God! Help me! I'm going to die!'

Whereupon two nurses rushed in and after looking under the sheet covering Bridget's raised knees, nodded their heads. One said, 'Yes, she's ready.' A wheelchair was then rolled in to whisk Bridget away to the Labor Ward.

In Bridget's absence Mary tried to read one of her magazines. But she couldn't concentrate. Her mind was awash with visions of all sorts of things that could go wrong. Would Bridget survive the birth? After all she'd had a dreadful pregnancy; once nearly losing the baby. Would the baby be delicate because of that threatened miscarriage? For that matter would the baby survive? She thought about the time when Lily was dying when she was convinced that God was going to take Lily and send her a grandchild as a replacement. Now that Lily was out of danger, maybe God had other plans for Bridget and her baby. Such were Mary's morbid thoughts when, an hour later, Bridget arrived back in the wheelchair carrying her new born, very vocal baby girl. One look at Bridget's luminous expression was enough to banish all Mary's fears.

Later holding the quieted infant in her arms, Mary said to Bridget, 'This is what life is all about; the miracle of creation.'

'You're so right, Mother,' Bridget said, tears of joy spilling down her face. 'It was worth every minute of the pain and suffering.'

'The Lord works in mysterious ways his wonders to perform,' Mary said. Then asked, 'What are you going to call her?'

'Oonagh, after Michael's grandmother.'

At that point Michael burst in the door carrying a huge bunch of flowers. 'I've a daughter! I can't believe it! I can't believe it!' he kept saying. He was like a two year old. Throwing the flowers on the foot of the bed, he clasped Bridget in his arms and smothered her in kisses. Mary turned away. This passionate display made her mildly uncomfortable.

Michael then turned his attention to his new daughter in Mary's arms. 'Can I hold her?' he asked.

'Of course,' Mary handed the baby over.

'She's absolutely beautiful,' Michael exclaimed. He put his finger through the infant's hand. 'Look at those little fingers,' he said in wonder. 'They're absolutely perfect.'

'Yes,' Bridget said from the bed, 'and there are ten of them.'

Mary could see that Michael was totally enchanted with his new daughter. He walked around the room chatting to the infant as though she was an adult; telling her about all the wonderful things she was going to accomplish when she grew up, while Bridget and Mary looked on, bemused. Mary couldn't wait to get home and break the good news to the others.

She found Jane and Eileen having supper in the kitchen. Whoops of joy greeted her announcement.

'How is Bridget?' Jane then asked, concerned.

'Mother and daughter are doing fine,' Mary said proudly.

'Can they have visitors?' Jane asked.

'Yes,' Mary answered. 'She can have visitors at any time; she's in a private room.'

Twitching with excitement, Eileen said, 'Imagine! I'm an Auntie!'

'You're already an Auntie,' Mary reminded her. 'There's Colbert and Heuston, remember.'

'Ach, it's not the same,' Eileen wrinkled her nose. 'We never see them.'

§

'You'd know she was a girl,' Jane said to Bridget when she held the baby in her arms at the hospital the following day. 'She's so dainty.'

'I think at that stage they all look the same,' Bridget said.

'Oh, no,' Jane said looking fondly down on baby Oonagh. 'Colbert and Heuston were big bruisers from the day they were born.'

'About the christening,' Bridget said. 'I wish to God I could have you as Oonagh's godmother. But, blast it! We have to stick with tradition and have the first bridesmaid in that role.' Bridget screwed her face up showing her antipathy. 'That means the Nancy wan is going to be her godmother.'

'Don't worry about it,' Jane said. 'I'll be godmother to the next.'

'Anyway,' Bridget continued, 'after the christening we're having a small celebration here in this room with whatever members of both families are available. Just cheese and wine, cups of tea and a few buns.'

'It's on Sunday?'

'Yeah, after twelve o'clock Mass,' Bridget said. 'I'm hoping yourself and Willie will come?'

'I'll be there,' Jane muttered dispiritedly. 'But I'm afraid Willie won't.'

'I thought he was free on Sundays?' Bridget said.

'He probably is,' Jane made feeble gestures as she spoke, 'but you might as well know,' she said dispassionately, 'Willie and I are finished.' Her face contorted with pain as tears welled up in her eyes.

Bridget stared at her in disbelief. She was so stunned by Jane's statement she couldn't speak for seconds. Finally she burst out, 'But you can't be finished; the two of you are madly in love.' Suddenly, she looked straight into Jane's eyes and asked, 'Or are you? Can it be that you don't love him any longer?'

'Oh, I still love him,' Jane said morosely.

'You're not going to tell me that he's out of love with you?' Bridget said. 'My God! He can't take his eyes off you when the pair of you are in the same room.'

'It's mostly my fault,' Jane said sadly. 'I wrote him a letter breaking everything off.'

'But why?' Bridget asked, mystified.

Jane remembered Bridget's kindness to her when herself an Willie first started walking out. Of course, she was entitled to an explanation. Trying to keep her voice on an even keel, Jane proceeded to tell her the whole story about their mother's involvement; how totally prejudiced she was against Willie because of his association with Collins. And how determined she was to break them up.

'Forget about Mother!' Bridget said blazing with rage. 'From what you tell me,' she went on, 'it sounds like Peter was quite prepared to help out; to mastermind secret meetings between the pair of you while he worked on Mother.' Her voice now became soft and conciliatory. 'And you know of old how well Peter can manipulate our mother. In the name of God, why didn't you wait for him to go into action?'

'There's more to it than that,' Jane said wistfully.

'Tell me,' Bridget urged.

'It's about Lily,' Jane said. Then suddenly she seemed reluctant to go any further.

'Well, don't keep me in suspense,' Bridget said with urgency. 'What about Lily?'

Once again Jane hesitated. 'I don't know whether I should be telling you this or not.'

'Jesus, Jane! You have me worried out of my mind,' Bridget spluttered. 'Will you for God's sake tell me.'

'When Lily was dying I made a pledge to the Almighty that if He spared her life, I'd make the supreme sacrifice and do what Mother wanted — give up Willie. So I wrote a letter to Willie calling everything off.'

Bridget, her face white and disbelieving, was struck dumb.

'I can't go back on my pledge,' Jane said, starting to cry.

Bridget finally got her voice back. 'Sweet Mother of God! Jane!' she burst out. 'And what do you think Lily would have to say about that?'

'She must never know.'

'Well, she's bound to ask for an explanation about why you've split up with Willie?'

'I have an answer ready for her,' Jane said.

'And what might that be?' Bridget asked. Then added flippantly, 'You're not thinking of entering the convent?'

'No, nothing like that,' Jane had to smile. 'I'll just say he has another girlfriend.'

Bridget looked at Jane suspiciously. 'Are you telling me the whole story?' she asked.

'Does he have another girlfriend?' By now she was feeling overwhelmed by this incredible disclosure of Jane's.

'It's a possibility,' Jane said, pursing her lips as if holding herself back from adding something else.

Bridget's eyes were now bulging in her head as she stared at Jane. 'Jane,' she entreated, 'don't leave me dangling like this. Does he or doesn't he have another girlfriend?'

'I'm not sure,' Jane said. 'There's a nurse in training in Jervis Street Hospital whom he met at a ceilidhe in the West of Ireland at Christmas; he seems to be very great with her ever since.'

At that moment Michael arrived full of beans. 'How are the most beautiful mother and child in the world feeling today?' he asked bubbling over with joy.

'See for yourself,' Bridget indicated Oonagh in Jane's arms.

Jane stood up and handed the baby over to Michael. 'I've got to go,' she said airily. Bending down to kiss Bridget's cheek, she whispered, 'Remember, not a single word to anyone about what I told you.'

FIOCRA

Chapter XXVIII

Collins said to Willie when he arrived into his office at the back of Little Strand Street, 'Did you know, Willie, that the British are intensifying their search for me? A considerable reward is being offered for my body, dead or alive.' He smiled in a self-satisfied way. 'According to the network, they've sparked off a manhunt throughout the length and breath of Ireland, the likes of which has rarely been seen. I'm described as a tall, well-built figure, who speaks with a strong West Cork accent. And according to my sources, the Castle is absolutely hell bent on breaking up my intelligence system too.'

'So what are you doing about it?' Willie asked, concerned.

'The same as I did with all their other threats: being my natural self, attempting no camouflage, riding my bicycle through the city as though I owned it. I wrote to Harry recently, in reply to his cautionary note from America, saying, *I'm in love with life as much as the next man.* The escapes of others often chill me to the marrow. But as for myself, I take a logical view of things and act in accordance with what would seem to be super sensitiveness.'

Joe O'Reilly arrived.

Collins greeted him with the words, 'How many days do I have to live, Joe?'

Joe smiled ruefully and said to Willie, 'Will ye look at him, you'd think he hadn't a care in the world.'

'Well now,' Collins said, 'I've many a care, not least of which is supplying ammunition to those 'flying columns' working their arses off in the South of Ireland.'

'Talking about the South,' O'Reilly said, 'there's some very bad news from there today: Thomas MacCurtain — the Lord Mayor of Cork — was shot dead yesterday.'

Collins let out a roar of horror. 'Jesus! You're serious?' he gasped.

'Never more.'

'Any details about how it happened?' Collins asked.

'Only that the ones who did it wore masks,' O'Reilly said. 'Apparently they tried to make it look like the IRA did it, but their English accents gave them away.'

'The bloody British bastards!' Collins spat the words, outraged.

'I suppose that means you'll be making the trip to Cork for the funeral?' Willie said.

Collins cogitated before he answered. 'Of course I should go to the funeral,' he said, 'but taking into account Quinklink, Jameson and Molloy's treachery of late and the fact that I'm carrying this price on my head, wouldn't I be an obvious target if I attended MacCurtain's funeral.'

Answering Willie's puzzled expression, O'Reilly explained, 'Mick trusted those three lads too much and it now turns out that they were informers.'

'I know, Joe,' Collins put in contritely, 'you distrusted them from the beginning and tried to warn me.' He turned to Willie. 'We had to give up Rathmines on account of those bastards'

'Oh! Rathmines is gone too?' Willie asked.

'Yeah, one of those bloody buggars informed on us,' Collins said. 'Just after Christmas, a party of British military conducted a house-to-house in the Rathmines area looking for me. But Joe there and a couple of his cronies intercepted the Captain of the party when he was on his own in one of the houses.' Collins screwed up his face and looked quizzically at Joe. 'I think his name was Captain Maynard?'

'That's right,' O'Reilly affirmed.

'Well, anyway,' Collins continued, 'Joe threatened him with a revolver and told him to call down his men from upstairs. As soon as the other three soldiers arrived, they were bound and gagged.

Then the bauld Captain Maynard, blindfolded, gagged and with hands bound, was taken outside the house and marched through a series of back alleyways to my office a few minutes away.'

Joe intervened. 'Mick orders me to remove Maynard's binding and his blindfold and, if you please, offers him a seat and a cigarette.'

Grinning, Collins continued telling the story, 'Maynard asks me what my intentions were towards him? I tell him it depends on how useful he proves to be to me. He says, 'The search parties will, no doubt, be looking for me at this moment.' To which I replied, they've been looking for me for a long time.'

Itching to finish the story, O'Reilly butts in, 'Mick then has the nerve to say to Maynard, how much do you think my life is worth? 'A great deal,' he says. 'How much?' Mick insists. 'Anything from five pounds to fifty,' he answers. Mick then informs him that he thinks it's a 'poor value' they've put on his life.'

'We smoked three *Castles* cigarettes together,' Collins said, 'before I ended the interview.'

Collins and O'Reilly could no longer suppress their laughter.

When the laughter subsided, Willie asked, 'So, what happened to him?'

'Joe bound his hands and put his blindfold on again,' Collins said. 'Then ushered him outside where the other lads took over. I believe they traipsed him through millions of back alleys until they released him somewhere near College Green.' Collins looked pensive. He then turned to Willie. 'Willie,' he said, 'how would you feel about being my deputy at MacCurtain's funeral?' For seconds, Willie was indecisive. Collins rushed on, 'I'll fix it with Finbar tonight,' he said. 'Being the staunch republican he is, I'm sure he won't raise any objections about letting you off to attend an ardent Nationalist's funeral.'

Though Willie had enormous sympathy for the MacCurtain family, he was inclined to be irritated by Collins tone of languid assurance. He didn't particularly want to make the trip to Cork or anywhere else at this time. But then when he realized the danger in which Collins could be placed were he to go himself, he decided the practical solution was for him to go. Besides he couldn't think of a plausible excuse not to.

Faking enthusiasm, Willie said, 'Right, if you can fix it with Finbar, I'll do it.'

'Good on you, By!' Collins said, looking very grateful.

'You'll be doing Mick a big favor,' O'Reilly said. 'Possibly saving his life. I can almost guarantee that the cemetery will be swarming with British intelligence expecting to nab him.'

'Well,' Willie said, trying to sustain an air of careless distraction, 'Mick's safety is sacrosanct.' Then added flippantly, 'You'll owe me, Mick!'

Despite the flippancy, Collins detected tension in Willie's face. 'Willie,' he said, with an inquiring look, 'you're sure it's convenient for you to go?'

Willie maintained his air of flippancy. 'Don't you know, Mick,' he said, 'that your wish is my command.'

'Right then, that's settled,' Collins said. 'I'll call into the Tivoli tonight to see Finbar and yourself. I need to write a special letter to the MacCurtain family, which I'll ask you to deliver by hand, Willie. Also, I'd like a wreath with my name on it to be placed on his grave by a member of the MacCurtain family. Could I ask you to buy this for me in Cork and have it sent to them?'

'On no account should you put the wreath on the grave yourself,' O'Reilly chipped in looking seriously concerned. 'There's no knowing who's going to be watching. So take no chances.'

'We should know the funeral arrangements by this evening,' Collins said. 'Most likely it'll be the day after tomorrow. Which means traveling tomorrow.'

'About money?' Willie said anxiously.

'Don't worry,' Collins said, 'I'll fix all that up with you this evening.'

§

As the train wended its way southwards, Willie had the feeling that the world was crumbling around him. He was hungry for the sight and sound of his lovely Jane. At the same time he realized he must not let his need take control. Now he must concentrate on his present mission. But try as he might Willie's mind kept wandering back to his beloved Jane. He was very consoled to hear from Aine a few nights ago that Lily had at last regained consciousness. Further, she assured him that provided there were no other complications, Lily should make a complete recovery. 'But,' she told him, 'Lily is very weak and her visitors are apportioned; she's still only allowed to see members of the family in ones.'

Willie thought this good news about Lily would be a great palliative for Jane; surely now she would be more approachable? But now all his great plans about seeking Peter's advice beforehand as to time and place to waylay Jane, had to be put on hold because of this mission to Cork. More than ever he wanted to talk to her. But here he was speeding further and further away. Why does life have to be so bloody perverse? he wondered.

At Mallow Station a familiar face got into Willie's carriage. It belonged to Fiocra, the Galway journalist he met on the train coming from the West that disastrous first Christmas he spent in Mayo with his family Fiocra recognized him immediately.

'Small world!' he exclaimed affably.

'Yes, indeed,' Willie agreed. 'We never did get around to having that jar in Flanagan's pub in Dublin.'

'No,' Fiocra said. 'Shortly after I met you, I got a full time job with the *Cork Examiner.*' Looking quite pleased with himself, he went on, 'I married a Cork girl and we're expecting our first child in June.'

'So things have worked out pretty good for you?' Willie said, feeling very envious.

'So far, so good.' They were quiet for an instant. Then Fiocra said, 'I take it you going to Cork?'

'Yeah,' Willie said guardedly. Collins' warning was ringing in his ears: *'The Country is rampant with informers, By,'* he said. *'Watch your every word to strangers.'*

'A visit?' Fiocra asked.

Willie stalled for an instant, then decided to play safe. 'Yeah, just a couple of days,' he said.

'The South is where the action is,' Fiocra said with acclamation. 'I've just been covering the story of an ambush that took place in the wilds of Tipperary. It was carried out by the 'invisible army' against a truck load of British military.'

Willie plucked up his ears. 'Any casualties?' he asked.

'Some,' Fiocra said. 'Three dead, six injured.'

'Any of ours?'

'No, thank God!' Fiocra said. 'As far as I could ascertain from my interviews, the 'invisible army' as usual, melted into the mountainous terrain.' Fiocra smiled triumphantly. 'That invisible army is doing a magnificent job,' he said. His face glowed with pride as he continued. 'I suppose you know that Cork City is home to a lot of Republicans in the South. It's where they plan most of their missions, raids, ambushes and the burning down of barracks. Situated as it is, on the perimeter of the most perfect countryside for guerrilla warfare, it's a hot bed of IRA planning and activity.'

'That more or less explains the reason for MacCurtain's assassination?' Willie said.

'Yeah,' Fiocra agreed. 'As Lord Mayor of Cork, the authorities blame him for not putting a stop to it.' Fiocra smiled wryly, 'but sure wasn't he the most ardent republican of them all.'

Fiocra was so frank about his activities and about where his sympathies lay, that Willie felt quite the hypocrite. He decided there and then to confide in him. 'To be honest with you, Fiocra,' he said, 'I'm deputizing for Collins at MacCurtain's funeral tomorrow.'

Fiocra looked surprised. 'He can't make it himself?' he said.

'Too risky,' Willie said. 'Presently he's the most wanted man in Ireland.'

'He's a wise man to stay away,' Fiocra said. 'If anything happened to him where would the country be?'

'Good question,' Willie said. 'As far as I'm concerned, he's made himself indispensable to this country.'

As the train pulled into Cork City Station, Fiocra asked, 'Have you arranged a place to stay?'

'Oh, I'll stay in some hostel or other,' Willie answered.

As they were taking leave of each other, Fiocra said, 'When you're settled in maybe you'd have that promised drink with me this evening?'

'Where would you suggest?'

'One of the finest nationalist pubs in the city of Cork.'

'Which is?' Willie asked.

'The Swallow in Patrick Street.'

'Oh! I know that pub,' Willie said with enthusiasm. 'I had quite a few drams in there when I was working on Collins' election campaign.'

'Good!' Fiocra said. 'I'll see you there then around eight.'

Willie found a room in the hostel he'd used during the time of the general election. Later he joined Fiocra in The Swallow Pub. Being a Tuesday night the place was relatively empty and they were able to find a nice, quiet table in a corner.

'So what have you being doing with yourself since we last met?' Fiocra asked Willie. 'Did you get fixed up in a job?'

'I have a job of sorts,' Willie said disparagingly. He then went on to tell Fiocra about his job as a film projectionist in the Tivoli Cinema at night, which paid a measly salary and his volunteer work for Collins during the day, which paid no salary.

'From the sound of it,' Fiocra remarked, 'you're in one helluva rut.'

'Aye,' Willie agreed. Then suddenly, emboldened by his creamy pint of Guinness, he found himself opening up to Fiocra who seemed so amiable and so easy to talk to. He told him things he wouldn't tell his own brother. Things as close to his heart as the situation with Jane, to whom he thought he was unofficially engaged, but the mother's prejudice towards his nationalistic affiliations put an end to it. 'I'm convinced,' Willie said, 'that it's all the mother's fault; she forced Jane to write that letter to me calling everything off. I love Jane dearly and I know she loves me,' he said with much bitterness. 'Since I got her letter, I feel I've nothing to live for, no interest in anything and I'm sleepwalking through the day most of the time.'

Fiocra looked thoughtful. He was deeply moved by Willie's down-to-earth frankness about his personal life. Eventually he said, 'Willie, I've an idea I think I'll throw at you.'

'What?' Willie asked, interested.

'You'll probably think first hand it's ridiculously outlandish,' Fiocra said. 'But here goes anyway.' He stoked his forehead stalling to find the right words. Then he came out with it. 'What would you think about starting up your own cinema here in Cork?'

Willie nearly choked with surprise. 'You've got to be joking! Fiocra.'

'Now, Willie, listen to me.' Fiocra said firmly. 'From what you're telling me about your present circumstances, don't you think that having your own business, as opposed to working for a pittance for somebody else, would make a big difference to your financial standing? It would……..'

'It's out of the question!' Willie appeared resolute in his dismissal of any further discussion on the subject.

But Fiocra was determined to have his say. Patiently he continued. 'Willie, just hear me out. Now,' he said very positively, 'in the beginning you could rent premises. You have the know-how to do the job; that's a big plus.'

'Where on God's earth would I get the money to rent premises,' Willie asked. 'For that matter, where would the necessary capital come from to equip such premises?'

'Ever heard of a bank loan?'

'Unfortunately, Banks need collateral; I don't have such a thing,' Willie said bleakly.

'Banks recognize a good, secure investmet when they see one,' Fiocra said, smiling. 'You couldn't fail, Willie. The Cork people would welcome a cinema with open arms.' Looking very serious, Fiocra continued, 'At this moment the idea probably sounds too daunting to even contemplate,' he said. 'But think about the benefits, Willie. First, there'd be the huge cash turnover, so in no time you'd be able to pay back the bank loan and still make a profit. Second, and most important, you'd be able to marry your Jane; get her away from the influence of that awful mother of hers.'

'What about Collins?'

'Chances are you could be very useful to him down here in Cork. As I've just been saying, Cork and its surrounds, is probably the most active nationalistic County in Ireland, bar none.' Fiocra pressed Willie's arm sympathetically. 'Think about it, Willie,' he said. 'You're in a black hole in Dublin at the moment, miserably trying to work things out.' Fiocra grunted. 'Sure it's no life for anyone. You need a break away from it.'

'I'll think about it,' Willie muttered not very convincingly.

'Look,' Fiocra said, 'if it's any help I could introduce you to my bank manager in Cork and put in a good word for you.'

'You'd actually do that for me?' Willie said, his face showing undiminished astonishment.

'Course I would,' Fiocra said enthusiastically. Then added with emphasis, 'Willie, you made a lot of sacrifices for your country, don't forget that.'

'Much good it did me!' Willie said dismally.

Fiocra smiled a slow smile. 'What you need is a good sympathetic Republican bank manager. And I think I can point you in that direction.'

'Do you mean your own bank manager?'

'Him and others.' Fiocra's grin was as sly as a fox's. Before they left the pub, Fiocra gave Willie his business card, saying, 'Now Willie, I want you to think positively about what we discussed. Meantime, I'll keep my eyes open for a premises that could be easily transformed into a cinema.'

'You think such a place exists?' Willie said, warming somewhat to the idea.

'If there is such a place, I'll find it,' Fiocra said. 'Working for a newspaper I have all kinds of privileges; including access to information that's normally not available to the public. Should I come across any suitable premises, I'll drop you a line giving you the details.'

§

After Willie's two failed attempts to contact Peter through his office, he was relieved to run into him on his own in Flanagan's pub at lunch time the following Sunday morning. Luckily, Collins wasn't around. So, after Willie secured his pint of Guinness, he joined Peter. The timing for a discussion about what was on his mind couldn't be more appropriate.

As if reading Willie's mind, Peter greeted him with the words, 'You're going to query me about Jane, aren't you?'

Willie smiled and nodded. 'How did you guess?' he asked.

'It's written all over you, Willie,' Peter said. 'You look the epitome of someone crossed in love.'

'Is it that obvious?' Willie let out an exaggerated sigh. 'So Doctor O'Dwyer what's the cure?' Willie asked. 'Dare I approach Jane now?'

Peter prefaced his words with, 'As things stand, Jane is still recovering from the shock of Lily's illness.' Then seeing Willie's harassed look, he hastened to add, 'Well, when I saw her at Bridget's baby's christening, she was still very hoarse and had little to say. I presumed she was preserving her voice.'

'Which was the result of her continual reading to Lily when she was in the coma?'

'Exactly.'

'Surely someone could have relieved her during that time?' Willie said irately.

'She wouldn't hear of it,' Peter said. 'No, our Jane can be very stubborn when she likes.' He managed a half-hearted laugh. 'She was convinced that as the member of the family closest to Lily, her voice would have a better chance of penetrating the coma and reaching Lily. And, of course, she was right.'

'So how is Lily doing now?' Willie asked.

'Still very weak. Not allowed visitors,' Peter said.

'But she's out of danger?' Willie said.

'We hope so.'

'So what about Jane?' Willie asked anxiously. 'Any chance I could talk to her? Tell me the truth before I burst wide open.'

Peter said, 'I'm afraid, Willie, for the moment it looks like you're a prisoner of circumstance; I did mention your name to Jane at the Christening, but all I could get out of her was a hoarse 'we're finished.'

Willie felt numb.

I'm sorry, Willie,' Peter said, 'but that's about the size of it.'

'I can't believe she said that!' Willie gasped.

Seeing his wretchedness, Peter hastened to say, 'But it's still early days yet, Willie. Just give her time. Remember, she's just come through a very traumatic experience. Think about it. For the past four weeks or so, she was expecting to lose her favorite sister and her best friend. I think she went through hell. She certainly looks it.'

'The fact that Lily is recovering,' Willie entreated, 'should be enough surely to make Jane change her position?'

Peter laid his hand sympathetically on Willie's arm. 'Like I said, Willie, give her time.' He pondered a while. 'Going on her demeanor last Sunday at the Christening, I'd say this is definitely not a good time to approach her.'

There was an awkward silence while Willie cast about in his mind for something else to talk about. Then came inspiration. He found himself telling Peter about Fiocra and the idea of him starting up his own cinema in Cork.

'Are you giving it any serious consideration?' Peter was unable to hide his enthusiasm.

'I'm thinking about it, all right,' Willie intoned solemnly, 'but I'm torn between so many things here in Dublin.'

'Jane topping the list?' Peter put in.

'That and Collins,' Willie said despondently.

'Well, Willie, it's your life,' Peter said. 'This fellow, Fiocra, sounds very genuine. If he can follow through on all his promises — the premises and the right bank manager — I'd say go for it.'

'It's a big decision,' Willie said, 'but I am thinking strongly about going for it.'

'Well, now, putting it bluntly,' Peter said, 'if you were to become the owner of a cinema, it would put a very different complexion on things with our mother. She'd have no option but to climb down off her high horse and agree to a marriage between yourself and Jane.'

'If Jane will still have me?' Willie said dejectedly.

'Of course she'll have you,' Peter replied without hesitation. Then added, 'Nonetheless, I must say, having a business in Cork could well solve all your problems.'

'Strange, I was thinking along the same lines,' Willie said.

'If you're strapped for money,' Peter went on, 'I can help you.'

'I wouldn't dream of taking it,' Willie said very definitely.

'Even if it was inadvertently the mother's money?' Peter said, grinning from ear to ear.

'What do you mean *inadvertently the mother's money?*'

'Well, I'm in the throes of buying a house in Clontarf; the flat is now much too small for the family,' Peter said. 'My mother has offered to help me out financially. So instead of asking her for three hundred pounds, I could up the ante to four.' Peter winked guilefully. 'That extra hundred could be passed on to you to help you with your business.' He took a fit of laughing. When the laughter subsided, he continued, 'Now wouldn't that be one for the books! Imagine it! My mother involuntarily helping you out financially. Done in the eye, so to speak, by the very person she doesn't want her daughter to marry.' Peter went into whoops of hysterical laughter at the very idea. Suddenly he realized that Willie wasn't laughing.

There was an awkward clanging silence before Willie angrily broke in with, 'Forget it, Peter. Not one penny would I take from your Mother.'

Peter was bewildered by Willie's anger. 'But she'll never know,' he protested.

The pain of poverty bit deep into Willie but he was determined not to show it. 'Even so,' he said with passion, 'there's no way I'll ever be beholden to your mother.'

For seconds Peter was silent. He was puzzled and hurt like a child who had offered a gift to a grown up and been rebuffed.

'Sorry, Peter,' Willie said. 'I've hurt your feelings. The last thing I want is to sound ungrateful.'

For a while conversation was forced. Eventually Peter chipped in with, 'When you hear from Fiocra, why don't you take a week's vacation. Go down to Cork. And find out what's what?'

'The job,' Willie said, 'I doubt—'

Peter interjected, 'Surely you've been working at that cinema long enough to warrant at least a week's vacation?'

'I'll see what I can work out with Finbar,' Willie said. 'Could be problematical; I hate deceiving the man, but there's no sense in trying to explain things, unless and until things are accomplished.'

'Quite understandable,' Peter said. 'But if you intend going ahead with the project, somehow or other you've got to get yourself down there to Cork and do a thorough investigation into the pros and cons of the business.'

'I think you're right,' Willie said.

'Course I'm right,' Peter answered.

'In case it doesn't work out,' Willie said, 'I think t'would be best if we kept it a secret between us.'

'Oh, definitely,' Peter agreed. 'Until such time as you're all set up, mums the word.'

'You seem confident that I'm going to succeed,' Willie said.

'Think positive, Willie,' Peter answered. His eyes wandered to the clock on the wall. He stood up. 'Now I'm afraid I have to leave. The ball and chain will, as usual, be on the war path.' As he was leaving he added, 'If you go to Cork, I'll be very interested to know how you get on. In case we don't run into each other, be sure and drop into the office and tell me about it. Because,' he said, with a rush of enthusiasm, 'despite your pessimism about Jane, I'm confident that one day you're going to be my brother-in-law. A favorite one at that.' At the door he turned back to add, 'and whether you like it or not that financial help will still be in the offering.'

§

Two things of significance happened in Willie's life the following Monday.

First, there was a letter from Fiocra telling him he'd found the ideal premises for a cinema —a small warehouse situated about a half a mile from the City center. He ended his letter saying, 'Could you get yourself down here in the next few days before the word is out and somebody snaps it up ahead of you. As yet it hasn't been advertised.'

Second, was seeing Harry Boland in Collins' office when he reported for work. Boland's arrival was unexpected. The fact that he too was on a wanted list meant he had to be smuggled into the country in a fishing vessel. He'd left DeValera behind in the States. Clearly Collins was over flowing with jubilation. When Willie arrived he was bringing Boland up to date on what was happening currently in the country.

'The latest from our intelligence net work,' Collins told Boland, 'is that reinforcements for the R.I.C. (Royal Irish Constabulary) have been recruited in England and are now pouring into Ireland. Needless to say, it's to suppress the guerrilla warfare.'

'I thought by now,' Boland said, 'the British might have mellowed a bit?'

'You've been away a long time,' Willie said. 'The word 'mellow' doesn't exist in the British vocabulary.' He smiled whimsically. 'If anything, this latest development shows they're more determined than ever to crush the little war.' That's the impression I got, anyway, at MacCurtain's funeral.'

Collins addressed Willie. 'Did you see any of those Black and Tans, as they're called in Cork, when you were at the funeral?' he asked. 'I understand the first contingent has arrived in the South.'

'I saw some of them around the cemetery,' Willie answered, 'but my understanding is that the majority are based in Tipperary for the moment; that's where most of the action is.'

'Why are they called Black and Tans?' Boland wanted to know.

'According to our lads in Cork,' Willie said, 'the British hadn't enough bottle green uniforms to go round, so a lot of the new recruits are appearing in trousers and tunics that don't match (such as black tops and khaki trousers.) It seems they've been nicknamed after a famous pack of hounds in Tipperary called Black and Tans.' Willie smiled gleefully. 'They look quite comical; our lads regularly liken them to a chorus from a Gilbert and Sullivan opera.'

'What is their role?' Boland asked.

'Simply to swell the ranks of the R.I.C.,' Willie said. 'They're not a special force.'

'So far, they're not,' Collins put in. 'But there's something else I've heard that I don't know whether to be worried or pleased about…'

Boland raised an inquisitive eyebrow. 'That's a very enigmatic statement,' he said. 'What have you heard and why are you mixed up about it?'

'According to sources it seems a special Auxiliary force is presently being recruited in England for the R.IC.' Collins said. 'It's a force compiled mostly of officers toughened up by their experiences in the Great War. Naturally, with all that experience, they'll pose a greater danger to the Irish.'

'We now know what you're worried about,' Boland said. 'But,' he added, puzzled. 'what in the name of God is there to be pleased about?'

'I'll put it to you this way,' Collins said. 'By sending in those special forces, Britain is at last recognizing the fact that a 'little war' still wages in Ireland.' He sniffed audibly. 'Up to now, they've done their best to ignore it. This was to play it down internationally. But now bringing in extra forces could well establish them as the aggressor. Hence Ireland's little war will get the attention of the whole world; something that's bound to constitute a slur on the British.'

'And they won't like that one bit!' Boland said drolly.

'Just my point,' Collins said.

Having amicably arranged for time off 'with pay' with Finbar the night before, Willie decided this was the best time to break the news of his impending holiday to Collins. Boland's presence should make it easier. Coming in on the tram this morning, Willie mentally rehearsed how he'd broach the subject to Collins without having to disclose any details.

'By the way, Mick,' Willie interjected offhandedly, 'I won't be around for the next week.'

'I hope you're taking a holiday?' Collins retorted cheerfully. 'Because you look like someone who could do with one.'

'You guessed right,' Willie said, smiling. He was grateful that there had been no awkward questions. Just as he had reckoned, Boland's presence deflected Collins' attention away from probing the whys and wherefores of Willie's holiday.

Shortly afterwards Collins and Boland left.

Chapter XXIX

'And how is the patient today?' Nurse Aine asked as she wheeled Lily's dinner tray towards her.

'Good,' Lily said, with a brilliant smile as she sprung up in the bed. 'And looking forward to this; I'm starving.'

'Makes a change,' Nurse Aine remarked as she plumped up Lily's pillows behind her to make her comfortable. 'A month ago you couldn't even look at food, don't mind eat it.'

'That was a month ago,' Lily said brightly. 'As you can see now, I'm fully recovered. So when are they going to let me out of this place?'

'You need a lot of convalescing,' Nurse Aine said. 'Do you realize we nearly lost you?'

Lily smiled and said jocosely, 'Like the proverbial cat, I have nine lives. But seriously, I feel as fit as a fiddle and I wish to God they'd let me go home.'

'Patience, patience,' Nurse Aine remarked. 'We don't want you having a relapse because you were discharged too soon.' She gave Lily a critical look. 'You know you're still very thin,' she said. 'You need fattening up.'

Nurse Aine was halfway to the door when Lily importuned strongly, 'Before you leave, Nurse!'

Nurse Aine stopped abruptly in her tracks. 'Yes, what is it?' she asked.

Lily's face went beetroot red. It was obvious to Nurse Aine that something was embarrassing her. She hastened back to the bedside. 'Is something wrong?' she asked, anxiously.

Lily swallowed hard before she spoke. 'I'd like to ask you a personal question,' she said.

'Sounds ominous.'

Rushing on, Lily said, 'I probably have no right to ask you this question.' She hesitated for seconds.

'Out with it, Lily,' Nurse Aine said coaxingly. 'You can ask me anything.'

'It's just that I need to clarify something I heard from my sister, Jane, recently.'

Nurse Aine could see plainly that something was really bothering Lily. 'Come on, Lily,' she said, 'what is the question?'

'It's how Jane heard that you were walking out with Willie since you two met at the Ceilidhe in Mayo,' Lily said. 'Is there any truth to it?'

The question came as a thunderbolt to Nurse Aine. 'In the name of God, where did she hear the likes of that?' she said, breathlessly. Then went on. 'Yes, Willie and I did meet at a ceilidhe at Christmas.' She nodded her head very negatively. 'But as far as walking out with him is concerned, I have my own boyfriend. If Willie's walking out with someone else, it's definitely not me.'

Lily made a wry face. 'I'm truly sorry if I offended you by asking,' she said plaintively, 'but I just had to know. At least now I can rule you out of the puzzle.'

'No offense taken,' Nurse Aine said spiritedly. Then made for the door where she ran into Bridget coming in.

'What a lovely surprise,' Lily cooed from the bed. 'So how's the new mother and my new niece?'

'Your niece is doing fine,' Bridget said leaning over Lily to kiss her cheek. 'Can't say the same for the mother,' she added. 'She's getting very little sleep.'

'Cross?'

'No, just hungry all the time,' Bridget said. 'And by gum, she lets me know about it.'

'It's a good sign.'

'I won't complain,' Bridget said. 'If she wasn't eating wouldn't I have something to worry about.'

'It's been such a long time since I saw you, Bridget.'

'Not since Christmas Day when I was as big as a mountain.' Bridget studied her. 'So how are you? You look splendid.'

'I look exactly as I feel,' Lily said. 'A sorry excuse for a patient, malingering here under false pretenses.'

'Ah now,' Bridget said, 'I'm sure the doctors know best. They'll discharge you as soon as you're fit enough and not a moment sooner.'

Suddenly Lily became very serious. 'What's all this stuff I'm hearing about Jane and Willie breaking up?' she asked Bridget ruefully.

'Seems to be the situation all right,' Bridget said casually. But her face was too impassive for Lily's liking. Lily looked accusingly at her. 'You know something I don't,' she said.

'How do you mean I know something?' Bridget asked, trying to look innocent and bewildered.'

'You know more about the situation than you're saying?' Lily was now thoroughly agitated. 'Jane comes in here and tells me that it's all off with Willie because he has another girlfriend; she even told me who the girl was.'

Bridget feigned surprise. 'She actually told you her name?'

'She did.' Lily's face was now red with anger. She nodded towards the door. 'By all accounts it's supposed to be that nurse you met at the door as you came in.'

'That one!' Bridget said, slowly exhaling the breath she had been holding.

'Yes. According to Jane, that's who it is — Nurse Aine.' Lily continued sounding quite piqued. 'Jane comes in here and gives me a cock and bull about how Willie met Nurse Aine at a Ceilidhe in Mayo over Christmas and they've been walking out ever since.'

'Maybe it's not such a cock and bull,' Bridget began tentatively. 'Maybe—'

'I know for a fact that it is a cock and bull,' Lily shot back at Bridget.

'You know! How do you know?' Bridget was holding her breath again.

'Because I asked Nurse Aine straight out if herself and Willie were walking out?'

'Good heavens! Lily!' Bridget gasped. 'You never did!' Her eyes practically popped out of her head with horror.

'Yes I did,' Lily was unwavering. 'She denied it, of course, saying she has her own boyfriend.' Lily scowled at Bridget. 'Bridget,' she fumed, 'what's going on? Jane looks like someone who's going into decline.'

Bridget began to get flustered. She looked at her watch. 'Lily,' she said, 'I have to go. It's the baby's feeding time.' She left in a hurry.

By now Lily was at screaming point she felt so frustrated. She wondered if Willie really did have another girlfriend? Or was Jane just guessing? When Jane told her the full story originally, she was vague to the point of being blasé; it was as though she couldn't care less. She even used the phrase, 'There's as good a fish in the sea as ever was caught.' But Lily could see she was very changed; her face was thin and gaunt, the light had gone out of her eyes and her smile was forced and artificial. In short, Jane was a shadow of her former self.

'Don't tell me,' Lily talked out loud, 'that Jane isn't brokenhearted about splitting up with Willie. I wasn't born yesterday.'

Suddenly the door was thrust open. Bridget stood on the threshold looking frenzied.

'I had to come back, Lily,' she said. She seemed to be struggling to find the right words. Finally they came out. 'I had to tell you the truth.'

Lily shot up in bed fearful and alarmed. 'Willie's dead!' she screamed. 'Jane wanted to spare me.' She thought, isn't Bridget's face saying it all: the dark secret is out at last. Before she could stop them, the tears were rolling down her face.

'No, no,' Bridget said, hastening to her bedside. 'Willie is very much alive; get that idea out of your head.'

'But,' Lily said, whisking the tears away with the sleeve of her bed jacket, 'what is the truth?'

'The truth is...' Tears came into Bridget's eyes. 'When you were dying, Jane made a pledge to the Almighty that if He spared you, she would do what Mother asked and give up Willie.'

It was now Lily's turn for her eyes to nearly pop out their sockets with shock. 'You mean to say that Jane and Willie split up because I survived?'

'For God's sake, Lily,' Bridget pleaded, 'don't put it like that.'

'But that's what you're telling me.'

Tears flowed down Bridget's face. Lily held her arms out to her. The two sisters hugged in sympathy. 'I didn't know what to do,' Bridget whispered. 'I'm the only one in the family who knows the truth.'

'She told you?'

'Yes, she told me and she swore me to secrecy.'

'Does Willie know the truth?' Lily asked.

'Course not,' Bridget said. 'He thinks Jane has allowed Mother to seduce her into submission.'

'Have you seen Willie?'

'I haven't, but Peter has,' Bridget said. 'Peter keeps telling him that it'll all blow over. But I don't know. Jane seems to be adamant about keeping the faith with the Almighty. She's so grateful to Him for sparing your life.'

'Oh, Bridget! I'm so glad you told me,' Lily let out a huge sigh of relief. 'I need time to think about what's the best thing to do.'

'Telling you has taken an almighty load off my chest,' Bridget said. 'But for God's sake, Lily,' she pleaded, 'don't do or say anything rash.'

'Bridget, we're dealing with the Almighty here; no small entity,' Lily said profoundly. 'Of course I intend to be very circumspect.' She winked wryly at Bridget. 'I'll have to come to an arrangement with Himself above before I can take any action.'

Bridget left with a much lighter heart.

§

As the Cork train trundled southwards, Willie reflected on revelations Collins shared with him before he left.

'With such a price on my head, Willie,' he said, 'people wonder why the British have failed to arrest me?' He smiled a smug smile. 'Well, I'll tell you now how I've managed to evade them — It's the strength of my network.'

'You don't have to tell me that,' Willie said. They're working miracles keeping you out of jail.'

'But did I tell you about the coup I brought off recently?' Collins asked.

'What coup?'

'Well, I'm calling it a coup, because it involves the gathering together of a handful of picked men which include Liam Tobin, Tom Cullen and Frank Thornton. Tobin is set up in an office in Crow Street within two hundred yards of Dublin Castle. That particular office contains the 'brain' of the British intelligence organization; files, dossiers of men — ranging from military officers to government leaders — captured documents and so on.' Truly Collins was in his element as he continued. 'Tobin — a natural expert in decoding cipher documents — is carrying on work of inestimable importance to me. Along with that my friends, Ned Broy, Kavanagh, Neligan and McNamara act as spies for me in Dublin Castle. So you see,' Collins said with a wily grin, 'apart from the value of the documents they bring me, my freedom depends to a large extent on the activities of those men.'

Willie was met at the Cork railway station by Fiocra who appeared to be bursting with enthusiasm. After showing Willie the key, he said, 'I hope you're going to like the premises?' The light in his eyes practically willed Willie to agree with him. It took twenty minutes for them to walk from the Station to the building. En route Fiocra filled Willie in on the bit of information he managed to ferret out the Agent. 'You can either buy or rent the building,' he told Willie. 'If you decide to rent, you'll have the option to buy at a later date.'

It was music to Willie's ears hearing that the place could be rented. He thought, maybe after all there's a chance that this venture might actually come to fruition.

The outside of the building was most unimpressive; it looked just what it was — a warehouse.

'Don't worry about the outside,' Fiocra hastened to tell him, 'a carpenter friend of mine told me that all that concrete can be camouflaged with paint, carvings and decoration. T'was the inside that struck me as being really adaptable and suitable.'

Fiocra was right about the inside. The potential was definitely there. Lots of space with an upstairs room at one end overlooking it. This upstairs room could easily be turned into a Projection Room.

Willie was sold immediately on the building. 'Yes,' he said excitedly. 'I think it would certainly make a good cinema. However, I'd have to think about renting it first rather than buying it.' Suddenly he became a shade less excited. 'There is, of course, the worrying matter of…'

'Money,' Fiocra interjected. It was as if Fiocra was reading Willie's mind. He said, 'I hope you don't mind, but I I took the liberty of approaching a Surveyor friend of mine.'

'You did?' Willie exclaimed.

'Yeah. I asked him could he give me a rough estimate of what the conversion would cost? He's presently working on it.' Fiocra took his pocket watch from his waistcoat pocket. After studying it, he said, 'Would you have time now, Willie, to come and see him?'

Willie was staggered, not only by the question, but by all the hard work Fiocra had already put into the project. Plus he was so humble about it. 'Of course I have the time,' Willie said. I'm here for a week. Lead on.'

Donal Hargodan, the Surveyor, was a gray-haired man with a plausible voice and careful manners. 'Certainly, I agree with Fiocra,' he told Willie, 'depending on how much you can afford, that building could easily be transformed into quite a nice cinema.'

At the mention of how much he could afford, Willie gave a choking laugh. He was thinking about his financial circumstances. He had the clothes he stood up in, a job that paid barely enough to cover room and board with a few shillings left over for lunches with Jane and the odd pint at the weekend. Putting it bluntly he was as poor as a church mouse.

Fiocra butted in. 'Just tell us the minimum amount Willie would need to spend at the outset?' he asked Hargodon.

Hargodon studied his figures. 'I'd say something in the region of four hundred pounds,' he said. 'That would include painting, renovating, carpeting and seating.'

'Seating for how many?' Willie asked the important question.

'Roughly two hundred,' Hargodon said. 'Of course, that sum would not include the cost of buying and installing the equipment.'

As they left the Surveyor's office, Fiocra said, 'I have an appointment with my Bank Manager tomorrow morning regarding my own account. What would you think about coming with me to meet him?'

Willie hesitated, then looked at Fiocra dubiously. 'My God Fiocra!' he exclaimed. 'I can't believe I'm even contemplating this venture. I haven't a bean to my name.'

Fiocra laughed heartily. 'It's many's the millionaire that started out the same way,' he said. 'Don't let the money put you off. Come with me to the Bank tomorrow.' Once again, Fiocra retrieved the watch from his waistcoat pocket and studied it. 'I'm sorry, Willie,' he said, 'but I have to leave you.' He wrote something on a small writing pad and handed the sheet to Willie. 'That's the address of my bank,' he said. 'Meet me there tomorrow morning at ten o'clock without fail.'

Willie acquiesced meekly. 'Right,' he said. 'As impossible as the situation is, I suppose there's no harm in talking to your bank manager.'

That night after registering at his usual hostel, Willie dropped into The Swallow. Here, he got talking to a group of IRA volunteers, some of whom he'd already came across during the Collins election campaign. They greeted him cordially.

'No fundamental changes despite the results of the elections?' a young man, named Jimmy, said to Willie.

'For all the good those elections did with the British authorities,' Willie said disconsolately, 'we might as well have left it alone.'

'Ah now,' Jimmy put in, 'that's not the way we look at it here in Cork. If nothing else, the British attitude has succeeded in uniting the country more than its ever been.'

'You're active I take it?' Willie queried.

'Along with everybody else,' Jimmy said. 'You know something, by unleashing those repugnant Black and Tans and Auxiliaries on us, the British left us no option but to fight on. Violent, vicious bastards, they are — those Tans — If you'll pardon my French. In the space of the short time they've been in this country they've succeeded in committing some appalling atrocities.'

'You're still using guerrilla warfare tactics?' Willie asked.

'None other,' Jimmy said. 'Despite the lack of numbers, the IRA make up for it by their courage, aggressiveness and discipline. Up to now we've been ambushing the big Crossley Tenders, relieving them of their ammunition. Killing individuals — sometimes police, sometimes military, sometimes informers. But here I have to tell you that a lot of the IRA's success is due to intelligence. For instance, recently I spent two days and two nights stuck in a ditch keeping the movements of tenders and battalions under surveillance. As soon as we're cognizant of their habits, we dig holes in the roads to facilitate our ambushes.'

'We also destroy bridges and interfere with British communications,' another of the lads, Sean, put in.

'And we'll keep it up till we get satisfaction,' Jimmy added.

'As I was coming here,' Willie said, 'I read a Notice on a tree to the effect that for every member of Crown forces shot, two Sinn Feiners will also be shot.'

'Yeah, that's happening too,' Jimmy said dejectedly. 'Reprisal and counter reprisal seems to be the order of the day.'

'But sure didn't those Tans burn down twenty-five houses in Balbriggan, outside Dublin, yesterday; driving people from their homes, making them homeless,' Sean put in. 'It was reported in this morning's *Cork Examiner.*'

'God between us and all harm!' Willie ejaculated. This was news to him. 'I understood the Tans were only operating in the South,' he said, his face gone a shade whiter with shock.

'Doesn't surprise me one bit,' Jimmy said. 'Just last week, those bloody Tans burnt down a Creamery in Wexford and a Dairy in Waterford. It's a means of hitting at the people through their jobs.'

'It now looks like they're doing the same thing in Dublin,' Sean put in.

My God! Willie thought, am I crazy thinking about setting up in business at a time like this? At this moment he was having grave doubts about going ahead with the cinema project.

But next morning Fiocra talked Willie out of his doubts. 'Don't be thinking about the flies in the ointment, Willie,' he said. 'Think about the advantages, the quick cash turnover, the small staff, the rewards generally.'

'If times were normal,' Willie said, 'I wouldn't hesitate for a second, but after listening to those volunteers last night, they put the wind up me crosswise.'

Fiocra smiled at Willie's funny expression. 'Willie,' he said with much determination, 'you can take it from me, there'd be no question of your cinema being burnt down. Its location couldn't be better: on the fringe of a housing estate, far enough off the beaten track to be inconspicuous. But best of all there isn't a police barracks within miles miles of it. And that's where all the action is.'

At the bank, Fiocra had a private interview with the Manager first. After fifteen minutes he reappeared and beckoned to Willie to join him in the Manager's office.

Hugh Consodine, the Bank Manager, a little man, middle-aged, with a face that radiated intelligence, said to Willie, 'Fiocra's right. Presently, a cinema anywhere in Cork would be God send for the morale of the people.' Opening a drawer in his desk, Consodine pulled out a number of forms and chose one. Then looking up at Willie, he asked, 'How much of a loan do you want?'

Before Willie could reply, Fiocra butted in. 'Five hundred pounds,' he said decisively. Turning to Willie he apologized, 'Sorry, Willie, for butting in.' After that he resumed talking to the manager. 'In Willie's absence,' he said, 'I dealt with the Surveyor. That was the figure he gave me.'

Willie thought, Fiocra's using the loaf asking for a larger sum.

Consodine played around with figures on his writing pad, then lifted his head. 'I think that could be arranged,' he said. Pursing his lips, he added, 'Regarding the terms of the loan, if it could be paid off within five years, the interest rate could be kept low. But in the event of it going over five years, the rate would automatically rise. How does that fit in with your plans, Willie?'

After Willie gulped deep in his throat, he said, 'The five years would be grand.' He felt that he mustn't let a hint of the surprise he was feeling at how easy it was, show on his face. Sounding very positive now, he remarked, 'With the a huge cash turnover peculiar to cinemas, it wouldn't be inconceivable for that loan to be paid off within a couple of years.'

'The cash turnover is what I'm banking on,' Consodine said as he handed Willie the form. 'Now if you'll just fill that out and sign it, I'll be able to make the necessary arrangements.'

As Willie was filling out the form, Fiocra asked the crucial question: 'How soon will the money be available?'

'Immediately,' Consodine answered.

Willie looked up from the form. He had a problem. 'Do I give my Dublin address?' he asked Consodine.

Consodine looked surprised. 'You don't have a Cork address?'

'Not as yet,' Willie said. 'I still have to go back to Dublin to finalize things.'

Fiocra looked quizzically at Consodine. 'Maybe he could use my address for the moment,' he suggested. 'Until such time as he has a permanent address in Cork.'

'How long will it take to finalize your business in Dublin?' Consodine asked Willie.

'Two weeks at most.'

'Right then,' Consodine said. 'Put Fiocra's address on the form and add 'temporary' after it. Then as soon as you have your own address in Cork, notify the bank.'

When Willie finished filling out the form, Consodine signed it.

Then standing up, he said, 'If you'll come with me now, I'll get our Loans Officer to process your loan.' With that he lead Willie and Fiocra to the Loans Officer's Office on the main floor of the building. 'Donal,' he said, handing the young man behind the desk, the form, 'will you process this loan for this gentleman?' Then turning to Willie, he shook his hand warmly and said, 'The best of luck to you, lad; remember you'll be doing the Cork people a great favor providing them with a cinema.'

'What did I tell you,' Fiocra said to Willie after they left the bank, 'simple, wasn't it?'

'Agreed,' Willie said, 'but we're not there yet.'

'No,' Fiocra said, 'we've still to see the Agent, sign a lease, pay him some money and get the keys.'

'Where does he hang out?' Willie asked.

'A short ride on the number ten tram.' On the tram, Fiocra mentioned, 'A word of advice, Willie: I think for the moment you should give that Swallow Pub a miss.'

'Agreed,' Willie concurred. 'Much too risky. If I was caught in there during a raid, they'd have my name on their records.' Then with a negative shake of his head, 'No,' he said positively, 'no sense in bidding the divil good morrow.'

After signing the lease, paying a month's rent in advance and collecting the keys, Willie decided that this had to be the route to a better life. The thought of owning his own cinema was exhilarating. As Willie had five more days to spend in Cork, he was keen to make a start on the changes to the building. But before anything could be done, there was the matter of a huge amount of leftover junk to be disposed of. With the help of a strong, young man, named Conor—recommended by Fiocra, who described him as 'someone who aspires to high standards'—between Willie, Conor and Conor's friend, Adrian (who owned a lorry), they cleared the place out in two days.

As it turned out, Conor, proved to be invaluable. He was a Cork man who knew his way around; the places where the necessary materials could be purchased at the 'right' price, the people who could do intricate jobs they couldn't do themselves, again, at the 'right' price. Presently unemployed, Conor called himself 'an odd jobs man.' Willie was more than glad to employ him. His wages came out of the extra money Fiocra managed to weed out of the bank manager. In many ways, Conor reminded Willie of himself—persistent and patient when he had his mind set to achieving something. After applying the primer to all the interior walls of the warehouse with Conor's help, Willie made a decision. As soon as the primer dried, in Willie's absence, Conor could carry on with the painting. All the walls would be painted black conforming to a realistic cinema environment.

When it came to the end of the week, seeing the interior of the Cinema begin to take shape, Willie was reluctant to leave. Working for himself, seeing results, was so satisfying. Not to mention being in control; his own boss. He couldn't wait to get back from Dublin to resume working on this project.

On his own in the carriage of the train, stark reality dawned on Willie. My God! he thought, the die is cast! Imagine me the owner of a cinema in Cork! It sounded so good he said it out loud to the empty carriage. 'Imagine me, Willie McNamee, the owner of a cinema in Cork!'

Then a few unpleasant thoughts encroached on his enthusiasm. The news still had to be broken to Finbar and Collins. He wondered how they would receive it? Would Finbar be willing to help with the technicalities involved? This was the next hurdle. To make this venture a success Willie would definitely need all the help and cooperation he could get from Finbar. Would it be asking too much? He wondered. Suddenly Jane came into his mind. He consoled himself with thinking that he might soon be in a position to offer her something of substance. That was, of course, if she still loved him. It was a sobering thought.

So many things needed to be sorted out in Dublin.

§

Jane picked her way up the steps of the Jervis Street Hospital. How well she knew those fifteen steps. Most of them were in good condition, but some were badly eroded from years of wear and tear. The top step in particular was a definite hazard. Cracked and broken, she wondered when the hospital would get round to having it fixed. She wondered, too, how many people had already become croppers on those dangerous steps? Such were Jane's thoughts on this miserable, wet Monday evening when she was on her way to visit Lily. She couldn't wait to tell her sister about the invitation she'd received to the Army's Annual Ball the following Friday night. However, she was under no illusions. It was patently obvious the invitation was initiated by her mother; not in a million years would our Nancy issue it of her own volition. She could just hear her mother saying to our Nancy, 'Poor Jane! Since she broke up with Willie, she never goes anywhere except to work and to see Lily. Why don't you find a partner for her for that Army dance you're so busy organizing?' And to be sure our Nancy would have milked he situation as much as possible; making sure she was handsomely paid for doing the needful.

Anyway, our Nancy had dropped into the Store that afternoon full of excitement—Mi ah!- (supposedly) to tell Jane about this Army Captain who needed a partner for the Ball. Then asking her if she'd consider being his partner? Jane had mixed feeling about it: one part of her wanted to go, the other couldn't bear the thought of being held in arms that weren't Willie's. At the thought of Willie that terrible pain jabbed at her heart. If only I was going with him, she thought despairingly. Oh God! Will I ever get over him?

Lily was up and dressed and sitting reading in a chair when Jane arrived. Though she still looked frail, Jane thought it was marvelous to see her out of bed. Surely it meant she'd be coming home soon.

'Surprise! Surprise!' Lily greeted Jane. 'I'm being discharged at the weekend.'

Jane threw her arms around her sister in a massive hug. 'That's wonderful!' she said. 'When did you hear?'

'The doctor told me this morning,' Lily said with a flashing smile. 'I can't wait to get out of here.'

'God! It'll be great to have you home, sharing the bedroom again,' Jane said excitedly. Then she looked thoughtful. 'Before I go any further,' she said, 'I need your advice?'

Lily plucked up her ears. 'Advice?' she repeated, 'About what?'

'I've been invited to the Army's Annual Ball this coming Friday.'

'What are you doing for a partner?' Lily asked, surprised.

'That's the intriguing bit,' Jane said. 'He's a stranger.'

'How did this come about?' Lily asked. Then lightening struck. 'Don't tell me the miracle happened with our Nancy,' she shrieked. 'That she actually invited you?'

'Just that,' Jane said, with a laugh that had a mystical sound to it.

'Well, I'm mesmerized,' Lily said. Then not bothering to hide the sarcasm, added, 'The bitch actually has a human streak in her after all.'

Jane laughed the mirthless laugh that had become the norm. 'Don't be so fast to give our Nancy all the credit,' she said. 'The more I think about it, the more I'm convinced that it was essentially Mother's idea.'

'Why would you think such a thing?' Lily asked.

'Well, she obviously feels very guilty about…' Jane stopped abruptly. Her face crimson.

'Guilty about what?' Lily importuned with puckered brow.

Jane realized she'd said too much. Since Lily came out of the coma, except to tell her that Willie had another girlfriend, she hadn't gone into any details. And the one and only time Lily brought up the subject of Willie, Jane explained that it caused her too much pain to talk about it. So thankfully Lily had respected her wishes and had not mentioned the subject since. Hoping she sounded more lighthearted than she felt, Jane adroitly changed the subject saying, 'So what do you think about me going to the Ball? Should I go?'

Lily was pensive for a moment. Then put in, 'It sounds great. But what do you know about your partner?'

'His name is Captain Bernard Skelly; he's a friend of Gerald's.

And like I said, he's stuck for a partner.'

'And you've never met him?' Lily said.

'No, I'd be meeting him for the first time on Friday.'

'Maybe he'll be a runt of a man, with a big, fat neck, a pot belly and a face on him that looks like someone sat on it when it was hot,' Lily said laughing. *Without a doubt,* Jane thought, *Lily's back to normal.* 'Of course, Lily continued, raising her eyebrows snobbishly, 'He might turn out to be a prince.' She now started laughing hysterically. Her infectious laughter got Jane going. For the first time in months she threw her head back and allowed the laughter to flow. It was a while before Lily gained control. 'You'll definitely have to go,' she chuckled, 'if it's only to see what kind of partner our Nancy dragged out from under a stone. Think about the fun we'll have afterwards talking about it.'

Nurse Aine arrived carrying Lily's medication. Seeing Jane about to leave, she stayed her saying, 'No need to leave; it's just a few pills.' While Nurse Aine concentrated on attending to Lily, Jane observed her closely. She had to admit she was very attractive. If Willie was consoling himself with her, who could blame him. The fact that he hadn't attempted to answer her letter or get in touch with her, confirmed her suspicions that himself and this lovely girl were now walking out. Once again that awful, sharp ache was back in her heart.

After Nurse Aine left, Lily blurted out, 'She's the one you gave me the cock and bull about: supposedly she's walking out with your Willie?'

Jane mustered a weak smile. 'Now that I've had a good look at her,' she said, 'I think she's very attractive.' She rubbed the back of her neck wishing to God they weren't having this conversation. 'And by the way,' she said with a very straight face, 'it wasn't a cock and bull.'

Lily grinned at her. 'Come on, Jane,' she chided, 'it's your sister, Lily, you're talking to here. Let's have the truth.'

'I told you the truth,' Jane said, doing her best to keep the tremble out of her voice. 'I have it on good authority that Nurse Aine is

Willie's new girlfriend.'

'But you and I know that isn't true,' Lily said. Jane shrugged her shoulders assuming insouciance. Lily went on sounding quite aggressive. 'Well, I know for a fact that Willie and that nurse are not walking out.'

'You do? How do you know?'

'I asked her straight out if Willie and herself were walking out?' Lily said.

Jane's eyes widened in horror. 'You didn't!' she gasped.

'I certainly did,' Lily said hotly. 'Why should she be held responsible for the break up between you and Willie when she has a boyfriend of her own?'

For a second Jane was stumped for an answer. Then said, 'You're serious?'

'I was never more serious in my life.'

Suddenly tears of joy began to trickle down Jane's face. Lily rose from her chair, crossed the room and joined Jane sitting on the bed.

'Jane,' she said in a solemn voice, 'I've been talking to Himself above,' she nodded towards the ceiling, 'and we've come to an understanding.' Adopting the mannerisms and the guttural voice of the Disciplinary Sister in Sienna Convent, she said, 'Do you realize, child, how much offense you've given to the good Lord by offering him a bribe? At your age you should know better. He has a particular aversion to bribes. He frowns on them.' Lily put her arm lovingly across Jane's shoulder and squeezed it. 'Anyway,' she said in her normal voice, 'he told me that as He fully intended to spare my life, it was a wasted bribe. So, in a nutshell, you can have it back.' Lily's eyes got misty. 'Putting it bluntly, Jane,' she said, 'you're completely absolved from that stupid pledge you made to the Almighty when you thought I was going to die.' Suddenly Lily felt such a rush of affection for Jane she threw her arms around her. With that the tears came. 'Jane,' she said in a choked voice, 'if it's only for my sake, will you please make up with Willie. Otherwise, I'll feel it's all my fault and I won't be able to live with the guilt.'

Jane clutched Lily tightly. 'Oh Lily!' she sobbed into her neck, 'you're such an angel. I love you so much. I did it because I couldn't imagine life without you.'

Lily pulled back from her. 'Well, if you love me that much, you'll do as I ask.'

Jane nodded her head in quiet submission. 'Oh! I will, I will!' she whispered. 'That is,' she sighed through her tears, 'if he'll have me back.'

'Don't be ridiculous! Of course he'll have you back,' Lily said. 'Get out there and find him. Between making pledges to the Almighty not to see him again and mistrusting him so badly, you've a helluva lot to make up to that poor fellow.'

Jane produced her handkerchief and wiped her eyes. Then handed the handkerchief to Lily to dry hers. 'Does that mean I'm not to go to the Army Ball?' she asked.

'Oh! Under no circumstances are you to miss the Ball,' Lily chuckled. 'Think about the fun we'll have afterwards dissecting it.'

'Big difference between a ceilidhe and an Army Ball,' Jane said. 'I wonder how Willie would feel about it? Would he give a damn?'

'Stop talking like that,' Lily said. As Jane was leaving, Lily stressed, 'Next time I see you, I want Willie to be with you.' Then forcefully, 'Do you hear me?'

Jane smiled nodding her agreement. Lily was in deadly earnest about herself and Willie getting back together.

The big question in Jane's mind now was, how she should go about contacting Willie? Should she write to him? How would she phrase the letter? What could she say by way of explanation? Should she voice her suspicions about him having another girlfriend? No. He think she was the jealous type. But then if she told him the real truth about her pledge to the Almighty, he'd probably think she was a raving lunatic; that is if he believed her at all. No, she decided, her best bet was to drop into the Tivoli Cinema casually and see him. It would be more favorable to meet face to face; that way she could see for herself his reaction when she suggested that they get back together. So much time had elapsed since she wrote that awful letter terminating their relationship. How could she be certain he still had the same feelings for her? Jane made the decision to go to the pictures in the Tivoli that night. Afterwards, she would lie in wait on the stairs leading to the Projection Room for Willie to come out.

Being a Monday night, the Tivoli was only half full. It seemed like a good picture, but Jane could hardly concentrate on it; her mind was in such turmoil thinking about what was going to happen afterwards. What if Willie didn't love her any more and didn't want a reconciliation? What if he did have another girlfriend? These thoughts tormented Jane throughout the picture. When 'The End' came on the screen and she realized the moment of truth had arrived, somehow her rubbery legs managed to get her out of the stalls and on to the stairs leading to the Projection Room. Filled with a mixture of fear and excitement, she waited for the door to open. Ten, fifteen minutes elapsed before the door eventually opened and a strange young man emerged.

Seeing what to his mind was a very ill-at-ease, attractive young woman, he asked her, 'Are you looking for someone?'

The only word Jane could rasp out was, 'Willie.'

'Oh, he's on vacation,' the young man said. 'I'm filling in for him.'

'For how long?' Jane asked.

'A week, I think,' the young man was vague. 'I couldn't be sure.'

'Has he gone out of town, do you know?' Jane asked in a quivering voice.

'Now, that I couldn't tell you,' the young man said. Then after locking the door of the Projection Room, he joined Jane on the stairs.

'Anything I can do to help?'

'No thanks,' Jane said, turning on her heel and scurrying away.

Stumbling down Francis Street, Jane thought miserably, God! can I ever get anything right? Tonight she'd got herself well and truly psyched up for an encounter with Willie. Now what should she do? I don't really have any option, she thought, putting a brave front on her disappointment, but to wait for Willie's return. Please God! don't let it be longer than a week. I can't wait to see him.

Jane's spare time for the rest of the week was taken up with preparations for the Army Dance. In many ways, it was a welcome distraction helping to keep her mind off Willie. The day following her visit to the hospital, our Nancy duly arrived into the Store to get her decision. After spending what she considered enough time hemming and hawing, Jane eventually indicated her willingness to attend.

'Have you a decent dress to wear?' our Nancy inquired querulously.

'I'll probably wear the bridesmaid's dress I wore at your wedding,' Jane said.

For seconds our Nancy looked apoplectic. 'You mean that awful taffeta thing the dressmaker made? You've got to be joking.'

'It's only one occasion,' Jane reasoned. 'The dress is there. It's handy. Why spend money on something I'll never wear again.'

'Nonetheless, we have to keep up appearances,' our Nancy said. 'The style at this Ball will blind ye. So whatever you wear has to be high fashion. I don't want you making a show of us,' she scoffed. 'For God's sake buy a dress in Switzers or in one of those exclusive boutiques in Anne Street.' Then waving her hand indicating the Henry Street store, she added, 'We don't want you wearing a dress from a two penny-halfpenny shop the likes of this one.'

Jane had to bite her tongue to keep from shouting at her, until you married Gerald, this two-penny-halfpenny store was good enough for you, particularly when you got your discount through me. But once again it was neither the time nor the place.

The search for the right dress was particularly frustrating. Lunchtimes, Jane tried Switzers and a number of boutiques in Anne Street and Grafton Street. But every dress that appealed to her was much to expensive. Imagine paying twenty-five or thirty pounds for a dress I'll wear once, she thought. It's all right for our Nancy: she's a social butterfly, flitting between army functions and soirées.

She finally settled on a dress she found in Clerys. Granted, it wasn't a classical model, like the ones she tried on in the upper class boutiques, but it looked fine on her. She liked the shade. Powder blue. It was quite flattering. More to the point, it was a reasonable price. Strangely during that time, her mother showed great interest in what she was going to wear. 'Now, if you're stuck for money,' she told her, 'don't hesitate to ask me. I'll give you whatever you need.'

On the night of the dance Jane took the tram to Beggar's Bush Barracks, carrying her new evening dress and her night attire in a small suitcase. The idea was she would dress for the dance in our Nancy's house and after the dance stay the night. As soon as they were all dressed and ready, around seven o'clock, Bernard would arrive and make Jane's acquaintance over drinks. Nancy was on her own when Jane, looking lovely in her new dress, eventually appeared in the drawing room.

Our Nancy's reaction was to stare incredulously at her. 'In the name of God,' she said, rude as you like, 'where did you get the dress?'

'In Clerys,' Jane said, feeling intensely annoyed at her fault finding. But determined not to show it. She wouldn't satisfy the bitch.

'It looks it,' our Nancy said derisively. 'Cheap!'

Just then Gerald, looking very handsome in his dress uniform, entered the room. 'My,' he said, looking admiringly at Jane, 'what a pretty dress; you'll have all the single officers chasing after you tonight.' Gerald made for the drinks trolley. 'What can I get you to drink, Jane?' he asked, as he poured himself a stiff one. Our Nancy was already holding a glass.

'Just a soda,' Jane said. Our Nancy continued to scrutinize Jane from top to toe. Jane knew she was doing her best to make her feel uncomfortable. When Gerald's back was turned, Jane couldn't resist the temptation to stick her tongue out right into our Nancy's face. What she couldn't say out loud, she could certainly show by action. Our Nancy wore a gold lame dress with a long gold feathery boa reaching down over her stomach endeavoring to disguise her pregnancy. This was news to Jane. As yet our Nancy hadn't announced this fact to the family.

Bernard duly arrived. He was a man of medium build, probably in his early thirties, Jane guessed. Personable and intelligent. Very English. Like Gerald, he looked particularly smart in his dress uniform. Inwardly Jane smiled. She couldn't help thinking about Lily's prediction: 'Maybe he'll be a runt of a man.' Mind you he wasn't a prince either.

Bernard looked with approval at Jane when they were introduced. After which he said, 'It's very kind of you to be my partner on such short notice.'

Before Jane could answer, Gerald at the drinks trolley said, 'Name your poison, Bernard.'

'Oh, make it a whiskey and soda; a small one,' Bernard said. 'As you know, I'm not a drinking man.'

After handing Bernard his drink, Gerald said to our Nancy, 'How about producing those savories I brought from the mess?'

'I thought they were for after the dance?' our Nancy said.

'We'll have no appetite for them then,' Gerald snapped at her. 'We'll be stuffed with a seven course dinner.'

'But I didn't put them in the oven to heat,' our Nancy pouted.

'Ach, bring them out anyway,' Gerald said garrulously. He was beginning to look the worst for drink. 'Dinner won't be served till after nine.'

With two more stiff drinks under Gerald's belt (the others having declined), the four left the house and walked the short distance to the building hosting the dance. To Jane's mind, the ballroom was like something out of a fairytale: a vivid and imaginative kaleidoscope, its ambiance festooned with decorations, iridescent lighting, multi coloured balloons in bunches and couples dancing (men in dress uniforms, ladies in high fashion.) Topping it off was a military band playing a wonderful Strauss waltz.

Standing at the door, Jane gawked awestruck. Until Bernard gently took her elbow and lead her to a table a distance away. The four joined two other young married couples. Very British. But nonetheless charming. However, straightaway Jane realized she had nothing in common with any of them. When the women, including our Nancy, weren't discussing cookery and gardening, the men were bragging about their drinking binges. Thankfully Bernard, albeit not much of a talker, was a keen dancer and a very good one. Jane and he danced most of the dances.

Meanwhile Jane noticed that our Nancy wasn't dancing. She put it down to the fact that she was pregnant. Until the music stopped for dinner and only seven of the people in the party assembled at the table. Gerald was missing. Then Jane spied him staggering from table to table chatting up people and generally making a nuisance of himself. This then explained why our Nancy wasn't dancing; Gerald was as drunk as a lord. He'd now arrived at a table occupied by officers bedecked in medals — the Army Brass. And just for good measure, he made advances towards one of the wives, pawing her in the process. Observing this, the husband —a Major General at least — shot out of his chair, furious. With a face filled with rage, he dragged Gerald physically back to his own table and pushed him into the empty chair. Undaunted, Gerald put his chin on his chest and fell asleep.

All of a sudden there was an outburst of chatter at their table. Everyone talked at the same time. The guests were obviously doing their best to cover their embarrassment. *The apple doesn't fall far from the tree,* Jane thought. Strange, though our Nancy wouldn't thank her for it, she couldn't help feeling sorry for her. But, for Jane, the big surprise of the evening was when Bernard asked her, during the last dance, if he could see her again? Though he had been particularly attentive to her throughout the evening, Jane had no wish to spend further time in his company. He was the strong, silent type; a type that didn't appeal to her. At her politest, she answered, 'My boyfriend will be back on Monday.' Then smiling sweetly to take the sting out of it, she added, 'I doubt he'd approve.'

Bernard's face dropped.

Chapter XXX

Due to the exigencies of the Cork project, on arrival in Dublin, Willie decided to seek Finbar out immediately. On the train the thought suddenly struck him that he knew precious little about the setting up and the running of a cinema. Granted, he was a good projectionist. But there was much more to it than that. In the first place, there was the business of purchasing a projector and lots of other equipment, all of which would have to come from abroad. That much he knew. Then there was the question of finding a specialist to install it. Many questions remained to be answered. For instance, where abroad did all this stuff come from? What was the situation regarding importation? He was annoyed with himself that he hadn't shown more interest or asked more questions when he worked for Finbar. God knows he had ample opportunity. But he failed to take advantage of it. But then, he thought, did I ever foresee owning my own cinema? Not in a million years. Finbar, who had organized and set up the Tivoli Cinema himself, would know about the complexities and difficulties facing Willie in his chosen career. He was, therefore, the obvious person to advise him. That was, of course, if he was willing? It was a big 'if.'

Being a Saturday night (the busiest night of the week in the cinema) Willie reckoned the place to find Finbar would be the Projection Room in the Tivoli Cinema.

Finbar greeted him with the words, 'What the hell are you doing back so soon? I didn't expect you till Monday.'

'I came back a bit early,' Willie said. 'I've something important to discuss with you.' Gazing around the room, he added, 'But this is not the place to do it.'

'What divilment have you been up to now?' Finbar asked, eyeing him suspiciously. 'Collins given you another mission?'

'No,' Willie said, 'it's nothing like that.' He moved towards the door. 'Please,' he entreated, 'have a pint with me in Nearys after the show?'

Finbar gave him a look that was hard to read. Then nodded acquiescence. 'Right,' he said.

As Willie nursed his pint at the counter in Nearys pub, he began to have misgivings. What if Finbar took his news the wrong way? What if he wasn't prepared to give him the help he desperately needed? If it was not forthcoming Willie envisioned a long drawn out process trying to learn the tricks of the trade the hard way. If he was to speed things up it was essential that he had Finbar's cooperation.

Finbar arrived. Willie ordered a pint of Guinness for him and they moved to a table.

'This had better be good.' Finbar fussed, looking at his watch. 'I've an appointment in O'Donovans in fifteen minutes.' Then more inquisitive, he asked, 'What's so important that it couldn't be discussed within the confines of the Projection Room?'

Willie got to the point immediately. 'I'm starting up my own cinema in Cork,' he said. There was a proud look in the set of his head and an immovable rectitude in the straight line of his lips.

For seconds Finbar was stunned. Then he came alive. Slapping Willie on the back goodnaturedly, he said, 'Well, good for you lad! When did this all come about?'

Willie proceeded to tell him, with relish, about the recent happenings in Cork. About the warehouse, the agreeable Bank Manager. In general, the whys and wherefores of the project. He held nothing back. Even included the fact that he was in love and wanted to get married. But concluded bitterly that the chances of this happening were very slim unless he branched out on his own. Though his body was stiff with tension, he spoke with conviction. He ended by saying, 'I don't have to tell you I'll need all the help you can give me.'

'Well, aren't you the secretive one!' Finbar said, smiling genially. 'I can't say but I have to admire your spirit and determination, lad.'

Willie found his words reassuring and relaxed a bit. 'I think a lot of the credit is due to my friend, Fiocra,' he said. 'If he hadn't pushed me so hard and done so much to help me, I doubt I'd have the courage.'

Finbar looked at his watch again. Pursed his lips thinking. Panic-stricken, Willie wondered, is he going to vamoose now and leave me dangling?

'Ah, feck him!' Finbar said more or less to himself. 'He can wait. This is much too interesting.' He lifted his head and addressed Willie. 'So tell me, Willie,' he said, 'how can I help in this most interesting enterprise of yours?'

Hearing his words, Willie's excited heart thumped in his chest. 'You're not annoyed with me for leaving the job?' he asked with a wry smile.

'Why would I be annoyed?' Finbar said without hesitation. 'Aren't you bettering yourself? And I've the greatest admiration for entrepreneurs: where would the world be without them?' Finbar scratched his head. 'So anyway,' he repeated, 'what can I do to help?'

'Well,' Willie said, 'I could do with your help, first, with regard to information about the technical side. How do I go about getting a projector, generator, films? Roughly what the cost is? After that I'd need an expert to set things up.' Then, with a wily grin, he added, 'Remember, I can afford to pay.'

Finbar pondered the questions, then said, 'I think it would simplify matters if you and I spent sometime tomorrow afternoon going through our files and making notes. We could then take it from there.'

Willie clapped Finbar on the shoulder, 'Gosh!' he said, 'you're a wonderful friend.'

'You're only discovering that now?' Finbar said, pretending surprise. He stood up. 'Got to go,' he said. 'Meet me outside the Tivoli tomorrow at three.'

Later, when Willie was leaving Nearys, he felt like he was walking on air.

Next day, Sunday at lunchtime, Willie dropped into Flanagan's pub hoping to run into Collins. But the snug was empty. Daniel, the barman, quietly informed him, 'He hasn't been here for the past two Sundays, because — surprise! Surprise! — we got raided by the Tans.'

'Any idea where I might find him?' Willie asked, disappointed.

'There's a list.'

'Give it to me,' Willie said.

'O'Donovans, Vaughan's Hotel, O'Sheas, Meaghers,' Daniel said. 'Take your pick.' Then more positive, he whispered, 'my guess would be Vaughan's.'

Willie took the tram to the Pillar and walked the rest of the way to Vaughan's Hotel on Parnell Square. When he came to the corner of Parnell Street, he wondered would fate ever be kind enough to allow him to bump into Jane? He wanted so much to see her lovely face again, to hold her in his arms and reassure her about the future; a future, hopefully, they would share together. But no such luck.

Trying to get into the bar in Vaughan's Hotel was like trying to get into the National Mint. Though he could hear lots of chatter coming from the bar, the door was locked. And when he inquired at the Reception, the Clerk told him the bar was open only to residents. Then adding insult to injury, when he failed to find Willie's name in the Register, he asked him to leave.

Trying to work a quick one, Willie said, 'But I'm supposed to meet Mick here.'

'Mick?' The clerk looked at him, baffled.

'Yes,' Willie said confidently. 'Mick Collins.'

The clerk consulted the register again. 'Sorry,' he said, 'there's no guest by that name registered.'

'Ach,' Willie said, looking very agitated. 'He's in there. I can hear his voice.'

'I'm sorry,' the clerk repeated, 'but you can't go in.'

Just then Harry Boland came out of the Men's Room. 'The hard,

Willie!' he said slapping Willie on the back. 'Did you have a nice holiday?'

The reception clerk addressed him. 'You know this man?' he asked.

'Course,' Harry answered enthusiastically. 'Isn't he Mick's right-hand man.'

Accompanied by Boland, Willie entered the bar through the back door. Collins hailed him, 'Home is the hero!' he said. 'Great to have you back. How was the holiday?' He was surrounded by a number of men, some of whose faces were familiar, some not. Willie could see that it wasn't going to be easy to get Collins on his own. Meantime Collins ordered a pint of Guinness for Willie from the bar man.

'I called into Flanagans,' Willie said by way of conversation. 'But apparently they've been raided the last two Sundays.'

'Tell me about it!' Collins said, waving his hand at the group surrounding him. 'Yeah,' he said, 'thanks to my friends here, we were tipped off in time.'

It was then that Willie realized that most of the people present were part of Collins' intelligence network. Hence the strict security outside.

Sitting beside Willie, Boland struck up a conversation with him. 'Did you go out of town for your holiday, Willie?' he asked.

'Yeah,' Willie said, 'I went to Cork.'

'So you don't know about the mysterious Lieutenant G?' Boland asked.

'No,' Willie looked baffled. 'Never heard of him. Who is he?'

'Mick is keeping that one close to the chest,' Boland lowered his voice. 'He's a recent addition to Mick's network. As far as I can ascertain, Lieutenant G. is a member of the British Military Intelligence in Ireland.' Boland then added slyly. 'As well as being one of Mick's chief Agents, it seems he's especially good at imparting information about the relevant and forthcoming activities of British military intelligence, Auxiliaries and the Black and Tans. Though none of us, except Mick, knows what he looks like, apparently he's a real ace in the hole.'

'It sounds like things are hotting up in Dublin,' Willie said. 'What with all those Balbriggan houses being burnt down.'

'That's just the start of it,' Boland said. Then went on to say, 'You've probably noticed the Auxiliary's Crossley Tenders in the streets of Dublin. It would seem their policy is to shoot first and ask questions afterwards.' Boland shook his head dolefully. 'Their atrocities are not far removed from those perpetrated by the Black and Tans — who everyone knows are mostly ex-inmates of the English prisons. But the fact that the Auxiliaries are ex-officers, you'd think their actions would be morally better.'

'It seems they're all tarred with the same brush,' Willie said sardonically.

'Right! You get the point,' Boland said. 'However, the good news is, this Lieutenant G. is doing a massive job keeping Mick out of trouble.'

'Why all the mystery about Lieutenant G. among Mick's friends?' Willie asked.

'According to Mick,' Boland said, 'he ranks very high among British spies. That means the less the rest of us know about him, the safer we'll be.' He hesitated a second then said, 'Enough about politics, how was your holiday?'

'T'was more of a busman's holiday than a recreational one.' Willie now made up his mind to take the plunge. 'I've decided to open my own cinema in Cork,' he said bluntly. There it was out at last.

'Well, good for you!' Boland said. 'I always felt you were wasted in that job; that you weren't fulfilling your potential. Take it from one who knows. There's nothing like owning your own business.' Boland turned towards Collins and let out a roar at him. 'Did you hear that Mick?' Collins stopped talking and turned his attention to Boland. 'Willie's been telling me he's opening his own cinema in Cork,' Boland said. 'Isn't that stupendous?'

That really got Collins' attention. He looked hard at Willie. For the first time he was seeing him in a different light. There was admiration in his eyes. 'Well, bully for you, By!' he exclaimed. 'I suppose that means we're losing you?'

'Fraid so,' Willie said.

'When?' Collins asked.

'As soon as I've finished clearing up a few messy situations here in Dublin; which include your office,' Willie said facetiously. 'As things seem to be moving faster than expected in Cork, I'm hoping to get back there in two weeks.'

Collins stood up, lifted his chair over beside Willie's. 'This is a bit of a shock, By!' he said in a low tone. 'Two weeks...that fast? How did you manage to get organized so quickly?'

'As you well know, Mick, I'm one of those who doesn't let the grass grow under his feet,' Willie said jokingly. 'The opportunity presented itself and I grabbed it.'

Collins called George, the bar man. 'Bring us a bottle of your best champagne,' he said to him. 'We've something to celebrate.'

§

As Willie was crossing Henry Street en route to the Henry Street Department Store, he saw Jane emerging through the entrance. His long, loping strides attracted Jane's attention. For a moment her breath caught in her throat. Her eyes met his. Her face crumbled into tears as she ran towards him. Willie barely had time to open his arms before she collapsed into them.

'It's Lily?' Willie asked fearfully. Jane was weeping too hard to answer. 'For God's sake tell me,' Willie gasped, 'is Lily all right?'

Jane's body began to shake. Eventually she looked up at him with anxious eyes. 'Lily's fine,' she said. 'It's what I did to you,' she sobbed. 'I'm so sorry! So terribly sorry!' she kept repeating it through her tears.

'It's all right!' Willie reassured her, stroking her hair lovingly. 'It's all right, darling.'

'Can you ever forgive me?' Jane asked. She looked so stricken, Willie grabbed her and kissed her hard on the lips. She kissed him back with fierce passion. At that moment the words reverberating in

Willie's mind were, she still loves me.

When he released her, he said passionately, 'Jane, I love you, I always will. I'm never going to leave you again, whether you like it or not.'

'Oh Willie!' Jane said exuberantly, 'you've no idea how much my heart overflows with love for you.' She wanted to freeze this moment in time.

Passersby stared thinking here was a spectacle worth watching. Gradually, Willie became conscious of their stares. 'Jane,' he said, taking charge, 'come with me.'

'To the ends of the earth!' Jane said. Suddenly she was radiant, glowing with that light that comes from within.

'No, not that far,' Willie said with a smile, effectively diffusing the situation. 'Just as far as Wynns Hotel.'

Jane's answer was a glowing smile so rewarding that Willie felt like she'd given him a present. They started walking. Suddenly Jane stopped dead. 'But it's after six,' she said. 'Shouldn't you be at work?'

'Not any more,' Willie declared. Then when he saw her expression of surprise, he added, 'Don't ask any questions till we get to Wynns Hotel.

Wynns homely Hotel, filled with old fashioned, upholstered furniture and lots of mahogany, was normally the favorite haunt of people from the country. But because of the 'troubles,' except for the odd British 'top brass' uniform, it was virtually empty. With the result that Willie and Jane were escorted by the Head Waiter to a choice table in the main dining room. After consulting the menu they ordered the 'set dinner.'

Jane looked around her in wonder. 'Willie,' she said, her eyes sparkling with curiosity, 'this is going to cost a fortune; have you come into money?'

'No, not necessarily,' Willie said casually. 'But I anticipate making a lot of money in the near future.' He couldn't hold back the avalanche of his eagerness to tell her. Words rushed over one another, he was so anxious to get it all out at once. He told her about the

Cork enterprise, from the day he met Fiocra on the train to yesterday afternoon (Sunday) when he got all the necessary information about the process from Finbar.

Listening to Willie, Jane couldn't help thinking that he reminded her of a schoolboy who'd just scored the winning goal.

Willie watched Jane's reaction as he spoke. Though her eyes sparkled with interest, her face gave nothing away.

As for Jane, though she was eager to ask countless questions, instinct warned her not to.

Willie grasped her hand. 'Jane,' he said, 'we can now be married.'

Before she could stop herself, Jane blurted out, 'Does that mean we'll have to live in Cork?' A shadow crossed her face.

Willie threw her a troubled look. 'Would you mind that?' he asked, the tremor in his voice betraying his nervousness.

'Course not,' Jane said expansively but not very convincingly.

'You're sure?' Willie asked with anxious eyes. 'Because my darling, if you're not happy about it, I'll give up the whole idea.'

'Oh! No! No! No!' Jane hastened to assure him. 'You're halfway towards achieving your goal already; you must go on.'

The waiter arrived with their soup.

After he left, Willie said, 'But I want you by my side, Jane. You're not only my love but my life.'

Jane raised her eyes from her soup. 'Willie, I love you so much it hurts,' she said, passionately. 'I've been through hell these past few months.'

'If we weren't in such a public place,' Willie said, 'I'd take you in my arms and show you how much I adore you. During our separation I realized I couldn't go on living without you.' Then impulsively, he said, 'Jane, let's do it! Let's announce our engagement!' As he waited for her answer, doubts gnawed at him. Was he asking too much of a sacrifice of her? Expecting her to leave her native Dublin, her family and her friends?

Jane cogitated before answering him. Then with a burst of laughter, she said, 'Willie, whither thou goest, I go with you. Let's announce our engagement immediately.'

§

Standing behind the counter serving a customer that morning, Mary was taken completely by surprise when she saw her sister, Jude, looking absolutely stricken, coming through the door. Before she had time to greet her, Jude burst into tears.

Eventually she moaned, 'Sweet Jesus! Mary, I'm in terrible trouble. I feel like I'm slipping down a cliff and I can't stop it. Please! Please! You've got to help me!' The muscles of her jaw twitched in anguish. Jude's statement got everyone's attention in the O'Dwyer Family Dairy; customers and staff alike. For seconds there was silence and business came to a halt. Never before had Mary seen her sister so upset. Normally, Jude was easy going and laid back. Something horrible must have happened.

Mary rushed out from behind the counter. Taking Jude by the arm, she lead her to the office at the back. 'In the name of God Jude,' she asked anxiously, 'what is the matter?'

Jude looked like she was drenched in panic. Tears welled up in her eyes as she answered, 'I don't know where to start.'

'Try starting at the beginning,' Mary said calmly.

'It's Dermot!' Jude said. Dermot was her nineteen-year-old son.

'What about Dermot?' Mary asked.

'I think he's in terrible trouble.'

'What has he done?'

'Himself and two other lads who work for Collins' secret army, stayed the night at my house last night,' Jude said. Then added, 'Once in a while, not very often, they hold meetings at my house that run late. On these nights, some of them sleep on the floor,' Jude hesitated.

'Well, go on,' Mary urged. Though she was shocked to the core by the revelation of her nephew's involvement with the IRA, she tried to act normal and not to show it.

'Around nine o'clock this morning,' Jude continued, 'There was an almighty hammering on the front door. The pounding was so loud I'd visions of the door caving in. When I eventually answered it, four of those Black and Tans nearly knocked me down rushing past me. One shouted, 'Where are they?' Three of them ran all over the house, into the back, up the stairs, out the back door. A fourth one stayed behind and ordered me out, at gun point, saying, 'for your own safety, Mam, get out of here and don't come back.' "

'Sit down for a minute,' Mary said. 'I'll get you a cup of tea.'

'No, I can't sit down and I don't want tea,' Jude said, now absolutely frantic with worry. 'I've got to do something about those boys, and do it soon.'

Mary spoke in a stern voice. 'The first thing you've got to do is stop being so panic-stricken,' she said. 'Chances are the three were taken into custody. The worst that can happen is they'll do a stretch in jail.' Mary was amazed at her own calmness. But first and foremost she had to put Jude's mind at ease. 'Whether you like it or not,' Mary said resolutely, moving towards the door, 'you're having a cup of tea. Afterwards, I'll accompany you back to the house.'

On arrival at Jude's house in Manor Street, they found both front and back doors bolted. So Jude's latch key was useless. Looking terrified, Jude said, 'The fact that the doors are bolted on the inside means the Tans are still in there. God only knows what they're doing to those lads, they could be torturing them?'

'On the other hand,' Mary said optimistically, 'maybe t'was your lads who bolted the doors. Why don't we knock the knocker really hard?'

'I wouldn't if I was you.' A voice came from behind them. It belonged to May O'Reilly, Jude's next door neighbor. She was standing at the bottom of the steps. 'I'm sorry to tell you this, Jude,' she said apologetically, 'but I heard shots ring out in your house sometime ago. To be honest with you, I was afraid to put my nose outside the door. Those Tans have a terrible reputation.'

'How did you know they were Tans?' Mary asked very curious.

'I saw them going in earlier: sure, you'd want to be stone deaf not hear the racket they were making banging on Jude's front door.'

'Sweet Jesus!' Jude said, visibly shattered. She would have collapsed there and then on the steps had Mary not caught her in time.

'I'll fetch some brandy,' May O'Reilly said, rushing away as Mary lowered Jude on to the steps. Within minutes May was back with a bottle of brandy and some glasses. Mary's face was chalk white with the shock of it all. 'You could do with a tincture yourself, Mrs.,' May said to Mary, as she poured the two glasses of brandy.

The brandy helped to restore Jude's strength enough to walk to her neighbor's house where the three women discussed what to do next. 'It's useless going to the police,' May O'Reilly said, nodding her head dismally. 'They won't lift a finger to help; they're in league with the Tans.'

Suddenly Mary remembered the nice, decent British Officer who helped her to get the Pass during the time of the Rising. Afterwards, he came into the shop a few times and they became quite friendly. His name was on the pass, which, thank God, she'd put safely away, just in case.

'Maybe,' Mary said out loud, 'I could talk to that British Officer who helped me to get a Pass during the Rising.'

'He'd be your best bet,' May O'Reilly said. 'With the lawlessness that exists in our city presently, the only dependable people left to approach are in the British Army.'

'Look,' Mary said to May, 'is it all right if I leave Jude with you for an hour or so?'

'Oh, certainly, certainly,' May said. 'She can stay as long as she needs.'

Jude, who up to now had been staring into space, put in, 'Our Peggy will be coming home from school soon; she mustn't go near the house.'

'Don't worry, Jude,' May reassured her, 'I'll keep an eye out for her.' She turned to Mary. 'You go, Mrs.,' she said, 'and do whatever you can.'

'I'll be as quick as possible,' Mary told the two women, 'but unfortunately I'll have to go back to Parnell Street to find that officer's name.' She left with a heavy heart.

Mary took the tram from Manor Street back to Parnell Street. On the tram she decided to enlist Peter's help in her search for this particular officer. Peter would know what to do. As Usual Peter wasn't in his office and wasn't due back till five o'clock. T'was no surprise to Mary. When was she ever lucky enough to catch him in his office when she visited in the past? Nevertheless, though she felt every moment was precious, she was prepared to wait for his arrival. She thought, God only knows what's happening to those three lads at this moment at the mercy of those awful Tans.

Thankfully, Peter arrived earlier than expected.

'Oh, thank God! Peter! You're here,' Mary vociferated when he came through the door.

Peter could see that his mother was in a frightful state of tension and anxiety. 'In the name of God,' he exclaimed, 'what's wrong, Mother?'

Mary explained the situation as best she could. As the story unfolded, she could see the blood draining from Peter's face.

When she finished, he flopped down in his chair, saying, 'God! This is terrible news.'

Mary then proceeded to tell him what she thought the solution might be; namely, that if she could contact this Captain Charles Garland, that he might be able to help.

Peter agreed with her. After finding the number in the telephone directory, as he lifted the phone, he said to Mary, 'Right, I'll put a call through to Army Headquarters and see if we can track him down.'

He gave the number to the telephonist, then waited patiently to be connected. There was a pause. Then Mary heard him introducing himself to the person on the other end of the line. After another pause, Peter went on to explain that he needed to get in touch with Captain Charles Garland. When Mary saw him write a number on a pad, she assumed that Captain Garland could be reached at that number. Peter thanked the person he'd been speaking to, clicked the phone and asked the telephonist to get the number he'd written on the pad.

After a few seconds Peter was talking to someone. 'Yes, I'd like to speak to Captain Charles Garland. Would he be there by any chance?'

As Mary listened, Peter put his hand over the mouthpiece. 'They're transferring me to his office,' he said with a bright smile. 'Yes,' he said into the phone. 'Is that Captain Garland? It is?' Peter couldn't hide his excitement. 'Well, my name is Peter O'Dwyer. I'm a journalist with the Independent Newspapers. You don't know me, but you do know my mother.' Pause. 'Oh you remember her?' Pause. 'Good. Well, she's here with me in my office. I'm afraid she's very much in need of your help. Could you hold the line, please.' Peter handed the phone to Mary.

'Hello, this is Mary O'Dwyer,' Mary said into the phone in a very strained voice.

'Yes, Mrs O'Dwyer, how can I help you?' Garland's voice came through the phone. Mary proceeded to tell him about her sister's son and his friends' predicament. It was no accident, however, that she left out the bit about their involvement with the IRA. 'It sounds really serious, Mrs. O'Dwyer,' Garland said, in a somber voice. 'But you must know that the Tans' procedures do not have the approval of the regular British Army. However, that's neither here nor there.' He paused, then went on. 'I'll first have to consult my Commanding Officer, who unfortunately isn't here at the moment. And I'm not sure when he'll be back.'

'Is he out of town?' Mary asked, trying hard to keep the tremble out of her voice.

'No, he's around, but he's not here today,' Garland said. 'Could I phone you tomorrow morning? Normally I see him in the mornings.'

'I'm afraid I'm not on the phone,' Mary answered. 'But you could phone my son, Peter O'Dwyer, here at the Independent newspaper office.'

'Right, I'll do that.'

'Is that the very best you can do?' Mary's voice did tremble this time.

'Sorry, Mrs. O'Dwyer,' Garland said, 'but I can't make decisions without first consulting my commanding officer. I need to have his authorization, you understand?'

'I do understand,' Mary said, 'but do you understand that my sister and her family are locked out of their home and afraid to go near it for fear of being shot by the Tans?'

'Your sister and her family have my complete and absolute sympathy, Mrs. O'Dwyer,' Garland said. 'Be assured that somehow or other we'll find a way to resolve this problem. Leave it with me.'

On the tram going back to Manor Street, Mary was worried sick having to tell Jude that nothing could be done until tomorrow morning. Meanwhile she was going to insist that Jude and Peggy came to stay at her home. However, when she arrived to the O'Reilly house her plans were incontrovertibly changed; May insisted that Jude and Peggy stay with her.

'It makes sense,' she asserted, 'that Jude would want to stay close to the house and watch developments.' She had a point.

First thing next morning, after Mass and breakfast, Mary was in Peter's office. He'd barely arrived.

'Did the captain phone yet?' Mary asked anxiously.

Peter looked at his watch. 'It's only eight o'clock, Mother,' he said. 'Give him a break.'

'Do you mind if I wait here?' Mary asked, indicating the spare chair.

'Be my guest,' Peter answered, starting to type. For the next hour and a half, every time the phone rang Mary, unnerved, jumped in the chair. With each call she kept telling herself, this has got to be it. The call eventually came just after ten o'clock. 'Yes, Captain,' Peter said answering the phone. When Mary heard the word 'captain' her heart practically jumped into her throat. 'Hold on,' Peter said into the phone. 'She's here now. I'll let you speak to her.'

Mary's hand trembled as she took the phone from Peter. 'Yes Captain,' she said, her voice practically reduced to a whisper. 'This is Mary O'Dwyer.'

'Well, now, Mrs. O'Dwyer, what my Commanding Officer recommends is that I take some of my men over to that address and demand to be allowed in. If they don't comply with the order, we'll be forced to break down a door; preferably the back door.'

'Oh, thank you, Captain,' Mary said. 'I really do appreciate you doing this for us.' Then she asked, 'Roughly what time do you think you'll be there?' Her voice quivered fiercely as she asked the question.

'Well, it's just after ten now,' the Captain said. 'We should be there in an hour or so.'

'The blessings of God on you, Captain,' Mary said fervently. 'I'll see you there.'

'I could do with His blessings all right,' the captain said, laughing.

'Not a sign of life next door,' May told Mary when she arrived at her house. 'I don't like the look of it at all.'

'Oh, now, please God,' Mary said, 'the British Army will be here soon and the mystery will be solved.'

Strangely when Captain Garland and twelve of his soldiers arrived, he insisted that all civilians stay indoors and stay away from the house. May, however — a nosy parker at the best of times — found a spot behind a bush in her garden where she could surreptitiously observe what was happening. After a while she charged back into the house and announced, 'They've broken down the back door. Soon we should know what's going on in there.'

Minutes later there was a knock on the hall door. May opened the door to Captain Garland.

'Is Mrs. O'Dwyer around?' he asked in a very solemn voice.

'Yes,' Mary said coming into the hall.

'I'd like to talk to you in private,' Captain Garland said.

'Come into the front room,' Mary invited him. Suddenly her stomach began to churn. Instinct told her he was the bearer of bad news.

After closing the door behind him, Captain Garland turned to Mary and said gravely, 'I'm afraid, Mrs. O'Dwyer, I've very bad news for the parents of those boys next door.'

Mary's hand flew to her throat. 'What is it?' she gasped.

'All three are dead,' Garland said. 'I presume your sister's son is one of them. Apparently they were shot as they tried to escape.'

'Oh my God!' Mary cried out. 'How am I ever going to tell Jude?'

The Captain sighed mournfully. 'I think neither she, nor any of the other parents, should see that sight next door,' he said emphatically. 'It's absolutely harrowing and will haunt them the rest of their days.' The Captain had a thought, 'By the way,' he said, 'where is Mr. McCarthy?'

'Peather, Jude's husband,' Mary said. 'I believe he's in Donegal; he's a traveling salesman. And he's not due back till the weekend.'

'You'll need to get him back immediately,' the captain said. 'In the meantime, if Mrs. McCarthy will permit it, I'll arrange for an ambulance to take the bodies away. That way she can return to her home.'

'Am I permitted to go next door before the bodies are removed?' Mary asked.

'Oh, I'm not forbidding anyone access,' the Captain said. 'I'm just trying to spare people suffering, particularly the parents.'

'Knowing Jude, I'd say she'd want to see for herself,' Mary said.

'I'll be guided by you, Mrs. O'Dwyer,' the captain agreed.

Mary now had the burden of breaking the grim news to Jude.

However, Jude had instinctively guessed already. She met Mary at the door on her way into the back room. 'I know,' she said desolately. 'Dermot is dead.' Mary put her arms around her and they both cried bitterly. 'Where is he?' Jude asked. 'I must see him,' she wailed.

'He's next door,' Mary said. 'But the Captain strongly advises against you seeing him.'

'I don't care what the Captain says,' Jude cried out, 'I want to see my son.'

To say the scene was gruesome would be an understatement. The three bodies, were positioned on different parts of the stairs, where they had evidently been shot as they tried to escape. Each of them had been shot in the head. The walls and the stairs were splattered with blood and brains.

Jude let out a piercing scream when she saw Dermot's body. 'Oh, Sweet Jesus!' she shrieked, 'How could you let this happen?'

Mary and May took her bodily away from the scene into next door. Shortly afterwards an ambulance arrived and removed the bodies.

§

When Jane arrived home, she had excitement written all over her. She couldn't wait to see Lily. She found her sister in bed fast asleep; obviously knocked out by her nightly sedative. After all, she was only home from the hospital three days. Jane was torn with guilt about disturbing her. But reckoned that Lily would be so thrilled to hear her marvelous news, she would undoubtedly forgive her. Nothing could interfere with Jane's radiance as she talked up a storm telling Lily the details of what transpired between Willie and herself. However, as she excitedly recounted the happenings of the day, she was ill prepared for Lily's reaction. There was no happy response. No throwing her arms around Jane congratulating her. Just a blank stare. Jane thought, of course, it's the effects of the sedative. Until she saw a tear trickle down Lily's face. Suddenly she felt very fearful.

Stopping dead, she said anxiously, 'My God, Lily! are you feeling all right?'

'I feel fine.' Lily pointedly grasped Jane's arm. 'I couldn't be more thrilled about yourself and Willie,' she said, 'but I take it you haven't heard the news about our cousin, Dermot?' Though her face showed terrible distress, she made an effort to be calm and factual.

'No, has something happened to him?' Jane asked, alarmed.

'Yes,' Lily said bitterly. 'Himself and two of his friends were found dead in Aunt Jude's house; each of them shot through the head by the Tans.'

'Oh, my God!' Jane was so horror struck, she felt faint. 'When did this happen?' she asked in a hoarse voice.

'It was discovered this afternoon,' Lily said. 'Apparently the Tans arrived at Aunt Jude's house yesterday morning looking for the lads and ordered Aunt Jude out of the house. Then,' Lily went on, 'when Mother and Aunt Jude went back to the house in the afternoon, they couldn't get in; all the outside doors were bolted on the inside.'

'You mean to say,' Jane put in, 'that all day yesterday Mother knew about Aunt Jude being locked out by the Tans and never said a word to anyone in this house.'

'Not a syllable,' Lily said, 'though I did notice she was acting very strange, continually pacing back and forth between the office and the shop; she seemed very disturbed.'

'Yeah,' Jane said. 'I noticed that too; t'was like she was disoriented. But tell me,' Jane said, 'how did Aunt Jude eventually find out about Dermot and the other lads?'

Lily went on to tell the whole story about Captain Garland and how he had assisted by bringing British soldiers to Aunt Jude's house and breaking down the back door. Finished telling Jane the facts, she suddenly burst out, 'Oh, Jane! Thank God your Willie is going into the picture business and getting out of the IRA.' Her face expressed the relief she was feeling. 'Those Tans are absolute devils.'

'Amen to that,' Jane said. 'This is dreadful news.'

'It seems a shame,' Lily said, giving a tremulous smile, 'that after all yourself and Willie have been through, you'll now have to keep quiet about your engagement. Because it's going to be an excruciating time for the family.'

'It's certainly not the time for announcing engagements,' Jane said sensibly. 'But who am I to complain?' She shook her head dismally. 'It's a minor set back compared with what Aunt Jude must be going through. Imagine seeing such a grizzly sight; her first son sprawled dead on the stairs. It doesn't bear thinking about.'

'Mother too,' Lily said. 'Telling us, afterwards, she was so upset; she looked absolutely traumatized. But despite the horror of it all, she was a tower of strength for Aunt Jude.'

'Uncle Peadar isn't around?' Jane asked.

'No, apparently he's in Donegal on business,' Lily said. 'One of the first things Mother did was send him a telegram.'

'Mother's staying the night with Jude?'

'She is.'

'It's bound to bring back memories of Jody's death.' Jane said mournfully.

'I suppose it is,' Lily agreed. 'But remember Jody's death was an accident. This atrocity was deliberate,' Lily said bitterly. 'It'll be much harder to bear.'

§

When Jane and Willie were having lunch in their retreat next day, after telling him the full story about her cousin, Jane said in somber undertones, 'Trouble is because of the fact that Dermot was shot by the Tans, the incident has to be kept quiet.'

'For security reasons?' Willie said.

'Aye, and not to attract unwanted attention,' Jane answered.

'They're not even publishing his death in the newspapers. The funeral will be private.'

'I understand,' Willie gave a pitying shake of his head. 'My God! It's a terrible tragedy for that family and the other families.'

'Thank God, Willie, you're getting away from Collins,' Jane blurted out. 'You could be next.'

'No, Jane,' Willie said very positively. 'The one good thing about working for Collins was that he was always tipped off in advance by his network about misfortunes that were about to befall him or his associates. I only realized recently that, in effect, while I worked for Collins I was safe as a house under the umbrella of his network.'

'It means we won't be able to announce our engagement for some time,' Jane said regretfully. 'But when I think of Aunt Jude''s agony, it's little to ask.' She was on the edge of tears.

'I fully agree,' Willie said. 'Considering that family's suffering at the moment, we should be thankful to God for what we've got.' He hesitated, then said, 'I imagine you won't be expecting me to attend the funeral or the house. However, I will send a Mass Card.'

Jane made a gesture of frustration. 'Yes, it might be best if you didn't put in an appearance,' she said, then uttered achingly, 'Oh Willie! I so wanted to let everyone know about our engagement. I was even thinking about an engagement party before I got this awful news.'

Willie grasped her hand. 'Darling, he said soothingly, 'we just have to be patient a little longer.'

Chapter XXXI

Though Willie was going to miss Jane desperately, he was glad to be getting out of the city and back to his pet project in Cork. It had taken him nearly three weeks to extricate himself. What with all the lists he had to make for Collins, to enable him to maintain the order Willie had established in his many offices. Along with that there was the daunting task of finding an Agent who could order and import the cinematic equipment. This proved a big problem: a case of being continually referred from one Agent to another. He and Finbar did the rounds for at least two weeks. It was slow and frustrating, not unlike a wild goose chase. But then, as Finbar ably put it, 'What can you expect? Ireland isn't overrun with cinemas; it's not every day of the week that Agents get this type of inquiry.'

Towards the end of the second week Willie was bordering on despair. Then suddenly Finbar's determination paid off. He found the right Agent. Thank God for Finbar! Not only had he found the Agent, but he was there to specify the requirements in detail. During the interview Willie was relieved to learn that the equipment could be delivered directly to Cork. But then came the bad news. 'However,' the Agent said, 'there will be at least two months delay in the delivery.'

Another reason why Willie was glad to leave Dublin was political. Not a day went by that he didn't hear of some atrocious incident in the city; incidents which invariably involved either the Tans or the Auxiliaries. People were being shot down in the streets, innocent bystanders killed in the crossfire. It was no longer safe to walk the streets of Dublin. His one regret was not being able to get Jane away from it all. He was worried sick about her safety.

Two days before he left, at Jane's request, he dropped in to say good-bye to Peter in his office. There a big surprise awaited him.

Barely in the door, Peter handed him an envelope, saying, 'Jane has been talking to me. She told me about your engagement and how the announcement has to be postponed. She also brought me up to date on how things are with the cinema in Cork. Sounds great, Willie!' he said with real enthusiasm. 'Congratulations.'

Willie opened the envelope. To his amazement it contained Peter's personal check for one hundred pounds. For seconds he looked at it spellbound, then declared defiantly, 'I can't take this.'

Peter laughed, ignoring Willie's remark. 'As promised, that's the mother's inadvertent contribution. Of course it'll have to be our secret: on no account must it be shared with anyone else, not even your bride-to-be.'

'I still can't take it,' Willie avowed, throwing the check carelessly on the desk.

'Not even to buy a pianola for Jane,' Peter said, coaxingly. 'When you're married and running the cinema would you deny her the opportunity to entertain the picture-goers, not to mention the picture-goers themselves, the pleasure they'd get out of it?' Willie was momentarily speechless. 'Oh, for heaven's sake! Take it, Willie,' Peter insisted.

Willie got his voice back. 'Sorry, Peter,' he said. 'I must sound very ungrateful.'

'As a matter of fact, you do,' Peter said trying to sound truculent, until his face broke into a grin. 'Think about Jane's surprise and joy when she finds a pianola waiting for her in your cinema; you know how much she loves playing the piano.'

'Well, if you put it that way,' Willie said, taking the check back off the table, 'how can I refuse.' For the first time in a long time, he felt a warm glow surge through him.

'You must let me have your address in Cork when you get settled,' Peter said. 'I frequently get assignments there.' He was interrupted by the telephone ringing. Before picking up, he extended his hand to Willie. As they shook hands Peter said with an exaggerated grin,

'So you haven' seen the last of me yet. Good luck, Willie.'

Another bright spot was Sadie's farewell party the Saturday night before he left. It was brilliant; the food was wonderful as was the company and the music. Best of all was the fact that it got Jane away for a few hours from the melancholia and the fear that existed in the family home since the cousin's tragic death. But saying good-bye that last night was heartbreaking for both of them.

On his arrival in Cork, Willie resolved to get his cinema up and running as quickly as possible. It didn't matter how much effort it took; he'd work day and night if necessary. Next morning he hardly recognized the warehouse: it had undergone such a metamorphosis. It transpired that Conor was a real workhorse. In addition, he had a team of two other work horses helping him.

'They don't want any pay,' Conor hastened to inform Willie with a wily grin, 'free passes to the pictures when the cinema is in business, will suffice.'

Bemused, Willie smiled and decided that the question of pay would be trashed out later.

The painting of the interior in black was complete. Further, to give authenticity to the place, the youngest lad—a schoolboy named Liam—had brought in a pair of heavily lined, rich, red curtains (about to be given away by his mother, he contended.) These curtains had been strung up by the lads on a track on the wall where they assumed the screen would be positioned. It was very effective. It made the interior look more and more like a real cinema.

Meanwhile, Niall—the other helper—a carpenter by trade, had done some rough sketches of what he thought needed to be done inside and outside the building. Included was a sketch of a Lobby Entrance, complete with Ticket Office. Besides that, he'd drawn sketches of how the front of the building could be enhanced and decorated to make it look more like a cinema. Willie was amazed at the progress the lads had made in his absence. More amazing was the fact that both Niall and Liam were determined to give their services free. It all boiled down to the enthusiasm they felt about having a cinema in Cork. However, Willie decided there'd be none of this no payment business. Whether they liked it or not they would be paid, not only in free passes, but in money. But when it came to the crunch of hacking out a financial arrangement with them, despite the hard work they'd put in during the past three weeks, they were adamant about not being paid.

Niall, the carpenter told Willie, 'I've a full-time job and can only work nights and weekends.' Then he added, 'my working part-time on this job might not be to you liking. Maybe you'd prefer to have a carpenter who works full time?'

'Do you think you could do the job in two months?' Willie asked. This young man was so hard working and sounded so honest, he felt he could trust him implicitly.

'Oh definitely,' Niall assured him, his eyes lighting up at the prospect. 'It's such a wonderful challenge.'

Niall and Liam, continued to stick to their guns about not accepting money. Until Willie finally said, 'All right, why don't we make it a lump sum payment when every thing's finished?'

Niall and Liam went into a huddle to discuss Willie's proposition. Then Niall, acting as spokesman, addressed Willie. 'As long as we get the free passes to the pictures, we'll accept the lump sum when the job is finished,' he said, sounding like he was doing himself a favor.

It was then Willie realized that these lads measured the value of their work in free passes, not in money.

'The free passes will definitely be yours,' Willie answered. Then shaking the two lads hands, asked, 'Do we have a bargain?'

'Sure,' they both answered in concert, looking very pleased with themselves.

Later when Conor joined the group, he inquired of Willie, 'Have you decided on a name for the cinema yet?'

Willie's face crinkled in a smile. He was remembering the many discussions he'd had with Jane about that very subject.

She wanted to call the cinema *The Princess,* But Willie wasn't mad about that name; he thought it a bit too effeminate. He was thinking more in terms of something that had a hint of Irish in it.

'What about *An Tarraige (The Sea)* ?' he had suggested. No, she didn't like that. They went through hundreds of names, writing them down and sounding them out loud. Finally, they settled on *The Emerald* as the name. Both were happy with that.

'*The Emerald,*' Willie told the lads, very decisively.

'*The Emerald,*' Conor repeated after him. 'Has a nice ring to it.'

'I'll second that,' Niall said enthusiastically.

'Yeah, me too,' Liam agreed with glowing eyes.

§

Dear Jane,

Just a quick note to bring you up to date on how things are progressing with the cinema. .The momentum established by my stalwart assistants, together with my own efforts, has continued to surge ahead to such a degree that I foresee The Emerald opening well ahead of schedule. We're now at the point where the team feels it will be possible to have the grand opening the beginning of August — the height of the tourist season.

There's much speculation about our cinema being a huge draw in Cork this summer; attracting tourists from all over the South.

Darling, what would you think about a July wedding? Not having you around is like my heart is missing. Please say yes?

In haste.
Your loving Willie.

§

Dear Willie,

Yes, yes, yes! How could I say no when all I've done since you left was think about you and long for you. Not a moment passes that you're not in my thoughts.

But now to the big problem — my mother. Do you think you could bring yourself to ask her for my hand in marriage, in person? Up to now I haven't said a word about our engagement. I was waiting for the right moment. Well, Willie, let's be factual. I'm chicken when it comes to Mother: she has me completely intimidated. Though according to Lily, after seeing what the Tans did to our cousin, her attitude towards a lot of things, including the IRA, seems to have softened somewhat.

However, there isn't much of a change in her attitude to me: I think she'll never forgive me for not going into the shop. That's why I think we should do everything right and give her no chance to throw a spoke into the wheels of our happiness.

Do you think you could come to Dublin and face the ogre?' Write soon.

All my love
Jane.

It was coming up to six o'clock and Jane was busy totting up her Sales Book, when instinct told her to look up. She saw Willie coming towards the Jewelry Department. The sight of him sent a torrent of excitement rushing through her. Her pulse quickened.

When he arrived at the counter, he leaned over it and whispered in her ear, 'just looking at you feeds my soul.'

Jane felt giddy with joy. 'Oh, Willie!' she gasped, 'What a wonderful surprise! I didn't expect to see you so soon.'

'Darling, my body aches to hold you,' Willie said, staring passionately at her. 'How soon will it be before you're free?'

Jane glanced at the big clock hanging in the center of the store. It showed ten to six. 'Ten minutes,' she said.

'Ten minutes too many,' Willie said. 'I don't want to compromise you by hanging around; I'll see you in our retreat in fifteen minutes.

Jane's heart soared and plummeted a dozen times as she went through the motions of getting into her street clothes. Never was happiness so close to being in her grasp as at this moment. There would, of course, be a number of stumbling blocks, her mother being the principal one. When Jane arrived at their retreat her cheeks were flushed and her eyes shone. Before Willie had time to stand up, that lopsided smile of his that turned her heart over, made her dash across the room to give him a lingering kiss. While they were eating Willie filled Jane in on the exciting developments with the cinema.

'The interior decoration is finished, the carpet is laid, the seating is in,' he told her eagerly. Continuing, he said, 'And Conor, the young carpenter I told you about, has shown incredible skill, building a Lobby which includes the Ticket Office,' Willie smiled with rich delight. 'In addition, he's produced sketches showing how the front of the building can be so transformed that you'd never guess it was ever a warehouse.'

'I'm dying to see it,' said Jane. 'Do you think it will be ready for an opening in August?'

'I don't think, I know,' Willie nodded his head with conviction. 'Those lads are so determined, they're working morning, noon and night.' He squeezed Jane's hand across the table. 'Now about our marriage?' he said.

The word 'marriage' made Jane's breath catch in her throat for seconds. Then she recovered. 'You'll talk to Mother first?' she uttered the words sounding extremely nervous.

Willie gave her an encouraging grin. 'Of course,' he replied airily. 'The sooner the better. If we're having a July wedding,' he said with a glint in his eyes, 'we need to be engaged for a respectable length of time.'

'Two months,' Jane mused out loud. 'Not very long.'

'To the outside world, it may not be long,' Willie said pointedly, 'but you and I know it's close to three years since we first became engaged. So,' he asked with a rueful grin, 'when do I have the pleasure of braving the ogre in her lair?' He could tell that Jane was troubled. He squeezed her hand a little tighter. She sighed — it was almost a groan.

'As bad as that?' Willie inquired anxiously.

'Oh, Willie,' Jane said passionately, 'not once has she inquired, even obliquely, about you or your absence; it's like you never existed.'

'Well, I intend to change all that,' Willie said firmly. 'Whether she likes it or not she's going to have me as a son-in-law. So lead on.'

'You mean now, tonight?' Jane couldn't hide her unease.

'Jane, I'll be guided by you,' Willie said soothingly. 'You tell me when is a good time in the next twenty-four hours to talk to your mother. Even if it's the middle of the night,' he added flippantly, 'I'll be there.'

As Willie waited for her answer, Jane seemed indecisive. Eventually she said, 'I think I should do some ground work first.'

'You mean prepare her?'

'Sort of,' Jane said. 'At least tell her that you're coming to visit.'

'Right,' Willie said sounding very determined. 'At what time do I pay this visit tomorrow?'

'Oh Willie!' Jane burst out, 'You will be prudent?'

'Jane, I'm asking for your hand in marriage,' Willie said with forceful lightness, 'not to recruit you into the IRA.'

Jane had to laugh. She could just imagine her mother's reaction if he said such a thing to her even in jest. Finally, it was arranged that Willie would come for supper the following evening. Hugging Jane goodnight, Willie thrilled to the warmth of her body, as he told her about his days and nights of longing for her to be there with him in Cork.

On the way home Jane felt weighed down thinking about the best way to break the news of her upcoming nuptials to her mother. Mary made no secret of the fact that she thoroughly disapproved of Willie. So, to say the least, the discussion about her marriage was bound to be tetchy, if not impossible. She'd have to pick her words carefully. But then, she wondered, will any words of mine impress her sufficiently to change her mind about Willie?

She found her mother as usual on her own in her office — the perfect place to say what she'd come to say. As she entered the office, Mary looked up from her writing.

'This is a surprise,' she said, 'you don't often pay me the compliment of visiting me in my office. What's the problem?'

'It's not a problem,' Jane said, her stomach in a knot with tension, 'it's just to tell you that I've invited Willie for supper tomorrow night.'

'Oh!' Mary raised surprised eyebrows. 'I thought he was past tense?'

Jane could see by her stern countenance that this wasn't going to be easy. 'No, Mother,' Jane protested. 'He's by no means past tense. He never was.'

'You mean to say that despite my feelings in the matter, you two are still walking out?' Mary remonstrated.

'Well, except for the fact that he's been in Cork for the past two months setting up his own cinema,' Jane said, 'you could say we're still walking out. Anyway, he's in Dublin presently making arrangements about supplies and I asked him to come to supper tomorrow evening.'

'That was nice of you,' Mary said sardonically. Jane fought back the angry retorts that sprang to her lips. 'So you're telling me he's based in Cork now,' Mary said. 'That's a relief.'

'I'm telling you that he's opening his own cinema there in August,' Jane said proudly.

'How interesting!' Mary sounded anything but interested; bored would be more like it. 'Right,' she said dismissively, 'we'll set another place at the table tomorrow evening.'

'It's like trying to climb Mount Everest on roller skates to get through to that woman,' Lily said to Jane later in bed. 'But look on the bright side. Regardless of what she thinks, when you're married and living in Cork, you'll be away from all that prejudice.'

'But in the meantime I need her blessing to get married,' Jane put in. 'There'll be all those preparations beforehand.'

'Have you set a date?' Lily asked.

'The second Saturday in July,' Jane answered. 'We want to have a bit of a honeymoon before the official opening of the cinema.'

'Which is when?' Lily asked.

'The first weekend of August.'

'Gosh!' Lily said with tumultuous excitement, 'I'd love to be there for the opening.'

'And you will be,' Jane said. 'That's a promise.'

'Well, then let's get down to the nitty gritty of the wedding preparations,' Lily said optimistically. 'Any ideas about who's coming and where you want to have the reception?'

'It's going to be a very quiet wedding,' Jane said resolutely. 'Just the two families.' Then she added, 'As far as the reception is concerned, it'll be nothing fancy. Because we'll be catching the train to Cork that afternoon, we thought about a breakfast in a small, local hotel.' Jane hunched her shoulders dispassionately. 'Whatever!'

'Where are you going to live in Cork?' Lily asked, agog.

'It'll have to be a flat for the time being,' Jane said. 'Then as soon as the cinema starts to make money, we hope to be in a position to buy a house.'

The following evening, from the very start of the meal, an aura of tension pervaded the room. Conversation was stilted. And despite Lily's courageous efforts to bring lightness to the situation — regaling the company with a stream of anecdotes about her stay in the hospital — there were periods of strained silence.

Until Eileen arrived on the late side. Letting out an exclamation of delight, she threw her arms around Willie and said with a heartening wink, 'Oh, Willie! You're back! I'm so glad! I've just learned how to play a new game of cards.'

Willie could have kissed her. 'Can't wait to beat you,' he said, with an ingratiating smile.

'I'll show you afterwards,' Eileen said.

Mary stood up and left the room abruptly. Consternation registered on the faces in the room. Willie looked at Jane in a what-do-I-do-now expression?

Lily interjected sarcastically, nodding towards the door, 'Give her a minute to settle into her bloody figures.'

It was then that Eileen's questions came in torrents. 'What's wrong with mother? Why is everyone so uptight? Is Mother annoyed because I was late for supper? Should I apologize to her?'

'No, Eileen,' Jane said in appeasement. 'It's nothing to do with you.'

'Well, what is to do with?' Eileen wanted to know.

'We'll tell you about it later on,' Lily said. 'Go and get your supper, it's in the oven.'

Thank God for Lily's presence of mind, Jane thought. The distraction of Eileen getting her supper afforded her time to furtively tell Willie, 'Just knock on her office door and walk straight in.'

Willie couldn't get over the look of incredulity on Mary's face when he knocked on the door and walked into her office without being invited.

'What is it?' she said, cloaking her disdain in a thin layer of good manners.

'It's about Jane and I,' Willie said, his voice muted to the silence of the room.

'What about Jane and you?' Mary asked, dropping her eyes to conceal a flare of antipathy.

'We wish to get married,' Willie said bluntly. 'We love each other.'

Mary flinched as if she'd been struck. 'And what have you to offer my daughter, pray?' she asked tetchily.

Willie found his breath coming fast as if he'd been running. But still he was determined to stay calm. 'Well, I'm hoping to open my own cinema in Cork in the not-too-distant future.'

'You're hoping?' Mary repeated derisively. 'I'm glad you put it that way. Is there any guarantee that this venture of yours is going to be a success?'

'Well, a lot of people have faith in me,' Willie answered and before Mary could question him any further, he over rode her, giving a painstaking analysis of what had taken place to date with the cinema. He spoke with remorseless determination, telling her about the bank loan, the help he was receiving, both physical and financial. He then went on to say, 'Of all people, you, Mrs. O'Dwyer, must know what it's like to start up a business? How without the faith and trust of others it would not be possible.'

Suddenly Mary's expression changed to one of interest. 'Oh! I know what you're talking about,' she said. 'But in my time things were very different; we weren't at war with Britain. Which brings me to a most important question, are you still associated with that demon Collins?'

'How could I be?' Willie answered. 'If I'm based in Cork and he's based in Dublin.' Willie felt this was not the moment to equivocate. 'In answer to your question, Mrs. O'Dwyer, I'm no longer associated with Michael Collins, though,' he added with deliberate emphasis, 'I cannot but admire the man.'

Mary looked vaguely jubilant. 'Well, that's a relief,' she said.

'So are you going to give us your blessing?' Willie asked, fear and uncertainty clutching at his heart.

Her answer was delivered in tones of reserved politeness. 'Well,' she hunched her shoulders, 'if both of you are determined to go through with this union, who am I to stand in your way?' She said it without a trace of excitement or emotion in her voice.

'Does that mean you'll give us your blessing?' Willie asked, staring her straight in the face, determined to get an answer.

Mary paused for dramatic effect. 'It seems I have no option,' she said begrudgingly. Then suddenly it dawned on her that she was being excessively insufferable. Willie couldn't help noticing the sudden change in her demeanor. 'Have you a date in mind?' she asked, sounding more agreeable.

'We thought about the second weekend in July,' came Willie's immediate reply.

'That soon?'

'Well, Mrs. O'Dwyer,' Willie said, 'Jane and I have been walking out, on and off for three years, mostly without your approval.' He gave a shaky laugh. 'I reckon we both know exactly what we're getting into.'

'Right, so be it,' Mary said, matter-of-factly. 'You have my blessing.' Standing up, she said, derisively, 'No doubt the others will be expecting a celebration, so let's go to the parlor.'

Three anxious faces greeted them in the parlor. Jane's face was very pale; she was sick with apprehension. So it was a great relief when Willie — towering behind her mother — winked triumphantly at her. The color then seemed to hasten back into her cheeks.

Mary addressed Jane. 'It's all right, Jane,' she said, in a chilly voice, 'your marriage to Willie will have my blessing.'

'Hooray,' Lily whooped standing up and clapping her hands. Jane jumped up and embraced her mother; which embrace was unceremoniously shaken off.

'No need to get all mushy and sentimental,' Mary asserted. She then turned to Eileen and directed her to go to the kitchen and get the bottle of port wine in the press over the sink. 'It's a cause for celebration, I suppose,' she said without a scintilla of emotion.

'Gee whiz! Another wedding!' Eileen exclaimed with delight as she rushed towards the kitchen. Meantime, Mary got the wine glasses from the cabinet.

Before leaving for Cork, Willie presented Jane with a beautiful ruby and diamond engagement ring.

From the beginning it was obvious to Jane that her mother hadn't the slightest interest in her wedding plans. Apart from saying early on, 'Right, Jane, go ahead and make your plans and let me have the bills,' no attempt was made to ask cogent questions about the details.

'It's just another date in her diary,' she told Lily. 'The bare words — *Jane's Wedding*. Nothing else. No elaboration.'

'Ach, to hell with her!' Lily said. 'Just do as she says; arrange the wedding and give her the bill. And,' she added with a mischievous grin, 'do your best to make it a whopping big one!'

'I can't get over her attitude,' Jane said, looking really hurt. 'It was so different for Bridget and our Nancy's weddings: in their cases, her diary had reams of details about the church, the reception, the number of guests, even down to the apparel everyone in the family was wearing.'

'Face it, Jane,' Lily said solemnly, 'she doesn't particularly like Willie. Talking about which, when are you going to meet his parents?'

'Looks like it'll be the day of the wedding,' Jane said. Then nodding her head doubtfully, 'That is, if they come at all.'

'You don't mean to say they're not coming?' Lily looked aghast.

'Could well be,' Jane said. 'Willie warned me that his mother and father have never been further than Galway. Once he tried to get them to come to Dublin to see the pictures in the Tivoli, but when push came to shove, they cried off.'

'Doesn't sound very hopeful,' Lily remarked.

'However,' Jane said brightly, 'his brother, Martin, will be acting as best man.' Pausing to reflect, she added, 'In a way, I'd prefer if his parents didn't come. Mother's is so cold and distant with Willie, it could be embarrassing.'

'You're right,' Lily agreed. 'Mother's attitude could be very off-putting for them.'

'Well, whether Mother likes it or not, Jane put in, 'both Willie and I are determined that the wedding will be small and intimate; just immediate family with spouses, no relatives, no friends.'

Lily started to laugh hysterically. 'Willie should invite Collins,' she said. 'That'd really give our sullen mother something to snort about.'

Lily's laughter was so infectious, it got Jane going. When she got it under control, she said, 'Maybe he shouldn't stop at Collins. Why not include his intelligence network?'

'Yeah,' Lily said, 't'would be good enough for her!' Lily then became serious. 'So to get back to the wedding arrangements, you've sent invitations to Peter and Nancy Pete, Bridget and Michael, our Nancy and Gerald, myself, Eileen and Mother, of course. After that who else?'

'Just Willie's parents, Ellen and Patrick and his brother, Martin. That's it!'

'That makes fourteen, including the bride and groom,' Lily said. 'Oh!' she exclaimed, 'What about the priest?'

'I've talked to Father Hanlon, the parish priest in Dominick Street. He's going to officiate. But apparently he's tied up afterwards with parish business and can't come to the breakfast.'

'Mother didn't insist on Father Vincent doing the honors this time,' Lily remarked.

'Not a mention of him; another snub,' Jane said bitterly. 'Why would she ask the Reverend Father Vincent to officiate at a wedding that has her daughter marrying an arch-traitor!'

'Feck her anyway!' Lily said vehemently. Then moved on to a more pleasant topic. 'So have you booked the hotel for the breakfast yet?' she asked.

'Yes,' Jane said, 'Vaughan's Hotel. Apparently it has a great reputation for wedding breakfasts and it's a nice, short walk from the church. So we won't have to rent carriages.'

'Not even for the bridal couple?'

'No, it won't kill Willie and I to walk.'

'What are you going to wear?' Lily asked. Then before Jane could answer, she added, 'More important, what do you want me to wear?'

'Well, I'm wearing the blue dress I got for the Army Dance. And I have my eye on a lovely cloche hat in the store; it's white covered in artificial blue forget-me-knots.'

'So, have you any ideas about what I should wear as your bridesmaid?' Lily repeated the question.

'Lily, I'll leave it to yourself,' Jane said. 'But if you want any help choosing a dress, a hat or both, I'll be more than willing to accompany you to the stores.'

'Well, considering the hullabaloo associated with the last two weddings,' Lily said, smiling, 'sounds like this one is going to be a very quiet affair altogether: no rows about priests, no rows about bridesmaids or flower girls, no rows about relatives who should and should not be invited and no embarrassment about drunken in-laws.'

Jane smiled back. 'Makes a change doesn't it,' she said. Then added facetiously, 'Sometimes it pays to marry a rebel.'

As Willie was working up to the last minute in Cork getting the cinema ready for the opening, understandably he had to leave all the wedding arrangements to Jane. When he eventually arrived at the O'Dwyer house the evening before the wedding and Jane brought him up to date about arrangements, everything was grand and to his liking. Until she mentioned Vaughan's Hotel for the breakfast.

'Jesus!' Willie let out an exclamation of surprise. 'Why Vaughan's?' He struggled to stifle the shock he was feeling.

'What's wrong with Vaughan's Hotel?' Jane asked curiously. 'It came highly recommended. I heard the food was marvelous.'

'T'would have to be marvelous to cater for their special clientele,' Willie said cryptically.

'Oh, so you know the place already?' Jane asked mystified.

Willie wasn't sure how to answer her so he quickly changed the subject. Looking at his watch, he gritted his teeth and tried to make his voice sound casual. 'I have to go,' he said. 'My brother, Martin is due to arrive at the Broadstone station in a half an hour.'

'But what about…?'

Willie was halfway out the door. 'See you at the alter in the morning, darling,' he said. Then over his shoulder, he added, 'you've done a magnificent job with the arrangements.'

Of all the places to pick for the breakfast! Willie thought, as he sat on the tram going to the Broadstone. She would pick Vaughan's Hotel — a hotbed of Irish republicans. A feeling of panic crept over him. After a while, he shook his head. He was thinking negatively; fretting and worry never achieved anything. Chances are, as the breakfast is early in the morning, Collins and his crowd won't be abroad. Meeting Martin was a welcome distraction. They had a lot to catch up on. Martin was particularly interested in hearing about the cinema; intrigued by the idea of a warehouse being converted into a cinema. How it was achieved? The work it entailed?

The wedding appeared to go off without a hitch. Jane looked radiant in her blue dress, cloche hat and bouquet of white flowers, while Willie looked handsomer than ever in his new navy suit, white shirt and white carnation in his buttonhole. Willie's parents didn't come: they excused themselves on the grounds that the cow was sick and couldn't be left. However, Martin did a good job in the role of best man and represented the family admirably.

A trembling joy surged through Jane as she said the words, 'I do,' on the alter. She almost had to pinch herself to make sure she wasn't dreaming. Not even her grim-faced mother could dampen her joy this wonderful day.

Contrary to Willie's hopes and expectations the night before, the first person he spied on entering the Vaughan's hotel dining room, was Collins. He was sitting having breakfast with a very comely young woman at a corner table some distance from the wedding table. Otherwise, the room was empty. As the bridal party was ushered in, Collins gave only a desultory glance in their direction, then continued giving his attention to his lady friend. (Probably his fiancée, Willie concluded.) A knot came into Willie's stomach and his palms began to sweat as he tried to decide what to do. Should I go over and greet him? he wondered. Or should I just wave to him if he catches my eye? He decided to wait and see. Obviously Collins hadn't spotted him coming in. But the way the wedding table was arranged, with himself and Jane at its head — fully exposed with no where to hide — sooner or later Collins was bound to catch sight of him. Then what would happen? His mind was eaten up with tension. Suddenly he found he'd no appetite. Except for drinking the glass of orange juice and eating the grapefruit, he just toyed with the lavish plateful of rashers, eggs, sausages, and black and white puddings. The only thing his stomach could tolerate was the home-made white soda bread.

Jane noticed his lack of appetite and put it down to wedding nerves. As for herself, she was ravenous. And now that the arrangements had worked out so well, she felt she could relax at last. In fact, she was getting the impression that this wedding breakfast with just the family, looked like being a huge success. It was like a unity; a unity that certainly didn't exist at any of the other weddings when the family was scattered all over the place. The informality was marvelous; they (the family) could talk frankly and openly about their lives without having to watch everything they said in case they ruffled feathers. It was noticeable too that her mother seemed to be really enjoying the exchange of family news. In the best sense of the word, this was a reunion where everyone relaxed and could be themselves.

Even Nancy Pete was agreeable: she surpassed herself socially regaling the company with hysterically funny yarns about the mischief Colbert and Heuston got up to. Like the tale she told about the day Colbert got hold of his daddy's razor and tried to shave Heuston. 'If Colbert hadn't cut his own little finger,' she declared gleefully, 'I swear to God, he'd probably have cut the child's throat.'

This brought bursts of laughter around the table. When she was in the mood, Nancy Pete could be as funny and as witty as the best.

'Heuston's archangel was obviously looking after him that day,' Peter put in.

Nancy Pete turned to our Nancy sitting beside her. 'You have it all before you, girl; the joys of parenthood,' she said, placing her hand on our Nancy's stomach.

If our Nancy's looks could kill, Nancy Pete would be dead on the spot. Our Nancy had gone to a lot of trouble to disguise the fact that she was pregnant.

Suddenly, Willie saw Collins make his way across the room and head towards where he was sitting. His stomach churned and he swallowed hard as he stood up to greet him.

Shaking Willie's hand warmly, Collins said in his best Cork accent, 'I just had to come over and offer my felicitations, By.' He grinned broadly at the rest of the company. They, in turn grinned back. Bending over Willie speaking behind his hand, Collins whispered, 'No introductions necessary, Willie, tigin tu (you understand?)' He then offered Jane his hand, which she willingly took as she smiled her most dazzling smile. 'But surely the bauld Willie knows how to pick a beauty!' he said, his eyes filled with admiration. Then digging Willie playfully in the ribs, he added, 'God! She's only gorgeous!' With that he turned to Mary, who seemed eager to shake his outstretched hand. 'And this must be the bride's lovely mother?' he said, at his most flattering. 'We don't have to ask where the good looks in this family came from.' Mary, full of smiles, lapped up the compliments. Collins then turned to Willie and slapped him on the back. 'Well, the best of wishes to yourself and your beautiful bride,' he said.

'Jesus, Christ!' Willie exhaled gratefully before he said to Collins, 'Care to join us in some wedding cake and champagne?'

'I'd love to,' Collins said, letting his eyes rove around the table, stopping to wink at Peter. 'Can't remember when I seen such a bevy of beauties in one group,' he said good naturedly, 'but unfortunately, I have to rush away.'

With that he was gone.

'He seems a very agreeable sort of man,' Mary said to Willie. 'Who is he?'

Before Willie could answer, Peter interjected. 'Mick Collins,' he said in a soft tone. He was tempted to add, 'Put that in your pipe and smoke it,' but desisted.

Mary's face went a deep shade of red.

Nancy Pete jumped up. 'In the name of God, Willie,' she said aggressively, 'why didn't you introduce him to us?'

'Well, I...' Willie didn't get a chance to finish the sentence, because Nancy Pete was on her feet running after Collins. She caught up with him before he reached the door where his lady friend awaited him. All eyes at the table were on her. Then Peter left in hot pursuit. Willie closed his eyes in relief and said 'Amen' silently.

Peter arrived at Nancy Pete's side just in time to hear her say to Collins, 'I just had to tell you how much I admire what you're doing for Ireland.'

On seeing Peter, Collins exclaimed, 'Ah Peter! Your lovely wife is here trying to flatter me up to the eyeballs.'

'It's not flattery,' Nancy Pete said, at her most dramatic, 'it's genuine.'

'I'll vouch for that,' Peter said. 'She's a staunch admirer of yours.'

'Well, thank you, Mam, for those kind words,' Collins said to Nancy Pete, 'but now, I have to go.'

The people at the table were flabbergast when they saw Nancy Pete companionably link arms with Peter as they strode back to the table.

Meanwhile, the waiter arrived with the wedding cake and the champagne. Willie, his stomach now gurgling with hunger, was forced to fill the void with wedding cake. Martin, acting as the best man, made a speech extolling Willie's virtues and welcoming Jane into the MacNamee family. Thankfully, it was short and sweet. He finished by wishing the couple a long and happy life. After which he asked the company to stand and raise their glasses in a toast to the newlyweds.

After that, Willie replied telling of his great love for Jane and how he would leave no stone unturned to make her happy. He finished by asking the company to drink a toast to the lovely bridesmaid, Lily. As glasses were raised to Lily, Jane thought, at last Lily is having her day in the sun.

Peter wrapped things up with a speech welcoming Willie into the O'Dwyer family and telling some funny anecdotes about their time together in Frongoch.

After that, as the couple were catching the afternoon train to Cork, it was time for them to leave.

As Jane went to embrace her mother, Mary drew her into her arms in an unusual loving hug. 'He's a good man,' she said tearfully into her ear. 'He'll be a wonderful provider.' Jane supposed it was the best her mother could do by way of a compliment to Willie. Releasing Jane, Mary said, 'I wish you every happiness, Jane. But I'm going to miss you.' Then whacking the tears from her eyes, she added, 'I have to compliment you on the wedding arrangements; they were absolutely wonderful. Between you and me, I've enjoyed this wedding much more than any of the others. Somehow you managed to bring harmony and accord to our family. Could anyone ask for more?' Mary then handed Jane an envelope saying, 'No sense in giving you a piece of furniture until you have your own home. Hopefully, this will come in handy.'

Later the couple were astounded to find that the envelope contained a cheque for five hundred pounds — an exceedingly generous wedding present.

Chapter XXXII

The Opening Night of the cinema was a huge success: a gala occasion with a full house.

During most of the day Willie felt exhilarated and frightened at the same time. But he need not have worried. The curious Cork people and tourists flocked to the cinema in their hundreds to see for themselves what these amazing pictures were all about. Jane, too, was walking on air anticipating the arrival of Lily and Peter from Dublin to join in the celebrations. Somehow, Peter managed to get permission to make 'the opening of the Cork Cinema' an assignment for his newspaper. In the middle of the afternoon when the orgy of preparations was at its height, who should arrive unexpectedly, but Willie's parents, the whole way from the West.

When Willie introduced them to Jane, she came close to apoplexy. Even so, she managed to keep the horror out of her voice as she said with forced lightness, 'Oh! you're so very welcome!' But, she thought, not at this particular moment when Willie and I and everyone concerned are up to our eyes battling against the clock trying to have everything ready by seven o'clock. This special introduction couldn't have come at a worse time. A hard knot of guilt formed in Jane's chest. By rights she should be making them a meal. They'd come such a distance. And being from the country, they probably hadn't eaten all day. But now Willie and herself were so involved with the preparations, they couldn't be away from the cinema even for minutes. Jane had in fact prepared a small celebratory meal in the flat for after the show: just a few drinks, light refreshments, sandwiches, savories and cakes. Then a paralyzing thought struck her. They'll probably expect to stay the night. That means Willie and I sleeping on the hard living room floor. Jane's first meeting with her in-laws was becoming more and more of a nightmare.

Willie took valuable time off to give his parents the grand tour of the cinema. While they were so doing, Peter and Lily arrived. Lily immediately detected the falseness in Jane's voice as she tried nonchalantly to explain the unexpected arrival of her in-laws.

'Great timing!' Lily spoke derisively, 'when you're both so tied up and unable to roll out the red carpet for them.' Then she added irreverently, 'I bet they're about as welcome as the measles.'

Jane was forced to smile at the way Lily put her finger on it. 'To be honest with you, Lily,' she said, 'their timing couldn't be worse.'

'Okay,' Lily said, 'let's see what Peter and I can do to take them off your hands.' She turned to Peter. 'Peter, he said, 'you and I are about to go and have a meal at our hotel. Why don't we invite Willie's parents, Patrick and Ellen, to join us?'

A huge sigh of relief gushed from Jane. 'You're a gem!' she whispered quietly into Lily's ear. As the four were leaving to get a quick meal, Jane said in a low tone to Lily, 'For God sake, Lily, watch your language; please, no cursing and swearing.'

'Don't worry!' Lily responded, 'I'll be the soul of discretion.' In the heel of the hunt, not only did Lily solve the problem of the food, but she announced at the celebration in the flat later on, 'believe it or not, Ellen and I are going to be sleeping companions tonight.'

Not to be outdone, Peter chipped in boisterously, 'As are Patrick and myself.'

'Yes,' Ellen said to Jane and Willie grinning sheepishly, 'I hope you don't mind, we won't be staying with you this trip. Your sister, Lily, talked us into sharing her and your brother's bedrooms at their hotel tonight.'

Eagerly, Patrick put in, 'They have two beds in each of their rooms.'

Jane's eyes brimmed with relief. Willie then said, 'I'll pay half the damage.'

'You'll do no such thing,' Patrick said. 'We intend looking after that ourselves.'

'The rooms are already paid for, Patrick,' Peter interjected. 'Each room cost the same for two as it does for one. So you can forget about paying.'

'Oh, that's very generous of you,' Patrick said.

'Be glad of the company,' Peter answered.

Ellen clasped Jane's hand in her's. 'Are you sure you don't mind?' she said, her face ridden with guilt.

Jesus! Jane thought, if she could read my mind. 'Not a bit of it,' she said brightly. She thought, the arrangement couldn't be more of a relief. Throughout the evening her mind raced with dread thinking about herself and Willie having their night's sleep on the hard floor. Now thanks to Lily and Peter, they could look forward to a decent night's sleep. God knows they'd earned it.

In the short space of time she spent with them, Jane developed quite a fondness for her in-laws. A fondness she felt was reciprocated. Because next day, at the railway station when the four guests were taking their leave of Jane and Willie, Ellen made a point of saying, 'Patrick and I can't remember when we enjoyed ourselves so much.' Then when Jane hugged her good-bye, she added, with eyes welling up, 'I'm so glad Willie married such a beautiful person and into such a lovely family.'

Like most Irish summers, this one was a long, soggy endurance test that had tourists fed up and frustrated. In August, gray skies, dripping rain and blustery winds drove many of them into the Emerald Cinema, together with the locals. People stood in long queues every evening waiting for the cinema to open. But the trouble was on Friday and Saturday nights many of them had to be turned away because the Cinema was jam-packed. Seeing the rush on the cinema, Willie decided to run daily matinees. Once again, people came in their hundreds; parents and children seeking refuge from the continuous rain.

Conor, now on salary, in charge of the Ticket Office, couldn't get over the amount of money he was taking in. 'Be gorrah!' he said to Willie, excitedly, 'Soon you'll be a millionaire.'

Jane too worked hard playing her marvelous new pianola. She

was an added attraction, not only playing for the pictures, but also giving recitals before each show. Relief and happiness swamped Willie. His leap of faith had paid off. The previous months' challenges and worries evaporated. His confidence was now so great, he felt, with his lovely Jane by his side, he could accomplish anything.

When the sun began to set earlier and the chill of autumn filled the air, the tourists began to disappear. It was then that Willie decided to stop running matinees. This gave himself and Jane time to enjoy each other. A thing that seemed impossible up to now; they were so busy with the business of the cinema. During the week's honeymoon in Kinsale, with Willie so tense and constantly worrying about the success of the cinema, consummating their love was not as euphoric as anticipated. But now it was different. Bedtime — when they could lose themselves in each other's arms without worrying — couldn't come fast enough. The success of the cinema too was sufficient to merit a celebration. This took the form of a mad spending spree. Flush with money, the couple bought all before them; clothes for Jane, which included a fur coat, a winter coat for Willie, bits of furniture and odds and ends for the flat. At the sight of Willie's happy face, Jane's heart was ready to burst with happiness.

They spent most Sunday evenings having supper with Fiocra and his wife, Betty, either at Fiocra's house or in their own flat. Jane and Betty got on like a house on fire. Though more handsome than pretty, Betty's real beauty lay in her warmness and consideration for other people. The couple were now the proud parents of a three-month-old baby boy named, Felim.

Meantime, Willie trained Niall as a relief projectionist. He was a quick learner. This meant that if Willie was forced to stay overnight in Dublin (where he routinely went on Mondays to renew the films) he wasn't unduly worried leaving Niall behind to run the show.

Though Willie had completely cut himself off from politics, he was very upset hearing about Thomas MacSwiney, the Lord Mayor of Cork, who died after seventy-three days on hunger strike in Brixton Jail in England. He'd been arrested on the 12th of August, 1920.

His body was brought back to Cork and his funeral, at which Arthur Griffith headed the mourners, was a massive display of national solidarity. Attending MacSwiney's funeral, Willie felt a sudden surge of nationalism, but then decided, no! — despite what they've done, I mustn't get involved. I'm now a married man with responsibilities. However, the vast amount of coverage given by the newspapers, local and international, to MacSwiney's ordeal, attracted lots of attention to Ireland from all over the world.

Early one Monday morning in November, there was a knock on the flat door. Willie, wearing night attire and looking totally mystified, answered it. He found Fiocra on the doorstep, his face frozen in pain.

'Something's wrong?' Willie said with surprising mildness despite the fluttering of his heart.

'Sorry to disturb you at this hour,' Fiocra said dolefully. 'But I thought you should know the bad news.' His face changed from pain, to contempt, to disgust.

'For God's sake come in,' Willie said. 'What is the bad news? It's not about the cinema, is it?' he asked, fear gripping his heart.

'No, no,' Fiocra hastened to assure him. 'It's nothing to do with the cinema. It's bad news from Dublin.'

Fiocra went on to tell Willie the facts.

'According to my sources, at 9 a.m. yesterday morning (Sunday) eight groups of Collins' men went into action executing fourteen British spies in their different lodgings. Reaction from the British was swift. Lorry loads of Auxiliaries drove to Croke Park in the afternoon where the Gaelic football match was in full swing. They opened fire point blank into a crowd of men, women and children, killing fourteen (including one of the players) wounding many others.'

'My God!' Willie gasped, 'that is dreadful news!'

'It's monstrous,' Fiocra said, the anger pouring out of him. But, this was just the beginning. Later Willie was to learn from Fiocra that the IRA had wasted no time with their act of reprisal.

On the 28th of November an entire patrol of eighteen Auxiliaries was ambushed by a flying column of the IRA at Kilmichael, County Cork; much too close for comfort for Willie.

Worse was to come.

A few nights later, when Willie and Jane emerged into the night air after closing the cinema, they were immediately struck by the nauseous smell of burning. Further on they could see the red sky in the distance. On the main road into the City, they ran into a group of people staring in that direction. Some held handkerchiefs and scarves to their faces.

A man said to Willie, 'That's the City of Cork being burnt to the ground by the Auxiliaries.'

'My God!' Willie exclaimed. 'You're not serious?'

'I'm bloody awful serious,' the man said. 'It seems they suffered the loss of eleven of their members at Kilmichael, and by God, they're determined to get their revenge!'

For Willie and Jane is was like history repeating itself. They were reminded of that night back in 1916 when the city of Dublin was on fire.

Next evening Fiocra, who was assigned to cover the big fire dropped in to see Willie in the cinema and told him the details. 'Apparently,' he said, 'the Auxiliaries stormed into public houses all over the city, helped themselves to drinks, then proceeded to ransack and loot the pubs and surrounding buildings and finished up sprinkling petrol and setting the whole lot on fire. Then,' he continued, looking very grave, 'because that wasn't bad enough, they prevented the fire brigades from reaching the scene, even went so far as to cut the hoses of the few who were courageous enough to persevere and get there.'

'Thank God we're based in the suburbs,' Willie said, aghast. 'But then, can you ever be sure?'

The following Sunday when Willie and Jane were visiting Fiocra and Betty, Fiocra showed Willie some International newspapers which carried front page banner headlines saying, CORK CITY BURNED TO THE GROUND.

'This sort of thing,' he said to Willie, 'is causing considerable embarrassment and disgust in England and throughout the world.'

'Let's hope they're disgusted enough to do something about it,' Willie said. He was grateful to God that the Cinema had survived, but like a lot of the Cork people, he had the jitters; he didn't know from one day to the next what to expect. Needless to say, the burning of the city affected attendance at the cinema; people were terrified to be abroad after dark.

Later during one of their many conversations, Fiocra told Willie, 'With every passing week the violence in the South and in Dublin is getting worse. Reprisals and counter reprisals flourish between the Auxiliaries and the IRA in Dublin and the Tans and the IRA in the South.'

Notwithstanding the violence, people gradually began to gravitate back to the cinema; they desperately needed a break away from news of killings and bloodshed.

The Christmas season arrived. Though it was Jane's first time to spend Christmas away from home, oddly enough, except for Lily, she didn't overly miss the family. She and Willie were deliriously happy. Nothing or no one could change that. As the cinema would be closed on Christmas Day, Jane determined to make this Christmas the happiest one possible for Willie. During the days coming up Christmas, she spent time buying lots of stuff to make the 'rabbit hutch' (the flat) as festive looking as possible. On Christmas Eve morning, when Willie was missing, with Conor's help, Jane surreptitiously installed a Christmas tree, dressing it with lots of ornaments and lighting the candles just before Willie was due for lunch.

On arrival, a look of wonderment came over Willie's face when he saw the transformation that had taken place in the rabbit hutch; a traditional Christmas tree, holly behind the pictures, colored paper chains strung from the ceiling. Jane had undoubtedly captured the spirit of Christmas.

Gathering her into his arms, Willie burst out in a rush of excitement, 'Darling Jane, this is a Christmas I'll cherish all my life.' Motioning towards the tree, he added, 'You've given me my very first Christmas tree.' Willie's reaction reminded Jane of baby Colbert's when he saw the family Christmas tree for the first time.

Fiocra and Betty (along with baby Felim) were guests at their Christmas dinner. To Jane's delight (except for the lumpy gravy) her culinary skills were a roaring success; the turkey, stuffing and all the trimmings tasted delicious. As soon as the main course was over and the dishes cleared away, while the ladies were preoccupied with domestic chores—Jane preparing the Christmas pudding and Betty breast-feeding baby Felim in the bedroom—the men got down to the important business of drinking port wine, smoking cigars and discussing politics.

Willie told Fiocra, 'Last week when I was in Dublin I had a Christmas drink with my brother-in-law, who told me that Collins now has the Royal Irish Constabulary practically reduced to a neutral force.'

'An amazing man, that Collins!' Fiocra declared, lighting up his cigar.

Willie continued. 'And what with the non-stop reprisals and counter reprisals it seems the state of the warring elements is at a general stalemate.'

'Doesn't surprise me,' Fiocra said. 'How much longer can the killings continue? Nobody's getting anywhere.'

'But here's the interesting bit,' Willie went on, 'it seems that secret attempts through intermediaries are being made by the British to talk to Dail Eileann about some sort of reconciliation. But guess who the fly in the ointment is?'

'Dev.'

'The very one,' Willie said. 'He refuses to negotiate unless it's on his own terms.'

'Bad cess to him,' Fiocra said in disgust.

Once in a while at the end of the day, Fiocra dropped in to see Willie in the cinema with a six pack of Guinness. Uninhibited, they would talk for hours. Sometimes heatedly, occasionally calmly, but never lightly. Their thoughts, arguments, doubts, discussions, persuasions were all well ventilated, discarded then ventilated again like jumbled dominoes. Though it meant going home on her own these particular nights, Jane was pleased that Willie had this outlet; it was a healthy one. He definitely needed someone — preferably a male — with whom he could have regular political discussions. Fiocra, so well informed, fitted the bill perfectly. He was the ideal person. Besides it didn't happen too often.

By arrangement Lily arrived by train the afternoon of New Year's Eve. She was there to ring in the New Year with Jane and Willie. She would sleep on the new sofa. Knowing how much they'd have to talk about, Willie made himself scarce. (Anyway there was no shortage of jobs to be done in the cinema during the daytime.) He thought: it's wonderful for Jane to see Lily again and hear all the family news.

Lily started by telling Jane about Christmas Day.

'We had Bridget and Michael, plus baby Oonagh and Nancy and Gerald for Dinner,' Lily said. 'Believe it or not, Gerald was well and truly sozzled when they arrived. And he acted like a stupid galloot for the rest of the day.'

'How did Mother react?' Jane asked.

'For a while she pretended not to notice,' Lily answered. 'But then as the day wore on she couldn't conceal her annoyance: it was particularly noticeable when her two grand sons arrived in the afternoon. Instead of the usual warm welcome, they were greeted with a wintry smile.

'Sounds like Gerald really ruined her day.'

'Precisely,' Lily said. 'Their only redeeming action was to leave early. Then we could all relax.' Lily looked hard at Jane, then said, 'But, oh dear God! Jane! How I missed you! How I wished you didn't live in Cork.'

'I'm afraid that's the way it has to be,' Jane sighed. Then added, 'after that experience with Gerald, maybe Mother might see Willie in a different light — a more favorable one?'

'If you ask me,' Lily said sagely, 'Gerald is now the 'back of her hand.' Your Willie could now possibly become the white-haired boy.'

'What about our Nancy?' Jane asked concerned. 'How did she

react to Gerald's carry on?'

'Like the proverbial ostrich,' Lily said. 'Though she's about to drop that baby any minute, everyone could see she already has her hands full with that fella. I certainly don't envy her.'

But Lily's big news was that she had a new boyfriend.

'His name is Matthew Walsh, he's twenty, not much to look at, but he's fun to be with,' she told Jane.

'Where did you meet him?' Jane asked.

'He's a regular customer in O'Grady's shop,' Lily said. 'Very much into horticulture: apparently has a beautiful garden and a heated greenhouse.'

'So how many times have you been out with him?'

'Gimme a chance! Just the once.' Lily said. 'He doesn't like coming into the city at night time because of the violence.'

'So where did you go?' Jane was all excitement.

'He took me to the Opera before Christmas,' Lily laughed. 'Well, you know me and opera!' She threw her eyes up to heaven. 'It's a pain in the arse! Still, when we had the tea afterwards, he was full of poetry and wit and had me in stitches laughing.'

'You definitely like him a lot?' Jane said, moved.

'Yeah,' Lily said. 'Put it this way, I feel very relaxed and at home in his company.'

'So when are you seeing him again?'

'He suggested his mother's house in Rathgar for tea sometime soon,' Lily said. 'The garden and greenhouse are located there.'

'You're meeting the mother already?' Jane looked surprised.

'It's not like that,' Lily said, screwing up her face. 'It's just that he wants me to see the stuff in his greenhouse. And sure, maybe I could give him some advice.'

'Are you sure it's stuff in his greenhouse he wants you to see?' Jane said dubiously. 'He may have something else on his mind.'

'Stop thinking like that,' Lily said. 'When it comes to market gardening, he seems to know his stuff. Anyway, I know him long enough coming into the shop to know he's not a chancer.'

'Be careful, Lily,' Jane entreated.

'Does Mother know about him?'

'Course not,' Lily laughed. 'Amn't I back to telling lies again.'

Jane pealed with laughter. She was remembering her own courtship with Willie.

The three (Willie, Jane and Lily) celebrated ringing in the new year — 1921 — In Fiocra and Betty's house. With all their hearts they wished it would be a peaceful one.

Later that night when they were on their own, Jane gave Willie her joyful news. 'Willie, I'm pregnant,' she said, her eyes aglow.

'You couldn't have given me a nicer present, Jane.' Willie said, hugging her. 'My cup runneth over.'

EPILOGUE

Late in May, 1921, the IRA launched their biggest operation of all in Dublin. It was the burning of the beautiful Eighteen Century Customs House on the Quays by the river Liffey; at that time the all-important Center of British Administration in Ireland.

It started with the Dublin Brigade of 120 men surrounding the building during working hours, pushing their way into the offices to turn out the Civil Servants. After they'd emptied the building, they sprinkled petrol all over it and set it ablaze. Soon afterwards, the Auxiliaries arrived to find smoke belching out of the building and rifle fire being directed at them by the IRA. But now it was the IRA's turn to be surrounded by the Auxiliaries and other Crown Forces. A couple of IRA men were shot dead, the rest, over 120 surrendered. It was not only the biggest operation the IRA had launched, but the greatest disaster they had yet to experience. Though the IRA was still powerful in the countryside and the morale and organization was good, in Dublin, Collins had lost almost all of his men as well as a considerable quantity of badly needed arms and ammunition.

Around this time of stalemate, both sides began to put out feelers towards each other. On July 9th, 1921, DeValera and other representatives of Sinn Fein and the IRA met British representatives (including the Commander-in-chief in Ireland, General Macready and the Under Secretary, Andy Cops) in England. Two days later a truce was signed between all the Crown Forces and the IRA. Not long before, *The Irish Times* newspaper had written, 'All Ireland streams with blood.' Now, quite suddenly and almost unbelievably, it was over. But a political solution which would turn the truce into a peace was going to be harder to achieve. There had been little opportunity in recent years for political maneuver. DeValera adamant for a sovereign independent Irish Republic — though possibly in 'external association' with the British Empire — and Arthur Griffith, less dogmatic on constitutional niceties, both went to London for preliminary negotiations with the British Government. But the man in whose power it lay to make or break a possible settlement, was the man who made this invitation from the British Government to the IRA possible in the first place — Michael Collins.

On his first visit to London after the truce he was still wearing the mustache he had cultivated for his days on the run. On December 6th, 1921, after months of difficult and sometimes deadlocked negotiations between the Irish delegation, headed, under duress, by Michael Collins and Arthur Griffith and the British cabinet, an agreement was signed at Downing Street known as the Anglo-Irish Treaty. The conclusion of that Treaty was regarded in a rather different light by both sides. The British regarded it as having solved at last the ancient problem that had bedeviled relations between the two islands for 750 years.

Michael Collins, soon after signing it, is reported to have said, 'I have signed my own death warrant.'

The effect of the Treaty was to give twenty-six of the thirty-two counties of Ireland the constitutional status of the Dominion of Canada at the time; with its own army and navy and total control of its own affairs at home and abroad subject to the King. The new state was to be called, not the 'Irish Republic,' which the IRA had fought for, but 'The Irish Free State.' For the present, at their request, the six Northern Counties of Ireland were allowed to opt out pending later negotiations. Another aspect of the Treaty which made the failure to unite Ireland seem less urgent was the oath to the King which in the minds of many nationalist Irishmen seemed to provide a more important issue still.

Clause 4 prescribed the oath to be taken by members of the Free State parliament (The Dail) as follows:

'I do solemnly swear true faith and allegiance to the Constitution of the Irish Free State as by law established...and that I will be faithful to H. M. King George V, his heirs and successors by law, in virtue of the common citizenship of Ireland with Great Britain and her adherence to the membership of the Group of Nations forming the British Commonwealth of Nations.'

This was anathema to many republicans. Dan Breen, the man who had begun the republican violence in 1919, was to say that the Treaty was 'the negation of everything I ever fought for. No way will I give allegiance to a foreign king.' In fact, Collins negotiating hard with Lloyd George had managed at the last moment to have the word 'allegiance' in the clause shifted as far away as possible from the word 'King.' He anticipated that many people, like Breen, who had helped him to the negotiating position, were going to think about it. And he argued that the oath can be seen as a mere symbol necessary to secure a constitutional position from which it could later be abolished.

As one of the IRA supporters put it, 'You'd take the oath to get rid of it.'

Thus, while among the ordinary population of Ireland the general reaction to the Treaty was one of relief and thankfulness that the horror of the last two and a half years had been ended, the IRA was split. Well over half of them, including DeValera and Cathal Brugha, regarded the Treaty as a betrayal, particularly where Northern Ireland was concerned. The fact that Collins himself had signed the Treaty made it easier for many of the IRA to accept it on his terms; namely that it gave 'the freedom to win freedom.' His continued control of the still existing Irish Republican Brotherhood enabled him to disseminate this argument forcibly, although the final IRB decision was to leave the matter to individual consciences.

DeValera, the titular head of the Republican 'Government' which earlier negotiated with the British, had conveniently remained behind in Dublin when it came to the actual signing of the Treaty. This was done principally because he knew that some compromise on the full republican demand was inevitable and that all his political skills would be required there to make it acceptable. He made the delegation in London his 'plenipotentiaries'; on the other hand, he had instructed them not to sign a final settlement without first referring it back to Dublin. They had, in fact, returned to Dublin to consult with him on more than one occasion of deadlock in the negotiations. But impressed by Lloyd George with a sense of critical urgency during the last tense night of negotiation, they eventually signed without resorting to the telephone.

Straightaway, DeValera disassociated himself from the Treaty and the split in the IRA was thus reflected among the republicans themselves.

A series of grim events followed in April 1922 when tension between the pro-Treaty and the anti-Treaty sections of the IRA ran high and sincere hopes on both sides that it might be resolved were beginning to evaporate. Leaders of the anti-Treaty elements occupied and set up their own Headquarters in the Dublin Four Courts. The most prominent of the republican leaders there, who regarded the Treaty Collins had signed as a sell-out, were Rory O'Connor, who had been Collins Director of Engineering and Liam Mellowes, one of the few Volunteer leaders to have taken action outside Dublin in 1916. They were backed by some of the most successful leaders of flying columns in the 'war' against the British: men like Liam Lynch and Tom Barry from the South, and in Dublin Earnie O'Malley, who had been one of Collins' principal IRA organizers.

Then there was the enrollment in the Free State Army of many Irishmen who had been officers and men in the British army. This confirmed the anti-Treaty elements' suspicions that the new State was merely a continuation of British rule in disguise. The fact that it was headed by their old leaders, Collins and Arthur Griffith, only increased their bitterness.

The split in the IRA had a desperate effect on Collins. His agony was further intensified by earlier developments in what was now 'Northern Ireland.' Fears among the Protestant population there that the Boundary Commission might undermine their new state, together with the fear of being overwhelmed by the Catholic majority, lead to serious rioting. There were 128 casualties in Belfast alone (three quarters of them Catholic) and 30 people killed in a single night. This lead to Catholic refugees streaming south of the Border.

The situation in the North continued to deteriorate. Deaths in communal violence in the first six months of 1922 amounted to 264 (most of them Catholics.) Meantime, paramilitary police forces, organized by Sir James Craig's government there, were asserting law and order in a manner very prejudicial to the Catholics. The IRA, both North and South, did what they could to protect their fellow nationalists, and Collins, though in honor bound by the Treaty to respect the integrity of the Northern State, equally, 'could not stand idly by' and leave nationalists to be murdered. He, therefore, found himself in the ambiguous position of supplying arms to the anti-Treaty IRA in the North while faced by a challenge to his authority and that of the Free State, from his old comrades in the Four Courts.

Despite these crises, the Dail, after a serious of agonizing emotional debates, finally ratified the Treaty by a small majority. The country itself ratified it by a larger, thought not an overwhelming one, in the first Free State General Election held in June 1922. An incident that further exacerbated the situation in Northern Ireland took place when British Field Marshall, Sir Henry Wilson — Craig's Security Adviser in the North — was gunned down by two IRA men on the steps of his home in London. This happened shortly after the elections in the Free State.

Their action now precipitated Collins into an even more painful phase of the crisis in which he was already enmeshed: though his conscience lead him to make strenuous but unavailing efforts with the British to save the two from the gallows. After this assassination, assuming that the anti-Treaty IRA was responsible for it, the Free State Government, which for months had watched with increasing anxiety the passive toleration towards the anti-Treaty Republican Headquarters in Dublin, now adopted a 'get tough' attitude towards them. They insisted that Collins take action against the Four Courts. Otherwise, they would regard the Treaty as abrogated.

After stalling for some days, Collins, provoked on his own account by the kidnapping of one of his Generals by the republican forces, eventually gave the Four Courts twenty minutes to surrender and, when they refused the Free State army began to shell them from the other side of the Liffey with two field guns borrowed from the British. The range was ridiculously short, but since the only available shells were shrapnel, it took two days to subdue them. Some of the anti-Treaty forces then took up positions in buildings in Sackville Street. A week later, Sackville Street was once again in ruins.

The Irish Civil War had begun.

After eight days fighting in Dublin during which 60 people were killed and 300 wounded, the anti-Treaty republicans in Sackville Street surrendered as those in the Four Courts had done. Cathal Brugha, refused to surrender and was mortally wounded. Rory O'Connor, Liam Mellowes and other top IRA men were made prisoners in Mountjoy jail. In other parts of Ireland, particularly in the South and West, the anti-Treaty IRA were strong. They had a big hold on the city of Cork.

One evening in August, Willie arrived as usual to open up the Emerald Cinema. To his great surprise he found Finbar, looking unusually grim, waiting for him outside. He knew immediately that something was radically wrong.

However, before he could open his mouth, Finbar rushed in with the words, 'Willie you're going to have to get out of Cork immediately.'

'In the name of God, why?' Willie vociferated.

'Terrible things are about to happen in Cork,' Finbar said. 'Collins sent me to warn you.'

'What sort of things?' Willie asked, looking puzzled as he opened the main door of the cinema and beckoned Finbar inside.

'No doubt you're aware of the fact that the anti-Treaty IRA are in control of Cork city?'

'Yeah, I know,' Willie said much dispirited. 'And I'm avoiding them like the plague.'

'Collins is sending Free State troops to take the city back,' Finbar said somberly. 'He's afraid you and your family could be in danger.'

'So you're telling me that Collins wants me to clear out of the city straightaway?' Willie said as he mounted the stairs leading to the projection room, followed by Finbar. 'How the hell can I leave when I have a business to run.?'

'That's just the point,' Finbar said. 'Collins is convinced that the anti-Treaty IRA will go on the rampage and hurt people like yourself. They'll target your cinema. Then go after you. It's their modus operandi in Dublin.'

'So you think my absence would save myself, my family and the cinema?' Willie asked earnestly. He was thinking about Jane and their baby girl, Enda. (Named after Saint Enda's College, which Pearse established.)

'T'would be a help,' Finbar said. 'You've no idea how bitter this civil war has become. Collins has a lot of enemies, particularly in Cork.' Willie could see that Finbar was acutely agitated. 'God, Willie!' he gasped, 'it's hell in Dublin at the moment with brother fighting brother, father fighting son, friend fighting friend. Those anti-Treaty lads have pledged their allegiance to Dev. They're dead against Collins.'

'And to think that they were once Mick's loyal friends.'

'I'm telling you Willie you're not safe staying in Cork at the moment. As Collins' friend you're in a lot of danger.'

Willie was thinking about the days when he used to fraternize with the IRA in the Swallow pub before he took up residence in Cork. They'd know where his loyalties lay. Finbar certainly had a point.

Finbar saw beads of sweat break out on Willie's forehead. 'I brought my van to transport you and the family to Sligo,' he said. Then added, 'I was thinking that maybe if you brought your projector and the necessary equipment, you might find a place over there where you could show the pictures.'

'Why Sligo?' Willie asked, puzzled.

'For the simple reason that that County seems to be reasonably peaceful for the moment. It's also a seaside resort, which means your prospects of earning a living would be more favorable.'

Willie plumped on to a chair. He held his head in his hand. In desperation he considered Finbar's proposition. He then came to the conclusion that if things were going to be as bad as Finbar predicted, he'd no alternative but to secure the safety of his family by getting to hell out of Cork.

Eventually he said, 'When does Collins intend to attack the city?'

'Tomorrow,' Finbar said. 'But for God's sake don't breathe a word of that to anyone.'

'As if I would.'

'Look Willie,' Finbar impressed on him, 'do you think I'd take the trouble to make the trip from Dublin to Cork if this wasn't an emergency?' Finbar now looked frenzied. 'I'm telling you, Lad, you've got to get going and get going quickly. If you value your life and your family's lives, don't open the cinema tonight. Get out of town as quickly as you can. I'm here to help you.'

This was how Willie ended up showing pictures in the Ballroom of the Empress Hotel in Sligo for the remainder of the Civil War. That night in August, Finbar whisked Willie and his family across Ireland to Sligo. Later, a letter from Fiocra told Willie that the cinema had suffered damage when anti-Treaty IRA forces sought refuge there and fought it out with the Free State troops. 'However,' he wrote, 'not to worry, the cinema is salvageable.'

A week after Cork had fallen, Ireland was shattered by the news that Arthur Griffith, only fifty, exhausted by overwork, had collapsed and died of a heart attack. Brokenhearted, Collins came from the military operations in the South to carry his coffin at the funeral.

A few days later he returned to the Cork area to tour the newly won Free State positions there. One of his military aides, Emmet Dalton, was concerned for his safety, but Collins, as a Cork man, replied confidently, 'Sure they won't shoot me in my own county.'

At about 7:30 p.m. on the 22nd of August, 1922, the convoy in which Collins was traveling ran into a set of obstacles placed across the road in a gully called Bealnablath, between Macroom and

Bandon in County Cork. A party of anti-Treaty republicans had been waiting for them there all day. Firing broke out as the convoy halted.

Half an hour later, before it got dark, Collins was dead.

Ireland was in shock. Within a week of each other, Collins and Griffith had gone to their graves. The Civil War continued well into 1923, during which time, a number of anti-Treaty IRA members were executed by the State. William Cosgrave, who had fought in the 1916 Rising and was condemned to death by the British, but reprieved, was at the helm as an Taoiseach — the Prime Minister.

Willie and his family stayed out of harm's way, showing pictures to the Sligo people and tourists until the Civil War was over in 1923. Then, much to Jane's delight, the family returned to her beloved city of Dublin. Willie, having been successful in the Civil Service Examination, ultimately became a Higher Civil Servant. As the country settled into a reasonable state of normalcy, fate smiled on Willie: he sold the Emerald Cinema in Cork for a sum far exceeding what he paid for it and made a handsome profit.

ACKNOWLEDGEMENTS

My father fought in the General Post Office during the 1916 Easter Rising. 'Whom God Loves' the book's genesis is a TAPE made by him telling his story to Veterans in 1966 — the 50th Anniversary of the Rising. This TAPE later surfaced when the family home was sold. My father's story, along with many others narrated by my parents to us children while growing up, was the inspiration of this, my first book.

I would like to thank some of the people who gave so generously of their help and support. The Writers Guild of Alberta. Leonard Davidchuk and Aiden Gately — the computer geniuses. Last but not least, my thanks goes to Victoria White my patient editor.

ISBN 1425105891